Forever Is Over

Calvin Wade

authorHOUSE®

AuthorHouse™ UK Ltd.
500 Avebury Boulevard
Central Milton Keynes, MK9 2BE
www.authorhouse.co.uk
Phone: 08001974150

© 2011 Calvin Wade. All rights reserved.

No part of this book may be reproduced, stored in a retrieval system, or transmitted by any means without the written permission of the author.

First published by AuthorHouse   03/18/2011

ISBN: 978-1-4567-7009-9 (sc)

Any people depicted in stock imagery provided by Thinkstock are models, and such images are being used for illustrative purposes only. Certain stock imagery © Thinkstock.

This book is printed on acid-free paper.

Because of the dynamic nature of the Internet, any Web addresses or links contained in this book may have changed since publication and may no longer be valid. The views expressed in this work are solely those of the author and do not necessarily reflect the views of the publisher, and the publisher hereby disclaims any responsibility for them.

This book is dedicated to my wife Alison, my two sons, Bradley and Joel, my mother Jacqueline, my father Richard, my sister Lisa and my grandparents Elsie (Rest In Peace) and Ernie.

Alison – my love for you grows stronger by the day, there is no stronger bond.

Bradley & Joel – for teaching me the meaning of parental pride and making me appreciate where my father was coming from!

Mum & Dad – for providing me with the perfect upbringing. I am very proud to have you as my parents.

Lisa – we were always different but we were always good friends (except for that time in Majorca!)

Nan & Pop – "behind every successful man, there is a wise woman"…..the only thing missing from my thirties, Nan, was you.

"Forever Is Over" was inspired by "Sunny Road", a song by Emiliana Torrini on the magnificent album "Fisherman's Woman".

I would to thank the following people for their support in putting this project together:-

David Allen (for the website www.calvinwade.com), Andrew Wharmby (for the cover photo taken near Obyce, Slovakia – the relevance to the book is artistic rather than geographical!!), Mark Sunderland (for friendship, trust and belief), Guy Cullen (for providing the motivation to start the book), Emiliana Torrini for making time to respond (several times) despite being pregnant and moving home, Adele Riley (for the offer of a helping hand), Dr. Rob Letch for medical guidance, Sara Griffiths (for friendship and proofreading). Kathryn Saxby at Fleetriver (for pointing me in the right direction). Jill Wildman (for the boundless enthusiasm and unwavering support). Ivone Gomes de Silva (for caring). Gareth Roberts (Editor of 'Well Red' Magazine) and Kit Loughlin (for honest feedback). Michelle Loughlin (for some new ideas). David Stuart-Capita at the BBC (for permission to use the chilling broadcast by Peter Jones on Sport On Two, Hillsborough 1989). Paul Rawson (for the very entertaining story that he allowed me to pinch!)

Thanks to the following people for their friendship, love and encouragement:-

Lisa, Vin, Olivia and Max ('The Vernons'). Paula & Barry Walker (for all your support since the day I met your daughter.) Jennie, Jon, Chloe and Emily Askew. Andrew & Sarah Moss. Andrew & Yvonne Berry. Phil & Joanne Holmstrom. Graeme & Jackie Gregory. Andrew Elkington (for the horseracing craic and the offer of help at a moments notice). Jo, Shaun, Ellie & Lucy McManus. Dereck, Joy, Tom and Ben Stagg. Dave & Gill Hughes. Chris Evans. Jon Evans. Jamie Lowe. Jay & Debbie Davy. Lee Rankin. Sean & Kellie O'Donnell. Carl & Katie McGovern. Tamsin & Paul Hawkins. Dave & Laura Barron. Gareth Jones. Anna & Paul Ponting. Ed Payne. Chris Ayres. Gordon, Hilary, Gavin, Alexin and Colin ('The McGraes' and Inksons). The Wades. Andy Sykes. Emma Millington. Rod & Heidi McKirgan. Nicola Guy Edgington. Phillip Hesketh. Howard & Pam Slack. Charles Canning. David Robinson. Sara Curtis. Iain Lindsay. Michael Walsh. Ian Sincock. John Ritchie. Gary Lugg. Tina Panayi. Vicky Ingham. Katriona Dixon. Caroline Carroll. Chloe Collins. Viv Kennedy. Matthew & Caroline Helme. Emma & Mark Butterworth. Rick Blanks. Nicky Harburn. Amy Stabler. Nadeem Iqbal. Stuart Napier. Amanda Bramhill. Ian Prowse. Dave Pinnington. Marie Grundy. Kevin Formby. Amanda Bramhill.

Sara Leigh Boyd. Cathie Hunter. David Prescott. Alison Coates. Ian Bates. Louise Dermott. Steve Collins. Laura Wright. All my Facebook friends who have spread the word to their friends! Andy Seel, Dave Pilkington, Alastair Mollon for helping me run Gregson Lane JFC U11s! All the lads at Metropolitan and Dingwall Football Clubs – the football was great and the laughter was always loud! Cheers!

I am sure I have left out a million and one other people… I apologise in advance!

Jemma – The Beginning Of The End

I really wanted him to open the door but he wouldn't. Perhaps he smelt a rat, I'm not sure. Perhaps he recognised some of the cars outside – I'd told them to park down the road and walk up, but it was a wet and windy night and some women would rather spoil the surprise than spoil the hair they have just spent hours putting into place.

"Go through", I said to him, trying to coax him in.

"Can you not open a door?!" he asked, in a tone that implied he may have clocked my unusual behaviour. I was not in the habit of standing on ceremony! Anyway, Richie was having none of it, so I made a grab for him, whilst simultaneously trying to push open the double doors.

As I opened the doors, I was greeted by about a hundred of Richie's nearest and dearest, party poppers at the ready, for when his frail but smiling face emerged. The DJ, sensing his moment had come, pressed play and the room was filled with Elbow's "One Day Like This". It was no good though, multi-tasking had never been one of my strong points and as I pushed the door open, Richie had wriggled his skeletal frame out of my grasp and somehow managed to summon enough strength to run as fast as his legs could carry him, out the exit and back towards the car.

"Just give me two minutes", I explained apologetically to the anxious crowd, as I turned on my heels to go after him. Richie's Mum, Dot, made a move to the door too, but I wasn't waiting and shot off after him in a Shaggy & Scooby styled run.

Back in his healthier days, Richie would have reached the car in a flash, but once I was outside, I knew he was not going to escape me, as his run had become a determined stride, still oblivious to the howling winds and rain that only Gene Kelly would want to be out in.

"Richie, what are you playing at? Everyone's here for you?"

I loved every single pore on that man's skin, every ounce of flesh, every strand of hair, every eyelash, every tooth, every finger, every toe, but he was as stubborn as a mule when he wanted to be.

"I'm not going back in there".

"Yes, you are." I replied without sympathy.

"Jemma, I'm not".

Richie's Mum was outside by now, but thankfully, for once, she kept her distance.

"Richie, people have travelled a long way to get here. They've arranged babysitters, booked hotels, bought dresses, had their hair done, your Helen, even looks like she's had a boob job especially".

Richie didn't laugh. Sometimes when he was trying not to laugh, you could see the sides of his mouth curling upwards, this was not one of those times.

"Jemma, I can't do it. I wish I could, but I can't".

"Yes, you can".

Tears started to well up in his eyes.

"I can't face it, Jemma. I can't face a "Pity Party"."

"Come on Richie, once you get inside you'll enjoy it. You know you will."

"Jemma, these people are here because I'm dying".

"They are here because they love you."

"No, they are here because I'm dying. What am I supposed to talk to them about? Where are you going for your summer hols, Dogger? Majorca, great. I'm going to the crematorium, its going to be bloody roasting, but don't worry, I don't really feel the heat or at least I won't when I'm dead!!"

I was going to rush in with a sentence that began with, "Stop being so bloody stupid…" and then I was going to let my anger and annoyance complete the sentence for me, but for some reason, I stopped to think. Richie was dying, we all knew that. I desperately wanted him to see all his family and friends, some of whom he hadn't seen for years. I wanted him to see them whilst he was still well enough to enjoy the night, but I was not the one who's life was slipping away. If it was too much for him, it was too much for him, I shouldn't push it.

"OK, Richie, just listen to me for a minute."

"Jemma, I don't want this".

"Richie, just listen. Don't interrupt, just listen…"

"Shit!", I thought to myself. "SHIT!"

I'm not one for swearing out loud, I very rarely swear, but, at that very moment, my brain was turning the word "shit" over and over like food on a barbeque. With good reason, I was wanting inspiration to arrive like an express train, but it had been delayed by leaves on the line.

This was supposed to be my moment. Our moment. I wanted to say something witty or brilliant. Something inspirational. Something that would make him see things in a totally different light. Problem was I had nothing planned, no start, no middle and no ending. I'd just have to blag it. Here goes nothing.

"Look Richie, your Mum and I arranged this for you. As you know, only too well, I am from a weird family. I've had "stepdads", "stepbrothers", "stepsisters", "stepcousins", I've had more steps than a John Buchan novel, but your family's different. From the moment we met, I loved you, but I was always jealous of you. You had a proper family. A Mum and Dad who adore you. Your Mum is an interfering old bat, but she's prepared to stand outside in the pissing rain in the middle of November for you. You've got a brother and two sisters, all from the same Dad and you all get on. You're like the bloody Waltons!

That's not all. You've got friends who you've known since infant school. People you would do anything for and would do anything for you. I wish I didn't have to say this, but these are friends you may never get the opportunity to see again after tonight. Now, if you want to miss out on an opportunity to see these people because you think they are so tactless that they'll talk about their summer holidays, then lets get in the car and go home. But we both know the real reason they are here. They're here because they know you're dying and it's destroying them like it's destroying me. They are here because they want to have a wonderful night with a wonderful man. They want to celebrate your life with you and not at your funeral when they can't hug you and kiss you and tell you how much they love you. They…."

"That's enough, Jemma."

Richie took a tissue out his pocket. Blew his nose, wiped away a tear and walked towards me. I wasn't one hundred percent sure whether he was going to slap me or hug me, but he wrapped those skinny little arms around me and held me tightly.

"I'm sorry, Jem. I want to be brave, I want to be positive, I want to live every moment like it's my last, but it all doesn't seem real. Nights like tonight, however well intentioned, just remind me of what lies ahead. I remember being on Sales courses at work and you'd get these really confident "life coaches" who would tell you to assess the problem, then gauge its importance from one to ten, with ten being death. This problem is a big, fat ten, Jemma. I'm dying. Our kids won't have a father next Christmas. I won't see Jamie score his first goal and I won't be there to walk Melissa down the aisle on her wedding day. I so wanted to do that. You won't believe how much I wanted to do that".

Richie broke down, sobbing and sobbing as all the fears and anxiety that had been built up since the diagnosis came spilling out. Richie's mother, Dot, a woman who would not normally go swimming for fear of getting her hair wet, shuffled towards us like a rat that had been drowned and revived several times over.

"Everything alright, love?" she asked from just further than slapping distance away, which is what half of me felt she deserved for asking such a stupid question. The other half understood though that she needed to be there for Richie and I managed to keep quiet, paving the way for a response from her son.

"Everything's fine, Mum. Jemma's just persuaded me to go back in and see everybody. You go and get yourself dried off, Uncle Billy would have a field day if he saw you looking like that! Get yourself dried off and we'll follow you in, in a minute."

Dot gave her son a re-assuring smile and headed inside, looking every single day of her sixty three years. She didn't deserve a daughter-in-law like me. She deserved better. She only ever saw the good in people, especially Richie. I don't believe all parents have a favourite child, but Dot's was definitely Richie and she was losing him. I'm sure people learn to live with loss, but I knew in those moments neither Dot nor I would ever learn to live with the loss of Richie.

Intertwined and emotionally battered, Richie and I went inside and the party began………

He said he hated every minute of it, but he said it with a huge smile! It was a fabulous night. A fabulous night for a wonderful man. Two months have passed since I lost him and I have yet to manage twenty four tear-free hours. I don't care. If I shed a tear in his memory every day for the rest of my life, I will go to my grave a proud woman.

This is our story. The story of Richie Billingham and Jemma Billingham (nee Watkinson).

Enjoy it, learn from it and more than anything, never take your health for granted. Don't just seize the day. Seize the moment. Every single one.

Richie

I was an early starter with women or should I say young girls. I'm talking about a long time ago here, back when I was six years old, in 1977, the year of the Queen's Silver Jubilee.

Anna Eccleston was the first girl that ever caught my attention. I don't think Anna started Aughton Town Green County Primary in first year infants, or if she did, I didn't notice her, as I was too busy pining for the school bell that signified my ordeal was over and I could venture out and seek my Mum's re-assuring hug. By six though, I'd very much settled in to the school routine and decided Anna Eccleston was the girl for me.

Looking back, Anna Eccleston wasn't an overly pretty girl, but she was an athletic, outgoing, tomboyish girl who liked chasing me and catching me during "Catch A Boy, Kiss A Boy". This was always going to find favour with me! I wasn't the only boy she chased, I could name half a dozen others too, but she devoted more time to chasing me than anyone else, so I did the decent thing and tried my damnedest not to be caught for a little while, but then somehow managed to appreciate when she was on the verge of moving on to chasing another boy and at that point, I would accidentally-on-purpose allow myself to be grabbed!

Faye Williams and Sophie Leigh were different, I would run to the ends of the earth and back to avoid being caught by them, especially after being caught by Faye once. Her kiss was all teeth, spit and bad breath, but Anna Eccleston was worth being caught by! I clearly remember the sense of anticipation after being caught. Around the perimeter of the playground was a wall, which must only have been a couple of feet high, or sixty centimetres in today's half-metric world, which was there for children to sit on. Behind the wall was the school field, which was only accessible after a three week dry spell, but the field sloped down to the playground which meant that, providing it was dry, you could sit on the wall, then lie back horizontally onto the grass. Anna Eccleston would therefore take you to the wall, sit you down, push you back so you were virtually horizontal, then jump on top of you and plant an almighty smacker on your lips! I don't really remember whether the kiss itself was pleasurable, the nastiness of Faye Williams kiss lingered longer, but the whole dominance routine was fantastic!!!

So, as far as I can recall, pretty much every day followed that routine and 1977 was a great year! In a sign of things to come in late childhood/early adulthood, this feminine feast was followed by a famine. Even though I say it myself, I was an adorable six year old, very blond, blue-eyed, very bowl headed, cute lisp and cuddly…what more could a six year old girl want?!

Problem was, I didn't stay cute. I probably didn't do myself any favours with my temper tantrums either which were generally followed by a flood of tears. In 1978, I was a proud member of the "Dennis The Menace Fan Club" but when I lost an eye off my Gnasher badge, all hell broke loose, especially when Miss Fletcher, our acoustic guitar playing teacher, would not stop the "Yellow Bird Way Up in Banana Tree" song to send a search party out to the playground. There were forty two kids in the class at the time and I still think to this day that if she had sent a dozen of us out on a playground mission to find the missing eye, she would have still been able to have a good singalong with the other thirty. OK, maybe I shouldn't have tried to smash her guitar, but she started it, I was just retaliating!

The "Well, she started it!!!" theme, or just as regularly "Well, he started it!!!" theme, was also a common one in our home. I had, and still have, two older sisters, Helen, who was two and a half years older and Caroline who was eighteen months older and one younger brother, James, who was ten months younger than me. The girls shared a bedroom, as did James and I. In our room, there was a battle for supremacy. We were regularly stealing each other's toys (footballs, Action Men, Bionic Men, darts, go-karts etc etc) or wrestling (I was Big Daddy, he was Giant Haystacks) . If we weren't battling with each other, James and I would be conspiring together against the girls, putting their dolls in the oven and baking them, drawing beards on the pin-ups they had blue-takked on their walls from Jackie or Tammy magazine, putting spiders or ants in their ice creams, pretty much anything we could think of to liven up the day!

The girls would often chase us around the house trying to kick or punch us and then Mum would chase them with a rolled up newspaper whilst they would shout,

"Well, they started it!!". We were the little ones, so often our crimes went unpunished!

With regards to the age gap between James and I, it dawned on me in my early teens that James must have been unplanned as I knew no woman on earth would think,

"Right, my baby is four weeks old now and my bits have just about recovered from having that enormous head coming out of them. Time for another! Come over here big boy and show me some spunk!"

I remember one evening asking my Mum in my own diplomatic style,

"Mum, was James a mistake?"

My mother, Dorothy, a lovely woman with less tact or diplomacy than any man or woman I have ever met, replied in her dulcet Scouse tones,

"Yes Richie, he was! A bloody big mistake! It was your father's fault, I had just returned to some semblance of normality downstairs,(at the time I thought by "downstairs" she was talking in terms of our home, so I thought she meant she had just managed to get the lounge and kitchen tidy again) when your father caught me in a weak moment and persuaded me that even Mary could not get pregnant again four weeks after giving birth!

Mind you, you were all bloody mistakes! Every single one of you! No-one would have planned to have four under fours and with your father being neither use nor ornament, its surprising I didn't have a nervous breakdown!"

Back to the barren years! As far as I can remember 1978 to 1981 did not bring a single kiss to my door unless it was delivered by a family member or an overbearing family friend. My swansong with Anna Eccleston was first year juniors when our class were on the school field playing "The Farmer wants a wife". Anna was the farmer and she chose me to be her wife, every memory points to Anna being the trouser wearer in our relationship! After that, nothing…. I had become less blond, my mother now described my hair colour as"ash blond", less cute, less lispy, just as bowl headed and more tempermental, but the main factor in my lack of success was a lack of interest. A new love had come into my life and that love was football.

Women say men cannot multi-task, but boys can't either. I didn't have room in my heart or my mind for both football and girls, so I went for the sensible option and it wasn't girls!! It was Everton FC!

Jemma

I was an Ormskirk girl, born and bred. I was the eldest of my mother's two daughters and throughout my single digit years, I have no recollection of being anything other than a little toughie. I was brainwashed into this both by nature and nurture.

I started my school days at Greetby Hill Primary School, the largest primary school in Ormskirk and soon found my tomboy manner was appreciated by the boys but less so by the girls! I could climb trees, kick a football and throw a punch better than any boy at Greetby Hill! I don't recall ever having a birthday party of my own, nor do I remember attending any of the girls parties, but I recall several five-a-side football parties at Burscough and Skelmersdale Sports Centres! Every party, I was the only girl, but whilst the other outsiders like the fat kid, the square one and the snotty nosed one were always the last to be picked, I was first choice or even the child that was doing the picking!

As my childhood progressed, I remained tough but lost the tomboy label. Once I hit eleven, my periods started, my breasts grew and the boys no longer treated me as one of their own. The girls did not welcome me into their fold either, so I became trapped in 'No Man's Land'! I remained there from aged eleven to fifteen, with only one true friend and a younger sibling around to retain my sanity. Fortunately for me, at fifteen, I did the ugly duckling trick and the boys began to sit up and take notice. I was once again the girl that every boy wanted to take to parties, but for entirely different reasons the second time around! I suspect they now wanted me to be doing other things to their balls rather than kick them!

I suppose, in every teenage girl's life, there comes a time when some shallow, brainless, infantile, adolescent lad, who has a penis for a brain, tries to pressurise them into forsaking their virginity. In my life, this time came at sixteen years old, in Fifth Form. It came in the form of Billy McGregor, heartthrob of my year and pretty much all the Sixth Form girls too. Billy McGregor was in Upper Sixth and was universally ranked "gorgeous"!

I was not stupid. I knew Billy was wanting to sleep with me for two reasons and two reasons only. The first was lust. As stated previously, boys think with their todgers and I had become a decent looking young girl, so naturally I understood my vagina had magnetic charms to a penis. Second reason was bragging rights. Billy McGregor was a cocky, self-obsessed, arrogant lad and wanted to share the intimate details of his experience with his spotty, less successful mates. Billy knew the girls liked him but what I reckon he wanted more than anything was for the boys to like him too. I don't mean fancy him, of course, I just mean admire him. As far as I remember, most lads in Sixth Form thought Billy McGregor was the ultimate dickhead. Some of them were jealous, some of them just wanted to be him, but mainly the reason most lads thought he was the ultimate dickhead was, quite frankly, because he was!!!

If this gives you the impression that I hated Billy McGregor, then it's the wrong impression, I didn't, I liked him. It was no teenage crush, 'liked' him was as far as I could stretch it, but I dated him for seven weeks largely because there were at least seventy five girls at school, who would quite happily have chopped my feet off with a cleaver so they could slip into my shoes. Billy was tall, dark haired and blue eyed, the perfect Rob Lowe combination. He was also athletic and pus free. Given most of the lads in our year and Sixth Form could have filled a two litre bottle of Coke with the pus from their foreheads alone, this was some achievement. God had dealt Billy McGregor a fine set of cards, it was just a pity that he knew it. He was used to getting what he wanted and what he wanted during our seven week relationship, was to take my bloodied sheets to "The Wine Bar" in Ormskirk and hang them over the first floor balcony for all to see. I kept feeling like I was the girl in that Meat Loaf song ("Paradise By The Dashboard Light") who was getting felt up by the guy who was trying to get to all the bases and then score a "Home Run". Difference was, in that song, the girl wanted the lad to love her forever and I certainly didn't want that from Billy McGregor! I knew that I didn't want to lose my virginity to him. In my life, things have always been done on my terms. I didn't want to be in the

"Billy McGregor Stole My Cherry Club" which at that stage probably already had about fifty three members or I suppose one member and fifty three broken hymens.

So, other than looks, I was simply going out with him because I could and I knew this drove the majority of the other girls at school mad! I would have won no popularity contests amongst the bitches of Ormskirk Grammar School, so I could not have thought of anything that would have given me more pleasure than the pleasure I derived from watching their collective faces when I walked out of school and down Ruff Lane, hand in hand with the person they most desired. I savoured the jealous rage cooked up by every female onlooker. The bitches of Ormskirk Grammar School had a cauldron bubbling over with hatred and resentment every time I kissed his honey lips!!I loved it!! Even writing these words now, many years later, about their displeasure, still sends a tingle down my spine!

Despite his over inflated ego and testosterone, Billy was pleasant company when it was just the two of us! I know I said he was "The Ultimate Dickhead" but I just meant he was the ultimate dickhead when he was in a gang of lads. He wasn't the sharpest of Rambo's knives, but even at the time, I liked him like a parent likes their three year old son…he was pretty cute, he was entertaining but he still had a lot to learn about life, so despite him stropping around and throwing tantrums, I knew it was unhealthy long-term just to give him what he wanted!

There were further complications. Even if I had wanted sex with Billy McGregor, I was not 100% sure I quite understood everything sexually, well enough to feel comfortable doing it and the last thing I wanted to do, was to close up like a clam or a Venus fly trap and lock Billy's willy inside! I could just imagine Billy and I having to waddle down to the pub, in some bizarre wheelbarrow motion, to tell my idiot of a drunken mother that we were off to hospital!

That was the problem, I had no-one to turn to for sexual advice. I had a no good, pisshead mother, who would have probably suggested bringing some of the lads back from "The Ropers Arms" to teach me a few tricks if I had been to her for sexual advice. I did not have a father, not one I had met anyway and although I had a grandmother, who I referred to as "Tut", as that's all she ever did when she came round to our house, I thought of her as a sourfaced old cow who despaired of my mother and thought Kelly and I would be better off in a foster home than being brought up by our Mum. To be fair, she was probably right, but in the same way I thought of "Paradise By The Dashboard Light" when I was kissing Billy McGregor, when I saw "Tut", I thought of that tune from the "Wizard of Oz" that plays when Almira Gulch (The Wicked Witch of The West) cycles by threatening to take Toto away from Dorothy. I always thought back then, that if I was ever allowed a dog, I would have called him Toto!

Incidentally, Kelly is my sister (probably half-sister as I can't see any man being daft enough to sleep with my mother twice – unless they were equally drunk and had blotted out the first time). When I was sixteen, she was thirteen years old. Kelly was loving, beautiful and a diamond in the field of crap that my family was. At thirteen, I had only just bought Kelly her first tampons (Mum was too hungover to make it to Spar) so obviously I couldn't have turned to her for sexual advice.

So, as a sixteen year old, what did I not know about sex? Obviously I knew the basics, I wasn't totally naïve! "Vomit Breath", as I had christened my mother when I was fourteen, had shipped enough men into and out of our house (and her vagina) over the previous few years, that I had had many eye witness encounters of forgettable (for them), fumbling sex. I had also had a bit of "hands on" experience of the warm-up act when necking Barry Pounder at an Aughton Tennis Club disco and become a victim of his infamous, wandering hands. Nevertheless, I did not know everything. At sixteen, I was still not quite sure where sperm came from or rather where they came out from. I know this sounds really, really, stupid, but let me try to explain what I mean……

Down below, girls/women had three entrance and exit points, but as far as I was aware, boys only had two. Each one of a girl's exit points has a specific duty, one to poo, one to wee and one for creative duties (blood, sex, babies).Thus, if boys only had two, I figured out one had to be a multi-tasker, either that or there was another hole I was unaware of. After giving it a lot of thought, I deduced that the hole at the end of the penis obviously had a dual role, but it struck me as very odd. How did the male body know when to release what? I was not sure. Was it size dependent? For example, erect penis = sperm, limp penis = urine? This would make sense, but I was not sure that was right. I really did not get it!

I cursed my luck. I thought I would probably be the girl who slept with the lad who's body malfunctioned and we'd have to dispose of a condom overflowing with wee. Obviously an additional complication that scared me was the condom "putting-on", but I expected the likes of Billy McGregor to have had plenty of experience on that score. When it was my time for sex, I decided I would pretend to look the other way when the condom was going on and then slyly glance back to watch.

For all I knew the sperm/urine thing could have been a common, unspoken problem, and concluded that potentially this was where the expression,

"He doesn't know whether he is coming or going" came from!

I suppose the simplest solution would have been to just ask Billy, but I worried that any talk about sex may have given him the impression that I was up for it and I was not . Definitely not! I knew I would not be comfortable until I knew what I was doing and how everyone and everything was functioning! I realised it was a bit of a chicken and egg situation though, how would I know what I was doing until I had finally done it!

Questions about male genitalia and questions like,

"Who's Fitter – Matthew Broderick, River Pheonix or Rob Lowe?"

Answer – Rob Lowe (dark hair, blue eyes – winner every time), took up all my thinking time at school and proper study took up very little. I just wasn't interested in schoolwork.

Questions about John Betjeman and friendly bombs falling on Slough were boring! How could bombs be friendly? I just didn't get that at all!

Betjeman was earth shatteringly dull, but Jane Eyre (and whichever Bronte sister wrote about her) was even worse! Who gave a monkey's whether Mr.Rochester had his wife stuck up in the attic and wanted to trade her in for Jane Eyre? I didn't! I concluded that even if it was true, it was hundreds of years old so they'd all be dead now anyway, so let's just move on. I applied the same logic to R.E! I only changed my mind on that when I was in my twenties. English Literature was my least favourite lesson though, as I found the teacher, Miss Caldicott, to be the mistress of monotony and dullness. I knew I was going to fail all my "O" levels, but Vomit Breath did not tell me to knuckle down, far from it, she encouraged me to leave homework and school work well alone.

"There's no way on God's Earth I'm putting you through two years of Sixth Form when you could be paying your way to help me and Kelly out".

She was a charmer my mother! Get a job, Jemma! Helps with the school uniform for Kelly and the large scotches and ciggies for me! Heart of gold? Sadly not. More like a big, fat,decaying black heart. I hated her. Hated her more than I can put down in words.

Richie

I was born an Evertonian. My Mum was an Evertonian, my uncle was an Evertonian, my Grandad was an Evertonian, so before I could walk I was a brainwashed blue. My Grandad started buying me a season ticket in the Lower Bullens from when I was seven years old until he became too old to go when I was twenty one. They don't ban Senior Citzens at Everton, he just found the walk to the train station and the climb up and down the stairs too much once he got to his late seventies! Bizarrely though, any real interest in going to the game was triggered by my first ever trip to a football match which was at Burnden Park, Bolton.

My Dad is originally from Bolton. Growing up I wasn't close to my father. I wanted to be, but from Monday to Friday he was working, he was a Regional insurance rep, Saturdays he was either at the bookies or watching the racing on TV, then on Sundays he would strop around, cursing his luck and re-counting his stories to anyone who would listen about the horse in his accumulator that let him down.

"If COMPLIANT LAD had a longer neck, our family would all be sunning it up in Barbados now".

My Dad wasn't a bad man. He was, in many ways, a good one, but he loved his horse racing and unfortunately, too often, he put his own vice before his family. Even more unfortunate for me was that I later discovered gambling was a genetic affliction.

In 1984, my mother decided enough was enough and issued an ultimatum, "the horses or me". I'm sure if it had been a straight choice, he'd have probably packed his bags and headed off to watch the 2.10 from Haydock in peace, but the "me" included four children he loved dearly. He may not have made a huge amount of time for us, but there was no doubting he loved us dearly so from that day forward he stopped gambling……. well, so my mother thought, anyway! In actual fact, all he did was gamble far more discreetly than he had ever done before! He spent more time at home, we did more as a family, Peter O'Sullevans commentaries stopped echoing around the house every Saturday afternoon and he learnt to hide his disappointments rather than share them.

Back in 1978 though, my Dad was still an open and honest gambler. Gambling came first, family second and Bolton Wanderers a close third. As a child, Dad was apparently a decent inside-half although I don't recall a single day he kicked a ball with me. I do, however, recall him being a massive Bolton fan.

"I promise one day I'll take you and James to Bolton", he used to pipe up. Even at seven, I knew not to believe him, this man made more promises than Noel Edmonds made swaps. For those of you too old or too young to remember, Saturday morning was Swap Shop time, in our house it was anyway, as my mother banned Tiswas which was on the other side, as she deemed it to be "too aggressive". James hated that decision, I wasn't bothered, I preferred Swap Shop! With Swap Shop, you had to phone Noel Edmonds and Keith Chegwin and tell them what useless bunch of crap you wanted to swap for something fantastic. I still remember the phone number. 01-811-8055.

Anyway, Dad made promises all the time that came to nothing.

"Father Christmas will be bringing Choppers for you and James this year and a bloody great big dolls house for your sisters." He didn't.

"Jimmy in the office was saying he's just bought his lad a goal with a net for the garden. I think I'll get one of those for you boys and I promise I'll come out there with you and we'll have a bloody good kickabout". No kickabout, no goal either!

Dad said things. He didn't mean them, he just said them, so even at that age, I didn't get excited as I knew it meant nothing....unless of course, the sentence was finished off with a,"'cos I've had a win on the gee-gees!!!"

If Dad won on the horses, he was the happiest, most generous man in the world. When he won, it was like God turned the egg-timer over and he evolved from a sour-faced grump, infrequently seen, to an all singing, all dancing, one man cabaret.

Helen, the oldest and wisest of his offspring, deemed it to be his "three hour happy window". Good things happened in the "happy window" and one Friday he must have nipped into the bookies after work, fortune must have been on his side, as he arrived home that Friday evening with three tickets to Bolton Wanderers against Wolverhampton Wanderers, for Dad, James and I. I remember James asking if it was a local Wanderers derby!

James wasn't into football much then, nor is he now and at the time, although I told everyone I was an Evertonian and collected Panini stickers, I didn't quite understand the older kids obsession with football either, but the most exciting part of the announcement was that James and I were going to be spending the whole day with our Dad. Our Dad, a man who generally focused five minutes of his day towards us, was going to focus his whole day on us – well, us and Bolton Wanderers anyway.

It's more than twenty five years ago now, so my memory of the day are a little fuzzy. I remember being in Dad's car, me in the front, James in the back. I remember it was a hilly journey and although it's only about thirty miles from Ormskirk to Bolton, if that, at the time it seemed like a huge distance. Dad parked a long way from the ground and he took it in turns to carry James and I. I remember when I was aloft, his face felt re-assuredly strong and stubbly. Even on this day of days though, he wasn't perfect. He stopped at a sweet shop and bought James and I some "Spangles", then told us to wait outside another shop, a smoky shop, because children weren't allowed in.

"I'll just be five minutes", he promised.

James and I talked. It was obvious to us that this was one of those "bookies" that Helen and Caroline had warned us about. The place where Dad's bad moods came from. We stood there, crunching our Spangles and pining for our father like a pair of abandoned toddlers. We knew that his mood for the day would be determined by the five minutes spent in this shop. Smacks and hugs were on the line with only one winner. Thankfully for James and I, Dad emerged from that bookies with a grin the size of Burnden Park itself, his lucky streak had extended into a second day and he proudly announced,

"Today has just paid for itself!!"

I didn't understand exactly what that meant. Today was Saturday. How could Saturday pay for itself? He must have won money but what did that mean? I didn't toy with the question for too long though, as Dad was so obviously happy, I just wallowed in his positivity. Me, my Dad and my brother were going to a real football match and didn't it just feel great!

I didn't know or care back then, that lucky streaks don't last. I was naïve to the fact that every gambler has a lucky streak at some point or other, but more often than not it is followed by an unlucky streak that lasts longer and costs more. Is gambling more or less harmful than smoking? Its hard to say. Ultimately, I suppose it depends on the individual, but they are both slow destroyers. Smoking slowly murders your vital organs whilst gambling attacks the brain, breaks down your self-control and sucks out your spirit. I wish I had known that back then. If only! Back then all I knew was that we were on the crest of a wave and I headed off to the match with a newly acquired black and white scarf and a rattle, full of the joys of spring.

Bolton were in Division Two back then. Division Two was a different league then to what it is now. There were no Premierships and Championships back in those days, just Divisions One, Two, Three and Four. Simple! Bolton, I think were near the top of the league and Wolves were the top, so it was a promotion battle. Bolton scored twice but they were both disallowed, whilst Wolves scored once and it counted, so that was that, Wolves won 1-0. I thought it was fantastic. Twenty thousand excited people captivated by the actions of twenty two. I wanted to go again and again.

Dad took footballing defeat better than horse racing defeats, probably because there was no money involved and I remember the three of us walking back to the car with Dad imploring us to tell the kids at school on Monday that we had been to the mighty Burnden Park. I did tell them, but we lived in Aughton, a village twelve miles from Liverpool and a mile from Merseyside so near enough everyone supported Liverpool, who at the time were European Cup holders, with a smattering of Evertonians for good measure, so the boys were about as interested in Burnden Park as I was in kissing Faye Williams (dog breath).

That Saturday was a turning point for me though. As my Dad twiddled the knob on his car radio, trying to get a good enough reception to pick up the racing results, I knew, as well as a seven year old could know, that my Dad was an unreliable sort. I knew this was a one-off and no matter how much I begged him, he would not be taking me to football matches every other weekend. What I also worked out on that car journey home, was where the window of opportunity could be found and the following morning I clambered through it.

By eight o'clock that Sunday morning, I was fully dressed and ready to go out. I skipped five doors along to my Nan and Grandads house to recount the story of the previous day. They were my Mother's parents and were not my Father's biggest fans, so the fact that my Dad had clambered up off his big fat arse to take us, was a shock to their systems. I didn't miss a detail, carefully dropping the bait, telling them how great Burnden Park was and how I loved every minute of the whole experience.

"Burnden Park, great?!" my Grandad scoffed, "wait until you see Goodison!"

"But my Dad won't take me to Goodison, Grandad, he supports Bolton not Everton".

"Of course he won't Richard, but I will! Next season you and I and your brother if he's interested, are all going to have season tickets at Goodison Park!".

For the following four years everything revolved around football. I started playing for cubs, (Aughton St Michaels 40th Ormskirk pack – "Tuesdays" – there were also 40th Ormskirk "Wednesdays", the rivalry was fierce!!) and the school team and every other Saturday, Grandad and I went to the Everton match. James was offered the opportunity too, but he turned it down. James was into other things such as Lego, Meccano and as he grew older, Dungeons and Dragons. I hated all of them with a passion. He was the practical one, I was the sporty one.

My lifelong love affair with Everton Football club started to gather pace in 1978 and over the following four years it became so strong, girls were not given a second thought. Then, in 1982, things changed. Rachel Cookson, seemingly overnight, grew the most fantastic pair of breasts I had ever seen in my entire life and football, for a while anyway, became a secondary passion!!

Jemma

School was boring, but school on Fridays was particularly boring, especially when you were going to a party after school and you just wanted the day to end in double quick time. First lesson was double English with Miss Caldicott. Now how was that meant to go in double quick time?

For our "O" level, we were doing one novel, Jane Eyre, which in my opinion was the dreariest book ever about the dreariest romance ever, one book of poetry by John Betjeman and a Shakespeare play, which for us was "Julius Caesar". Betjeman and Shakespeare were boring too. The other English sets got to do Oscar Wilde, which sounded more exciting, although Miss Caldicott could have turned a trip to the moon into one big yawn. Anyway, the Friday of party night was Jane Eyre, so I spent half the lesson trying to carve my name off the desk with a compass. Just to explain, in a previous English lesson, I had carved a heart with my name and Billy McGregor's into the desk and as we were now finished, it was time to get rid of it.

Billy and I had split up on the previous Thursday. A mutual decision of sorts. The lack of sex had become more and more of an issue for him, so much so that I was expecting his head to pop off like a cork and his body just to fizz out millions of gallons of sperm like a massive ejaculating firework. He had just passed his driving test so he had this newly found freedom he wanted to exploit, as well as me. His Mum and Dad, Mr & Mrs Middle Class, had bought him a Vauxhall Chevette for his eighteenth, so he had wanted to take me out on the previous Friday to the Astra cinema in Maghull, to see "Beverly Hills Cop". No doubt he had some elaborate plan to take me to Clieves Hill, or somewhere equally desolate afterwards, but Vomit Breath put paid to his plan as she would not let me go, well not unaccompanied anyway.

Vomit Breath, as you could probably guess, was not the world's most protective mother. If I had told her I was off to play chicken on the M58 motorway, she'd have just said,

"Well, don't you be expecting me to come up to A&E to see you when you get run over, its quiz night at The Ropers tonight."

The Ropers is about two hundred yards from Ormskirk hospital.

So, when I asked her on the Wednesday night if I could go to the cinema on Friday, she surprised me when she said,

"Course you can, love".

I wasn't expecting that. I threw in another line.

"I'll be back about eleven".

She just kept dragging away on her Marlboro Lights, unconcerned.

"No problem, love", her voice rasped out in between inhales.

Shocker! Oh my god, what was going on!! Then reality bit, small chunks at first, then bigger ones.

"Who are you going with?"

Vomit Breath didn't do niceties. The air was now full of suspicion and vomit breath. We traded questions.

"Billy McGregor. Why?"

"Who's he?"

"My boyfriend. Why do you want to know who I'm going with?"

"Is he a nice lad?"

"He's OK. Why?"

And then the answer,

"Because if he's a nice lad, he won't mind taking Kelly too. I'm off to the Kingsway on Friday night. There's a coachload of us going. We're getting picked up at the Kwik Save car park at nine. You've got Kelly."

"I'm not taking Kelly on a date!"

"Jemma, you either take Kelly with you or you don't go, simple as that."

This was never going to work. How many cool points would Billy lose if he took his sixteen year old girlfriend and her thirteen year old sister to the cinema? If he was spotted, it would look bad. Furthermore, devious plans to go to Clieves Hill or any other "Lovers Lane" would be out the window if a thirteen year old was tagging along. I knew next day at school, crisis talks were needed.

Ormskirk Grammar School in the 1980's, was still stuck in the Victorian era. Boys and girls were not allowed to play together at break times or lunchtime. There was a designated area for boys, the playground and a designated area for girls, the mud and tarmac that divided the school buildings! How sexist was that?! That was just one of many strange rules. My favourite was that girls were not allowed to step over puddles in case the boys should happen to see the reflection of their knickers in the water!! Classic! There were plenty of others too, like girls were not allowed to roll up the sleeves on their shirts as this would have mentally, sexually energised the boys! They were teenage boys, did the staff not realise they were already mentally, sexually energised?!

The girl/boy divide was not really a deterrent to seeing Billy though as he was in Sixth Form and they were handed special privileges. These included not playing out at break times and just hanging around the Sixth Form block. The block was pretty much slap bang in the middle of the girls designated area, so it was easy for me, at Thursday morning break, to get a message to Billy via Liz Malthouse, who had nipped out for a sly fag in Coronation Park, that I wanted to meet him outside the Sports Hall at one o'clock.

One o'clock came and went. No Billy.

Ten past came and went. No Billy.

Twenty past came and went. No Billy.

The bell was due at half past and I needed to see him, so I just marched into the Sixth Form, which was "Out Of Bounds" to Fifth Formers. We were easily spotted by teachers as we had to wear a proper uniform, Sixth Formers just had to dress smartly, but this lunchtime, thankfully, no teachers were around.

I pushed past a few of the plebs in the cloakroom and there, sat in the middle of the Common room, was Billy McGregor playing poker with about four mates. I was livid.

"What are you doing?"

"What does it look like I'm doing? I'm playing Poker."

"I wanted to meet you at one o'clock."

"I didn't want to meet you."

"Why?"

"Cos we're finished."

"I know we are. That was why I wanted to meet you. To tell you it was over". I lied.

"Too late".

"Tosser!"

Out I stormed. Turns out the smoke signals about Kelly playing gooseberry had reached Sixth Form. Kelly had told her mate, Jenny McManus and she had told her Sixth Form sister, Georgina McManus and she had probably blabbed to everyone, including Billy McGregor, who was no doubt trying to maintain his reputation as universal heartthrob by finishing with me. Billy had decided credibility was everything. So, Friday night was spent babysitting Kelly, rather than being felt up by Billy McGregor, which was probably a better option anyway. Good looking lad but he had dirty, jagged fingernails.

When she was thirteen, Kelly was great. I could already tell that she was going to break hearts when she was older. My eyes are pale blue and lifeless but Kelly's are really green and sparkle like diamonds. She has really long eyelashes too. Even at thirteen, she was stunning and I knew if she was all dolled up, she could get away with being sixteen. Her hair was a bit mousey but I told her I'd pay for blonde highlights for her once I was working full time. I knew she'd be even more beautiful then. She was intelligent too and was mature enough to have an adult conversation too, unlike Billy McGregor. The Friday of the cancelled date, we had a great evening, we stuffed our faces full of Maltesers and watched loads of great stuff on TV like Cheers and The Word.

By the time that Friday night was over, Billy McGregor was out of my system. I tended to categorise people into two teams, those I loved such as, Kelly, Rob Lowe, Amy Perkins, my best mate,....and those I hated, Miss Caldicott, most of the girls at school, Vomit Breath, "CC" - Deputy Head at School, real name Miss Turnbury, Tut and Billy McGregor. I vowed that when I was older and rich and famous, Billy McGregor would watch me on the TV and think,

"if only I'd met her that time outside the Sports Hall and taken her and her sister to the cinema!"

Actually, I realised it would probably be Kelly that was famous, I thought maybe Kelly would be a famous model and I would be her manager and Billy McGregor would think,

"I could have taken both of them to the cinema, if I hadn't been such an idiot!"

Vomit Breath was a nightmare that weekend. In the early hours of Saturday morning, I heard her stumble out of the taxi. I looked out my window and there was some fella with her and he was probably intending on coming in to see what he could get (VD probably!), but when she zig-zagged out the taxi, took four steps and threw up, he was back in the taxi before you could say "gonorrhoea".

So, on the Saturday, my mother well and truly lived up to the "Vomit Breath" title and a "Bear with a Sore Head" was putting it mildly! She didn't get up in the morning, so I took Kelly into Ormskirk to have a look around the market, but there was nothing that took our fancy. I did bump into Amy though. She was off to Dorothy Perkins with her Mum. Amy was my best friend at school and, if I'm honest, probably my only REAL friend. She was one of those girls that everyone likes, unlike me, because she was very tactful and would not say a bad word about anyone (again unlike me!) They say opposites attract and Amy was definitely a calming influence on me. Her surname was Perkins so I asked her if she was going to Dotty P's to keep the business in the family, but she looked confused so I had to explain.

Amy told us that she had been invited to Joey Birch's party in Halsall on Friday night. Joey Birch was in our year, he was in 5 Left. There were six classes in total in our year, North, South, East, West, Left and Right. I was in 5 North. "Left" and "Right" was our school's very tactless way of branding two classes as "not quite as bright". Joey didn't try much at school. He wanted to be some sort of mechanic that worked on motorbikes, his two older brothers each had bikes and he had started riding them too, as he had been sixteen the previous month. His Mum and Dad had gone to Canada for their Silver Wedding anniversary, so the three lads had decided to have a massive party the following Friday! Not to celebrate the Silver Wedding I wouldn't have thought!! Joey and Amy used to get on really well, so he told her to come along and bring some (and I quote) "fit mates"!

My first thought when Amy told me this, was that I wouldn't be allowed as Mum would be out with her mates and I'd have babysitting duties for Kelly.

Kelly must have thought this too as she said,

"Jemma, if Mum's going out, I'll make arrangements to stop over at a friend's, so you can go out too."

She was a little star, Kelly. The problem was, for many years after, I wished she hadn't been so kindhearted and I had never been to that stupid party!

On the basis that Kelly was sorted, I agreed to go. The rest of the weekend was spent keeping out of Vomit Breath's way. Despite staying in bed all Saturday morning to sleep off her hangover, on Saturday afternoon she tried to get rid of it, by drinking her way through it, but this just meant that Sunday was a carbon copy of Saturday, except it started differently, as some ugly, bearded bloke left her room on Sunday morning.

It was back to school on Monday and as Friday grew nearer, Amy and I talked about nothing else other than Joey's party. So, in Miss Caldicott's lesson on Friday morning, I wasn't paying much attention (surprise, surprise!!), I was just trying to get my name off the desk and thinking about the party that evening, what I would be wearing, what make-up I'd put on, how I was going to get back from Halsall to Ormskirk before "Vomit Breath" etc etc.

At one point, I was carving away on the desk and I somehow felt the glare of thirty pairs of eyes on me or forty really as there was about ten kids with glasses in our class, so they counted double. Then, I felt an icy shadow over me and looked up to see a very unimpressed Miss Caldicott. It's hard to describe Miss Caldicott. I suppose the best way is to say that if there had been a competition for "World's Ugliest Woman" in 1987, she would have come a close second to Vomit Breath! She wasn't that old, thirtyish, but had greasy black hair, glasses and lots of moles and warts with hair coming out of all of them. Someone once said she looked like she was "spawned by the Yeti" and that's just about the perfect description!

Anyway, Miss Caldicott, half English teacher, half Yeti, growled angrily at me,

"What do you think you're doing, Miss Watkinson?"

"Don't know, miss".

"You don't know!! Surely you know what you were doing, you have a compass in your hand".

"I was cleaning the desk, miss".

She didn't like that. Steam came out her ears and if you'd have tipped her head to one side, with a mug and a teabag beneath her, you could have made a fine cup of tea.

"It didn't look like cleaning to me! It looked like vandalism to me."

I never knew when to give up on something. I told you Amy was tactful and I was not.

"Someone has written about me on this desk, miss. I was just trying to get it off."

"Save your breath, Watkinson! Go and explain it to Miss Turnbury. NOW!!!!!!!!"

Shit! Miss Turnbury (or "CC" as we called her) was Deputy Head and also Head of Girls. She was about one hundred and six years old. The school was founded centuries ago and she was probably teaching back then. She hadn't updated her teaching methods either. They were still PRE-Victorian. Anyway, off to her office I went. I knocked on her door, praying she'd gone roaming somewhere, seeking out misbehaviour like Supergran gone wrong. No such luck. She was in.

"Enter!"

I entered. She was sat there behind an old oak desk, writing something with a fountain pen. No doubt it was some sort of lecture, as Miss Turnbury was forever lecturing. She gave me a cold stare.

"I guess, Miss Watkinson, that you are not here on a social visit?"

"No, miss."

I would have loved to say,

"Well, actually, I am as it happens. Miss Caldicott's lesson was boring me shitless so I thought I'd come and rescue you from 1834. I'm going to a party tonight to lose my virginity, fancy coming with me and losing yours?"

Obviously, that's what I would have loved to say with hindsight anyway. I wasn't exactly planning to lose my virginity that night. If I had said something similar, Miss Turnbury probably would have re-introduced hanging to Ormskirk Grammar or even beheading.

Still, as much as I would have liked to, I didn't say any of the above other than,

"No, miss".

"So, why are you here then, Miss Watkinson?"

She said this with the superiority complex that she had evidently spent centuries perfecting.

"Miss Caldicott sent me, miss".

"Why though? Why did she send you?"

"I was carving something off the desk, miss".

"Carving something off the desk or carving something on?"

"Off".

"You don't strike me as a "Good Samaritan", Miss Watkinson".

I tell you, I would have enjoyed striking her on her grey haired top lip. I didn't though!

"No, miss. Someone had written something on the desk about me, miss. I was just taking it off. It's not fair that…"

I thought I was really beginning to sound like the innocent victim, sometimes I was so good at it, I manage to persuade myself I was hard done by! Miss Turnbury wasn't falling for it though!

"STOP!"

They were all the same, teachers, they didn't like elongated excuses.

"Miss Watkinson, I don't care whether you were carving something ON the desk or carving something OFF the desk. The fact is, you were carving. Miss Caldicott was taking a lesson and you had a compass out and you were carving on the desk. It's vandalism. Pure vandalism. I have absolutely no choice but to punish you. Luckily for you though, young lady, I can swiftly administer this punishment. I have a number of school reports to sign off tonight, so you can join me in the office, after school and complete your lines here. I expect to be here until eight o'clock so you can now expect to be here until eight o'clock too."

This wasn't a detention! This was a date! She had no-one to keep her company in her sad and lonely life so I was being punished to fill the void.

"But miss, my Mum will be expecting me home".

I was hoping that Miss Turnbury was unaware of Vomit Breath's reputation.

"I shall get the school secretary to ring your Mother and explain your late arrival home."

You'll have to ring the pub, I thought. Then it dawned on me…. the party!

"But miss, I'm going to a party tonight!"

"Well, you will just have to go to the party after eight o'clock then won't you Miss Watkinson? Now get back to your class and I shall look forward to seeing you at half past three."

I left that office in a state of shock. Was it legal for teachers to keep you back at school until eight o'clock at night? That's not an hour or an hour and a half, that's bloody ages! I went back to Miss Caldicott's class in a stunned silence and didn't catch another word she said as the only thing that went around and around in my head was how I was going to get to Joey Birch's party. I had made arrangements to meet Amy, at seven, at her house and her older brother, Martin, was going to give us a lift to Halsall, for four quid! How was I going to get there now? Vomit Breath couldn't give me a lift as she didn't have a car and even if she had, it would have been useless because she was never sober enough to drive nor kindhearted enough to do me a favour. I don't even know if she could drive! At break, I spoke to Amy about my dilemma.

"So CC has given you detention until eight o'bloody clock?!"

Amy and I thought "CC" was an entirely appropriate nickname for Miss Turnbury, it had travelled down from one set of schoolchildren to the next. It was short for something very rude! Something to do with her virginal status! The first word was cobweb and the second word rhymed with blunt!

"Yeh, can you believe it?! I'm screwed now, I'll never get to Joey's party. I'd get a taxi but I've got no money, Vomit Breath borrows, or should I say steals, all my money for fags and booze."

"Of course you can still go," Amy responded in her calming tones, sounding scarily like the fairy in Cinderella.

"No, I can't. If I get out of detention at eight, I've got to go home, get changed and then get to Halsall. I don't even know if buses go to Halsall, there's only about six people, three cats, a dog and several hundred sheep that live there."

"We'll wait for you."

"Amy, you can't do that! It starts at half seven! "

"Get to mine straight from detention. Let's go and find your Kelly now, I'll go to yours straight from school and get some clothes for you to wear from Kelly and take them to mine. You leg it to mine after detention, quick change, slap on a bit of make-up and lippy, have a few glasses of Thunderbirds with me and away we go!"

"What about Martin?"

"He doesn't wear make-up and I don't think he likes Thunderbirds either!"

"You know what I mean! He thought he was taking us at seven not half past eight.

Is he not going anywhere?"

"Martin?! Are you talking about my brother, Martin?! He's a geek! He just spends his evenings playing some game called "Elite" on his computer. He'll take us any time we want."

"Are you sure?"

"Of course I'm sure!"

"And you don't mind?"

"Jemma, I'm not going into Joey's house alone! If I had to wait until midnight for you, I would. You're my best mate and we're going to this party together."

Richie

Matchmakers. Can you still buy Matchmakers these days? I'm not sure if you can. They've probably ceased to exist along with Dip Dabs, Mojos, Texan bars, Spangles and the likes. Matchmakers were long, spindly sticks of chocolate that came in at least a couple of flavours. Mint & Orange I think. From the day it happened to the day I die, orange Matchmakers will always remind me of Rachel Cookson.

Town Green was a decent sized primary school with over three hundred children, all told. Every school year had two classes and Rachel Cookson had never been in mine, so she pretty much escaped my attention, until fourth year juniors.

Fourth year juniors at primary school is a great time of life, but also an uncertain one too, its like a sunny day with a big, black cloud in the distance. You are eleven years old and for the very first time, you are the senior pupils, big fish in a small pond, but in the back of your mind, you know you need to make the most of it, as the following year it will all change, everyone moves on to various Secondary schools and you revert back from frog to tadpole, butterfly to caterpillar.

As I had grown older, my temper tantrums had lessened, then pretty much disappeared, in school anyway and by third year juniors, I was almost a model pupil. I still had a fixation with Everton Football Club which would often lead to arguments and the occasional fight with the Liverpudlians, but only in the playground. In lessons, I was well behaved and academically bright. Thus, when we started fourth year juniors, Mrs. Hawkins, our fourth year teacher and Deputy Headmistress, chose me as the House Captain for Windsor. A proud moment! At Town Green, the children were separated into four teams, named after Royal residence, so we had Balmoral, Clarence, Sandringham and Windsor. Every week children were given team points for good work or model behaviour. I remember once a lad called Nick Thompson was given a teampoint for honesty because he confessed, in assembly, to only brushing his teeth once a day, every one else put their hands up for two or three times! You could also lose team points for bad behaviour like fighting in the playground over football!

Every Friday afternoon, two of the House Captains would collect the team point books from the teachers in each class, tot up the scores and the following Monday morning, in assembly, the House Captains of the winning team would receive a trophy in assembly. There were also sporting events too, where you represented your House, the boys did football, the girls netball and the games were played at lunchtime so the rest of the school could watch and cheer their House on. Then, at the end of the school year there was Sports Day. Competition was actively encouraged and thank goodness, non-competitive events had yet to raise their politically correct head.

I was the Male House Captain of Windsor, the female House Captain was Rachel Cookson. We had some intelligent and sporty kids in Windsor, so we pretty much cleaned up, which meant every Monday morning in assembly, Rachel Cookson and I would be holding a trophy proudly aloft at the front of the assembly hall. For several months we rarely spoke, but testosterone was spilling into my body and oestrogen into Rachel's, so every Monday morning I was confronted by her ample breasts and the infants on the front row, who happened to look in the wrong direction, were confronted by rather a large bulge in my short trousers.

After Christmas, Rachel and I were beginning to say "Hello" to each other in the playground and by Easter, I had confided in several friends that I wanted Rachel Cookson to be my girlfriend. What you were expected to do as "boyfriend and girlfriend", I didn't really know, but I knew the more time I spent with her, the more time I would have to look at her amazing chest. With hindsight, maybe I should have just asked to take a photo of her from belly button to neck, as other than saying "hello", I had no idea what to say to her. I was incredibly confident in a group of boys, but add a girl into the equation, particularly one I was attracted to, I just clammed up and went a distinct shade of pink. Girls, as a whole, didn't really know much about football, Everton FC and the failings of Gordon Lee, our manager, but other than that, my conversation range was pretty limited. I knew a little bit about netball as Helen and Caroline, my sisters, had both represented the school when they were at Town Green, but I could probably only eek out a three minute conversation about Goal Attacks, Wing Attacks and Goal Shooters.

Nevertheless, despite painful shyness and the inability to converse, I did have a determined streak and decided I must ask Rachel out. I had to ask Helen what exactly this meant as I thought you just said,

"Will you go out with me?"

Then the response would be a "Yes" or a "No", but Helen informed me you had to ask the girl out on a date and if she enjoyed it, you would go out again and then you would be classed as "going out". She leant me a few magazines of hers and after a Saturday afternoon of flicking through these romance fests, I got the idea! I was also a shrewd cookie and seeing as though all the dates in Helen's magazines involved the cinema, the local swimming baths or a disco, I had a mental picture of what Rachel may look like in a swimming costume, so the "Disco Swim" at Park Pool Swimming Baths on a Saturday afternoon (a Saturday afternoon when Everton were away, of course!) seemed like the ideal option.

So, one lunchtime, I left the rest of the boys to "British Bulldogs" and wandered over to the skipping area. I watched, mesmerised, as Rachel Cookson skipped up and down, her breasts bouncing like a pair of Space Hoppers, whilst the rest of the girls sang,

"On a Mountain.
Lived a lady,
Who she is,
I do not know,
All she wants is,
Gold and silver,
All she wants is,
A very best friend,
So call in my very best friend,
My very best friend,
My very best friend
My very best friend
So call in,
My very best friend,
Whilst I go out to play".

Then Rachel shouted, "Anna" and the pair of them skipped together as the song started again. Before they got through it a second time, Rachel's foot clipped the rope and she was out. My moment had arrived! I approached her nervously. James apparently watched me from afar and told me that night that I was all hunched up and he was expecting me to start saying "Esmerelda" and "The Bells, The Bells!". I was terrified. What would I say to her? News travels fast in primary school and I guessed she knew I wouldn't be approaching her to talk about team points. My head was still in a bit of a spin after watching her blouse bouncing, but somehow I kept my nerve for a brief conversation.

"Hi Richie!"

"Hi Rachel." Her "Hi" was more enthusiastic than mine, mine was filled with trepidation.

"You OK?"

"Yes".

"Did you want me for something?"

"Yes".

"What was it?"

She was better at talking than me.

"Doesn't matter".

I felt a fool. I turned around to walk away but she called after me.

"Whatever it was you wanted, the answer's yes".

I should have thought this through. Here was a golden opportunity the likes of which I had never had before. The answer's "Yes", Richie Billingham, you just have to make up the question. Not untypically though, I fluffed my lines.

"Pardon?"

"Whatever it was that you were going to ask me, Richie, the answer's yes".

"Oh!"

"What was it then?"

"What was what?"

"What was it you were going to ask me?"

"Oh."

"Come on Richie, spit it out, it'll be my turn to skip again in a minute!"

She said this in a jovial, amused tone that gave me the impression that she was taking this in her stride. I wasn't. I was just about managing to breathe!

"Will you come to the disco swim with me at Park Pool on Saturday?"

"No".

"I thought you said, whatever I asked, the answer would be 'Yes'?"

"Well, it would have been, but I can't swim".

I was shocked. Surely those breasts would keep her afloat. I should have taken stock, then gone on to suggest an alternative venue. The cinema, maybe. If I was nineteen or one of those super cool blokes in

Helen's magazine, that's what I would have done, I wasn't though. I was an eleven year old idiot.

"Bring armbands".

Of all the stupid things I could have said, that had to be number one! I knew it was stupid the second it left my mouth. Whoever heard of anyone going on a date with armbands on? There were no pictures in "Jackie" of some gorgeous fourteen year olds splashing around the swimming pool in their rubber rings and armbands.

"I don't like swimming".

"We could go in the little pool. You can stand up in there."

Rachel took a moment to reflect.

"OK then. I'll bring my brother. What time shall I meet you?"

"Two o'clock".

"OK."

Off we went in our separate ways. Rachel back to skipping, me back to "British Bulldogs". I had to be the chaser because I'd skipped a game. As I chased the boys around the playground, I reflected on what had just happened. Success. Of sorts. I was now going on a date with Rachel Cookson and her six year old brother, Barry. He was in second year infants. He was a bit mad, he once broke his leg when he jumped out his bedroom window in his Superman costume, but he was OK. I guessed he probably couldn't swim either. Knowing Barry though, he'd probably turn up thinking he was "The Man From Atlantis" and I'd probably have to keep fishing him out from the bottom of the pool. Still a date with Rachel and Barry was better than no date at all, so I went home that night feeling pretty darn pleased with myself, until James burst my bubble with his "Hunchback of Notre Dame" jibes.

I asked Rachel for a date on the Wednesday, by Friday, I was a nervous wreck. All told, I was a nervous child. Before a football match, whether it was playing for Cubs or watching Everton, I would get nervous to the point where I could not sleep. This was similar, but a hundred times worse. It wasn't just nerves, it was pure, unadulterated fear. What was I going to say to her? What would she be wearing? If she just wore a bikini, what would I do? Could I be trusted not to stare at her bust? Could my ding-a-ling be trusted to stay in my Speedos? If I didn't stare at her bust, would I be able to look at her at all? I mean if I was looking at her face, her bust wasn't very far away and I know I'd want to have a sneaky look. If I just looked away from her the whole time, would she think I was a weirdo and would she be able to hear me when I spoke? Was this a date? What would we do after we got out the pool? Her Mum would probably have to pick her up if she had her brother with her. What would I do then?

There were too many questions I just didn't have answers for. I liked to be in my comfort zone, not that I knew what a comfort zone was when I was eleven and this was taking me very much outside of it. Friday night, I hardly slept. Saturday morning came and I resorted to new tactics. Safety in numbers tactics. Rachel was taking her brother, so I would do the same. After breakfast, I found James in the corner of our room, building aeroplanes out of Lego.

"What are you up to today, Jim?"

Some of the older kids in the road had started calling him, Jim and I thought it suited him, as he was such a serious child, so I had started calling him Jim too. Not in front of my mother though, she hated it. If anyone called around and asked,

"Is Jim playing?"

My Mum would say,

"I am afraid you have come to the wrong house. No-one by that name lives here."

Jim didn't raise his head from his Lego.

"Basically this".

"Fancy going to Park Pool?"

"Now?"

"No, this afternoon."

"But it's disco swim on Saturday afternoons. I hate the disco swim".

Jim at ten was not cool. At twenty, he was cool because he didn't want to be, nor try to be, but at ten, Jim was square.

"Its not disco swim in the small pool though".

"Why would we want to go in the baby pool?"

"We're meeting someone there. Two people actually, one's little, the other can't swim."

"Who?"

"Rachel Cookson and her brother, Barry".

Jim's shoulders started to twitch, he then started giggling and eventually he broke out into sustained laughter. Hysterical laughter. He laughed so hard the sound eventually stopped and tears rolled down his cheeks.

"The Hunchback is having a date with Esmeralda in the baby pool! Only babies and toddlers go in that pool, you'll look ridiculous! You have to be a non-swimmer too! How are you going to get the rubber ring over your hunchback?! And Esmerelda's brother will be there too! What a date!"

"And you", I said, almost pleading, knowing anger would not help me, "I want you to come too."

Jim sort of grunted sarcastically.

"I'm not going! There's no way in the world I'm going on a date with you, Rachel Cookson and her little brother! Not a chance!"

James, despite being an intellectual, had an Achilles heel. He was a money grabber.

"Jim, I've got ten pounds in my money box. If you come with me, it's yours."

"Richie, you've got £12-38. If I come with you, you give me a tenner, you pay for the train and our tickets into Park Pool".

"Deal".

"Deal".

We shook hands and the weirdest foursome in the history of dating were now in place.

The afternoon soon came around. If Rachel, Barry, Jim and I were going to be, as I have just said, "The weirdest foursome in the history of dating" then the date itself could accurately be described as "The Worst Date In The History Of The Universe". Twenty five years on, Jim still reminds me of the infamous date with Rachel and Barry Cookson at Park Pool or in fact to be more accurate, he calls it,

"The Infamous Date That Wasn't With Barry and Rachel Cookson".

For boys, Jim and I had always been pretty sensible and Mum trusted us from about the age of eight to tell her where we were heading and then return back at a time she specified. We, therefore, were pretty much able to play at the park in Winifred Lane whenever we wanted (I did this a lot, Jim didn't, he'd be stuck at home gluing Airfix models) or head off to friends houses or go on bike rides or whatever we wanted to do. Obviously, there were some boundaries. One Saturday afternoon, Grandad was laid low with the flu and I announced that I'd be fine going to Goodison to watch Everton on my own. Mum didn't buy into that one, she took me, but spent the whole game saying stupid or irrelevant comments such as,

"The wind is playing havoc with my hair!"

"Did you say Everton are the blue team or the black and whites?"

"What do you mean we aren't supposed to cheer when the black and whites score, that man with the black perm scored a nice goal!"

She even put her hands over my ears when the Gwladys Street started chanting a song with an "f" word included. It was our one and only joint visit to Goodison! Nevertheless, when Jim and I told her we were off on the train to Ormskirk, this was fine. She even gave us the money for the return train fare (36p each) and entrance to the baths (35p each). Jim looked unimpressed with this, as he was looking forward to making a further dent on my financial reserves.

"You pay for the hot chocolates out the machine when we get out then", he said.

I was OK with that. They were 9p each, Mum had saved me £1-24.

From midday, I was impatient to leave and at one o'clock, I literally pushed Jim out the door. We were far too early, Town Green train station was only two minutes walk away, the train came five minutes later, the train journey was less than ten minutes and the walk from Ormskirk station to Park Pool was only five minutes too, so after a quick change into our trunks, we were in the pool by half-one. The "big" pool. The "little" pool, as Jim predicted, was full of young mothers and under twos. We agreed we would change pools at five to.

Jim started annoying me from the start. We went to the deep end and were doing various jumps and dives into the pool and Jim kept saying,

"No, Richie, you do it like this…" and would then do the crappest dive or biggest belly flop, get out and say,

"See!"

He thought he was ten years older than me rather than ten months younger.

My blood, at that stage, just bubbled occasionally under the surface. Jim was relentlessly antagonising though.

"Do you know why the little pool's so hot?" he asked, just after correcting my starjump.

"No idea. To keep the babies warm?"

"I doubt it. I reckon its something to do with boiling the water to disinfect the pool. Look at how many babies there are in there! Weeing away happily no doubt. In half an hour's time we will be swimming in a pool of piss…. and shit probably!"

I was already nervous. Now I was angry too. I was going to strangle him in a minute. He continued,

"I can't believe you have arranged a date in there!"

For a ten year old, Jim had an annoyingly smug manner. I knew he was jealous too. No girl with boobs would agree to go on a date with him. As we clung to the side of the deep end, we began to verbally joust.

"Shut up, Jim. At least I've got a date."

"When I get a date, I'll take her somewhere decent. Not the babypool!"

"Like where, Jim? Like our bedroom so she can help you glue bits on to an Airfix model?"

"At least there'd be no babies in our room, wetting themselves. Unless you were there! Does Rachel Cookson know you're a bedwetter?!"

In our teenage years, Jim learnt when it was time to back off. He would still light the fuse, but would make sure he was standing a thousand yards away by the time I exploded. At ten, he was standing right over the firework, peering down as it sizzled underneath, saying "Its not going off! Its not going off!"

I mentioned earlier that prior to important football matches I struggled to sleep. What I didn't mention was that, when I did get to sleep, I would sleep very heavily, so heavily that sometimes I wouldn't hear my bladder calling and I would wet the bed. As we shared a room, Jim knew this. Him mentioning this now, just before my first ever date, was below the belt.

"Shut it, Jim!"

He wouldn't listen.

"Maybe you need to give me another tenner or I'll tell Rachel Cookson why you have to go in the bottom bunk!"

This was the final straw. As soon as he finished the sentence, I let go of the side of the pool, bent my right arm straight back, clenched my fist and catapulted it straight into his smug little face. I caught him square on the nose.

"Owww!!" he yelped.

He was about to hold his nose, then thought better of it and lunged at me instead. He was a rubbish fighter and not the greatest swimmer either, so we sort of thrashed around manically, trying to stay afloat whilst wrestling and throwing in a few weak punches. Halfway through our synchronised brawl, Jim's nose started bleeding. We kept on wrestling though, oblivious to the fact that we looked like shark attack victims. A lot of kids around us got out to watch and eventually the DJ of the disco swim turned the music off. The first time we became aware that our water wrestling had become a spectator sport was when we heard the shrill sound of a whistle.

You two! OUT!"

We looked up and about fifty kids were watching us, as well as a very angry looking lifeguard.

"Out!"

We clambered out sheepishly and were then frogmarched out the pool with my left ear in the lifeguard's right hand and Jim's right ear in the lifeguard's left. The lifeguard took us to the changing rooms, gave us the biggest rollocking I have ever had, about safety in the water and told us that he had worked there for fifteen years and had yet to witness anything quite like this. He also said that if he ever clapped eyes on us in the next fifteen years, he would strap us to a rock and throw us to the bottom of the deep end. Needless to say, for the rest of our childhood, we didn't return. Twelve months later, Mum booked us in for swimming lessons and we paid Helen to phone up, pretend she was Mum and cancel them. Mum booked them and we cancelled them about four times before she told them they were "hopelessly inadequate" and booked us in Skem baths instead. Twenty years later, when I took my own kids swimming at Park Pool, the first thing I did before I got in the water, was check that lifeguard wasn't still there!

With my adrenalin pumping from the fight and the rollocking, my thoughts did not return to Rachel Cookson until we were turfed out the front entrance. Just as we hit the pavement, Ormskirk Parish Church bells tolled for two o'clock and Jim could not help himself saying,

"The Bells! The Bells!"

I administered a quick kick between Jim's legs but did not stay around long enough to see whether he shouted "The Balls! The Balls!", as I was running around Park Pool, into Coronation Park, to the glass window round the back, where you could see into the swimming baths. When I peered in, all I could see were a load of happy teenagers in the "big pool" and a lifeguard who was blowing his whistle more than a referee in a Merseyside derby. My date had finished before it had begun.

I went back round to the front, picked a tearful Jim up off the pavement and headed home.

Halfway to Ormskirk train station, we started scrapping again. Once again, it was Jim's fault. Nursing a sore nose and aching testicles, you would have thought he would think before he spoke, but he just kept opening that smug gob! I was walking to the station distraught, I knew I probably wouldn't ever get a chance for a date with Rachel Cookson again and for all I knew, maybe no girl would ever touch me with a bargepole if they thought I had deliberately stood Rachel up. I decided I would try to repair the damage at school on Monday with a grovelling apology, but just as I was deciding what to say, Jim still dabbing his nose with a tissue, piped up with a,

"I still want that tenner, Richie".

Jim's nose bled worse second time around!

Patience was not a virtue I possessed. I couldn't wait until Monday as Rachel would have had to spend forty eight hours trying to figure out what had happened to me, which just wasn't right. I woke up on Sunday morning, full of remorse, not for my three separate attacks on Jim, he deserved more than he got. He knew it too, because when we got home, Mum spotted that his nose was bloodied and he said he had been looking for his train ticket in his pocket and had walked into a lamppost! My remorse was for letting Rachel down.

The tenner I had refused to give Jim was now put to use (part of it, anyway). I took that crisp, brown and pink note out my moneybox and headed down to Mitchells Mace, the local convenience store and bought Rachel a box of orange Matchmakers. I then trudged the two miles to her house, in the pouring rain, only to find that she wasn't in. I had forgotten her family were churchgoers, so would no doubt be out until lunchtime. I managed to find a pencil in my jeans pocket, scribbled, "Sorry Rachel" on the Matchmakers box, left them in the porch and headed home. At least on the way home, the clouds parted and the sun came out, so I was able to dry off in the sunshine and started to feel good about myself again.

On the Monday at school, Rachel and I kept an embarrassed distance apart. I discovered from third party sources that Barry and Rachel had witnessed the concluding scenes of the ear grabbing incident from the safety of the little pool. Rachel had also arrived home from church on Sunday, to find a box of melted Matchmakers in their sunny porch! Apparently, she still thought I was "nice" but had decided I was probably "too immature" for her. No doubt she was right!

It took me another three years to arrange another date, again it was a group event, this time with Emilia Laudrup. Her father was Danish and the boys nicknamed her "Danish Dynamite", she was a real sweetheart, fair haired, blue eyed and had the boys wrapped around her little finger. It, therefore, appeared to be a major triumph when she agreed to go to the Astra cinema in Maghull with me to see "Mask". When I arrived at the bus stop to meet her though, she had invited half the girls in our class and Katie Robertson sat in between us during the film. The gap between Emilia and I turned out to be a blessing as I cried my eyes out when Rocky Dennis died at the end! We didn't date again, although I did phone her up a few times to ask, but it was in that uncomfortable phase when my voice was breaking, resulting in my tones varying between Olive Oil and Barry White, so I had lost my nerve well before popping the "date" question. I soon gave up on Emilia Laudrup and two further unsuccessful years followed. All in all, it can safely be said that before I reached sixteen, my lovelife was either non-existent or a complete disaster! I remember thinking on my sixteenth birthday, though, that the tide was turning. For some bizarre reason, the image of King Canute sitting on his throne, on the beach, as the incoming tide splashed around him, now springs to mind!

Jemma

3.25 p.m. The bell rang. The weekend had arrived! One thousand one hundred excited pupils made a dash for the exits and spilt out onto Mill Street and Ruff Lane. One thousand and ninety nine did anyway. The solitary other one trudged up the stairs in "A" block and once again knocked on CC's office door.

"Enter!"

Déjà vu.

CC's office was bleak. It had a very high ceiling and the windows were high up too, so you couldn't see anything when you looked out of them other than sky. I noticed it was raining.Apt.

CC sat me down, lectured me about irresponsible behaviour, told me it had no place in modern society and then gave me a line that she wanted me to write out five hundred times. It was, "Chewing The Cud Is An Activity Best Left to Cows In The Field."

I looked at her, confused.

"Miss, why do I have to write this, miss? I wasn't chewing gum!"

"No, you weren't, were you! That was Julie Loughlin, wasn't it?! That was lunchtime detention. You were carving your name on to a desk, weren't you?"

"Off, miss. Carving my name off, miss!"

Small point but it needed re-iterating.

"OK, Watkinson, you can write this…Acts of wanton vandalism are unacceptable at Ormskirk Grammar School and all methods should be used to prevent their escalation". CC said it slow enough for me to write it down, but she looked very proud of herself after she dictated it.

"How many times, miss?"

"I beg your pardon?"

She obviously misunderstood me. Perhaps she thought I was asking her how many times she'd had sex. I didn't need to ask that, the answer was obvious.

"How many times do I need to write that line, miss?"

"Five hundred."

"That's not fair, miss! "Chewing the cud is an activity best left to cows in the field" only has…(I counted them on my fingers)…thirteen words, miss…and they're short words. "Acts of wanton vandalism are unacceptable at Ormskirk Grammar School and all methods should be used to prevent their escalation has…(again I counted)…twenty words…and they're long words, most of them."

CC was not one for turning. No doubt Mrs. Thatcher was her hero. She gave a political answer.

"Miss Watkinson, punishments must fit the crime. Chewers get thirteen words, those who vandalise desks get twenty words. That seems fine to me, does it not seem fine to you?"

I should have shut up and just got on with it, but I couldn't help myself.

"I think chewers are worse, miss. You can get chewing gum all over your skirt when they stick it under the desk, miss. If someone carves something on the desk, miss, it can't ruin your skirt."

"Watkinson, do you think we live in a democracy?"

"Yes, miss."

"And in a democracy can people give their opinions without fear of repercussions?"

"Yes, miss."

"Well you're wrong, Watkinson! You only live in a democracy outside of school hours! Society may well be democratic, but this school is not! Pupils should not be spouting their views off to teachers in this school, they should just accept whatever punishment comes their way…. To prove to you that this isn't a democracy, you can now do six hundred lines. Only once you have completed this task, can you go home and I don't care if that means we are here until midnight!"

I kept my mouth shut after that. Half of me knew CC was right. I was a gobby little know-all who had got what was coming to her. I needed to knuckle down, do my lines, then get out of there.

It took me three hours, my hand ached, but by half past six, I was done.

"Finished miss!"

"All six hundred, Watkinson?"

I don't think she wanted to be left on her own. A spinster's life is, I would imagine, a lonely one.

"Yes, miss".

"Off you go then. Enjoy your party, but be careful, boys these days cannot be trusted".

Never a truer word spoken.

"Ok miss. Have a nice weekend, miss!"

Off I ran. Why I was exchanging pleasantries with CC, I have no idea. She had just given me the longest detention in history. As I was going down the stairs, I was half-expecting Roy Castle and Norris McWhirter to spring out on me and tell me I was a "Record Breaker"!

When I got to the exit by "B" block, it was absolutely pouring down. Amy lived in Calder Avenue, which was at least a mile from school, it was dark and I had no coat and no umbrella. I knew I was going to get soaked but I ran like Mary Decker (except I didn't fall over a barefooted South African), all the way to her house. I reckon it took me less than four minutes, I had visions of Roger Bannister, in his prime, trying but failing to keep up with me and shouting as he toiled behind me,

"Hey Jemma, slow down!"

Roger Bannister didn't have to carry a schoolbag either!

As I gasped for breath outside the Perkins house, Amy opened her front door.

"Quick, come in, you look like a drowned rat! Mum can you get some towels for Jemma, she's absolutely soaking!"

Ten minutes later, after a good rub down from Mrs Perkins, a cup of tea and a Chocolate digestive, I was ready to get myself dressed up for the party. Amy and Kelly had already sorted out my clothes and make-up earlier. Kelly had given Amy my pink leather mini with black leggings, my cropped white lace blouse and my white lace fingerless gloves. Amy crimped my hair and she must have put a bottle of mousse and a bottle of hairspray on it. I remember thinking that it looked "mega"!

"How come you're here so early? I was so shocked when I saw you running up the road! I wasn't expecting you until eight?!"

"CC gave me lines and said I could go as soon as they were done!"

"Well, I'm not complaining! I can tell Martin we can go a little bit earlier now! Do you want some Thunderbird?!"

"Be rude not to!"

So, Amy rolled out a bottle of blue Thunderbird from under her bed and the pair of us took turns to swig it out the bottle! Not very ladylike! By the time we told Martin we were ready to go, in drinking terms, we were already well on our way!!

Amy gave her Mum a hug goodbye and promised her she would be back by one. Mrs P even gave her the money for a taxi home. Vomit Breath would never have offered me money for a taxi and if I had dared to ask her, she would have given me a clip round the ear for insolence. Mrs P was great, Vomit Breath was a complete nightmare.

Martin took his "X" reg blue Ford Escort out the garage and Amy and I clambered in. We both got in the back. Amy wouldn't have been one of the prettier girls in our year, she was only tiny with red hair and freckles that gathered together in clusters below her eyes and over the top of her nose, but she looked really stunning, she had a navy blue floral dress on with a loose black tie and white and black striped trousers. Her outfit really suited her. Martin was a pretty fast driver and as he sped along the back lanes of Ormskirk, Amy and I squeezed each other's hands in drunken excitement. We were going to a party and it was going to be absolutely awesome!

We passed St Bede's school and took the second left at the roundabout at the bottom of Holborn Hill, by the fire station, into Asmall Lane. Ten minutes and we'd be there and the real fun would begin! It was still a wild old night, the wind blew, the rain continued to fall and Martin's wipers squealed out in exhaustion.

All of a sudden, I had a sense of unease. It's difficult to describe the feeling that came over me, but something, a sense of foreboding, made me look out of Amy's side of the car. A split second later, I was yelling out in a drunken, high-pitched scream that temporarily lifted Martin out of his seat,

"SSSTTOOOPPPP!!!"

Martin hadn't long passed his driving test so he was used to doing emergency stops but given the conditions, it was impressive how quickly we came to a standstill. I suppose his car had been trying to fool us that it was shifting along, but we were probably not doing more than thirty.

"What's the matter", Amy asked concerned, "have you forgotten something?"

I pointed. Within a second, the colour drained out of Amy's face. Our evening was about to take a dramatic shift in direction and we both knew it.

Richie

Five years after the date that wasn't at Park Pool swimming baths, my success rate with girls remained zero since the glory days of 1977!! This was more to do with lack of confidence than ugliness. Despite a daily battle with acne, which involved TCP, Clearasil, Acnidazil, dry skin cream, tablets from the GP and two carefully positioned fingers around any protruding yellow heads, I had matured into a tall, reasonable looking, blond haired teenager, with a gold stud earring (left ear only) and a flick in my hair that Tony Hadley and Simon Le Bon would have been proud of. The blond hair was thanks to my sister, Caroline – otherwise it would have been greasy brown hair. In 1986, my other sister, Helen, had done something none of the Billingham clan, to my father's knowledge, had ever done before. She had gone to University. Helen had always been mature beyond her years, she was a female version of Jim, without the smugness and had, therefore, not been dazzled by the bright lights of Southport and Liverpool, once she had hit alcohol consuming age. She would sometimes head out drinking with friends, but she liked the quiet, local pub, finish at eleven, environment of Ormskirk, rather than the busy, nightclub, finish at two with a kiss or a kebab, environment of Southport. To put it bluntly, Helen was very pleasant but a little unadventurous. A bookworm. The studious type. She passed nine "O" levels with "A"s and "B"s and then four "A" Levels with B's and C's. She was accepted at Lancaster University to read Economics.

Lancaster University was ideal for Helen, as it appeared to me to be pretty much Ormskirk on campus. A close knit community of people (in this case, students) without the bright lights of a major city.

In October 1986, as my mother sobbed heartily, we all squashed into the Sierra Estate, with Jim in the boot and took Helen up to Lancaster. On the way home, Caroline was brimming over with excitement, she had lost a sister, but for the first time in her life now had a bedroom that she could call her own.

Caroline and I were the closest siblings. Growing up, we hadn't been particularly close, but once she hit fifteen, Caroline developed a wild, independent, rebellious streak and I just thought she was fantastic! Much to Mum's dismay, she had each earpierced several times, wore more make-up than Boy George, had a steady flow of weird looking boyfriends and a record player that Spinal Tap would have been proud of as she played everything at volume eleven.

When Helen shared her room, Caroline would spend a lot of time out of the house, at friends or boyfriends, but once Helen went, the friends and boyfriends came to us. Dad was a little bit intimidated by Caroline, so he used to send Mum in to battle.

"Go and tell her to switch that bloody rubbish down, Dot!"

"Dot, that new boyfriend's been up in Cal's room for ages, go up will you and check he isn't giving us a grandchild!"

One of the things Caroline and I had in common, was an interest in music, or even a passion for music. Caroline had an eclectic taste, which meant some of the stuff she was into, was brilliant, but some of it was bloody awful! Amongst her particular favourites were Scorpions, Depeche Mode, The Smiths, INXS, Throwing Muses, Pink Floyd, Marillion, 10,000 Maniacs and Al Stewart ("only the early stuff"). I thought they were all great, but she also liked T'Pau, It Bites, Terence Trent D'Arby, Leonard Cohen and Tom Waits, all of whom I thought were absolutely terrible! To be fair, with Leonard Cohen and Tom Waits, I just didn't get them when I was fifteen and reluctantly had to admit to Caroline, later in life, that I had become a huge fan of both.

With Jim being a super nerd, I used to wander into Helen and Caroline's room pretty frequently just to get away from him and my bond with Caroline just strengthened from when I was fourteen onwards. Caroline was a mousey blonde like me, but had gone a lot fairer, which she initially explained was down to the summer weather (Dad had barred her from having her hair highlighted, saying it was a complete waste of money – the words pot, kettle, betting slips and black, spring to mind!). One day though, I was in her room with her, listening to Al Stewart's "Love Chronicles" (which Caroline told me was the first ever song to mention the "f" word!) when the true source of the colour change was revealed.

"How come your hair used to be the same colour as mine and now its really blonde?"

"The sun's been on it."

"Get lost…do you not think the sun would have reached mine too?! I haven't been wearing a bandana!"

"Yeh, but I've been squeezing lemon juice into mine!"

"No, you haven't!!"

"I have. Look next time I'm sunbathing, you'll see a raw lemon next to the sunbed!"

I started sniffing.

"What's that smell?" I asked.

"What smell?"

"Oh, I know! Bullshit! Heaps of it!"

I smiled at her.

"Come on, Cal, what's made it so blonde? Billy Idol's hair's darker!"

Caroline smiled back at me.

"Promise you won't tell?"

"Promise!"

"Cross your heart and hope to die?"
"Cross my heart and hope to die."
"Do it!"
I crossed my heart.
"THIS!!"

Caroline went to her wardrobe that was decorated in posters from Smash Hits and all the rest of her magazines and under a mountain of scrunched up clothes, she scooped out a red and white plastic bottle, which said "Sun In" on it.

"Every couple of weeks, when I wash my hair, I put this in it."

I looked at her puzzled. I washed my hair every day.

"Do you only wash your hair every two weeks? Do you donate grease to the Acropolis?" (the Acropolis was Ormskirk's finest fish and chip shop).

"No, dimwit, I wash my hair three times a week, but I only put "Sun In" in it every two weeks".

Now I understood.
"Right!"
"And that stuff makes you go that colour?"
"Its just gone a bit lighter every time I've used it. You should try it!"
"Me?!"
"Why not? You're the same colouring as me, you just said so. Next time you have a shower, come in here before you dry your hair and I'll put it in for you! You'll be a blondie like me, Richie! The girls will be chasing after you!"
"Why do they chase after you?!!"
"You know what I mean."
"Will Mum and Dad not wonder what's going on, if we both end up blonder than Debbie Harry?!"
"Who cares?!"

I thought about it. I didn't care. Mum wouldn't say anything anyway, she'd probably tell us we looked great. Dad would moan at us, but that's what Dad did. If we were blond haired, he would moan, if we were brown haired, he would moan, if our hair was black and had white horses painted into it, he would probably back us to win the 4.30 at Goodwood. Then, when we lost, he would moan at us!

I had an adrenalin surge, I was ready to explore my wild side!
"OK, I'll do it! Shall I have a shower now?"

"You might as well. You smell ready for one…B.O boy!"

"Sod off!"

I trotted off for a shower. After a quick soaking, I put on my dressing gown and headed to Helen and Caroline's room with wet hair and an appetite for my first taste of "Sun In". Blond hair could definitely make a difference with the girls.

Caroline went through the safety procedures like a Sun-In hair hostess.

"If you start putting this on yourself, don't put it on your pubes".

She wrapped a towel over my dressing gown.

"Why would I put it on my pubes? No-one will see them but me!"

"I tried it."

"You're mad!"

"I know. It turned them bright red!"

"You're a loony!"

"You haven't heard the best bit yet! Don't you dare tell anyone this, but after I did it, I shaved my bikini line into a heart shape, so I've got a big red heart down there now!"

I don't know why Caroline told me that. I wish she hadn't. I wasn't 100% sure what a female looked like naked. I had never seen a porn film and had only really seen pre-teenage girls with nothing on. When I was conjuring up an image of a naked woman, I didn't suddenly want to get a mental picture of my sister's red heart. At the time, it made me feel a bit nauseous, but I have to admit, a few years later when Nirvana released a song called "Heart Shaped Box", it made me erupt in a fit of giggles.

"Kurt Cobain's written a song for you, Cal!!" I joked.

I'm sure that song must have been about something dark and serious and intense, but even now when I hear it, despite everything, it brings a cheeky smile to my face!

Still, back in the moment, the Sun-In went in, the hairdryer went on, the brown hair went a shade lighter and a few months down the line I was as blond as Caroline, but never as red. Red was Liverpool, I couldn't have done that!

As the 1980's prepared itself for the 1990's, Caroline and I confided in each other about every romantic development in our life. This pretty much meant that Caroline confided in me about everyone she did anything with and I confided in her about everyone I would like to do something with.

When Caroline lost her virginity to Andrew Cullen, one summer evening in Coronation Park, ("to the tune of rats scurrying"!), I was the first person she told. I guess Andrew Cullen knew before me, but I was the first third party.

"How did it feel?" I asked intrigued.

"You know sometimes when you have a poo and it's a really big one and you wonder how you'll ever get it out? Well it was like that but the other way round."

Not exactly the description I was hoping for! If the porn industry ever wanted to sell the sexual concept to teenage boys, they would be well advised to steer clear of employing my sister.

"Does that mean it felt good or bad?"

"It was a relief. Nothing special, I guess it's like wine."

No-one but Caroline could describe your first sexual experience like poo and wine. She was talking rubbish. I didn't have a clue what she was on about.

"What ARE you on about?"

"Well, have you ever tasted wine?"

"Yes."

"Did you like it?"

"No, it was horrible."

"And what did Mum and Dad say when you said it was horrible?"

"They said it was an acquired taste."

"Exactly! I reckon sex is an acquired taste. Not great at first, but after a while you get used to it."

That made sense.

As I said, as time elapsed, Caroline had lots to tell me. I fantasised. She fulfilled. There were loads of other boyfriends. Caroline didn't sleep with them all, but she did sleep with a few and she added to her wine analogy, saying sex was also like wine because there were some fine wines that tasted great and others that stank! That made me feel as nauseous as her red heart. If the only sex you know about is your sister's, it is not good.

None of Caroline's boyfriends really lasted longer than a few weeks. She also once said (as you can see she was a girl for analogies),

"Lads are like pick and mix sweets to me. I just want to taste every one!"

In the summer before Caroline went into Upper Sixth, things changed. She started dating a lad called Nick Birch, who was to become a long-term boyfriend. Nick was a year older than Caroline, he was a Grammar school kid like ourselves, but had left after Sixth Form. Caroline ran into him again at the "Rock Night" at the Floral Hall in Southport and they both quickly fell "Head Over Heels" in love.

Nick had a mass of black, frizzy hair and always wore his denim jackets with his Metallica, AC/DC and Motorhead patches. He was heavily into motorbikes too and him and his older brother, Mike, were often seen and heard biking around Ormskirk. I have no idea how he managed to get his helmet over that mass of hair!

As well as Nick and Mike, there was also another brother, Joey, who was in my year at school. Joey wasn't one of my mates, but he was OK. At school, there were the trendies, the nerds, the in-betweeners and the D-Gas boys (D-Gas stood for "Don't Give A Shit"). I was an in-betweener, not really a nerd, not really a trendy, Joey was a D-Gas boy. He was into his bikes, like his brothers and just wanted to leave school as soon as he'd done his C.S.E.s. I often remember him sneaking through a broken panel at the back of a part of the school called Ashcroft and smoking in the garden there with the rest of the smokers. Rumour had it that he also smoked a bit of weed too. Our paths didn't cross too often, but I quite liked him and I'm sure he could tolerate me too, we just didn't have much in common. That was of course, until his brother and my sister started dating, but even then, we didn't speak much.

In March, nine months after Caroline and Nick started dating, his Mum and Dad buggered off on holiday somewhere for their "Silver Wedding" and stupidly, left their house in the "safe" hands of three mad biker boys, who were low on intelligence but high on pot. When Caroline told me the Birch boys were going to have a massive party one Friday, during their Mum and Dad's holiday, I wasn't the least bit surprised. I could just imagine about three hundred bikes and mopeds parked on the front lawn and three hundred crash helmets in the hallway.

For some reason, Caroline wanted me to go to Nick's party with her.

"No thanks, Cal. It won't be my scene at all."

"Come on Richie, it'll be a laugh".

"House parties are never a laugh. They normally involve gatecrashers, pissheads, fights and broken glass."

I was old before my time! Caroline sometimes called me "Dad" as I had a greater sense of maturity than our biological father and was forever warning her to be careful, particularly sexually, but I also warned her to be careful with drugs and when riding on the back of Nick's bike. Caroline loved danger whilst I steered away from it.

After some gentle persuasion though, I agreed to go to the Birch's party. Although I initially had reservations, the fact was, it was a party, there would be girls there and no "proper" adults. Realistically, I guessed it wasn't likely to be my scene but any opportunity whatsoever to meet a decent looking girl, was always one I wanted to grasp with both hands.

Rumour had spread like wildfire around Ormskirk Grammar School that the Birch's were having a party, it was the worst kept secret since Charles and Di's engagement or since Emma Marley in fourth year was pregnant the previous year (she was really skinny then it looked like someone kept blowing a balloon up in her stomach). Loads of people said in Fifth Form and Sixth Form that they were going to check out the Birch's party. In our year, only the nerds opted out, the "trendies", the "inbetweeners" and the D-Gas boys were all up for it, the latter were always going to go as it was Joey's party, but the "trendies" presence was going to have a positive effect on the quality of girls present.

The Birch's party was a massive turning point in my life. I don't believe in fate, I do believe that every decision we make in life impacts on the next and then the next and so on and so forth. My decision to go to that party definitely shaped the rest of my life. Little did I know the two greatest loves of my life (or only loves really) would be at that party and through the course of the evening, I would have an incredibly positive effect on one of them and an incredibly negative effect on the other!

Jemma

I was over the road in a flash. It was my second soaking of the evening, but once again, events took priority over vanity.

"What the hell is going on?"

The policeman was massive, there must have been seven feet dividing his shoes from the tip of his helmet. I wasn't talking to him though, I strode straight past him…

"Kelly, I said what the hell is going on?!"

My sister stood, head to head with the policeman or head to chest given the height differences, under a bus shelter on Asmall Lane. Kelly looked wet, flustered and annoyed. Predominantly annoyed. I was used to seeing Vomit Breath annoyed, Kelly was used to seeing me annoyed, but Kelly was placid. The policeman kicked off our three way conversation.

"This young lady is in serious trouble".

"What for?"

I don't even know why I asked that, the evidence for the prosecution was in her right hand.

"Underage drinking", replied the policeman, "it's an epidemic round here, it really is!"

Kelly continued to look like she wanted to knock the policeman's hat off, stuff it with Tiswas foam pies, then plant it forcefully back on his head and twist it.

"This is a joke!" Kelly ranted. "An absolute joke!"

"Not to me, young lady. Not to me!" replied the not so jolly blue giant.

As the sole member of the jury, I had already found her guilty. A smoking gun in the form of a can of cider was in her right hand. The irony of me standing there, between Kelly and "Dibble on stilts", judging her, when I was guilty of an identical crime, somehow escaped me.

"Kelly, you've got a can of cider in your hand! Who does that belong to then, the invisible man?"

I'm not quick witted when I'm sober, I couldn't really expect to be when I was half drunk.

"It was just on the floor! I do my bit to "Keep Britain Tidy" and end up in Bizzy bother!"

Had Kelly gone mental?! Using Scouse slang to describe a policeman was pretty normal in Ormskirk, but not in front of them! I was half expecting her to start oinking. Kelly was not endearing herself to Lou Ferringo in uniform and this set him off with a lecture that "Tut" would have been proud of.

"Young lady, spare me your phony stories. The fact of the matter is, you were drinking it as I drove past. It is my role to keep the streets of

Ormskirk free from crime and you were committing a crime, so if you would kindly like to step into my car, we can discuss this down at the station".

"Whoah there!! Hang on a minute!"

This was bad! This was very bad! A trip to the station would kill my party plans once and for all. I'd come too far for that.

"Listen, before you take her down to the station, can I just talk to her? Maybe if I could get her to apologise, would that make things better?"

I looked up at him hoping for sight of an ounce of human decency. I didn't see it.

"Would a murderer be let off with a murder if he said "sorry" or a rapist or a thief? Of course not! A crime is a crime. And who are you, by the way?"

"I'm her sister."

"And how old are you, Herr Sister?"

He was saying it as though I was German.

I lied. No point me joining Kelly in the cell.

"Nineteen".

"As a responsible adult then, should you not have been looking after this one?"

He was starting to annoy me now too.

"I spend my life looking after her."

"Perhaps you should start doing a better job".

"It's not my fault she's drunk!"

Kelly protested,

"Jemma! I AM NOT DRUNK! Even nipple head isn't saying I'm drunk! You're making this worse!"

"I am not!"

"Yes…YOU ARE!"

The policeman sighed. He turned his hand over so his palm was collecting rain, then used it to gesture at me and then at Kelly.

"Older sister. Younger sister. Both arguing. Both not wearing much. Both smelling of alcohol. Both probably under age…. In my eyes, not a good example! I have no choice in the matter, we all need to go to…"

I was ready to flip. I was all set to push him over and shout "RUN!", I could mentally picture Martin screeching up the road pursued by a gigantic copper waving his truncheon…then it happened…the god of disastrous sex must have looked down at me and decided he had his own plans for me, that it was time to intervene. The police car of our favourite law enforcer was parked up on the opposite side of the road to Martin's Escort, Ormskirk facing. Despite the rain, the window of the passenger side door was open and all of a sudden the control desk came calling. "Blue Ferringo" stopped mid-sentence, ran over to his car and stuck his head through the window. We couldn't hear a word that was said to him, but he muttered an extended version of "F in scum!" to himself, took a few steps back, then ran full pelt at his car, jumped through the open window like a stretched out version of a Duke of Hazzard, clambered over to the driver's side, switched his sirens on and sped off.

Kelly and I stood for a few seconds under that bus shelter in stunned silence before she spoke,

"I'm as innocent as the Birmingham Six!"

"Well you could have been introducing yourself to them, if that copper hadn't been called away! Come on, Kelly, get in the car! There's a group of disappointed lads in Halsall worrying that I may not be turning up!"

On the way to Halsall, Kelly would not shut up! Her adrenalin was obviously still pumping after her brush with the law and she recounted her whole tale to Martin and Amy from beginning to end. Vomit Breath was off out to the Kingsway in Southport, clubbing as usual, so Kelly had already known that she would have to make plans to avoid me babysitting. She had arranged to go to Kirsty Murray's, a friend from school, who lived near the Eureka pub, just off Asmall Lane. The arrangement had been for Kelly to stay for her tea, then at about ten o'clock when Vomit Breath would definitely be out, she was going to return home in a taxi. She knew I would be back before Vomit Breath and that VB would be too drunk to check on us when she came in, so no questions would be asked. Working in conjunction with Kelly, I had already told Vomit Breath that I was going to the cinema and that I had made arrangements to pick Kelly up on my way home. I trusted Kelly so had no concerns that she could not look after herself for a few hours.

Kelly's side of the plan did not run smoothly. After passing my clothes and make-up to Amy, she headed to Kirsty's and had her tea there as intended. She was all set to stay there until ten, but Kirsty's Mum had taken a call from her sister to say their Mum, Kirsty's Nan, had taken ill. Her Nan had angina and she was complaining of chest pains so they were all concerned her eighty five year old body might be calling time. Kelly said there was a lot of anxious scurrying around the house and although Kirsty's Mum said Kelly was welcome to accompany them up to Burscough, Kelly felt she would be surplus to requirements and lied convincingly that her own Nan would be more than happy to see her in Aughton. "Tut" didn't live in Aughton, she lived in West Kirby, thirty miles away, but obviously Kirsty's family didn't know that!

So, as Kirsty's family all sped off in their Vauxhall Astra GTE, Kelly decided to sit down at the bus shelter, fifty metres from Kirsty's house, collect her thoughts and decide where to go. It was too early to go home just in case Vomit Breath was still there having some pre-night out drinks with her mates, the "Halitosis Horrors", as we had christened her fat, ugly friends.

Kelly says that as she ran into the shelter to avoid the wind and rain, she knocked over a can of cider that had been left there by a drunken litter lout. She picked it up and gave it an inquisitive sniff, but as she was about to put it in the bin, the copper collared her. To be honest, as far as I was concerned this was the biggest cock and bull story since Foghorn Leghorn (the Looney Tunes Rooster) went to Spain to become a matador! There is no way in the world Kelly would have just been sniffing a cider can. She was probably drinking it in Kirsty's bedroom and then smuggled it out when she left. This was the least of my concerns though. I was more concerned with what to do with her now. Martin pulled up about a hundred metres from the Birch's house, windscreen wipers still working overtime, as we weighed up our options. A thirteen year old girl did not belong at a party held by three lads aged between sixteen and twenty one.

"Amy, do you think your Mum would mind if Kelly stopped at your house?"

"No, she'd be fine."

"Shall we send her back with Martin then?"

Kelly wasn't impressed. She was in the front and turned around and gave us daggers.

"Hey you two! Stop talking about me as if I'm an overnight bag! I don't want to go back to Amy's! Can I not just come to the party with you?"

Amy and I both replied in tandem,

"NO!"

Kelly was blossoming into a crafty bitch.

"Well you two will have to come back with me then."

"Why?"

"Martin's a bit creepy. I don't fancy the idea of a twenty minute car journey in the dark with him. No offence, Martin."

"Kelly, you can't say that!"

Neither Kelly or Martin appeared perturbed by her statement.

"I just have! Sorry Martin, I don't really know if you're creepy or not but you do look a bit creepy! Now if I go back to yours in the car, I'll probably find out you're very nice…but what if I don't? No-one will hear my screams on those lonely back roads!"

Again Amy and I, in tandem, exclaimed,

"Kelly!!"

I think we were both shocked she had the gall to come out with something like that but also, deep down, we were aware she had a point! Martin was a bit weird! He was probably just quiet but, hand on heart, I wouldn't like him to drive me home to Ormskirk from Halsall either. Like Amy, he was small and red headed, but he wore glasses, had severe acne and had one continuous eyebrow that stretched across his face like a foxes tail.

Amy whispered to me,

"What should we do?"

"How do you think it will look if she comes into the party with us?"

"Very uncool!" Amy stated

"What if we smuggle her in?" I suggested, but Amy was not pleased.

"Smuggle her in!! Are you joking? What in? A dustbin?! What are we going to do, get Ted Rogers to come with us and distract everyone with his 3-2-1 hand signs?"

"Don't be daft. She could just follow us in a couple of minutes after we go in."

"And what would she say? That she was just in the neighbourhood?! What the hell would she be doing in Halsall! Maybe she could say she just popped over to milk the cows and shear the sheep!"

Amy's tone was now full of sarcasm, irritation and annoyance.

"Amy, I have no idea. I am just trying to think what to do. Getting annoyed with me is not helping a single bit. I wasn't planning for us to bring Kelly"

We hadn't even reached the party and already it had been a weird night. Two of the kindest, most laid back people in the world were completely losing their cool. I hadn't seen Amy or Kelly lose control before and here they were, both losing it on the same night.

Amy sighed,

"Jemma, I know it's not your fault. I'm just annoyed we didn't think to take Kelly to my Mum's when we found her in Ormskirk rather than bring her all the way out here and then try to decide what to do with her."

Martin, normally a man who, if he said a few words, would have been described as having a talkative day, now decided to join the debate.

"Do you want to know what I think?"

Amy looked at him as if his bowels had just moved. I was more receptive, we were stuck in a hole and if Martin had a spade that was fine with me.

"Why not, Martin? Hit us with it!"

"Ultimately you have no choice. Kelly doesn't want to come back to ours with me, so you've got to take her in. Everyone there will be fifteen or older but that doesn't mean they will look fifteen or older. How old are you again, Kelly?"

"Thirteen. Fourteen next month."

Martin digested this, paused a moment, possibly because he had never spoken this much in his entire life, then continued.

"OK. Kelly's pretty much fourteen. There'll definitely be people there who are twelve months older who look younger. Have you two got any make-up with you?"

We checked our handbags. We knew what we had but we were double checking.

"Only a lipstick and a spot cover-up between us."

"Well, I'll drive up to the Birch's, drop one of you off at the door, go in and find one of your friends who has some make-up, borrow it, come out, put it on Kelly, then all three of you can go in and enjoy yourselves."

We thought for a second. Amy was only too pleased to rain on Martin's parade.

"Two problems, Einstein. One, most of the people in there go to the Grammar, so they'll know Kelly, so even if she had loads of make-up on, they'd know she was thirteen. Secondly, even if you do drop one of us outside the house, we still have to go up the drive and back again, look at the weather out there! It's pissing down! I'm not volunteering to get drenched and I bet Jemma won't either. Will you, Jemma?"

Wanting to and having to, are two different things.

"I'll go, if one of us is going to get soaked."

Martin was ready to deal with any objections that came his way.

"Amy, stop thinking about how uncool Kelly is going to make you look! If she was almost six, it would make you look daft, she's almost fourteen. She's just going to look like a rebel! You encouraging her to come with you is just going to make you look cool. As for the rain, there's a black brolly in the boot. I'll get it out."

On the basis there was a brolly, Amy volunteered to go into the house. She also admitted later that although Martin was a square, he was a smart one. He turned his engine back on and drove up the road to the Birch's path.

Armed with a brolly, Amy went in, said a few quick hellos then took some blusher, mascara, eyeliner and lipstick out of Sophie Leigh's handbag. The lipstick was nicer than ours and Sophie had left her handbag in the lounge whilst she was sucking the blood out of Dereck Baxter's neck, like a cider fuelled vampire, on Mr & Mrs Birch's king-sized bed. Dereck Baxter later claimed it wasn't the only place she sucked, but boys are liars so I didn't believe him. Anyway, Amy returned to the car laden with make-up and within fifteen minutes Kelly was looking like an English Debbie Gibson.

"OK girls!" I said as I puckered up to Martin's passenger side mirror to check out Sophie Leigh's lipstick, "let's go and show those boys what they're missing!"

Before quickly adding,

"Not you, Kelly! You keep your legs crossed and the only things I want to see you doing with your mouth involve talking and eating! If you as much as smile at a lad over sixteen, his dick will get the 'Fatal Attraction' bunny treatment."

After Kelly and I both gave an embarrassed Martin a peck on the cheek, we were off. I entered that house full of nervous anticipation and left eight hours later with a hangover, a carrot filled perm and a horror story about a misplaced virginity

Richie

It was pouring down. The bonnet of Caroline's Mini Metro was keeping my upper body from a soaking, but my lower body was as wet as "Walter & The Softies" from The Beano. We were on our front drive, Caroline all dolled up, banging her steering wheel in frustration and I was under the bonnet trying to fathom out what was wrong. I gave up.

"It's no good, Cal! I reckon it's a flat battery! Just give it another try now."

Caroline turned the key and the car gave out a mild wince, like it could barely be bothered trying.

"Shit Richie! It's half seven! We should be at the bloody party already!"

"Can't you ring them up and see if someone will give us a lift?"

"Ring the Birch's!! They'll all be pissed or stoned or both! Even if they weren't, would you get on the back of their motorbike from here to Halsall?"

"I'd rather have a three in a bed romp with Maggie Thatcher and the Queen Mum!"

"Exactly!"

Things weren't looking good. Mum and Dad had gone out with friends to see a play at Southport Little Theatre, that Mum's mate, Jacquie, was in. Only Jim was in the house and given he was only fifteen, he wasn't going to be driving us. Maybe we could get a taxi.

"How much money have you got, Cal?"

She checked her purse.

"37p".

"37p !!!!!!"

"I didn't think I'd need money! How much have you got?"

I checked my pockets.

"£2-56. We won't get to Halsall in a taxi with less than three quid. We'll barely get to Ormskirk!"

"Jim might have some money. He never spends any Grandad gives him!"

"Good thinking!"

We ran back into the house. As per usual, Jim was in our room, on his bed, reading some weird science fiction book. Jim was smaller than me, but stocky, bordering on tubby. The curse of acne had struck him too. Worse than me. The Elephant Man would not look in the mirror at our house and say,

"I am not an animal", he'd say,

"Still, at least I'm better looking than Jim!"

I think Jim's borderline tubbyness was due to boredom, in that he stuffed his face with crisps and chocolate ("Starbars" were his favourite and "Worcester Sauce" crisps) when he had nothing much else to do. He did have a very small, select band of friends. Two in total! They were

Warren Walker and Russell Jones. Both "rectangles" (ie. odd shaped squares). Jim rarely saw them out of school though, as all three of them seemed to retreat to the privacy of their own rooms out of school hours. They took boring existences to a new level.

"Jim, how much money have you got, mate?"

I never called Jim, mate, but if he had the potential to lend Caroline and I some money, he was my temporary mate now.

"Loads, thank you!"

"Can you lend us twenty quid then, please?"

"What for? Are you paying someone to take that crap out of your hair?"

Luckily for him, I needed the money. Otherwise, I'd have jumped on top of him on that bed and punched his lights out. Jim was stocky but still a crap fighter. He still threw punches like a girl throws a tennis ball.

Caroline joined in.

"We are going to a party, James. My car won't start. We need to get a taxi."

"Where's the party?"

"At Nick's in Halsall."

"It won't cost twenty quid to get a taxi to Halsall!"

Jim must have guessed this. As an anti-social animal, I am sure he had not been in a taxi in his life. Jim lecturing us on taxi fares was like the Pope lecturing us on sexual technique. I kept calm as I needed his money.

"No, you're right, Jim, it won't cost twenty quid but I want to buy a few beers and we'll have to get a taxi back too."

"OK then."

Jim started looking for his wallet. Something smelt vaginaery. Jim being decent and helpful was not normality. There must be a catch.

"I'll lend you twenty quid on one condition."

There was a catch!

"Which is?"

"I come too."

I wasn't impressed.

"What would you want to go to Nick Birch's party for?"

"It might be interesting."

"Warren and Russell won't be there."

I don't know why I said that! I'm sure at no stage during negotiations would Jim have ever thought that his two odd ball chums would be going to Nick Birch's party. I was just trying anything to put him off.

"I know that. I've just never been to a party other than children's birthday parties. I'd like to sample a wild party for myself".

Caroline, despite her own wild nature, thought it was necessary to be Jim's surrogate Mother.

"If you come, James. You're not drinking."

"I wouldn't want to drink. I'm fifteen. I act my age, I don't act younger by trying to act older."

This was a pop at me. Jim had perfected this art.

"And you may see things you've never seen before", I added. I meant like glue sniffing and pot smoking not breasts and naked women. If there were any of them about, I was confident Jim would not be sampling their wares.

"That would be a good thing!" James replied with a smile.

Damn!

"I'm not sure this would be a good idea, Jim".

Caroline pulled rank and made the decision.

"Ok, James. You can come. Be careful though. No pot. No beer. No smart arse comments and if there's any sign of trouble, get out of the way fast!"

"No problem."

My memories of Park Pool 1982 came flooding back.

"And Jim…"

"Yes, Richie."

"If you mention to anyone…anyone…that I wet my bed until I was ten, I swear I'll kill you.

Jemma

The Birch's house wasn't massive. It was a reasonable sized semi, but if everyone at school who said they were going to this party had turned up, in addition to Joey's older brothers mates, we'd have been like sardines in a tin (without the brine and the tomato ketchup). Everyone didn't turn up though. Whether it was the bad weather or parents banning them or kids talking the talk but not walking the walk, I don't know. It turned out there were only about fifty people there, probably about forty lads and ten girls, including Amy, Kelly and myself.

Going into that house felt like how I would imagine it would feel if you were a singer on "Top of The Pops", as you had to wade through a massive cloud of smoke, only difference being that the BBC had smoke machines whilst the Birch party had massive spliffs. Pot was fairly rife around our way, but the dealers must have made a tidy sum from the Birch's and their invited guests, as there was more weed there, than in the garden of a derelict stately home. I'm not kidding you, the fire brigade probably inhaled less smoke on a busy shift than Amy, Kelly and I inhaled in our first two minutes at Chez Birch. Everyone just seemed to be rolling up, smoking pot or giving the impression they had had too much already. Of the three of us, Kelly looked the least shocked as we surveyed the downstairs rooms for signs of sobriety. We didn't find it. The only sober people we came across, were those who arrived after us and the majority of them were stoned before you could say "wacky baccy"!

We found Joey Birch sat at the kitchen table, spliff in one hand, can of lager in the other. There were several other D-Gas lads gathered around the table with him, they were all singing along to Pink Floyd's "Wish You Were Here" or at least they were singing it, there was no music to accompany them. Joey looked the least ill, which wasn't saying much as he looked wrecked! He stood up uneasily, in an attempt to greet us. He looked like he had just twizzed round in circles twenty times at full pelt.

"Hello Amy! Hello Jemma!"

He was puzzled by Kelly, a think bubble came out of the top of his head which said, "I know you from somewhere but I am too wrecked to work out where!"

So he just mumbled,

"Hello thingermebobby!"

Joey then allowed himself an embarrassed giggle.

I explained.

"Joey, this is Kelly, my sister…Kelly, this is Joey. He's normally not quite so off his head!"

"Hi Joey!"

"Yes, I'm high! Very, very high! Can you tell?"

It wasn't hard to tell, his eyes were pink like someone had been using them as pallets to mix their red and white paint. His speech was slow and slurry. Amy looked concerned.

"Joey, sit back down! Take it easy!"

He was embarrassing! He tried to make two peace signs, one with each hand, but as he did it, he dropped his can of lager and his spliff onto the kitchen floor and then got down on all fours as he retrieved the spliff from the pool of lager. When he shakily stood back up, moving like Trevor Berbick at the end of his bout with Mike Tyson, Joey's jeans had two large, wet, circular patches around the knees. He berated himself jovially.

"Man, I'm gone!!!!!!"

I didn't tolerate potheads and pissheads well. Perhaps its because of a childhood spent having to deal with Vomit Breath and her alcoholic misadventures. I didn't have the appetite to make small talk with drunks and druggies. I hadn't written six hundred lines and helped Kelly escape arrest to giggle uncontrollably about pigeons. As Amy transformed into Florence Nightingale, collecting up abandoned half-full cans, pouring their contents down the sink then pouring a glass of water for Joey and dabbing his forehead with some damp kitchen roll, I slipped out the kitchen, pulling Kelly out with me. The lounge looked more inviting. There were more familiar faces in there, but these lot were Sixth Form "Groovy Gangers", the type who would smoke pot but not inhale and drink just a few cans rather than a D-Gas member who would drink until it returned as projectile vomit. Thus, the "Groovy Gangers" looked relatively sober in comparison with the D-Gas kitchen boys.

There were about a dozen people all told in the lounge, about seven or eight were sprawled out on the Birch's two settees and the rest sat cross legged on the floor with the exception of Eddie Garland, an Upper Sixth Form mate of Billy McGregor's who was stood up, centre of attention, finishing some crude joke about golf, prostitutes and business men on a trip to Japan.

"What do you mean, wrong hole??!!"

Half the lads laughed, the other's smiled and the two girls in there, Sally Park and Jane Makerfield from Lower Sixth, looked at each other like they didn't understand but would rather not ask for an explanation.

Eddie Garland was from Billy McGregor's card school gang. Equally cocky, equally good looking and to-night reeking of Kouros. His hair was petrol black and slicked back with Brylcreem like Bono's on the front of "The Joshua Tree" CD. To still look good with a hairstyle like that, said a lot. If everyone was an animal and their height was based on their levels of arrogance, Eddie Garland would be a giraffe.

"Wonderful to see you, ladies. John, Max, budge up on that sofa and let Jemma and her mate sit down."

I was concerned the vultures would swoop if the "Groovy Gangers" thought Kelly was my mate.

"She's not my mate, she's my little sister. You don't have to budge up, we're fine on the floor."

Kelly whispered, "Thanks a lot, Jem!"

We sat on the floor. My backside and particularly my thighs immediately felt wet. Eddie smirked.

"You'd have been better on the sofa! Everyone else on that floor has been like a cow protecting a dry patch! I've lost count of how many drinks have been spilt on there!"

"Thanks for telling us after we sat down, Eddie!"

Eddie ran his hand through his hair.

"Don't blame me! I told you to sit on the settee! If you want anyone to dry your arse, Jemma, let me know!"

I smiled at him sarcastically,

"I thought you only kissed Billy's arse, Eddie!"

There was a collective, "OOOOHHH!!!"

Eddie ignored my retaliatory attack.

"Right…who's got any good jokes to tell?"

Eddie Garland and his modesty-challenged mates then preceded to bore us senseless for the next three quarters of an hour with some appalling jokes. Amy briefly popped her head in, a couple of times, to pass me a glass of wine and Kelly a coke in a plastic beaker, so at least I could drown my sorrows as Eddie told countless tacky jokes about penises, periods and "puppies" (breasts). I felt like that 19th Century woman on the postcard being bored to tears by some bloke, with a caption saying, "Absinthe Makes The Heart Grow Fonder". A pint of absinthe at that stage would have gone down a treat!

Through boredom and the re-emergence of a slight light headache, I stood up, no longer caring if my backside was wet, my leather skirt had protected me to some degree and wandered into the study. Kelly said she was going back in the kitchen to see Amy, so I left her to her own devices, knowing she was in capable hands. In my mind, Joey Birch's house was like a life-sized version of a Cluedo board and I suppose, sub-consciously I was searching for someone, not a murderer though, just a good looking lad. I had been in the kitchen, then the lounge (is there a lounge in Cluedo? I'm not sure) so next stop was the study. From the shouts and laughs that were filtering down the stairs, there were evidently a fair few people upstairs, but I wanted to check all the downstairs rooms out first before venturing up there. So, I went through a third door downstairs into Joey's Dad's study.

The study was compact. It was crammed full of people, the majority of them standing. I had to wait for a couple of people to move out, before I could squeeze in to see for myself, what was going on in there. The room itself looked like it normally contained little more than a desk with a computer on, a chair, a few framed photos of the Birch children looking innocent, well before they were gripped by motorbikes and marijuana, and a drinks cabinet. After the karaoke Pink Floyd in the kitchen and the Bernard Manning gags in the lounge, it was surreal that the entertainment in the study was being provided by a game of chess. Sitting around the desk were four people I recognised, James, Richie and Caroline Billingham and Joey's brother, Nick Birch. Paul Murphy from Upper Sixth, an overweight boy with dark greasy hair and eczema, was stood next to the Birch's drink cabinet, mixing various drinks from the cabinet into a large glass.

"What's going on?" I asked Paul, who was trying to look like Brian Flanagan (Tom Cruise) in Cocktail but with his hefty frame and glasses, looked more like a younger version of Fred from Coronation Street.

"Its "Killer Chess", loser has to drink this!! James Billingham is beating everyone that takes him on! Nick's taking him on now but he's getting stuffed! He'll have to down this in one in a minute!"

He pointed at the glass which was a frothy mix of Pernod, Baileys, whisky, vodka and brandy. Paul Murphy seemed incredibly excited by something incredibly unexciting.

"What if he refuses to drink it?"

Paul Murphy looked at me as though I was the bastard child of Adolf Hitler.

"There is no…"What if?" He just has to…it's the rules! The reason everyone is staggering around here looking totally battered is because Jim Billingham is like one of those Russian or American Grandmasters!

Joey Birch fancied himself as a bit of a chess player but Jim has beaten him three times already! You should have seen Joey, he took his forfeits like a man! Stick around and in a couple of minutes you'll get the chance to see Nick following in his brother's footsteps!"

That explained a lot. It explained why Joey was smashed out of his skull and it explained why Caroline Billingham had a very concerned look on her face. Nick Birch and Caroline Billingham were boyfriend and girlfriend. Nick was one of Joey's two older brothers, along with Mike. I didn't really know Nick, but I knew Joey idolised him and Joey's motorbike obsession stemmed from Nick and Michael's interest in bikes. I knew Nick was a heavy metal fan and I remember a rumour went round school once that he masturbated in the smoking carriage of the Ormskirk-Liverpool train, when he was going to see Slayer at the Royal Court and he fired the sperm onto the ceiling, but I don't know if that was true. Probably not.

I thought Caroline Billingham was pretty cool. Given 99% of the girls in Sixth Form were so annoying, I'd have liked to have thrown them all into the Mersey in a massive rock filled sack, this was some achievement. The reason I liked her was that she didn't try to conform to any stereotypes, she just did as she pleased. Of all the girls I knew, if I could have been like anyone it would have been Caroline Billingham. Not too hip. Not too square. Not too swotty. Not a complete layabout.

I was aware that the older of her two brother's, Richie, was in our year at school. The year before Miss Caldicott inflicted Jane Eyre upon us, we had a great English teacher called Mrs. Illingworth. We read "Pride and Prejudice" which was pretty alright really, especially when you compare it with Jane Eyre. The male hero was Mr.Darcy. The reason I am telling you this, was because Richie Billingham reminded me of Mr. Darcy. He was a strong, silent type. His hair had gone really blond (probably dyed), he had a stud earring in one of his ears and was tall and muscular.

Richie wasn't a Billy McGregor or Eddie Garland type though, full of their own self-importance, he was pretty humble, modest and unassuming. Most of the girls in our year and Fourth Year, had a crush on him, but because he was so quiet, no-one really made a move on him as they didn't know what to say. I thought he was too young for me, but thought that if he got a bit of confidence and came out of his shell, then maybe in the future something might happen.

Richie's younger brother, James, however was ODD with a capital everything! He was sarcastic. He was greasy. He was a bit whiffy. He talked to everyone like they were intellectual inferiors. Odd, odd, odd, odd, odd. What he was doing at a party in the first place was anyone's guess, as he would have been more at home in his bedroom listening to depressing music like The Smiths and Spear of Destiny and drinking a cup of tea out of a pot with a self-knitted tea cosy. The fact that he was at the Birch's party was surreal (he would never have been there if Caroline hadn't been with Nick) but the fact that he was at the Birch's party playing chess with Nick Birch, a biker pothead, was even more bizarre.

I knew enough about chess to see Nick was in serious trouble. He was blacks and he had a King and two pawns left, James had a queen, a castle, two bishops, a knight and several pawns, one of which was about to be crowned and his King. Nick was just moving his king around the table buying time like a rabbit in a snakes cage.

"Who's up next?" I asked Paul.

"No-one, he's beaten everyone who can play and most of them are now too pissed and stoned to play again!"

Nothing ventured, nothing gained.

"I'll play him then!"

Paul looked at me like I had just announced I was third in line for the throne.

"Can you play?"

"Of course I can. That one with the cross on its head, is that the prawn?!"

"That's the King! The prawn!! Did you hear that, Caroline, Jemma called the King, the prawn! Do you not know anything?!!"

Caroline gave Paul a richly deserved condescending look.

"She's joking, Paul!"

Paul looked hurt. Idiot.

"No she wasn't! Were you?"

"What do you think?!"

It was meant to be a rhetorical question, but Paul answered anyway.

"I think you said it by accident!"

"Suit yourself. Maybe I did."

There must have been an unwritten law somewhere that said if you were a lad at Ormskirk Grammar School, when you went into Sixth Form, you had to do a large turd, your brain must then be removed and the turd must slot into the void where the brain once was. I reckon the teachers then probably did a test, whereby they sliced off the top of your head until there was a small hole at the top, dipped their fingers into the brain, took it out and smelt it and if it didn't smell of crap, you were sent to King George V College in Southport! This had to be the case as every single boy in Ormskirk Grammar School's Sixth Form had shit for brains!

I was just reflecting on this when James Billingham spoke.

"Checkmate!"

James grinned like a baby filling his nappy.

"Looks like you're up!" Paul said to me in a tone that indicated my drink was likely to be laced with his phlegm. He pushed his way into the hall.

"Oi! Everyone! Nick's turn to down his drink!"

Loads of people suddenly emerged out of nowhere like old people on a sunny day in Southport. They all started jostling for position, the glass was passed to Nick and someone, probably Paul, started a chorus of,

"Down in one! Down in one! Down in one!" to the tune of "Here we go!"

Nick Birch had obviously mastered this art as he tilted the glass vertically upside down and before you could say,

"Paul Murphy, complete tosser!" Nick had slammed his glass back on the desk with a smile.

He won't be smiling when he's spewing up, I thought to myself, then realised I was next and began to panic.

Paul announced me as though he was a boxing compere.

"Ladies and gentleman, make way for the next contestant, all the way from Ormskirk, Lancashire, please give a warm Halsall welcome to …..Jeeemmmmaaa

Wat - kin – son!"

Shit! Why have I volunteered for this, I asked myself, then I remembered where the drunken bravado had arisen from. In one of Vomit Breath's many past lives, she had been married to a geezer called Tony. Tony was a plasterer from Leighton Buzzard and he definitely was a geezer. He had moved up to Ormskirk after he was divorced from Tonya, his first wife and his mate, Charlie had suggested Tony should follow him up here for a fresh start. Charlie was a labourer and had had a brief affair with a redcoat from Pontins in Southport and had stayed up here, as there was plenty of building work going on in the nearby cities.

Tony came up, married Vomit Breath and quickly moved back South, a few years later, when he got to know the inner VB. Anyway, whilst Tony and Vomit Breath were married, his three kids, Tony Jnr, Vanessa and Marcus would come up to stay at our house for a few days in the summer holidays. The youngest, Marcus, was a couple of years older than me and he got through the pain and boredom of stopping up here by teaching me how to play chess. I was pretty good too, but that was several years ago and I had hardly played since. A heady mix of Thunderbirds and Piesporter had briefly persuaded me that I could beat James Billingham. As I sat down at the desk, reality was now telling me that I couldn't. At first, I couldn't even remember properly which of the knight and the bishop moved diagonally and which moved one step forward and two to the side, jumping over other pieces, then I remembered the knight looked like a horse and horses jump. It was lucky I did remember that as Paul Murphy would have had a field day if I'd have asked which piece moved where!

As I was getting mentally prepared, something from the depths of my subconscious memory banks came to me, the "four move mate"! No doubt there is a "Two Move Mate" and a "Three Move Mate", but I didn't remember them, at least I had managed to remember the four move mate though!

As the guest on the table, I was able to choose which colour to be, so I chose white. Not sure if there is a black four move mate, but I certainly didn't know it. Whites always start in chess. I was nervous. I was a one-trick pony and the one-trick was dependent on the other player making completely the right (or "wrong") moves. Luckily, James wasn't really concentrating, so sportingly fell into my trap.

First thing I did was move the pawn in front of my king forward two places. James mirrored my move and moved the pawn in front of his king forward too. Good news so far! I then moved my bishop out (diagonally I remembered!) to attack what my one time stepbrother called the "King Bishop Pawn". I don't know if that was the correct terminology or whether he just made that up. I remember saying to him,

"It's just a pawn! That's a king! That's a bishop! AND THAT is a pawn! If it was a kingbishop pawn, it would be a special looking pawn that looked like a king and a bishop…it doesn't, it just looks identical to its seven little friends!"

Marcus hated this! It really pissed him off. He was, like James, a misunderstood intellectual type who had no time for a sense of humour. Anyway, James then made some random bad move, I got my Queen out, James started saying something to Caroline and Richie, I could tell he wasn't concentrating as he made another random move without really looking, so I moved my Queen all the way forward diagonally, took the aforementioned

"KingBishopPawn" and announced in an unattractive yelp, "CHECKMATE!!!!!!!!!!!"

Thirty seconds and it was over. Fantastic! I stood up and did a celebratory bum, arms and breast wiggle. As sore losers go, James was good.

"Hang on! Hang on! That's not fair! I was talking!"

"Seems fair to me, James. You've lost! Fair and square. The King is Dead!! Long live the Queen!!"

Paul Murphy was temporarily stunned, he hadn't even mixed a new drink after Nick's defeat. He let out a,

"Bloody hell! I don't believe it! Jim's not only lost but lost to a girl! A girl!!"

James was still moaning,

"She must have cheated! Was anyone watching? Did she cheat?"

James looked round the audience. Silence. There were a few shaking heads. At the best of times, I am as cool as a freshly baked cucumber.

"Why must I have cheated? Four move mate. Oldest trick in the book. My stepbrother taught me that when I was seven!"

"You cheated! I know you cheated! Play again!"

"Not a chance!"

"Come on! Scared you'll lose?"

"I probably will lose, but that's not the point. The point is, you lost this time, so stop sulking like a baby and drink the forfeit!"

James muttered under his breath,

"Fucking bitch!"

Not a good move.

"I beg your pardon?"

Aware of his audience, James repeated himself, much louder second time around, "I said, FUCKING BITCH!".

At this point, I lost it! I dived across the desk, grabbed him by the scruff of the neck, then rose up, lifting him up off the floor, whilst all the time staring right into his eyes. We were so close the tips of our noses collided but this was no Eskimo kiss. I thought I could smell urine.

"Just because you forgot your mask, Phantom of the Opera boy, does not mean you can start calling me a bitch! You need to learn some manners and start taking defeat like a man. Apologise."

"Get lost!"

He was scared. I tightened my grip on his neck.

"Apologise".

Caroline felt the need to protect her little brother,

"Let go of him."

"As soon as he says, "Sorry!".

James just about managed to speak through the vice like grip I had on his throat,

"Not…saying…sorry."

I smiled at him. Hannibal Lecter would have been proud of that smile.

"Jimbo, if you want to go home without a broken jaw and a party straw to drink liquidised meals through for the next six weeks, I suggest you quickly say sorry and then down that drink."

Amongst the weak, self-preservation always beats pride.

"Sorry!"

I let go. James made pathetic choking and gulping sounds. Caroline still had more to say.

"Leave him alone now".

"He needs to drink the forfeit."

"Jemma! That's not on! He's fifteen years old!"

"So?"

"He can't be downing massive shots of alcohol at fifteen. It'll kill him!"

"Rubbish! I'm sixteen, if he'd have beaten me, do you think he would have saved me?"

"Probably."

"Don't lie, Caroline, you know he wouldn't."

James had his voice back.

"No, I wouldn't! But I wouldn't have cheated either!"

It was Caroline's turn to lose her cool.

"James will you just shut up and change the bloody record!"

The altercation had given Paul Murphy time to mix the forfeit. Once again, the crowds had gathered.

Paul spoke,

"Show her what you are made of James. Take the forfeit like a man!"

To the renewed chant of "Down In One!", James attempted to down the drink Paul Murphy had mixed. It was a smaller, less potent mix than the one for Nick Birch as I think Paul had taken heed of Caroline's words and did not want to be facing a manslaughter charge before the night was out. He need not have worried as its impact was greatly diminished by the fact that the majority of the drink ran off the sides of his mouth, down his spotty chin and onto his clothes. As he put the glass down, Caroline shook her head at me and said,

"You're tight". I thought a lot of her, but I was very aware the feeling was not mutual! Not that I was bothered, I was not intending on changing my spots for anyone. Brimming with confidence after my chess victory, I headed back into the lounge and my romantic positivity began to return when I noticed a new group of lads in there who were about nineteen or twenty. There were four of them altogether and thankfully amongst them were a couple of lookers. Catching my eye, one of the two strutted over like a featherless peacock.

He smiled,

"Alright?!"

I am now, I thought, I am now!!

Richie

Caroline gave me a dig in the ribs with her elbow. A chess room is like a library, you have to communicate in whispers,

"Cheer up! What's the matter with you?"

I gave her a look like she was Screaming Lord Sutch's crazier sister.

"What's the matter with me?! Do you really have to ask "what's the matter" with me?! We are at a party and there are about fifty lads to every girl, pretty much every single girl belongs in the "Gardens of Babylon" because she is so hanging and we are sat in Nick's bloody study watching our prat of a brother beating a load of imbeciles at chess! I don't even know how to play chess! Do you?"

"No!"

"Does Nick?"

"By the way James keeps taking all his pieces off the board, I seriously doubt it!"

"Look how many people are in here! It just shows how crap the party is when there's a big bloody crowd crammed into the study to watch a chess match."

As James was taking yet another one of Nick's pieces off the board, the study door opened and Jemma Watkinson slithered in through the crowd. Jemma was, without doubt, the prettiest girl in our school year. She was tall, model slim, dark haired, blue eyed and full lipped. She ticked all the right boxes apart from the crucial personality one.

I hissed at Caroline, "Bloody marvellous!"

"What now, Richie?"

"Jemma "Bloody" Watkinson. I hate her."

"Why?"

"There's nothing more annoying in life than a great looking girl with a crap personality."

"What's wrong with her?"

"Easier to tell you what's right with her, her looks, other than that nothing!"

A penny dropped on Caroline's brain,

"Is she the one that went out with Billy McGregor?"

"Yes!"

"You're right. She's horrible! She's a strutter."

"Pompous, obnoxious loudmouth."

Jim was becoming agitated,

"Can you two shut the fuck up with your whispering?! I'm trying to concentrate here!"

Caroline whispered again, this time directly into my ear,

"Shall we go somewhere else in the house then, after this game?"

I nodded, "Definitely!"

Caroline and I had sat for almost an hour and a half in that study, bored senseless. When we were agreeing terms and conditions of Jim's loan to us, in the taxi on the way to the Birch's, one of the conditions was that up to ten o'clock, Caroline and I would stick with Jim and he would decide what we would all do. After ten, the night was our own.

On arrival, Jim surveyed every room downstairs and discovered a chess board and pieces in the study. He set up the board. Nick came over.

"Are you any good, James?"

"Absolutely brilliant!"

"Great", Nick said, "we can make this into a drinking game. We'll get some drinks out my Dad's drinking cabinet and whoever wins the game of chess stays on the board and the loser has to down a mix of drinks."

Caroline wasn't happy,

"I've told James he isn't drinking!"

Jim was as cocky as ever,

"Chill out sister. I won't be losing!"

"I'll go and find Murphy," Nick said, "he can referee and mix the drinks".

Nick shot off excitedly in search of Paul Murphy, his friend who character and looks wise could be mistaken for Jim's older brother as he was ugly, intelligent and juvenile.

Within minutes the chess games began. An hour passed and without getting out of intellectual first gear, Jim had taken on and beaten all challengers. Nick's brother, Joey, who had apparently been smoking weed with the D-GAS boys in his bedroom all afternoon, turned up three times to mount a challenge and each game lasted a shorter amount of time as Jim brushed him aside. Six or seven others wandered in, took Jim on, lost, then wandered out with a bellyful of shots to send them on their way. A crowd had gathered, not to watch the chess, but to see the victims down the Paul Murphy mixed cocktails. For the first few games, I must admit, it was mildly amusing, but after that it became tedious.

Nick had now decided to have a game himself and was faring just as badly as all those that had come before him.

"As soon as you beat Nick, that's it, we're out of here and you can fend for yourself!"

Caroline whispered to Jim.

"It's not ten o'clock yet!" Jim replied as he took yet another one of Nick's pawns, leaving him with just two and his King. I didn't know much about chess but knew enough to know Nick was stuffed.

Paul Murphy was mouthing something to Jim and pointing at Jemma Watkinson.

"What's he saying?" I asked Jim.

"Jemma's up next."

"No, come on James," Caroline pleaded, "this is so boring. Can you not just finish off?"

"No!" insisted Jim, "you said ten o'clock! It's only half nine!"

Jim moved another piece and announced proudly,

"Checkmate!"

Nick, as a token gesture, tried to move his King in all directions, but he knew he had lost. He wasn't the least bit bothered, he just wanted a turn on Paul Murphy's specially mixed cocktail, but Paul had insisted he couldn't have one unless he played a game against Jim.

To the cheers of a mass of onlookers, Nick downed his drink in about three seconds flat, then headed out the room happily. I am sure he had better things to be doing at his own party than playing chess.

Jim was putting all the pieces back on the board in their starting positions as Jemma Watkinson was taking Nick's seat and being announced to the crowd by Paul "Prat" Murphy.

I can't properly describe how I felt about Jemma Watkinson at that point, as I didn't really know how I felt. I knew one part of me hated her. As I had said to Caroline, she was a "pompous, obnoxious loudmouth" who I am sure would face a five minute delay every time she passed her own reflection, but there was an intelligence about her and a sense of sadness that was almost tangible. Add into the mix that she was physically stunning with porcelain features and pale blue eyes that were somewhat hypnotic, all I knew for sure was that she made me feel uneasy.

Once, in school, when a group of us in Biology were talking about the previous nights, "Three Of A Kind", I had said that Lenny Henry had a look of Sidney Poitier. Jemma overheard.

"What?!" she mocked, "just because they are both black you think they look alike! Do you think Maryam D'Abo and Esther Rantzen look alike? For starters, they're both white! What about Bob Geldof and the Pope, do you think they both look alike? They're both Catholic?!"

This was one of the reasons I hated her. We didn't speak to each other, ever, but she could butt into one of my conversations and make me sound like a racist!

To be honest though, I also had reasons to like her. If I locked myself in the bathroom and wanted a mental image to bring my "teenage kicks" to a conclusion, Jemma Watkinson often appeared in my mind wearing only a navy blue set of bra and knickers, she sometimes even consented to slip on a pair of suspenders. It was complicated!

My comments to Caroline were pretty much spot on, I thought Jemma was stunning but her personality wasn't and I hated her creator for screwing things up. As Jim's new game with Jemma Watkinson kicked off (or whatever the start is called in chess, moved off, pieced off…whatever), Caroline was still nagging him.

"James," she whispered, "this is getting beyond a joke now! How much longer are we going to be stuck in this bloody study?!"

"Five minutes, that's all, five minutes, Jemma will be crap!"

Jemma may have been crap but she wasn't deaf, they were whispering too loudly, I'm sure she must have overheard.

Caroline persisted,

"Can you not let someone else take over?"

"NO!!!!!!"

Jim wasn't concentrating at all. As I say, I don't understand chess, but Jim wasn't watching the board, he was letting Caroline wind him up and he wasn't paying attention to what was happening to his pieces.

"CHECKMATE!!!" Jemma announced triumphantly!

I slid down in my chair! This could only mean one thing. Trouble! Jemma did a rather sexy little celebratory dance and I knew she should enjoy her moment in the sun because things would soon turn nasty. Jim was a terrible loser. He thought he was unbeatable and he had just lost in twenty seconds! Jim would not take that well! Sure enough, he kicked off! All hell broke loose. Jim accused Jemma of cheating over and over again. From previous experience of her at school, I did not expect

Jemma to placate matters and it didn't take her long to flip out too! At one point she even started to strangle Jim! I sat and watched thinking that if I was a sado-masochistic masturbator, Jemma Watkinson had just given me a moment to focus on for ever and a day! She was strangling my brother! Pity kinky stuff was not my style! Nevertheless, I was enjoying the fact that Jim was getting a taste of his own medicine, the cocky little tosser needed to reap what he sowed!

Jemma wanted Jim to down the forfeit drink and despite Caroline turning all motherly again and trying to protect him, he eventually succumbed to pressure and downed an almighty mix of cocktails in one awkward go. His jumper absorbed more than he drank.

"Thank God that's over!" I said to Caroline.

"It's near enough ten o'clock, Caroline, come on, let's get out of here!"

Caroline felt the need to give Jim a consoling hug and then disappeared off somewhere with Nick. I needed another drink, so headed straight to the kitchen. There were now about twenty people in the kitchen. Joey Birch looked in a sorry state, but he sat on a chair with an acoustic guitar on his lap, leading a chorus of "American Pie" followed by "Daydream Believer". All the D-GAS lads from our year were joining in with lager fuelled gusto. I stood and watched for a while as I drank my cold beer and spotted three others who weren't singing at the top of their lungs, Amy Perkins and Eddie Garland, who stood facing each other, deep in conversation and a younger girl who sat backwards on a kitchen chair, legs astride, in a Christine Keeler pose that would have had Lewis Morley reaching for his camera.

Time stood still. Joey and the D-GAS boys seemed to stop singing or at least I became oblivious to their droning sound. Amy and Eddie just stood and gazed. The fridge stopped opening and shutting, spliffs stopped burning and smoke stopped appearing from drunken mouths and nostrils. My complete focus was on the "younger girl". For the very first time in my life, a feeling grabbed hold of the entire length of my body and sent shockwaves and shivers up and down me, as though I was one massive pinball machine and a five hundred ball, multi-ball, had just begun. My heart didn't just do somersaults, it did triple somersaults that Nadia Comaneci would have been more than proud of. Call it fate, call it love, call it instinct but whatever it was, something drew me towards this girl. She was only petite, Jim later harshly described her as having "shrew like" features, but she radiated beauty. She had long, straight brown hair, amazingly green eyes and full lips that Jim would later in life call her "CSLs" (if you don't know what that stands for the last two words are sucking lips!) Her teeth were a dentist's wet dream and the thing that attracted me more than anything was her aura, which is so difficult to describe but the best I can manage is a sexual "Ready Brek" glow. I knew it was probably wrong to feel physically attracted to this girl who could not have been more than fourteen at the very most, but something within me wanted to love her and protect her.

I sat down next to her, not at all nervously, I felt like this was my destiny and a huge smile overtook my face like a joyous revolution.

"Hi!"

"Hello," a reciprocal smile came back.

The world started turning again, but as soppy and clichéd as this may sound, I knew my world would never be the same again.

"Enjoying yourself?!"

"I'm just people watching. Its very entertaining. I was sitting here with Amy but her attention has been caught by someone far better looking than me!"

Not true, I thought, no-one is better looking than you. No-one.

"Well, I'm glad Eddie Garland's grabbed her attention, it gives me the chance to sit down!"

Next to you, I meant, but luckily I stopped myself saying it.

"Well as long as you don't start singing along to Joey's music, I'll be happy to have you here!"

I smiled. Kelly blushed. There was a brief awkward silence. I broke it.

"How do you know Amy Perkins then?"

"She's my sister's best mate."

I was puzzled.

"Your sister's?"

"Jemma Watkinson. I'm her sister. Do you know her?"

Once again the words I thought and the words I said were a little different.

I thought, "Yes she helps me sleep at night."

I said, "Yes, she's in my year."

"I know she is! I knew you knew her really."

"Just teasing me?"

"A little! Sorry, I'm Kelly. Kelly Watkinson."

She extended her hand. It was soft and graceful. Holding it was a privilege.

"I'm Richie Billingham."

"I know who you are, Richie! I see you around at school all the time!"

"Kelly, if I'm being really honest, I really can't say the same. I'm sure I would have noticed you if I'd seen you around."

Mild flirtation, I thought. Test the waters!

Kelly swept her hand through her hair.

"You will have seen me, but just been oblivious to me. I'm in the third year."

My heart sank a little. I expected as much but confirmation was still a bitter disappointment. A two year age gap is nothing for two adults, but at this point it was a barrier. In my mind, if you were thirteen or fourteen, you were a child. If you were fifteen or sixteen, you were virtually an adult. I changed the subject from age.

"So how come Jemma and Amy brought you here?"

"Long story!"

"You might as well tell me. I'm not going anywhere!"

"I won't bore you with the whole story, but the shortened version is that Jemma caught me drinking cider at the bus stop in Asmall Lane."

Kelly stopped and giggled to herself.

"Actually no, that's not right, Jemma saw me getting grilled by a policeman after he caught me drinking cider at the bus stop on Asmall Lane!"

"Not as innocent as you look then?!"

"No! Not at all. My middle name's Risk!"

We smiled right at each other again. This was becoming a habit! This time though we shared a look too. A long look into each other's eyes.

"Mills & Boon", I thought to myself, "Mills & Boon!"

My romantic intentions towards Kelly were temporarily put to the back of my mind, however, when Nick Birch burst into the kitchen, sliding along the linoleum like Marty McFly in Back to the Future. He was looking for me.

"Richie, you need to get into the lounge!"

"Why?"

"It's your brother."

I sighed, "Bloody typical!" Anything involving me and girls, Jim had a tendency to ruin.

"What's he done now?"

"It's that girl who beat him at chess! There was a big argument, things turned nasty, she threw a punch…..you best get in there quick mate, I think he's dead!"

Jemma

I remember thinking, "Michael Birch, you are a lifesaver! You may look like one of Whitesnake and smell like 'Stig of the Dump', but you have some gorgeous friends!" Whether they were actually gorgeous or just appeared gorgeous as the alcohol kicked in, destroying brain cells and heightening libido, I can't really be sure. I just know that at that point, if girls had penises and boys vaginas, I could have picked my nose with mine.

I was one-on-one with the guy with the "Alright?" chat up line. What he lacked in opening gambits, he more than made up for in looks. If God had put a young Patrick Swayze and a young Richard Gere into a melting pot, to create teenage perfection, Matthew Coughlan would have been the finished article. God's masterpiece or the masterpiece of Mr Coughlan Senior's scrotum and Mrs Coughlan's ovary, depending on your religious perspective. To put it bluntly, he was mega fit!

I discovered Matthew was studying Chemical Engineering at Warwick University. Normally, swots were as big a turn off to me as a power cut on a winter's night, but if they looked like Matthew Coughlan, I was willing to discard the rule book! I feigned interest in his intellectual conversation but despite nodding and smiling, all my drunken mind was trying to formulate was how long it would take Sophie Leigh's lipstick (on my lips) and Matthew Coughlan's tongue to ignite with passion. The answer to that question, should have been, in all probability, six minutes, because, after five minutes, Matt (for his name had been shortened as we had grown closer), had taken my two hands in his, started stroking them gently and whispered in my ear,

"Do you fancy coming upstairs to find somewhere a little quieter?"

My brain answered, "Do babies crap in their nappies?!" but luckily this thought never reached my vocal chords and I just nodded and smiled sweetly as he led me by the hand to the stairs.

Teenage parties are weird things. When adults have parties, all the people tend to congregate in the lounge and kitchen, when teenagers have parties, the prudent couples gather outside for a snog, the adventurous couples find whatever room they can upstairs (bathrooms often being number one choice due to the inside lock), the confident singles mingle downstairs in the lounge and kitchen and the undesireables sit on the stairs! Not surprisingly, the Birch's stairs were full. Still holding hands, Matt and I plotted a route up the stairs, trying not to stand on the parties flotsam and jetsam.

It was pretty dark on the stairs so I smelt him coming before I saw him. In an instant, fear gripped me and my body turned goose pimply. There was a reason for this, the rancid smell of a mixture of ouzo, whiskey, brandy and vomit normally signalled the arrival of Vomit Breath. For once in my life, Vomit Breath would have been a better option. Staggering down the stairs was Billy McGregor. Why had I not detected his presence earlier? Mrs.Marple would not have been so stupid when presented with the evidence before her. For starters, Eddie Garland was there. Sidekick Eddie. Siamese twins had more alone time than Billy and Eddie. Eddie wouldn't fart without Billy striking a match. The only time they spent apart was when they circled around their female prey, like lions around bison. I have no idea where he'd been throughout the party, but based on reputation, location and smell, I am sure Mrs.Marple would have deduced it involved copious amounts of alcohol and perhaps (pre-vomit) a sexual encounter. As we encountered Billy, Matt was leading me by the hand up the stairs. Billy fixed me with a gaze that "Tut" had spent fifty years perfecting and then slurred out his thoughts.

"Good luck mate! You've got more chance of winning the pools than you have of getting into her knickers. I'd wear gloves, pal, they'll protect you from the icicles down there!"

Matt may have been blessed with the looks of Swayze and Gere, but he was not blessed with their Hollywood characters ability to fight to protect their lady's honour. He looked like he wanted his mother to appear at the top of the stairs armed with a brolly and a handbag to clobber Billy with and to tell him to leave her poor son alone. Weak men are a turn off. If we had ever reached the top of the stairs, Matthew Coughlan would not have reached first base let alone fourth. His grip on my hand tightened and he tried to pull us to safety as quickly as he could. Unfortunately for all concerned, Matt may avoid confrontation to protect his moisturised beauty but pacifism isn't a trait I have managed to learn. I may try and calm a situation down which involves my sister, Kelly and a trip to the police station, but when it involves Billy McGregor, bring it on! As Billy and I met on the same step, he looked at me with scorn and said.

"I hope you get AIDS!"

What a wanker! One minute he was implying my vagina was cold enough to store freshly opened bottles of champagne in and now he was hoping my promiscuity would get me a terminal illness. The insult took a couple of seconds to register and then I pulled away from Matt's grip, ignored his cry of,

"Hey! Where are you going?!" and followed Billy McGregor into the lounge. I am not one to worry about causing a scene. I followed the scent of vomit, caught him up in seconds and gave him rather a large shove in the back. This caught Billy unawares, which nearly resulted in him being spreadeagled across the drink sodden carpet but after a few corrective steps, he managed to maintain his equilibrium then turned to face me. In the clearer light, I could see his eyes were redder than a heavy flow tampon.

"You're a bitch, Jemma Watkinson!"

"You're a wanker, Billy McGregor!"

He smiled at me like Shane McGowan with teeth.

"Not at the moment, I'm not. Go and ask Faye Williams upstairs!"

No surprise to hear he'd been bonking.

"Is she the reason you threw up?!"

"No, I threw up after I finished screwing your sister and she reminded me she was only thirteen."

Now Matthew Coughlan may have failed to protect my honour but I was not going to make the same mistake when it came to Kelly. I knew it was a lie. I wasn't quite sure where Kelly was, but I knew for certain she would not be having sex with Billy McGregor. It sort of half crossed my mind that she must have been upstairs though, otherwise how would Billy have known she was here? I suppose all it would have taken was one person to mention her presence and for Billy to overhear, but maybe it was the wine that stopped me rationalising the information properly. I just took it in, digested it and then attacked, throwing an almighty punch that Mike Tyson would have been proud of. Mike Tyson would have been impressed with the power and the venom in that punch anyway, perhaps less impressed with its accuracy. It was a semi-circular swing that started behind my back, swooping around the front in a 180 degree motion, totally missing Billy but catching the nearest bystander square on the jaw. In a split second, my emotions went from shock to horror to amusement, when I realised it was James Billinghams face that had collided with my fist. Amusement only lasted for a few seconds though before it was replaced by panic, as I watched James Billingham's shocked torso crumple to the floor like a Thunderbird who's strings had been cut. I was pretty sure I'd killed him.

Richie

Kelly and I looked at each other. This time though, it was not flirtation, it was fear. Nick Birch was not one for elaborate hoaxes and if he thought Jim may be dead, I had no doubt something serious was going down. The irony of the fact that Kelly's sister may have killed him had not escaped me.

I stood up and legged it into the lounge, Nick and Kelly not far behind. Jim was poleaxed. He was laid out on the floor like a Russian leader at a state funeral. A few kids were kneeling down next to him, trying to wake him up and I even heard Sophie Leigh suggest we should ring for an ambulance. Jemma Watkinson stood over him, rubbing her right knuckles, she didn't look triumphant though, she looked pale. I bundled my way through the on-lookers and do-gooders.

"Let me get to him! He's my brother!"

The crowds dispersed like the sea for Moses.

"Jim! Jim! Wake up!"

Nothing. He was out of it. Where the hell was Caroline?

I shouted in panic, "CAROLINE! CAROLINE!"

I heard her shout back from the distance,

"Hold on, I'm coming!"

Caroline raced in looking flush. She surveyed the scene.

"Shit! What's happened?!"

Caroline kneeled down next to me.

"Bloody Jemma Watkinson punched him!"

"It was an accident." Jemma murmured from above.

Caroline slapped Jim's face gently.

"Come on now Jim, wake up!"

"Where have you been?" I questioned Caroline. It wasn't really a convenient time to begin the blame process, but I was doing it anyway.

"For a wee! Can you not wake him up?" Caroline asked.

"What does it look like?!" I replied before slapping Jim far harder than Caroline had.

"JIM!! JIM!! Wake up you dickhead!"

I turned to Caroline in panic.

"Does he need the kiss of life?"

I was desperate for help. Fear was overcoming me. How were we going to explain to Mum and Dad that we took Jim to the party, left him to fend for himself and he died. Luckily Caroline then had a "Eureka!" moment.

"Anyone got a mirror?"

Admittedly my first thought was what sort of crazy fool wanted to check out how she was looking whilst her brother lay on the floor dying.

"What?" I asked.

Nick was already on his way upstairs. He understood.

"A hand held mirror. Check he's breathing."

I held my hand out near his mouth, he didn't seem to be breathing. In a flash, Nick was back down, he stretched out the mirror to Caroline like it was a relay baton.

"Here Caroline. It's my Mum's."

Caroline took the circular mirror and placed it next to Jim's face. The do-gooders had already put him in the recovery position. After an anxious wait, which can only have been a second or two, Jim's breath created a mist patch on the mirror.

"He's breathing!" I squealed, "Thank God for that! He's still alive!"

I don't know whether I said this out of relief that a brother who annoyed the hell out of me, but deep down I loved, was still alive or that Caroline and I were now likely to escape the sort of bollicking the likes of which neither of us had ever witnessed. Jim sighed,

"Of course I am still alive! You don't die from a girl's punch to the jaw!"

Jim put his hands down and started pushing himself up. Caroline was unimpressed.

"Whoah James! Hang on! Take it easy. Just stay still for a minute."

Jim laughed quietly to himself, as he got to his feet,

"Cal, I'm fine. I just wanted to shit her up a little."

Jim gestured towards Jemma Watkinson.

"The stupid cow cheated at chess to beat me and then punched me in the face, I just thought it was payback time. Thought I'd scare her a bit!"

"You had us all scared, mate," Nick Birch piped up, "now are you sure you are OK?"

"I could do with some ice on this jaw."

Caroline and Nick went either side of Jim and helped him into the kitchen. Jim couldn't help having a dig at Jemma Watkinson as he passed her.

"If I was a lesser man, I would sue your tits off for this!"

I think he'd been watching too many American law shows! For the last fifteen years, Jim had driven me mad, personality wise we were poles apart and I had often resorted to overcoming my intellectual weakness by using physical force against him myself, but I felt genuinely sorry for him this time. He was trying to put a brave face on events, trying to spin it all in his favour, pretending it was all an act, but in reality he had been laid out by a punch from a girl and was no doubt hurting physically and emotionally. It's one thing being beaten up by your older brother but another entirely being beaten up by a girl, in front of an audience, at your first ever party, especially seeing as though it was the same girl that had humiliated him at chess only ten minutes earlier!

Jemma Watkinson was still stood there and I was all set to jump in with both feet and launch a volley of verbal abuse, then I noticed Kelly was at her side and this lessened my anger a little. Still, irrespective of who her sister was, I still felt duty bound to say something. I composed myself and then calmly walked over to the two of them,

"What happened?"

Kelly spoke on behalf of Jemma, who, to be fair, did look a little crestfallen.

"He," she pointed at Billy McGregor who was on his way into the kitchen, "said to our Jemma that he'd been having sex with me upstairs and that he'd thrown up when he remembered I'm not fourteen yet. Jemma lost it, tried to belt him, missed and caught your brother. It was a total accident, Richie."

Did I believe this? I'm not sure. If Jemma hadn't threatened to beat Jim up ten minutes earlier, it would have sounded more plausible. At the same time though, having spent all of five minutes with Kelly, if Billy McGregor had said to me that he had just slept with her, I would have wanted to knock his block off too. I thought Kelly was fascinating, beautiful, innocent, friendly, warm, honest…and

thirteen….why did she have to be thirteen? I mentioned earlier that I had felt an urge to protect her and if that had meant punching Billy McGregor, I would have done it without a moment's hesitation. I sought clarification from Jemma.

"Is this true?"

"Yes," she seemed distant, "can you just leave me alone for a while, I just need a bit of space?"

Jemma wandered off into the study. It was strange seeing someone as cocksure as Jemma being as humble as this. It was not a side of her character I had ever seen. I was delighted Jemma was like this though, as it gave me another opportunity to speak to Kelly again, just the two of us.

Kelly tried to go after Jemma but I took her hand and pulled her back.

"Let her go, Kelly! Give her the space she says she needs."

"I'm worried about her. She doesn't normally act like this."

I felt like saying "she's acting far nicer than she normally does!" but if Risk was Kelly's middle name, mine was probably Tact, so instead I responded with,

"She'll be fine. Just give her some space."

This no doubt came across as logical, caring advice but I wasn't being caring or sensitive at all, my motivation was purely selfish, I wanted Kelly to myself. Kelly was obviously a compassionate sister and had I been a compassionate brother, I would have gone into the kitchen at this point, to see how my brother was doing, but frankly Jim seemed

OK, so he was a long way down my list of priorities. I just wanted to be alone with Kelly.

"Do you fancy going for a walk?" I asked.

This plan had two motives. One was that it would prevent further distractions and secondly it gave me an opportunity to gauge Kelly's interest in me. It was a blatant move. I knew it was a move, Kelly, although only thirteen, was pretty intelligent and I am sure she knew it was a move too. If she was interested, she would say, "Yes", if not she would make an excuse.

Kelly smiled again and stared right into my eyes. A return to flirtation, I thought. A good sign! I hoped so anyway, suddenly I felt nervous. How ridiculous, a man of almost sixteen worrying about the reaction of a thirteen year old girl!

"OK! Let me go and tell Jemma we're heading out!"

It didn't seem like an excuse or a delaying tactic, after all she said it in an excited tone. I was pretty sure she was being genuine, but I was no expert. If I was a girl and I wanted to fend a lad off, I would make my delaying tactic sound pretty genuine too. Kelly headed into the study.

I twiddled my thumbs and watched the world go by. At one stage, Amy Perkins and Eddie Garland went past, Amy leading Eddie up the stairs. Continuing to have a sense of nervousness and a knot in my gut, I did a bit of minesweeping of half drunk beer bottles abandoned in the hallway. As a minute turned into two and then into five, I concluded a romantic walk was not going to happen. I was even tempted to follow Kelly into the study and ask her what the hell was keeping her, but once again my newly christened middle name got the better of me. Making a scene did not appear to be a good long-term move. I felt like I wanted Kelly to be around for a long time, not just someone I could French kiss and window clean her backside. If I started trying to call the shots, it may put her off me and I didn't want that. Why did she have to go and check on her sister anyway? I thought her middle name was Risk?! After what must have only been about five minutes, but seemed a lot longer, especially because I had guzzled four or five half-bottles of lager in that period and was now needing a wee, Kelly emerged looking both concerned and frustrated. I had already convinced myself that our walk would not be happening, but Kelly's look was the rubber stamp.

"I'm so sorry, Richie, I'm going to have to stay here and keep an eye on Jemma. She was already pretty drunk before we got here and she's in even more of a state now. She apparently just poured herself a massive mix of drinks from the cabinet and necked the whole lot in one, when that kicks in, she'll be in serious trouble! She's slumped down in there like a boxer who has had one fight too many, come and look".

Given the way Jemma threw her punches the boxing analogy was somewhat appropriate. Kelly grabbed me by the hand and steered me into the study. I'm so glad she did because if I hadn't seen Jemma for myself, I'd have just presumed she was making polite excuses. When I went in there, however, Jemma was sat down with her back propped up against the wall, looking like someone who had just been given several thousand volts of electricity from a cattle prodder. If that was Caroline, I must admit, I would not have left her either. Jim maybe, Caroline, definitely not.

"Sorry, Richie!" Kelly repeated.

"Forget it, Kelly. Its not your fault." I re-assured her.

"Can we do something another time?" she asked.

What was she doing now? Brushing me off or asking me out?

"I can stay with you now, Kelly, it's OK. You may need someone to grab the other side of Jemma if she's going to spew."

"Richie, I don't want you to stay. Jemma will be OK, I just need to keep an eye on her, you don't. Go and enjoy the party."

I wanted to tell her it was a crap party until the moment I saw her. I wanted to tell her I wouldn't enjoy the party one bit without her, but I didn't. I needed to be cooler than that and I wanted to retain some pride. I clung on instead to her penultimate statement.

"Are you serious about doing something another time?"

"Of course, I am!"

"Like a date?"

"Not like a date, Richie. A DATE!"

"And your parents would not have a problem with you going out with someone my age?"

"How old are you, Richie?"

"Fifteen, sixteen in August."

"Well, I'm fourteen next month. We aren't exactly Mandy Smith and Bill Wyman are we?!"

Kelly had a point.

"I know that! I know you haven't got an issue with it, but what about your Mum and Dad? Your Dad may think Fifth form lads are only after one thing!"

"I haven't got a Dad."

Great! My shoulders sagged. Trust me to put my size elevens right in it.

"Sorry. Did he die?"

"No idea. I have never met him. He's probably better off."

That struck me as a weird thing to say. If I had a daughter as beautiful as Kelly, I would stride down the street with my head held high. How could anyone be better off without her? This time I couldn't stop myself blurting something out.

"You're wrong, Kelly. He definitely isn't better off without you!"

I was immediately embarrassed I'd said it. It was cheesy and uncool.

Kelly smiled at me, not a flirtatious smile this time, a re-assuring, don't you be worrying type smile.

"Come to mine next Saturday, at six o'clock. We can go to the cinema but I'll introduce you to my mother. Then you'll understand!"

"OK", I replied, "whereabouts do you live?"

"Wigan Road. At the bottom end, one house up from the Ropers, near the hospital."

"I'll be there."

Maybe I'll get the chance to kiss you then, I thought, those lips look like they really need kissing. I was starting to feel more than a little drunk.

Out of the blue, Kelly reached up and kissed me on the cheek.

"I shall look forward to it, Richie! It's been lovely speaking to you tonight, now go off and enjoy the party! I'll see you around at school and see you properly at six o'clock next Saturday!"

"OK. See you Saturday!"

I blushed, smiled and then shot up the stairs. I needed to join the queue for the toilet as quickly as I could as my bladder was fit to burst. I stood in the queue which was about ten deep and cursed that it was mainly girls in front, which was a pain as they took much longer. I needed to take my mind off how close I was to peeing my pants so found an obvious solution by reflecting on my introduction to Kelly Watkinson. She was only thirteen years old but was far more mature than some of the girls in my year and miles ahead of most of the lads. She seemed calm and sensible, the middle name of Risk didn't seem to suit her at all. Some of my mates would probably take the mickey about me "going out" with a girl in third year, but I knew it would be worth taking any stick to spend time with Kelly. I already felt there was a strong chance we would stay together for the rest of our lives. Maybe that was the drink talking but I didn't think so. My future seemed, for the first time, to have some clarity and that future was with Kelly. The only problem was, I thought, if I ever married Kelly, I would have bloody Jemma Watkinson as a sister-in-law.

"What a nightmare!!" I said to myself out loud. No doubt the rest of the queue thought I was passing comment on the time it was taking to have a wee.

"I think she must either be throwing up or having a crap!" responded the girl in front of me.

If I married Kelly though, I suppose I would just have to handle Jemma. Every silver lining has a cloud! Ten further minutes passed with more thoughts about Kelly and then it was my turn. I ran in, ignoring the smell and whopped out my semi-erect willy and sprayed as much wee as I could manage into the toilet bowl. I struggled but I was certainly not the first of the evening to consistently miss the bullseye. As I was missing, I remember thinking that girls just don't understand how boys manage to miss such an easy target, but they should try putting their finger over a garden hose when it is full on and then try to spray the whole lot into a bucket. It's bloody hard!

After a very fulfilling wee, I headed back downstairs, avoiding the temptation to return to the study. I was sure Kelly thought I was pretty cool and I did not want to soil this impression. I headed to the kitchen and on reflection, this was the point that a near perfect evening began to head into a totally different direction.

I had headed to the kitchen to check on Jim and Caroline. Jim had a big plastic bag of ice placed under his chin and Caroline had become so concerned about Jim's jaw that she had ordered a taxi and was debating whether to go straight home or to casualty.

"Do we all have to go, Cal? It's not half past ten yet!"

I was showing my true colours. If there was a colour called selfish bastard, it would have fitted me well!

Jim was evidently annoyed that I was not being more sympathetic. If his eyes were daggers, I'd have been nursing two stab wounds to the heart.

"Look, Richie, you can stay if you want but I'm in bloody agony here. I need to go home and don't forget, I'm the one with the money".

Jim explained this in his typically diplomatic way. Basically he was saying come with us or walk six miles home along unlit country roads with no pavements. I didn't appear to have a huge amount of choice.

"You don't have to go, Richie!" said a now hugely inebriated Joey Birch, as he put his arm around me,

"You can stay here! Kip down on the floor with a few of the D-GAS boys! Come on man! It'll be a laugh!"

If I was any sort of brother, I'd have left in that taxi with Jim and Caroline. Caroline was a good sister, she left her boyfriend behind to show solidarity with a wounded sibling. A wounded sibling who later that night, after three hours in Casualty, was diagnosed as having a fractured jaw. I was a crap brother, accepted Joey's invitation, cracked open another beer and didn't have a moment's regret until six hours later when I was watching my vomit run down the insides of the taxi window, hoping beyond hope that no-one had witnessed my final party trick.

Jemma

I needed some space. Once James Billingham was floored by my knockout punch, everyone congregated in the lounge to get a view on the transpiring events and it felt awful. My knuckles ached and more disturbingly, hate was in the air. I could feel a sense of hatred being directed at me. I was used to people not liking me, but generally it was for reasons I could handle, I was too smart for them, I was too pretty for them or I had a boyfriend they wanted. A dislike based on jealousy was something I thrived on. This was different though. When James Billingham was flat out on the floor in the Birch's lounge, the impression I had, was not that I was hated because of looks, intelligence or having a boyfriend they wanted, I was now hated because I was horrible. My worst fears were starting to be realised, I was turning into Vomit Breath! Vomit Breath was the type of woman who would throw her fists around, in fact, she had a history of committing that very same crime. If a woman looked at her the wrong way, she would punch her. If a man spurned her advances, she would punch him ("for being gay") and if boyfriends did not comply with her every demand, she would punch them. I remember one poor guy called Duncan, a carpet fitter from Maghull, was picked up at the Kingsway and rolled back to ours and then at four in the morning all hell broke loose, as you could hear Vomit Breath release a series of punches into his face. His crime, breaking wind accidentally during the sexual act. Vomit Breath was that type of woman, pure evil and I was not wanting to become a carbon copy.

Once James came around, Kelly and Richie Billingham gathered around me like detectives at a murder scene, wanting to know what had happened and why. Kelly, ever the doting sister, was defending me and putting it down to being a bit of an accident, but that was missing the point. The point being, I threw a punch and although it had not connected with my intended victim, there was still a victim. I was not proud of my behaviour, I was appalled by it. The year before, one typical Friday night when Vomit Breath had disappeared on one of her weekend pub crawls, Kelly and I had watched a brilliant film on video called "Dangerous Liaisons". Glenn Close played the Marquise de Merteuil and at the very start, she is seen admiring her own beauty in the mirror, knowing how this beauty is envied. At the very end, she is looking at herself again in the very same mirror, but this time as a broken, ugly and despised woman. I felt like I had been through the same transition, from someone people envied to someone people despised.

I needed to get out of the Birch's lounge and like my mother's daughter, the only friend I wanted was in a bottle. I headed to the study, which was now empty and poured myself the biggest combination of shots I could fit into a glass. The sense of loathing had numbed my senses, within a minute my glass was empty. I knew this would mean trouble was around the corner, but for now I just wanted something to numb the pain. As expected, my senses were soon attacked by this alcoholic juggernaut. I felt like I was on a waltzer that was being relentlessly spun by a teenage gypsy boy. My eyes could not keep pace and my legs ached. I slowly and deliberately sat on the floor, making sure I propped my back up against the wall to prevent me from slumping into a heap. If I curled up into a foetal position, I had mental images of everyone coming in from the lounge to take turns to kick me like a football. I felt the world's all time most hated figures were Adolf Hitler, Charles Manson, Peter Sutcliffe, Joseph Stalin, Pol Pot and me.

My saviour then arrived. I could barely see her because my eyes were now moving like a washing machine's fast spin cycle, but I heard Kelly's comforting voice.

"Jemma, Jemma, are you OK?"

"Everyone hates me, Kelly".

"No-one hates you, honey!"

"They do! Billy McGregor hates me! James Billingham hates me! Amy hates me!"

"Amy doesn't hate you!"

"She must do! I haven't seen her all night!"

"Jemma, Amy's been with Eddie Garland all night! She's not avoiding you, she's attaching herself to him!"

"Tell her not to! Go and find her, Kelly, and warn her to keep away from him! He's a pretty boy! An arrogant pretty boy! I don't like him. Go and tell her I don't like him!"

"Jemma, I can't do that!"

"Yes, you can!"

"I can't! For all you know, Amy may have hated Billy McGregor, but she wouldn't say that to you because she's your best friend!"

"It's because she's my best friend that I need to tell her to keep away from Eddie Garland!"

I persisted, I'm not sure for how long but eventually Kelly relented and said she would go and tell Amy for me. I was relieved. I had been an idiot falling for Billy McGregor, I didn't want Amy to be equally stupid by falling for his sidekick.

Kelly soon returned. My spin cycle was now on that speed at the end of the cycle where everything whizzes around at several hundred revs a minute.

"Bloody hell Jemma! You look awful!"

"Thanks Kel! What did she say?"

"Who?"

I couldn't see her properly, but Kelly sounded confused.

"Amy!"

"Oh! She said thanks for the advice!"

Kelly was a terrible liar.

"You didn't tell her, did you?"

"No!"

"Did you even see her?"

"No! She's busy!"

"What have you been doing then?"
"Talking to Richie Billingham."
"About me?"
"No, about me actually. He's taking me out."
"Out where?"
"On a date."
"Oh!"
"Did you not see the pair of us staring at you a minute ago like you were a zoo animal?"
"No!"
"Why does that not surprise me?"
"Hang on", I said, "did you say you were going on a date with Richie?"
"Yes. Next Saturday!"

Kelly was too young to be going on dates, especially with lads my age, but I was drunk and she felt like the only friend I had in the world at that moment, so I concluded I would have to postpone my lecture for now.

"Kelly, do you think there's somewhere I can go to lie down?"
"Jemma, if you are feeling as bad as you look, do you not think we should just get a taxi home? I'll go and find Amy and tell her we need to go."
"No, no, not a taxi! If I went on those back roads to Ormskirk now, I'd be sick."
"Let's go outside then. The fresh air will do you good."
"OK. If I can get outside."

I stood up. I tried to keep my eyes focused on my feet so I could manage one step in front of the other. Kelly lead the way, opening the front door and then steering me to the end of the path, past a few necking couples and then on to a sheltered bus stop. It had now become a pleasant night with a breeze that eased my alcohol induced illness slightly. There was a wooden bench that ran around the perimeter of the shelter. Kelly sat down.

"What is it about us and bus shelters tonight?!" she asked rhetorically.

I attempted to park my backside on that bench too, but as I slid drunkenly down, I missed the bench completely and my bum hit the concrete slabs below.

"Ow!"

"Jemma!" she laughed a little, "are you OK, honey?"

She picked me up and positioned me carefully on the bench.

"How weird is this?! I'm used to looking after Mum when she's off her face, but not you!"

"I'm so sorry, Kelly! I should be looking after you!"

"Jemma, I'm fine, I don't need looking after."

I was drunk, I couldn't help saying what I thought.

"You might do soon though."

"Why?"

"If you start dating Richie Billingham."

"What's wrong with Richie Billingham?"

"I don't know what's wrong with him. I don't really know him. I just know he's sixteen and sixteen year old lads are only after one thing."

Kelly sort of half laughed, half snorted.

"Are you my Dad?"

"What?!"

"Doesn't matter. Just something Richie said earlier. Anyway, he's not sixteen, he's fifteen and next month I'm fourteen."

"Just be careful."

"Jemma, now is not a good time for you to be giving me advice! You look like a beardless Oliver Reed! How can I take advice off you when you can't even plant your bum on a seat in a bus stop properly?!"

"I won't mention it again. Just remember I told you to be careful."

We were silent for a while. Kelly was probably lost in thought, she was the deep thinker and I was quiet because I was now so drunk, I could not manage to string a word, let alone a sentence, together. The fresh air must have done some good though because after a period of quiet contemplation, I managed to say.

"Take me back to the Birch's now, Kel. I really do need to lie down."

That conversation was the last thing I remembered for an indeterminate period of time!

I don't remember walking back to the Birch's, I don't remember going in, I don't remember Kelly sorting out somewhere for me to sleep, it is all a complete blank! The first thing I remember was being in a lovely, comfy bed, a double bed, in total darkness and then the door opening slightly, light and noise flooded in, followed by a male figure, I couldn't see who, creeping in, closing the door behind them and then sitting on the edge of the bed.

"How are you feeling?"

I recognised the voice but the world was still spinning, albeit at a slower speed than before, so my brain failed to put a face to it.

"A bit better, I think. How are you?"

I was doing my Miss Marple bit, trying to get clues.

"Pretty pissed!"

Great! That ruled no-one out.

"Do you mind if I lay down on the bed too? To be honest, Jemma, I'm hammered."

"No problem."

I felt him getting in under the sheet and continental quilt then I drifted back off to sleep……

How long I then slept for, I have no idea, but it couldn't have been long. I woke up and me and the mystery man were huddled together or at least I had snuggled into his back. He was definitely asleep. I edged myself away from him a little. I wanted to know who it was. I wanted to get up, go to the door, open it slightly so the light from the landing came in and I could see his face, as all I could see was a very vague silhouette. I sat up in bed, ready to get out of it but my body objected, I was still in a right state, my body parts had gone on strike and were failing to respond to commands from my brain. I gave him a nudge.

"How are you doing over there?"

He groaned a little and then replied,

"I'm OK. Still drunk, but OK."

I was going to have to ask.

"Who are you?"

He laughed. I half recognised that laugh.

"Do you not know?!"

"No! It's bugging me, tell me!"

He laughed again and then put a smooth hand on the side of my face and gently kissed me. I could have pulled away, struggled up to the door and the game would have been over, but to be honest, I didn't want it to be. The whole issue I had with myself was that I felt unloved and unwanted. At the very least, I was wanted now, I kissed him back! "Not Billy McGregor then!" I thought mid-kiss. Billy was a crap kisser, clumsy and wet, this guy knew what he was doing. For all I knew, I could be kissing a frog, but in that moment, I didn't care! As we kissed, my left hand moved down towards his crotch. He had jeans on (which again ruled no-one out!) and my fingers, although on the outside, knew that things were livening up down there. I felt stirrings of my own too. This was bizarre! As soon as we finished, I wanted to know who this was! We stopped kissing momentarily when our teeth clashed. No brace anyway, that ruled out a few geeks on the stairs!

"Sorry!" he whispered.

Whoever he was, he was really polite! I started kissing him again, throwing my tongue into his mouth with wild abandon! Funny how my body could do what it was told when it was getting some benefits! I couldn't help thinking though, when I turned the light on, I was in for a massive disappointment! I put that to the back of my mind though and kept on kissing, when I put my hands in his hair, it felt silky and clean, which probably ruled out the whole Birch family and the majority of their friends. Then, when his hands worked their way round my back and expertly undid the clasp on my bra, I was relieved,

"Its not James Billingham either! Thank God for that!" I thought. I was half-expecting it to be him!

As our kissing marathon continued, one of his hands touched my left breast in a tender, inquisitive fashion. He circled my nipple which stood to attention like a guard at Buckingham Palace! The fact that I had no idea who I was sharing caresses with was driving me wild! My right hand, emboldened by the drink and circumstances, left the safety of the outside of his jeans and crept under his boxer shorts, through a forest of pubic hair and then on to his now erect penis. My fingers gripped it like a gaggle of pornographic fingerbobs!

Mystery man responded in kind, his free hand working its way under my leather mini, on to my thigh, then moving my knickers to one side and awaiting an invitation in. Now was not a time to be prudish, my left hand took his and encouraged his fingers inside. I was wet, really wet. This felt so different to being with Billy McGregor, with Billy's clumsy ways and dirty fingernails, I could be as dry as the Sahara!

Clothes started coming off. My top, his top, his torso felt teenage boyish but attractively so, he was muscular, toned and hair free, then his jeans came off, followed by my mini-skirt. I wanted him inside me now, properly inside me. I made a move on his boxer shorts. He stopped me, which was unexpected.

"Are you sure you want to be doing this?" he asked.

Did boys ask questions like that?

"Have you got any johnnies?" I asked. Not the most romantic question ever, but it needed asking.

"No! I only came in here for a lie down. Shall we stop?"

Damn! I didn't want that! This was all mysterious and sexual, it was now becoming sensible. I took the lead and kissed him again.

"Just make sure you are out before the dynamite explodes!"

After that, the passions were soon re-kindled. I eased his boxer shorts down, he tugged gently at my knickers, they had reached my knees when the door opened slightly.

"Oops, sorry!"

I looked up to see who our intruder was and just before the door shut again, I realised it was Amy.

"Shit!" I thought, if my eyes hadn't been drawn to the door, I could have seen who he was.

This time the interruption didn't upset our rhythm, I took my own knickers the remainder of the way down, then turned so he was below me, pressed his shoulders down and in the darkness slipped on top of him, shuffling around a little to allow him inside. I was expecting it to hurt, but it didn't. He thrust into me a couple of times, my body tingled, then all of a sudden he stopped.

"No Jemma! Stop! I'm so sorry, I need to get out of here!"

He wriggled beneath me. Embarrassed I clambered off him and buried my head in the pillow, I heard him gathering his things together, putting his boxer shorts on and searching around in the darkness for the rest of his clothes. Within seconds, he had gathered them up and was out the room. Gone! I still didn't know who the hell he was! Then a thought occurred to me. I didn't know who he was, but whoever was outside the door, in the landing, would definitely know. It was my turn to scramble for clothes. Quickly finding my knickers and bra, I was ready to unmask "The Phantom Fucker"!

"Amy!" I shouted. "Amy! Quickly come here!!"

Richie

I was in serious trouble. Hiccupy burps were a bad sign. Hiccupy burps that rose up through your body, leaving you with a vomit-smelling halitosis, such as I had just had, were your body's message that the last train to porcelain was just about to leave and would be depositing carrots, lager and the lining of your stomach at its final destination. My body was telling me that I needed to get on board quickly, as it was likely to be an express train, journey time five minutes and if I didn't act quickly it would be re-routed and be the last train to "Carpetsville".

I ran up the stairs. The stairs that had been crammed full earlier were now almost empty, like supporters leaving five minutes before the end due to their team's five-nil defeat, partygoers en masse had decided they had gleaned all they could from this party and it was now time to head home. Only the optimistic and the desperate, the drunks and the copulators remained. To my horror, the majority of them had gathered in an orderly queue outside the bathroom, no doubt to relieve their bladders, to return their lager from whence it came or to flush away their condoms filled with millions of children they would never have. My body did not empathise with their need to queue.

In total, there must have been a dozen queuing and based on a turnaround time of three minutes per head, my stomach could not empty its contents for thirty six minutes, it had already conveyed the message that this was an impossibility. I needed to beg favours,

"Excuse me, I'm not feeling too good, any chance I can go before you?"

I pleaded in my drunken, but well mannered, style. I only remember three people in that queue, the rest are just faceless memories, but they no doubt took one look at me and deduced, for their personal safety, it would be wise to let me pass. Within a very short space of time, I had edged from the very back of the queue, to fourth in line to the throne, but once I laid eyes on the front three, I decided to retain a modicum of dignity and stop begging. The front three just happened to be Amy Perkins, Jemma Watkinson and Kelly. Bloody typical!

Amy, Jemma and Kelly must have had a predicament of their own to contend with, with Jemma as the central character, as Amy and Kelly were floating around her like wasps around an unwrapped lollipop. All three of them were wittering away excitedly, especially Amy who was like Minnie Mouse on speed, at a bionic pace that only girls can manage. Luckily for me, this meant they were oblivious to the people around them. Only the backs of their beautifully maintained hair, faced towards me. This was great as I did not want Kelly to be introduced to the pale, edge of vomit, version of me. All of a sudden it came. No stationmaster blew his whistle. No starter said "On your marks, get set…". The vomit just rose up out of my body like a volcano or one of those waves at Rhyl Sun Centre that you were half-expecting but it still managed to knock you off your feet. I was immediately aware of the dangers, so I locked my jaw tight and put my hand to my mouth, but about a third of a pint of carrot-laden vomit managed to beat the trap door closing and squeezed through the gaps in my fingers, spraying gently on to the back of Jemma Watkinson's hair, like a vile smelling lacquer. I watched in slow motion and awaited the turning of heads and the slap in the face, which was a particular concern as most of the vomit was still in my mouth. To my immense relief, Amy, Kelly and Jemma were too immersed in their own conversation to realise my sick was hanging off the back of Jemma's hair like a bizarre collection of Christmas decorations inspired by "Carrots R Us". Just as I was about to thank my lucky stars and focus on what to do with the litre of vomit that had filled my mouth, Kelly somehow sensed my presence and turned.

"Oh! Hi Richie! I didn't realise you were behind us! Are you OK? You look awful!"

I nodded and attempted to smile with my eyes and with one of those grins you manage for school photos when you are seven and have no front teeth. The difference being when you are seven, you do not tend to swill a litre of vomit around your mouth.

"Jemma's a bit upset about something and she's still not feeling great, so Amy and I are looking after her!"

I put both my thumbs up at her.

'Jemma'll be even more upset when she sees the back of her hair', I thought to myself, whilst cursing myself for looking so ridiculous.

"What's wrong with your voice?!" Kelly asked, amused by my hand signals. I had no choice now. Someone had cruelly massacred Jemma Watkinson's hair and the murder weapon was still within my mouth. It needed to be concealed in a better hiding place than this because, if it wasn't, my guilt would soon be revealed to everyone. Not that anyone knew that a crime had been committed but it was only a matter of time.

I had to be brave and swallow. I pulled a face, scrunched up my eyes and threw down what moments earlier I had thrown up. I gagged as the chunky bits caught in my oesophagus. Kelly was perplexed.

"What's going on with you, Richie? You look like you've just drunk a bottle of vinegar!"

She obviously didn't have a great sense of smell, either that or the lingering smell of vomit from the bathroom acted as a decoy. If only I'd swallowed a bottle of vinegar! I am sure that would have been far more pleasurable. Covering my mouth to hide the smell, I came out with some random nonsense,

"I think I'm allergic to marijuana! It keeps catching in my throat!"

"Really! I hate that smell too. My Mum and her mates tend to smoke it. It reeks! We've obviously got even more in common than I thought!"

Kelly smiled at me, a radiant smile, I smiled back sheepishly, hoping there was no carrot on my teeth.

The smile was followed by the wonderful sound of the lock on the bathroom door moving back and forth, as its occupant tried to come out. After thirty seconds effort, Andrew Cullen emerged.

To my relief, Amy, Kelly and Jemma all made a forward motion to the bathroom. They were all going in together.

"Sorry about the stench girls," Andrew apologised wholeheartedly, "its bitter, it plays havoc with my bowels!!"

The girls continued on their journey to the bathroom, shut the door behind them, locked it and literally a couple of seconds passed before there was a collective,

"Eeuuuurrrrgggggghhhhh!!!"

Whether this sound was reflective of the gases extracted from Andrew Cullen's backside hitting their nostrils or the discovery of vomit in Jemma Watkison's hair, I have no idea. Once the bathroom door closed, I decided I had chanced my luck enough for one evening. With the threat of vomit no longer imminent, I headed downstairs, bade a stoned looking Nick Birch farewell, did a D-Gas handshake with Joey and jumped into the taxi at the end of the drive, that had been booked in the name of Watkinson.

Karma soon catches up with you. I regurgitated my vomit over the taxi's passenger window halfway home. I was so drunk I thought I had wound the window down! I hadn't! On arriving home, I was escorted to my doorstep by a fuming taxi driver who demanded the full fare from my mother plus an additional £25 fee to cover cleaning and subsequent loss of trade as he was going to have to head home to find something to clear up the smell. As I was in such a drunken state, my Mum did not shout and scream at me that night, she just helped me up the stairs and put me to bed. The following morning, however, I had to sit in front of my Mum and Dad for an hour, as they had set up a kangaroo court in our kitchen and they introduced various family members, namely Jim and Caroline, to testify against me. I was sentenced to imprisonment within the family home for a month, only gaining parole to attend school.

If I had been sentenced for the "boomerang vomit" and the damage incurred by the aforementioned taxi driver, I would not have had cause for complaint. I was however, found guilty of a crime I did not commit, due to falsification of evidence by my siblings. Jim and Caroline had decided it would be creating a whole host of trouble for all concerned if they had told Mum and Dad that Jim's jaw had been broken by some drunken girl at a party, so they concocted a story about Jim and I falling out over some Dungeons & Dragon figure, me punching him and then swanning off to the party leaving Caroline to take Jim to hospital. In their fictional world, I was the only one that attended the party, they spent the whole evening at Casualty. Neither Jim nor Caroline had appreciated my lack of solidarity the previous night so they were doing me over good and proper. On reflection, I suppose I deserved everything I got.

As a consequence of my imprisonment, my date with Kelly Watkinson did not take place the following Saturday. Fate had intervened. Nevertheless, she had found a way into my heart and like a tattoo, there would be a place for her there until my dying day.

Jemma

There was a knock at the door.

"Who is it?"

"It's Amy!"

"What are you knocking for then, you daft cow, come in?!"

Amy entered.

"Is that you, Amy?"

I suppose it was a stupid question but I was struggling to see.

"Of course it's me! When did you turn into Stevie Wonder?!"

"Since I started drinking with you! I don't feel quite as drunk any more, but my brain hasn't told my eyes that yet!"

"Well you didn't look that drunk when you were flashing your naked bum at me before, you dirty cow! Who was that you were getting it on with?!!!"

"I was going to ask you the very same question!"

"Eddie Garland!"

I did not process this information properly. My heart sank. That was going to make life difficult. Billy McGregor first, now Eddie Garland. The two best looking but most arrogant lads in Sixth Form and I had been out with one and now, sort of, slept with the other. Then, my memories of my encounter with "The Phantom Fucker" and previous conversations with Kelly started slowly dripping back into my brain. This guy was polite and Eddie was plain cocky and did Kelly not say Amy was with Eddie before and had I not sent Kelly out to tell Amy to keep clear of him.

"Hang on, Amy! Who was with Eddie?"

"Me, you dozy mare! I thought you said you weren't still pissed! Who do you think was with him?! YOU??!!!"

"I didn't want to know who you were with, Amy! I wanted to know who I was with?!"

I was confusing her.

"That's what I want to know!" Amy replied.

"Amy, I don't know who the hell it was! After you came in here before, did you see anyone come out? A lad, dressed only in his boxer shorts and carrying the rest of his clothes?"

"No. I was busy with Eddie!"

"But you came in here! Did you not see him then?"

"No, I was dazzled by the light reflecting off your bum!"

"Amy, I'm being serious. At no point did you see who it was?"

"No, I only came in because Eddie and I were looking for a spare room. This one was taken so we found another empty one……are you trying to tell me that you were stripped off naked with someone and you don't even know who it was?!"

"That's exactly what I am trying to tell you!"

"OH….MY….GOD!!! JEMMA! Have you seen the amount of freaks that are here?! Did you sleep with him?"

"Depends what you mean by "sleep with", we both fell asleep when he first came in."

"You know exactly what I mean by "sleep with", Jemma Watkinson! I mean "birds and the bees" sleep with! Did he dip his wick?!"

"Not for long!"

"Oh my god, Jemma! You lost your virginity and you don't even know who to?! Imagine how bad this could be! Imagine if you had a baby and blood tests and stuff revealed someone really sad like Jim Billingham was the father!"

"I know it wasn't Jim! When I was here with "The Phantom Fucker", I was thinking for a second it could be Jim Billingham and if you want to know the gory details, that thought was tightening me up a bit, but then I remembered I punched him in the jaw! He couldn't possibly kiss me, let alone, as you so eloquently put it, "dip his wick"!

"It could be someone equally bad though!"

"Thanks for making me feel better, Amy! You really are working wonders! Anyway, someone will have seen him coming out of here so we'll know soon enough. Where's Kelly? She might know."

"She was in the kitchen before. I'll go and find her."

Amy disappeared. There were plenty of mysteries still to be solved, including where Eddie Garland had got to and how far Amy had gone with him, but for now, the only one I wanted solving was, "The Mystery of the Phantom Fucker!"

I continued getting dressed and within a few seconds of finishing, Amy was back, now accompanied by Kelly.

My eyes were beginning to focus a little better and thankfully Kelly still looked a lot better than me. I was setting a terrible example to Kelly, I was almost as bad as Vomit Breath, but luckily Kelly seemed to be showing no interest in following in my footsteps, well, except for the incident earlier with the can and the copper, but maybe she was innocent after all.

Kelly was looking me over quizzically.

"How are you feeling, Jemma?"

If I had a pound for every time I had been asked that question in the course of that evening, I would have had enough money for the taxi ride home.

"A bit better. Still a pile of crap though."

"You scared me before. I sat on the side of your bed for an hour to check you didn't choke on your own vomit. Like we do with Mum."

"Sorry babe!"

"No, no, I wasn't looking for an apology or any praise, I was just worried."

"I'll be alright now."

"Good!"

I now needed to see if Kelly could provide me with any clues.

"Kel, where were you five minutes ago?"

"I don't know. I've just been downstairs to book us a taxi, it'll be here in fifteen minutes."

"You went down, where were you before that?"

"Having a wee!"

"So were you in the queue on the landing for a while?"

"There wasn't much of a queue, but yes, why?"

"Did you see anyone coming out of this room?"

"No. The toilet queue faces the wrong way for this room. My back would have been facing it. Why, did someone come in and do something to you, Jemma?"

Amy butted in.

"Less a case of doing something, more a case of taking something!"

Amy laughed at her own "witty" comment, Kelly looked confused and I glared at Amy. We normally got on so much better than this. I felt like telling her to stop being so bloody cocky, but stopped myself as I knew I was teeing her up for another stupid innuendo.

"What's happened?" Kelly was both concerned and inquisitive.

"I was having a lie down, someone came in here, a lad, got into bed with me, we had a bit of a kiss and cuddle and then all of a sudden he scarpered."

"How long was he in here?" Amy asked.

"I'm not sure. We both fell asleep."

"Good kissing then! Instead of the kiss of death, it was the kiss of the coma" Amy jibed once more.

"You know I meant before the kissing, Amy!"

"You couldn't have been asleep long. I kept checking on you every fifteen or twenty minutes." Kelly said.

"It's a pity you didn't come in whilst he was here, I could have done with knowing who it was!"

"I went in, Kelly, but all I saw was your sister's bum mooning at me!!"

Neither Watkinson laughed.

"What were you doing in bed not clothed and kissing someone, if you didn't even know who it was in the first place?! Are you mad?!" Kelly wanted to know.

"I don't know. It felt right. I suppose I am mad!"

"And drunk and horny!" Amy added for good measure.

"Anyway, I can't turn back time, it's done now. Can one of you two help me up, I'm bursting for a wee and I'm still not sure how well my body will cope with a walk?!" Kelly and Amy both helped me out of bed, then out the bedroom and into a now massive queue for the bathroom!

"I thought you said there wasn't much of a queue!" I said to Kelly.

"There wasn't before!"

"That would be the icing on the cake and the cherry on top if I now wet my knickers!" I moaned.

"I thought your knickers were already wet but for entirely different reasons!" Amy added.

Maybe it was the drink that transformed Amy into this right royal pain in the arse, whatever it was, it was getting on my tits.

"Will you just shut up, Amy!"

Amy's cocky side now took a backseat as her sensitive side came to the fore.

"That's not fair speaking to me like that! I thought we were best friends?"

I still couldn't see all that well, but it sounded like Amy was about to burst into tears. Tough, she had brought it on herself.

"We are best friends, Amy! I've just hardly seen you all night and when I have, you've been making stupid comments!"

"I have not!"

"Hasn't she, Kelly?"

Getting my sister on side was a little cruel, but necessary. I could always count on Kelly to take my side, but also to be diplomatic.

"Once or twice, Amy, you've had a few little digs, which isn't like you at all."

"I'm so sorry, honey!"

Amy gave me an apologetic hug.

"I've just been so excited about tonight and with the wine and Eddie Garland and

everything, I think I've just got a little out of control. You don't hate me, Jemma, do you? Tell me you don't hate me!"

"Of course I don't hate you!"

We had another hug. It was at this point I realised Amy was probably not a great deal more sober than me.

We waited in that toilet queue and we waited and waited. Amy excitedly related her evening to us in minute detail, whilst stopping every thirty seconds to check I was still OK. Thankfully french kissing was as far as she had been with Eddie Garland, who had then sloped off dejectedly to catch a taxi into Southport with Billy McGregor. After about ten minutes, my bladder had taken a turn for the worse and even more worryingly, I felt it was time to throw up. Knowing I would be sick soon, I kept focusing on the bathroom's door handle, as it became the centre of my world and everything else revolved around it. My sick was so near at one stage, I could almost smell it. Just as I was about to give in to Biology and pebble dash the landing, I heard a familiar voice,

"I think I am allergic to marijuana! The smoke keeps catching in my throat!"

That voice! That familiar voice!! THE PHANTOM FUCKER!!"

I wanted to turn around to make doubly sure but I was too paralytic to turn. He was standing behind us in the queue, chatting to Kelly! Who was it?

Then I realised. Richie! Richie Billingham.

Polite? Yes.

Good body? Yes.

Drunk? I think so.

Guilty about screwing me? Probably.

Kelly said he had asked her out, so that would make sense. That would explain the jump out of bed, the gathering of clothes and the bolt out the door. Guilt.

I was mulling this all over when the bathroom door opened and Kelly, Amy and I flooded in. I only got about two steps into the room when the combination of a previous near vomit condition and the rancid smell of Andrew Cullen's crap, hit me. I was sick before I could get to the toilet.

"Euuuurrrgggghhhh!" shrieked Kelly and Amy in unison.

I ignored it and plugged on towards the toilet, battling against the elements like Scott in the Antarctic, reaching my destination just before the second wave of sick arrived. I hate being sick. Retching and the stench of puke are not pretty and things went from bad to worse when Amy, who had sympathetically kneeled down beside me to stroke my hair observed,

"Jemma. Now may not be the best time to tell you this, but it looks like someone has spewed in the back of your hair."

I ran my hand through my hair and it emerged full of diced carrot. I threw up a third time.

I hated Richie Billingham. He had crept into my room, taken my virginity and then at some point, puked all over the back of my head and then cleared off before I realised. How did I not realise that someone had been sick in the back of my head?! To make matters worse, he'd also asked my thirteen year old sister out. How could I tell her what he'd done, she was only a child, it would break her heart.

I owed Richie Billingham big time. I'd make him pay for this. No doubt about it, I would make him pay.

Richie (two years later)

Ormskirk's nightlife wasn't the greatest. Everywhere shut down at 11pm and then until midnight, half the town's drinkers congregated outside a fish and chip shop called the Acropolis, either to soak up their alcohol with fish and chips or sausage and chips or to scan around desperately looking for an available member of the opposite sex. When

Helen and Caroline were younger and were first heading out into Ormskirk in

the mid 1980's, the pavement outside the Acropolis also doubled up as a boxing ring, as many bare knuckled fist fights took place amongst Ormskirk's inebriated. By the end of the Eighties, however, a healthy police presence had minimised the outpourings of testosterone and if it began to kick off, the aggressors were bundled into the back of a police van.

Ormskirk is a market town in West Lancashire, located approximately halfway between Preston and Liverpool. Half its occupants are the offspring of "Scousers" who have moved out of the city and the other half are the offspring of dyed in the wool Lancastrians. The former were known as "plastic Scousers" and the latter "Woolybacks". Our family were pretty much a combination of the two. "Plastic backs" or "Wooly Scousers"!

Unless alcohol was involved, there was no animosity between "Scousers" and "Woolybacks", generally a small town spirit of togetherness had been created with everyone knowing everyone or, at the very least, knowing someone who knows someone. Good people are created in Ormskirk but very few famous people. The only one I can think of is Tony Morley, the former Aston Villa left winger. I'm not even sure he grew up in Ormskirk, I just know from my Panini sticker albums that he was born in Ormskirk. Ironically, Tony Morley once scored the "Match of The Day" Goal of the Season, but it was for Aston Villa against Everton in about 1982 and I was there to witness it! Being a goal against Everton, it was a painful blow, but it wasn't as painful as every other goal scored against Everton by non-Ormskirk folk!

Amongst the older generations, Ormskirk is noted for having a Parish Church that has both a tower and a steeple and a market that takes place every Thursday and Saturday. It also had a teaching college called Edge Hill, which supposedly had about ten female students to every male, but none of these women ever came looking for me. Ormskirk was a wonderful place to grow up, but it wasn't London.

At half eleven on a Friday and Saturday night in my late teens, I would generally stumble out of "The Chelsea Reach", "The Brahms & Liszt" or "The Buck I'th Vine" and stagger down to the Acropolis with my mates. "The Chelsea Reach" was directly opposite the Acropolis, so we often planned our night with strategic precision to ensure the drinking part of our night out concluded there, so we had minimal staggering distance to the Acropolis. Every Friday and Saturday was much of a muchness, I would buy a portion of chips, chat to a few schoolfriends, friends from old football teams I had played for, or fellow Evertonians, then wander back home to Aughton, my home village, two miles away.

Educationally, I had surprised myself and passed seven "O" levels, so had stayed at Ormskirk Grammar School for "A" levels too, so home life, school life and night life all centred around Ormskirk. I was happy with my routine, I had a 100% record of romantic failure on nights out in Ormskirk during my first two years of drinking, but this was through a lack of trying rather than trying and failing.

One Friday night, in late summer 1988, everything changed. It was in the middle of the summer holidays, I was about to go back into Upper Sixth and had just had a few pints in "The Buck" with my mate, Dogger before wandering down to the Acropolis on my own. Dogger was in Sixth Form with me, but he lived in Westhead, and the Acropolis was five minutes walk in the wrong direction for him, so he had forfeited chips and walked home. I had bought chips and stood outside, unravelling the paper and surveying the scene. I spotted her instantly. Crossing the road from "The Chelsea Reach", linking arms with three of her friends, was Kelly Watkinson. Back at the Birch's party, when I first noticed her, Kelly was a pretty young girl, but now, nearing sixteen, she was a stunning young woman. If there had been an agent for some massive modelling firm out in Ormskirk that night, Kelly Watkinson would have been the one and only girl that would have been worthy of his attention. To my mind, Cindy Crawford and Naomi Campbell were languishing miles behind Kelly in the beauty stakes, Linda Evangelista ran Kelly close, but Kelly had a slight edge on her too! Her hair was now long, straight and blond, she had grown taller over the two years since the Birch's party and now must have been 5 feet 7 or 5 feet 8. With heels on, she towered over some of her friends. This was not new information to me though, every school day for the past two years I had been tortured by her presence. The thing I did notice that night, more than ever before, was her bum which was packed tightly into a white pair of jeans and a fine pair of breasts that were only partially covered by a silver silk shirt that had its top few buttons undone. Where had those beauties sprung up from? They weren't massive, but weren't bee stings either. "C" cuppers, I concluded.

I watched Kelly and her friends go into the Acropolis. I watched her queue and then watched her come out, armed with a portion of chips and gravy. Kelly was the first of her friends to come out, I took advantage of the opportunity and rushed over,

"Had a good night, Kelly?!"

"Brilliant until about ten seconds ago."

This wasn't fair.

"This is getting boring now!"

"You brought it all on yourself, Richie!"

"That's where you're wrong!"

"How do you figure that one out?"

Kelly's friends were coming to join her now, I took it as a positive that she was prepared to continue to argue with me rather than just walk away.

"I haven't done anything wrong! Give me one good reason why you and I should not go out on a date?"

"Because you're revolting!"

I knew she didn't mean that!

"A real reason!"

"Richie, if seven legged aliens arrived on the planet and killed off every single male with the exception of you, I still would not go out with you."

"That's not a reason!"

"Ok. I'll give you three reasons. One, we had a date arranged two bloody years ago and you didn't show up!"

"Hang on…I didn't stand you up, I cancelled! There was a reason…."

"Hold on! I said three reasons. Let me finish."

"OK."

"Secondly, you virtually raped my sister!"

"Bollocks!"

"And thirdly, you threw up in the back of her head!"

"When exactly?"

"That same night in the bedroom at the Birch's party!"

"That's bollocks too!"

Not complete bollocks, but I wasn't going to tell Kelly that! I threw up in her hair on the landing not in the bedroom!

"How you ever expect me to forgive you for asking me out and then sleeping with my sister, on the very same night, I will never know!"

I sighed.

"Look Kelly, how many times are we going to go over this. I DID NOT and I repeat DID NOT sleep with your sister. She was very drunk, she either dreamt it…"

"Why would she dream of sleeping with you?! My god, how vain are you?!!"

"Or she slept with someone else."

"She is 100% sure it was you."

"It was not me!"

"Well Jemma says it was and I know who I believe!"

"Kelly, for the hundredth time, I swear it wasn't! When are we ever going to draw a line under this and move on? Jemma's moved on."

"She hasn't, she still wishes you were dead."

"She's left school, she's got a boyfriend, she's happy. Why can't you be happy?"

"I am happy. Very happy. Thank you!"

"You would be even happier if you were "going out" with me!"

"I would not. Anyway, how do you know Jemma's got a boyfriend?"

"She's always with some lad from the bank."

"Stalking her now are you?! Not satisfied with creeping in and bonking her. Now you are stalking her too."

"I am not interested in Jemma. I'm just interested in you. The only reason we did not go on a date two years ago, is because your sister broke my brother's jaw and because he did not want to tell my mother that a girl did it, so he blamed me. I was grounded for a month because of your sister. I had to cancel our date, you were upset, Jemma then told you not to worry about it because I was a complete toerag, who had sneaked into her room when she was drunk, slept with her and then puked in her hair, right?"

"Pretty much."

"And I have spent the last two years insisting I did not sleep with her and asking you to give me another chance to take you out. Also right?"

"Yes."

"If I was interested in your sister, why would I spend my whole time chasing after you?"

"I don't know!"

Kelly blushed. This was going well.

"So what would I have to do now to wipe the slate clean and get you to give me that chance?"

It was the perfect time to ask, only because her three friends were watching events take shape and I got the impression they liked me. Her friends decided to start setting the necessary tasks.

Claire Northover chipped in first.

"What if he came to your door every day for two weeks and sang a song by your window, like they do in films?!"

I didn't like that idea.

"I can't sing!"

"That doesn't matter!"

"That'd be too easy," Kelly replied.

Once again though, I took heart. This was Kelly's opportunity to say,

"No, I'm just not going out with him and that's that!!"

but she wasn't saying that at all, she was giving me hope.

"What if he had to come and sing at six o'clock every morning for two weeks?"

Sammy Wickes added with a giggle.

"I'm not up at six!" Kelly pointed out.

"You could just get up for a few minutes and then go back to bed!" Sammy responded.

"Still too easy!" Kelly pointed out.

"What if he was only dressed in Speedos?" Claire Northover suggested.

"Still not enough!" Kelly replied, "Even if he came at six o'clock every morning for two weeks, wearing Speedos and his Mum's bra, that wouldn't be enough!"

"Good one, Kel!" added Helen Kumar, "Speedos and his Mum's bra and then on the last day, he could do it naked!!"

"Girls, this is ridiculous!" I moaned but in a playful way. There was definitely a window of opportunity here.

Kelly decided at this point to define the task.

"OK. OK. I tell you what, if you come to my house at six o'clock every morning, for the next two weeks, starting tomorrow, dressed only in a pair of Speedos and your Mum's bra and sing a different love song to me every day and the last morning you do it naked, I will go on ONE date with you. Providing you do one other thing."

"What's that?"

"Apologise to my sister."

"What for? She should be apologising to me!"

"Richie, that's the deal!"

Kelly and her mates then all turned and walked off, heading up Aughton Street into Ormskirk, towards the clock tower, linking arms and singing a song. I had it in mind that they sang En Vogue's "Never Gonna Get It" because that would have been entirely appropriate, but it must have been something else as that song didn't come out until a few years later!

"Kelly!" I shouted after her, "I don't have any Speedos!"

Kelly turned her head around, her body was still linked to the other girls.

"That's not my problem, Richie! If you want that date, I expect to see you in the morning in Speedos and your Mum's bra. Don't be late!"

Jemma

The Birch's party was an epiphany for me. If there was one thing in life I did not want to become, it was a clone of Vomit Breath. She spent her entire life either drinking, drunk or hungover and men were used, not as a tool for a relationship, but basically just for their tool. If they liked drink as well as sex, that was an added bonus, but sex was the key. If I had taken Vomit Breath with me to the Birch's party, her behaviour would have mirrored mine, get drunk beforehand, turn up, strut around like you own the place, getting progressively more drunk along the way, find a random man for sex, throw up, miss your taxi and arrive home at five in the morning, waking at midday feeling like Timmy Mallett had attacked you in your sleep.

Richie Billingham had taken advantage of my situation but on reflection, I was a more than willing partner and if he had wanted to continue on an orgasmic journey, I would have let him. I was still annoyed with him for throwing up in my hair and in the days after the party, I did everything I could to sabotage any chance he had with Kelly, but the desire to buy a shotgun and paint a target on Richie Billingham's forehead soon passed.

With regards to sabotaging Richie's chances with Kelly, he pretty much did this himself. On the Wednesday night after the party, Kelly came into my room, sobbing her little heart out. She came over to me and hugged me tightly. After Kelly had spent the majority of the Birch's party looking after me, it felt good that I was reclaiming the senior sister role. I stroked her hair.

"Honey what's the matter? What's happened?"

Kelly stopped hugging to take a tissue out her pocket and blow her nose.

"Oh, I'm being ridiculous!"

"Let me be the judge of that." I said, "Who's upset you?"

"Richie's cancelled our date on Saturday."

A wave of relief swept over me. I was tempted just to say,

"Good! That lad's an arse!" but I needed to regain some credibility with Kelly, so for once, I actually thought before I spoke.

"Why has he done that?"

"He's grounded."

"Well, can't you just arrange it for another time?"

"No, you don't get it. He's not been grounded for one night, he's been grounded for a month! Outside of school, he's under house arrest!"

"Bloody hell! What did he do to deserve that?"

"Nothing! That's why it's so upsetting!"

Kelly blew her nose again.

"You don't get grounded for a month for nothing, Kel!"

Then she hit me with a verbal sucker punch, unintentionally I think, but it hurt all the same.

"He's been grounded for a month for breaking his brother's jaw!"

"How did he do that?"

I asked the question but I knew the answer.

"HE didn't, Jemma! You did!"

So much for reclaiming the senior sister role! I felt humiliated.

"I'm so sorry, Kelly! I was an idiot at that party, but why has Richie taken the rap for me?"

Maybe Richie wasn't as bad as I thought.

"His brother and sister stitched him up. They said he did it."

"Do they not like him?"

"They were annoyed because he stayed at the party instead of going to Casualty with them."

"No wonder they were annoyed! If you broke your jaw, I wouldn't stay at a party whilst you went off to hospital!"

I know you wouldn't but I'm not Jim Billingham, am I?! Jim Billingham's an arsehole!"

"Kelly!"

I hated her swearing. Vomit Breath was a foulmouthed tramp. I didn't want Kelly to be.

"Sorry, but he is!"

"Who are you upset with, Kelly? Are you upset with me?" "You, Richie, Jim, Caroline, Richie's parents, everyone really….we have a crap life with Mum and finally something good was happening in my life and now it's been snatched away. It's not fair, Jemma! It's really not fair!"

I felt like a parent who had grabbed her child's ticket to Disney World off her and set it on fire. A lot of the time, Kelly seemed a lot older than her tender years, but at this moment, she seemed like a little girl.

"Kelly, if I can put this right for you, I will. If you want me to go round to Richie's house and tell his parents the truth, I will."

"You would?"

A cloud appeared to temporarily lift from above Kelly's head.

"Of course I would. It's more my fault than anyone's that your date has been cancelled. I'll go around to Richie's after school, speak to his parents and tell them that I broke Jim's jaw."

Kelly wiped her eyes and then the maturity that she so often displayed kicked in.

"No, I don't want you to Jemma!"

"Why not?"

If you tell Richie's parents, they aren't just going to say "Thanks for telling us!", they'll call the police. You'll be in serious trouble. You might be charged with GBH like Mum."

Kelly had a point. Throughout our childhood Mum had always been fighting. A couple of times she had to attend court, once she got off on a technicality, the other time she received a suspended prison sentence. Social services were involved at one stage and "Tut" came to live with us for a while to provide the moral guidance we were lacking from Vomit Breath. "Tut" spent six months treating our house like a 19th Century orphanage and even Kelly and I were glad when she moved back home. Vomit Breath is horrible to have around but its even worse having her mother as well. Kelly was thinking of me by worrying about police charges, but it was self- preservation too, if I was taken away to a "Young Offenders Institute", Kelly would be home alone with Vomit Breath.

"It's your call, Kelly."

"My call is to leave things as they are. I'll just to have to go out with Richie next month!"

"OK, if that's what you want."

It must have been the way I said it or maybe my body language failed to mask my disappointment, but Kelly sensed something instantaneously.

"Jemma, why do you hate Richie?"

"I don't!"

"The other night you weren't happy about me going out with him and I can tell now you still feel the same. He's a lovely guy, why can't you just give him a chance? If it's the age thing, that's just daft! He's less than two years older than me! Mum has dragged blokes back here that are half her age and others who are twice her age!"

"Don't use Vomit Breath as your example of how things should be done!"

Kelly smiled. Her tear soaked green eyes sparkled. She was and still is so beautiful!

"I know, bad example! Is that why you don't like him though, because he's in the

Fifth Year and I'm in the Third Year?"

"No. There's more to it than that."

"Like what?"

I have a big mouth. It's not a good trait, but sometimes, most of the time, I just can't help myself.

"When you mentioned the other night that you were going on a date with Richie Billingham, my concerns at that point were all about his age and your age, nothing more than that. I swear."

"It's two years, Jemma! Less than two years!"

"I know. The age is no big deal but I have other reasons to be concerned now."

"Like what?"

"I don't want to go into the details, but let's just say I have every reason to feel concerned about you dating Richie Billingham, that's all I'm saying!"

Sadness returned to Kelly's face. Sadness with a hint of anger.

"No, it isn't! You can't just leave it like that! What has someone told you about Richie that you don't like? It might be rubbish anyway! Some people are just born liars!"

"Just leave it, Kelly!"

I knew she wouldn't leave it. I suppose we both knew I would tell her eventually, but I wanted it to feel like she had dragged the information out of me!

"No-one has told me anything, Kel. I just have my own reasons for not liking him."

"New reasons?"

"Yes."

"Tell me!"

"NO!"

"I'm your sister. You need to tell me."

I sighed, then got up and closed the door. Vomit Breath was a nosey bitch, I didn't want her earwigging on our conversation. It would give her ammunition in future battles. I sat on my bed.

"You won't like what I am going to say."

"I don't care. Tell me."

"OK….", I hesitated, "you know at the Birch's party, someone sneaked into the bedroom when I was really drunk and slept with me?"

The tears welled up again in Kelly's eyes then one popped out and rolled down her cheek. She wiped it away.

"No it wasn't! It wasn't!"

"Kelly, it was Richie!"

"You're wrong Jemma! You didn't hear how he spoke to me that night. You didn't see the love in his eyes! It wasn't Richie! I remember, you said you didn't know who it was!"

"I didn't at first! It was only when we were in the queue for the bathroom. I heard his voice again and I knew, straight away, that Richie Billingham was "The Phantom Fucker!"

"You were really drunk, Jemma. You threw up seconds after!"

"Kelly, I wish it wasn't Richie, but it was!"

Kelly was determined to try to change my mind on this one or at least plant a seed of doubt in my brain. She was like one of those wives who didn't want to believe their husband was a rapist or a murderer.

"You think it was or you know it was?"

"I know."

"100% sure?"

"Pretty much. 99%."

"So there is some doubt in your mind then?"

It was my turn to get annoyed now! I reckon our fathers were probably Italian, I had always had a Latin temperament and now Kelly was getting one too.

"For fucks sake, Kelly! The only reason there is even the slightest of doubts is because I was so pissed I couldn't see properly, but it was Richie. Definitely. Same voice. Same mannerisms. He even legged off mid-shag because he felt guilty!"

"And it was Richie that threw up in your hair too?"

"Yes."

"Have you got a tissue?"

I dug a box of tissues from under my bed and passed them to Kelly. She blew her nose hard.

"Be honest, Jemma. Do you hate him?"

"No, I don't hate him, Kelly."

"How do you feel?"

"I just don't want Richie Billingham to start dating my sister. If you want to, I can't stop you, but at least you know everything now and you can make a decision based on all the information."

Kelly started laughing. Not proper laughing though. The type of laughing women do in the movies when their husband has just died in a car crash but they have some silly flashback about how he used to make dogs out of balloons and give them to little girls.

"I can make a decision now! Well THANK YOU VERY MUCH!"

"It's not my fault, Kelly."

Kelly put her head in her hands.

"I know. I know, but there is no decision to make, is there?"

"I don't suppose there is."

"What about you though, Jemma?"

"What about me?"

Kelly was looking at me in a way I had never seen her look at me before. Suspiciously.

"You snuggled up to him, you kissed him, you even started having sex with him for a bit. Do you want me to keep away from Richie Billingham because you want him for yourself?"

"Kelly, if he was the last man on earth and I was the last woman, I would let the human race die out before I'd go anywhere near him."

Richie

It was raining. Where Kelly lived on Wigan Road was a fairly busy main road, but thankfully not all that busy at 6am on a Saturday morning. It was almost three miles from my house to Kelly's so I had set my alarm for five, stripped out of my pyjamas and into the designated speedos, but then added a T-shirt, tracksuit bottoms, trainers and a long winter's coat (despite it being summer it was a cold morning) before heading off.

There are two pubs within half a mile of Kelly's house, "The Ropers Arms" and "The Windmill Inn", I reached "The Windmill" first, so when I got there, I nipped round the side, took off all additional layers, put them into a plastic bag and from the plastic bag, I withdrew a lacy, white bra that I had stolen from the drawer next to my Mum's bed. Worryingly, I had mistakenly gone to my Dad's side first and there were condoms in his top drawer! Surely my Mum was too old to get pregnant and surely she was too old to be having sex with my Dad! The Speedos were Jim's. They were a bit small, but I took comfort in knowing this would make my sleeping anaconda underneath look bigger. I left the plastic bag at the side of the pub and headed up to Kelly's, tying the bra around my left thigh as I went, at no point had Kelly stated it was to be worn on my chest.

Within two minutes, I was there. I knew exactly where they lived and exactly which room was Kelly's. I had spent many weekends in the last two years, walking past, hoping to co-incidentally bump into her, but had met with no success. The Watkinson's house sloped down to the road, so I went up the stairs on her front path and then stood below the window of her bedroom, it was at the front of the house, which was good, if it had been around the back I may have had a dog or the police to contend with. Her curtains remained drawn, not a major shock given the time. I picked up a couple of small stones from the pathway and threw them at her window.

I waited a minute but the curtains did not twitch. Second time around, I picked up a couple of bigger stones, but they were still small enough not to threaten the glass. I tossed them up gently but they still made a hefty sound when they rapped against the pane. This time, within twenty seconds, the curtains were pulled apart, the window was opened and Kelly looked out with ruffled hair and a fluffy pink dressing gown.

"Good morning!" she croaked.

I wished I was up there, in her bedroom, rather than stood on the wet grass, barefooted, making a fool of myself in the rain. I cleared my throat and began to sing. I sang "A Small Fruit Song" by Al Stewart, the song is probably about two minutes long, but the acoustic guitar covers about the first ninety seconds, which meant I only had to sing for thirty seconds. Good job for all concerned as I can't sing. It was a cringeful rendition, but sometimes it's the destination that counts, not the journey. Once I finished, Kelly shouted down,

"Nice speedos, Richie! I haven't clue what the song was but I like the words! The singing wasn't great but that doesn't matter! Tomorrow, wear the bra where it should be worn, not around your leg, the sight of your nipples is too much for me at this time of the morning!"

Did she mean she was disgusted or turned on?! I wasn't sure. I started to head back down her path thinking I would like to see Kelly Watkinson's nipples any time of the day! I would like to see her nipples, her full breasts, her little tuft of blonde pubic hair (I visualised it as being blonde and well groomed!), her smooth, silky bottom, her vagina, I ached to see every inch of Kelly Watkinson's body! I wasn't standing there, making an idiot of myself just for a laugh!

Just as I reached the bottom of the path, I noticed a taxi had pulled up and a fierce looking woman stepped out. My first thought was that she had missed her vocation in life, she should have been in Hollywood as she could definitely have stolen the lead for "Throw Momma From The Train".

She probably said her first thought which was directed at me with vengeful eyes,

"Who the fuck are you and what the fuck are you doing on my front path?"

I could hear in the background Kelly's window shutting and her curtains being drawn.

"I came to see Jemma, but I couldn't wake her!"

Jemma had caused me no end of trouble over the previous two years, revenge was going to be sweet. I was more than happy to drop her in the shit!

"Have you been here all night, shagging my daughter?"

Why did everyone always think I had been shagging Jemma?! Even Jemma!

"No, I've just arrived."

"Look at my face," said the ugly woman who was obviously Mrs. Watkinson, "does it look to you like I was born yesterday?"

She didn't. She looked like she was born around the same time as Queen Victoria. Her breath smelt disgusting. I kept expecting some green gas to ooze out when she spoke.

"No, but I have just arrived!"

"I don't believe you!" she then smiled which probably damaged her looks still further as she had chipped, gold and black teeth mixed in with normal ones. I guess she had run out of money for the dentists half way through the job.

"I hope you have been shagging her," she continued, "about time something put a smile on that miserable bitches face! That ugly boyfriend doesn't!"

She looked at the bra around my thigh.

"Is that her bra, is it? I bet she's a kinky little minx, isn't she? It runs in the family!"

If a captured soldier had to have a kinky sex session with this woman during a time of conflict, I am sure the United Nations would go after Britain for committing war crimes. I decided not to continue the conversation, I just ran off towards "The Windmill" like a scolded cat. As I arrived back there, there was a stray mongrel sniffing around my clothes. It would have cocked its leg on them if I had arrived a second later. One down, thirteen to go. I spent the walk home wondering how that monster of a woman had managed to create perfection. Kelly was like a pre-Raphaelite model which was a miracle as her Mum looked like a Picasso. Life was strange, I thought, as I walked back with my Mum's bra now being tested around my chest. Life was very strange indeed!

Jemma

Kelly never did re-arrange the date with Richie Billingham for the following month. She told me she had a right go at him and despite his protestations of innocence, she refused to take pity. I was relieved and life moved on.

My "O" levels were largely unsurprisingly, convincingly failed and in June 1987, I left Ormskirk Grammar School with a "B" in "O" Level Art, a "C" in English Language, (Kelly said Vomit Breath would have got an "A" in "Foul Language"!) and a CSE Grade One in Biology. Despite the results, I somehow managed to fluke my way into a cashier's job in the Middlelands Bank in Ormskirk, on the proviso that I re-took my Maths "O" level. I started in July and actually enjoyed the job, enjoyed the interaction with adults and even managed to put some proper effort in, when it came to studying for my Maths re-take. In November 1987, I passed my Maths "O" level with a "B". It was an unusual feeling, feeling proud of myself and even stranger having other people, other than Kelly, feeling proud of me too. Everyone at work was delighted for me, in particular, Ray Walker, my "Branch Manager", who had stayed back after work to tutor me on any areas of the Maths syllabus I did not understand. Ray even drove me to Hugh Baird College in Bootle the day I sat the exam.

Ray was a kindhearted, gentle, educated man. He had started working at the Middlelands as a Graduate Management Trainee, two years earlier, having taken an Accountancy degree at Exeter University and prior to that he had been privately educated at Merchant Taylors school in Crosby. Two months before I started, Ray had been made "Branch Manager", he was only twenty three at the time and became one of the youngest branch managers in the country. I was sure he would go on to bigger and better things, so his interest in me was flattering. Ray was almost seven years my senior, so initially I thought his interest in me must be purely work related, but as the months passed it became evident there was a romantic interest too. Ray spent more time with me than any of the other girls at work, called me into his office more, complimented me more on my work performance and smiled at me in a way that indicated there was a place in his heart for me.

One Friday night, just after my seventeenth birthday, everyone went for a drink into Ormskirk after work. We used to go to the "Bowlers" which suited our mixed age group more than some of the other pubs I typically frequented. I was also safe from "Vomit Breath" in there, as she called it a "Yuppie's Wine Bar" and refused to go in. Ray and I ended up as the last two there as everyone else had partners and after a quick drink or two, had headed home to their husbands, wives and partners. Ray offered to walk me home, but we only made it fifty metres along before he wrestled me into the layby next to "A Passage To India", cornered me against the wall, bumping my head slightly in the process and we had our first kiss. It was a Billy McGregor type kiss rather than a "Phantom Fucker" kiss, awkward and sloppy and hinting at a lack of experience on Ray's part. I wasn't concerned by this though, I was just delighted that someone of Ray's intelligence, confidence and maturity was interested in me. I was sure with practice his kissing would get better.

Ray was not a stereotypically handsome man but I found him attractive. He was very tall, over six feet, but was very slim, skinny even. A high jumper's frame. He probably weighed less than ten stone. He was dark haired and freckled, his hair was curly too which helped cover up his ears as they protruded. I remember an old school friend of Ray's once came into the Middleland and called Ray, "Plug". I presumed the reason for this was because he bore an uncanny resemblance to the character in the Dandy. Luckily for Ray, it was not a nickname that had followed him into adulthood.

Over the next twelve months, Ray and I grew closer. I always felt as though Ray enjoyed the fact that he thought he was dating an intellectual inferior, so he could lead and I could follow. He enjoyed the relationship being on a teacher and pupil type basis. He did teach me a lot, I had absolutely no understanding of politics or world affairs and I did became a better informed individual through Ray. Ray was a true blue Conservative, but from what he told me, I think my political views were moderate, SDP seemed like the right party for me.

At work, Ray decided the relationship should be kept under wraps from our colleagues, as the bank tended to frown upon relationships between two staff members within the same branch. With the branch performing well in Regional tables, Ray did not want our relationship to be the cause of him moving on. I am sure a few of the staff guessed, but we remained colleagues only at work. For my part, I decided to keep Ray away from my house and, in particular, Vomit Breath. If he walked me home, I avoided inviting him in. If we were going out somewhere, like the cinema, I would watch out of Kelly's window until he arrived and then run out down the path before he had an opportunity to make it to the door. I gave him a full briefing about Vomit Breath, so he knew she was a nasty piece of work, but in the early stages, I did not want him to see for himself. After six months of dating though, Ray decided he wanted to meet Vomit Breath "in the flesh" as "she can't be all bad". So, we agreed that one Saturday evening, Ray would come to our house and I would do something for our tea before heading out for a couple of drinks.

There was plenty to like about Ray but he was a stubborn man, very opinionated and seldom admitted he was wrong. After his encounter with Vomit Breath that Saturday evening, he was quick to retract his statement that Vomit Breath "can't be all bad". He admitted people, or Vomit Breath anyway, could be "all bad"! Ray was very keen for a first visit, but not so keen for a second. After that first encounter, I stopped having to use Kelly's room as a lookout point, Ray would just sit in his car and await my arrival. Once bitten, twice shy as they say!!!

Richie

By the thirteenth morning of standing outside Kelly's bedroom window, I was pretty sure she had no romantic interest in me whatsoever and just wanted to get back at me for cancelling our date, puking on her sister's hair and having sex with her sister (a charge I strongly deny), by humiliating me. On Morning Two, it was not Kelly that opened the curtains but Claire Northover and I had to perform "My Funny Valentine", a Frank Sinatra classic, in a howling wind, pouring rain and an over-sized bra. Thank goodness it was another short song!

On Morning Three, it was dry, but a pensioner up early to walk his dog, stopped on the pavement below me to check what on earth was going on and hear my rendition of U2's MLK. I had deliberately incorporated my three shortest songs into the first three days, as I had deduced that my confidence would increase as the days progressed so needed to get a few short but sweet songs in first.

Morning Four was another dry one, but I had my biggest audience to date - four (or five if a dog counts). The pensioner from the previous day had now brought his wife and Kelly had invited Jemma in to spectate. Having Jemma watch me was very unnerving. I liked to think Kelly was on my side and probably found my efforts a little charming but with Jemma watching, I could just feel the "what a dickhead!" vibes. I sang "Have I Told You Lately" and if Van Morrison had been watching, I am sure he would have dragged me off well before the second verse.

On Morning Five, the rain was back, it was absolutely belting down. I had decided if Kelly had even a shred of decency, she would stop me even before I started singing and invite me in for a nice warm cup of tea. It didn't happen, so I changed my Stevie Wonder song from "I Just Called To Say I Love You" to "For Once In My Life". It was an attempt at irony that I am sure Kelly didn't appreciate, but I was pretty sure now that, in contrast to the song I was singing, Kelly did not need me at all. I should have just told her where to go, there and then, as there was no-one else around, the pensioners were obviously put off by the bad weather and Kelly had not invited anyone else along to wallow in my misery.

Morning Six was actually brilliant, the only day I really enjoyed. I sang The Beatles "When I'm 64", at the time, I sang it because I liked it, we used to sing it in primary school, but now the fact I chose that song makes me feel incredibly sad. It was a bright, sunny morning, even at that early hour and once I finished Kelly smiled her beautiful smile in my direction. I skipped home that day and I even found time to shake the hand of the pensioner who had brought his dog out to watch once more.

It was all downhill from there! On Morning Seven, the second Saturday, I imagine Kelly must have stopped out as her curtains never opened. She either slept through my rendition, heard it from bed or woke up elsewhere and laughed at my expense. I began by singing, "Something" by The Beatles, but when it was evident that I was performing to an audience of zero, I swopped over to "Unforgettable" by Nat King Cole. Once again, I sang this for its ironic value. The pensioner didn't show up either. I was expecting an apology somehow, a phone call or a call at the door but it did not come. What was I supposed to do now? Keep on calling or just call it quits? I decided I would arrive on Morning Eight and if Kelly was still not there or could not be arsed getting out of bed again, then that was it, I was going to pack in.

I won't bore you with all the details from the following five mornings, Morning Eight to Morning Twelve, but needless to say, Kelly was back and I sang my love songs with an ever decreasing amount of gusto. I must also have lost my novelty value as far as the pensioner was concerned, as he had stopped attending.

On Morning Thirteen, I sang "Songbird" the Christine McVie, Fleetwood Mac classic. Once again, I sang a song that's lyrics were totally unsuitable for the circumstances, because by now I was utterly and completely pissed off with the whole thing. I just felt like I was making a complete fool of myself and when Kelly popped her head out the window after I'd finished, I was ready for her.

"I'm looking forward to tomorrow, Richie! Just the final, naked performance and then I am happy to draw a line in the sand and go on that date with you!"

"Piss off Kelly!"

"Pardon?"

It was starting to rain. Black clouds gathered together in an almighty huddle.

"I'm not coming back tomorrow, you can forget it. I've made myself look a complete arsehole for the last thirteen days and you've stripped me of any dignity that I used to have. There's no way I am stripping off all my clothes too. You may think it's worth putting me through this to pay me back for sleeping with your sister, but I have never slept with your stupid sister! I don't even like your sister, she's an arrogant bitch! The only reason I've allowed myself to look this stupid, Kelly Watkinson, is because I love you. I have wanted to go out with you for the last two years, but if you don't feel the same, frankly I don't give a shit any more! Find some other poor sod you can humiliate!"

I took my mother's bra off and threw it at her window, then I stormed down the path and back to "The Windmill" to collect my clothes. By now, it was really throwing it down and I arrived back at the side of the pub just in time to see that stray mongrel from the other day, cocking its leg up on my clothes. Bloody typical!

By the time I was halfway up Prescot Road in my piss stinking clothes, I was completely soaked. Thunder came, followed by lightning, followed by my tears. I felt like jumping on someone's roof, borrowing their TV aerial, strapping it to my back and seeing if one of those lightning bolts could come and finish me off. Why had I allowed myself to look so stupid? I hated myself for this and, for a short while, I hated Kelly just as much.

I arrived home feeling cold and miserable. As I walked in, my Dad was sat in the kitchen, drinking a cup of tea and listening to Radio Two.

"Good morning, son! Where have you been? Out trying to impress that girl again?!"

Bloody Caroline! Sometimes I thought I could trust her, but she had a big mouth!

"That was the last time. I've made an idiot of myself, Dad."

My Dad took a sip of his tea.

"Son, you're not the first lad to make a fool of himself for a woman and you certainly won't be the last! A little bird tells me she's called Kelly. A very nice girl so I'm told, she certainly sounds very nice!"

How much had Caroline told him? I was going to kick her in the shins when she
woke up!

"I thought she was nice, Dad. I've changed my mind now!"

"Why's that then?"

"She's made me do things I shouldn't have done."

"What sort of things?"

Dad must have been interested, he even got up and switched his radio off.

"Just things, Dad."

I didn't want to tell him.

"Legal things? She hasn't had you out robbing cars for her, has she?"

Dad smiled. He knew the last thing I would be doing was robbing cars. He had taken me driving once on Southport beach. I was hopeless, I kept stalling the bloody thing! Obviously, he had promised we'd keep going until I got the hang of it, but we never went back!

"Of course legal things! Silly things that's all. Silly things that made a mug of me."

"Why did you do them then?"

"Because I thought I loved her."

As soon as these words came out, they seemed very strange. It seemed OK to tell Kelly I loved her, but it seemed wrong to be disclosing this fact to my Dad, a man who shared very little with me. Anyway, how could I love Kelly? This wasn't love, for two years I had just longed for her, from afar.

"Does she not love you then, Richard?"

"No, she just loves me to look stupid!"

"So you don't think she'd like to go to the cinema with you tomorrow night, then?"

"Unless I was naked, probably not."

I think my Dad was trying to do the confusing, but now he was the one that was confused.

"What?!"

"Kelly just likes to see me make a fool of myself, if I went naked, I'd be making a fool of myself. She'd like that."

"Well, as I said, she sounds very nice to me and she told me she wants you to know she'd love to go to the cinema with you tomorrow night, if you'll find it in your heart to forgive her."

My heart started pounding. It would just be my luck to have a heart attack now, I thought to myself.

"She told you?"

"She just telephoned five minutes ago! Got me out of bed, she did, but as I say she sounded very nice so I'll let her off!"

This was one of those moments when I didn't know whether to laugh or cry. I had pursued Kelly Watkinson for two years and just when I had decided enough was enough, she had decided to reciprocate. Whoever said the chase is always better than the kill, had obviously not spent two years chasing Kelly! Wild horses would not stop me going on that date! I felt euphoric! I managed a smile. A big, fat smile.

"Thanks Dad!"

Dad grinned right back at me. This was a novelty in itself, sharing smiles with my father.

"She said something else too."

"What?"

Here came the catch! Kelly had said two weeks ago that I would have to apologise to Jemma. Bad news was on its way, I was sure of it, I bet Kelly had insisted that I had to make a grovelling apology to Jemma. No chance! I wasn't going to! Typical, I thought, just when I thought I had finally cracked it, here came the bad news!

"She said to tell you she'd wash your Mum's bra and bring it with her! Best not tell your mother that one, son! She might start worrying about you!"

Fair play to my Dad. He could tell when I walked in, that I was upset, knew he had been given the power to put everything right and had delivered his lines to perfection, even managing to share a joke with me to finish off. As I was getting older, I was growing to like him more and more. He still had all the same faults and bad habits he had had when I was a child, but as I grew older, I was learning to accept them.

"Is the hot water on, Dad?"

"It is."

"I think I'll go and jump in the bath."

"Good lad. You look like you need a good, hot bath!"

"And thanks, Dad."

"What for?"

"For being a good Dad."

Dad and I didn't hug. We didn't kiss. We didn't generally tell each other how much we meant to each other, so it felt good praising him and I knew it would mean a lot to him receiving praise from me.

I jumped in the bath, feeling back on top of the world again. As I sat there though, warming back up, thinking how life could change from bad to good in an instant, I felt something. Something odd. I was just there, messing with the soap, slipping it up my left groin, across my stomach and then down the other side, under my testicles and back around. I just felt something wasn't right. I dropped the soap and felt with my hands. It was on my left testicle. Was it a lump? I wasn't sure. What did my balls normally feel like? I wasn't sure.

Was it something to worry about? No, of course it bloody wasn't! I worried too much about everything. It was probably nothing. Life was on the up and I needed to keep smiling, a sunny disposition, that's what I needed. Tomorrow, I would be going out with the most beautiful woman in the world and I was the luckiest lad alive.

Jemma

The doorbell rang. I opened it almost instantly and there stood Ray brandishing a small bouquet of flowers.

"For your Mum!" he explained before I had the chance to thank him.

Ray had obviously not heeded my warnings about Vomit Breath. Arriving with flowers was a daft move, she was about as interested as flowers as she was interested in poetry.

Vomit Breath wandered into the hallway to see who had arrived.

"For you, Mrs. Watkinson!" said Ray, extending his arm out and passing Vomit Breath the flowers. If he had passed her a plastic bag, full to the brim with dog poo, she could not have looked less enthused.

"What am I supposed to do with these?"

"I'm sorry", Ray said in his upper middle class tones, "do you not like flowers?"

"Say that again!" Vomit Breath urged.

"I'm sorry, did you not hear me? I said, do you not like flowers?"

"I heard you first time, love, I just wanted to hear your voice! You're dead posh, aren't you? Pity you're so ugly, you could have been a James Bond if you hadn't been so bloody ugly!"

I gave Ray one of my "told you so" looks. I told him to expect a barrage of insults. Vomit Breath was not letting me down. Not unusually, she was also drunk.

"Take a look in the mirror before you start calling people ugly, Mum!"

Vomit Breath ignored me.

"Come through". I said to Ray, we were still standing in the hallway.

"I'm going to make Ray something for tea. Can you make everyone's life easier by clearing off to the Ropers?"

When I spoke about my mother to anyone, I referred to her as Vomit Breath but for about five years, in her company, I refused to call her a name. Mum was a term of endearment that Vomit Breath did not deserve. Vomit Breath looked at Ray as though I had just cut her nipples off with a pair of scissors.

"That's charming, isn't it?! Do you speak to your mother like that, lad?"

Ray shuffled uncomfortably.

"No".

"Ray's mother isn't a drunken troublemaker." I added.

"Is that your name is it? Ray?"

"No, his name's Simon. I just call him Ray for a laugh!"

Again Vomit Breath ignored me.

"I've met a few nice fellas called Ray. Better looking than you, mind! Always good in bed, Ray's are. Big dicks normally! Last fella I had called Ray had a dick so big, I called him Sting Ray!"

"Go away, will you?!" I begged.

"Are you good in the sack, Ray? Does Jemma close her eyes? Wouldn't want that ugly mug of yours looking down at me!"

I'd had enough. I dragged Ray up the stairs to the sanctuary of my bedroom. He'd been at our house less than two minutes. I slammed the door behind us.

"She's a bit of a character, like you said!" Ray commented.

"A character! I didn't say she was a character, Ray! I said she was a total nightmare and she is!"

"Surely she's not as bad as that when she's sober?"

I thought about that.

"Probably not actually, no. She doesn't tend to do sober though, just drunk or hungover. When she's hungover, she just stomps around angrily. Its better though as she hardly opens that big, fat gob of hers. Gives us some peace."

"Does Kelly not get on with her either?"

"No, Kelly tolerates her better than me, but we both hate her. What is there not to hate?"

"Is Kelly in?"

"Yes, she's in. Hang on! KELLY!" I shouted, "Kelly! Come in here!"

Within a few seconds, Kelly arrived at my door. She knew I had company so she knocked. I guess Amy's story of my backside glowing back at her at the Birch's party still haunted Kelly!

"Come in!"

Kelly entered with a towel wrapped around her head. Even with a towel on her hair and a pink dressing gown on, she still had the capacity to look stunning. I wasn't concerned that Ray might find Kelly more attractive than me because even if he did, he would be wasting his time. Kelly would not be the slightest bit interested in Ray. She was too good for him.

"Ray, this is my sister, Kelly. Kelly this is Ray."

Kelly smiled. Ray pouted in a macho fashion.

"I take it Mum's been trying to cause trouble again?"

"Would you expect anything else?" I replied.

Ray was looking serious. Thinking about it, he always looked serious.

"Kelly, I believe you are taking your GCSEs this year."

"Yes."

"Now I don't want to sound patronising, but make sure you do everything you can to get good grades. Going to University was the best thing I ever did, if you have the chance, work hard and get there. Jemma says you're a clever girl. Make sure you take the opportunity, you'll never regret it."

I think Kelly found Ray's advice useful but she was aware of an issue that perhaps Ray had overlooked.

"Mum would love that, wouldn't she, Jemma, if I went to University?! She keeps moaning on about Sixth Form and not wanting me to stay on. She keeps saying its about time I went out and earned a living. She said she'd break my neck if I went to University!"

I explained the situation to Ray.

"Ray, I'm sure you have been raised by good people and although I would love to say that Vomit Breath has a soft and cuddly side, the reality is that she hasn't. She's a selfish, drunken cow who only ever thinks about herself.

Because Vomit Breath has been spawned by the devil, I've said I'll fund as much of Kelly's education as I possibly can. Kelly works in Woolworths too on Saturdays, so she is putting most of her own money away too, aren't you Kel?"

"Yes. No point relying on Mum to fund me!"

"You'd get a grant too, of course!" Ray added, "I'm sure it would be the full amount too, given the circumstances."

"Well," Kelly said, "it all seems a long way off just now. Anyway, I need to go and blow dry my hair. Nice meeting you, Ray!"

"Nice meeting you too, Kelly! Don't forget what I said. Work hard. Control your destiny!"

"OK. Thanks Ray!"

Kelly left. I was amused. I thought Ray just saved those pep talks for work, but obviously not. I liked Ray a lot, but he took himself very seriously. He was twenty three going on fifty.

Ray and I stayed and talked in my room for about half an hour, about people at work, about Ray's ambitions, he wanted to be an Area Manager then National Branch Manager, then on the Executive, he had it all mapped out. We also talked about his family, his mother was a hygienist at the dentists and his father was a dentist, but at a different practice to his Mum. He had one sister, Verity, who had studied law at Manchester University and was now working in a solicitor's office in London. Ultimately she was going to be a barrister. That's something I noticed about Ray, his singlemindedness. Ray said "she was going to be" not "hoped to be" or "wanted to be". I liked that about Ray, he was focused on progression and obviously his sister was to.

After half an hour, we ventured back out from the safety of my bedroom like a pair of soldiers emerging from the trenches . I had bought a couple of lasagnes that I could just put in the oven, so we headed to the kitchen for me to pop them in. I knew Vomit Breath would come and pester us, but I was past caring. Sure enough, when we walked into the kitchen, she was sat at the table, half-smoked cigarette in her left hand and a vodka and a smouldering ashtray on the table.

"Can you go and smoke somewhere else, I'm putting our tea in now."

"No, I can't. I own this house!"

"You don't! Mr Bukhari owns it."

"Well I pay the bloody rent! What are you cooking us?"

Vomit Breath knew full well I would not be cooking her a thing.

"I'm not cooking you anything. Ray and I are having lasagne."
"When did you make that?"
"I bought it."
"Real hostess you, aren't you? Would you have made more of an effort if he", she pointed at Ray, "wasn't so ugly? You should see what she makes her handsome boyfriends, Roy. Three course meals. Roast dinners and everything!"
"Take no notice of her, Ray. I have never had anyone here before. Probably won't have anyone here again, after today."

I turned the oven on and went to the freezer. I had left the lasagnes in the first compartment, they weren't there. I checked the second, third and fourth compartments. No lasagnes.

"Have you taken my lasagnes out the freezer?" I asked Vomit Breath sternly.

Vomit Breath dragged on the remaining stub of her cigarette.
"I didn't know they were yours. I had them at lunchtime."
"Both of them?"
"I was hungry. I'd had no breakfast."
"Well what are we going to have now?"
"There's a bit of cheese in the fridge."

I went to the fridge. It was virtually empty other than a small slab of cheese which a small mouse would regard as a morsel. I then checked the cupboards. All that was in there was a mouldy loaf. Old Mother Hubbard was an alternative name for Vomit Breath.

"Right, Ray. Looks like we are going out."

Vomit Breath finally gave up on the remnants of her cigarette and stubbed it out.

"Take a key, love. I'm off out myself in half an hour. If I play my cards right, I might be out all night. If you two come back here, make sure you put a nodder on, Roy. Last thing I want is an ugly grandchild! Do you want me to see if I have got any spare nodders before you go? It would make things right, wouldn't it, after me eating your tea."

We ignored her. Ray left the house as quickly as he could. Only stopping briefly to shout a quick goodbye up the stairs to Kelly.

"Fair play to your father for going anywhere near that!" Ray said as we walked towards town, "He should be knighted for bravery!"

It was the funniest thing I had ever heard Ray say, which wasn't saying much. Comedy and lighthearted banter were not Ray's strong points.

"Do you know what? I've seen pictures of Vomit Breath from twenty years ago and she used to look like me. If I went on one continuous piss up from now until I was thirty eight and smoked my way through it, I could turn out like that!"

Ray was stunned.

"Don't tell me your mother is thirty eight!!!"

"She looks older, doesn't she?"

"My grandmother looks younger and she's seventy! Don't ever do that to yourself, Jemma. Beauty is important for a woman, it's a way of getting power. Your mother has obviously been a fool but she can't turn back the clock now. You have your whole life ahead of you, value it and make the most of it."

I smiled to myself. Ray made me smile., he didn't mean to, but he made me smile. He talked a lot of well meaning crap! Ray noticed my suppressed laughter.

"What are you giggling at?" he asked.

"Ray, are you sure you're twenty three and not sixty?! You talk like an old man sometimes!"

I could tell I had offended him.

"I talk sense Jemma, that's what I talk. Complete sense."

I took Ray's hand. I felt safe with Ray. In my life, safe was not a word I had been too familiar with, I liked it. Vomit Breath would not go near a man like Ray, he didn't drink and the craziest thing he had ever done was close the Bank two minutes early on Christmas Eve. He was definitely a safe pair of hands. In the future, I thought he would be a good family man. Maybe our future would be together, who knows? I was just relieved that my wild days were behind me and I was now more responsible, a better person. I'm sure Kelly was proud of me.

Richie

We were on the bus going to Maghull to the Astra Cinema to see "Rain Man". It was a double decker, Kelly and I were the only ones upstairs. We had met at Ormskirk bus station and ten minutes into our date, we were chatting away like old friends.

"You know you said you had seen our Jemma out and about with her boyfriend, what did you think of him?"

I cast my mind back. Although I was infatuated with Kelly, at bedtime, sometimes, I still visualised Jemma when I needed a sleeping pill of sorts. When I had seen Jemma out and about in Ormskirk with her boyfriend, it was not the boyfriend that I tended to look at. I thought hard.

"Tall, skinny…that's about it really."

Kelly became impassioned.

"Ugly and boring would be my two words! I met him the other week and he gave me a lecture like my Nan would, about the importance of education and all that crap. I was looking at him and thinking, 'What the hell is our Jemma doing going out with this wazzock?!!' Excuse my French but he's a fuckwit!!"

"He works with her, doesn't he?"

I sort of pretended I only half remembered, just so the accusation of stalking did not return.

"Yes, at the Middlelands. He's her boss!"

"Maybe it's in her interest to 'go out' with him, then!"

Kelly shook her head. Not in disagreement with me, more in disbelief at her sister's boyfriend choice.

"She's changed since she started there. I know you described her as an arrogant bitch the other day, but at least she used to be feisty! This Ray is just making her really, really boring!"

I was enjoying every second of our date so far. Kelly was lively, energetic and fun. I was proud to be seen with her too, every male downstairs on the bus wanted to be me, I could tell. I deliberately went up the stairs before her, it probably seemed like a lack of chivalry, but she was wearing a cream dress above the knee and if I'd have followed her up the stairs, my eyes would have followed the inside of that dress up to her knickers and I would then have had to sit their uncomfortably, waiting for things to shrink!

"Kelly, I don't ever want to mention this again, but can I just say one thing?"

Kelly looked right into my eyes. Inside I shivered, her green eyes were just wonderful. I was right the other day, I was the luckiest man alive.

"Richie, you have my permission to say whatever you want!"

My mind then played tricks with me. Having permission to say what I wanted was a teenage boys dream come true, my mind wanted to say,

'I really, really, really want to shag you, Kelly Watkinson!!' but luckily I didn't say that, I said what I had initially intended to say,

"Whatever Jemma may think, it was not me that slept with her at Joey Birch's party."

Kelly took my hands in hers.

"I believe you."

"You do?"

That shocked me, I just thought Kelly had forgiven me for sleeping with Jemma, I didn't think she actually believed that I hadn't.

"I think Jemma will always be unsure whether it was you or not, but I know now that it wasn't."

"Great," I held her hands even tighter, "that means a lot to me, Kelly."

I leaned over and kissed her. It was just meant to be a peck on the lips at first, but it naturally developed into a full blown snog. No tongues, just a lovely, lingering kiss. Her full lips were amazing to kiss. It was the nicest kiss I had ever had. Without a shadow of a doubt. When I pulled away from her, I could see the bus driver looking at us through his reflective mirror.

'Jammy bastard!' he was probably thinking!

"Wow!" Kelly said as she came up for air, "I wasn't expecting that just yet!"

"I've waited very patiently for two years to have an opportunity to do that, Kelly, I couldn't wait much longer!"

Every second of that whole evening was perfect. "Rain Man" was a brilliant choice of film, although I couldn't help wondering how attracted Kelly was to Tom Cruise. We even managed to keep our lips off each other throughout, although our hands remained sweatily clenched. After the film finished though, we went for a walk rather than catch the first bus home as neither of us wanted the night to end. We walked along for a while comfortably silent before Kelly asked,

"Do you think you'll go to Uni next year?"

"I hope so."

"Will you go far away, do you think?"

I hoped this was a leading question. I hoped this meant Kelly was thinking we would still be together in twelve months time and she didn't want me moving too far afield.

"Probably not. I want to go to Manchester."

Thirty five miles away. A grin covered Kelly's face. I was right, this was what she had been thinking!

"To study what?" she asked.

"History."

Kelly smiled even more, "I hate history!"

"How can you hate history?!" I asked. "History covers everything! Tomorrow this date will be history!"

"I don't think you'll study this date for your degree!"

"No, but every major event that has ever happened is history! How can you hate history? History is knowledge!"

Kelly smiled yet again, I smiled too. It was the night of smiles.

"I like you, Richie Billingham! I like the way you think!"

"Well that's good, Kelly Watkinson, because I pretty much worship the ground you walk on!"

If there had been any earwigging bystanders, this would have been the point at which they would have stuck two fingers down their throat, but there wasn't, we were well and truly alone and anyway, there was no point playing it cool, I had spent two years chasing Kelly. I think she had a good idea about how I felt!

Kelly laughed.

"Do you think you are the cheesiest man that ever lived?!"

"Well, remember you once said that Risk is your middle name?"

"Yes."

"Well mine is Cheddar!"

"Richie Cheddar Billingham", Kelly said, "I like it!"

Kelly reached over and kissed me. This was a dream.

"Pinch me, Kelly!"

This was not a mild sado-masochistic request.

"Why?"

"Just pinch me."

Kelly gave me a gentle pinch on my left arm. She knew what I was going to say but I was justifying my middle name. Live up to your billing, that's what I say!

"No, I'm definitely not dreaming!"

"I knew this date would go well!" Kelly said "I'm psychic you see! We'll go well together you and I, you're cheese and I'm crackers!"

We caught the bus home, shared a lovely kiss at the bottom of Kelly's path, I promised to ring her in the morning and then I ran the three miles home, it didn't seem far at all. It was a perfect summers night. The stars illuminated the sky and lit my pathways home.

Once I got home though, I couldn't sleep as I kept replaying the date in my head, over and over again. It had been absolutely brilliant. Eventually, growing tired but with an active mind, I decided the solution may be to have a little play. I checked over on Jim, he was flat out, not quite snoring but breathing noisily. I slipped my hand under my pyjama bottoms, closed my eyes and pictured Kelly. I pictured us reaching her front door and her saying,

"Come in! No-one's home, my Mum and sister are on holiday, it's just you and me…"

Pictured us climbing the stairs to her bedroom, pictured Kelly laying down on her bed, hastily removing her clothes until she was left with just her bra and knickers. Pictured me falling hungrily on top of her, kissing those lovely full lips over and over and over again……….

I stopped. I had felt it again. That lump. There was definitely something strange about that lump. There was definitely a lump on my left testicle. No doubt about it. If it had always been there and my left ball had always just had a weird lump on it, surely I would have felt it before? Wouldn't I? Maybe not. Maybe it had always been there and I was just more aware of my body now I had a girlfriend. I decided against playing around. I tried to go to sleep but my mind was now thinking about health related issues rather than romantic ones. Maybe your privates were a bit like your face, whereby you could get a lump for a few days and then it would just go away. Testicular acne. I had never heard of it but no-one was going to come to school and talk about "Ball Zits"! I couldn't really think of who I could ask about it without feeling embarrassed, so I just made a mental note to keep an eye on it, then I went to sleep dreaming of Kelly Watkinson and re-living that perfect date.

Richie (six months later)

"What do you think it is?" I asked Jim, I had pulled my boxer shorts down in front of him.

"It's a bollock! A hairy bollock!"

"I know it's a bollock, you stupid knobhead! That on it. What's that?"

"It's a lump. Does it hurt?"

Jim went to prod it. I backed away.

"It does a bit, yes. It'd hurt if you shoved your fingernails into it!"

"How long has it been there?"

"I'm not sure. I noticed it a few months ago."

"Have you shown anyone else?" Jim enquired.

"No, you're the first."

"Aren't I the lucky one?!" Jim sarcastically noted.

"Do you think it's something nasty?"

"Richie, I've no idea! Thankfully big lumps on my bollocks are not something I have experience of. Go and ask your Doctor."

"I'm not lobbing my meat and two veg out in front of my Doctor! What if it's nothing? I'd look like an idiot."

"Don't go then. When you're in a hospital bed dying of cancer, see how much of an idiot you look then!"

Trust Jim to put it so succinctly! Did he think it was cancer? I thought it was, Jim obviously did too.

"Anyway," Jim added, "you quite happily lobbed them out in front of me!"

"That's different, Jim. We share a room, you've had seventeen years of seeing me naked."

"As I said 'Lucky Me!'"

"I'm not going to the Doctor's!"

"Show Kelly then. See what she thinks."

I was getting flustered with Jim now.

"Jim, that's an even worse suggestion! I want Kelly to be attracted to my balls and knob, not scared by them."

"She'll have seen the one eyed white ghost and goolies before though?!"

I didn't reply. My silence said everything.

Jim continued, "She's not seen them yet then?!"

"NO!"

"You're a fast mover, aren't you?!"

Jim had a bloody cheek! Up until six months ago, he had not even been anywhere near a girl, then he started wearing black clothing and announced he was a "Goth".

Dad kept saying Jim looked like a young Johnny Cash, which pissed Jim off no end, he knew Johnny Cash was a decent looking lad in his prime but Jim wanted to look like a Goth not a country and western singer. Nevertheless, the "Gothettes" seemed to like him. Several weekends he had come home, woke me up and related his sexual encounters to me in a little too much detail. Jim thought he was a "Gothic Casanova" now.

"Jim, I'm not like you. 'Every hole is a goal' and all that crap! I'm not in a desperate rush to sleep with the girl I'm with before she discovers what an arsehole I am!"

I pulled my boxer shorts back up.

Jim cupped his hand to hear his ear.

"What's that's sound I hear? Oh, I know, it's envy! You're just jealous, Richie! At least I'm not a hunchback with a lump on my back and a lump on my balls!"

Bloody hell! Of all people, why had I thought it a good idea to speak to Jim about this lump? He had now picked up a newspaper and was rushing around our bedroom trying to squash a fly.

"You know what I don't get?" Jim asked.

"What?"

"Flies. If I was a fly and someone was trying to squash me into a million little pieces, I wouldn't just fly from here to here."

Jim indicated about three inches.

"What I would do," he continued, "is fly as far away as my little wings would carry me so the big oaf with the newspaper would not get a second chance to smash my brains to smithereens. It's a stupid creature with a stupid name! "Fly"! We don't call sheep "Baa" or "Grass Munchers" or dogs "Woof" or "Sniffers", because that's what they do, so why do we call a creature that flies a "fly"? Madness!"

I shook my head. Another pearl of wisdom from my lunatic of a brother!

"What do you suggest we call them?"

Jim sneaked up on a fly and smashed his newspaper down, missing it by a split second.

"Annoying twat!" he muttered.

"Can't see it catching on!" I replied. "Just imagine mothers teaching their kids, this is a bee, this is a wasp and this is an annoying twat!"

"You're an annoying twat!" Jim moaned, putting his paper down and accepting the fly had defeated him.

"Look who's talking, Jim! I asked for some advice on my lumpy ball and all I get is the hunchback insult and some nonsense about re-naming flies!"

I had sat down by this time on my bed and Jim now came and sat next to me. I felt uncomfortable as we normally granted each other a lot of personal space. I'd have told him to move but I realised he was about to launch into some brotherly advice.

"Richie", he began, "excuse the pun that's on its way, but you need to grow some balls and get down to the doctors and let them have a look at that ball sack. As I said I'm by no means an expert, but I've seen a programme on TV about testicular cancer and on that, they said most of the time, lumps are just harmless cysts. They'll probably just drain it away. That's not for me to tell you though, Richie, that's for a Doctor to tell you. Do yourself a favour, Richie and go and see a Doctor! He's not going to bite it!"

"OK, ok! I will! I will!"

Miraculously, Jim had actually helped. I felt better about it now. I'd never even heard about cysts in your privates, but according to Jim, that's what lumps normally were. I thought I had cancer, without a doubt, but in all likelihood, it was a cyst. A harmless cyst! Not sure if I fancied a Doctor draining it off though, that didn't sound pleasant, it sounded humiliating! If it was harmless, maybe I could hold off visiting the Doctor, I decided, for now anyway. If it got a bit bigger or more painful, I would definitely go to see the Doctor, but not just yet. I would probably have to listen to Jim's jokes about odd shaped balls for fifty years, but that was OK. At least now I felt confident, I would be around to hear them.

Jemma

Richie Billingham was back on the scene! To give him his due, as far as I was aware, he had not been near another girl in two years, the only girl he had eyes for was Kelly. It was hard to know how to feel about him though, he was obviously smitten with Kelly. If he had just held his hands up though, admitted to sleeping with me and apologised, both to Kelly and myself for what he did, I think I could have at least partially forgiven him. An apology, however, was not forthcoming. Thus, I would have been happier if Richie had withdrawn from the scene and left Kelly alone, but it appeared very unlikely that this was going to happen.

One Monday night, just before I was about to get into bed, Kelly came into my room.

"Are you alright, honey?" she asked.

"Fine thanks, Kelly, just off to bed."

"What time are you up in the morning?"

"I normally get up about seven, have a shower and do my hair before work. Why?"

"Fancy getting up at six?"

Kelly was not one for asking daft questions. I would not want to get up at six just for the hell of it, there was obviously something going on.

"Why?!"

"Last Friday, I set Richie a challenge. He had to come here for fourteen days on the trot, just in a bra and speedos and sing me a love song from below my window at six a.m! He'll be here in the morning! Fancy watching?!"

"You are making him wear a bra and speedos?!!"

"Yes! I'm testing him! I want to make sure he's true to his word when he says he'll do anything for me!"

Suddenly I had a flashback to a bizarre conversation I had with Vomit Breath on Saturday afternoon.

"How long has he been doing this?" I asked.

"Three days so far. It's really funny, you should see him. He's really cute!"

"Kelly, you bitch!!"

Kelly looked hurt despite me saying it in a tone that implied I was only joking.

"I'm not a bitch, Jemma! I'm telling you, I'm just testing him. He says he'll do anything for me, I want to see if he really will.."

This did not sound like the best of plans to me.

"Kelly, you can't do that! You decide whether you like them by gauging how strongly your heart beats when you see them and how much you miss them when they aren't there. You don't put people to a test to see how much they will endure for you. You're just tormenting the poor lad!"

For a split second, it looked like Kelly was going to cry.

"I can't believe what I'm hearing! Are my ears deceiving me? Are you calling Richie Billingham a poor lad? You, of all people!!"

"It just sounds like a mean thing to do. Vomit Breath was calling me a slag on Saturday because she reckoned she'd come across some hunk on the path who she'd caught red handed leaving my room, post-shag apparently! She even mentioned that I'd tied my bra around his thigh! I presume this was Richie?"

Kelly's head bowed a little.

"Yes. Am I awful, Jemma?"

Kelly looked at me, her face flush with embarrassment.

"Do you really want to know what I think, Kelly?"

"Please."

"On the one hand, I do think its harsh, but on the other.... I think it's bloody hilarious!!"

Kelly looked at me and we both cracked up. I laughed so hard, I nearly wet myself. When we finally calmed down, Kelly asked,

"So do you want waking for tomorrow's performance then?"

"Absolutely!!! I wouldn't miss this for the world!"

Kelly woke me at 5.45 with a cup of tea. Five minutes later, I was sat on her bed as she peered through her curtains, awaiting Richie's arrival and five minutes later again, she excitedly announced,

"He's here! He's here!"

It felt like she was announcing the arrival of a beardless Father Christmas in speedos! Kelly pulled her curtains apart, then opened her window.

"Good morning, Mr.Billingham!"

I peered out besides Kelly.

"Morning", replied Richie, he appeared a little downtrodden, perhaps because I was there or perhaps it was because some old couple and their dog had stopped at the end of our path to watch him. Whatever the reason, I did feel sorry for him. Despite the "Phantom Fucker" episode, despite laughing my tits off the previous night when I heard about this bizarre routine Kelly was subjecting him to, I truly felt for him. I just wanted to run down the stairs and give him a hug. Not a romantic hug, just a sympathetic one. He looked so silly in his speedos and white bra that had obviously been manufactured to prop up a bosom far more ample than Richie's! He looked pale, but his body was really attractive, long, muscular legs and an athletic, young man's torso with just a hint of a six pack. For me, this was just confirmation that Richie was indeed "The Phantom Fucker", but my insides did not well up with hatred, there was just calmness and acceptance.

Richie sang, "Have I Told You Lately", a beautiful Van Morrison song, but he sang it like a cat that was having its tail rammed up its own backside with a broom!

"He's crap!" I whispered to Kelly.

"I know," she whispered back, "he knows too, he's just doing it for me! How sweet is that?!"

"Very!" I replied honestly.

I considered for a second whether Ray would do the same for me, it only took that second to dispel it as a preposterous notion, with the answer most certainly being,

'Not a chance!' Ray took himself far too seriously to agree to such a stunt.

Once finished, Richie gave us a little bow and then he was off back down the path and we watched him slowly disappear into the distance down Wigan Road.

"Do you still really think, Richie, with the way he feels about me, crept into your room and screwed you that night at the Birch's?"

I knew why Kelly was asking. It was the same reason she had invited me into her room to witness Richie's devotion. Richie's feeling for Kelly were being reciprocated but Kelly felt she needed my consent before anything happened.

"I'm not sure now," I replied, "his body certainly seems different to the one in the bedroom. I was really drunk Kelly, I can't be 100% sure, maybe I have made a massive mistake."

"I think you did!" Kelly said like a girl excited to be on the verge of a great romance.

"I think you definitely did!"

I gave Kelly a hug. Tactfully, I had given Kelly my blessing to begin a relationship with Richie Billingham. There was nothing I wanted more in life than to see Kelly happy and that morning, I realised Richie would do anything for her and he had the ability to make her happy. Bizarrely, one of the feelings I had to suppress, as I went to have my breakfast, before getting ready for work, was a feeling of jealousy. It wasn't because I was attracted to Richie, far from it, it was just because big, romantic gestures were not really Ray's style. He might change though, I told myself, as I finished my cup of tea and toast and besides, nobody's perfect.

Richie

It was a beautiful summer's day. There were a couple of big, fluffy, cumulonimbus clouds in the sky and up in the heavens a few whispy cirrus ones, but other than that it was just a mass of blue sky. Just the weather I had hoped for, or so I thought, until I was halfway up Holborn Hill between Ormskirk and Aughton, then I started wishing it was not quite so hot!

I had told Kelly I would meet her at her house and, weather permitting, we would go on a picnic. My Mum had bought a brilliant straw picnic basket which contained everything you could possibly need for a picnic – plates, plastic glasses, cutlery, a picnic rug, salt and pepper pots, condiment pots, the only thing missing was the food itself, so I had been up early and begged a lift off my Mum into Ormskirk to buy that. I even managed to get away with being eighteen in order to buy a mini bottle of champagne. I was only a few months off eighteen and with being tall, no-one ever requested documentation from me.

Despite the heat, I eventually managed to make it up to the top of Holborn Hill and then by Christ Church we crossed over Northway, the dual carriageway that ran from Ormskirk to Liverpool. After criss-crossing along a couple of back roads, we ended up on Clieves Hill, our picnic destination point. This was the side of Aughton that I loved best, small, quaint, nineteenth century cottages, old narrow roads that wound their way to Formby and Southport and a mass of greenery. From the hill, you see for miles in all directions. I was in my element, perfect place for a picnic with perfect weather and perfect company too. Fantastic!

"Look at the view!" I said excitedly to Kelly as we finally stopped walking and opened the basket to lay down our rug.

"That's Liverpool over there and just beyond it, that's Wales and if you look across the other way, you can see Blackpool. Can you see Blackpool Tower there in the distance?" I asked Kelly.

"Yes. I can see it! It's wonderful up here, Richie! I bet it's great on New Year's Eve when all the fireworks are going off. Imagine it on New Year's Eve 1999! It'd be amazing!"

"Maybe we can come back here with our kids that night!" I suggested.

"Maybe! All five of them!"

"Six", I corrected her, "don't forget Looby Trixy Lix!"

Kelly and I had now been dating for twelve months and both of us were guilty of making statements presuming we would remain a couple for the rest of our lives.

'When we get married, I'd like it to be at St. Michael's in Aughton', Kelly would say, 'it's such a beautiful church'.

Or I would say, 'When we go on our Honeymoon to Tahiti, which island will we go to? Do you fancy Bora Bora?!'

Everything was going so well, it just didn't seem natural to think one day it would come to an end.

We sat down on our rug, looking out across the miles and started to tuck into our picnic.

"So when did you say you used to come here?" Kelly asked with her mouth full of a chicken drumstick.

"Pretty often when we were kids. My Dad used to bring us here. Mum raised us without much help from my Dad really. My Dad was a gambler, still is, so his Saturday's were spent engrossed in the horse racing on BBC 1. If he wasn't gambling, he'd go to watch Bolton Wanderers with a few of his mates, so sometimes on Sunday mornings, Mum would be tearing her hair out because she'd had us all week, so she'd say to my Dad, something along the lines of,

"Can you take the kids out for a couple of hours just to give me some peace?"

So Dad would reluctantly bundle us all into the car, buy a newspaper and take us somewhere. If it was a nice, pleasant day, he would get Mum to make us a picnic and bring us here. If it was raining, he'd normally take us to Southport and let us loose in the Amusement arcades. He'd normally end up on the fruit machines too!"

I paused, looking around, taking everything in again, as childhood memories came flooding back.

"I loved coming here though. My Dad used to call this place 'The Sunny Road' because we only ever came here on sunny days. He told us whatever the weather was on the other side of Aughton, it was always sunny here. It took me a few years to realise he was lying!

On a lovely summer's day, he'd just sit here, with a flask of coffee and a paper and we would just play in the fields and run up and down the lane before stuffing our faces full of sandwiches and Wagon Wheels! I've a lot of happy childhood memories of this place."

Kelly put her arms around my neck and kissed me.

"We should keep coming here then!" Kelly decided. "Then you'll have happy adult memories of this place too. On a Saturday or Sunday in the summer, if its sunny, we should do what we've done today, make a picnic and then say, 'Right! Let's go to the Sunny Road'!"

"OK, let's do that!" I agreed. "It can become our place then, rather than just my childhood place."

"Then," Kelly added, "if we ever split up, when you drive past here in your Volvo with your wife and three kids, you'll think,

'I used to go there with that girl. What was her name again?!'"

I didn't like the way this conversation was going. A few seconds earlier, I was having six kids with Kelly, now Kelly and I were splitting up and I was being allocated a Volvo, a random wife and three kids. We hadn't ever talked about splitting up before. Every conversation about the future was about our future together.

"What makes you think we'll split up?" I asked in a sullen fashion.

"I'm not saying we will split up, I'm just saying 'if we ever split up'. Hopefully we won't."

"We won't!" I stated firmly. "Unless you finish with me!"

Perhaps I wore my heart on my sleeve too often but I couldn't help it, that was me.

Kelly ran her hand through her hair and then fixed me with an intense look. A serious look rather than an annoyed one.

"Richie, I don't know whether I will ever finish with you and…."

I was about to butt in with 'I know I'll never finish with you!' but sensing that, Kelly verbally marched on, acknowledging my interruption as she went.

"Let me finish, Richie! I don't know whether I will ever finish with you and I don't know whether you will ever finish with me. Saying we won't is basically promising things will stay exactly as they are now and we will stay exactly as we are now. Things change, Richie! People change. Who knows how you will feel when you go to Uni? You may meet someone on your course or you might study miles away and we may try everything in our powers to stay together but the distance may intervene. We just don't know! We just have to make the most of our time together and hope fate is on our side and we stay together for a very long time."

"Or forever." I suggested.

I was beginning to notice that my determination to stay with Kelly may be interpreted by her as desperation. This was not good. Caroline once said in one of her more profound moments that it takes two people to drive a relationship, one to steer and the other to change the gears and work the pedals. If either person wants to do all the driving, the other will just go and buy another car! Although I loved Kelly and wanted us to stay together, I would never become a doormat and hoped she realised this, despite my statements of everlasting love! Just to be on the safe side, I warned myself to ease off a little!

Kelly reached over and kissed me again. She was very tactile, I could be too but sometimes I would debate, inside my head, whether it was the right moment whilst Kelly would just do whatever she wanted to do!

"Let's just keep making the most of our time together, that's all I'm saying!"

Kelly was smarter than me. She talked about things on a level I didn't. My natural tendency was to worry about simple things and problems that existed in the moment, like whether it was a good time to kiss or whether I should put my hand down her top or what we should do for the rest of the day, whilst Kelly would naturally think about the meaning of life and whether there is a God or not and how a lifetime is a short time and we should do and see as much as we can whilst we are here. We were different animals but I could throw myself into her world and she could slot into mine. Kelly knew though that her little speech had dampened my spirits, derailed my emotions, so she tried to get things back on track.

"I know what we should do!" she announced.

"What?" I replied, not quite snappily but certainly moodily.

"Whatever happens we should meet on the 'Sunny Road' for the rest of our lives. Once a year, every year, on New Year's Eve, we should make a pact to meet up, irrespective of whether we are together or not!"

This was one of those rare occasions that Kelly was in such a rush to make me feel better, she had not properly thought through her suggestion. I started to laugh a little.

"Kelly! If you and I weren't together, soon enough you would have a new boyfriend and I would have a new girlfriend. Eventually you would get married and have a husband and I would get married and have a wife. Do you not think they would get a little suspicious if we kept disappearing on New Year's Eve?! Anyway, it wouldn't even be a 'Sunny Road' at the end of December!"

Kelly was ruffled! I was not used to seeing her ruffled!

"Don't laugh at me! It doesn't have to be New Year's Eve, I was just thinking aloud! We could meet any day of the year you wanted. If it had to be sunny, we can say we will meet every 4th July, American Independence Day, for the rest of our days, but if we get close to 'Sunny Road' and it is not a sunny day, we will leave it for another year."

I liked this now. It was becoming a big romantic gesture.

"That's a better suggestion! What would we do when we got here? Kiss, cuddle, bonk?!!"

I was half-joking, but half-serious, I was trying to picture the scene a few years down the line and wanted to know whether Kelly would be clambering into the back of my car for a quickie or whether we would just formally shake hands or share a peck on the cheek. I was almost eighteen, I was dictated to by testosterone, any thoughts always came back to sex!

Kelly's brain was as sharp as a politician's, she was ready with an immediate response.

"It would depend on what our circumstances were. If we were both happily married, it would just be an opportunity to catch up on each other's lives. We would probably give each other a tender, informal hug or perhaps a pleasant kiss on the lips, but then just sit here in the sunshine and talk. Talk about how our children are doing or air frustrations that maybe we couldn't talk about to our husband and wife. I might moan that my husband never changes the babies nappies or that he pees on the floor around the toilet and you might moan that your wife is always out buying designer shoes or has a headache every time you want sex! We wouldn't tell anyone we were going, only you and I would know and this would carry on as we got older and older until one day we are sitting there with our walking sticks, plastic hips and false teeth!"

The idea was continuing to grow on me.

"What if we were both single?" I enquired.

"As long as we were both single and neither of us was cheating on anyone, then we would just sneak off to that hay field over there and screw each other's brains out!!"

Kelly had this amazing ability to shock me and she had done it in fine style here! We were not sexually active and I had no idea when we would be, but here she was talking about random sexual encounters for the rest of our lives! The mood clouds that had been lingering above my head, immediately blew away.

"What time on 4th July?!" I needed to know this now!

"Midday."

"OK." I said. "I'll see you here, on this very spot, at midday on 4th July, for the rest of our lives. Deal?"

"Deal." We both spat into our hands and shook like two kids out of an American kids TV programme.

"Only if it's a sunny day though, remember!" Kelly reminded me.

"Fine. No point shagging in that hay field if it's peeing down!"

"That's true." Kelly agreed. "Muddy bums aren't very attractive!"

"I beg to differ, Kelly Watkinson!"

I am sure Kelly's bum would look fantastic whether it was muddy or not!

"Well I hate to disappoint you but it doesn't do it for me! Let's hope for some good summers for the rest of our days!" Kelly concluded.

We sat there, on 'The Sunny Road' for several hours that day, before making the long walk back. Kelly suggested, after a small glass of champagne, that we should stay to watch the sun set, which we were going to do, but we were both struck down by, "numb bumitis" and eventually decided to make our way home early in the evening. To go from 'The Sunny Road' to Kelly's house to mine was probably a six mile trip, but that was no problem for a lovestruck teenager.

I hoped the 'Sunny Road' would become our place, but not for a once a year get together, just a summer picnic spot for us and our children. That's if I could have children. I'd had my lump for twelve months now and had still not done anything about it, I still hadn't been brave enough to go and see the Doctor. The lump was definitely still there, but it didn't seem to be getting any bigger and it didn't really hurt either, which I told myself was surely a good sign. I kept meaning to go to the Doctor's just in case, but for whatever reason I hadn't got round to it.

A few days after this first trip to the 'Sunny Road' my hand was forced. I was getting dressed one morning and Jim sat up in his bed.

"Did you ever go to the Doctor's about that bollock lump?"

"No." I replied as I shuffled into my jeans.

"Does that mean it's gone then?" Jim asked.

"No. It hasn't gone. It's not sore though and no bigger. I think you're right, I think it's just a cyst."

Jim was unimpressed.

"Is that what you are going to have on your gravestone,

Here lies Richie Billingham, died aged 20, much loved son of Dorothy and Charles, brother to Helen, Caroline and James. Beloved boyfriend of Kelly Watkinson. Famous last words, 'I thought it was just a cyst'!!"

"You said it was a cyst, Jim!"

"I did not! I said it could be a cyst. How do I know? I'm not fucking Quincy!"

"Well, I reckon it is just a cyst!"

I was trying to persuade myself as much as Jim.

"Look Richie, you've had it for ages now, if you don't get it checked out, I'm going to blab."

"Judas!" was my response.

"I don't care!" Jim replied. "It's for your own good. If you don't get to the Doctor's by this time next week, I'm telling Mum and Dad and I'm telling Kelly what's lurking there in your underpants!"

Jemma

I wanted to punch her. Punch her in that stupid, fat, drunken mouth. My pre-disposure for violence had eased since I had started 'going out' with Ray, but at the very least I wanted to hire Mohammad Ali, in his prime, to come to our house wearing boxing gloves and put a George Foreman mask over Vomit Breath's head. We were mid argument.

"Yes, she is…" I again stated.

"No, she is not." Vomit Breath replied.

It was a verbal rally of positives and negatives that had gone on for some time.

"Not whilst she's living in my house, anyway." Vomit Breath re-emphasised.

Kelly just stood there and observed, like the referee in the aforementioned Ali-Foreman fight. As far as I was concerned, it was not her prerogative to maintain a neutral stance, she should have been in my corner, fighting this battle with me. It was a battle for her future after all.

"Look, I'm working now. I've been putting some money away, I'll help pay for her to stay at school. She got nine GCSEs, for God's sake! If you just let her study, she'll be earning twice as much in five years time."

Vomit Breath did not appreciate the lecture in child rearing. She was a know all. A thick know all, if such a thing existed. I was by no means a Mastermind Grand Champion myself, but I was a lot smarter than Vomit Breath. It felt like a five year old in armbands refusing to take swimming lessons from Duncan Goodhew.

Normally, when Vomit Breath felt she was being intellectually challenged, she resorted to violence. She liked her leopard spots and whilst there was air in her lungs, she would not be changing them. It came as no surprise, when she charged at me, grabbed me by the collar of my blouse and pressed me against the kitchen wall. My mind immediately flashed back to the time I did something similar to James Billingham at the Birch's party and, despite my own predicament, I did not feel fear, I just felt consumed by guilt.

Vomit Breath's nostrils flared like a dragon's. 'Puff The Magic Vomit Breath'.

"Listen you!" she growled, "I don't know how much you get paid in your hoity-toity little job in the bank, with the Elephant Man's grandson, but at a guess, it wouldn't come anywhere fucking near paying for your sister's education."

"Let me try!" I pleaded.

"No, it's ridiculous! You don't know a thing about putting food into people's mouths! I'm a single Mum, I've had eighteen years experience of having to scrimp and save to make sure you and Kelly can make the most of your lives. I can't do it forever though! I've done it for eighteen years now. Eighteen fucking years!! Enough is enough!"

This was a joke. Of all the words I could think of to describe Vomit Breath, I think I could use a high percentage of the dictionary before I got to altruistic. I sneered at her. Given that she had me backed up against a wall, what I said next was pretty foolish.

"That's right! Eighteen fucking years! 'Cos that's what you have spent the last eighteen years doing, fucking any Tom, Dick or Harry who is stupid enough to share their seminal fluids with you! Don't make me laugh about giving us opportunities to make the most of our lives! You've spent eighteen years trying to wangle every possible benefit you can possibly get your grubby little hands on, then you've pissed most of it away on booze and fags! Voles make better mothers than you and they eat their offspring! You're a disgrace, an absolute disgrace!!"

My only surprise was that she let me get through my whole speech before she hit me. As soon as I finished, Vomit Breath walloped me with a backhander that made my cheek throb like it had been stung by a wasp. My adrenalin was pumping through my veins though and there was no stopping me now.

"You hate the idea of her making something of her life, don't you? Kelly's everything you are not and you resent her for it. She's intelligent, beautiful and warm hearted and you're stupid, ugly and cold blooded, so you are desperate for Kelly to have as miserable an existence as you, but I'm not going to let that happen. I'm not! Do you hear me, I'm not! That girl is going to make something of her life and once she escapes from your clutches, you evil bitch of a woman, she won't ever be back until we both trample the dirt down on your grave!"

Vomit Breath turned away from me as if she was going to walk out the kitchen door, but all of a sudden, she spun round on a sixpence, in a 180 degree turn that George Best would have been proud of, catching me full in the mouth with a forearmed smash. I slid down the wall like melted butter, then for good measure, Vomit Breath decided to take the George Best analogy to the next level by using my head as a football. She kept kicking, left foot then right, then left again. I covered my head in my hands, but made no attempt to stand back up, just allowing the barrage of blows to come my way. There was a reluctant acceptance on my part, but I had said what I needed to say and the resultant beating was worth it. After over a dozen kicks to the face and ribs, Vomit Breath stopped kicking, regurgitated some phlegm and spat it on to my snail shaped, curled up body. My nose and top lip bled heavily and both eyes ballooned. Vomit Breath gasped for breath. A slap, a punch and twenty seconds of relentless kicking takes a lot out of you when you are a chain smoking alcoholic.

"You're an ungrateful bitch, Jemma! I've a good mind to kick you out, right here and now, but despite everything I've got too much heart to do it!"

Perhaps the fact that I now paid two-thirds of the rent, which included an element to repay the arrears Vomit Breath had accumulated, may also have been a contributory factor.

"You," Vomit Breath now turned her attention to Kelly who had frozen rigid in fear throughout the argument and my subsequent beating, "you can forget any ideas of "A" levels, young lady. There'll be no scroungers in this house, no more. As soon as you can, you get a fucking job. Do you hear me?"

Vomit Breath must have made herself exempt from this no scroungers ruling. Kelly did not say a word but nodded.

"Now pick your smart arsed sister up off the floor and get her cleaned up. Don't make a mess of the fucking bathroom either, 'cos if you do, I ain't fucking tidying it!"

Vomit Breath strode towards the kitchen door, as she passed me, she sneered down at me like an upper class lady on her way to Royal Ascot, looking down at a pile of dog poo that obstructed her path. She could not resist aiming one last kick into my back, as I lay prostrate on the floor, dripping blood onto the kitchen linoleum.

"Kids," she muttered to herself as she went in search of the dual comforts of fags and booze, "who'd fucking 'ave 'em!"

Jemma

Kelly and I just stood at the top of the stairs like pyjama clad mannequins. We looked at each other and then looked at Vomit Breath sprawled in a heap at the bottom of the stairs. My emotions were everywhere. Panic, fear and joy were all jumbled together, it even crossed my mind to throw a bucket of water down to see if the 'Wicked Witch' theory had any mileage. Panic ruled though. Since she had toppled down the stairs in a series of rolls and somersaults that Mary Lou Retton had spent ten years perfecting, there was silence. Vomit Breath had uttered none of her customary "f" words, she did not moan or groan or even move, she just lay there, as still as a snowman on a wind free day.

Kelly broke the stunned silence.

"Oh my god!" she exclaimed anxiously, then repeated it in a more drawn out fashion,

"OH…MY…GOD!"

"Quick!" I replied.

I don't know what I wanted Kelly to do quickly or, for that matter, what I should be doing quickly, I just felt a sense of urgency should be demanded

"What do we do?" Kelly asked.

"I'll go check on her." I suggested, feeling a sense of duty once more to take the

senior role.

"What should I do?" Kelly demanded.

"Go and get a mirror."

"Why?" Kelly asked.

"Remember the Birch's party. Caroline Billingham got a mirror to check if James was breathing. Go and get one!"

I ran down the stairs. My heart beat twice on every step. Vomit Breath was still out cold. Once I reached the bottom, I wasn't sure what I was supposed to be doing, she was face down, arse up. I had seen on television that you weren't supposed to move people in case of paralysis, but it seemed wrong to leave her upside down. I leaned over Vomit Breath and gently rolled her over, so her head was facing up on my lap. There was blood, thick blood, oozing out of her nose and ears.

Kelly looked down from the top of the stairs, her hand mirror clutched tightly in her hand. She was in tears.

"I can't come down there, Jemma! I can't!"

I tried to be comforting. I spoke softly and slowly.

"Kelly, leave the mirror there at the top of the stairs. I will come and fetch it. What you need to do now is to go back to your room, get back into bed, go to sleep and pretend nothing has happened. Once you hear anyone arriving, turn over, let them come and wake you."

Kelly was incredulous.

"You seriously expect me to go to sleep?!"

"No, Kelly, but I need you to get back into bed. Once anyone arrives, you need to at least pretend you have been fast asleep. Wait for them to wake you. As far as they know, you slept through everything. You're a heavy sleeper, you didn't hear an argument, you didn't hear a thud, just ask them what's happened. OK?"

I needed her to be strong for me. Kelly needed to keep everything together.

"Jemma, I'm not leaving you on your own with her."

"Kelly, you can't just stand there procrastinating, either get back into bed or bring me that mirror now!"

The word "procrastinate" took me back to the halcyon days of Ormskirk Grammar School and English lessons with Miss Caldicott. I think we were in for more than a detention this time.

"Is she dead, Jemma?"

"I really don't know, Kel. If you bring me that mirror, I'll have a better idea."

Kelly ran down. Whilst she had been deliberating, I had been frantically, but tactfully, searching for some sign of life from Vomit Breath, she didn't appear to be breathing, so I checked for a pulse. I couldn't find one. This did not unduly concern me as I often tried to find my own pulse, but couldn't find that either. I searched for a heartbeat on her chest, nothing. By now, my own heart was beating like the hooves of Desert Orchid galloping on a concrete road. There had been so many times I had wished this woman dead, but given the circumstances, this time I wanted her alive. I would be quite happy if she died some time soon, in a pool of her own vomit, on some kerbside outside a nightclub, but just now I did not want her dead. Please not now. Kelly passed me the mirror.

"Shit!" I cursed.

"Does that mean she's dead or alive?" Kelly pressed.

I suppose all things considered, it was a lose-lose situation. Damned if she's dead, damned if she's not.

I didn't say a word, I didn't need to. I just looked up at Kelly. We were sisters. We had both had to endure this woman throughout our lives. Not any more though. Vomit Breath had died. No more drunken men pumping away at her groaning body at four in the morning. No more punishments for failing to conform to her wishes. No more insults. No more Vomit Breath. We should have been putting our red shoes on and partying on down with the 'Munchkins', and we would have done, we really would, if only the circumstances had been different. As Kelly and I stared at her lifeless body, we knew the nature of that evil woman's death would haunt us for the rest of our lives.

Richie

Sleep deprivation had become a by-product of the lump. Every waking second its existence was there, somewhere in my sub-conscious mind. Masturbation, the dosage of choice of teenage male insomniacs, failed to assist. Even when I did manage to doze off, I would wake in the middle of the night and instinctively reach down to check the lump was still there, which it always was, like a scrotal Quasimodo. That was the first thing I would do upon waking. The second thing I would do, was panic.

I was almost eighteen years old. My mortality should not have been at the forefront of my mind, I should have been thinking about drunken nights out and sexual encounters. The only lumps that bothered me should have been squeezed out forcefully into bathroom mirrors. Before the lump, I thought I had a bit of depth to my character, but in reality I had as much depth as the shallow end of a toddlers swimming pool, but that began to change. I pondered the unanswerable questions,

"Where would I go when I died?"

"Would there be a heaven? If there was, had I done anything in my eighteen years to qualify for an entrance pass beyond the pearly gates?"

Two jumble sales for "Guide Dogs For The Blind" was the best I ever managed to come up with! What about Hell? Anything warrant my inclusion on the Devil's guest list? I suspected there was more on that list than on Angel Gabriel's. I spent many a pre-teenage summer frying flying ants on my Mum's electric hob or putting insects into pans of cold water then boiling them. I had also kept creatures in Tic-Tac boxes until they starved or suffocated. Ming the Merciless had nothing on me!

Not only had I done bad things, I had failed to do the good ones. I hadn't prayed, I hadn't attended church, most importantly I hadn't believed. I wanted a faith now, even more than that, or perhaps linked to that faith, I wanted courage. Courage to go to the Doctor's and courage to deal with whatever news he delivered. I felt like the lion in the Wizard of Oz.

My mind was constantly working overtime. As soon as I visualised solutions to certain questions, new questions emerged. If I did get the courage to go to the Doctor's and he decided I had six weeks to live, what would I do and who would I tell? Would it be courageous or selfish to run away and die alone like a sick old cat? I decided, until it came to a stage that my illness became evident, the only person I would tell would be Kelly. I could mentally picture her holding my hand as I slipped tragically away like a scene in an Australian soap opera, even to the extent that I had some white coated Aussie running in as the flatline sounded, shouting,

"Strewth! The flaming gulahs copped it!"

The others I considered telling were my Mum and Dad, my two sisters and Jim, but I decided, Mum, Helen and Caroline would suffocate me with kindness before the cancer got me and Jim would spend my final few weeks saying,

"I told you so!"

As for Dad, I concluded that he would probably put every penny the family had on a 66-1 shot running at Brighton, on the basis that if it won, he would pay for me to trial some miracle cure.

It wasn't hard to decide that confiding in Kelly was my only real option. Kelly was smart and tactile, so she would say the right things and provide the necessary amount of hugs needed. That was the intention anyway. Sometimes though, where you set off towards and where you arrive at, can be two totally different destinations.

Richie

It was never my intention to go to the match with him. I had always had the impression that he was a token Evertonian, that maybe his Dad had supported us and he had just followed suit and feigned an interest, but Ray was Kelly's sister's boyfriend and Kelly's sister still didn't like me, so it felt like I was duty bound to agree to it. It wasn't just any old game either, it was Everton against Norwich, FA Cup Semi-Final and the winner, in all likelihood, would face Liverpool in the Final, as it was widely anticipated that they would overcome Nottingham Forest in the other semi. I had been to the Final in 1986 when Liverpool had beaten Everton 3-1, despite Everton leading 1-0. Since then, Liverpool had probably become even better and Everton were no longer as good, but another Merseyside final would give the blue side of Merseyside an opportunity to avenge this defeat.

FA Cup Semi Finals were always played at neutral venues, ours was Villa Park, Birmingham, the other one was at Hillsborough, Sheffield Wednesday's ground. I had a season ticket at Everton, so managed to get hold of a couple of tickets for our Semi, but having failed my driving test three times, I was intending to head down to Villa Park by bus. That was the plan until Kelly's sister managed to overhear a conversation Kelly and I were having about me trying to flog my spare ticket so I could afford to pay for an Eavesway coach down.

It was early one Saturday evening and Kelly and I were watching Noel's House Party in their lounge. After the bra around the thigh incident, during my karaoke sessions at Kelly's window, Kelly used to keep me away from her mother, as I think she decided her Mum would have me for supper, like a praying mantis, if our paths ever crossed within their four walls. According to Kelly, her Mum referred to me as "F.K" (short for "Fit Kid"!), so to protect my personal safety, I was only ever invited around on one of the regular nights her Mum was out on the lash!

On this particular Saturday, I had just related my tale of poverty, as if I was a modern day Jack from the beanstalk story, with the FA Cup Semi-Final tickets replacing the cow, by being the only thing I had of value. Jemma must have been earwigging in the hallway as she popped her head in. I shifted uncomfortably on the settee, hoping Jemma did not have a strong sense of smell, as we were at the stage of our relationship where foreplay tended to be the end play, as it had been ten minutes earlier. I made a mental note not to play these games when Jemma was also in, she arrived unannounced too frequently and I did not fancy the idea of being caught mid-spurt.

"Did I hear you talking about FA Cup Semi Final tickets?"

There was no "hello", no "how's it going?", or "how are you doing?", just straight in with the question, blunt as ever. Kelly reckoned Jemma was a changed woman, but certain things remained the same.

"I've got two," I replied, "I'm selling one though".

"I'll have it!" Jemma proclaimed.

It was Saturday 1st April, I looked at her face to see if there was any indications that she was taking the piss. It appeared not.

"How much do you want for it?"

"Just what I paid for it. Face value. Fifteen quid."

The smell of sperm was not the only thing making me feel uncomfortable now. Jemma appeared deadly serious but I really did not like the idea of going to this game with her. I presumed she could drive and that she would drive us down. If she did and I gave her the wrong directions, I could imagine being accused of looking for a lay-by so I could screw her again, like in her imagination, I already had. I bought time as I thought of an excuse to turn down her offer.

"I didn't know you were into football, Jemma? Kelly's never mentioned it."

This was a genuine question. Nothing had ever given me the impression at all, that Jemma was into football. If Colin Harvey, Everton's manager, had knocked on their door at that very moment, I still suspected that she would have given him the milk money.

"I'm not!"

Phew!

"Ray is though…"

Damn!

"….he's a big Evertonian! He'd love to go! You wouldn't need to get a coach down either. Ray could drive."

Brilliant!

So, at 7am on Saturday, 15th April 1989, Ray's shiny, metallic blue Ford Escort with spoilers, revved its engine outside our front drive and Ray impatiently beeped his horn.

"Who the bloody hell is that, tooting his horn at this time of the morning?!"

I heard my Dad say through the bedroom wall that divided us.

"It's my lift to the match, Dad!"

I shouted back through, as I gathered my scarf and headed out my door and down the stairs, grabbing my jacket off the peg in the hallway, although I guessed I wouldn't need it, as there was every indication that it was going to be a beautiful day. The sun had appeared from the horizon with a smile on his face and a steely determination to stick around.

"See you later!"

I shouted up the stairs.

"Tell that lad he's not a taxi driver and he can get up off his fat arse next time and come to the front door, like a normal person!"

"OK, Dad! See you later!"

"Hope they win, son!"

I would love to tell you I climbed into that car and over the course of the next two hours, my opinion of Ray totally changed, that Kelly and I had got him all wrong, that the journey was thrilling and I had never laughed as much in my entire life and from that day forth, Ray became a close friend. I would love to tell you that but I can't. I can manage the odd white lie on occasion, but not out and out lies. Kelly had Ray down to a tee. Ray Walker was a wazzock. A bigger tit than either of Sam Fox's! He was a complete and utter banker!

At the end of that two hour journey, if Magnus Magnusson had stopped Ray's car, taken both of us out, whisked us both across to the Mastermind studio and insisted our specialist subjects had to be each other (Ray answering questions about me and me answering questions about Ray), Ray would know nothing at all about me, not one thing, other than my name and the fact that I was dating Kelly, which he already knew before the journey, yet I had an encyclopaedic knowledge of Ray! Every conversation was geared around Ray and if it threatened not to be, Ray was quick to ensure he steered it right back.

For example,

"Have you ever been to America, Richie?"

"Yeh, once. I went to Florida when I was ten."

"Right. I've been about a dozen times now. When I was four, we went with my parents to Vegas, then when I was seven, my parents bought a holiday home in Fort Lauderdale. North East 22nd Way, number 5950 it was. It was fantastic! Most years we would fly over to Miami, head over to the house, stay there for a week or so, just watching TV or swimming in our pool, then, after a week, we'd head off in the car and make our way up to Orlando and do the whole Disney thing. I remember going to the Epcot Centre when it had just opened. Fantastic! Sea World was amazing too! My parents sold that house when I was seventeen and bought one in L.A...."

He then went on and on about L.A and his time spent in California, before finishing with,

"Yes, it's a great place the USA, pity you've never been! You really should go!"

Ray had managed to forget at some point in his fifteen minute monologue that I had actually told him that I'd been to Florida! He probably didn't even register the information in the first place, he was just teeing himself up with the initial question. Every conversation was the same.

"How are things going with Kelly?", was followed by ten minutes talking about his relationship with Jemma. How they met in the bank, how he was concerned about how his bosses would view the relationship so he had kept it from them, how Jemma hated her mother and referred to her as "Vomit Breath". Every possible piece of information I could possibly be told about Ray, he managed to squeeze into that two hour trip. I'm surprised he didn't tell me how many strips of toilet paper he used when he had a crap. He was happy to bore me with everything else. When we finally parked up, about a mile from Villa Park, it felt like I had endured three days verbal torture. If he'd been around, the Viet Cong could have used him during the Vietnam war to torture US soldiers.

Ray is officially the most boring man I have ever had the misfortune to meet. As well as being the most boring, he also wins prizes for being the world's best talker (about himself) and the world's worst listener. I'm surprised he ever managed to open an account for anyone in the bank, because I imagine he would just start telling each and every customer about his own three hundred accounts and how half the world's money was stored in them. My only consolation was that I didn't much like Jemma and there was some sort of perverse justice that she had been lumbered with this idiot!

On the walk to the stadium, Ray must have sensed his capacity to irritate had not quite peaked so he managed to annoy me even further by showing a complete lack of footballing knowledge.

"Hope Kendall puts a good team out, today!", was irritating statement number one.

"Howard Kendall's not here any more, Colin Harvey's the manager!"

"That's what I said," Ray responded, "Colin Harvey."

Followed by,

"We were great that year we won the League when Gary Lineker was here."

"Ray, we didn't win a thing the season Gary Lineker was here! It was the year before and the year after."

"That's what I said, Richie! The year before Lineker came, it was great when we won the League! Bloody hell, mate, are you deaf or what?!! I reckon you might need your ears syringing! A few years ago, I had problems hearing and when I went to the Doctor's, he syringed my ears. It was wonderful! You know when you go swimming and you get water in your ears and then eventually it pops and hot water gushes out and all of a sudden, you can hear, well that's what it was like. Are you a decent swimmer, Richie?"

"No." No point me elaborating, he wasn't interested. He was off again.

"When I was a child, I used to swim for the county. I used to go swimming seven days a week. Every day before school and after school, I used to swim. I used to start at six o'clock, every day for seven years, I did a couple of miles before school and a couple of miles after."

Ray was really, really winding me up now. I should have just let him go on, but I found myself displaying my annoyance.

"Ray, that doesn't make sense!"

"Of course it makes sense! What are you on about?"

"You said on the way down, when you asked if I played badminton, that you represented England at badminton and you used to have badminton coaching every day before and after School."

Ray was temporarily taken aback, but soon managed to wriggle his way out of this awkward spot. He was adept, probably from experience, at piling new lies on top of old ones.

"Why doesn't that make sense, Richie?! I did swimming six until seven every day, then badminton seven until eight. Then after school, swimming four until five and badminton five until six. It was hard work, but I did it, I was dedicated."

I was going to ask Ray whether he swam in his badminton kit with his racket in his hand and played badminton dripping wet, but didn't bother as he would no doubt have said he did, as a handicap, as he was so much better than everyone else.

"Did you do any sports at school, Richie?"

"Just rugby."

"Right. I played for the school at football. Centre midfield. I played for the school, Town Green Boys, Craven Minor Representative side and Lancashire. Scored fifty goals from midfield one season. Liverpool and Everton were both after me."

They probably didn't sign him as the first team would have been embarrassed that they were nowhere near his level. It would have knocked Kenny Dalglish's confidence if Ray Walker had arrived at Anfield in his speedos, badminton kit and football boots and run rings around him!

I was relieved to finally get into the ground as at least the cheering and the singing managed to drown the arsehole out!

Kelly

My feelings towards my mother, all things considered, were pretty neutral. Other than the fact that she brought me into the world and somehow kept me alive until I was old enough to fend for myself (or at least old enough for my older sister, Jemma, to care for me), my mother was not an easy mother for a daughter to have a fondness for. I appreciate that for a lot of mother's and daughter's, there is a special bond, but in our family that bond was between Jemma and I, not Mum and I and most certainly not Jemma and Mum. On the whole, Mum was just not a likeable person, unless of course your raison d'etre was partying hard. Mum lived for her Friday and Saturday nights out and if there wasn't booze, fags and sex involved, the night was deemed a disaster. There is apparently an Asian saying which translates as,

"If your head's at the top of the bed or at the bottom, your bellybutton is still in the middle", which pretty much means "things balance out in the end".

Jemma had learnt this from a friend at school, taught me it and then developed a similar phrase which she felt suited Mum. Jemma's phrase was,

"Whether her head is at the top of the bed or at the bottom, there's always an arsehole in the middle," which I took to mean that whether Mum was up on a high or down on a low, in Jemma's eyes, she was always an arsehole!

Jemma hated Mum. I remember someone once said to me that you should not hate anyone as that means you wish them dead. Hate was therefore a good description of Jemma's feeling towards Mum. She wished her dead, absolutely despised her and she had every right to. Jemma had virtually brought me up single handedly, certainly from the age of eight or nine, but she was never a beneficiary of Mum's kindness, just a victim of her selfishness. She learnt to live with that, as did I. Even before we were teenagers, most of our weekend mornings were spent unblocking our sinks or toilets of Mum's vomit, whilst she lay comatose in bed. Due to being comatose, we lived in a house that stank like wet nappies and changing urine soaked bed sheets was also a weekly chore. Heartfelt gratitude or embarrassment were never expressed.

We grew accustomed to strange men watching TV with us on Saturday and Sunday mornings, making themselves a cup of tea and a piece of toast (or sometimes cereal) before heading off. Rarely did we see the same face twice and if we did, she tended to allow them to move in, and sometimes even marry them, so for short periods, stepbrothers and sisters would arrive. Looking back, it was all very strange but for Jemma and I, at the time, it was normality. It was only when we became young adults that Mum changed from being a drunken idiot to an aggressive, drunken idiot. That was when the problems really started.

My "GCSE" results probably spawned the aggression. I took nine GCSEs and to Mum's horror, passed nine. This meant that as far as the school, Jemma and I were concerned, Sixth Form and subsequently University, were options. This was not an option Mum entertained though, as all Sixth Form meant to her was that less money would come into the house and more money would go out.

Jemma only ever wanted the best for me. She knew I was intelligent enough to go to University, to get a degree and for her, this was my ticket out of there. An escape route. Jemma wanted me to pursue this dream. Perhaps it was not an altogether unselfish strategy. Perhaps Jemma thought if I left Ormskirk, went to University, got a degree and a good job then created a home elsewhere, at some point in the future she could follow. I think Jemma's dreams were dependent on my success.

At sixteen, Jemma had started working in a bank in Ormskirk, which kept Mum happy as it meant that Jemma contributed to the household expenditure. Jemma viewed it that the State paid the bills and she paid for Mum's piss ups! As a financial contributor, Jemma felt this gave her a say in matters in the house, which in effect meant she felt she had the right to question Mum's authority. Mum was a strong minded woman who did not like to be challenged, so when Jemma, at eighteen years old, stated that she thought Mum was completely ridiculous for not allowing me to stay on at Sixth Form, a heated row ensued which culminated in Mum punching, kicking and spitting on Jemma. It was hideous. Mum scared me when she went off on one and I went into self-preservation mode, keeping out the way and doing anything she asked. I was disgusted with myself for being such a coward. Jemma would do anything for me, but I was so intimidated by Mum, I didn't have the strength of character to help her. Mum had often related tales of her fist fights on the streets of Ormskirk and Southport. Women only had to look at her the wrong way and a full-on hair pulling, rolling along the ground, fist fight, would often ensue, but prior to this attack on Jemma, she had never used her clenched fists on her own offspring. This, by no means, is meant to cast her as a fairytale mother, as we grew up she had often administered a severe smacking on any occasion we were deemed to be a nuisance, but this kicking and punching incident was the first of its kind, but unfortunately not the last.

The incident seemed to offer Mum, a woman of limited intelligence, an opportunity of clinging on to some control over her eldest daughter, who had long since become her intellectual superior. On a weekly basis, once the beatings started, Jemma took one beating after another and every time, I am ashamed to admit, I just looked on and did nothing.

The single most horrific beating was one that was delivered on a Saturday morning at 4am. It transpired that this was the final beating Mum ever delivered, although we were obviously oblivious to this statistic at the time. That night, Mum must have staggered in from whichever watering hole she had tarnished, probably feeling frustrated that she had been unable to snare a man, she stumbled into Jemma's room, clambered onto her bed, straddled her and whilst she was still sleeping, Mum punched her square on the nose. Jemma shot up like a tortured Jack-In-The-Box and as she did so, Mum smashed into her again with a second right hook, knocking her straight back down. I was woken by Mum drunkenly slurring,

"My fucking knuckles are killing me!"

Did I go to Jemma's aid? No, I buried my head in my pillow and cried myself back to sleep.

Jemma arrived in my bedroom the following morning looking like a Formula One racing team had borrowed her face to use as a crash test dummy. It was the final straw.

"If Vomit Breath lays her fingers on me one more time," she promised, "I'm going to fucking kill her!"

That Saturday afternoon, Jemma's boyfriend Ray, having witnessed the mess that Jemma previously called her face, came round to our house to remonstrate with Mum, threatening to get the police involved. To be fair to Ray, despite being charmless and probably hiding a tattoo of a penis somewhere underneath his hairline, he loved Jemma and it was honourable that he was trying to help her in her battle with Mum. It made me feel even guiltier that even an arse like Ray was doing right by Jemma when I was failing her.

As far as defining moments in my life go, whatever happens in the rest of my life between now and my dying day, nothing will ever cause such a seismic shift in my life, as the moments in the early hours of Sunday 16th April 1989. The day before had witnessed an afternoon of unparalleled tragedy for supporters of Liverpool Football Club. There was no final figure on the death toll, but by Saturday evening, it was widely known that many, many people had died at a football match at Hillsborough, Sheffield. The dead were all Liverpool fans. Men, boys, women and girls. All just football fans enjoying a day out, following their team.

Mum didn't understand tragedies that didn't directly effect her. If she didn't get a shag on a Saturday night or had no money left to go out, that was a tragedy in Mum's selfish world, people who she did not know dying, that was someone else's tragedy. Mum went out that night into Southport, there was probably a sombre mood around the town, understandably given the massive tragedy that had taken place that afternoon, but Mum would not have empathised so she arrived back, earlier than normal, aggressively drunk. Jemma and I were both still awake, we had spent the evening together, as our boyfriends, Ray and Richie, had gone to the other FA Cup Semi-Final, involving Everton. I was in Jemma's room, just chatting, when we heard the door slam.

"What a fucking shit night!" Mum muttered to herself, the words drifting up the stairs like a putrid odour.

Jemma looked at me, her face displayed a mixture of fear and a determination not to allow herself to be Mum's punch bag any longer.

"I'm telling you, Kelly, if she lays a finger on me, I'm going to kill her, I mean it, Kel, I'll kill her!"

As if to prove her point, Jemma put her hand under the mattress and pulled out a bread knife.

"I'm ready for her this time, Kelly."

This was crazy. I could hear Mum banging around downstairs, no doubt fixing herself a drink. If recent history was anything to go by, the drink would not take long to down and pretty soon she'd be heading up to take her aggression out on Jemma.

"Jemma!" I whispered to avoid detection by Mum. "Put the knife away! I'd like Mum out of our lives, just as much as you, but you can't just stab her to death! Where do you think you'll be spending the next fifteen years if you kill Mum?"

Jemma gave me a look of disgust, the likes of which she had never diverted my way before. Still clasping hold of the knife, she spat out her words, in a barely audible diatribe,

"You want Mum out of your life as much as I do, Kelly?! Do not make me laugh! Can I just remind you only one of us has the balls to confront her, only one of us pays her rent, only one of us gets introduced to her fists, EVERY FUCKING WEEK! What are you doing whilst all this shit is happening to me? I tell you what you're doing, little sister…. NOTHING. You are just keeping your nose clean, agreeing with every request that witch sends your way, sitting back, saving your skin whilst I take all the crap."

Jemma's eyes were welling up with tears but her grip on that knife did not loosen.

She continued,

"I do everything for you, Kelly, everything. Always have. You would have gone to school with a shitty little backside at primary school if it wasn't for me, because that bitch wouldn't wipe it. Now, despite everything, when all I want is a little help back, you don't deliver. I used to think you were the most beautiful person that walked this earth, Kelly, but not any more. Now I'm just thinking I've got you all wrong. You're not the girl I thought you were. These last few weeks, Kelly, I've needed you, really needed you, to be strong for me and you haven't been. You've been weak. So don't you dare start lecturing me on what to do and what not to do. I'll sort this out MY way."

Mum, a creature of disgusting habit, had finished her drink and was heading our way, she must have been aware that something was going on as she slurred as she shouted up,

"Are my darling daughters still awake, are they? Don't fret my babies, Mummy's home. I'll come and tuck you up in a minute. You first, Jemma, you know how much I love to tuck you up!"

Jemma passed the knife from hand to hand. A tear rolled down her cheek.

"Bring it on, Vomit Breath! Bring…..it….on!"

I started to cry. Not a composed tear like Jemma, floods of tears.

"Jemma, I'm begging you, don't do this."

I could hear Mum double locking the front door, within seconds, this was all going to kick off.

Jemma was pumped full of adrenalin. She gestured at me with the knife.

"Get out of here, Kelly! Get into your room, close your door and do not move until I tell you to come out."

I pleaded with her, tearfully.

"Jemma, please don't do this! Please!"

"OUT!!"

I ran across the landing into my room. Everything Jemma had said was right. I had badly let her down. Mum wouldn't have been a match for the two of us, but without a united front, she was too physically strong for either of us, on our own. I had just protected myself and let Jemma take Mum on alone. A battle she was never going to win.

Mum was in the hallway. She must have seen me run across the landing. I heard the floorboards creak as she drunkenly began to climb the stairs. I was petrified, this was turning into a horror movie that I did not want a part in. I pushed my back into my closed door to barricade it shut. Once again, self-preservation was priority number one. Mum spoke in tones of foreboding doom,

"What's going on, Jemma? You upsetting your sister? Naughty children are answerable to me. Your mother doesn't suffer fools gladly."

I heard Jemma's door open. I guessed Mum was halfway up the stairs by now.

"Have you had a nice evening, Mum?"

Jemma had not referred to Mum as anything other than "Vomit Breath" for some time, it was even longer since she had called her Mum.

Mum growled back,

"Like you care!"

Once Jemma began talking again, there was a quiver in her voice, a quiver that told me the knife was now on show. Jemma was trying so hard to sound calm and in control,

"Of course it matters to me if you've had a good night, Mum, because we both know what happens when you have a bad one. You come and show me just how bad it is, don't you? You're thoughtful like that, aren't you mother? You like to share. If you've had a shit night, you make damn sure that I have a shit night too."

Mum laughed. A laughing "at you" not "with you" laugh.

"Well, honey pie, you'll be glad to know, Mummy's coming again. To-night was crap. Fucking shit! Everyone was miserable. I feel as sorry as the next person for all those Liverpool fans, but what can I do about it now? I can't bring them back, can I and neither can anyone else, so why let it spoil the whole night out?"

Mum paused for a few seconds to let her sympathetic views on the Hillsborough tragedy be digested, before adding,

"What's the knife for, Jemma?"

"Protection."

"Don't blame you. Nasty world out there these days. Does no harm to protect yourself. Sensible kid. Who are you protecting yourself from?"

It was Jemma's turn to laugh sarcastically.

"A bully."

"I see. Let me tell you something, Jemma. A word from the wise. You shouldn't allow yourself to get bullied. It's a dog eat dog world where only the fittest survive. If you allow yourself to get bullied, that's a sign of weakness. The strong don't get bullied, just the weak."

"That's not how I see it, Mum. In my eyes, it's the weak that bully. They bully because they're scared."

"Scared?"

"Something scares them, something they don't know how to cope with. They lack the intellect to adapt, so they resort to physical force. The physically weak though, may not be weak mentally and they start thinking about things. Thinking about how, in the end, they will triumph over physical force."

I could tell Mum was becoming increasingly vexed.

"That's how it works in fairytales, Jemma. Not real life. In the real world, the poor are always poor, the rich are always rich, the weak are always weak and…."

"The drunk are always drunk!"

"Very funny, Jemma. Let's give you a round of applause for that."

Mum clapped slowly.

"Pass me the knife, Jemma. We both know we could stand here until we're both grey haired old biddies and you would never find the nerve to use that knife. Do you know why?"

"Educate me."

"Because I've brought you up to be middle class! That ugly shit of a boyfriend of yours would certainly not want a jailbird girlfriend. How would that look amongst his snooty banker friends, if he had to piss off to Walton prison every lunchtime to see you? He was all brave when he came round here the other day, reading me the riot act, but he wouldn't be so brave at Walton. He would visit you once and that would be that. Wash his hands of you, that's what he'd do….so let's stop pretending you're tough, Jemma. Pass me the knife."

"Not a chance!"

"Look Jemma, if you pass me that knife, we'll just forget this little incident, both say sorry, give each other a nice, big hug and go back to being family."

"Family! Who do you think we are, mother, the fucking Waltons?! Think about this. I've got a knife out. Now if I don't use it, I'm not stupid, I know exactly what will happen. You'll beat the living daylights out of me, even more than you do already, for ever and a day. My life will not be worth living. So now this knife is out, my cards are on the table. I have absolutely no choice but to use it.

If I were you, Vomit Breath, I would start a very quick, drunken run, because you have got me all wrong. I hate you and using this knife on you, does not scare me at all. Think about it for a second. If I kill you, which incidentally I am going to do. If I kill you, what do you think would happen to me? I'll tell you. I'd get hauled up in front of a judge and jury and charged with your murder. Then, Kelly, Ray and everyone else at the bank, would testify that I've been battered and bruised recently, at your evil hands. The judge would take one look at my innocent little face and take pity on me. I'd be sent down for eighteen months, serve six, then I'd be smelling of roses whilst your rotting corpse would be pushing up the daisies and your sorry soul would be Lucifer's."

Listening to this was unbearable. My head was in my hands, my face was now drenched in tears and my knickers were wet with urine. It was like two tom cats squaring up. I knew them both too well. I knew neither would back down. There was a disaster heading their way, impending doom and all my tears and fears were for Jemma. I loved Jemma, she was everything a sister should be, but she was in a situation now whereby it was impossible to emerge victorious. She was going to be a murderer or murdered. The verbal sparring was relentless.

"How fucking stupid are you, Jemma? Do you really see me running away from you? Knife or no knife, what makes you think for a second, I would run away from a snobby little bitch, like you? I'd rather die!"

"RUN MOTHER!"

"NOT A CHANCE!"

I could hear the slow creaks of the stairs and could just tell Mum was slowly edging her way up towards Jemma.

"I'm warning you, do NOT come any closer!"

"You don't scare me Jemma, not one bit!"

A futher creak of a stair. They must have been so close now that they could almost touch.

"Back off, MOTHER!"

Jemma spoke in panicky tones. Mum spoke in an aggressive, assured tone. The experience of a million stand-offs.

"Jemma, I am warning you. If you don't put that knife down, I'm going to rip your head off and dip soldiers in your neck!"

"MOVE….AWAY!"

I suddenly flipped. I stood up, opened my door, put my head down and screaming as loud as my lungs had the capacity to scream, I ran along the landing towards Mum, who was barely a few feet away, a couple of steps from the top of the stairs. I caught her off guard, seeing me hurtle towards her, she took half a step back and then I put my two hands out and PUSHED. She instinctively reached out to grab me like a woman teetering on a mountains edge, but the drink inside her meant her reactions were too slow. Mum fell backwards, flipping over and then tumbling. Our hall was tiled rather than carpeted, so when Mum hit the bottom, there was an almighty thud. Then silence. I broke it.

"Oh my God!!"

Jemma dropped the knife.

"Quick!" she said. I couldn't do anything quickly now. Shock had kicked in. What had I just done? I had pushed my mother, with all the might I could muster, down our stairs. Mum was going to kill me. I was the little sister again.

"What do we do?" I asked.

I needed an answer. I needed Jemma to make everything right. When Mum got up, Jemma was going to have to protect me. Jemma was not going to be the sole victim any more.

When I was in primary school, Jemma would come into my room, when I was having nightmares, hold my hand, talk soothingly and wipe my brow. I wanted Jemma to do that now, hold my hand, comfort me, give me a big sister kiss, stroke my hair and tell me not to worry. Let me know it was all going to be OK. Please God, let it all be OK.

Richie

Throughout the first half, stories were spreading, emanating from men with portable radios, about trouble at Hillsborough.

"Bloody Liverpool fans!" was the initial reaction, "I can't believe they are doing it again after Heysel."

Football violence had overshadowed football itself in the 1980's and the tragedy at Heysel, four years earlier, where thirty nine Juventus fans had died, following riotous scenes pre-match, had led to English teams being banned from European competition. Wrongly, many Evertonians assumed, based on the first radio reports, that this was another incident of football hooliganism. The cursory words aimed at Liverpool fans soon eased though, as news slowly spread, that it was not violence on the terraces but an incident triggered by overcrowding.

"They've called the game off," someone reported, "they are saying one person may have died. On the radio they are saying it may be a young lad."

There was universal concern. Football loyalties in Merseyside and the surrounding areas often divided families in two, half blue for Everton, half red for Liverpool. The vast majority of Evertonians would have had friends and family at Hillsborough. Several of my friends from school had gone, as well as a couple of Uncles and many close friends of my Mum and Dads.

"These things get blown out of all proportion," one middle aged man said as he switched off his radio, "no-one will have died. Remember when Liverpool won the League at Stamford Bridge in '86, when Dalglish scored? Rumours went around Goodison that Chelsea had equalised, then gone 2-1 up, 3-1 then 4-1. One nil it ended. I've heard it myself, there's been some overcrowding in the Leppings Lane end, everyone's really worried, but the police, the stewards and the paramedics will sort it out. It'll be something and nothing. Might just teach the FA a lesson. Liverpool should have been in the home end, not that away one."

Minds that had temporarily been drawn away from events on the pitch in front of us, were soon focused back on our game. Everton were on top for most of the game, but it was a nervy match, full of mistakes with Everton eventually squeezing home one-nil with a scrambled goal from our Scottish winger, Pat Nevin. A bundled shot hit the post and Pat tapped in the rebound from about two feet out. It was never going to win "Goal of The Season", but at the time it was our "Goal Of The Season" and when it went in, I hugged the stranger on my left rather than prostitute myself by hugging Ray.

When the final whistle went, I was elated, even high fiving Ray. FA Cup Final here we come. A chance to avenge the 1986 defeat against Liverpool. I was so pleased, I almost hugged Ray at the end, then came to my senses and settled for that high five. I skipped, child like, all the way back to the car.

"Put the radio on," I implored Ray, "you'll catch the match report and see if there's any truth in that story about the other semi-final being called off."

Amazingly Ray switched it straight on without even a hint of a bullshit story about the day he played in a Semi-Final that was abandoned because he had to rugby tackle three dozen lions that escaped from the back of a passing circus lorry. I immediately twiddled the dial to find "Sport on Two". I found it in an instant and the sombre voice of the presenter, Peter Jones, painted a horrendous mental image,

"….well I think, the biggest irony is the sun is shining now and Hillsborough is quiet and over there to the left, the green Yorkshire hills…who would have known that people would die here, in the stadium, this afternoon.

I don't necessarily want to reflect on Heysel, but I was there that night, broadcasting with Emlyn Hughes and he was sitting behind me this afternoon and after half an hour of watching stretchers going out and oxygen cylinders being brought in and ambulance sirens screaming, he touched me on the shoulder and he said, "I can't take any more," and Emlyn Hughes left.

The gymnasium here at Hillsborough is being used as a mortuary for the dead and at this moment, stewards have got little paper bags and they are gathering up the personal belongings of the spectators and there are red and white scarves of Liverpool and red and white bobble hats of Liverpool and red and white rosettes of Liverpool and nothing else………….and the sun shines now."

"Fucking hell!"
We swore in unison.

The dead. How many dead? As Ray drove home, initial figures were discussed, it was thought that over seventy had lost their lives and by the time we reached Stafford, that estimate had risen to over eighty. Men, women, boys and girls, out for the day to cheer their team on, would never return home. It was impossible to take in. This was not young men going to war, this was a football match. Rivalries existed but for most people they weren't real, it was all just banter. Radio reports indicated that there were definitely several children amongst the dead.

At a petrol station on the East Lancs Road, the enormity of the tragedy kicked in. Some of the delayed Liverpudlians had stopped to re-fuel and to grab a quick hot drink or a sandwich, still wearing their hats, scarves and badges. The red of Liverpool and the blue of Everton all mixed together, some relieved families who that morning had gone to their separate Semi-Finals were meeting back up. Everyone was united in grief for those less fortunate than them. I could not control my emotions any longer, my tears flowed.

People are shallow creatures and to an extent I think grief is a selfish emotion. We do not cry solely for the dead, their family and their loved ones. We cry through empathy, often a selfish empathy, that, "it could have been me" feeling. Here I was, returning from the other FA Cup Semi-Final with a strange lump lurking in my ball sack. I sobbed from the depths of my soul, for the red half of my nearest city, for the families who had been or would be told of losses they would never learn to live with and I cried because I was one of the lucky ones at the "safe" Semi-Final and I cried because I did not know how long my luck would last.

Throughout that day, my loathing for Ray had grown as quickly as a beanstalk in a fairytale, so at that precise point, I did not think it possible to hate him more, but Ray rose to the challenge. He put a consoling arm around me.

"Don't upset yourself, mate! Just think of it as karma."

My emotions shifted. Hairs stood up on my neck. Sadness was replaced by anger. I could not believe what I was hearing, even from him.

"What?"

"It's karma, mate. For those Italians that died at Heysel. For us Evertonians that missed out on a European Cup campaign because of their hooligans. Do you know what this is? It's a higher power levelling up the score, that's all."

Of all the stupid things I have ever heard in my entire life, this one wins. In fact, it does not just win, it ranks as a billion times more stupid than anything else I have ever heard before or since. For me, Ray's words were the pinnacle of tactless stupidity in the aftermath of an almighty tragedy. When I look back at my reaction, I have always thought, considering who I was dealing with, I did exactly the right thing. I could have punched him in the face. I could have spat in his face, but I didn't. I just leaned across the car, put my right arm around his neck, pulled him towards me and kissed him, throwing in a little tongue for good measure. Ray had just made me feel sick to the pits of my stomach and now I was making him feel the same.

Pulling away forcefully, Ray looked at me in horror, bemusement and shock.

"What the hell are you doing?!! That was disgusting! What are you playing at?"

I opened my car door.

"No, Ray, you are disgusting."

I closed the door behind me. I didn't slam it, to make a scene, just gently pushed it to. As I walked towards the petrol station, I heard his engine start. I kept walking. As he got level with me, he rolled his window down.

"What are you doing?" he asked.

I looked straight forward, ignoring him. I had no intention of speaking to Ray that minute, that hour, that lifetime. I was not getting back in his car!

"Are you getting back in this car so we can go home? Answer me, you weird little shit! What are you on?"

Ray's questions were met with silence. I just kept walking. Millions of people were united in a collective grief that day, yet I was stuck with one man who's head was so far up his own arse, he did not understand.

"Sod you then, Richie! Find your own way home!"

Ray let his foot off the clutch, slammed his other on the accelerator and wheel span off.

It wasn't hard to get a lift back to Ormskirk. Half the supporters travelling home virtually passed by Ormskirk on the M58, which runs through to North Liverpool. I managed to get a lift off a married Liverpudlian couple, in their thirties who were very shaken up, particularly the lady, as they had been together in the Leppings Lane end when the tragedy had happened. They had been away from the main incidents as they had stood by one of the corner flags, but they had seen the events unfolding from only twenty metres away.

"There are a lot of people tonight with blood on their hands." Gary, the male half of the couple explained as he sped along the M58,

"Think about it, Richie, there's a multitude of people who deserve to take their fair share of responsibility for this. Do you believe in God, Richie?"

I shook my head. "No."

"Neither do I mate, neither do I. I think that makes it worse to be honest, mate. Just thinking these people had their lunch somewhere in Sheffield today, all excited about the game, talked tactics, talked scorelines, eagerly arrived early to get a good view of the pitch, then, because of a string of mistakes by bureaucrats, people they didn't even know, their whole existence has been snuffed out. "

Gary clicked his fingers.

"Just like that, gone. Just imagine going to the match with your mate today, getting separated by the surge, getting out and discovering your mate never did. It doesn't bear thinking about."

Gary obviously had a lot running through his head, there were various people he held responsible for the tragedy, a lot of the time we sat in silence, but once in a while he thought about another section of society who played their part in creating this disaster and wanted to vent his anger. He dealt with the Football Association and the Government and then moved on.

"You know who else I blame, Richie? I blame every single football hooligan in this sorry nation of ours. I'm not talking about today, I'm talking about violence on the terraces and outside the grounds over the last ten years. These pricks think it's clever to fight in the name of eleven men they don't even know against some other daft fuck who's fighting for his eleven men, who he doesn't know either, just because they kick their ball at his ground and he decided at five years old that he liked their football shirt. Think about it, Richie, it's ridiculous, isn't it?! But as a result of these stupid thick twats fighting with each other, the rest of us are all caged in like animals every time we go to a game! Then tragedies like todays happen because innocent kids and young men and women are trapped in the cages these knobheads have caused to be there.

I also blame the police. They just stood there and watched dozens and dozens of people die in front of their eyes. Collectively, could they not have done something more? Why did they not delay the kick off or talk to each other on their walkie-talkies and stop people getting in or put them into our section, by the corner flag, which wasn't even full? How could they have got it so wrong?

You know what, Richie, you know what I think would be a tiny piece of justice?"

"What?"

"If every single person and group I've mentioned was forced to attend as many of the funerals as it was physically possible to attend.

Let them witness first hand what their stupidity and incompetence has done. See the families they've destroyed. See the heartbreak they've created. They should all be made to line up in front of the mourners and made to say,

'I am responsible for the death of your father…your mother…your husband…your wife…your daughter….your son…' whoever. Because I tell you what, Richie, over the next few weeks, mark my words, no-one will take their share of responsibility….everyone will blame everyone else . I hope I'm wrong, I hope all these idiots come forward and carry the can for their mistakes, but they won't, mark my words, Richie, they won't."

Gary let go of the steering wheel then simultaneously slammed both arms down onto it.

"How can something like this be allowed to happen? It's just insane!"

I asked Gary to drop me off at the Little Chef in Skelmersdale, by the exit of the M58, but he wouldn't hear of it. He took me all the way to Aughton, dropping me off outside my door.

Mum and Dad were in the lounge watching TV when I came in. Mum came up to me and without saying a word kissed me on the forehead. I knew exactly what she meant by this. It was a way of saying we were the lucky ones.

I struggled to sleep that night. Peter Jones' commentary kept going round and round in my head, **"who would have known that people would die here, in the stadium, this afternoon."**

As I finally drifted off, my mind bade farewell to the horrors of the day, selfishly relieved it was no-one I knew. Little did I know, four hours later an all together different grief would be heading my way.

Richie (24 hours earlier)

I hate going to the Doctor's. Always have. Give me the Dentist's any day. At the Dentist, they'll tell you that you need a filling or a tooth out, they won't tell you that your arteries are clogged and your tickers knackered or chances are you have cancer. I'm sure 99% of the time, GPs don't deliver nightmare news but Dentists never do, so I know which one I'd rather visit.

I sat in the waiting room nervously. To me, the sound of multiple coughers is like nails on a blackboard. Excruciatingly annoying! I looked around. A Doctor's waiting room is a mixture of the old and the new. For the old, its like a fitting room for the undertakers,

"Could you get up on the bed, please."

"What for? I only came in with a cough."

"I know. We just need to measure you up for your coffin."

I mentally berated myself. I was not in a position to be taking the mickey out of anyone who may be edging towards death, for all I knew these old guys might be out lasting me.

It was just impossible not to notice though that the surgery was full of old people and paranoid parents who bring their babies down because they have a runny nose and Mummy's bored, looking for something to do as toddler classes don't start for another twelve months.

I was the odd one out. As I gave my name to the receptionist, I felt like the "townie" ordering a pint in a small village pub. I could feel the looks. I was half-expecting someone with a West Country accent to tap me on the shoulder and say,

"You ain't from these parts, are you?"

As I gave the lady my name, babies stopped crying, coughers stopped coughing and the coffin dodgers who had hitherto been facing away from me, managed to muster 180 degree mobility in their necks, probably for the first time in years. Everyone wanted to know who was gatecrashing their early morning moan fest.

I'm sure a dozen regulars played "Guess The New Boys Illness" in their own minds. It was time. The lump had outgrown its scrotal nest and was now seeking a wider audience. I could hold it back no longer. It had been around now for twelve months, it wasn't a baby any more.

Despite a 9.30a.m appointment, I had to sit in the waiting room collecting germs until gone ten. Readers Digest, May 1987, had never seemed so interesting. At five past, I was all set to have a word with the receptionist but her demeanour was off putting. Dr.Whiteside had obviously borrowed her from a Victorian orphanage and frozen her in time for a hundred years as she was extremely adept at denying anyone access to the Doctor. I imagine Oliver Twist would not even have got his first bowl of gruel off this tyrant. She seemed fascinated with the phone, which I suppose was only natural given her Victorian background,

"Well, I don't care if your three year old has contracted rabies, Mrs. Funnell. Dr.Whiteside is extremely busy until a week next Friday, bring him in then. I bid you good day!"

At ten past ten, nerves in tatters, I got the call,

"Richard Billingham…Dr.Whiteside will see you now."

I crept over to the receptionist to avoid disapproving looks from the pensioners, who by now, en masse, had buried their heads in the magazine offerings of the surgery, the aforementioned Readers Digest, Woman and Lancashire Life.

"Excuse me," I timdly began, "whereabouts is the Doctor?"

The receptionist fixed me a look from above her spectacles, balanced on the tip of her nose, as though I had passed her a second hand instrument from an Ann Summers catalogue, with a wiry hair still attached and asked her to demonstrate it to the whole waiting room. Disgust was not the word.

"Second door on the right, you fucking idiot!" she said, but the last three words were silent, they just passed from her brain to mine telepathically.

I walked out the coughing/coffin room, into a creaking hallway and along to a second door on the right. I knocked and waited,

"Come in!" replied the rather jovial voice from the other side.

I pulled the door to me. Nothing happened so I pushed. Doors were always "push" in that scenario, with the exception of toilet doors which were often "pull". I cursed my unconscious incompetence. Nerves, I figured.

Dr.Whiteside sat behind a large mahogany desk, looking like he had been there since he had been in short trousers, placed in Ormskirk to provide prescriptions since the end of World War II. He dressed in a rare mix of colourful shirt, dickie bow and a cardigan containing an array of browns and greys.

"Take a seat," he gestured.

There were two. I was unsure if this was a psychological test, but concluded it was more likely a spare for anxious mothers. I suddenly had visions of childhood. Mum dragging me down to the Doctor's, describing my ailments as if I was mute. On reflection, this was the first time I had ventured to the Doctor's alone. I felt very alone. I sat.

"And what appears to be the problem?" Dr.Whiteside probed.

I started to blush. I knew within a few minutes he would be inspecting my scrotum. I prayed to the God that I did not believe in to save me from an inopportune erection. Throughout my teenage years, I was always in fear that it would decide to stand to attention when I least wanted it to.

"I have a lump on one of my testicles."

By now my face was crimson. I felt like Dr.Whiteside was going to take an egg out his pocket and fry it on my face.

Dr.Whiteside began to take notes.

"When did you first notice it?"

To avoid sounding like an idiot, I made a reduction. A year sounded too long.

"A few months ago, I thought it may just clear up by itself, but it hasn't."

"Does it hurt when you touch it?"

"No, not really."

"Does it feel uncomfortable?"

"It's hard to describe, it just feels strange. Like a small piece of wood is trapped in there."

Dr.Whiteside put his pen down.

"OK. Take yourself behind that screen, pop your trousers off, then once you're done, climb on that bed over there."

Five uncomfortable minutes followed. Thankfully when Dr.Whiteside asked if I could just take my boxer shorts down, nothing stirred, in fact, it probably shrank a little. Sometimes you just worry that if your brain is saying,

"Don't have an erection! Don't have an erection! Don't have an erection!"

Your willy might just think,

"This'll be a laugh!"

Luckily, this was not one of those occasions. After a minute or two of inspecting, Dr.Whiteside told me I could pull my boxer shorts back up and get myself dressed. When I came out from behind the screen, I felt strangely liberated. I now felt I could ask him anything. Dr.Whiteside had seen my lumpy bollock, the only person to see it other than my brother, Jim. What else could there be that would be anywhere near as embarrassing? I thought I may as well ask the $64 000 question.

"Do you think it's cancerous?"

I fixed him a glance. I was looking for Dr.Whiteside to shift uncomfortably in his chair or develop a nervous tick, which I concluded would be a give away, but he did not flinch.

"That's not something I can rule out at this stage, Richard. All I can tell you at this stage is that cancer is a possibility. What I will need to do, is write you a referral to go to see a consultant urologist."

I was disappointed. I was expecting answers today.

"How quickly will I get to see the consultant?"

It had taken me months to get the nerve to go to the Doctor's. Now I had managed it, I wanted to ride on this rare wave of bravery. I wanted to get to see the consultant as quickly as possible, get the whole humiliating period out of the way as fast as I could. Dr.Whiteside twiddled with his dicky bow.

"Richard, given your age, the fact that a number of months have elapsed since the lump came to your attention and the very natural concerns I appreciate you must have. I will get a letter written up today for the consultant urologist and will ensure it is marked as urgent. Within a couple of weeks, you will be notified of your appointment date."

Standing up, I was going to reach across and shake his hand but I could not recall whether Mum had done that and not knowing if it was the done thing or not, I awkwardly extended my arm and then pulled it back about halfway into the stretch.

"OK. Thanks Doctor! Thanks very much!"

I was out of there in a flash. My second one within minutes. I felt relieved that I had at last made my first step towards a diagnosis, but was annoyed with myself for not challenging Dr.Whiteside with regards to the appointment date. OK, I would get a date within a fortnight, but that date could be 1999 for all I knew. I suppose I just had to accept it would be dealt with as quickly as the urologist could manage. From then on, it would be "Phase Two" – rather than worrying about what it could be, I would be dealing with cold, hard facts. My anxiety could then be over or my concern may be multiplied as I would be dealing with what the lump actually was, not what it could be, what it was.

In life, there is nothing more scary than the things you cannot change. I decided, on my way home from the Doctor's surgery, that although I could not change the diagnosis, at least I could change how I was dealing with the lump. Bottling things up, not sharing my fears and worries with Kelly, was surely the wrong way forward. I was off to the Everton-Norwich FA Cup Semi Final the following morning, which would provide a twenty four hour distraction, but had arranged to see Kelly on Sunday. I would break the news to her then. Little did she know change was coming.

On Sunday, Kelly would discover the person she thought was perfect was anything but, his body was malfunctioning and his mind was struggling to cope. I was scared what this would do to her. As far as sixteen year old girls go, Kelly was pretty street wise but it was a big thing for anyone having a boyfriend with cancer…if that's what it was or at the very least some sort of cyst on his privates. For my own sanity though, I needed to share this with someone, someone other than Jim, who was a better brother these days but still not exactly the perfect confidant. I needed to unburden myself. I'll tell her Sunday, I told myself. I'll tell her Sunday, no matter what.

Jemma

After I was 100% certain Vomit Breath was dead, I gave myself ten minutes before ringing the emergency services. The first thing I did, was make my way through to the kitchen to see what Vomit Breath had left behind. Unsurprisingly, there were several cans of special strength lager scattered around the work surfaces and a topless vodka bottle on the kitchen table alongside a lipstick marked crystal glass. Not a huge amount of the vodka had been drunk, it was a half-bottle and three quarters still remained, so I put on some oven gloves, picked the bottle up, poured the majority of it down the sink and then returned it to the table. Mum was a drinker, a massive one, but I just needed to emphasise the point to anyone from the emergency services who may be heading round.

I then went back upstairs to see Kelly. The sound of sobs could be heard before I climbed a stair. Some tough love was called for here, otherwise Kelly was digging a big hole for herself, a big hole that led directly into a prison cell.

As I went into her room, she was sat upright on her bed sniffing and sobbing.

"I'm a murderer Jemma! Nothing can ever change that now! For the rest of my life, whatever happens, I will always be a murderer."

I didn't say a word. I just walked over to Kelly and slapped her face. I was careful not to slap her too hard, as the last thing I wanted was Kelly to have a hand print on her face when the ambulance arrived, but hard enough to sting.

"Oww!! What are you playing at Jemma! That hurt!"

"Kelly, do you want to go to jail?"

"Of course I don't! But I will!"

"What for?"

"Murder. We've both just seen me kill our mother."

"I didn't see a thing, Kelly."

"Yes, you did!"

"No, Kelly, I didn't. I heard a thud, which woke me up. I went to investigate and that was when I saw Mum, at the bottom of the stairs, in a heap. I didn't see a thing."

"Jemma, they won't believe us!"

I grabbed Kelly. Not aggressively. I just brought her towards me, stressing a point.

"Kelly, remember what I said before. You didn't even hear anything, did you? You're a heavy sleeper. The first thing you knew about all this was when the paramedic woke you up."

Kelly did not look convinced. She began to shiver and when she spoke her voice was frail.

"Jemma, if we lie about this, we'll only make more trouble for ourselves. Maybe it'll be like you said before to Mum. Maybe if we tell them how she used to beat you up and make our lives a misery and explain that I just ran at her impulsively, to protect you from another beating, maybe then I won't go to jail for too long."

"Kelly, shut up! Our future is dependent on you. I'm no genius, I'm never going to get a fancy job that pays a load of money…"

Kelly interrupted,

"You've got a good job in the bank."

"I know but where's that going to take us? If I'm lucky in a few years time I might get a supervisors job, but that won't make us a fortune."

"We'll be OK."

"Kelly, I don't just want us to be OK. You are the brains in this family. You could be anything. You could be a Doctor, a Dentist, a vet, a surgeon, a scientist, you could be whatever you want to be. The world is your oyster. Do you think it will still be your oyster after a couple of years in a young offenders institute? Of course it won't! So let me say this one last time. I heard a thud which woke me up. You slept through. We went to bed at 11.30, after a night in together. OK?"

"OK…" Kelly was still unconvinced, "but what if they catch me out?"

"Kelly, no-one's going to catch you out. You went to bed at 11.30, you heard nothing, you were woken up when people started arriving. It's not difficult to remember."

"What if they ask about my little accident?"

Earlier I could not help noticing that Kelly had a wet patch between her legs. It appeared that she had reacted to the bedlam in the manner of a nervous puppy on Bonfire Night. There was no crime in that, sixteen year old girls should not be subjected to this sort of ordeal.

"Just say you are a really heavy sleeper and its really embarrassing to admit, but on occasion you have a little accident. Anyway, no-one will ask you about that."

"Well, what if they start asking questions about how we got on with Mum?"

"Just say she was a pisshead but she was our Mum and we loved her."

Kelly started to get a bit of colour back in her cheeks. She was finally starting to believe we had a viable alternative to confessing.

"OK."

"Kelly, they may even get me to wake you, to break the news. Just act like you normally would if I came into your room and woke you up at five in the morning. Cranky!"

"OK…Jemma?"

"Yes."

"She is definitely dead, isn't she?"

"Kelly, she is definitely, definitely dead. She was a horrible, horrible woman, Kelly and I owe you big time for helping me when I needed you. Please just do as I've said, don't panic and everything will be OK."

I gave Kelly a hug, tucked her into bed, kissed her cheek, squeezed her hands and then left her room, praying she would be strong enough to get through this. On the landing, I collected the bread knife I had dropped earlier and took it down to the kitchen, stepping over Mum's body on the way and putting it back in the cutlery draw. The knife had not been used in anger and my fingerprints on the family bread knife were not going to arouse suspicion. No-one was even going to look for fingerprints, because there was no murder weapon. Vomit Breath fell down the stairs. There was no mystery. Vomit Breath was a drunk, she came home, drank a load of neat vodka, staggered up the stairs, then fell. I'm sure police throughout the UK deal with a host of drunken tragedies every weekend. I picked up the phone and pushed the nine button three times.

"Good morning! Emergency services! Which service is it that you require?"

"I need an ambulance. It's my Mum, she's fallen down the stairs, she's out cold and I can't wake her up. Please send someone around as quickly as you can. PLEASE!"

Richie

I struggled to get off to sleep on the night of the Hillsborough disaster, but once I eventually fell asleep, I slept heavily. Too deep for dreams. Under normal circumstances, if my Mum ever had to wake me up, as soon as the door swung open, I was aware of her presence and would be fully alert immediately. This time though, Mum came into my room at 5am and a door opening, followed by some softly spoken words apparently failed to make me stir, so Mum resorted to a good old fashioned shake.

"What are you doing, Mum?! Leave me alone!"

"Richard, you are going to have to get up. There's a policeman downstairs waiting to see you."

That did the trick! Suddenly, I was awake! I staggered down the stairs in my pyjamas to find a solemn looking, uniformed but helmet free constable sitting on our settee. The missing helmet comforted me as I'd heard that arrests were only made by policemen in helmets. What exactly he was going to arrest me for, I was unsure, although a public act of indecency towards an insensitive idiot, sprang to mind. I was further comforted by the police constable's opening gambit,

"I'm sorry to get you up in the middle of the night, Richard....", was how he began.

I was off the hook! I didn't know much about the criminal underworld, but I suspected that when thieves and no goods were arrested in the middle of the night, the police did not start their arrests with an apology.

"...its just that I have a very upset young lady in the car and she mentioned to my colleague that she needed to see you. She just wanted to tidy herself up a little before she came in. I'm afraid she's had to deal with some very bad news to-night."

I drew my own conclusions straight away. It was Kelly, there was nothing more certain than that – who else would ask for me in the middle of the night? And the bad news? There was only one person, other than me, that meant anything to Kelly. I was 100% sure something must have happened to Jemma. Something serious. Without adding anything further, the policeman stood up and led me through to the porch. We looked through the double glazing and as soon as I saw Kelly being escorted out of the patrol car, wrapped in a blanket and being comforted by a young policewoman, my detective work was concluded on the spot. Jemma Watkinson was dead.

The policewoman helped Kelly up the drive, like a uniformed crutch. Kelly was unsteady and tearful. In my mind, it was now odds-on that Jemma was the unfortunate victim, the only thing left to hear was how her death had come about. My mind kept working its way back to Hillsborough. Could Jemma have been there? It was a stupid question, Jemma didn't even like football. Two separate tragedies within such a short period of time was too much for my brain to comprehend.

Once Kelly was halfway up the path, she spotted me. I opened the door and she broke into something faster than a jog but slower than a sprint, a three-quarter pace dash into my arms. I ran to meet her, reaching out and enveloping her into my chest. Kelly just sobbed, big, tearful, shoulder shrugging sobs. She could barely speak but managed to stammer,

"Sh sh she's dead, Richie! I can't believe it! Sh sh she's dead!"

'I knew it!' I thought to myself, 'Jemma's dead!'

Whilst comforting Kelly, in my mind I was applauding the powers of my sub-conscious mind and its ability to sense this tragedy. When we stepped back into the porch, my Mum suddenly re-appeared from nowhere, clad in white dressing gown and fluffy pink slippers.

"Can I make you a nice cup of tea, Kelly love?"

Kelly nodded.

"Go and have a seat in the lounge then love, whilst I make you a nice cup of tea and a biscuit!"

My Mum thought a lot of Kelly. Their paths had not crossed more than five or six times, as I would spend most of my time around at Kelly's, once her Mum headed out on the razz, but when she came to my house, Mum would repeat continually after her departure,

"She's a lovely girl that one! You make sure you take good care of her!"

There was a strange bond between my Mum and Kelly, maybe it was because my Mum mothered Kelly, whilst her own Mum just acted like an older sister you were ashamed of. Maybe the police had already told Mum what had gone on. I was probably the only one who didn't know. I felt like I was missing out. I needed to find out. I took command.

"Come in to the lounge, Kelly."

I began to guide her through. The police did not follow her out of the porch. The policewoman began to speak in a calm but assertive tone. Being a teenage boy, I wondered how often her husband managed to coax her into wearing that uniform in the bedroom, handcuff him to the bed and then punish him for being a naughty boy. Probably never, I decided as I came to my senses and the cynic within me arrived.

"We're not coming in, love," the policewoman said to me.

"Look after her and see how she goes. If she wants to go back home, ring this number," she passed me a card with Ormskirk police station's number on, "and

Lisa at the station will send a patrol car around to pick Kelly up. If she stays with you, can you ring the station and just let them know if she's still here by the afternoon, as at some point today we'll just need to ask Kelly some routine questions…."

The policewoman turned to Kelly, "nothing for you to worry about, Kelly, we just have to follow procedure."

Kelly managed to half-smile at the policewoman.

"Thanks Gillian! Thank you so much for everything."

"It's alright, love. You take care now and I'll see you again soon. Just to check you're OK."

The coppers left. I took Kelly by the hand and guided her through to the lounge, sitting her down on the settee, then sitting down next to her and giving her a cuddle. I was desperate to find out what had gone on, but Kelly wasn't speaking and I didn't want to push it, so we sat in silence until Mum's silhouette could be seen through the glass panels of the lounge door.

"Let me in, Richard. I can't open this door with a tray in my hand!"

As I got up to open the door, the neon blue light on the video recorder revealed that it was 5.13am.

On opening the door, Mum came in with a tray containing a teapot, two mugs, a sugar bowl and an assortment of chocolate biscuits.

"How are you feeling, love? The nice policeman told me everything. He was ever so nice, wasn't he? Must have been a terrible shock for you, love. Put plenty of sugar in your tea and take a biscuit. Sugar's good for shock!"

What the bloody hell had gone on! This was torture, I was unable to sustain my diplomacy any longer!

"What happened, Kelly?"

I asked in my softest, most compassionate voice. All of a sudden, Kelly shot up out of the settee, like a spring had catapulted into her backside.

"I need to go out, Richie, will you come with me?" she said this with some urgency like a drunk would just before a vomit.

"Of course I will."

As I stood up, I could see the disappointment written all over Mum's face, I had inherited my inquisitive nature from her bloodline.

"What about your tea?" she protested.

"Sorry Mum, we'll have a cup later. Let me just throw on some clothes over these pyjamas, Kelly, and then we can go. Do you just want a quick walk around the block?

A breath of fresh air?"

"No," Kelly replied, "I want you to walk me up to the "Sunny Road."

"The sunny road?" Mum was confused. "It's not going to be sunny now, love, it's still pitch black out there. Stay and have your tea!"

"It's fine, Mum. The "Sunny Road" is just a name we gave a road over on Clieves Hill and anyway, it's starting to brighten up already, by the time we get over there, it will be daylight and by the looks of things, it might even be sunny."

I threw some clothes on and despite Mum's protests we headed off on our walk. From Mum and Dad's to Clieves Hill and the "Sunny Road" is no more than a mile and a half, a half hour walk, but we left in lamppost lit dusk and arrived in daylight. On the journey, sketchy details of Kelly's ordeal began to emerge and the real victim was revealed. Initially though, my assumption that Jemma was dead, led to mutual confusion!

"…so Jemma and I pretty much knew she was dead straight away."

"Whoa! Whoa! Whoa!" I needed to grasp this, it was all a bit too freaky for me.

"Kelly, you're saying both you and Jemma knew she was dead."

"Yes. She wasn't breathing."

Assuming there's an afterlife, which I don't believe there is, but assuming there is, when you die, you know you're dead, but I didn't understand how Kelly could say that both her and Jemma knew Jemma was dead.

"I don't get it."

Kelly looked at me like I was as bright as a black button at midnight.

"Richie, what is there not to get?"

"How did you know, Jemma knew she was dead?"

"She told me."

"She told you?!"

I looked at Kelly like she was some sort of freak.

"Yes. Jemma told me she was dead. I've told you this."

"How did she tell you then? Using some weird telepathic, spiritual power?"

"No, she moved her mouth."

Kelly had lost it. Speaking to the dead! She was well on the way to the Psychiatric Ward! I was just playing along now for a laugh.

"Go on then, tell me when Jemma told you that she was dead."

"Whilst Jemma and I were waiting for the ambulance to come and collect her body."

I smiled.

"Right! You spoke to Jemma whilst you were waiting for her body to be collected!"

"Yes! So?"

Who did she think she was? Mary Magdalene?!

"Does that not strike you as being completely insane?!!!"

"It was insane that she was dead, but it was not insane that I would be speaking to Jemma. We're sisters, she brought me up, we had been through this together. Why would I not be talking to her?"

"I can understand why you would be talking to her, but I don't understand why Jemma would be speaking to you."

This question seemed to freak Kelly out even more.

"What do you mean? What are you trying to say, Richie? Why would Jemma not be speaking to me? Are you accusing me?"

"Kelly, I'm not accusing you of anything."

This was the most bizarre conversation I had ever had.

"All I'm asking is whether Jemma spoke back to you?"

"Absolutely. It was Jemma that stopped me completely freaking out!"

At that very moment, I must admit, I wanted to wash my hands of Kelly. Jemma had tragically died, but even after her death, Kelly was having a two way conversation with her. It was all too weird for me. Kelly was scaring me. I imagined grief had the capacity to do strange things to the mind, but I wasn't expecting Kelly to be the type of girl who would embrace the paranormal so readily.

A random question only asked to break an eerie silence, was the one that solved the mystery.

"Where was your Mum whilst all this was going on?"

"Out for the count at the bottom of the stairs. We didn't move her."

"Drunk?"

"Probably Richie, but I think the fact that she was dead was more important than the fact she was drunk!"

"Your Mum's dead?

"Of course she's dead! What's up with you, Richie?! The police car, the uniformed officers, the tears, this whole strange conversation – are they all not one big clue?"

"So Jemma's not dead?"

"NO! Why would Jemma be dead? I just told you I was talking to her!"

"Well why are you crying then?"

This was not meant to be heartless. If my mother or father had died unexpectedly, I would be a total wreck, but there was a major difference here, I loved my Mum and Dad with all of my heart. OK, my Dad was a gambler and more than a little unreliable, but he was a loveable rogue. From all accounts, Kelly's mother was a nasty piece of work, always drunk, uncaring, selfish and promiscuous. Until Kelly muttered her response, I was still in the phase of thinking none of this added up.

"Because…." Kelly half-choked on her line, "I killed her."

The penny dropped faster than a freefall skydiver. We stopped walking.

"How? How did you kill her?"

"She was going to attack Jemma again. I was cowering in my room, hating myself, wishing I had the bottle to do something, then, all of a sudden, I did have. Someone or something took over my body and I just ran at her screaming. She was at the top of the stairs, I pushed her, she took a step back, lost her balance and fell."

To an extent, I felt relieved. I thought Kelly was going to say she stabbed her or poisoned her or something equally first degree.

"Kelly, you can't blame yourself for that. You said she lost her balance and fell. You were just pushing her away from Jemma. It sounds like it was an accident, Kelly. A tragic accident."

"Richie, it wasn't! OK, I didn't mean to kill her but I pretty much pushed her down the stairs. Mum would still be here now if I hadn't. The police are going to send me to jail for this or at least some young offenders unit. My Mum is dead and I killed her….as soon as the police cotton on to that fact, I'll be heading behind bars for a very long time.

"Don't be ridiculous, Kelly. It was an accident. You won't go to jail."

"Richie, you're right, I won't go to jail. I won't allow them to do that to me. I'm leaving, Richie. I am going to pack a bag and go. Disappear. The thing is, Richie, I don't want to do this on my own. I want to run away with you, Richie. I need you to come with me. Please, come with me. Show me how much you love me and come with me. Please Richie, I don't think I can do this without you"

Jemma

"It doesn't make sense."

Ray was annoying me now. I had gone to his house for a bit of 'TLC', not to be subjected to questioning from Ray, who all of a sudden thought he was Britain's answer to Columbo.

"What doesn't make sense, Ray?"

"How your Mum died. It makes no sense whatsoever."

"She fell down the stairs."

I wished he'd give it a rest.

"Yes, Jemma, but you said she was coming up the stairs. I have fallen when running up the stairs and all that happens is that you fall forward, face first into the stair, you don't topple backwards."

"Ray, I wasn't there! I just heard a thud. I thought she must have fallen when she was coming up to bed but maybe she forgot something, started going down, then fell and that's when I heard the thud."

Ray had a smug expression on his face.

"Now that makes more sense. What you need to do, when you speak to the police tomorrow, is explain that you have been talking to me and I have worked out that the victim obviously fell whilst heading down the stairs. If they don't understand, tell them to ring me."

"Thanks Kojak! They've probably worked that one out themselves!"

"Well, you hadn't!"

I humoured him.

"Yes, but I'm not as intelligent as you, am I, Ray?! Anyway, can we not just talk about something else. For the last twenty four hours, all I have done is talk to people about the accident."

The smugness had not yet left Ray's face.

"I know what I've not told you! Something weird happened to me yesterday!"

I loved Ray but a drama without him being central to it, would only interest him for so long. I'm sure he felt genuinely sorry for me, that I was having to deal with the crisis created after Vomit Breath's death, but ultimately he knew I wasn't in the depths of despair, so he was happy to change the subject to one where he was the central character. As I say, I loved the man, but Ray's favourite subject was always, "RAY". I was happy to allow him to talk. At times, his incessant talking could become a little irritating, but following on from Vomit Breath's death and the countless questions I had been asked, it was a welcome distraction.

"Someone kissed me yesterday!"

I think Ray was hoping I would be furiously jealous, but after the twenty four hours I had been through, all I could manage was to feign minor interest.

"Really? Who?"

"You're not going to believe this!"

Only Ray could try to trump the unexpected death of my mother by a story about someone kissing him! I was bored already.

"Just tell me, Ray!"

"Honestly, Jemma, you won't believe it!"

"I'm sure I won't. Who?"

"Guess!"

"Ray, at this moment in time, if it was Madonna or the Pope, I'm really not bothered. Just tell me."

"Richie!"

"Richie?! Kelly's boyfriend, Richie?"

Still smug.

"The very one!"

This sounded odd. Then again, I suppose Richie was odd. He had slept with me and then denied all knowledge. Kelly loved him dearly, but he was odd.

"When did he kiss you? Was it when Everton scored?"

"No, no, it wasn't a celebratory kiss, Jemma, it was a romantic one. He must have a bit of a thing for me. It was mad! He pulled me to him in a vice like grip, started kissing me, tongue and everything and when I pulled away, you should have seen his face. Furious he was. Got out the door, slammed it and stomped off. We were at a petrol station just off the M6 and he wouldn't even get back in the car, I had to leave him there!"

"Is this the God's honest truth?!"

"Swear on your life, Jemma! He told me I was disgusting for repelling his advances. He must be one of those pro-gays who thinks everyone who is not gay is weird!"

All things considered, it was probably an inappropriate time to be laughing, but I couldn't help myself. It sounded ludicrous!

"Ray, there is no way that Richie is gay!"

"Well he was doing a very good impression yesterday! He started crying about the Hillsborough disaster, I started comforting him and he obviously read my signals all wrong and started kissing me. He's gay, as sure as a puff is a puff!"

"So are you not interested then?"

"NO!"

"He's a good looking lad!"

"Don't be ridiculous, Jemma, I'm no arse bandit!"

"But you think Richie is!"

"I don't think Jemma, I know. If I'd have kissed him back, he'd have been up my bum like a rat up a drainpipe!"

Richie

Kelly and I sat in the early morning sunshine on the "Sunny Road" only speaking intermittently. We both had a lot to take in. As I thought, questions were raised in my head so I would occasionally break the tranquillity by asking Kelly for explanations. I needed to fill gaps in my understanding. One of the biggest shocks for me was learning that Kelly's Mum used to regularly beat Jemma. I knew she was an idiot, I just hadn't realised she was a psychopath.

"Why did you not tell me all this had been going on?"

"I couldn't, Richie. I was ashamed of myself for not doing anything to help."

There was also the shock of coming to terms with the simple fact that my girlfriend had ended someone's life. My girlfriend who seemed to me like the most beautiful and gentle girl you could possibly hope to meet, had killed someone. Finally, I had to deal with the shock of being asked to run away with the aforementioned killer.

"Kelly, where we would we run to if we ran away?"

"Abroad. They would find us if we didn't go abroad."

"Whereabouts are you thinking?"

"We'd need to keep moving. Anyway, there's loads of places I'd like to go. Places that are culturally a million miles from here, places like Saudi Arabia and Egypt."

As I was no stranger to home comforts, Egypt and Saudi Arabia did not exactly appeal. I managed to smile.

"I can't imagine us there, Kelly!"

"Why not?"

"I'm too used to my Mum making my bed, cleaning the dishes, putting the TV on for me and making me a pot of tea. Can you see me riding through the desert on a camel?!"

"No, but I could picture us riding through the desert on horseback, like in Lawrence of Arabia!"

"I think you've watched too many films, Kelly! I wouldn't even be able to get on a camel or a horse, I'd probably end up facing the wrong way!"

For the first time all day, Kelly giggled a little to herself. It was a sweet giggle.

"OK. You win! Egypt and Saudi are out. Where do you want to go?"

I wanted to stay in Ormskirk but I knew that was not what Kelly wanted to hear.

"Somewhere they speak English. My French is crap and I can't roll my "R"s so anywhere Spanish speaking is out! Somewhere like Australia or America would be great."

After I said Australia, I cringed as I thought Kelly may latch on to the ancestral convict link, but luckily she didn't.

"I'd be happy going to either the US or Oz, I just need to get away from here."

"Today?"

"No, but soon."

"How soon?"

"This month."

"I don't think we could get into Australia that quick, you need a visa. You might need one for America too." I was trying to slow things down. Ultimately, I was going nowhere, I just didn't want Kelly to either.

"I need to go this month, Richie."

"Kelly, that's daft."

Kelly's bottom lip quivered a little. I could tell she was offended.

"No it is not!"

"Kelly, it is! I saw that policewoman with you earlier, there is no way in the world that she thinks that you killed your Mum. If you try and leg it this week, then all of a sudden, you are looking guilty."

"When do you suggest we go then?"

This was another surreal conversation. I had a lump in my scrotum the size of a marble and pretty soon I'd be listening to a urologist tell me whether or not I had cancer. Going on the run with a sixteen year old killer was not high on my list of priorities, despite her being the prettiest girl in the world.

"Let it all die down. We could go in a few months time."

I didn't mean this. This was a halfway house that was meant to placate her. It didn't work.

"I might be in jail by then," Kelly complained.

And I might be lifting hot coals with your mother, I thought.

"There are too many reasons that we can't just up and leave."

"Like what?"

"I've already mentioned two. One is the fact that we'll need a visa to get in any decent country and the other is that if you make a run for yourself, you may as well tattoo, 'I killed my mother' on your forehead."

"Those reasons aren't enough to stop me." Kelly stated.

"Well they're enough to stop me! So a third reason is that if you go now, you go alone."

"What else?" Kelly was mad now. Not mad crazy, mad furious.

"Money, for starters. How could we survive as runaways, we're skint!"

"I'm not. I've been saving the money I made in Woolies in case I stayed on into Sixth Form."

"How much have you got?"

"Two and a half grand!"

I thought she was lying.

"Two and a half grand!! From working at Woolies?!"

"No, most of it came from my Grandad before he died three years ago. He gave me a passbook from a building society with my name on and two thousand pounds in it. He said to keep it away from Mum because she'd just fritter it away on drink and drugs. He did the same for Jemma."

Inadvertently, Kelly had just handed me my 'Joker'!

"There's my final reason."

"What?"

"Jemma. Could you leave Jemma to deal with all this crap on her own?"

I knew I had her. Kelly thought long and hard about this conundrum, before eventually replying,

"No, you're right, Richie. I couldn't. I've let her down too much already to leave her on her own. In a lot of ways, Jemma relies on me. If we ran off and left her here, on her own, she'd never forgive me……………So I'm trapped, aren't I?"

"You're not trapped, Kelly, you just have to sit tight. No-one will ever suspect you of killing your Mum. They may suspect, Jemma, but you, never!"

I felt guilty saying that but it was true. If the police suspected anyone of killing Kelly's Mum, it would be Jemma. Problem was, if Jemma was arrested, Kelly would confess. There was no way Kelly would let Jemma go to jail for a crime that Kelly had committed.

I started to panic. Maybe I had this all wrong. Maybe Kelly was in more danger of being caught for doing this than I thought. On the TV, no-one gets away with murder. Maybe it's the same in real life. Maybe Kelly should be making a run for it. Maybe I should be encouraging her to do just that.

Having convinced myself this would all blow over and a new normality would emerge, now I suddenly felt a lot less secure. Everything was falling apart. Kelly's life, my body. That's right, I remembered, I had convinced myself this would be the day I told Kelly about the lump. Nothing was going to stop me telling her. I looked at Kelly. Her face was pale and she looked crestfallen. I couldn't break the camel's back with this one. It would have to wait. Wait until the good times returned, which if I got the all clear, could be just around the corner, it would be an insignificant news item then. On the other hand, if I had cancer and the truth about Kelly came to light, those good times might be light years away.

Jemma

"She was great your Mum! Life and soul of every party! I'm going to fucking miss her! Saturday nights will never be the same again!"

This was a universal eulogy for Vomit Breath from every druggie and alcoholic, aged over thirty, within a ten mile radius of Ormskirk. Each and every one of them turned up for the funeral, probably scenting the smell of free beer. They all wanted to share their stories of nights on the lash with Vomit Breath! She was the patron saint of dipsomaniacs! I refrained from adding my own eulogy as it would have shattered their allusions.

"She crammed several lifetimes of partying into her thirty eight years, your Mum did! Burnt the candle at both ends! She was generous too, always the first to the bar!"

Being first to the bar was not generosity as far as Vomit Breath was concerned. It was a shrewd tactic. Buy the first round in the local whilst drinks were cheap, then avoid paying later when they hit the bars and nightclubs where prices were almost doubled. As the night progressed, Vomit Breath's mates were always too smashed to keep track of who had bought the last round, so she always said she had bought the round before last. At home, she used to brag that in over twenty years of partying, she had never bought two rounds in the same night. Very generous! To a fault!

All in all, there were about fifty mourners. Over forty drunken friends of Vomit Breath's, plus myself, Kelly, Ray, Richie, Vomit Breath's mother "Tut" and my school friend Amy, who I hadn't seen a great deal of since working in the bank and dating Ray, but she came to provide some emotional support which was really good of her.

"Tut" was on typical form.

"Look at these people! Jemma, if you ever needed proof of what a mess your mother made of her life, you would just need to look at the quality of her friends. The lowest of the low! If the caste system existed in this country, these lot would be the great unwashed! How on earth did your mother screw everything up so badly? I feel sorry for your poor Grandad, he'll be turning in his grave tonight, he really will."

I pictured what a body would look like after three years of decaying. Not fit to turn, I wouldn't have thought.

Over the course of the day, Ray and 'Tut' had formed an alliance. It wasn't the most unlikely alliance in the world, as other than Amy and I, he wasn't really left with too many people he could talk at. Ray and Richie were maintaining a healthy distance apart throughout the post-crematorium knees up and I knew full well that Kelly was not Ray's number one fan.

By nine in the evening, both Ray and 'Tut' had had enough and they looked at the drunken revellers downing whiskey shots in Vomit Breath's memory, with more than a hint of disdain.

"We need to kick this lot out soon," Ray commented to 'Tut' looking at his watch,

"I have experience of dealing with drunks. They'll wreck this place if we don't get them out soon!"

"I'll tell them to go," Tut replied, "and if they don't leave, I'll be calling the police."

'Tut' considered this statement for a moment before re-considering.

"Actually, no. I'm sure most of these reprobates have spent plenty of time in a prison cell, maybe the threat of the police will not be enough to get them out. More drastic action is called for!

I tell you what we could do, Ray. We could pour the rest of the alcohol down the drain, that would send them packing!"

So, 'Tut' and Ray began the process of discreetly trying to empty the house of booze. To be fair to 'Tut' this was one of her better ideas and I have to confess throughout the day she had been unusually tolerable, even making me smile with some of her acidic comments.

At the crematorium, when Vomit Breath's coffin slowly disappeared from view, on it's way to the incinerator, 'Tut' muttered,

"Dear Lord, that woman has so much alcohol inside her, when she hits the fire, she'll go up like a flambé!"

Prior to that, when the funeral hearses arrived at our house, Kelly, more through guilt than sentiment had started to weep. 'Tut' was unsympathetic.

"Pull yourself together, Kelly! You weren't even fond of the woman!"

"It's not that, Nan," Kelly replied, "I'm just not feeling too well today."

'Tut' huffed.

"Well, I wish you'd have told me," Tut replied, "I could have made a two for one deal with the undertakers!"

Vomit Breath's funeral service was held at St.Michael's church in Aughton. The Vicar only consented to the service taking place as 'Tut' had been a regular member of the congregation there for many years and at one point was even the Church treasurer. Vomit Breath, however, had not stepped in that church or any other, throughout her adult life and I'm sure if she had had time to plan her own funeral, it would not have included a church service.

The Vicar read from Matthew Chapter 19 verse 26,

"But Jesus beheld them and said unto them, with men this is impossible, but with God, all things are possible."

I think this was the Vicar's way of saying, in his kind hearted way, that no-one could sort Vomit Breath out on earth, so it was now God's job to get her on the straight and narrow. Personally, I was convinced Vomit Breath's escalator would be heading in completely the opposite direction.

The Vicar mentioned in his speech,(it was definitely a speech not a eulogy), that Vomit Breath had "her own quiet faith".

"Silent more like," I whispered to Kelly, "the only faith Vomit Breath had was faith in her ability to get tanked up every Friday and Saturday night!"

Kelly did not laugh, she was taking the whole ceremony very seriously. From St.Michael's, the funeral procession headed to Southport crematorium. There were two hearses and about eight other cars, four of which were taxis, all crammed to capacity as Vomit Breath's mates were permanently unfit or unwilling to drive. Then, after the crematorium, 'Tut' had arranged a buffet at the Comrades Club in Ormskirk. The room was far too big for the amount of mourners but 'Tut' had chosen it as there were plenty of bar staff and she thought it would be the only place in Ormskirk capable of managing the demand for drink!

Once the Comrades function finished, we were followed back to our house by about twenty of Vomit Breath's friends, who had decided to honour her memory by getting paralytic. By ten o'clock, through a combination of the endeavours of 'Tut' and Ray who poured drink down the sink in vast quantities and the revellers who poured it down their throats in equal measure, the house was dry. Once they became aware of this, the alcoholic locusts moved on, en masse into Ormskirk town centre, leaving the three family members, plus Amy, Ray and Richie, to clear up their mess.

The following morning, we realised that several CDs had disappeared along with bed clothes, pillows, jewellery, cuddly toys, a collection of Vomit Breath's sex toys and £40 in cash. At one point, Kelly and I reckoned that there must have been one thief in Vomit Breath's bedroom whilst their accomplice was in the back garden catching everything that was thrown out of the window. Classy friends!

Once everyone had departed that night with the exception of Kelly, 'Tut' and myself, 'Tut' sat us down and asked how we intended on paying the bills now Vomit Breath had died.

"I was already paying the majority of the rent, Nan," I explained, "and Kelly's going to ask for more hours at Woolworth's, between us we'll cover the rent."

"Well that's a good start, but what about the utility bills and supermarket shopping and everything else. Life's not cheap you know."

"Nan, stop stressing. I know. I've had to chip in for years. Remember, I used to work at Freeman, Hardy & Willis before the job in the bank? Your daughter has not exactly grafted to pay for us to live like pigs in mud. We will manage. No doubt about it, we will manage."

"Well, I hope so Jemma otherwise you will have to move in with me."

"Seriously, it'll be fine!"

"I'll give you three months, Jemma. I'll come across every week to check how you are getting on. If you're not keeping on top of everything and I mean everything, I will be making you pack your bags and move to mine.

I expect the washing and ironing to be done, every room to be tidy and I also expect boyfriends just to visit for the evening, not stay the night. If I find either of you young ladies turning this house into a brothel, I will guarantee you, I will pack your bags myself and drive you both over to the Wirral.

At your age, I am not expecting you to show the level of maturity necessary to run a household on your own, but you have three months to prove me wrong!"

When 'Tut' was saying this, I was 100% certain everything would work out fine. I expected Kelly and I to work together to make it all happen. I thought three months would pass without incident and the dark days were over. I was totally wrong. Within that three months, everything changed. The relationship I held dearest was totally torn to pieces and as a direct result of the events that triggered this breakdown, Kelly and I did not see or speak to each other for the next ten years.

Richie

As dawn became morning on the "Sunny Road", I felt it was time for Kelly and I to head home, to my home anyway. We had talked through everything we could possibly talk through, the Hillsborough tragedy, Kelly's mother's death, Kelly's bizarre childhood growing up with a drunk, the strong bond she had established with her sister, the possibility of running away, our love for each other and what we thought the future would bring. We re-emphasised our plans to meet up right there, on the "Sunny Road", every sunny 4th July for the rest of our lives, no matter what and, in that moment, I was convinced it would not be necessary as we would be together for the long haul. The fact that I was totally in love with Kelly, despite her mother's death, seemed like confirmation that nothing was ever going to come between us.

For the first time that morning, the sun hid behind a fluffy, white cloud and I took this as a sign that it was time to go.

"Come on, Kelly! Time to head off!" I said as I stood up, knocking the grass off my backside. Two handed, I gripped Kelly's hands in an attempt to pull her up, but she resisted, pulling back against me.

"No, please Richie, can we not stay a little longer?"

"We need to head back, Kelly, you're going to have to get that visit to the police station out the way at some point, you may as well get it done before you get too tired, whilst you are still on your toes and can concentrate properly."

"I know! I know! Just not yet! Please just sit down with me."

"OK."

I sat back down.

"Give me a hug," Kelly requested.

We hugged. I loved hugging Kelly, just holding her tightly used to give me goose pimples. She always smelt divine and no matter what the circumstances, I would always drift off to a world that was uncomplicated and negativity no longer existed, just joy and happiness. I was savouring every second of that hug, when Kelly pulled away.

"Richie, can we make love?"

This caught me off guard. My first thought was that I was wearing pyjamas under my clothes, not altogether sexy.

"Now?"

"If you want to."

I started to twitch a little. We had done a lot of the stuff that girls magazines describe as "heavy petting", but had always avoided taking things that one step further. I suspected that I was somewhat unusual for a male, but it was probably me that had been reluctant to make that final step. We had never discussed our avoidance of sex, but I knew that if I had orchestrated it during those heated moments, Kelly would not have stopped me.

I was just scared of that next step. The fear emanated from a myriad of sources, including "the lump", potential premature ejaculation, potential pregnancy, potential lack of size and the potential of things changing in our relationship, once it became a sexual relationship. Sometimes the journey is better than the destination and I was scared in case this is how things turned out. I wasn't a virgin, but I wanted everything to be right the first time with Kelly, as I pretty much knew she was.

Given how stunning Kelly was, with those porcelain features and mesmerising green eyes, I am sure 99.9% of teenage males in my position would have asked no further questions, unbuckled their jeans, whipped down their pyjamas and got going, but I was more than a little apprehensive.

"Why now, Kelly?"

"Do you not want to?"

"I desperately want to, I just want it to be right. I love you more than you'll ever know Kelly Watkinson and because of that, I only want to do this if it's going to be perfect."

That was as honest as I could be.

Kelly took my hands and played with my fingers as she responded.

"Richie, this is perfect. Look at this place! The view, the sunshine just creeping back from under the clouds…..this is our "Sunny Road", Richie, it always will be our special place, if we did this, it will be even more special to us."

I was still hesitating.

"Should we be doing this now though? After everything that has just happened?"

"Absolutely! Once we leave here today, no matter what, our world will continue to change. I have no idea how things will turn out, but I know my world changed forever last night when I charged out my room. In many ways, I wish I'd have just continued to be the coward and left the heroics to Jemma, but it's too late to change that now. What is done, is done. All I want now, is to leave here having lost my virginity to the only boy I have ever loved. I adore you, Richie and whatever happens, if we make love now, I will never forget how much you meant to me.

You said you wanted it to be perfect, well if we make love here, this morning, on the "Sunny Road", if it lasts three seconds or half an hour, I can guarantee, in my eyes, it will be perfect."

They were the last words spoken on the "Sunny Road" that morning. I could have said,

"What if someone sees us?" or

"There's something I need to tell you first," but I held those words back.

At first, we just hugged. Long, meaningful hugs. Then we kissed, slowly and passionately. When I felt ready, I undid the button on my jeans and as I undid Kelly's, she pulled keenly on my top and then slipped my jeans off. The undressing process was like the kisses, slow and tender. Pyjamas are easy to take off at the height of passion! I did fluff my lines a little when I failed to unclasp Kelly's bra after three or four attempts, but silently and methodically, Kelly took the lead and slipped her bra off as though it was as easy as flicking a switch. Kelly's breasts were wonderfully pretty and she rested her head back on the grass as I caressed them. Then, as the silence was broken by soft moans, I headed downwards.

I know this is a soppy confession and not in the least bit masculine, but when my tongue ventured inside of Kelly's body I had tears in my eyes. Everything about Kelly whispered perfection and I felt humbled that she loved me enough to allow me to be the first. Sensing my tongue could not maintain its involvement without other areas calling a halt to proceedings, Kelly guided me upwards and I held her face in my hands and caressed her soft, wet lips as I lay on top of her. With a little guidance, our two bodies became one.

I would love to say that with our bodies entwined, I thrust deeply into Kelly, time after time, providing her with wave after wave of orgasmic pleasure, as she wept tears of joy, but life is not like that. I did, however, manage to bite into my bottom lip long enough and hard enough to last for a couple of minutes, before being overcome by a series of shakes that McDonalds or Elvis Presley would have been proud of.

As we dressed in the spring sunshine, we exchanged smiles, with Kelly being the first to speak as we held hands on our walk back home.

"I told you it would be perfect!" was all she said.

Kelly

Adapting to life as a murderer is not easy. Every knock at the door, every telephone call and every tap on the shoulder generates a feeling of impending doom. For several weeks, I could see no way forward other than confessing to the police and serving the time that my actions warranted. The only two people who were aware of my guilt, Jemma and Richie, both argued that a confession would be nonsensical. My mother was dead, I had only acted instinctively to defend Jemma and there was no intention for my actions to result in her death. Time is a healer though and the urge to confess, although never completely disappearing, diminished by the day.

The fact that Jemma and I continued to live in the house where Mum died, did not aid my emotional recovery. The staircase was a constant reminder of that fateful night and every room brought back memories of my mother. I pleaded with Jemma to join me in looking for somewhere else to live, but although she was extremely sympathetic, Jemma explained that we had re-negotiated the tenancy agreement with Mr.Bukhari after Mum's death and we had to stay there for six months, after which we could move on. If we didn't stay for six months, future landlords would not look upon us favourably. I understood, but understanding and liking something can be world's apart, so I ended up spending as little time as possible in that house and every possible moment I could with Richie.

I had become totally besotted with Richie Billingham. In a sea of uncertainty, I saw Richie as my life raft. Richie had a tendency to worry about minor things, but when it came to the major ones, inexplicably he had an aura of calmness. Despite knowing exactly what had happened to my mother, in those first few difficult weeks, it appeared his love for me was unfaltering. We were both totally convinced that we would be together forever, that Richie would father my children and our love would never die. The morning after Mum's death, we made love in the fields on the "Sunny Road". It was my first time, our first time and it was gentle and delightful. In the days that followed, as spring headed towards summer and the daylight hours lasted longer, the "Sunny Road" became our sanctuary and we would spend hour after hour there, talking, hugging, laughing, crying and making love.

Something deep within me should have warned me that it was not going to last. When Richie and I first started dating, I was struck by his unwavering faith in our ability to stay together. Having been raised in a world of negativity and pessimism, I found it difficult to buy into this world of fairytale endings. At that stage, Richie was convinced we would stay together, whilst I thought at some stage things would change. If I'm honest, I thought his love for me would die. The more time I spent with Richie though, the more I found his faith in our collective destiny was warranted and I too found myself believing, or being convinced, that we belonged together.

I don't remember the exact moment things changed, it wasn't a gradual process, it was a quickfire one, but around a month after Mum died, all of a sudden, Richie's behaviour changed. We did not row, we did not bicker, there was no defining moment that seemed to signal the end, Richie just changed. It was like someone else had taken over his body and we suddenly became strangers. It would be wrong of me to say he went cold on me, but without a shadow of a doubt, the full on, passionate, all consuming relationship that we had became less intense.

Relationships to some degree are about life patterns. If your boyfriend buys you flowers every Saturday, then one Saturday he arrives at your house without them, it is only natural to wonder why. If, like in my relationship with Richie, he wants to spend every spare minute with you, then all of a sudden he wants to spend his spare moments alone, its only natural to question why things have changed.

Spare moments alone were not the only sign, our trips to the "Sunny Road" were suddenly avoided and the times we did spend together were less tender, some nights were totally passion free with just a peck on the cheek at the end of the evening. We had been so close for so long, there was no way I wasn't going to question Richie about the changes in his attitude. I took his hand in mine one evening at his Mum's and came right out with it,

"What's going on, Richie?"

Richie immediately wriggled out of my grasp, his body language contradicted his response.

"What do you mean, 'what's going on?' – nothing is going on!"

"Richie, you've changed. You just don't seem to feel that same way about me that you used to."

"I haven't changed!"

"Don't deny it, Richie. I was the one who used to say that this might not last forever and you were the one that was offended by that statement. Now though, when I want to see you in the evening, you often say you are stopping in. When I go to kiss you, you turn your head. It's like you feel guilty about something. Do you feel guilty because you don't love me any more?"

Richie hugged me. A genuine hug, not a token one. He looked hurt that I had said this.

"Kelly, I love you as much as I have ever loved you. If not more."

"What's changed then? Is it anything to do with what happened to Mum?"

Richie shook his head.

"Kelly, your Mum dying did not change how I felt about you one bit."

"Then why the change of attitude?"

"I've just got a lot on mind, Kelly. I thought I was hiding it from you, but obviously I was not making a very good job of it."

"Richie, you aren't the only one with things on their mind, you know! I'm still petrified that the police will send me to jail, but that hasn't changed how I treat you. What is it on your mind that has you acting so differently?"

Richie audibly gulped.

"I just haven't wanted to burden you with it, with everything you have on your plate, right now."

"Tell me."

"It's just…….it's just that I'm scared that I…."

Richie could not get his words out. I could tell he was on the verge of something major. He seemed like he was going to break down in tears and confess something to me, something incredibly important. Richie then took a deep breath and after he did that his composure returned. I am 100% sure, what he eventually said was not what he had originally planned to say.

"It's just that I'm scared that you might move to your grandmother's. I can't drive. How would our relationship cope if I was in Ormskirk and you were on the Wirral?"

This was drivel. I did not believe him.

"And that's why you've been acting so strange?"

"Yes…."

Poppycock!

"…I didn't realise I had been acting strange, but I guess so. Maybe I've been inadvertently trying to prevent myself getting too used to seeing you all the time, because if you move to the Wirral, I won't get to see you every day." It didn't seem too much of an issue to me. It was a forty minute train journey away. I started to think perhaps this was the real issue after all. Richie did sometimes worry about inconsequential things, maybe this was a big deal to him. I took his hands again.

"Richie, don't be so silly! Jemma and I are doing just fine at our place and if everything continues like it is right now, we won't be moving anywhere. We're paying the bills, we're keeping the place spotless, Nan's delighted with us. She threatens to ship us over to the Wirral, but she doesn't want us there really, we'd get in the way of her trips to play bowls and her coffee mornings. She just says it to make sure we behave ourselves!

"Don't worry, Richie! I'm not going anywhere!"

"Phew!"

As soon as he said, 'phew', I flipped right back to not believing him. It was just said without any conviction. I could not put my finger on what it was, but there was certainly something the matter with Richie. At that point, I had no idea, but soon enough I thought I had discovered the root of the problem and when I did, the love that we had built up came crashing down quicker than a Fred Dibnah chimney.

Margerita McGordon

Majorca is fantastic in the Spring. Wally and I are both in our seventies now and although in our younger days, we loved the intense heat of July and August, as we were both real sun worshippers, these days warm is wonderful. We have had a villa in Costa D'En Blanes, for seventeen years now and have headed out for a six week holiday there from mid-April to the end of May, for the last nine years. Karen, one of our daughters and her husband, Andrew, often head over for the last week of May and then stay there for a further couple of weeks after we head home. Our other daughter, Paula, rarely comes over, she has an olive skinned complexion and since she was a child has avoided the sun like a bat. Paula's always there to pick us up from the airport though!

For those six weeks, we just love sitting on the balcony, smelling the sea air and reading a good book, or at least I do, anyway! Wally tends to find odd jobs to do around the villa whilst listening to the BBC World Service on the radio. I don't think I've ever seen Wally read a book, he'll read The Daily Bulletin or The Sun, but after the awful tragedy at Hillsborough, which happened just the day before we went away, he made a stance to never read The Sun again, so he read The Daily Express this time.

I think he misses the half-naked, glamour pusses on Page Three, but he was so disgusted with them after Hillsborough (the bosses at "The Sun", not the Page 3 girls), that he was willing to forsake Sam Fox and the likes in the name of common decency. I admire him for that. He is a good man, my Wally.

The six weeks away were perfect. We had two cloudy days and the rest of the time, it was wall to wall sunshine, about as hot as British summertime but with sun! Costa D'en Blanes is ideal for us, it's very quiet, but if we fancy a coffee in the day or a beer and sherry at night, we are only a couple of miles away from Portals Nous and Palma Nova. We tend to get a taxi now as Wally gets a little nervous about driving over there as the Majorcans are mad drivers. We mainly go to Portals Nous now, we're getting too old for Palma Nova, it's for the young ones.

Last Sunday, our six weeks were up, we had a Sunday afternoon flight back from Palma to Manchester with Dan Air. It was a great flight, just a little bumpy once we began our descent, as it was raining in Manchester. Paula picked us up. Paula has been living on her own for the last three years, since her and Gerry divorced and I worry about her. She's thirty eight now and I doubt very that she'll have children, at that age. It's very sad.

Wally had not wanted Paula coming all that way from Ormskirk, to pick us up. He wanted us to leave the car at the airport, but once I told him how much car parking would have cost for six weeks, he quickly changed his mind! Paula is a safer driver than Wally now anyway, his reactions are not what they were. She was there five o'clock, on the dot, just like we asked. She's marvellous, our Paula!

Paula did not break the news to us until halfway home. The first half of the journey was just filled with the normal chit-chat, how were the cats, did we eat at Friar Tucks much and how was Puerto Portals getting along and were there bigger and better boats there this year? Had we seen anyone famous? Just Nigel Kennedy, we told her. Only when we were half way home did Paula break the sensational news about next door.

"You know what I completely forgot to tell you on the phone, Mum?"

"What?"

"Your noisy neighbour…"

"Don't tell me she's been fighting again! We saw a police car there the morning we left to go to Majorca and I said to Wally, 'I bet that womans been up to her old tricks again!' Didn't I, Wally?"

Wally nodded.

"She died, Mum!"

"She died! When?"

"It must have been that Saturday night, when you went to Majorca on the Sunday. That will have been why the police car was there. It was in the Ormskirk Advertiser. She fell down the stairs, probably drunk, one of her daughters was woken up by the noise and when she went to look, she found her. Dead."

When your next door neighbour dies, you should feel sadness, shouldn't you? I should have felt awful, but I had been praying to God that she would move away and now, in a way, she had. I thought back. The mother and the eldest daughter were always arguing, Wally and I could often not hear Corrie because of the din through the walls. Often we had to turn the volume up. We felt sorry for the youngest one, she was a sweet, beautiful young thing, but it must have been dreadful for her, living in that house, with her mother and sister screaming at each other the whole time.

"We heard them rowing that night, didn't we Wally? As per usual, the mother stumbled in drunk and her and the oldest girl had a right row again, didn't they?"

Paula did not believe me at first.

"It couldn't have been that night, Mum. It said in the Advertiser the girls were asleep. They only woke up when she fell down the stairs."

Wally backed me up.

"The local rag have got it wrong, Paula. They woke us up, about one o'clock, didn't they, Rita? Your mother was in a right state saying they had ruined her holiday already, as they just had no consideration and she went on and on about how she was going to be jetlagged for the first few days of the holiday, because of next door. If your mother had not been with me the whole time, Paula, I would not have been surprised if she had gone round to next door and pushed that woman down the stairs!"

"Wally!"

"It's true though Rita, isn't it?! You were fuming, weren't you?"

Wally was right.

"Well, Wal, she has made our life a misery every since they started renting that place."

"I know she has, dear."

This conversation seemed to concern Paula. I could not help but notice that she was frowning. It was the same troubled frown she had when she discovered that Gerry had been having an affair with Holly, the Avon lady.

"Mum, Dad, are you 100% sure about this? It was definitely that Saturday night?"

"Paula," I said, "we are old, but we aren't senile! It was definitely that Saturday night. The day before our holidays. We were already upset because of what had happened to all those poor people at Hillsborough, then the foghorn came in and that was it, pandemonium, as per usual!"

"Could you make out what they were saying?"

I am not good with details like that. Luckily, Wally is.

"Can you remember what they were saying, Wally?"

Wally scratched his head like he was trying to get to his brain, to tap into his memory banks.

"The two girls were arguing at first, in the bedroom. Remember, Rita, we woke up when the older one shouted "GET OUT!" at the younger one. Then the older girl and the mother were arguing for ages, about a knife, I think. Remember Rita, the older girl said something like,

'Run, mother!' and then the mother said something like, 'No chance!' then there was an argument about backing off and not backing off and then someone screamed, then there was a load of banging, then it went quiet. Didn't it, Rita?"

Wally's attention to detail is just first rate. When he was describing it to Paula, I could just picture the two of us lying there, listening, as if it was yesterday, not six weeks ago. I wish my mind was still as sharp as that.

"That was it, Paula. Exactly like that."

Wally continued.

"After it went quiet, I got up, went for a wee, I am a slave to my prostate these days, Paula, I really am. Went for a wee, then I went downstairs, made your mother and I a drink of water, then we went to sleep. The following morning, we were up at five and we headed off to Majorca."

"Did you not think of ringing the police?"

Wally and I laughed a little, Wally explained.

"The police! We tried that when she first moved in, but it didn't stop her. The police would have been around here pretty much every night if we had reported that woman every time she rose her voice! Bloody nightmare she is!"

"Bloody nightmare she was!" Paula corrected him.

"Well, we're going to have to contact the police now." Paula stated.

"Why love?" I asked. Admittedly I am not always the quickest to appreciate the significance of certain things. Petrocelli, Columbo, Murder, She Wrote…I would never get the murderer, never.

"Because Mum, by the sounds of it, you and Dad may very well have witnessed a murder!"

Wally did not see Paula's logic either.

"Those girls won't have killed their mother," he said, "they haven't got it in them."

"Dad, that's not for us to decide. Let's ring the police, tell them what you heard and let them decide what to make of it. You might be right, it might be nothing, but why would the girls say they were fast asleep, if they were awake the whole time? I think they will have some serious explaining to do, at the very least."

Kelly

As long as it's not raining, market days in Ormskirk are always busy. If the sun comes out, it can be like a mass gathering for a Val Doonican concert. On this particular sunny day in early June, it was total bedlam. Having passed my GCSEs, I had taken a year out of Further Education, to help contribute to the household bills, but also to save some money, so I could go back to school and fund myself the following year. Jemma was helping too. She worked at the bank and I was getting as many hours in as I could at the Woolworths in Aughton Street. I started there as a Saturday girl at fourteen, then after my GCSEs, I did Thursdays, Saturdays and Sundays before stepping it up to full-time after Mum's death. For this, I was paid £105 per week, by no means a fortune, but enough to put a bit away, as well as helping Jemma with the rent.

My supervisor, Kathryn, had pinched first lunch that day, as she wanted to nip down to 'The Buck I'Th Vine' for a celebratory drink with her boyfriend, Gaz, as it was her 21st birthday the following day, so I was left in the CD department on my own for a crazy hour and a quarter. Barry Manilow and Dolly Parton had new albums out, so the older generations were buying them, whilst all the rockers were buying the Sepultura album "Beneath The Remains", so it was a bizarre looking queue!

By the time Kathryn returned, a little giddy for booze at quarter past one, I was tired and hungry. Every day at lunchtime, I would walk the hundred metres up the Aughton Street slope to the Middlelands Bank, to see if Jemma was around, to share my lunch hour with, but when I ventured into the branch that day, Jemma was not there but Ray was, looking like someone had forced a stick of dynamite up his bum and lit the fuse. He was ready to explode. He was striding around the front office, apologising to a snake like queue, twenty deep, for their delay. The cashiers looked harassed. I gently tapped his shoulder as he was about to brush past me, oblivious to my presence.

"Is Jemma not about, Ray?" I asked in cheery tones.

"No, she bloody isn't! She's the cause of this chaos! Twelve o'clock she went on her lunch and she's twenty minutes late already. I've had to get Margaret to go on the tills and Margaret isn't a cashier, she's a current account adviser. Its slowed the whole thing down. Look at the size of the bloody queue! If my Regional Manager stepped in here now, I could forget any plans of promotion. If you see her, Kelly, wandering around the shops merrily, can you send her back, straight away. She's dumped us right in the shit!"

Ray whispered the last sentence so the irritated pensioners in the queue did not overhear.

"OK. I'll tell her."

Jemma had a tendency to be late for things. I was always the punctual one. I knew five or ten minutes was the norm with Jemma, but twenty minutes was taking the mickey! I was dazzled by sunshine as soon as I left the bank. The weather, on the whole, was promising a decent summer and I wanted to enjoy my hour before the chaos continued at Woolworths in the afternoon. I headed up Burscough Street and decided to treat myself to a portion of fish and chips, then headed over to Coronation Park to sit on a bench and eat my dinner under blue skies.

When I arrived at Coronation Park, I found an empty bench almost straight away which was a right result, as pensioners out on sunny days normally seek out the benches to rest their weary legs. There were hundreds of people in the park and they were not all pensioners, there were mothers and fathers pushing children on swings in the play area, teenage boys with their tops off displaying their skinny, milk-bottled, hairless torsos and shop workers and office workers mingling with shoppers, sitting on picnic rugs having lunch.

As I ate my lunch, I scoured the masses, looking for a familiar face. I was popping my last chip into my hungry mouth, when I spotted Jemma in the distance, sat on the grass. Spontaneously, I stood up and headed towards her to warn her that she needed to head back to the bank, as Ray was fuming.

Within a few strides of setting off, I relaxed a little. I could see that she was sat with Ray, they were cross-legged, holding hands and she was lovingly touching his face. They were deep in conversation. Ray had obviously calmed down a lot since I had seen him in the bank. As I took a few further steps, it dawned on me that although it was definitely Jemma, it was definitely not Ray! Jemma's lawn companion hung his head so it was difficult to make out features, but he was too thick set to be Ray. No doubt he was too good looking to be Ray too, but I was unable to confirm this from such a distance. This was beginning to amuse me! No wonder Jemma was not rushing back to work!

I instinctively took a few steps back, re-tracing my footsteps, not wanting to intrude. If Jemma had another man in her life, was this my business? After everything that we had been through together, it did seem bizarre that she had not let me know about this development in her personal life, as we had always confided in each other about everything.

As the man re-adjusted his posture and straightened, I caught sight of him more clearly. My body sagged in desperation. I forced my eyes to blink over and over again, anticipating proper clarity, willing my brain to remove this mirage. Surely, I was mistaken. I forced myself to look again. Jemma was stroking the cheeks of a handsome man, then kissing him softly. I started to pace forward now, angrily. As I advanced, what I hoped was an apparition continued to remain real and constant. It was Richie. My Richie. The man I had spent eighteen months with. MY BOYFRIEND! How could this be happening? He was with MY sister. Despite everything.

Richie had never had a decent word to say about Jemma. Not one. The whole incident at the Birch's party, that had driven a wedge between us for so long, that I had dismissed as a simple case of mistaken identity, no longer appeared to be just that. I had been hoodwinked, but for what purpose? Why had I become embroiled in this? I wanted answers.

I suddenly found myself within touching distance of Richie and Jemma, having come at them from an angle to avoid detection, from over their shoulders. They looked like they were re-enacting the Peter Gabriel and Kate Bush video for "Don't Give Up". A seated version anyway.

Jemma caught sight of me first.

"Kelly!"

Cowardice was not a word I would use lightly when applying it to Jemma. For every single day of my life up until that point, it was a word that was the polar opposite to how I perceived Jemma. She had not shirked her responsibility in any matter, ever, and truthfully, a lot of the problems that Jemma had encountered in her life, were more down to an abundance of bravery rather than a lack of it. This was different though. My eyes bored into her, filled with hatred. Jemma averted my stare, turning to Richie to resolve an uncomfortable position. They let go of each other and stood up.

"Richie!" she begged. "Tell Kelly what's going on. She needs to know."

Richie was immediately tearful which struck me as a little pathetic.

"I can't, Jemma! Not after everything that's happened. I can't!"

"Just tell her, Richie, or I will."

To give Jemma some credit, her cowardice was temporary. Not that she deserved much credit, I had just caught her kissing my boyfriend!

"No!" he refused.

Six weeks earlier, a short burst of bravery on my part had been responsible for our mother's death. I think that moment had sapped away any steely determination that I had within me. The last thing I wanted to do now was stand in front of the only two people in the world that I loved, sobbing my heart out, as they attempted to make their peace with me about their betrayal. Before the tears began to flow, I managed to cry out,

"How could you do this to me?!"

Then I turned and ran. I heard Jemma shouting after me,

"Kelly! Wait! Please wait! Let me explain."

I did not receive that explanation. I ran determinedly towards home. I could not bear to hear their excuses. That "the only thing we did wrong was fall in love" excuse. I needed to clear my head first. I needed to try in some way to rationalise this and decide how I would go forward in life without Jemma and Richie's love. I ran from the park into Ormskirk town centre, past the crowds in Aughton Street, checking out the market stalls, past Woolworth's (there was no way I was heading back to work in this state) to the clock tower then headed right into Moor Street, constantly running, all the way out of town and up to Wigan Road. I only broke into a walk when I spotted the police van outside our house. As I crossed over, to the opposite side, I noticed the van was actually not outside our house, but outside next doors. The adjoining house. Mr. and Mrs.McGordon lived there. They were a sweet couple in their seventies, they had had a few run ins with Mum, but then who hadn't and if I had retired, the last place I would want to live, as I saw out my days, was next to us. Both of them were standing at their door, speaking to two male police officers. One was the guy who had dropped me off at Richie's on that miserable night. Their garden, like ours, sloped up to their front door. The volume of traffic meant that I was too far away to hear their conversation. When I reached a point that I was parallel to the police van, I knew I was out of sight. The police officers had their backs to me anyway, but I had visions of Mr. and Mrs. McGordon pointing at me and shouting,

"There she is, Constable! Get her!"

I was under no illusion that the police were visiting the McGordon's to invite them to a social evening at the Civic Hall. They had been away and now they were back and the police were no doubt checking if they had heard anything when Mum toppled to her unsavoury end. Unless they were both deaf or very heavy sleepers, our statements would be blown out the water. I crossed back over, hiding behind the police van at first, then crawling on all fours under it and keeping horizontal below the wall at the end of their garden. I could now pick up their conversation.

"Would it be possible we could come in Mr. & Mrs. McGordon? Just to take some further details, perhaps?"

"Of course, please come in."

Everything was collapsing around me. I knew exactly what was happening. This was God's way of punishing me. I had ended a life and he was making sure my sins would find me out. I was getting what I deserved. Jemma and Richie were obviously in love, that was evident from the tenderness they were displaying, I was just an unwanted obstacle in that love triangle now and if I didn't act quickly, it looked like I would soon be heading to jail for my mother's murder. Next door must have heard me screaming as I ran at my Mum and then the sickening thud that followed when she hit the tiled floor. They were probably telling the police officers that right now.

With the McGordon's door closed behind them, I gathered myself up from my cowering position, ran up our path, went in through the front door, up to my room, threw as many random objects of clothing as I could into a bag, dug out my passport, Yorkshire Building Society passbook and any cash I could find, stuffed them into the side pocket of the bag and bundled the bag down the stairs. I crept out the front door, checked that no-one was emerging from the McGordon's and then shuffled along in a lopsided run, down the path and all the way down to Ormskirk train station. The Merseyrail train to Liverpool was already on the platform when I arrived. I bought a single ticket to Central, rushed on board, avoiding the smoking carriage and bade Ormskirk farewell.

My stay in Liverpool was a short one. I decided to get off the train at Moorfields, went across to the Yorkshire Building Society in Castle Street and closed my account, withdrawing every penny I had. I then went to the bottom end of Lord Street, re-investing some of my cash in a flight to Amsterdam. I wanted to go that evening from Manchester Airport, but there were no flights out of Manchester that I could book on to that night other than to Arecife and Palma and now was not the time for a suntan, so I ended up booking a flight from Heathrow toAmsterdam. It was an ideal destination, as I knew you had access to most other airports in the world from there. Having booked my flight, I walked up to Lime Street station and booked myself on to a train to Euston. From there, I went on the tube, taking the Southbound Victoria line to Green Park and then swopping on to the Piccadilly line, westwards, all the way to Heathrow. By 10.30pm, I was in Amsterdam. My life as a fugitive had begun.

Richie

"It's not good news, I'm afraid, Mr.Billingham. The test results show that the tumour on your testicle is cancerous. What we need to do now, is look at how we are going to treat it……….."

That's as much as I remember hearing. The talk continued but it never reached my brain. There was no point kidding myself any longer that it would all turn out to be something and nothing. This was my reality now. My cancerous reality.

As I left Ormskirk hospital after my second meeting with the consultant urologist, Mr.Davenport, within a week, my mind was everywhere. As promised by Dr.Whiteside, my initial appointment had come through within a fortnight. The date of the appointment though, was another four weeks down the line. Initially, I had forgotten all about it, but as it crept ever nearer, I struggled to keep up the pretence that everything was OK. I suppose the easiest solution would have been to tell Kelly about it, but I just felt that I would be burdening her with too much after the death of her Mum. I opted to tell Jim instead, but all he responded with was,

"It's about time. Hope it all works out OK for you, bruv."

Jim was pleasant enough but he was not designed to provide emotional support. At least Jim knew though and if my behaviour was short tempered or erratic, he understood. With Kelly, it was more difficult, I had no justifiable reason to take any of my worries out on her, so just found myself starting to avoid her.

In the six weeks between the GP appointment and urologists appointment, I wanted to develop a better understanding of the beast that lay within. If it was cancer, I wanted to know exactly what cancer was. I knew it was a serious killer, up there in the causes of death league with heart disease, but that had been the extent of my knowledge. I went to Ormskirk library and took out six books on cancer and testicular cancer and spent several evenings over the next month trying to comprehend what could possibly be going on with my genitalia.

I found out cancer is just the name given to loads of different diseases all over the body. They are grouped together as they are all abnormal growths of cells acting in an uncontrolled way and sometimes spreading. What I discovered my lump could be was a malignant tumour of the testicle. Testicular cancer, to a great extent, is a young man's illness, with the majority of those diagnosed being under forty. I was certainly not unique in suffering from this illness at my age. By the time I went to see Mr.Davenport, although I had read most testicular lumps are not cancerous, I had diagnosed myself as a testicular cancer sufferer. I suppose, to an extent, I was playing mind games and was opting for a worst case scenario, in the hope of being proved wrong, but that did not happen. All Mr. Davenport did was confirm my assumption.

On the basis that I had already assumed that I had testicular cancer, I don't really know why I was in such a head spinning state of shock when I left Ormskirk hospital late that Thursday morning. I guess it was down to the fact that Mr.Davenport had now eradicated all doubt and it was perhaps that element of doubt that I was clinging to. I walked through to Ormskirk town centre in a daze. I don't really know where

I was heading, perhaps sub-consciously I was heading to Woolworths, to see Kelly, to reveal the background to my peculiar behaviour. In an attempt to shield Kelly from my troubles, I had already alienated her, as she had concluded that my separation from her illustrated a diminishing interest in our relationship. Nothing could have been further from the truth, but how was Kelly supposed to know that? All Kelly was aware of, was a boyfriend who was keeping his distance.

I never reached Kelly. It was market day and Ormskirk town centre was jam packed. You needed your wits about you to manoeuvre through the throng, but I had left my wits back at the hospital. Solely due to a lack of concentration on my part, I collided with a lady who had just bought a cheese filled baked potato from a van on Moor Street, that had parked up next to the market stalls. The potato and its cheesy contents were knocked from her grasp and landed upside down on the concrete flags below.

"YOU STUPID IDIOT!!! Why did you not look where you were going? I've just spent ten minutes queuing for that!"

I looked at the enraged woman. With typical misfortune, I had only managed to walk straight into Jemma Watkinson! That pretty much summed up a miserable day! I was in bits. I put my left hand up on to the top of my forehead and into my hair and just stood there for a moment, silently. By this time, I was on auto-pilot. I could not control my hands. My left hand brought itself down to cover my face and then my right hand joined it. The tears then came. Jemma, unaware of the background, probably thought this was more than a little dramatic following the death of a cheesy potato!

"Richie! Are you OK? What's going on? Sorry, I over-reacted! It's only a potato! The world's full of them. The potato famine is no more! Richie! Richie! What's the matter?"

I took my hands away from my face. I needed someone to talk to about this. Not Jim and not Kelly, but someone else. I wasn't sure Jemma was the ideal candidate, we had never exactly hit it off, but sometimes fate intervenes in your life in mysterious ways.

"I'm OK!"

I said as I kneeled down in a vain attempt to salvage Jemma's potato, before realising it was a lost cause and standing back up.

"Are you sure you are OK?" Jemma enquired again.

"Actually I'm not. Do you have a few minutes to spare, Jemma? I have a problem, I really need to talk to someone about it."

I think people just ask if you are OK to seek their own personal reassurances. They want you to say yes so they can get along with the rest of their day, guilt free. My negative response caught Jemma out.

"I've got the time, Richie, but is it something you really want to be sharing with me? We hardly know each other. Is it something Kelly knows about? Maybe she'd be a better option?"

I shook my head.

"No, no, I don't want to drag Kelly into this."

"But you don't mind dragging me into it?!"

Jemma smiled. I did not like her much but she had a beautiful smile. I smiled back.

"No, Jemma, I don't like you nearly as much so I'll quite happily drag you into anything!"

I said this in my dry, sarcastic way but there was more than an element of truth in this statement and both Jemma and I knew that. Jemma must have sensed I was desperate. She gave me a half-hug, one of those uncomfortable hugs that two thirteen year old boys would do.

"I thought that was the case!" she said. "I tell you what, you buy me another baked potato with cheese, buy yourself something too, then come down with me to Coronation Park and we can sit in the sunshine on the grass. We can talk through your troubles there. How does that sound?"

It sounded fine to me, so that is exactly what we did. I bought Jemma another baked potato with cheese, bought another with a tuna mayonnaise filling for myself and we headed off to Coronation Park. Once there, I related the whole story of the lump, from initially discovering it right through to the diagnosis. I was pleasantly surprised by Jemma's capacity to listen and to empathise. For a bigmouth with a prat of a boyfriend, she listened attentively, just throwing in the odd pertinent question from time to time.

"Does the tumour hurt you then, when you touch it?"

"How big is the tumour?"

"Does Kelly know anything at all about this?"

"How will they treat it?"

Once I had finished the whole tale, Jemma beamed that huge smile at me again.

"Well, I must say, Richie, that was not what I was expecting!"

If she had smiled at all during my whole confessional piece, it would have seemed more than a little tactless and odd, but having listened with rapt attention through a detailed monologue from me, with just the occasional interruption, I think Jemma was now smiling to lift the sombre mood.

"I don't suppose you were going to guess I had cancer, but what were you expecting?"

"Honest answer?!"

Of course I wanted the honest answer, I was intrigued to know what she was expecting to hear.

"I thought you were going to say you were gay!"

"Gay?"

I smiled at Jemma. I looked at her intently. Jemma avoided eye contact.

"Jemma, given that you once accused me of sneaking into a bed with you and having sex, you are the last person I would expect, to believe I was gay!"

"You did kiss Ray though, didn't you? I thought maybe you were confused about your sexuality, had decided you could no longer cope with the guilt and were going to live an open gay life from now on!"

"Interesting theory, Jemma. Ludicrous, but interesting!"

"It's not that ludicrous! You kissed my boyfriend!"

"Yes, but only to piss him off!! He made some sickening comment about Liverpool fans deserving to die at Hillsborough, so I kissed him to piss him off."

Jemma shook her head as if she didn't believe me.

"Ray said 'Liverpool fans deserved to die at Hillsborough'?"

"Well not exactly. He said that it was karma that Liverpool fans were dying as they had killed a load of Juventus fans at Heysel."

"But he didn't say they deserved to die?"

I had no idea why Jemma was defending this arsehole! Blind loyalty was the only possibility.

"Excuse my language, Jemma, but it was still a fucking thick thing to say!"

"OK. But why did you not just say, 'Shut up, dickhead!'? Why kiss him?"

"I told you, I did it to piss him off! It worked too! If I'd have told him to shut up, he would have just continued with his incessant wittering about how fantastic he is. A kiss had more impact. It was a big, sloppy kiss too! It was impossible to ignore. I just wanted to disgust him, like he had disgusted me."

Despite herself, I could tell Jemma was trying to suppress a smile!

"Well, you achieved that, but Ray now thinks you fancy him!"

I chuckled.

"Good! I'll blow him a kiss next time I see him!"

Our tone was now most certainly jovial, but Jemma still had questions she wanted to ask. Questions that could only return the mood to serious.

"So, explain to me again, why you haven't told Kelly?"

"About the kiss?"

I wanted the jovial tone to continue.

"No, you know what I mean. About the cancer. You may not think much of Ray, but if I had cancer, I would tell him and he would be there for me. I know for a fact, Kelly would be there for you too, so why not tell her?"

"What would it have achieved?"

"It would have been less of burden for you. A problem shared is a problem halved and all that."

"Yes, but Kelly was already burdened by her own problems. Jemma, you and Kelly have been through so much recently, I didn't want to weigh Kelly down with even more problems."

"Why did you not tell her before Vomit Breath died?"

Ray was honest about one thing. Jemma did refer to her mother as 'Vomit Breath'!

"I didn't see the point. It could have been something and nothing. Most lumps in the scrotum don't turn out to be cancerous."

"And you were embarrassed."

"Yes, that too!"

"Well, just say that then! You don't have to lie to me, Richie. I'm your friend."

That sounded strange. Jemma Watkinson was now officially my friend.

Jemma may now have classed herself as my friend, but one thing I was still not comfortable telling her about, was the fact that I knew how 'Vomit Breath' had met her maker. I did not want to tell Jemma that I knew Kelly had pushed their mother down the stairs. I suspected Jemma thought that would remain a secret between her and Kelly until their dying day. Presumably, she would have been horrified to know that Kelly had confessed all to me.

"Are you scared?"

I was ill prepared for this question, as my mind was still picturing the scene at Jemma and Kelly's house that night, when their mother returned home.

"Of what?"

"Dying."

Jemma was nothing, if she was not blunt.

"I'm not expecting to die, Jemma. I'm expecting to have treatment, chemotherapy, radiotherapy, whatever it takes, but I'm expecting to come through this."

"Will you lose your hair?"

"I don't know yet. I've got appointments with a urologist and an oncologist. I expect I'll find out after I've seen them."

"What's an oncologist?"

"Someone who deals with people with cancer. People like me."

It was that final sentence that started me up again. 'People like me'. The conversation continued, but my insides suddenly felt very vulnerable. I was shaking inside.

"So, how are you going to keep it from Kelly when you turn up at our house looking like you've stuck half your arse on your head?"

"If that's going to happen, I'll tell her before it does, Jemma."

"You have to tell her now, Richie! It's not fair keeping something like this from her. Kelly loves you."

Here we go again! Tears welled up. I was on an emotional tightrope anyway and the 'Kelly loves you' statement felt like an electric prod.

"I will tell her. At some point, I will tell her. I just need to find the right time. Kelly means everything to me, Jemma. Everything. I'm not keeping this from her for any other reason than because I love her. I want to protect her from this for as long as I can. She's just a young girl, Jemma. She's just lost her mother, she doesn't need to be worrying about whether she's going to lose me as well."

"Richie, you're wrong! She does need to worry about this too, because its happening.

Like it or not, Richie, its happening. You must tell her."

By this time, I was ready to just curl myself into a ball and sob uncontrollably! I know Jemma was just looking after Kelly's interests, but I was too. Kelly's and my own, anyway. I did not feel emotionally strong and if Kelly needed to lean on me, I didn't think I had the strength to prop her up.

"I can't.……this thing is destroying me, Jemma. I won't let it destroy Kelly, too."

The tears started. I reverted to sobbing like a new born baby with a needle in his nappy! Crying my heart out. I think Jemma felt guilty for steering us towards an emotional blub-bath and tried to comfort me as best she could. She spoke soothingly as she gave me a sympathetic cuddle.

"Come on Richie! Don't cry! It sounds like you've been so strong through this so far! You've just got to keep it going. Keep battling. You were right when you said this lump is not going to beat you. You'll conquer this. I know you will…come on now, don't cry!"

When you are in emotional turmoil, someone being kindhearted does not stem the flow of tears, it just makes them flow more. I felt like a radiator that was being bled, I filled up, full of water inside and then whoosh, it all became too much and it sprayed out everywhere. As the tears trickled down my face, Jemma gave me a few re-assuring pecks on the cheeks. Everything unkind I had ever said about Jemma Watkinson was now wiped clean from the slate. She had been brilliant to me this afternoon and I would always be grateful for that. I was thinking about my gratitude to her when Jemma cried out.

"Kelly!"

I didn't even think how this must have looked to Kelly. Here I was, caught in a clinch with Jemma. That did not cross my mind at all. All I could think about was that my tears were a give away. Try as I might to protect her, Kelly was now going to find out that I had testicular cancer. Jemma, probably understanding better than I did how this must have looked to Kelly, tried to cajole me into a confession.

"Richie. Tell Kelly what's happened. She needs to know."

I felt that I was naked with a finger pointing at my lumpy ball, but still could not bring myself to get the right words out. I pathetically refused. I had once told Kelly that my middle name was Cheddar. It wasn't. Stubborn was my middle name.

"I can't, Jemma! Not after everything that's happened. I can't!"

Jemma, at this point, probably realised the irony of the situation, I may have had a dodgy, cancerous ball, but I did not have 'the balls' to tell Kelly.

Jemma offered to do my dirty work for me.

"Just tell her, Richie, or I will".

The penny dropped. There was no way back now. I had testicular cancer and it was time I faced it like a man. I was not going to let Kelly find out from Jemma about this. I needed to tell her myself about this, right here, right now.

I was about to say,

"No, let me tell her!"

But as soon as I said, "No….," I paused, taking a huge intake of breath, ready to spill it all out, but Kelly did not give me that opportunity. She ran off like a scalded cat. Jemma shouted after her,

"Kelly! Wait! Please wait! Let me explain!"

It was too late, Kelly was disappearing into the distance. I think Jemma was going to make one last ditch attempt to bring her back, she had one final thing to shout, but just as she was about to yell it, she recognised the significance of what she was going to say. Jemma could not broadcast my illness to the surrounding masses, so instead she just spoke the words, she had been about to scream.

"He's got cancer, Kelly. Richie's got cancer."

Jemma

As a couple, when you meet new friends in life, at some point, they want to know how you came together as a couple. With Richie and I, the questions tended to follow the same path.

"How did you meet?"

Followed by,

"When did you get together as a couple then?"

Then finally,

"If there was such a long gap between when you met and when you finally got it together, when was it that you first realised that you had feelings for each other?"

This is an interesting one as our answers were always different! I don't mean the answers we gave were always different (although admittedly Richie did vary his answer a bit!) but we definitely recognised our feelings for each other at a different point in time. For me, the day I discovered Richie had testicular cancer was the day I realised that I had some sort of feelings for him. I didn't fully understand what those feelings were, I just understood how I was feeling was not how I should be feeling about my sister's boyfriend.

When we were at school, it was undeniable that Richie was a good looking lad, but he was always outside my age radar. I was always after lads two years older to five years older, so Richie Billingham did not overly interest me. I thought he was too young for me and too old for my little sister. I chose to ignore the fact that he was less than eighteen months older than Kelly! Using my own criteria, Richie was actually too young for Kelly!

As they became a couple, I grew to know Richie better and grew to like him. My initial doubts about him were down to "The Phantom Fucker" incident at the Birch's party, but putting that to one side, there was no doubting that he adored Kelly. As my feelings for my own boyfriend, Ray, began to ease, I developed a thought process of,

"why could I not have a boyfriend like Richie?" which eventually became,

"why could I not have Richie?"

On the weekend of Vomit Breath's death, Ray and Richie went to an Everton football match together. It turned out also to be the day of the Hillsborough disaster. Ray was not someone who was overly sporty, nor was he someone with any real social circle, outside of work he was not a good mixer other than with older women, as he had grown accustomed to them from working in a bank. To compensate for these social inadequacies, from all accounts, he really tried to sell himself to Richie by talking about himself and exaggerating his sporting prowess. This was forgivable, I could totally understand why he would do this, but the fact that he then went on to say something abhorrent about the victims of the Hillsborough disaster was indefensible. I imagine he did it to try to look tough in front of someone he was trying to impress, but all the same it was indefensible.

Once Richie told me about Ray's idiotic Hillsborough comments and his subsequent reaction to being kissed by him, I could only see Ray as an egotistical, homophobic idiot. On the other hand, the fact that Richie had reacted to Ray's comments by grabbing hold of him, pinning him down and kissing him, I thought showed a strength of character that was excitingly individual. During those moments that Richie and

I talked in Coronation Park, I knew my time with Ray and as a knock on effect, my time at the Middlelands Bank, were over. Ninety minutes after Kelly ended Richie's testicular cancer confession by turning up unannounced and then running off, I had managed to finish with Ray and hand my notice in at work. Ray had flown off the handle when I had returned to the branch following my two hour lunch break and as I was not in the right frame of mind for an argument, I just told him what to do with our relationship and the stupid job! My arrogance did not serve me well! I did not have another job after that for more than two years and never had the opportunity to work in a bank again! It wasn't just down to a row with Ray though!

For a young woman, an escape route from a relationship is an important thing. If your relationship is on its knees, it is always good to know what Plan B is. A few times during that long conversation at Coronation Park, especially when I felt compelled to hug him or cradle him and kiss his salty tears, Richie seemed like the ideal candidate to be Plan B. It was only really when I mentioned Kelly's name, that I came to my senses and dismissed this notion as the thoughts of a moron. The way Richie spoke, you could just tell he was smitten by Kelly. I also reflected on what Kelly had done for me, she had probably saved my life the night Vomit Breath died and I was repaying her by having romantic thoughts about her boyfriend. I concluded this was all wrong and attempted to redeem myself by going out on a limb for Kelly, by drumming home to Richie that he should tell Kelly about his illness.

I was doing a great job convincing myself that I was acting solely in my sister's interests, until Richie broke down in tears for the second time that day. When I comforted him, I just could not help myself appreciating that Richie had a warmth to his soul that Ray would never have. The fact that Richie was bloody gorgeous and Ray was bloody ugly was also a factor, even Vomit Breath had noticed that one, but the main thing that struck me was how passionately I felt about caring for this man. I wanted to take this journey with him. I wanted to be his shoulder to cry on. I wanted to be his confidant, to hold his hand in times of joy and times of trouble. I wanted to mean everything to Richie and for Richie to mean everything to me. All this was running through my brain when Kelly showed up and I expect I had guilt written all over my face.

The moment Kelly found Richie and I together was still a debating point between the two of us fifteen years later! In my opinion, if Richie had no feelings for me at that moment, he would have just blurted out,

"Kelly, I've got cancer!" and Kelly would have immediately forgotten about the suspicious clinch she had found us in. He didn't though. He said nothing. Nothing about his cancer anyway. He just froze on the spot. In my opinion, although Richie puts a different slant on it, this was because he knew, deep down in his soul that he felt something for me. Richie argued that he was only aware of those feelings much, much later although he does confess that he was physically attracted to me from the day he started secondary school (he just thought I was a bit of a bitch)! Choose to believe him if you like, but if you do, he's conning you!

For my part, I think I did what I genuinely felt was the right thing to do. I tried to encourage Richie to tell Kelly about his cancer. When he stalled though and Kelly ran off, there was a moment when I was going to stop her by shouting that Richie had cancer. Just as I was about to shout, I stopped myself and just said the words, out of Kelly's earshot. I was unsure how to interpret the events of the afternoon. By not telling Kelly about his cancer, but telling me, was there something between us? Some sort of chemistry? I wasn't sure, but if Richie had avoided telling Kelly, why should I win her back on his behalf? Maybe he wanted to lose her.

They say true love never runs smooth. It certainly didn't for Richie. Within a few hours of discovering he had testicular cancer, his girlfriend had fled to Amsterdam and within a few days, there was an even more dramatic development, his future wife was arrested for the suspected murder of her mother.

Kelly

Despite everything I had to ring him. Twenty four hours into my time in the Netherlands, I could not help myself phoning Richie. I was a sixteen year old girl who had never been abroad before and my first experience of a foreign country followed on from my mother's death at my own hands and my boyfriend cheating on me with my sister. Not exactly the perfect ingredients for a relaxing trip away!

The first night, I had stopped in a Youth Hostel in the city centre called the Hostel Orfeo, but the lady at reception pointed out as soon as I checked in, that they only had a bed for one night. They were fully booked throughout the weekend. I slept well that first night as I was shattered after a traumatic day, but the following morning, on checking out, they should have given me a donkey and a bearded man called Joseph to accompany me around the city, as every bed and breakfast and every hostel was fully booked. I decided to visit Anne Frank house as I had read her diary when I was thirteen and whilst in the queue for the museum, I befriended two American girls, Lauren and Madison, who were eighteen. They were heading over to Rotterdam on the four o'clock train, as they could not find vacant accommodation for love nor money either, so I decided to head across with them. There was something about Rotterdam that really appealed to me, it did not have all the canals running through it like Amsterdam, but as soon as you come out of the Rotterdam's Centraal station, there is a buzz about the city which I found infectious. The Youth Hostel was pleasant too and I even had a few beers with Lauren and Madison from the bar, all three of us excited by the fact that we were deemed old enough to be served. I did not want to be sharing adventures with two girls from Boston though, I wanted to be sharing adventures with Richie and emboldened by alcohol, I decided to use my remaining guilders that I had allocated for the day, to phone him. Given that I had bought three beers for the two girls and I, there was not a huge amount of coinage left in my pocket but a quick conversation was definitely better than no conversation at all.

As I was feeling a little tipsy, I was determined to get to the bottom of exactly what was going on between Richie and Jemma. I had spent all my alone time up until I reached Anne Frank house trying to figure it all out in my head and the urge to solve the mystery had come back to me now. There was just no way Richie and Jemma could have been an item before Mum died, as Richie had spent every second with me, but perhaps something had gone on subsequently. The more I thought about it though, the less likely that seemed. When I thought back to the evenings over the last few weeks when Richie had opted not to see me, I had spent the bulk of them with Jemma, so he had not been making excuses to enable him to see her, that logic just did not stack up at all. So why had they been together in Coronation Park? I had to find out. Richie's Mum answered the phone.

"Hello Dot. Is Richie there please?"

"Kelly, is that you? Are you OK, dear? My goodness we've been worried about you! He's been so upset, my love, so upset. Do you want to speak to him?"

Had I not just said that!

"Yes please, Dot!"

Dot's high pitched shout almost made by ears bleed!

"Richie! Kelly's on the phone!"

Richie must have run down the stairs at full pelt, as, after a few seconds of silence, he arrived at the phone breathlessly, either that or his Mum had interrupted him mid-bonk with my sister! I gave Richie the benefit of the doubt this time and presumed it was the former. As well as being breathless, Richie sounded confused and annoyed,

"Kelly! Where the hell are you?"

"I'm in Rotterdam."

There was a shocked pause.

"Why?"

"I had to go, Richie."

"To Rotterdam? Why?"

"No, I just had to go from Ormskirk. From England. Believe me, Richie, I just had to go."

"Because Jemma and I were together? Jemma told me you probably thought something had gone on between us, but it hadn't Kelly, I swear it hadn't."

It felt like we had come full circle. Here we were again, Richie pleading with me to believe that nothing had gone on between him and my sister.

"Something was going on, Richie. I watched the pair of you for a while, it all looked very intimate."

"I was upset."

This annoyed me.

"Richie, this is the bit I don't get. Why would Jemma be hugging you if you were upset? Hugging one of your sisters or your Mum, that would make sense, but why Jemma? You don't even like each other!"

"I don't dislike her."

I was still annoyed. More so now.

"I know that NOW, Richie. I saw that for myself yesterday! Before yesterday though, you had always said to me that you didn't like her, you said she was annoying."

"Kelly, I literally bumped into Jemma in Ormskirk. Knocked the baked potato out of her hand…."

"And your telling me that's why you were upset!! You must think I was born yesterday!"

"No that's not what I said, Kelly. I bumped into Jemma because I was upset, I wasn't upset because I bumped into her. I was upset and Jemma was a shoulder to cry on. Literally, a shoulder to cry on."

"Well, what were you upset about?"

There was another uncomfortable pause before Richie answered.

"Come back, Kelly. I need to tell you this face to face. I don't want to tell you over the phone."

If you can imagine a garden at this point. A garden with two trees in it. One with thirty cats in, the other cat free. If I was a dog, I would now be jumping up at the catless tree barking.

"You've shopped me in, haven't you?"

Richie did not have a clue what I was talking about.

"Pardon?"

"To the police. It all makes sense now. You've told the police what I did, haven't you?"

"Kelly, why would I do that?"

"I don't know. Maybe you thought you could get into trouble for not telling them what you knew. That you could be charged with withholding information. That's why the police were round at the McGordons and that's why you were crying to Jemma….because you shopped me in. That's why I've come away, Richie, not because of things going on between you and Jemma, but because the police are after me, Richie and now I understand why."

I was talking hurriedly. I always talked quickly when I was nervous or excitable. At this point, I was both.

"Kelly, slow down. I did not speak to the police about you. I love you, I would never do that, I promise you, I would never do that. Never."

Richie was either telling the truth or he was a bloody good liar.

"Promise?"

"Kelly, I just did but I swear on my mother's life, I would not tell the police about your Mum and what happened to her."

I could tell he was being guarded in case his Mum was earwigging. She had a tendency to do that, Dot, I had seen her do it to Richie's sister, when she'd been on the phone. I believed him.

"OK."

"Who are the Gordons?"

"The McGordons. They live next door. The police were there yesterday, talking to them. I saw them."

"That doesn't mean anything. Their car might have been robbed or they might have had a funny phonecaller…there's a million and one reasons why the police may have been at their house."

"I don't agree, Richie. It was about Jemma and I. I could tell."

"How?"

"I don't know. I could just tell. They will have heard us that night. I'm not coming back, Richie! Can you not come out here? I don't like it on my own."

"I can't, Kelly."

That's right! He still hadn't told me why he was upset. If it wasn't because he had shopped me in to the police, why was it?

"Why?"

"I've got no money for starters! Look Kelly, if you think its right to lay low for a while, you lay low for a few days, but ring me again and if nothing is happening, come back. It's 4th July next week, Kelly. We could meet on the 'Sunny Road'."

Perhaps I was being paranoid. I imagine murderers often were. What Richie was saying, seemed to make sense.

"OK. I'll ring you in a couple of days, Richie."

"Yes, do that, Kelly. And you believe me that there was nothing going on between me and your sister?"

I probably did, but with everything going on, I wasn't quite sure what to believe.

"Yes, but you still haven't told me why you were upset."

I was out of money. The phone started beeping.

"Kelly, we'll sit down on the 'Sunny Road' next week and we'll talk this through."

"I love you, Richie!"

Shit! Why was I saying that?! Twenty four hours earlier I had seen my sister kissing him.

"I love you too, Kelly Watkinson. Trust me, everything will work out fine."

Richie

At eighteen years old, when cancer enters your life, you cannot be expected to know how to deal with it. I treated it like it was the grim reaper. It had come along uninvited and ruined everything. All my hopes and dreams lay in tatters because of cancer. Kelly and I had sat on the 'Sunny Road', planning our future together, our full lives were mapped out as was our happy family home, filled with offspring. Once I had been diagnosed with cancer, it felt like we had been looking at the flower but had failed to see the stem which was laden with thorns. When Kelly had sat on that hill and warned that things change, people change, little did she know that within months, I would be aware that I was a cancer sufferer and she would be aware that she was a murderer.

Now though, many years later, if I could find a time machine that could transport me back to that diagnosis day and I could pause time, before having a choice of two pathways, one diagnosing me with cancer, the other giving me a clean bill of health, I would choose to have cancer rather than not to have it. Does that sound crazy? It probably does, but what I'm trying to say is that cancer was an awakening for me. It taught me to live life better. To treasure life more. Not at first, I suppose, but as I grew older it did. I am not saying that ultimately I would not have wanted to be cured and to have lived to see my great grandchildren grow up, but I would have rather had cancer for a short while than not to have had it at all.

Jemma often talks about the day of my diagnosis as being the day she fell in love with me. I guess a little bit of me was in love with Jemma Watkinson from the moment I laid eyes on her, but that was purely a looks thing. Personality wise, at first, I did not like her. I think children sometimes find fault before they find positives and I could not see beyond her brashness and eccentricities. All that happened that day was that I finally began to see Jemma's positive side, her tactile side, her loving side, her caring side, but with regards to my feelings for her, there was nothing romantic that day, my feelings just moved from the negative side of neutral to the positive side of neutral! The falling in love process for me probably started up, in some sense, that day, but it was a continuous development over the next few years, which also had to link in, I suppose, with the steady process of falling out of love with Kelly. I know Jemma disagrees with me, but at that stage in my life, both consciously and sub-consciously, Kelly was everything.

When we discuss this now, Jemma argues that I had ample opportunity to stop Kelly leaving Coronation Park that day. All I would have needed to say was,

"Kelly, I've got cancer!" and Kelly would probably have stayed with me then until my dying day. On reflection, I'm glad I didn't say it. I'm glad Kelly left when she did. I am a firm believer in the butterfly effect, that every decision we make has a knock on effect on the next and so on and so forth, so if I had said or done anything different at any point, my children would not have been born. So, by letting Kelly go, it ultimately led to the creation of my children! I definitely did the right thing! The reason I kept quiet though, was not because of any sub-conscious passion for Jemma, nor was it exactly because I did not want to tell Kelly I had cancer (although it is linked to that). The reason I kept avoiding telling Kelly I had cancer was down to a fear that had sprung into my mind the second I originally felt the lump and had been exacerbated by my visit to the urologists that day. I had not heard a lot of what the urologist said after the cancer was confirmed, but three words he mentioned, three words I did not understand at first, were the words that scared me the most. The words were "radical inguinal orchidectomy". In layman's terms, this is the medical procedure to remove a testicle. I could not face telling Kelly I had testicular cancer, because I could not face her knowing that I may have to go through life with one ball.

Even before my diagnosis and before I had read any books on cancer, I had an idea that a lump on my testicle might ultimately lead to the removal of said testicle. In my naivety, before reading the medical books, I presumed this could lead to a life without erections, a life without sperm and a life without children, so pre-diagnosis I always dismissed the idea of sharing this secret with Kelly. Once I had read the books, it became more of a cosmetic thing. I remember the childhood songs, sung to the tune of the Colonel Bogey March,

"Hitler, has only got one ball,
The other is in the Albert Hall,
His mother, the dirty bugger,
Chopped it off when he was small."

This conjured up the image of ugliness and a real stigma attached to having a testicle missing. So, I was scared a one-balled boyfriend may have been as unattractive to Kelly as a one breasted woman would have been to me. I was doing Kelly a disservice by thinking she would have been as shallow as me and to be fair to me, if Kelly had been diagnosed with breast cancer and had needed a mastectomy, I would not have stopped loving her for a second.

Once Kelly ran away from the park that Thursday afternoon, I ran after her but I wrongly deduced at some point she would head back into Woolworths, so sat on a bench on Aughton Street, for an hour, before venturing into the branch in case I had missed her. Kathy on the CD counter was hurrying around trying to alleviate a mounting queue so I did not even have to ask if she was there.

Only then did I head to her house on Wigan Road. I certainly have no recollection of a police van being there and I am sure if there was, I would have clocked it. Jemma had opened the door, anguish all over her face and she told me Kelly had packed some clothes and disappeared even before Jemma had arrived home. I walked back to Aughton and rang Jemma several times that day and again the next day, just in case Kelly had come home. Caroline, my sister, had a new boyfriend that she was very keen to have long, romantic telephone conversations with, so I had to bring her up to date with a basic overview about Kelly running off, packing a bag and disappearing, otherwise, if Kelly had tried to phone me, she would have had to contend with a constant engaged tone. I knew there was a sacrifice involved here, by telling Caroline, in all likelihood, the news would spread throughout the Billingham household, but the constant sympathy from Mum that followed was worth it, as I did manage to speak to Kelly the following night.

When I spoke to Kelly, I assured her everything would be alright. Who was I trying to kid?! Her or me! I probably said it with as much conviction as Clarice Starling did in Silence Of The Lambs when she arrived at the house of the serial killer alone and found Catherine Martin stuck at the bottom of an almighty pit!

Kelly

I had decided I was on my way home. I had spoken to Richie, pretty much every day whilst I was in Holland and my fears with regards to Mr & Mrs McGordon appeared to be unfounded. On the evening of the 2nd July, after speaking to Richie, I decided I was being completely ridiculous hiding in Europe. I was missing him and wanted to get back to Ormskirk for some serious making up! I decided I was going to surprise him. I knew he was a real romantic and without a doubt, on the 4th July, he would be there, on the "Sunny Road", hoping I would arrive to run into his arms with mine outstretched. Without telling him, I decided that was exactly what I would do. I would head back on the 3rd, go back home, not tell Richie, then I would turn up the following day on the "Sunny Road". He would be elated.

In my absence from home, Jemma only knew that I was safe through Richie. I had once again forgiven Richie and was still eager to discover what he had been so upset about, but I was finding it harder to forgive Jemma. I'm not sure why, maybe it was because she looked so guilty when I turned up at Coronation Park. Whilst I was in Holland, I had not phoned her at all. Once I had bought my foot passenger ferry ticket that Tuesday morning, to go from Hook of Holland to Harwich, I had an hour to kill before I needed to get on the ferry, so I thought I would phone Jemma. Richie had told me that she had finished with Ray and left the job at the bank, so I presumed that she would be at home. I wanted to clear the air before arriving back. I could feel my heart pounding as the phone rang but luckily, I did not have to wait long before it was answered.

"0695-402907".

Damn! Guilders wasted. I had rung the wrong number. It wasn't Jemma, it sounded like an elderly woman. Then I realised the number the woman said was our number.

"Who is this?" I asked.

"What do you mean, who is this? You rang me! If you are a newspaper reporter, you might as well hang up, because I'm telling you nothing."

Now I knew who it was, it was Nan!

"Nan, it's Kelly!"

"Kelly, where are you?"

"I'm at the ferry terminal at Hook of Holland. I'm coming back in an hour. Why would newspaper reporters want to speak to you?"

"Kelly, listen to me. Do not get on that ferry. Do you hear me, do not get on that ferry!"

Nan was scaring me. My heart was pounding like crazy now.

"Why Nan, what's the matter?"

Nan started whispering down the phone.

"Look, I can't speak for long. There's a policewoman in the hall who's just let me in and if she hears me I'm in all sorts of trouble, but do not come home. Don't even come to England."

"Tell me why Nan, you're scaring me now!"

"They've arrested Jemma, love. If you step foot in this country, I guarantee they'll arrest you too. She's been charged with your Mum's murder. Keep away, Kelly! Please just keep away!"

The phone went dead.

I was shaking. I needed to make a quick decision. I had forty five minutes to decide whether I should do the honourable thing, get on the ferry, go back to England and turn myself in or follow Nan's advice and disappear. Impulse told me to ring Richie, see if he could shed some light on things, but then fear took hold. What if Richie pleaded with me to come home? I could spend the next twenty years in jail. Richie would never wait for me then. By the time I was out, I would be a middle aged woman. Either way I was screwed. God was definitely out to get me. The doors to heaven had been firmly shut.

I started to think things through. Jemma was tougher than me. She would cope with it better. I wouldn't cope, jail would kill me. It took me all of two minutes to rip that ferry ticket up and run. Back to Rotterdam, then later to Amsterdam and back to Schiphol airport. Don't ask me why, because I don't really know why, but that night I flew on a Singapore Airlines flight to Singapore! A week earlier, I had left Ormskirk thinking I could never forgive Jemma and Richie for what they had done. The tables were well and truly turned now.

One thing was certain. My childhood was over. Life would never be the same again.

Richie

When Kelly decided to take a year out from her education after Fifth form, I jumped on the "year out" bandwagon too, deciding to work for a year too, once my "A" levels were completed. As I was two school years above Kelly, our years out had coincided. Amazingly enough! It made sense though. My Mum and Dad were permanently skint, mainly due to Dad's gambling habit, so although I had managed to knuckle down to some serious last minute cramming and secured a place at Manchester Polytechnic, I thought a year at work would help finance three years at Poly so I deferred my entry. Mum and Dad did not try to persuade me to do otherwise, as they knew I was taking some of the burden off them. They had just funded Helen through her years at Lancaster University and they were probably cursing me for doing unexpectedly well in my "A" levels! They probably wished I had failed them all like Caroline had managed to do! Jim, who was probably a little smarter than Helen, would be heading to University too the year after, so I was reducing the double whammy by paying my way, to some degree anyway.

Kelly had worked on the CD counter at Woolworth's in Ormskirk, since she was fourteen, as a Saturday girl and I had always thought that job would be better suited to me, as my interest in music and knowledge of it, was far more extensive than Kelly's. Problem was, there were no jobs going at Woolies, nor at the other record shop in Ormskirk, Quirks, even the bloke who had a small store in the 'Indoor Market' said he was unable to take me on, so I ended up applying to every other record shop I could think of in the North West of England! The pay was unlikely to be great and even less so if I had to travel to get there, but if I was going to have a year out working, I was going to find a job I enjoyed. I ended up landing a job in a place called Andy's Records, on a road called Cheapside in Preston town centre. They were a reasonable sized independent chain that had grown from a market stall in Cambridge or Bury St Edmunds or somewhere equally far away to about twenty branches in certain pockets of the United Kingdom, the North West being one such area with branches in Bolton, Warrington, Southport and Preston. Andy's prided themselves on having CD's in their stores that the major record retailers would not stock, so rather than having the odd CD by the likes of Leonard Cohen, Bob Dylan, Al Stewart, Billy Bragg and Jethro Tull, they had the whole back catalogue. I was in my element as I was working with like minded music enthusiasts and generally serving like minded music enthusiasts too. A female tramp once took a crap in there, but that was a one-off not a daily hazard and anyway, the assistant managed cleaned that up!

The only drawback other than pay that I can think of about working at Andy's Records was that you had to work near enough every Saturday. I threw the odd Saturday sickie due to having an Everton season ticket, but sometimes it worked well having a day off in the week. My urologists appointments, for example, were arranged for a Thursday as that was my regular day off.

In the whole scheme of things, the fact that I worked at Andy's Records in Preston whilst Kelly worked at Woolworth's and continued to work there after Kelly ran off (my year sabbatical becoming a two year sabbatical!),would have no great significance but for one thing. That thing being fate. When Jemma was arrested and charged with her mother's murder, where did the trial take place? You guessed it, Preston Crown Court! Two hundred yards from Andy's Records!

It was Caroline who had broken the news to me that Jemma had been arrested. She had heard on the Ormskirk grapevine, a form of communication that at times could spread news faster than the telephone. Initially, following her arrest, Jemma was taken into custody at Ormskirk police station. It had been an early morning arrest that had caught Jemma off guard. Apparently it had been her time of the month, but because everything had happened so quickly, Jemma had forgotten to take a change of tampon with her to the station. Perhaps she had thought she would only be there a short time. Jemma had telephoned her grandmother, who lives on the Wirral, broke the news of her arrest and requested a number of toiletries from her house, including the aforementioned tampons. Jemma's grandmother did not have a key, as Jemma and Kelly had refused to give her one, so she went to the police station first, collected one from Jemma's belongings and a policewoman went across with her to the house.

As Jemma's grandmother could not find the tampons, she popped into Boots in

Ormskirk to buy some. In Boots, she ran into Amy's mother who she had known for a number of years and whilst explaining to her why a woman of her age was purchasing tampons, her conversation was overheard by Janet Rimmer, who works as a Sales Assistant at Boots. Janet ran into Petra Sawyer at lunchtime and told her. Petra worked at H.Samuel, as did my sister, Caroline! The word was out!

When I arrived home from Preston that night, Caroline was waiting for me, as soon as I walked in the porch.

"Kelly's sister's been arrested!" she blurted out.

"What?"

"Jemma Watkinson! She's been arrested!"

"How do you know?"

"It's all around Ormskirk! She's been arrested for killing her Mum!"

"Who told you that?"

"Petra at work. She saw Janet Rimmer in Sayers at lunchtime and Janet had heard Kelly's Nan telling Amy's Mum in Boots. She was taking some tampons to Jemma in her cell at the police station."

I felt sick straight away. Physically sick. The world started spinning, I felt dizzy and had to brush past Caroline, into the downstairs bathroom, splashing cold water on my face. It was July 3rd. I had a horrible feeling Kelly may be heading back the following day, to meet me, on the "Sunny Road". If she found out that Jemma had been arrested, she would confess to everything, I knew she would and that would mean Kelly would be heading to jail too or at least some sort of juvenile correction centre, where did under eighteens go? I had no idea.

"Are you OK?" Caroline shouted through from outside the door.

"I'm fine, Cal! I'll be out in a minute. I just felt a bit sick on my way home. I'm OK though."

I came out the bathroom. Caroline wanted information from me. I felt like an adulterous pop star being pursued by a tabloid journalist.

"Do you think Kelly knew?"

"Knew what Caroline?"

"That Jemma did it! That Jemma killed her Mum!"

"She's been arrested, Caroline, not sentenced."

"Yes, but the police must think she did it, that's why she's been arrested."

"Shut up Caroline! We don't know what's going on!"

"I do! Kelly always said Jemma hated their Mum. I reckon she killed her!"

"Caroline! I said shut up!"

Caroline was annoying me now.

"You're a bit touchy, aren't you? Why are you defending her anyway? You've always hated Jemma Watkinson!"

"I don't hate her. I actually think she's OK."

Caroline did a double take.

"Since when?"

"Since recently."

"Well you've certainly changed your tune! You've always slagged her off! I can remember several times when you've been telling me how much you hated her! I can still remember the look on your face when you saw her at Nick Birch's party! It was a look of disgust!"

"I never used to like her, but now I know better. She's OK."

"For a murderer!" Caroline added for good measure.

"She's not a murderer, Caroline!"

"She might be."

"She's not a murderer."

Jemma

I was in prison for five months before my trial. Five long months. After twenty four hours at Ormskirk police station of intense questioning, I was charged with Vomit Breath's murder. My solicitor argued that the police case was purely dependent on the statements they had taken from our elderly next door neighbours, who claimed they had heard a lot of the commotion in our adjoining house that night. I protested my innocence, as I had every right to do, as I was innocent, but still felt like a Hollywood actress, as my argument was that I was asleep throughout. I feigned disbelief that I was being charged for a death that I slept through. I was charged though and I was transferred to Risley Remand Centre in Warrington.

What can I say about Risley? It was no five star hotel. The year before I was there, a senior official in the prison service had allegedly described it as "barbarous and squalid" and "dirty and dilapidated". He wasn't wrong! Just weeks before I was sent there, there had been an uprising by the men in "D" Wing. Fifty four men stayed on the roof for three days to protest about conditions. There were over eight hundred men in a facility built for five hundred. I obviously never visited the men's side of Risley, but I imagine the women's side was on a par with the men's. I managed to get nits within days of being there and in my five months awaiting trial, I was literally (to quote a Billy Bragg song of the time) "Rotting on Remand", as I lost two stone in weight, as I thought the food was just about fit for pigs and rats.

Only three people visited me during my time at Risley. Amy, bless her cotton socks, came twice, but she was a middle class girl from a lovely family and I think it was all a bit too much for her. Tut, who had always been as tough as old boots, so could cope fine with Risley. She used to come every week, sometimes even two or three times a week. Kelly and I had not liked Tut when we were kids but she was undeniably a good, strong woman and she was instrumental in sorting everything out for me, including my solicitors, Cooper, Taylor and Brighouse. I don't know whether she thought I was innocent or not, but she certainly gave off the impression that she thought it was a miscarriage of justice, if I was jailed for killing Vomit Breath. My third visitor was Richie. I held out no expectations of him visiting, although I was obviously attracted to him, we hardly knew each other, so his visits were a massive boost. We did get to know each other better during the six visits he made and the more I got to know him, the more I liked him. Women, as a sex, tend to say, we are attracted to a man's sense of humour more than anything else, but I don't think my local thirty stone binman is inundated with offers from skinny beauties just because he knows a few good jokes. As a rule, we like looks, we like power, we like confidence and a sense of humour is a bonus. Richie had the looks, he had no power whatsoever but he had a quiet confidence and a dry sense of humour, so three out of four was pretty good. After all, I had been out with Ray and the only one of those four he had really was power!

The first time Richie came in, he caused a major stir amongst all the female population of Risley, even some of the lesbians said he was so sexy he could turn them straight, as a one-off anyway!

"Now there's a mystery, who would I rather fuck, the sleeping assassin or her boyfriend?" said Julie, a crackhead streetwalker who was so ugly I'd have expected her punters would have wanted paying.

"He's not my boyfriend, Julie!"

"Why not love? Like the taste of muff, do you? If you ever want a ladies tongue between your thighs, pretty girl, you know where I am!"

"Piss off, Julie!"

"Why, what will you do if I don't? Push me down the stairs?! I hear you've got form for that! Poor Mummy!"

Richie told me he had lost contact with Kelly and I explained to him that she had rung our house on the day of my arrest and Tut had told her not to come home, because she would be arrested if she did, as I had been. Richie sat in stunned silence as I related the story to him, then admitted he was flabbergasted that she had not come back from Rotterdam, despite any consequences, as soon as she knew I had been arrested. It did not shock me. Kelly had run off in the first place because she was petrified of going to jail, so there was no way she was going to come back, own up and condemn herself to a life in prison. I thought Richie's view probably stemmed from the fact he thought she would return as a supportive sister not knowing that she had committed the crime.

As time passed, Richie would make regular visits, normally visiting every four to six weeks. I grew to have mixed feelings about Richie coming to Risley. On the one hand, each time he visited, he would break the news that there remained no contact with Kelly, so as time went on, I began to view him more and more as a single man. This was the good news, the positive aspect to his visit. I felt sad for him that Kelly had not at least phoned, but I had found myself thinking more and more about him and was totally aware that my feelings for him were deepening. If Kelly returned though, even if I was released, I knew my chances were non-existent.

On the other hand, I questioned why I was seeking this relationship. Could any relationship be more doomed to failure than one between Richie and I?! He had dated my sister, who would never forgive me if I subsequently went out with him, he also had testicular cancer and here was I, in prison awaiting trial for murder, my hair full of nits, skeletal frame and generally looking like a bag of shite! Why did I even entertain the idea of us getting together?!

Still, on balance, despite me looking uglier than the offspring of John Merrick and a sister of Cinderella, I was happy for Richie to visit me. We had never really been friends. Until I had left school and started at the bank, I had been a nightmare child really and Richie had not needed a friend like me. Once he had spilled my baked potato though, things had changed! We had clung on to each other that day like lifelong friends and I for one, was hoping that's what we would become. At the very least, I wanted us to become lifelong friends. I could not help Richie through his illness though from the insides of a prison cell, so that became the million and first reason why I wanted to get out of there.

The court case was to take place in Preston Crown Court. Twelve people on a jury would decide the future direction of my life. If I was found guilty, they would be getting things horribly wrong, but those twelve men and women had not been there when Vomit Breath had died, not witnessed the scene and would not be receiving the accurate version of events from the only eyewitness. If they sent me to jail, I could not blame them, I was just hoping my brief would be able to muddy the waters enough for the jury to have an element of doubt and ultimately find me innocent. If they did find me guilty, they had to decide whether it was pre-meditated, as I also faced a charge of manslaughter.

On Richie's final visit to Risley before the trial, he was surprised to find me in jovial spirits.

"Does nothing phase you?" he asked.

"What do you mean?"

"Well, here you are in this dirty, stinking hellhole of a place, awaiting trial for murder, surrounded by some of the toughest looking women I have ever had the misfortune to lay my eyes on, yet you're in a good mood! I don't get it! Does it not bother you being in here?"

"Of course it bothers me, Richie! There's just not a great deal I can do about it."

"Have you cried since you came in here?"

"No."

"Have you cried since your Mum died?"

"With relief, perhaps!"

Richie's face looked a picture. Stunned was not the word! I had grown up a lot since leaving school, but I still enjoyed having the propensity to shock.

"Jemma! Don't let the guards hear you say that!"

"They can hear what they like, Richie! I didn't like Vomit Breath, in fact, I hated the bones of her, but that doesn't mean I killed her. I didn't, I swear I didn't!"

"Jemma, it's not me that you have to persuade., it's the twelve people on the jury."

"But do you believe me, Richie?"

It was important to me to hear that he did. I was slowly falling in love with this man and his response would either apply more weight on the accelerator or shift everything into reverse. I might have learnt to be tough having spent my whole life living with Vomit Breath, but I was not a cold blooded killer. If Richie thought I was, I had him all wrong.

Richie stared into the depths of my eyes.

"Jemma, I have never thought for one second that you killed your Mum."

Fantastic!

"Why not?"

Life had taught me to be cynical. I was not just going to accept that answer on its merits. I needed to ask. Richie shifted uncomfortably in his seat. He paused before his response. I was nervous. Would his answer allow me to believe that he would have faith in me under any circumstances? It was only once Richie spoke that reality bit. He spoke in a whisper. A barely audible whisper.

"Because I know who did. Jemma. We both know who did."

Richie

It was pouring down. July and there wasn't a cloud in the sky, not one you could see anyway, as they all just mingled into one massive, grey sheet. The sky looked like it was sobbing heartily, leaving puddles everywhere. I was sat on a bench on the "Sunny Road", in a t-shirt, kagool, trainers and shorts. The road was not living up to its name! It was midday on the 4th July, but I was not even supposed to have been there on a rainy day. All bets were off on a rainy day. I had taken a day's holiday off work for this too and in total, I only had a miserly fifteen days a year to take! I knew before I arrived that it was highly unlikely that Kelly would turn up, but I felt duty bound to visit, like putting flowers on a grave, no-one that matters knows you've done it, but you feel better inside knowing that you did.

Two days had passed since I had last spoken to Kelly. My mind had jumped to hundreds of conclusions in those forty eight hours – she had been mugged in Rotterdam and was now stranded in Holland with no money, she had somehow heard that Jemma had been arrested so had confessed to the murder and was now in some holding cell awaiting paperwork to ship her over to Britain or maybe she had been picked up by a Dutch pimp looking for pretty, fresh faced young girls, drugged up and forced to work in Amsterdam's notorious red light district.

Something must have happened, I knew that much. Since we had started "going out", we had spoken every day, without fail. Now, two days had passed and Kelly had not tried to contact me at all. Another conclusion I played with, was that she had met someone new. I was 99% sure it was too early for that, but for all I knew, some fine looking Dutch bloke or American backpacker, could have swept her off her feet. She could be in some pot café now, rolling a joint with Ruud or Marco or Tyler or Brandon. Although I had kept telling myself, over and over, that Kelly was not going to show, I kept persuading myself to wait, just in case she arrived just after I left and then castigated me later for not loving her enough to stick around. Three hours after I arrived, at two thirty in the afternoon, I knew with absolute certainty that Kelly would not be coming. Midday was the agreed time, it had long since passed. I headed home feeling like that place was now off limits, I would only ever go back with Kelly or on the 4th July. I was a stupid, sentimental old fool before my time! I liked being me though. I was Kelly Watkinson's lover, no-one else in the world could say that….unless she was in Amsterdam taking guilders off drunken visitors to fuel her newly acquired heroin addiction…or was in some five star hotel with Marco, who had suddenly found fortune since the last time my mind had created him….it was a nightmare, I needed to hear from her, just to put my mind at rest.

As I trudged back from a wet and miserable "Sunny Road" with a damp bottom and a broken heart, I started running, running home just in case Kelly was phoning me right that minute. Just in case that two minute time saving could make all the difference between answering Kelly's call and missing it.

Once I arrived home, I begged the phone to ring but when it did it was Uncle Billy or Helen or one of Mum's friends, it was never Kelly. Kelly did not phone that day, not that night, not that week, not that month, not that year. Kelly had gone. Eventually she would write, but when she did, a different Richie Billingham opened that letter. A married man. A father. A veteran of fighting battles. A man not so emotionally needy as that boy on the "Sunny Road", no longer desperate for the return of his one true love. Is there such a thing as one true love? Was I destined to be with Kelly as I thought back then? All my teenage romantic notions were put to the test when that letter finally arrived and implored me to meet her again on the "Sunny Road".

Richie

All six of us were sat around the dining room table. No boyfriends, no girlfriends, no aunties or uncles or grandparents, just Mum, Dad, Helen, Caroline, Jim and myself. It was a rarity. A rare opportunity not to be missed. Mum had arranged for us all to meet up, as she had concluded that we were not spending enough time together as a family.

Helen had recently become engaged to her boyfriend, Tristan, a fellow Lancaster University graduate and was living down in Henleyon-Thames, with his parents, as they both looked for Graduate Trainee roles.

Caroline had been spending less and less time in the house. She was working in H.Samuel in Ormskirk, but her weekends were spent in North Yorkshire at her mysterious new boyfriend, Don's house. Unbeknown to the rest of the family, I knew a little bit more about "Don", than they did. Don was in fact Donna! It transpired that Caroline's boyfriend was a girlfriend. It was all hush hush. Donna was a student at Edge Hill College, in Ormskirk, on a teacher training course, but had returned to her home town of Boroughbridge for the summer. Caroline and Donna had met in the Golden Lion on a Monday night. Donna had been on a student pub crawl, Caroline had just been out for a few drinks with a couple of friends. Caroline told me she had always been "bi-curious" and once Donna approached her in the "Lion", she knew almost immediately that her first same-sex relationship was about to begin.

"Don't tell Mum and Dad!" she demanded of me one night in July, "Dad would have a heart attack and I have no idea what Mum would do. Probably have a panic attack about telling Grandma!"

After the revelation, I met Donna. From the start, we hit it off. She was only a small girl, slightly overweight with short bleach blonde hair and dark roots. She was reserved but had a dry wit similar to my own. Musically, she was into Joni Mitchell, Bob Dylan and Leonard Cohen, so if there was ever a hint of an uncomfortable silence, we could always fall back on music.

Jim was still screwing his way around Ormskirk. I joked that he would have to move soon as there were not many single women he had not been with! I was shocked what confidence and perseverance could get you, as he was not blessed with the greatest of looks.

The conversation that day was originally all about the events of the night before on the River Thames. A pleasure boat had been hit by a dredger and the boat, the Marchioness, had been sunk. The people on the boat had been on the River celebrating a birthday and it was uncertain how many people were still unaccounted for, but many of the hundred plus on board had drowned.

"Those poor families!" Mum commented., "I don't know how I would cope if something happened to any of you."

This comment made me shudder. I had already concluded, this was the time to break my news. It didn't deter me, though. They needed to know and with my cancer battle about to begin in earnest, there was no way it could remain a secret.

I let the meal pass in jovial fashion. Mum did her speciality starter (prawn cocktail) and speciality dessert (trifle) as well as a Roast Turkey main accompanied by all the trimmings, ham, stuffing, roast potatoes, sprouts, carrots, the works. It was only once dessert was finished that I decided to say my piece.

Jim and Dad were sat next to each other, with me opposite Dad, Caroline opposite Jim and Helen and Mum at the two ends. Helen and Caroline were chatting about something, I couldn't hear what as the conversation between Jim and Dad was far louder. Jim had never really been a sportsman, but he had followed in his father's footsteps and developed a love for horse racing. They were arguing over which was the horse of the year.

"It has to be Nashwan, Dad. Won the 2,000 Guineas, won the Derby. What more could it do to persuade you? Horse racing is all about speed and Nashwan's top speed is not fast, it's "whoosh"!!"

Dad loved it that Jim was now into the horses. They suddenly had a common interest.

"I know what you're saying son, don't get me wrong, I love Nashwan, that horse has won me a few quid, I can tell you. I backed it when when it won its maiden at Newbury, last August."

Mum interrupted.

"I beg your pardon! I thought you didn't bet any more!"

"I don't at the bookies, love, just the odd fiver against the guys at work, that's all. If they say a horse won't win and I say it will, I'll bet them a couple of quid that I'm right. More often than not, I am!"

"Well, you were wrong more often than not when you used to bet at the bookmakers, so I hope that's all it is!"

"It is love! It is!"

When Mum wasn't looking, Dad winked at Jim.

"But the greatest horse of the year, Jim, has to be our Dessie! Just for pure emotion and the race that had the whole nation talking, not just the racing world, the whole nation, it was Desert Orchid's win in the Gold Cup! When Yahoo took it up three out, I thought Dessie had no chance and even at the last, when Yahoo and Dessie were alongside each other, I didn't think for a second that Dessie would outstay him! Yahoo's a mudlark!! Out stay him he did though, I wish I'd been at

Cheltenham for that! It wasn't just the highlight of the year, it's up there as the highlight of the century!"

"Up there with what?" Mum asked, "Your wedding and the birth of your four children?!"

"Absolutely," Dad said with a smile, "sixth behind those five!"

"My vote's still with Nashwan." Jim said.

"Come off it, Jim! I've got Dessies win on video, after tea, I'll put it on!"

"His name is James." Mum angrily stated.

"Yours is Dorothy. We call you, Dot. Name's get shortened, love. No point fretting about that. You don't mind our Richard, being called Richie"

"I just don't like the name, Jim. It's common! If I'd have known our James would get called Jim, I'd have called him something else."

"Like what, Dot?"

"Like William."

"He'd have got called Bill then, or Willie, like Nashwan's winning jockey, Willie Carson!"

Horses! They had been the reason why Jim had always had to wear my hand-me-downs as we had grown up and yet he was still prepared to go down that wallet emptying route. Right, the four legged friend debate was obviously finishing, this was my cue.

"Dad, before you retire to the lounge to watch Desert Orchid," I began, "there's something I want to say."

You would expect a bit of hush. What you expected and what you got from my family tended to differ.

"Listen up everyone, Richie's going to tell us he's pregnant!" Dad joked in that 'I'm a Dad so I'm automatically not funny' kind of way.

"No, that's not possible, Kelly's not around to provide the sperm!" Caroline added.

"Maybe she froze the sperm and sent it over in a freezing test tube from the Bermuda triangle!" Helen added.

My family had found Kelly's disappearance concerning at first, but after a while, they had just seen it as an opportunity to make fun of me. They all continued taking pot shots. Well, the three of them did anyway. Mum didn't because Mum wasn't the type to poke fun at anyone, especially one of her sons, and Jim didn't join in either. Under normal circumstances, Jim would have been there, handing the stick out with the rest of them, but not this time. This time, he had a faint awareness of my situation, so he refrained from joining in. In fact, he did the opposite. He quietened everybody down.

"Listen you lot! Just hush a minute will you! Let Richie speak!"

"If you are pregnant, Richie, remember to run the babies name past your mother first! Don't be choosing anything common!"

"Dad!" Jim chastened, "Just shut up, will you!"

"When did you get so bossy?" Caroline wanted to know of Jim.

"Just be quiet! Please." Jim repeated in a serious tone.

Silence. There was silence. I cleared my throat.

"I need to tell you all something…" I started.

"I told you, he's pregnant!" Dad added. It wasn't even funny the first time.

"Let him speak, Dad!" Jim demanded.

"Sorry!"

"Right. Where do I start?"

"At the very beginning." Helen chipped in and then by way of explanation added,

"Sound of Music! Do-re-mi!"

I continued unabated.

"OK. You all know Kelly's gone away, don't you?"

There was a collective nodding of heads.

"But you don't know why? Do you?"

Collective shaking of heads.

"It was partially down to me." I explained. "You see, Kelly saw me with her sister in Coronation Park…."

Dad could not help himself.

"No, don't tell me, you were knocking off both sisters! Stupid boy! The other one's a murderer son!"

"She's not a murderer, Dad!"

"That's not what the police think, Richie!" Dad replied.

"I said that!" Caroline added.

"Look everyone! Let me finish. Kelly saw me in Coronation Park and I was with Jemma and she was giving me a hug. Kelly saw us and thought something was going on, but it wasn't!"

"Why were you hugging Kelly's sister?" Mum asked. Mum could keep quiet when they were all poking fun, but not when there was gossip to be gleaned.

"I found out some news. Jemma was trying to make me feel better."

"What news?" Caroline asked.

"The news that I've got cancer."

The words hung in the air like smoke on a windless day. The world stopped. The door could have swung open and tumbleweed blown by. Everyone's brains gathered the information presented to them.

"Sorry, what did you say?" Mum was already in denial.

"I've got cancer, Mum."

I had been brave to this point, but my voice began to quiver. I did not want to start crying again. Since the lump, I felt like I was always crying.

"Are you sure?" Helen asked.

"Yes, I'm sure. I've been to the doctor's, then to see a urologist who did an ultrasound. It's been confirmed. I've got cancer, Helen."

"What sort of cancer?" Mum wanted to know.

"That's not important right now. It's just important I get treated and I get rid of it."

"No, Richie, it does matter" Mum was like a dog sniffing out a bone or in this case, sniffing out a ball, a cancerous one, metaphorically speaking of course!

"It matters a lot." Mum said. "Some cancers are worse than others, if you've just got a bit of skin cancer, I believe, as long as it hasn't spread, that it's easily sorted. What cancer is it, Richie?"

"Please, Mum. Leave it. It's not important."

"Is it bowel cancer?" Caroline asked, concluding it was a cancer I would be embarrassed to have.

"No."

"Testicular cancer?" she guessed again.

I said nothing.

"Shit, Richie!" Dad exclaimed.

Helen and Caroline started crying. Mum stayed composed. Angry but composed.

"How long have you known?" Mum asked.

"A few weeks."

"You've known for a few weeks and you could not find it in your heart to tell me! Your own mother! Why?"

"I'm sorry, Mum."

"I'm not looking for an apology, I'm looking for an explanation. Why did you not tell me?"

"I just needed to deal with it, myself, first!"

"No, you didn't! You told that girl! Kelly's sister. You just said she was there for you. She hugged you. After everything I've done for you, Richie, I can't believe you didn't tell me!"

"Does it matter, Dot?" Dad asked. "The lad's telling us now."

Mum lost it.

"It matters to me! You may have been out every day, frittering away your hard earned money on some useless donkey, only fit for the knackers yard, but whilst you have been doing that, I have been raising our kids. Teaching them right from wrong. If any of them ever had a bump on their head or fell over and cut their knee, they would always come to me and I would fix it."

"You can't fix testicular cancer, Dot."

"Well I could have tried!" Mum was getting really upset now.

"And I still will try, but Richie's given it a few weeks head start on me now. There's people I need to speak to, Doctors, nurses, consultants. I just wish I'd known sooner, if I'd have known sooner, I'd have spoken to everyone by now. Richie would be getting the right treatment now."

"Mum! I am getting the right treatment! They're going to take it away!"

"The cancer? They're going to take the cancer away?"

"Hopefully. They're going to remove my testicle."

I hated saying that. It felt like I was saying I was incontinent, that I was sitting there having soiled my pants. Stupidly, I felt ashamed.

"Do they have to?" Mum asked.

I laughed through the first sign of tears.

"Believe me, Mum! I would not be agreeing to it, if they didn't have to. I don't want to be on the morticians slab with two testicles. I'd rather be here with one."

Mum sobbed now. I surprised myself by managing to recover my composure. She stood up and moved towards me. Kneeling down besides my chair, Mum hugged me hard. I hugged her hard back.

"You'll be OK, son. You'll beat this! I know you'll beat this!"

"I know I will, Mum. I'll be OK."

Helen and Caroline stood up. They came over tearfully, to create a mass emotional hug.

Jim looked on. He told me later that Dad looked crestfallen, I couldn't see through the hugs. Jim stood up.

"Come on, Dad. Come and show me, Desert Orchid. Let's leave them to it. We'll speak to Richie later."

Moments later Peter O'Sullevan's excitable commentary could be heard above the tears. Brave Dessie. I hoped his trainer had bottled that bravery because I felt that I could do with borrowing some. I knew right then, that I would need tons of it in those testing weeks that lay ahead.

Margerita McGordon

I was always uncomfortable about giving evidence at a murder trial. Wally was fine with it, he just felt it was our duty to testify, but from the moment Paula, our daughter, urged us to phone Ormskirk police station to the moment I stood down from the dock at Preston Crown Court, several months later, I had butterflies in my stomach. When I complained to Wally, he just laughed it off and said,

"They can't be butterflies, Rita, butterflies only live for a couple of days!"

From what the police said, there was additional pressure knowing that our statements were pivotal to the case against Jemma Watkinson. I felt very peculiar about the whole thing. Wally and I could be responsible for sending this young girl to jail, yet neither of us really knew whether she was capable of murdering her mother or not. She was certainly capable of rowing and shouting, but murder? It's hard to think of anyone that you would think is evil enough to commit a murder. All we were certain of, was that Jemma had been awake when her mother had returned that night, yet her statement to the police insisted she was asleep. She was certainly hiding something.

Paula bought me a new outfit for the trial. After giving evidence to the police, Wally and I both had to sign statements. A few days later, we read in the Ormskirk Advertiser that a nineteen year old had been arrested and charged with the murder of Carole Watkinson, we subsequently received letters saying that we may or may not have to testify at the trial of Jemma Watkinson at Preston Crown Court in December 1989. We were told to be mindful of the trial dates and be available if required. Once we received those letters, Paula said there was absolutely no way that we would not have to go to court and she took me to Sophie's, a ladies dresswear shop in Ormskirk, next to the bus station, to get a smart new outfit. Paula paid for a white blouse and a grey and black checked skirt for me, which was knee length. I could wear black tights underneath it. Both the lady in the shop and Paula suggested I may want to try trousers with the blouse, but ladies of my generation are just not comfortable in trousers and I certainly did not want to be up in the dock with everyone on the jury thinking I was mutton dressed as lamb. Smart, intelligent lady was the image I wanted to convey.

Why the police needed both Wally and I to testify, I'm not really sure. Our statements were virtually the same, we had been in bed next to each other when Carole had died. We had both heard the same things, but Wally remembers detail so much better than me, I just wish he could have sorted it all out. I just kept hoping they would only ask Wally to court and not me. When the letters arrived though.my heart sank, they needed both of us.

Wally was called to give evidence before me. When he came out of the court he did not look in the slightest bit phased. He looked more flushed when he had been around to our Karen's to sort out her electrics, the previous week. Wally re-assured me that it was all very straightforward and that everyone in court had been really polite and courteous.

"All we are doing Rita is confirming what we heard. It's not a test, no-one is trying to catch us out. We are just here to tell them, what we heard. Let the judge and jury draw their own conclusions."

The following day, it was my turn. When the 'Clerk of the Court' announced me, Margerita McGordon, I felt more nervous than on my wedding day, forty nine years earlier. I had worn white that day and I just felt everyone was looking at me thinking, 'Wearing white at twenty nine years old! How ridiculous!'

My cystitis had become a hundred times worse because of this ordeal and the fact that I might need to go to the 'Ladies' at any point made me feel even worse. Obviously I am not saying the trial had caused my cystitis, but the nerves made me go to the loo even more than I was doing already. My GP, Dr.Whiteside, had advised me to drink plenty of water too, which increased the odds that the trial would need to stop.

I took my oath to God and then Mr.Hodkinson, the prosecuting barrister, began to question me. Mr.Hodkinson was in his late fifties, he was grey, balding, had reddened, veiny cheeks, like a man who had enjoyed an affluent man's life. He was the consummate professional and although I was visibly shaking when I took the stand, within a couple of minutes, Mr. Hodkinson had put me at ease. His style of questioning was very calm and matter of fact and I felt comfortable relating the events of that Sunday morning in April to him. The court was packed, I suppose a murder trial brings more interested observers in than any other type of trial, but that did not bother me at all because of how Mr.Hodkinson made me feel.

Mr. Hodkinson wanted to know exactly what I had heard on that Sunday morning. I ran through the events of the whole night, packing, retiring to bed early, due to our very early morning trip to Manchester Airport and then relating how we were woken by the two sisters next door arguing. I told Mr. Hodkinson how the older one, Jemma had sent the other one away, how Jemma's mother and Jemma had argued and Jemma, in some form of head to head confrontation had warned her mother to back off, which was followed by banging and then it went quiet. Mr. Hodkinson seemed satisfied with this, thanked me and returned to his seat.

Mr. Cole-Crallen then questioned me too, on behalf of the defence. Mr Cole-Crallen was a lot younger than Mr Hodkinson. He was in his early forties, with a full head of wavy, dark brown hair, poshly spoken, as Mr Hodkinson had been, it was probably a pre-requisite for barristers and like Mr. Hodkinson, Mr. Cole-Crallen did everything in his power to keep me at ease. He sauntered up to the witness box.

"Good afternoon, Mrs McGordon. I apologise in advance for asking this question, a gentleman should not be asking a lady this, but would you mind telling the court how old you are?"

I didn't mind telling people my age. I would rather shock people by revealing my true age than say a younger age and have people think I look every day of it.

"I am seventy eight years old."

I am sure I heard a gasp from the public gallery.

"Really?" Mr. Cole-Crallen seemed genuinely surprised. "You don't look a day over sixty, Mrs.McGordon."

"Thank you! Wally….I mean Mr. McGordon, my husband, tells me that. Thank you!"

A double thank you to underline my gratitude.

"Now I understand having to testify in a murder trial can be an ordeal for anyone of any age, but I listened intently to the questions Mr. Hodkinson posed to you and I think your responses were incredibly insightful. I must admit, prior to hearing you testify to Mr. Hodkinson, I thought there may be some doubt about whether or not you could have confused the date of the incident next door. Now though, having listened to your answers, am I right in thinking you are one hundred per cent certain that you heard Jemma, her sister Kelly and her mother Carole, in the early hours of Sunday 16th April?"

"Yes."

"Of this you are certain, because you were going on holiday the following morning and they were disturbing you. Am I correct?"

"Yes, that's correct."

"And there is no way it could have been the previous weekend?"

"Absolutely not, no. We were not going on holiday the previous weekend."

"Good! So we now know for certain you heard voices from next door in the early hours of Sunday 16th April."

"Yes."

"Let's move on from that then, Mrs. McGordon, I don't feel it necessary to labour that point any longer. May I just ask how well you know the Watkinson family? How long have they been your neighbours?"

Wally calls me Ronnie Corbett sometimes, as I have a tendency to go into unnecessary detail with certain questions posed of me. I go off at tangents somewhat. On reflection, this was one of those times.

"Wally and I moved to Wigan Road in the summer of 1987. We lived in Granville Park in Aughton prior to that for twenty nine years. We had a lovely house there, with an acre of land and a heated swimming pool, but our two daughters, Karen and Paula, have long since flown the nest and Wally was struggling to keep on top of the garden and I was struggling to keep on top of the cleaning in the house, so we felt it was time to downsize. The state pension is next to nothing as well, so it seemed sensible to utilise some of the equity tied up in the property. Wally said it would allow him to continue to keep me in the manner to which I am accustomed. Granville Park is a very much sought after location, so our house sold in a matter of days and within six weeks, we had moved to our current home in Wigan Road, which is pleasant but a lot smaller than Granville Park. Still, it feels like home now."

"Were the Watkinsons already living next door when you moved in?"

"Yes, our house is semi-detached. The Watkinsons live in the adjoining house."

I suppose this was a bit of a faux pas. I should have said "lived" seeing Jemma was in prison, Kelly had, by all accounts disappeared off the face of the planet and Carole was dead. As things stood, the Watkinsons did not live next door.

"OK. Thank you. As far as neighbours go, have you been close to the Watkinsons over the last two years? Would you pop around there if you were short of coffee?"

"No. Wally and I hardly know them. I would have been tempted to call around if we were short of alcohol though. There never seemed to be a shortage of alcohol there."

"What makes you say that?"

"Jemma's mother, Carole, the deceased, was always waking us up. This incident on the 16th April was not, by any means, a one-off. Carole Watkinson was a dreadful neighbour. Utterly thoughtless. Every weekend there was singing and dancing and shouting, normally in the early hours of the morning and often this would be followed by other noises that Wally and I really did not want to hear."

"May I ask what sort of noises?"

"Sexual noises. Carole was very noisy when she had male guests. I think she wanted the whole of Wigan Road to know what she was up to, not just Wally and I."

"So, throughout the course of your two year period, living next door to the victim, you were subjected to this every weekend?"

"Pretty much. Sometimes week days too. Obviously, we go to Majorca whenever we can, so at least that gave us some sort of break from it."

"So Carole Watkinson was generally unruly?"

"Yes, especially when she had a drink, which was often."

"So, we've established Carole Watkinson liked to let her hair down...."

I thought to myself that it was not just her hair that she liked to let down but if I'd have mentioned her knickers in court, I am sure I would have found myself in serious trouble.

"….but a lot of independent young women like to enjoy themselves, this does not make them bad people. Did Carole Watkinson give you the impression that she was a good mother?"

"Absolutely not."

"If you don't mind me saying, Mrs. McGordon, that seemed a very firm response, given you have previously told the court that you did not know the Watkinsons very well."

"I could not think of a worse example of a mother."

"Why would you say that?"

"Mother's need to raise their children in a way that leads by example. Her example was a drunken, noisy, aggressive and promiscuous one."

"Aggressive? Why would you say aggressive?"

"Wally and I would often hear Carole threatening those girls. Excuse my language, but we would hear her say things like,

'If you girls don't make yourself scarce when Johnny comes round, you'll feel the full 'f'ing force of my right hook'..she did not say 'f'ing though!'

"Would Carole Watkinson say things like that or is that exactly what she would say to her children?"

"Exactly what she would say except it obviously wasn't always Johnny, it could be Frank or Ken or Peter or whoever."

"Did you ever hear her hitting the girls?"

We heard noises. Wally and I presumed they were the noises of Carole striking her children, but as we could not see what was going on, we couldn't exactly be sure."

"So you thought the victim was striking the defendant but you cannot be sure?"

"No."

"How often did you presume she was hitting her children?"

"Recently. At least once a week."

"But you cannot be sure."

"No."

"OK. So just to re-cap, how well did you know the defendant, Jemma Watkinson and her sister, Kelly Watkinson?"

"As I said earlier, I did not know the family very well at all. We did not socialise with them. We often saw them coming up and down the path and not long after we moved in, there was a memorable, amusing period, when a young man in swimming trunks, kept singing at one of the girls windows every morning., but that soon stopped and he then started to arrive fully clothed. He appears to be the younger girl, Kelly's gentleman friend."

"Would you know Jemma and Kelly to speak to?"

"Only to say hello to."

"Could you differentiate between their voices?"

"I beg your pardon."

Wally had advised me if I was asked any question that I was unsure how to answer, just to pretend I did not hear it properly. Wally said it would allow me some thinking time.

"Could you differentiate between Kelly's voice and Jemma's voice? If I blindfolded you, Mrs McGordon and played a tape recording of Jemma's voice and then Kelly's voice, could you tell them apart?"

"Yes."

"Could you really? I must congratulate you on having the capacity to do that, because I can't. I had to listen to the playbacks of their statements many, many times to enable me to tell the two sisters apart. They have very similar voices, don't you think?"

"Yes, they do, but Jemma's the older one, she tends to have more authority. We could often hear them and Jemma tended to mother Kelly somewhat, as an older sister does. Wally and I found Paula used to do that with Karen."

"So, given their voices are so similar, how can you be sure it was Jemma who confronted her mother, not Kelly?"

"Jemma told Kelly to get out of her room."

"How can you be sure it was Jemma telling Kelly to get out though, not the other way around?"

"Because it sounded like Jemma."

"But we've just established the two girls sound very similar."

"Yes, but I also said Jemma was the bossy one."

"So your judgement was formed on the basis that you could hear one girl bossing the other and as Jemma was normally the bossy one, she was probably doing the bossing on 16th April?"

"Yes."

"But you couldn't see the events taking place, could you?"

"No, we were in bed."

"And you said before that you could not be sure that Carole Watkinson used physical force on her children, because you could not see her. How could you be sure Jemma was the bossy one because you could not see them?"

"Because she was the older one and they referred to each other by name."

"OK. That makes sense. Just suppose though, on the night in question, Kelly bucked the trend. Just suppose it was Kelly that was annoyed with her mother. Would it not have been possible for Kelly to have told Jemma to go and then confronted her mother?"

"It's unlikely."

"Why? Did you clearly recall the sisters referring to each other by name? Did you hear Jemma say 'Get out, Kelly!'?"

"No, I don't recall that, but Jemma was always arguing with her mother."

"Yes, I appreciate that Mrs. McGordon, but I am asking you whether it was possible on the 16th April, for you to have jumped to the conclusion that it was Jemma confronting her mother, because, as you said it had always been Jemma arguing. Could you and Wally not have been woken up, in the early hours of the morning, and naturally presumed, based on past history, that it was Jemma arguing, even if it was actually Kelly?"

"I suppose so. It seems very unlikely though."

"But not impossible. There were two girls in that house, two girls who sounded very much alike. Is it possible that it was, in fact, Kelly who confronted her mother, not Jemma?"

"It's possible, but…."

"Thank you, Mrs. McGordon. You've been very helpful. No further questions."

Richie

Mr. Davenport, the urologist, told me the operation would be pretty routine. He indicated that I would have the operation on Thursday morning and all being well, I could even be home that evening. It turned out that I only returned home on Friday morning as I had a bit of a reaction to the anaesthetic, when they were taking me to Philip

Ward from surgery, I was taken back in an ambulance. In my drugged up state, I saw Andrew Prescott, an old neighbour of mine who had moved to Elland when I was five. Andrew was sitting next to me, as I was sprawled out on the trolley and he had a white rabbit on his lap that he was stroking. A white rabbit that developed, Kelly's head and it began to speak to me.

"I'm watching you, Richie Billingham! Never forget, I'm always watching you! You wouldn't grass me in, would you?! Of course not, you've got no balls!! If you'd have eaten more carrots, this would never have happened! Never!"

I'd obviously watched too many horror films as a kid! The hallucinations and general feeling of grogginess continued into the evening and my random incoherent mutterings towards apparitions were enough for the Senior House Officer to deem me unfit to return home. By the following morning, the drugs had worn off and I was just left to contend with an aching groin, a sore scrotum and a throbbing pair of balls, a real one and a sparkly new false one.

The week before the operation, Mr. Davenport had sat me down and explained what the procedure was and provided me with a couple of options on how we would take things forward. The operation itself was a unilateral inguinal orchidectomy. Mr.Davenport explained that he would be making a three inch incision into my groin to remove the testicle and that he would also be removing the entire spermatic cord too. I had no option but to trust him as I was totally oblivious to what spermatic cord was, it sounded like something you'd buy at a DIY shop or an Ann Summers party or was a technique learnt by a lecherous guitarist.

I would never have asked why the spermatic cord had to go, but Mr. Davenport obviously felt a duty to explain, as he went into great detail about how it was absolutely necessary to remove it, as often testicular cancer would spread from the cord into the lymph nodes near the kidneys. In total, he thought the operation would not last much more than hour. I expect it didn't, but as I was as high as a kite, I didn't have an opportunity to start and stop my stopwatch.

Despite knowing very little about the spermatic cord, I had, at this point, developed a vague comprehension of my illness. Mr. Davenport always went to the trouble of trying to explain it and coupled with the books I had been getting from Ormskirk library, my understanding was gradually improving. Mr. Davenport had explained that the tumour will have started from one abnormal cell. He said it was impossible to explain why that cell had become cancerous, but once it had, it basically went out of control and kept multiplying. My analogy, which I did not share with Mr. Davenport, was that it spread like the news of a teenager's house party when their Mum and Dad were away. It seemed to be a good one as both scenarios involved sex, wankers, pricks and knobs! A juvenile analogy perhaps, but I was little more than a juvenile at the time.

Mr. Davenport had gone on to say that there were certain groups of men that were more likely to develop testicular cancer than others. Men with undescended testes were one group, a group I did not belong to. A second group were men with a family history of testicular cancer. As far as I was aware, I did not belong to that group either. Mr. Davenport explained though, that because of my illness, Jim would now be deemed as being more at risk than someone who's brother did not have testicular cancer and on that basis, Mr. Davenport felt that it would be sensible for Jim to be screened. He would love that news, I thought at the time, but to be fair to Jim he took it in his stride and was given a clean bill of health. The third group, was the one I did fall into, this was the geographical one. For some reason, young, white men in Northern Europe tend to develop a higher rate of testicular cancer than anyone else in the world. I concluded there was, therefore, some truth in the phrase, "Freezing your balls off!" Once again, I did not share my witty sexual observations with Mr. Davenport!

That meeting, the week before the operation, almost passed with me having total faith in Mr. Davenport. Almost! Just before I left, however, having gone through everything in the finest of detail, Mr. Davenport explained that following the operation, my removed testicle would be sent to a pathologist for him to confirm it was cancer. Up until that point, I had every faith that this man knew what he was doing and I let everything go with a reluctant acceptance, but all of a sudden, I felt perhaps I was not challenging him enough. Had he not just said he would send my testicle to a pathologist TO CONFIRM IT WAS CANCER! Hang on a minute!

"Sorry! What was that, you just said? Why does my testicle need to go to a pathologist to check it's cancer? Surely if you are removing my testicle, you are removing it because its cancerous, not to see whether its cancerous or not. I take it, if the pathologist confirms it is not cancerous, you don't just open the stitches up on my groin and pop it back in?"

Mr. Davenport shook his head.

"No."

"So why do we need confirmation its cancerous?"

Mr. Davenport could see my calm exterior had now evaporated and the fearful child I was, was now truly laid bare.

"Mr. Billingham, trust me, I would not remove your testicle if everything did not point towards your tumour being cancerous, but we will only know with complete certainty, once the testis is out. The ultrasound scan we did indicated that your lump is a solid mass, which is likely to be a tumour, now if it had been a benign cyst, which is more common, it would have shown on the ultrasound as a fluid filled lump. Once the testis is out, the pathologist will have a look at it under a microscope and in all likelihood, confirm cancer."

"Will I need to have chemotherapy?"

"As yet, Richard, we do not know. Remember the blood test we gave you?"

I did. I hated bloody needles and the nurse had to sit me down on a bed as I had warned her that I may faint.

"Well, testicular cancers can often show the presence of certain chemicals in your blood. Your blood sample, did show these chemicals, so what we'll do, after your operation, is take another blood sample. If it remains positive, it means some cancer cells have spread to somewhere else in your body, if it comes back negative, the cancer was probably contained to the testis. If it is positive, then we will have to look at radiotherapy or chemotherapy. Hopefully, it will be negative."

"Could the cancer come back in the other testicle?"

"In a small number of cases it does, but it's uncommon."

My faith in Mr. Davenport was restored.

"Now then," he continued, have you given any further thought to the prosthetic testicle? As we discussed, it will be very similar in size and movement to your natural testicle."

I squirmed.

"I don't know if I'm being daft, but I'd like to have it."

"Why is that daft?"

"It just seems a bit pathetic having to have a pretend testicle put in there as a replacement, but I've thought about it and for some bizarre reason, I would feel better having it."

"You don't need to justify yourself to me, Richard. We would not offer prosthetic testicles if it was not common for people in your situation to want them. You are not pathetic. You are not bizarre. It's natural to want this, don't beat yourself up about it."

"OK."

"In most cases, Richard, testicular cancer is a cancer that is diagnosed, treated and then the sufferer returns to back to the life they had previously. If a prosthetic testicle helps return you to normality, then surely that's a good thing. Try and retain a positive outlook. Keep thinking after the operation, we will get good news back from the pathologist and other than regular checks, that will be the end of the matter. Alright?"

"Yes, fine."

"So, we'll see you next Thursday."

Mr. Davenport shook my hand.

"If you could give yourself a good shave and get rid of all your pubic hairs before the operation, that would be wonderful, saves someone else having to do it for you when you come in. On countless occasions, young men have arrived at hospital with a cleanly shaved face and have had an awful shock when someone has arrived to chop their pubic hair off, so I tend to pre-warn people these days!"

"Fine. I'll do it myself."

I left Ormskirk hospital that day just wanting next Thursday to come and go as quickly as possible, so I could bring my plucked meat and two veg to surgery, swop a ball, get the all clear and get on with my life. I was trying to be positive, but the way things were going, it seemed certain a fresh disaster would be just around the next corner and sure enough it was! What I didn't know though, was that when I finally managed to reach the light at the end of the tunnel, it would shine more brightly than the sun.

Richie

Jemma often says that she fell in love with me on the summer's day in Coronation Park when my urologist, Mr. Davenport confirmed that, in all likelihood, we were dealing with testicular cancer. That was the point that Jemma says that she realised her feelings for me were more than just those you would naturally have for your sister's boyfriend. I have always said that my feelings for Jemma changed from negative to positive around that time, but the first time I realised that I was starting to fall in love with Jemma was during her trial.

I was fortunate to be working at Andy's Records in Preston during Jemma's trial, so once it began, I would spend every lunch hour in the public gallery of Preston Crown Court. On a Thursday, which was my day off, I would travel up to watch the whole day's proceedings. Looking at things retrospectively, the fact that I would spend my day off watching Jemma's trial and had previously visited her at least once a month at Risley Remand Centre, showed my thoughts and feelings for Jemma were escalating, but at the time, I justified it as a way to maintain a link with Kelly.

Throughout the trial, there were only two other people providing moral support to Jemma, her grandmother, who was in attendance for every second of the seven week trial and also Jemma's friend, Amy Perkins, who I knew from school. Amy probably attended a couple of times a week, perhaps a little more often as the trial neared an end. Amy's Mum sometimes attended too, so I suppose you could argue that there were three people, other than myself, lending moral support.

As far as I could make out, as often the legal jargon was well beyond my comprehension, there did not appear to be a strong case for the prosecution. When Carole Watkinson had died, there were only two eye witnesses, one was on trial and was denying that she had seen the ill fated fall and the other was the defendant's sister, who had vanished. I was in a select band of people who knew that Kelly had left the country, other than Amy, Jemma, myself, my family and Kelly's grandmother, no-one was aware that Kelly had been in Rotterdam. The police had apparently been tracking activity on her bank accounts, but as far as I was aware they had not, at that stage, managed to trace her plane ticket to Amsterdam. If they had, it would, I imagine, have been mentioned in court, but it was not. It was just commonly known that she had disappeared. The defence team had tactfully latched on to the fact that Kelly had not stayed around and the impression I was certainly given, was that Jemma's barrister was indirectly pointing a finger of suspicion Kelly's way, just by dwelling on her absence.

The only other witnesses were "ear" witnesses rather than "eye" witnesses. One Thursday, Wally McGordon, a charming, confident, old man in his late seventies, took the stand and succinctly described how he had heard Jemma send her sister to her room, then threaten her mother with a knife, before hearing a crashing sound, which could well have been the sound of Carole Watkinson being pushed down the stairs. Wally seemed such a genuinely good man that if I had been on the jury, I may have started to believe that perhaps Jemma was guilty after all. This man did not stand to benefit from lies, Jemma did though, so the fact that his statement contradicted Jemma's, was certainly not re-enforcing her innocence.

When I returned home to Aughton, the Thursday night after Wally McGordon's testimony, I was extremely concerned that Jemma would end up imprisoned for life for a crime I knew she had not committed. I felt particularly guilty as Jemma was aware that I could make a statement to police that would prove her innocence beyond reasonable doubt. As I sat and watched the trial turn against her, my feelings grew, more out of admiration than love initially, as she had never pleaded with me to make a statement shedding light on Kelly's role. Jemma understood my loyalty was to Kelly, as was hers, and we both sought to protect the individual who had abandoned us.

The following lunchtime, when I arrived at court, Amy Perkins was in the public gallery, so I sat next to her. Every time Amy attended court, I would always seek her out. As had become customary in the previous five weeks when Amy had attended court and I had arrived at lunchtime, she brought me up to date with the events of the morning. Amy told me Margerita McGordon, Wally's wife, had been questioned and was totally out of her depth. Jemma's barrister, Amy believed, had certainly cast doubts about the accuracy of her statement and from what I could make out, had managed to discredit Wally McGordon's statement from the previous day, by suggesting it would be impossible to differentiate between Jemma and Kelly's voices.

Amy thought that the impression given was that of a nosey pair of elderly neighbours who had heard a commotion and assumed it was

Jemma rather than Kelly that had been central to events. The barrister had highlighted that they were wrong to assume. As Amy recounted this story, as a whisper into my ear, I began to appreciate how I was beginning to feel romantically for Jemma. I was almost euphoric that she was likely to be found innocent and I started to think about ways to build on our friendship. I felt a need to know Jemma better. If truth be known, I knew there and then that I wanted to date Jemma if Kelly did not come back.

The feeling of certainty that Jemma would be found innocent lasted for around a week. It lasted until the prosecution called Jemma to take the stand. They probably called her as their case was looking increasingly flimsy and they had nowhere else to go. It was a stroke of genius on their part. Jemma is a wonderful woman, she would fight a lion for someone she loved, but as I knew only too well, her Achilles heel is that first impressions are not always good. Despite being aesthetically pleasing and honest, Jemma was, and still is, blunt, abrupt and a terrible liar, not the perfect attributes for a young woman standing trial for murder, when first impressions are everything. Jemma, in trying to save her sister, was not in a position to be honest and in compromising herself, gave a shambolic performance, that could not have looked worse if she had set her pants on fire.

The thing I did not understand, as I watched her stumble through her answers, and still to this day do not understand, is why Jemma persisted with the "Sleeping Beauty" tale. Jemma's elderly neighbours, the McGordons, had totally discredited this line of defence and to gain some sort of empathy from the jury, Jemma would have been far wiser holding her hands up, admitting being awake, but insisting she played no part in her mother falling down the stairs. The fall had just been a tragic accident that had befallen an inebriated woman. Jemma could have just said she had originally lied in her statement because she was frightened and was fearful that the police would put two and two together and get seventy eight. Jemma's stubborn insistence that she had just slept through her mother's death just did not seem credible. Luckily for Jemma, her barrister continued to imply that the awkward nature of her responses was in some way linked to her blind loyalty to her missing sister. I was fairly sure at the time, and Jemma has confirmed since, that Jemma's barrister knew nothing about Kelly's role in her mother's death, he was just re-introducing the element of doubt after Jemma's cringeful testimony.

I was in court when the jury reached their verdict. Technically, I should not have been, as the jury of seven men and five women retired to consider their verdict on a Monday lunchtime, but when they failed to reach a verdict that day, they were sent back to a hotel to deliberate overnight, so I swopped days off with Stuart in the shop, to enable me to be in court the next day.

It is often argued that juries reach a quick verdict when the accused is found innocent. If there does not appear to be a strong prosecution case, it negates the need to deliberate. A counter argument, however, is that if a trial is an open and shut case and the accused is blatantly guilty, then there would be no need for deliberation either. Thus, I made no assumptions in relation to the delay, to me it did not point towards an innocent or a guilty verdict. I could not call it.

At 11.15 a.m on Tuesday 7th November, 1989, the court came back into session for the jury to announce their verdict. As the jury filed back into court, Amy grabbed tight hold of my hand.

"I can't bear this." she said as her voice wavered.

"It'll turn out OK." I replied, remembering I had re-assured Kelly in a similar fashion and as yet, everything still seemed a long way off turning out OK.

If Jemma went to jail for the murder of her mother, I knew the guilt would weigh heavily on me. She did not deserve this. Jemma's barrister had portrayed Carole Watkinson as a drunken, abusive mother but Jemma seemed too streetwise and battle hardened to come across as the poor, defenceless victim. In reality, Jemma was the victim, she had been beaten by her mother relentlessly over weeks and months and when Kelly finally did something to protect her, Jemma ended up being charged for the murder.

As well as being nervous, I was excited about the arrival of the verdict. If Jemma was found innocent, she would walk free from court and our friendship would be free to develop. There had been coy smiles, prolonged looks into my eyes and a shared sense of humour, during my visits to Risley, which hinted that Jemma may have begun to notice feelings for me. I would have to tread very carefully, as I could not afford to make a complete fool of myself by making unwanted advances towards Kelly's sister, but the more I got to know Jemma, the more I liked her and I was really interested in seeing where this would lead.

As everyone took their positions, the 'Head Juror' passed the verdict of the jury to the judge.

"Ladies and Gentleman of the jury, have you reached your verdict?"

"We have, 'Your Honour'," declared the 'Head Juror'.

"On the charge of murder, do you find the defendant, Jemma Louise Watkinson, guilty or not guilty?"

"Not guilty."

I grabbed Amy's hand tighter and with my other hand clenched my fist in a victorious manner! Fantastic! Justice had been done! She was innocent! They had found her innocent!

The Judge continued.

"On the charge of manslaughter...."

I cursed to myself. I had forgotten about the manslaughter charge.

".....do you find the defendant, Jemma Louise Watkinson, guilty or not guilty?"

"Guilty."

The colour drained from Jemma's face. There had been a mix of contented murmurings and shaking of heads when the 'not guilty' murder verdict had been returned, but when the 'guilty' manslaughter verdict was returned there was a moment were there was a stunned silence. As far as my recollection goes, this was broken by Amy sobbing and blowing her nose. The judge thanked the jury, then announced at the end of a rambling summary that Jemma would serve three years in prison for the manslaughter of Carole Watkinson.

Jemma was led away, not screaming and shouting like in an American TV drama, just quietly, head bowed, handcuffed to a tough looking policewoman who looked like she was more than capable of giving Mike Tyson a run for his money. Thistles and bulldogs sprung to mind.

Selfishness is an undesirable trait, but as Jemma was being led away, I must admit, I was not thinking of how she would cope locked away in a prison cell for the next three years, that thought came later, all I could think about was how the verdict affected me. My gorgeous girlfriend, who I had adored had left me, through no fault of mine and had made no contact with me for almost six months. Her current location was unknown. I genuinely thought she loved me but it seemed like I had that one wrong. Her sister, who was equally stunning, a completely different specimen but a rollercoaster ride I was keen to get on, was now going to be spending three years eating porridge at 'Her Majesty's Pleasure'. I sat there in Preston Crown Court, ignoring Amy's tears, making no attempt to console her, just dwelling on my own, personal misery. I felt well and truly cursed.

I reflected that I needed to move on now. Forget about the Watkinsons. Forget about the missing testicle and move on. A life less complicated would be the best option now, I concluded. Back then I was a fickle soul! I went home that night and played every melancholy CD that I had. I was looking for a song that seemed to sum up my situation. When I couldn't find one within my own collection, I raided Caroline's. After a lot of flicking through utter tripe, I stumbled across two songs, both by a band (or more accurately two ladies) I had never even heard of before that night. They were called the Indigo Girls and the two songs, that perfectly summed up everything I was feeling were called, "Blood and Fire" and "Crazy Game". I played those two songs over and over that night, on low volume so as not to wake Mum and Dad (fortunately Jim was stopping the night at Warren Walker's or Russell Jones' house, I wasn't sure which). They both felt that they had been written especially for me, all about the power and emotion love generates.

By the time I finally succumbed to sleep that night, I knew I was not prepared to give up on Kelly Watkinson just yet. She had gone away, but there were major reasons why. After six months, maybe I should be moving on, maybe the world was full of potential new girlfriends who could make me feel like Kelly had, but I did not want them, I just wanted Kelly back. I was doing a complete about turn but what I wanted more than anything else was to find Kelly, see how she felt about me now, six months down the line. Had our love been as real as it appeared to me? I was going to find Kelly, I vowed and I was going to find out.

As Jemma settled down to spend her first night in prison as a convicted killer, I went to sleep on my feathered pillows and comfy mattress, with my dreams all about her sister! The first time I fell in love with Jemma Watkinson, it was just for a fleeting moment, the second time, two years later, I vowed it would be forever.

Richie

As I entered Mr.Davenport's office, he stood up, walked around his desk and came towards me with an outstretched right hand. We shared a firm handshake and exchanged pleasantries.

"Hello again, Mr.Davenport!"

"Richie! How good to see you! Please take a seat. How are you?"

Under the circumstances it seemed a strange question. Given three weeks had passed since my operation, I was returning to see Mr.Davenport to hear the news from him about my state of health following blood tests and microscopic examinations of my lumpy, extracted bollock.

"I'm very well, thanks!" I replied, hoping that Mr.Davenport would not be following this with a pantomime, 'Oh no you're not!'

"Good! Good! Stitches come out OK?"

"They oozed a bit, but they were fine."

"So how's the groin now?"

"It feels perfect. It was very sore for a while, but its all good now."

'Get to the point, Mr.Davenport!' I thought, 'get to the point!'

"Excellent. Obviously you know why we are here today…"

It was a rhetorical question, but I gave an answer anyway.

"Yes, to review the results."

Surprisingly enough, I wasn't there to play tiddlywinks!

"Absolutely and I'm sure you don't want me to beat around the bush, so I want to tell you straight away that it's very positive…."

'Great!' I thought, "very positive" sounded a whole lot better as a starting gambit than 'I'm sorry there's no easy way of saying this…'

"Mr. Gray, the pathologist," Mr.Davenport continued, "confirmed, as we had thought all along, that it was indeed testicular cancer that we were dealing with."

Not very positive so far, I thought, although at least my testicle and spermatic cord had been taken out for a reason. I would have felt more than a little aggrieved if it had just turned out to be a boil!"

"The good news though," Mr.Davenport went on, "is in relation to the blood tests. Remember me telling me you that there were chemicals in your blood that gave us an indication of whether there were cancerous cells? Well, following the operation, your bloods are no longer indicating the presence of these chemicals, as they had prior to the operation. My concerns had always centred on the fact that, due to the delay between your initial awareness of a lump and your subsequent trip to your GP's, that the cancer could have spread to the lymph nodes. The indication is that the cancer has not spread. We will obviously continue to monitor you, to ensure everything continues to remain positive, but the operation appears to have gone very well. Very well indeed!"

In all my days, that minute was the best minute of my life. To hear you have beaten cancer is the greatest feeling. I am sure people react in all types of ways when hearing this news, I am sure consultants get bombarded with hugs and kisses from patients, luckily for Mr.Davenport though, I left him alone. I was just positively beaming! It felt like the guillotine had stopped halfway down and the executioner had announced it would take many years to fix.

I wanted to make sure though, that I was not jumping to conclusions,

"So does that mean that I won't be needing chemotherapy?"

"Not at the moment, no, and hopefully it won't be needed at all."

The next few minutes passed with Mr.Davenport and I chatting like old friends about the regular check ups I would need, about my missing girlfriend, about Mr.Davenport's wife and three children and how his oldest, Giles, was a ski instructor in Morzine. I then thanked him, bade him farewell, left his office and excitedly ran around the hospital in search of a payphone like Anneka Rice on "Treasure Hunt", to ring home. The whole family had wanted to come with me to the hospital, to hang around outside the office like last generation expectant fathers, but I had banned the lot of them, wanting to deal with the initial verdict alone. I found a phone and there was no-one on it and no queue, it was definitely my lucky day. I punched in the digits and once I heard Mum's voice, the pips started to go and I had to force my ten pence in, like the red telephone boxes of old.

"Mum, it's me! They don't think its spread!! They think they've got the cancer out!"

I heard Mum telling everyone and the shrieks of delight from behind her and then she broke down with relief.

"Don't cry Mum! It's all good! It's not quite over but if this was a boxing fight between me and cancer, Mum, the referee would be stopping the fight and declaring me the winner!"

I love analogies! I did then and still do. That boxing analogy was wide of the mark though. I was a long way off winning the fight. A retrospective analogy was that the cancer was doing to me what Ali had done to George Foreman in the "Rumble In The Jungle" in '74. The cancer was lying back on the ropes, taking my punches and pretty much everything I could throw at it, letting me think it was beaten all ends up, before it finally retaliated with a sucker punch. Cancer was not my real opponent, like everyone else my real opponent was time. Time is the heavyweight champion of the world, it defeats everyone in the end.

I was certainly fighting though, back then, blissfully unaware of what lay ahead. I was definitely not being knocked out in Round One. That day, the day of the results, changed everything. The overwhelming feeling was now relief not worry or concern. There were still subsequent days, around that time, that I felt all was against me, especially during Jemma's trial, but on the whole, moments became more precious, life became more precious, my family, even Jim, became more precious and sentimentality reigned. I hugged the whole family more, kissed them more and always remembered to tell them that I loved them. The same was true the other way around with Caroline, Helen and Mum, in particular, never missing an opportunity to hug me. It was like my outlook on life had been myopic and someone had given me glasses. You don't always remember to wear them but when you do everything is crystal clear – life is short and fragile, make the most of every healthy minute.

Jemma

I served twenty one months in Her Majesty's Prison, Styal. Originally built as an orphanage back in the nineteenth century, to house destitute children from the Manchester area, it was now home for the morally destitute. It was certainly not the type of place Judith Chalmers would have covered on "Wish You Were Here"! As much as I would have liked to see it, I just could not see a bronzed Judith and her television crew, waking up in a cell and inviting her ten million viewers to handle stolen goods so they too would get the opportunity to stay there.

Styal was a female only prison originally opened for young offenders in the early 1960s, but by the time I arrived it accommodated female prisoners of all ages. During my time there, about a fifth of the time, I had a cell to myself which was great as I had peace and quiet, the rest though was time spent with the type of people you would cross the street to avoid, a lot of prostitutes and petty thieves, who were regularly self-harmers and drug addicts. I do not condone drug use and thankfully I have not taken a drug in my life and have no intention of doing so, but from a self-preservation perspective, in my twenty one months in Styal, life was easier when there was a drop. Sharing a cell with a druggie needing a fix was a lot harder than sharing a cell with a druggie who had just had one.

Bizarrely, Vomit Breath actually went up in my estimation whilst I was in Styal. She was a drunk, she lived for the weekend and found children to be an unwanted distraction, especially lippy kids like me, who she could only control towards the end by administering a beating but those beatings were nothing compared to a couple I received in Styal, just for a perceived dirty look or for the indecency of being "clean". As a rule, prisoners at Styal were a hugely fucked up bunch, dragged into prison from the dregs of society. The large majority of inmates were addicts of some description, some alcohol but mainly drugs. Some of them you just avoided speaking to, but the ones that I was able to speak to, would tend to tell tragic stories how their lives evolved into the messy state that led to their arrival at Styal. Some of the prostitutes checked into Styal like a businessman would check into a hotel, back every few months, as they had to walk the streets to fund their habit. Lots had been brought up in orphanages and foster homes, many had a mother who was an addict or a stepfather or family "friend" who liked nothing more than carrying out a regular sexual abuse habit on them. They had all had torturous lives and although middle class society may turn their noses up at them, it was hard not to sympathise as most of them had fallen off the rails because they had no moral guidance. Try digging your way out of hell with a spade made from ice.

Compared to this lot and their families, Vomit Breath was not exactly Mother Theresa or Florence Nightingale but she wasn't Attila the Hun either. Vomit Breath did not deserve to die, but then I suppose no-one had wanted to kill her, Kelly and I just wanted her to leave me alone.

Fifteen or so years later, I only tell people in my inner circle about my time at Styal. Others probably know because rumours spread at school gates like colds in a classroom, but the only people who hear it first hand, are those I implicitly trust. When I tell them I was wrongly convicted for a murder (or manslaughter) that I did not commit and that as a result I spent almost two years in Styal, the common reaction is to suggest that I should write a book about my experiences. This is one of the most ridiculous things I have ever heard! Who would read it? People who want to cheer themselves up?! Not a chance. My time at Styal was the lowest period of my life and I would rather forget every second of it than delve into it in great detail. I made no friends there, I partook in no drugs or sexual relations, although both were as accessible as chocolate at Willy Wonka's factory, I just tried to be friendly enough to avoid a beating but distant enough not to get dragged into any cliques. This was not "Porridge" or "Prisoner Cell Block H" where inmates were friendly, loveable characters who were just a little rough around the edges. This was Styal where inmates had been pushed out the normality tree at a tender age and then been beaten by every shitty stick in the surrounding forest.

Fifteen years on, I remember no names. Not the wardens, not the governors, not even the woman's who I shared a cell with for three months, although having thought about that one for an hour, I think it was a Glaswegian self-harmer called Rosemary. It is all just a blur. I hated the place, I hated the people but I do remember the one thing that did eat away at me most in my time at Styal. It was not the twenty hours a day in a cell, it was not the beatings or the vile food. The thing that destroyed me in my first six months at Styal was visiting time. Four weeks after being sentenced, I received a letter from Amy telling me that my Nan ("Tut") who had been so supportive, had passed away in Arrowe Park hospital, three days after having a massive stroke. She was 72. After that, for six months, no-one else came. They left me to rot. My first visitor, six months after "Tut's" death was Richie Billingham. When he came, I had to decide whether I wanted to thank him for coming or reach across the table and punch him for abandoning me there for six months!

Amy

Richie Billingham was fit. Fact. Some things in life are debatable. Is Da Vinci's 'Mona Lisa' a masterpiece? Do you to go to heaven when you die? Are ugly people attracted to other ugly people or are they just getting by? Of all sexual persuasions do gay men have the most sex? There are people who will debate opposing viewpoints on each of these, but try and find a girl from Ormskirk Grammar School in the late 1980's who thought Richie Billingham was unattractive and honestly, you would have more chance finding that elusive needle at harvest time.

When Richie started 'going out' with Kelly Watkinson, I must admit, at first, I found it really, really weird. It was a bit like Patrick Swayze going for Jennifer Grey in "Dirty Dancing" or Richard Gere going for Debra Winger in "Officer and a Gentleman". If you had the pick of absolutely anyone, why would you choose them?

This is not to say that Kelly wasn't stunning, she probably turned out to be the prettiest woman I have ever met, she has mesmerising green eyes, wonderful skin and a smile that would cost a Hollywood actress a small fortune, but at the time, I did not appreciate any of that. All I could see was Richie Billingham, the heartthrob of our year, who could have trounced Gere and Swayze in any "Best Looking Male" competition, was "going out" with my best mate, Jemma's, kid sister, Kelly. She was just a baby. Kelly was two years younger than us. At that point in your life, a school year is a gulf, two years is a chasm.

Truth be told, I always had a bit of a thing for Richie Billingham. There were other fit lads at school, Jemma went out with one called Billy McGregor and I "got off" with his mate, Eddie Garland, once, but they were full of it. Nothing mattered more than their reflection. Richie was different. He had the smouldering good looks, he looked like Jude Law did in his early twenties, when he was married to Sadie Frost, but he just did not have that teenage boy ego. Richie was mature beyond his years, a true gentleman, which made it seem even more bizarre that he was dating someone who looked like she'd only just returned from Candy Land on the 'Good Ship Lollipop'.

Years later, when I went to see Les Miserables, the character Eponine reminded me of myself with Richie. I certainly did not have scheming, penny pinching parents like Eponine, but I was totally besotted with Richie, just like Eponine was besotted with Marius and in return, their feelings were purely platonic.

I remember once being at a party over in Halsall, at Joey Birch's house and being in Joey's kitchen when Richie Billingham walked in. That night actually turned out to be the night I 'kopped off' with Eddie Garland and when Richie walked in, I was already halfway through Eddie's best lines on me. I cursed my luck. I hadn't realised Richie was coming and now I knew he was here, what did I do, blow Eddie out and go for the star prize or stick with what I had? I remember standing there, not really listening to what Eddie was saying, as I kept glancing past him to see what Richie was up to. I must have tried to catch Richie's eye one hundred times in that kitchen, but he did not look my way once, he just sat there talking to Kelly, so after twenty minutes or so, I decided, by chasing my dream, I could end up with nothing, so I cut my losses and "kopped" with Eddie.

Later on that night, I was standing in the bathroom queue, with Kelly and Jemma and Richie came and stood behind us. I was drunk but Jemma was far, far worse and we were trying to get her to the toilet quickly. I remember when Richie was behind us, I daren't turn around as Eddie Garland had had a pretty stubbly face and I had a red rash all over mine where his stubble had been brushing up against my face during our more passionate moments! I stood in that queue pleading that Richie did not to say anything which made me turn around to reveal my face, it would take my already limited chances down to zero! I remember trying to keep the conversation going with Jemma and Kelly, without pausing for a second's breath, in case Richie should start talking to us. Kelly started chatting to him at one point, but I just kept yapping to Jemma until Andrew Cullen came out the bathroom and Kelly and I bundled Jemma in.

All through school, Jemma and I had been like soul sisters, we spent all our time together, mainly Jemma coming over to my house, because her Mum was a bit of an alcoholic fruitcake, but we were pretty much inseparable. Instead of calling us by our names, some of the catty girls at school used to call us "Siamese". Instead of saying,

"What are Amy and Jemma doing?"

They would say,

"What are Siamese doing?"

It didn't really bother me, but it used to wind Jemma up good and proper! Jemma always used to have an edge to her, that 'too cool for school' swagger and I don't think she liked being seen as part of a double act, after all she probably had the strongest personality of all the girls in our year. Like most girls, I just wanted to be liked, but Jemma wasn't like that, she did not care tuppence if she was liked or not, I just think she wanted to be remembered.

I loved Jemma. I thought she was great. A lot of the girls in our year, could not stand the sight of her, but I thought she was fantastic. I wished I could be as confident as her, as witty, as good looking. Mr. Redworth, our History teacher, described her as Ormskirk's Audrey Hepburn.

I do remember being completely cheesed off with her once though. It was that night at the Birch's. I had inadvertently walked in on her in bed with some bloke. I didn't see who it was, as all I saw was Jemma's perfectly formed backside riding on top of an obscured figure. Jemma later claimed it was Richie and I just could not get the vision of them together out of my head. It was an unwanted mental picture that I would have to carry for the rest of my life, like a tattoo of Jesus on an atheists arm.

I had probably had a thing for Richie for eighteen months by then. I had never confessed this passion to Jemma though, simply because she was far better looking than me. I feared by letting Jemma know how I felt, I may draw her attention to him when her sights had always been on older boys. So, despite hoping beyond hope that they would never be an item, it looked like their beauty had drawn them together.

I felt sorry for Kelly too, she was all happy to have secured a date with Richie, blissfully unaware that he'd been screwing her sister. Jemma told her later though, not that night, I don't think, but a few days later.

My teenage friendship with Jemma was never quite the same after that. It was probably not really down to that night, as I am a forgiving sort, but more down to "O" level results. After "O" levels, I stayed on at "The Grammar" Sixth Form, whilst Jemma left school and started work at the Middlelands Bank in Moor Street. We kept in touch, but not long after starting at the bank, she started dating some real gorky looking older bloke called Ray. He must have felt like all his Saturdays had come at once to be dating a girl like Jemma when his mirror told only horror stories. Once he arrived on the scene though, Jemma changed and our friendship faltered. We went from speaking a couple of times a week on the phone and seeing each other every Friday and Saturday night, to just the occasional phone call. I felt let down and I wrongly blamed Ray for taking her away from me, which was daft really as Jemma would have kept in touch more had she really wanted to. We both just moved on. I started going to Disraelis, Bowlers and The Buck at weekends with my Sixth Form mates, whilst Jemma did whatever she did with "Triple Sacker", as I called him – he was too ugly to be a 'double bagger', three sacks over his head to hide that ugly mug seemed about right!

Communication between Jemma and I just faded away like an echo until one weekend in April 1989. The weekend of the Hillsborough disaster. I was in Ormskirk that Saturday afternoon, trying to pick up a bargain or two off the market, when I noticed there was a crowd gathering outside Rumbelows window. Being of curious nature, I wandered over to see what was on the TV that was grabbing everyone's attention.

"What's happening?" I asked some tall guy at the back who was peering over everyone else's heads with his three year old daughter on his shoulders.

"I can't really tell. It looks like something has happened at the Liverpool game. Not football violence though, more like too many people on the terraces in the Liverpool end."

I managed to squeeze my way into gaps and found myself virtually at the front. The scenes were awful, Liverpool fans, policemen, paramedics and the men from St.John's were working frantically to help the injured. People in the stand were hoisting up the fans underneath, whilst the aforementioned groups were running backwards and forwards on the pitch, carrying away the injured on advertising boards. You could see the crush but it was hard to comprehend why it could not be instantly resolved just by opening the gates at the front or making everyone at the back take a few steps backwards. A white ambulance weaved its way through to the crowds to the terrace were the main casualties were. I walked away concluding some people must have been seriously hurt. It was only later, when I was at home in the lounge with Mum, that I appreciated the gravity of the disaster. Moira Stuart was on the BBC News and announced that seventy four people had died. I remember my Dad walking in as the news started and correcting her as she said they died at the FA Cup Final and it was the semi-final and then he felt guilty about picking up on something so trivial amidst such an almighty tragedy and he just sat on the sofa, watched and cried. We all did.

I went out that night but Ormskirk was quiet. Understandably. Bucking the tranquility trend were Jemma's Mum and the rest of her pathetic bunch of loser mates, who I remember seeing as I walked past the bus station and up town towards Disraelis. They were all coming out of the Golden Lion shouting "F" words to each other as they crossed the road to the taxi rank, clippity clopping on their stilettos like barebacked two legged horses looking for a ride. I remember putting my head down and increasing my walking pace in the vain hope that Jemma's Mum would not see me, but she did. I walked on, feigning deafness now as well as blindness as Jemma's Mum shouted over,

"Amy! Amy!"

I kept going but heard her yell,

"Ignore me then, you cheeky little bitch! No wonder you're mates with my daughter. Stuck up pair of tarts you are! FUCK YOU!"

It's funny how life works, isn't it? I remember at Jemma's Mum's funeral thinking that they were her final words to me! I also remember thinking that in my own very small way, I was responsible for her death that night.If I'd have stopped to talk to Jemma's Mum, she would have more than likely been later in the queue at the taxi rank and then taken a different taxi to Southport, arriving at different places at different times, come across different people. Who knows, she may even have met some random horny bloke with no self-respect, who may have taken her back to his house or flat and then she would never arrived back home in the early hours of Sunday morning and fallen to her death down her stairs.

I could have saved her life that night. Do I wish I had? Not really. I suppose I could have saved Jemma from jail, that's my only regret. I could have stopped Jemma from going to jail.

I woke up late the following morning, probably around eleven. When I went downstairs, Dad was in the kitchen dining area, on our old circular kitchen table, with a mug of coffee ("World's Best Dad" mug) in the midst of several papers, tabloids and broadsheets, with several horrendous images of crushed faces against the perimeter fence at Hillsborough. It seemed impossible to comprehend how photographers could just stand there, taking photos, whilst people were crushed to death in front of their eyes. If I had been a photographer at Hillsborough that day, I would have put my camera down and gone to help in any way I could. Sometimes there is more to life than just doing your job.

"Jemma called," Dad announced without raising his head.

"What did she want?" I asked.

"I don't know. I just said you were asleep and that you would ring her back when you woke up."

I grabbed the phone, dialled Jemma's number, expecting her to just have phoned for a chat or to tell me it was all off between her and "Triple Sacker" or something equally trivial and bland. Once she uttered the words, "Vomit Breath's dead!", my world entered spin cycle mode and kept spinning for several months. I did not know whether I was coming or going. I was a middle class Ormskirk girl, my world was supposed to be about hair highlights and fingernails, not remand centres and murder trials. I grew up a lot over those next few months, but still managed to make a holy show of myself in front of Richie Billingham, which haunts me to this day, even more than that vision of Jemma's bouncing backside!

Richie

I was officially smashed. Jim was at the bar and I was trying to focus on him from the table but it was a struggle. Jim was debating some point or other with the barman and then they shook hands, Jim handed him a note and the barman then took the optic off the upside down vodka bottle with its right way up label and gave Jim a tray, two glasses and the bottle of vodka. I looked at the mass of empty pint glasses on our table and groaned as I watched Jim proudly zigzag across the room with his newly acquired booty. He plonked it on to our table, pushing the empty pint glasses to one side.

"We will die if we drink that!" I protested.

Jim, still standing, put his arms around my neck and leaned into me with his head, displaying a level of affection never previously seen between us.

"Richie, you have had a shitty time recently and its made me realise what you mean to me. Sometimes, just sometimes, you are a right royal pain in the butt, but most of the time, you are a great brother and I'm proud of how you have dealt with everything that's happened to you. Cancer, Kelly disappearing, it's been crap for you hasn't it, but things are getting better now, aren't they? It's all uphill from here."

Maybe I wasn't the most inebriated!

"You mean downhill, Jim!"

"I mean downhill." Jim agreed. "There was a time there that I thought everything could turn really nasty and I thought about what life would be like without a brother. We aren't the closest brothers in the world, we like different things, we move in different circles, I have a lot of sex, you don't because you are into the romantic side of things and its all flowers and love songs and things I don't get, but we're brothers and the thought of being without you, just did not bear thinking about."

Jim stopped wrapping himself around my neck, sat down and poured two generous measures of vodka into our glasses.

"So, I want to propose a toast," he said lifting his glass, "to a great brother. May your days of dodgy girlfriends, lumpy balls and bedwetting be behind you! Cheers!"

Jim and I clunked our glasses and downed our drinks. There was that nice burning sensation in my throat that straight vodka brings.

"You always bring it back to the bedwetting, don't you, Jim?!"

"It would be wrong not to," said Jim with a smile, "I play the role of annoying little brother very well!"

Not so much of the little! Jim was built like a tank.

We were in Disraeli's. A virtually empty Disraeli's. It was generally a popular spot in Ormskirk, amongst all ages under forty, but not at six o'clock on a Friday evening. Three hours later, you would hardly be able to move in there, but at six o'clock, it was all ours, other than a couple of estate agents having a pint together before heading home to their families.

Jim had planned this drinking session with almost military precision. He was on a "Study week" off from Sixth Form, prior to taking his "A" levels and I was on one of my three weeks a year off from Andy's Records, so Jim had suggested we head out together for an all day and all night session. This was a good idea in principle, but Jim was built like a gigantic bullfrog and I was built like a high jumper, so he was always going to have the capacity to out drink me!

Jim had planned our route. We had started at "The Cockbeck" in Aughton at twelve o'clock, had a couple of pints there, before walking up Town Green Lane to the appropriately named "Town Green Inn", which was over the road from my primary school, which meant all those memories of my halcyon days of kissing Anna Eccleston in the playground, came flooding back.

We squeezed in a few rounds in the "Town Green" whilst having a quick game of darts (Jim won as I could not keep my hand steady enough to hit the doubles), before heading up Parrs Lane to the "Dog & Gun" on Long Lane, passing the house where I had left the orange Matchmakers for Rachel Cookson when I was eleven. My brush with death and Kelly's disappearance had definitely made me look back at any romantic moments with nostalgia!

Several more pints followed at the "Dog and Gun" and despite already being halfway to Ormskirk town centre, we decided against making the rest of the pub crawl on foot and ordered a taxi to take us in to Ormskirk. Jim wanted to hit Disraeli's whilst it was quiet, once it busied up it was a bit too "trendy" for Jim and then he wanted to move on to "The Golden Lion", "The Railway", "The Windmill" (where I had dumped my stuff when I was doing my Wigan Road karaoke outside Kelly's bedroom window) and "The Ropers Arms". Thanks to me, we did not get any further than Disraeli's! Jim poured us another large vodka each.

"We are not drinking that whole bottle, Jim," I said, in what I would imagine would have been very slurred tones by then.

"Chill bro! I know that, but I paid twenty quid for the whole bottle, if we'd have just had single measures, we would have only been able to have had about six each for twenty quid!"

"Which would have been about five too many!"

"Come on, Richie!" said Jim making a poor attempt to give me a dead arm.

"We're celebrating!"

I spotted something.

"Jim, take me round there."

I pointed to the far side of the bar. There was an area of Disraeli's that was an extension to the main bar area, a conservatory of sorts with a plastic roof, white tiles and decked out in comfy sofas and soft cushions.

"Why?" Jim asked suspiciously.

"I need to have a sleep."

"Sleep! Richie, you can't sleep, we're celebrating!"

That was the second time in a minute Jim had mentioned the fact that we were celebrating, he knew I was on my knees and was trying to provide me with a motivation not to give in. He was wasting his breath!

"Jim, I need a sleep. Let me just have half an hour and I'll be raring to go!"

"No, you won't Richie! I share a room with you remember? I've seen what you are like when you have a drink! If you fall asleep now, that will be it, game over. Come on, Richie, drive hard! It's only six o'clock!"

"I can't Jim! I'm gone. Just give me half an hour! I promise you it will just be half an hour!"

I stood myself up and weaved my way to the far side of the bar, to the empty Conservatory. It was like I was being hypnotised, I just shut my eyes, put my head back and within seconds, I was asleep………..

"Is he OK?" a woman's voice asked, what seemed like seconds later although I knew it wouldn't be.

I recognised the voice, my eyes were still closed, but I recognised that voice.

"He's fine, just sleeping the drink off, we've been hard at it all afternoon and Richie has never been the best at holding his drink." Jim replied.

I could tell from the general buzz in Disraeli's that it was no longer six o'clock, I opened my eyes and stretched like it was first thing in the morning. I looked up to see Jim and Amy Perkins staring down at me.

"How are you feeling?" Amy asked in the tone of a post-operation nurse.

"Great!" I lied. I still felt drunk but 'ill' drunk not 'on top of the world' drunk.

"What time is it?" I asked despite having a watch on.

"Half past ten." Jim replied with a tone which hinted at more than a little bitterness.

"You're kidding me!"

"I wish I was, but straight up, it's half past ten!"

"I've been asleep for four and a half hours! What happened to waking me up after half an hour?!" I asked trying to shift the blame back to Jim.

"I kept trying to wake you up, Richie and you kept telling me to piss off!"

"You did!" Amy agreed.

Perhaps to level things out, Jim piped up with,

"Amy was just telling me, she's heard from Kelly."

Jim said this in such a matter of fact way, as though he thought I probably wouldn't really be interested, when he knew damn well I would be. He said it as though it would have had little bearing on my life, like if him and Amy had been discussing England's recent performances in the "World Netball Championship".

"Did you hear, we won the netball today against Australia, eight-four, the goal shooter scored six points, the goal attack two?"

In reality, I was about as interested as I would be in the Ashes score or the World Cup Final score in football (if I had been locked in a cupboard whilst England were in the final). I was desperate to hear more. I shook my head from side to side like a rain soaked dog in a monsoon, in an attempt to sober up and then stood myself up like a labyrinthitis sufferer.

"You've heard from Kelly?" I enquired of Amy.

"Yes. Last week. She phoned up."

"Where did she phone from?"

"Singapore."

"Singapore?"

"It's in Asia."

"Amy, I know where it is, I just don't know what Kelly's doing there!"

"I don't know either," Amy explained, "she just phoned last Sunday afternoon.

She didn't have much money, so I only spoke to her for two minutes."

"Is she OK?"

"She said she was fine."

"Why is she in Singapore? That's just crazy, she's seventeen years old, on her own in Singapore."

"I've no idea what made her go there, she just rang to see what the situation was with Jemma."

I could feel a disaster coming.

"Amy, please tell me you did not tell her that Jemma has gone to jail for three years!"

Amy pulled a face.

"Well what was I supposed to do, Richie?! Tell Kelly that Jemma got off?! Just suppose Kelly had headed home on the basis that she thought the coast was clear and was then arrested the second she stepped on British soil, for being accessory to murder. How do you think I would feel then?"

My heart sank. Amy had a point, but it was not a point that I wanted to hear.

"She'll never come back now."

"Richie, that's not my fault! She asked me a question and I gave her a straight answer."

I was annoyed with Amy, or to be brutally honest, I was just drunk and annoyed so it was convenient to blame Amy.

"Why didn't you tell me last week that she'd phoned you?"

"I haven't seen you."

"Ever heard of a phone?"

"I'm telling you now, aren't I?"

"A week too late."

"A week too late for what, Richie? What could you have possibly done in the last week?"

"I could have stopped thinking she was dead for starters!"

Things were getting heated. Jim decided to bale.

"Right," he said poking his head between the warring factions, "I'm going to leave you lovebirds to sort out your differences. I hate it in here. I'm heading down to 'The Lion'."

"Hang on!" I said. "Is this not supposed to be my celebration night?"

"Yes, but given you have just left me alone for the last four hours in a bar I hate, whilst you slept the drink off, I really don't think you are in a position to get too mad with me, if I slope off to somewhere I actually fit in."

Jim was right. Goths and Disraeli's were not a great mix.

"You're welcome to come with me if you like."

For some reason, I looked at Amy, as if she was now part of our crowd. Amy shook her head.

"I'd rather stop here. My friends are here."

"Ok. Thanks but no thanks, Jim. We'll stop here."

"No problemo. See you back home, Richie. Nice speaking to you, Amy."

Jim kissed her hand and headed off. The distraction provided by Jim gave me ample time to calm down.

"Sorry, Amy. Kelly's been gone forever, I'm just annoyed that she rang you and not me. It's not your fault."

"It's alright, I understand. You need to move on now though, Richie. Kelly will come back when she's ready, the file on her Mum's murder is probably closed now that Jemma has been convicted anyway, but I just didn't want to keep anything from her. From your perspective, you can't just put your whole life on hold, waiting for that day. If she had wanted to, she could have phoned you, but for whatever reason, she is choosing not to."

Amy was right. I knew she was right, but I was struggling to move on. I went to the bar and bought myself a pint of blackcurrant and soda and Amy a glass of red wine. We then stood and chatted until last orders. Amy was out with a load of her old school mates, my old adversary from "Catch A Boy, Kiss A Boy", Fay Williams, was amongst them, but Amy hardly spoke to the rest of the girls, as she seemed content to just have a good old chinwag with me. We were kicked out of Disraeli's by twenty past eleven and given neither of us could be bothered stopping at the Acropolis fish and chip shop, I suggested I walk Amy up to her house. Amy's house was virtually on my walk home and she was a bit of company for me as I continued the slow sobering up process. The alternative companion for the two mile walk home would have been Jim, but I had no inclination to search for him as he was a big boy and would find his own way home, even if found his way into a ladies bedroom first.

As we walked up Prescot Road, Amy and I continued to chatter away comfortably. I found some girls difficult to speak to as they were pretentious and conversations became banal, but Amy was just a really pleasant, 'girl next door' type. There were no airs and graces about her, she was friendly, warm hearted and quick witted. We talked about the trial and how we imagined Jemma would be finding life in jail and discussed our reasons for not visiting her. Amy said that having visited Jemma at Risley, she did not think she would cope emotionally visiting her at Styal. Instead of being the tower of strength that Jemma needed, Amy said she would just be a blubbering wreck. She was racked with guilt for not going, especially as Jemma and Kelly's grandmother had recently passed away. This meant no-one was currently visiting Jemma, which was appalling.

"What about you, Richie?" Amy queried. "You visited Jemma in Risley and you went to the trial, how come you have suddenly stopped visiting too?"

I lied and explained that when I had visited Jemma in Risley, I had slowly developed the impression that I was not welcome, that I was only her sister's ex-boyfriend after all.

"I'm sure she'd have been delighted to see you." Amy said. "I'm sure she'd have been delighted to see anyone!" she suggested, before apologising for the way that had sounded!

I felt uncomfortable lying to Amy, but did not want to share the truth with her. The truth being that I had kept away as I felt Jemma and I were becoming too attached and I needed some time to work out what I really wanted. The problem was that I wanted to either be with Jemma or be with Kelly and neither of them was exactly readily available at this point in time.

Once we reached Amy's house, she asked me in for a coffee, 'to warm me up for the rest of the journey home'. I ventured in and her little Cocker Spaniel, Daisy, came to greet us, wagging her little tail, ten to the dozen. As I got down on my hands and knees in the hallway to stroke Daisy, Amy's dressing gown clad parents arrived to greet Amy and check that she had had a good night. They were a "touchy feely" family, without, I imagined, a cancer ordeal forcing them into it.

On reflection, I should have seen what was coming, but I did not. At that age, I could quite easily have shared a single bed with two naked Page Three girls without realising sex was on the cards.

Amy's parents soon went to bed and left Daisy, Amy and I in their lounge. I should have realised something was afoot when Amy sat herself down ever so close to me on a massive settee. I should have understood that the intent gazes I was receiving from Amy and the sympathetic advice to forget Kelly and move on, were all leading somewhere, but I was painfully oblivious. The penny only dropped when Amy put her hand on my knee as I was talking about Kelly's disappearance. I was more than a little uncomfortable with that, so, with my coffee finished, I began to make my excuses.

"Thanks very much for the coffee, Amy. I've really enjoyed speaking to you tonight, but I suppose its time I'd better get going. Let you get to bed."

Amy just pounced like a venus fly trap on an arachnid. Before I had chance to move from the settee, she pinned me down and started kissing me. I pulled away for a second. This was surreal, I had not had a romantic or passionate thought about Amy in my life. She was pretty in a pleasant way, but when you were friends with Jemma Watkinson, it went largely unnoticed.

It was at this point that I should have walked away. I should have apologised to Amy for giving her the wrong impression and walked straight out the door, but that is not what happened! I was a sex starved, drunken teenager who's girlfriend had turned invisible, nine months earlier and had not seen, felt or tasted a vagina since. I wasn't cheating on anyone.

"Sod it!"

Recalling this moment, I still have doubts whether I just said it in my head or out loud, but I do know subsequently, once that thought had crossed my mind, I dived back into that tongue sandwich.

Ignoring Daisy's presence and the fact that Amy's parents were only a drink of water away from coming back down the stairs, we began hurriedly undressing each other. My prosthetic testicle had its first public outing, although I don't think Amy noticed it, as her attention was drawn to the tip of the iceberg rather than the bits below the water. Five minutes after I had made my excuses, I found myself on my hands and knees naked on Amy's Mum and Dad's lounge carpet, pulling Amy's knickers off her ankles, as she lay now naked on the floor. Just as those knickers flew over her parents settee, like a horse over Beecher's Brook, I came to my senses. It was as if the hypnotist had clicked his fingers and I had come out of a trance, to find myself naked on stage with a woman I had never met, with six thousand people looking on. This was all wrong, I had to go.

"Amy", I said to my naked companion, who was laying, legs slightly parted and eyes closed, on the lounge floor, "I'm going to have to stop."

It was Amy's turn to be embarrassed. She sat up looking like she needed to grow an extra arm, as three arms were necessary to cover her two breasts and her pubic hair. Amy was understandably confused.

"What's the matter?" she asked.

"It feels wrong." I explained.

"It's just a lay," Amy replied, revealing that she would have gone the whole hog if I hadn't brought things to an early conclusion.

At this point, I had three choices.

Firstly, I could have taken the cowards option and blamed the whole thing on my testicular cancer. This was a lie, but would have gained me a huge amount of sympathy in Amy's eyes. I could have just said I wasn't ready for this after my operation and cancer ordeal. This was an automatic forgiveness pass.

Second choice was to just forget we had ever stopped, return my now less excited penis, back to its former glory and make the most of this rare opportunity or thirdly I could tell the truth!

Amazingly, I told the truth, not the truth about the cancer and the orchidectomy, just the truth about how I was feeling. These days, when I play the "Soundtrack to my life," over in my head as I relive moments, this moment is definitely Billy Bragg's "The Price I Pay." If you've heard it, you will know what I mean, if you haven't its about loving a lost lover too much to move on.

"Amy, it's not just a lay," I confessed, "it feels like I am cheating on Kelly!"

Amy was dressing herself again by this point. She had not seen her knickers leaping over the settee, so had slipped her trousers back on without sending a search party out for her knickers. It was not an appropriate time for her to be crawling around on all fours saying "Where's my knickers?! Where's my knickers?!"

I had stripped her of a certain amount of dignity and that would have just been the final straw. I started putting my boxer shorts on as she responded.

"Richie, for all you know, Kelly could have had a new boyfriend for the last six months. You are not being fair to yourself."

"But I was happy with Kelly."

They were the words I said, but I remember thinking how horrible they sounded as soon as they came out my mouth. To me, they sounded glib.

"You'll be happy again, if you could just move on."

"I'm sorry, Amy. I'm just not ready to move on."

I gathered the rest of my clothes together, put them on and Amy also dressed herself. I remember having a sneaky last glance at her breasts, they were attractive breasts, similar to Kelly's, pert and properly rounded, perhaps a little smaller than Kelly's but pleasant. If Kelly had been out my system I would have been suckled in like a hungry baby! My desire was now so low, it felt like I had released my bodily fluids on that carpet already. The continued process of getting dressed was carried out in an awkward silence.

Once dressed, I spoke,

"I'm going, Amy. I'm so sorry this got awkward."

Amy moved towards me. I was dubious about where this was leading but Amy just took my hands in hers. I was a coward and a procrastinator, Amy was quite simply a lovely person. Lovely people struggle in this world, they find the good in people less worthy than themselves, who in turn find fault in their perfection.

"Richie, we were friends before this, weren't we?"

"Yes."

"And we'll be friends after this too. If you want me to, we'll forget this ever happened. If you want this to happen again, but to actually happen next time, let me know."

That was twice in one night, Amy had pointed out her sexual availability to me. This time though, she was handing me the key to the chastity belt. I knew I would not be using it.

Just as I was making my way to Amy's front door, I heard Amy mumble something behind me. I thought I heard her right, but not understanding, I turned around.

"What was that?"

I knew the comment was obviously not intended for me, which made it all the more interesting.

"Doesn't matter." Amy said, turning back to the crimson shade she had been in before, during the heat of passion.

"Go on! Tell me!" I pushed pleasantly.

"I just said to myself 'Phantom Fucker'!"

I thought that was what she had said but was confused by its meaning.

"Eh?"

"Don't worry about it, Richie. It's a private joke between Jemma and I."

"You should go and visit her and share it face to face, Amy. It's not right her being in there and no-one visiting."

"I will, Richie, I definitely will," Amy said as she led me out the door,

"I'm sure she'd have a chuckle at my expense."

I had no idea what Amy was on about but was still too drunk to care. I set off home thinking things over and cringing to myself from time to time, screwing my face up to reflect my torture. How complicated was I making things?!

First, I fell in love with Kelly, who ran away to Holland then Singapore after pushing her mother down the stairs and killing her. Then, I developed an interest in her sister Jemma, who has now been jailed for the manslaughter Kelly committed. Finally, as the icing on the cake, I find myself naked in the lounge of Jemma's best friend, Amy, despite the fact that I had never been physically attracted to her in my entire life! Add into the mix, a cancerous and subsequently removed scrotum and it all adds up to one fine mess!

All I could conclude from the whole sorry state of affairs was that I wanted Kelly back. I remember breaking out into another Billy Bragg song that night on the journey home. A song called "The Only One" as that was what I wanted Kelly to be and by the time I reached home, I felt in utter turmoil. I had let Kelly slip through my fingers and I knew if I didn't get her back, I would regret it for the rest of my life.

Amy

"Come on big boy! Come to Amy!"

I closed my eyes, lay back on the carpet, the soft hairs tickling my naked back and told myself the more I relaxed the less this would hurt. There were too many things running around in my mind though to allow me to chill. The day before had been day five of my period and I would have just died of shame if Richie had been witness to the last of the blood. Blood was fear one, fear two was pregnancy. Should I stop before we start and suggest he put a condom on? Would Richie sort that out himself? If he didn't, could I get pregnant at this time of month? Claire Rayner was always saying no time in the month was safe, but the girls at school reckoned if you had just been "on" then it would fine. I trusted Claire Rayner more, but since I had leaped on Richie, we had just kissed and tore at each others clothes in silence, would it ruin the moment now if I spoke?

All this was going around in my head, when Richie suddenly started breathing like a Doctor had a stethoscope to his chest. On his second deep exhale, he came out with,

"I'm going to have to stop."

The first thing I thought was that he must have "come". Maybe, during all the passionate kissing and fondling, he had got himself over excited, overheating and then completely refusing to do any further work like a car engine in a traffic jam.

'This is going to be embarrassing', I remember thinking, 'especially for Richie!'

I opened my eyes and thought I had best keep my own frustrations under wraps.

"What's the matter?" I asked.

"It feels wrong." Richie replied.

What did he mean? Did he mean his big 'attention seeker' felt wrong? It had certainly looked alright before! I had never really seen a male 'attention seeker' in its proudest form before. I had felt a few in the darkness, but I had only seen my brother's at bath time when we were really little and I certainly had no recollection of it looking like Richie's just had!

Is that what he meant by 'it felt wrong' or did he mean, as I suspected he did, that it 'felt wrong', as he was still obsessing about Kelly and therefore rolling around my Mum and Dad's lounge naked did not seem like the best laid plan.

'Come on Richie!' I thought, 'This is my best ever chance of losing my virginity, don't bloody ruin it! You just don't understand how much I need to lose my virginity to you!'

"It's only a lay!" I said as if I was ever so laid back about the whole thing! I wasn't! This was a momentous occasion for me, or at least it could have been, if Richie had not backed out! Why was this happening? Boys always said that it was alright for girls, we could just have sex whenever we wanted it, we just had to make ourselves available. How much more available could I be?! I was laying naked on the floor with my legs as wide apart as a labouring mother in stirrups! I started to feel humiliated and within seconds I felt so small that Thumbelina would have loomed large over me.

Richie's next two sentences confirmed my virginity was to remain intact.

"Amy, it's not just a lay to me. It feels like I am cheating on Kelly."

At this point, I could have thrown a wobbly, accused Richie of unnecessarily stringing me along, but I was still clinging to the hope that once he got over Kelly, Richie might still want to be with me, so I just remained all sweetness and light. I had had too much to drink in Ormskirk though, which resulted in the 'think before speaking' switch in my brain turning itself off.

My first 'faux pas' was to pretty much say to Richie that although he had not wanted to nail me there and then, if he ever wanted to, he could just come around and do it.

I'm sure I did not put it quite as tactlessly as that, but I remember standing there cringing thinking,

'Amy, you are just making yourself look like a desperate slut! You should be playing hard to get, not "Open All Hours!"'

My second 'faux pas' was saying my drunken mutterings too loud. As Richie was all dressed and ready to go home, I was looking at him and thinking 'This Man Is Gorgeous!', I must be the only girl in the world who could manage to get both myself and Richie naked and still not have sex. Then, I thought,

'Hang on a minute! Maybe not! Jemma did that too! Back at the Birch's party! I think she managed to get further than me, but Richie still fled before everything got going! What was it Jemma called him again?

Dracula Dick? No, that wasn't right.

Fucking Frankenstein? No.

GOT IT!

Phantom Fucker!!!'

Problem was, when I said the right answer I meant to just mumble it to myself but I've always struggled to gauge my decibels one I have had a drink and through drunken excitement that I still had an active brain, I must have mumbled it far too loud.

Richie, who at this point was heading for the door, swivelled around with an offended look on his face and asked me what I had just said. I think he thought I was insulting him, as he probably only heard the word 'fucker', but I was just delighted to have remembered Jemma's nickname for the man who had crept into her room that night at the Birch's. Jemma had never been 100% sure it was Richie, but after this I would have bet my mortgage on it, if I had not lived at my parents at the time!

I made some lame excuse to Richie about it being a private joke between Jemma and I, which he did not appear to believe for a second, but we made some awkward, forced conversation before he finally left.

As soon as Richie headed home, I closed the door and slumped onto the floor like an exhausted marathon runner, one step beyond the finishing line. I knew every time I saw Richie from that day forth, he would not just think, 'Lovely girl Amy!', he would think,

'Lovely girl Amy, I've seen her boobs and fluffy bits!', which was just the most embarrassing thought!

As I lay on the floor, tearfully slapping the hall tiles with my fists, my Dad must have come down the stairs to see what all the commotion was about. Being face down horizontal, I wasn't aware of his presence, so I am not sure how long he witnessed my theatrical outburst for, but by the time he spoke, he had sat himself down, halfway down the stairs.

"Has that boy done something to upset you, Amy?"

It was more a case of what he had not done rather than had done, but there was no way I was going to tell Dad that. Still horizontal, looking like a drunken swimmer in an empty pool, I looked up at Dad. I knew how stupid I must look, so pulled myself up and dusted myself off. Being found fornicating in the lounge with Richie would probably only have been slightly more embarrassing.

"It's not Richie, Dad, it's me."

"What's you?"

"I've done something to upset myself. I keep chasing a dream and somehow I keep managing to turn it into a nightmare."

"How do you mean, love?"

"I fall for lads that are out of my reach, Dad. The one's that everyone wants. Why would someone like Richie want to 'go out' with someone like me? He's out of my league? I need to start looking for someone at my own level."

"And what do you consider to be your level, Amy?"

"Average".

Dad smiled. That knowing smile that parents do, which says 'you're so young!'

"Amy, in life, don't ever just 'make do'. Now I'm not saying don't compromise, because you will have to do that in life, but keep chasing dreams, because one day they will come true."

"That's not how it feels right now, Dad."

Having managed to compose myself temporarily, I was now staving off tears again.

"Amy, you will have heard the saying 'you have to kiss a lot of frogs before you find your prince'."

"Of course I have!"

"Well, that's probably how you feel right now, that there's a horribly long journey for you before you meet Mr.Right, but that is not necessarily true. I found my princess, your mother, very early in my adult life. She was my first real girlfriend. We started 'courting' when we were only seventeen. We met at "The Cavern Club" in Liverpool, one night at a Rory Storm & The Hurricanes gig. Their drummer, Ringo Starr, ended up in "The Beatles."

I had heard this story a million times before.

"I know, Dad. You had to borrow a shilling off Mum to get home and Mum always says it's the best shilling she ever spent and you say that was the dearest loan in the history of banking as you borrowed a shilling and it cost you a fortune!"

"That's right love, but the point is, I did not kiss a lot of frogs and you may not have to either. Your prince may be just around the corner or it may be you don't find him for a while yet, but I'll tell you something, Amy, you certainly don't need to drop your standards, because which ever young man ends up marrying you, will be the luckiest man alive. You are beautiful, Amy, inside and out, and there aren't that many people in life, who are that blessed. There is no-one less average than you."

I headed upstairs to bed, kissing my Dad on the way up and giving him an almighty hug. I didn't believe a word he said, it was just 'Dad speak', but the reason that I pretty much remember every word he said, was because he turned out to be right!

The following afternoon, the phone rang. Mum and Dad had taken Daisy to Formby beach for a run around the sand dunes. My Mum had already had a quiet word with me that morning about leaving knickers around the house, as Daisy had apparently found a pair somewhere and Dad had had to pull them from the back of her throat as she had been choking! Martin was out too, at some geek convention, so I answered.

"Hello".

"Is that Amy?" the voice of my future husband asked. I recognised it vaguely but could not place it.

"Yes."

I was going to ask who it was but I figured if I continued to let him speak, I'd be able to figure it out.

"I just wanted to ring to tell you that my brother is an absolute fool."

Nope, still no idea. Maybe if I established who the brother was.

"Who's an absolute fool?"

"Richie! He told me what happened last night and I told him he was a complete and utter idiot!"

I blushed so hard that I thought my cheeks would explode with the heat. I hoped Richie had not told Jim explicitly what had happened last night. Maybe he had. Maybe Jim was phoning to cash in his brother's "Shag Me Whenever You Want" voucher.

"He told you what happened? What exactly did he tell you, Jim?"

"That's between me and my brother!"

"Not if its about me, it's not! I just want to hear whether my version of events and your brother's are the same, that's all."

"Well, after I left you I went down to "The Golden Lion" and then to "The Ropers" as they sometimes have lock ins and I was in the mood for a few beers. When I got down to "The Ropers" though, there were about six pensioners there and that was about it, so I headed home. I saw a few mates at the Acropolis though, so stopped and had a bit of a chat. Richie made it back before me, but only just as he was sitting having a cup of coffee, when I came in.

I asked him if straight away if anything had happened between the pair of you. I know the two of you were having a row when I was in Disraelis, but it was a real husband and wife type row, a row between people with feelings for each other, so that was why I had made a discreet exit. I had sensed some sort of chemistry."

"You're obviously a good brother."

"Not always, I'm not! Richie could tell you a few stories!"

"So did he tell you a few stories about me?"

"Not really. He just said you had a bit of a snog and then he regretted it, because he's still got the hots for Kelly. I told him he was mad, you're much cuter!"

Jim was massaging my ego, but I knew he was building up to asking me out, he wasn't telephoning to check my lips were OK. I began to quickly think of excuses. There was no way I was going on a date with Jim Billingham. There were countless reasons. He was ugly and I was a bit of a looks snob. He dressed weird, like a 1920's throwback. Jim looked and dressed like 'Fat Sam' from Bugsy Malone! He was a school year younger than me, which felt like ten years and finally, and probably most importantly, I was madly in love with his brother. All told this was a lethal rejection cocktail.

"Thanks Jim!"

"Amy, I'm not being complimentary here just for the sake of it, I'm dealing in fact. You are an incredibly fine woman and you need someone who would love you and respect you for the wonderful specimen that you are!"

I knew it! I knew he was angling for a date!

"Jim, are you suggesting to me that you could be that man?!"

"I certainly think that I have all the qualities you need, Amy. I may not be blessed with my brother's good looks, but I make up for it in personality. If you come on a date with me, Amy Perkins, I guarantee you will not be disappointed."

I smiled. Jim was certainly not lacking in confidence!

"I may not be disappointed, Jim, but I'm afraid you might be. I'm not going on a date with you."

"Give me one good reason why, Amy."

I could have given him a hundred, but they would have seemed very cruel.

"I just don't want to!"

"That's not a good reason, Amy! Just one date. Why not? If you hate it, just don't have a second date!"

"You're too young for me!"

"One year, Amy. When you're ninety, I'll be eighty nine!"

Cruelly, I remember thinking that with a body like his, he'd have a heart attack long before he got to eighty nine!

"I'm happy single."

"So?! I had an Auntie Elsie who apparently said in the early 1970's that she was not going to swop to a colour television because she was happy with her black and white one! Once she got a colour one, she realised what she'd been missing!"

"What's that got to do with anything?"

"I'm just saying I could put some colour into your life!"

"No matter what I say, Jim, you are not going to accept it as a good reason!"

"Absolutely not!"

"So, basically what you are saying is, that you are going to force me to go on a date that I really don't want to go on, by persisting when any normal bloke would just take the rejection on the chin and slope off feeling sorry for himself."

"Amy, let's get a few things straight. Firstly, I am not a 'normal' bloke. I am unique.I am not part of the herd, nor would I ever want to be. I do things that I want to do. Linking in with that, I wouldn't dream of forcing you into doing something that you don't want to do, all I am trying to point out, is that your decision making process is flawed. If you want to come on a date with me – "great!", if you don't, then don't, but don't turn me down because of a twelve month age gap or pretend you would rather be single than have a boyfriend or because my external features aren't as pleasing on the eye as my brother's, that just makes you look shallow."

"Ok."

"OK you'll come on a date with me?!"

"No, I was just agreeing not to be shallow."

"So, will you come on a date with me? Just a drink in Ormskirk, tonight. It doesn't have to be Ormskirk, it could be Southport or Liverpool or Preston or Wigan, or wherever you like."

"Hawaii?"

"As long as you're paying!"

"Jim, another reason I don't want to go on a date with you, is because you have a reputation for trying to screw anything that moves!"

There was an element of irony in that statement. The previous night, I had not exactly been trying to avoid sex myself. At least I was selective though.

"Amy, I am not going to insult you by denying that I have a past, but that's all it is, a past. It would be far, far easier for me to ignore your obvious charms, go back out into Ormskirk tomorrow night and manipulate some Edge Hill College student who is just looking to feed her libido now that she's moved away from Mummy and Daddy's.

I'm not looking for easy though, Amy. I want to go on a date with you, as I think you are the only girl I have ever met who I truly believe I could fall in love with."

That line got me. Despite the age gap, despite his looks,despite who his brother was…that line got me. No-one had singled me out as the special one before and I knew he was genuine. There was just one more thing I had to check.

"If you feel as much about me as you say you do, why did you not stick around last night? Why did you leave me with your brother?"

"Richie's had a rough time recently. He deserves to have someone great in his life. He is the only person in the world I would have left you with last night. If it had been anyone else, I swear on my mother's life, I would have stuck around and fought tooth and nail for you."

Jim had bought himself a date. I fully expected it to be only the one date, but it wasn't. That night, we went to the Saracens Head in Halsall. A quiet pub next to the Leeds-Liverpool canal. Not exactly where you would expect an eighteen and nineteen year old couple to go, but Jim did say he was unique! I found Jim charming and very, very funny, but I did not feel any sort of spark. He just seemed to manage to do enough to get another date. We didn't kiss until our fifth date and I don't think I fell in love with Jim until about our twentieth date, but fell in love I did.

Seventeen years later, we are married with four amazing daughters and I have not stopped loving that crazy man for one second in our thirteen years of marriage. Every day is different with Jim, I wake up every morning excited that I get to spend my time with him and the daughters that we have jointly created.

I only regret one thing. That thing being that I ever had feelings for my brother-in-law! Richie was so not my type! I love him dearly as a brother, but wish I'd gone home with Jim that night in Disraelis and Richie had been the one that had moved on elsewhere! I suppose it was all fate though and everything happened the way it did for a reason. I just found it hard to accept that the best man at my wedding and the godfather of our first daughter, Gracie, saw me naked before my husband!

My Dad was right that night. Jim often tells me he's the luckiest man alive and I always tell him we are the luckiest couple. I didn't drop my standards, I raised the bar and no-one in the world could have sailed over it like Jim. The years have been kind to him and he is trimmer now than he was when we first met but he would still not win any competitions based on looks alone. Who cares?! Looks fade as personality continues to shine and anyway, these days Jim seems to gorgeous to me. He is an entertaining, caring, compassionate, intellectual man and I still burst with pride every time I introduce him as my husband.

Richie

"Richie, you want ME to lend YOU money?"!
Dad could not contain a smirk.
"ME!"
"Dad, I'm just asking whether you could lend me any money, what's so funny about that?"
"I'll tell you what's funny about that! This whole family spends it's whole together time giving me stick about not being able to look after money and now you are asking me if I will lend you some! Who else in the family have you already asked?"
I looked at him sheepishly.
"Everyone." I mumbled.
"So no-one else will lend you anything, so as a last resort, you come to your old Dad, eh?"
This conversation was taking place in the garden shed at the bottom of our garden. I had spotted Dad sneaking out there to read his "Racing Post" and thought it would be a good moment to approach him, before the losing bet rather than after. The fact that he was hiding in a shed, to read his Racing Post, indicated that most previous experiences of betting had not proved fruitful.
"Dad, I know you never have any money, but I thought I might as well ask."
"What do you need it for?"
"I want to go and find Kelly. I know round about where she is?"
"Where?"
"Singapore."
"SINGA-BLOODY-PORE! I thought you were going to say Manchester or somewhere like that! Not SINGA-BLOODY-PORE!"
"It wasn't my idea for her to go there."
"Yes, but you're the daft pillock who's going to follow her out there, like a lost puppy! How much is that going to cost you to get there?"
"In total, I reckon I'll need a grand."
"And how much have you got?"
"I had £300 myself and….."
Dad interrupted.
"How much have the rest of the family given you?"

"Caroline said she can give me £50."

"And the rest of them?"

"They're all skint."

"So you'd need £650 from me. Hang on whilst I write you a cheque!"

Dad motioned as if he was going to go in search of a chequebook. I started to get excited.

"Really?"

"No, of course not you daft git! Where would I get £650 from?!"

"I thought you may have had a win on the horses."

"The most success I've had on the horses recently, Richie, was when Doncaster was waterlogged and I got my stake money back!"

I thought as much. Tramps held on to money longer than Dad.

"Never mind," I said.

Dad realised I was disconsolate and stopped joking.

"So there's no way you could get there with £350?"

"I might be able to get a flight, but then there's food and lodgings to pay for when I'm there. I many not be able to find Kelly straight away."

"Right."

Dad had a little goatee beard at this point. He ran his fingers through it.

"What if I were to invest the money for you?"

"Invest it? That would need to be a good investment to go from £350 to £1000 within weeks."

"It could go from £350 to £1000 in the space of forty minutes. It could also be worth nothing in forty minutes too."

Now I understood.

"Dad, are you suggesting I put the whole £350 on a horse?"

"Not exactly!"

"Good! You just said you were having no luck and then I thought you were going to try to spread your bad luck to me! I've enough of my own, thank you!"

"Not one horse. Two horses! A short priced double!"

"Bloody hell! What sort of father are you?"

"Look son! Can you get to Singapore and stay there for £350? No, you can't. So, as things stand, that three hundred and fifty quid of yours is pretty worthless. Now if you gamble it, you'll either win and everyone is happy or alternatively you will lose and you won't be able to afford to go, which is pretty much the position you are already in!"

"Who's picked the horses?"

"I've had a couple of tips from a reliable source."

"Who?"

"Dave at the Dog & Gun."

"Dave at the Dog & Gun! How is he a reliable source, Dad? He's not exactly Lester Piggott!"

"His son is a stable lad at an up and coming trainers down in Shepton Mallet. His son's called Joe and Joe reckons they have two really smart horses who are going to have their first outings for the yard this week. The whole yard are really, really confident that both horses will win. Their star jockey, "Fingers" Marling, who rides mainly in Ireland, is coming over just for these two rides."

"He sounds like a safebreaker not a jockey. When are they running?"

"Tomorrow afternoon at Wincanton. I'm putting a hundred quid on the double myself!"

"I thought you just said you had no money!"

"I haven't! I've borrowed it off Dave! I'll pay him back out the winnings!"

"Dad, you are just a complete nightmare!"

"Don't tell your mother!"

"As if I would!"

Richie

I spent the whole evening in my bedroom debating whether I should gamble everything I had on two horses that Dad had recommended. Dad had spent my entire life skint, so it was not as though he had a history of tips that had made him a small fortune. If Dad was backing them, they were more than likely doomed to failure. Nevertheless, what choice did I have? As Dad rightly said, £350 was getting me nowhere, so why not gamble? Should I just pick my own horse though rather than rely on two of Dad's? I thought the best thing to do was sleep on it, see how I felt the following morning and hope that I woke up feeling lucky.

That fateful Thursday morning I woke up feeling desperate rather than lucky. Desperate to find Kelly. I needed that extra money and I knew I was going to have to take the risk. I just hoped fortune did favour the brave. I came down the stairs for breakfast, to find Dad at the kitchen table, not surprisingly his Daily Express was open on the racing page. Dad was always one of those blokes who read his newspaper from the back page to the front and unless something was happening at Bolton Wanderers, he would skim through the football, cricket and rugby headlines and keep moving inside until he got to the racecards.

"Morning!" Dad greeted me cheerily, "It looks like Paul Mullins horses are both running!"

I could tell Dad was excited, he had managed to convert Jim to the joys of horseracing, now I'm sure it felt like an opportunity to convert me too.

"What are they called?"

"Quartz Starr and Florida Diamond."

I must admit, I liked the names. They sounded like winners.

"So, if I decide to put my money on them. What do I do?"

"I'll juggle my appointments and make sure I'm in Ormskirk this afternoon. I'll show you how to put the bet on and guide you through the world of gambling. Now let me see, the races are the third and fourth races on the card. Florida Diamond goes first in the novice hurdle and then Quartz Starr goes next in the novice chase…."

I had to interrupt!

"Dad, if you'll excuse the pun, can you just hold your horses! Slow down a bit, will you! I can hear the words coming out of your mouth, but they mean nothing to me, you might as well be speaking Cantonese!"

"What bit did you not understand?"

"Novice hurdle. Novice chase. There's no point going into detail, Dad, it doesn't mean anything to me and I'm sure, win or lose, this will be a one-off. I will not spend every weekend for the rest of my life trying to sneak off to the bookies."

Despite saying I did not want specific details, Dad decided he would tell me anyway.

"OK. Novice just means they are new at it or crap at it, the horse can't have won a race in that sphere before the start of that season. Chase races are over big fences, like the Grand National and hurdles are just little baby hurdles that they skip over. The hurdles are probably not as high as the ones the sprinters leap over in the Olympics."

"What happens if one of my horses falls?"

"Then you lose. It's a double, Richie, they both need to win. If one wins and one comes second, you've lost."

This sounded like a long shot to me. Both horses had to get around the whole course without falling and even if they managed that, they had to win. I had seen the Grand National on the tv, horses fell pretty often!

"Is that not a bit hopeful, Dad? You hardly ever get one winner, let alone two!"

"These horses are really good horses though. Something a bit special, by all accounts. They'll both go off as favourites."

"Which means people like them?" I guessed.

"Sort of. It means the bookmakers and the punters think they are more likely to win than anything else in the race, so they pay worse odds on that horse than the rest of the horses in the field. They are both evens favourites."

He'd lost me again. 'Worse odds', 'horses in a field', 'evens favourites', I was pretty sure Dad was talking in jargon just to confuse me.

"Are you doing this deliberately, Dad?!"

"What?"

"Speaking in tongues!"

"Every Tom, Dick and Harry in any bookies up and down the country would understand what I've just said, it's basics."

"I'm not a Thomas, Richard or Harold that lives in the bookies though, am I? I'm a Richard who watches Everton and listens to music and falls in love with good looking girls. Horses and ponies are for girls and idiots with even less money than sense."

"You won't be saying that when you're counting your wedge later on."

I started to laugh.

"I hope you're right, Dad!"

Dad closed his paper, took a slurp of his tea and stood up.

"Richie, I'm going to have to get ready for work. Meet me outside the Brahms at one thirty and I'll take you over to Stanley Racing and show you how to put the bet on."

"OK."

"How much money have you got again?"

"Three hundred and fifty quid."

"Right, two evens favourites in a double means that if you put £350 on, when the first one wins, you have £700 going on to the second one. If the second one wins too, you double up again, which means you have £1400 in total, including the £350 you started with.

So you wouldn't just have a grand to get you to Singapore and get you somewhere to stay, you would have four hundred quid left over to buy Kelly some flowers and take her to Raffles Hotel for a Singapore sling and even book a room there! See you later, son! It's going to be one hell of a day!"

Dad slapped both my cheeks simultaneously and then ran up the stairs like an excited teenager.

What did I have to lose? I could have continued trying to save some money and I'm sure eventually I would have raised enough money to fund a plane trip through hard graft, but by the time that day came, Kelly may have moved on to Australia or New Zealand or Japan or anywhere else. Amy's lead was a hot one and I needed to get to Singapore sooner rather than later. The more I thought about it, the more I persuaded myself that this bet was the right thing to do. One way or the other it would seal my fate.

I can understand why gamblers gamble. The adrenalin that pumped through my veins that morning was not something I was used to experiencing. In a way, it reminded me of the euphoria I had felt when I had been told my cancer appeared to have been removed. This time the feeling was not euphoric though, it was excitement and fear all rolled into one. I had fallen in love with someone so beautiful and she had become so precious to me, that to lose the opportunity to see her again based on certain horses not running around the field as fast as others was just plain daft, but I was not in a position to look for logical and practical solutions. Within nine hours, I knew I would be buying a plane ticket to Singapore or cursing my idiotic decision and my idiotic father! Florida Diamond and Quartz Starr were probably in their horseboxes now, I thought, totally oblivious to the fact that their performance that afternoon would decide the future direction of my life.

"Fingers" Marling probably didn't give a second thought either to how his performance could impact on the punters who funded his sport. I knew there was no such thing as a cert, bookmakers shops managed to pay their rent, their staff wages, their electricity, their satellite televisions and their race sponsorships from the money they took off people like Dad, but I felt I was going to be different. My share of bad luck had been used up, it was good luck's turn. I kept picturing myself in Stanley Racing after the second winner, counting my huge wad of cash. All £1400!

I was at a loss what to do that morning. I distracted myself by watching a Laurel and Hardy film of Dad's called "Sons Of The Desert". I laughed hysterically at anything remotely funny as my nerves were taking me to the edge of insanity. I took my mind off things a little, but not a lot and throughout the film I must have wound my watch up half a dozen times as it felt like it had stopped. Eventually time consented to pass. Funny how when you want time to stand still, it is swallowed up like doughnuts but when you want it to proceed, it was almost statuesque.

At about half past twelve, I was gathering my things together, I had dug out my jacket and was searching for my scarf and gloves when I heard the front door slam. I tucked my wallet into my jeans pocket and went to investigate. I met Caroline in the hallway looking cold and flustered. She was supposed to have been in Durham for a week's holiday, but after twenty four hours, she had returned.

"What's up with you, Cal?"

"Are you the only one in?" she wanted to check before providing details.

"It's all over between Donna and I. We're finished!"

"Why?"

"She's too possessive. It seemed fun having an intense relationship at first, but I can't even get stuck in traffic without her thinking I'm off screwing another woman. I've had enough of it, I've told her we're finished. Where are you going?"

"Ormskirk."

"What for?"

"I'm meeting Dad."

"Does he know?!"

"Of course he knows!"

"Why are you meeting him?"

"To put a bet on a horse. Two horses in fact."
"Jim, give Richie his body back!"
"Funny!"
"You don't bet on horses!"
"It's a one-off. I need the money to get to Singapore to track down Kelly."
"How do you know she's in Singapore?"
"Amy Perkins told me. She had a phone call from Kelly."

The revelation of my good news did not seem to act as a fillip for Caroline. If anything, it turned her mood even more sour. The puss felt threatened.

"I wouldn't bother if I were you, Richie. If she'd phoned you, then maybe, but if she's phoning Amy rather than you, what does that tell you? It tells me, she's moved on, Richie. No offence, but you've had cancer, make the most of your life, don't go chasing cute fannies in Singapore when there's plenty to be found round here."

"Don't hold back Caroline, say what you think, sis!"

"The truth hurts sometimes, Richie."

"I know that. It's just my head is saying 'Forget Kelly' but my heart is telling me that I still love her and I need to go to Singapore to find her and see how she feels about me. I'm about to put every penny I own on Dad's tips and if I win, I'm booking a flight to Singapore straight after."

"Can I come?"

"To Singapore?! I'd rather you didn't. I need to do this alone and you would only try to split us up anyway."

"I meant to Ormskirk, soft lad!"

"Why? Do you need to go shopping?"

"No, I fancy coming to the bookies with you, it sounds like fun."

"Dad might not be happy."

"He'll just have to be unhappy then! I know he's a male chauvinist pig and he'll love you going in with him and hate me going in, but tough shit, I'm coming!"

We walked down to Town Green train station and jumped on the Merseyrail train to Ormskirk, a ten minute trip with just one stop at Aughton Park. Caroline wanted to let off steam about Donna, but the way she wanted to constantly divert the conversation back to her lovelife, seemed to me to indicate that this was more a lovers tiff than a break up.

We met Dad as arranged outside the Brahms & Liszt wine bar, which was literally just across the road from the bookmakers. Dad was surprised to see Caroline walking up Moorgate with me.

"Hi love," he said to Caroline, "what are you doing back?"

Dad kissed her cheek.

"I just decided I would spend my holidays with the family, Dad. I wanted to have some quality time with you all."

"Good. Your Mum will be pleased. What are you doing with Richie?"

"I just thought it would be fun to spend the afternoon with him."

Dad pulled a face.

"It's just that Richie and I have some business to attend to, love. You may have to go to Taylor's for a coffee for an hour and then he'll be all yours."

Caroline smiled.

"Dad, calm down! Richie's told me what's going on! I will be the soul of discretion. The rest of the Billinghams won't hear anything about this from me, especially Mum. I've never been into a bookies before, it sounds like fun!"

"It's not a place for young girls, love. It's full of old men smoking."

Caroline looked like she was seething inside, but managed to control her temper. She was determined to come with us and knew if she lost her temper and stormed off, Dad would be getting what he wanted.

"Dad, it's a bookmakers, not a strip joint or a peep show. I wouldn't have thought there'd be any women in there firing ping pong balls out their jacksies! I'm sure I'll be able to handle it! Come on, let's go!"

Caroline lead the way over the road to Stanley Racing. Dad rolled his eyes and whispered to me,

"What did you bring her for?"

I whispered back,

"I couldn't stop her!"

The bookmakers, as Dad had forecast, was a cloud of smoke. There were about twenty people in there before us, nineteen men and one old woman who was chain smoking her own roll-ups. She was smoking them until they almost burnt her tongue. She was probably younger than she looked, which wasn't hard as she looked like she was about one hundred and thirty. Her face had more wrinkles than the skin of a hot chocolate. The men were all ages from eighteen to eighty eight, but all looked like desperation to escape poverty was their motivator. I'm sure the wealthy gamble fortunes at Cheltenham and Royal Ascot, but that type of gambler was not visiting Stanley Racing in Ormskirk on a drizzly, damp Thursday afternoon. The Stanley threw its arms wide open to Society's outcasts. Those who questioned evolution by asking where were the transitional phases between monkey and man, only had to witness the reprobates in Stanley Racing on a Thursday afternoon.

The only smartly dressed man in Stanley Racing that afternoon was my father. Despite not obeying the dress code of torn top and paint splattered jeans or charity shop rejects perfumed in body odour, Dad was a fully accepted member of this oddball clan. Everyone greeted Dad warmly or nodded their hellos and the cash assistants and manageress all greeted Dad by name.

"Hi Charlie! How was the steak and kidney pie?" Sheila, the manageress asked, revealing that this wasn't Dad's first visit to Stanley's that day. Dad looked uncomfortable with this revelation, but Caroline loved it.

"Is this your first visit here too, Dad?" she mocked.

It was now ten minutes to two, Florida Diamond was running at two o'clock. There was another race at Uttoxeter taking place, so everyone gathered around the screens as an excited commentator belted out his commentary. There was a tight finish, so half a dozen punters came to life as three horses jumped the last fence (or hurdle, I can't remember which) in line.

"Go on 'End Of Reason'! Give him a crack O'Leary!" yelled one bloke.

"Whip his arse, McKenzie!" urged another.

These guys were unlikely to be paid up members of the RSPCA!

Once the horses reached the winning post, one guy jumped up and down, the others cursed and ripped up their betting slips. Dad pulled me over to a corner.

"Listen Richie, if we win these races, whatever you do, do NOT celebrate like old Welby did there. The guys know him and will let him have his moment of glory, but they know he'll have only had a couple of quid on. If you start celebrating like a fool and they see you picking up over a grand, it just takes one of them to decide he needs it more than you and they'll have it off you before you can say 'Red Rum'."

"Thanks Dad!" I replied. "Here was I worrying about losing and now you've got me worrying if I win too!"

"Just keep your mouth shut son and you'll be fine. Come on, I'll show you how to write the slip out for the double."

I was expecting some sort of complex bet completion process, but it was just a case of writing £350 win double on Florida Diamond and Quartz Starr and the times of their races, Wincanton 2.00 and Wincanton 2.30. The only complicated bit was the taxation.

"Are you going to pay the tax, son?" Dad asked.

"I get taxed for betting on a horse!! There'll be a toilet tax soon or a fresh air tax! I can't believe they tax betting!"

"Well, they do." Dad responded not empathising with me at all. "You've got a choice, you either pay tax on your bet, 10% of your stake, or you don't pay the tax at all and they take 10% of your winnings off you."

I did a quick calculation.

"£35 tax on the bet or a £140 tax on the win! It'll have to be on the win, I haven't got £35!"

"You could lower your stake." Dad explained.

"No. Let them tax me if I win. I'd still have £1 260. I can handle that."

"You say that now, but I haven't met a winner yet who hasn't wished he'd put more on and paid the tax!"

Once I'd completed the slip, I went to the queue to put my bet on. There was one person in front of me….CAROLINE!"

"Cal, what are you doing?"

"What's it look like I'm doing? I'm having a bet!"

"How did you know what to do?"

"Margaret showed me!"

Caroline waved over to the old dear with the face like the skin of hot chocolate. Margaret waved back with her yellow fingers and roll-up.

Five minutes later, despite the warnings from Dad, I was shouting on 'Florida Diamond' at the top of my voice, as 'Fingers' Marling came out from the slipstream of the grey horse that had been in the lead the whole way and suddenly told 'Florida Diamond' to "GO!" The horse reacted like it had been injected with bionic powers and scooted clear.

"GO ON THE DIAMOND!!" I yelled, as it left the rest of the field eating dust, "YOU BEAUTY!"

I did a victory dance as it crossed the line, too fuelled with delight to remember my instructions.

"Did you have that one then?" asked a bearded bloke next to me with a beer belly big enough to store sextruplets.

I remembered my responsibilities.

"Me? No." I replied. "My sister did though."

IVF man looked over at Caroline who was tearing her betting slip up and mumbling to herself about two quid going down the drain.

"She backed two horses," I explained.

Once again, Dad dragged me to a corner of the shop. Even Dad was getting excited.

"What did I tell you, son, what did I tell you?! Just less of the Hokey cokey, Richie, remember what I said about playing it cool?!"

Cool? I thought. How can I keep it cool ?! In just over half an hour, I will be collecting over a thousand pounds and heading out of here with pockets stuffed with notes, to book my trip to Singapore! Raffles Hotel here I come! In forty eight hours, I would be ordering a Singapore Sling and a bottle of champagne with two glasses for me and my gorgeous girlfriend!

Miss Watkinson

"Oh my God! It's Richie! I can't believe you've come! Thank you so, so much! You've come all this way to see me, how can I ever thank you?!"

Richie

Thirty minutes between races when you have seven hundred quid rolling on to an evens favourite is too long. Twenty nine minutes and fifty nine seconds too long! As soon as 'Florida Diamond' flashed past the winning post, I wanted the next race to start. I was on a high and wanted it to continue before reality kicked me in my surviving testicle.

Ten seconds after 'Florida Diamond's' victory, I was convinced it was my lucky day. Ten minutes later I was not so sure. In fact, I had gone from one extreme to another quicker than an Eskimo on a rocket to Dubai.

"Quartz Starr's going to lose, Cal, I know it."

"Whatever it does, you can't do anything about it, so stop stressing. What will be, will be."

"I can't help stressing. I've got seven hundred quid on a horse!"

Dad, who had been having a chat with one of his fellow punters, headed over to provide some fatherly advice.

"Richie! Pack in the pacing up and down the shop! Someone's going to kick your head in, in a minute and if you don't cut it out, it might well be me. They'll have all clocked you putting that big, fat wad on before and if shouting and screaming for 'Florida Diamond' wasn't bad enough, you're pacing up and down saying,

"Come on, Quartz Starr! I need this for Kelly! Singapore's waiting!"

Then I hear you say in a big, loud voice,

"I've got seven hundred quid on a horse!"

How thick are you, Richie?! It's like cutting your own arm off and then jumping into a pool full of malnourished sharks…I am warning you, Richie, cut it out!"

I suddenly had a vision before my eye's of Jemma's old boyfriend, Ray. I hated him because he was a loudmouthed show off, not interested in anyone else's situation but his own and I immediately understood Dad's point. I was only acting the way I was through nervous excitement, but from the perspective of my fellow gamblers, who may have just gambled away their wife's housekeeping, they would not want to see some young upstart pacing round excitedly with a fortune at his fingertips.

"Sorry Dad, I take your point."

"I understand how you're feeling son, but I've got £200 riding on Quartz Starr too and I'll be in more of a mess than you if it doesn't win, as I'll owe £150 to a man you wouldn't want to owe a pound too."

"I thought you said Dave at the Dog & Gun lent you the money."

"I lied son, Dave wouldn't lend me a penny. He's lent me money in the past and had to wait until my next win to get it back, which sometimes was several months. Dave did give me the tips but the money came from Kiffer. He wanted 50% back, but I figured if I was going to turn £100 into £400, I could afford to give him £50."

"Bloody hell, Dad!"

I had only heard of Kiffer but his reputation was well known in Ormskirk. He was a loan shark. A man who had apparently inspired dozens of soap storylines. The body in the attic of the disused semi, that was a Kiffer killing. The body in the gigantic ice cube in the ice cream factory, that was a Kiffer too. The human kebab, you guessed it - Kiffer! He didn't kill people himself, but it was rumoured his henchmen did, but nothing could ever be proven. I doubt he would kill my Dad over £150, but I certainly wouldn't want to be the one trying to explain why I didn't have it.

Dad could see that I had gone a whiter shade of pale.

"Don't worry son, Quartz Starr will romp home. I'll give him his £150 and still have £250 in my arse pocket."

I shook my head. I would never end up like Dad. Quartz Starr was definitely going to be my first and last bet. I would not be venturing into Stanley Racing again, there was enough drama in my life without this!

Two thirty eventually came around. Dad commented that Quartz Starr "looked immaculate". I had no experience of judging how well turned out a horse was, but Quartz Starr looked like he knew he was something special. He looked like an Olympic athlete whilst one or two of the others looked like they had an addiction to hay and sugar lumps! They were the horseracing version of the sextuplet IVF man from earlier. I made this point in a whisper to Dad.

"Quartz Starr looks much fitter than the rest of them."

"He should do, Richie! Apparently this is his prep race for the Cheltenham Festival. Him running against this lot, is like Seb Coe challenging me and you to a 1500 metre race. It'll be no contest, he'll piss this easier than Florida Diamond won the last one!"

"I hope you're right, Dad!"

"I will be."

The race was over two miles and the first mile and a half went like a dream. It was going so well, I had to ask Dad why the other jockeys looked like they were trying really hard, bouncing up and down on their saddles like they were backside trampolines, whilst 'Fingers' Marling was not moving an inch.

"It's all about the amount of horse you've got under you," Dad explained, "the rest of the jockeys know their horses are knackered, so they are trying to cajole them to go faster, whilst 'Fingers' knows Quartz is still in first gear, so he is just steering him around."

I was managing to contain my excitement but if what Dad was saying was right, this was virtually all over, there was just one other horse that looked like it could muster any sort of challenge.

The bookies had been relatively quiet, with just a few mutterings, when out of nowhere, the tranquillity was broken by a high pitched shriek that no doubt attracted the attention of any canines situated within a five mile radius.

"COME ON MISTRAL FLAGSHIP!!!"

It was bloody Caroline!

For a split second, I covered an ear with one hand and my eyes with the other, as I daren't look at Dad after this. His worst fears were just being realised! I opened my eyes, but now used my cupped left hand that had protected my eardrum to blinker me from Dad's stare. I turned to my right to face Caroline, who was jumping twice as high as I was in the previous race. It was bizarre, it was like she had borrowed a pogo stick! If Caroline had jumped any higher, she would have needed a motorbike helmet to protect her from the ceiling.

"Caroline! We haven't backed Mistral Flagship!"

"Speak for yourself bruv, I have! I've got a fiver on it, at 33-1! Margaret picked it out for me! GO ON MISTRAL!"

Caroline's horse was in the lead, but 'Fingers' was doing what he did in the previous race, just shadowing the lead horse, just waiting for his moment to pounce. I don't know whether it was horse or jockey, but with half a mile to go, one of the two decided enough was enough. To use Dad's analogy, it would have been like Seb Coe jogging along behind Dad and I for 1100 metres of a 1500 metre race thinking,

"I've not trained every day of my life for the last ten years to amble around at this pace!"

Then hearing the bell and thinking,

"Right! Now I'll show them what I'm really made of!"

Quartz Starr did just that. He probably only went into the second of his gears but in the blink of an eye, he left Mistral Flagship for dead, then moved further and further clear so his backside became like a speck in the middle of a TV screen to Mistral Flagship. Caroline stopped jumping and screaming. I was going to Singapore!

I guess in gambling the most dangerous thing you can do is to count your money before a race is over. I was doing just that. I was counting every twenty pound note in my head when all of a sudden the wheels came flying off our Formula One Ferrari. Approaching the second last fence, Quartz Starr was ambling along, he was so far ahead that 'Fingers' had now slowed him right down, to a pleasant trot no faster than a donkey on Blackpool beach. I am sure after the race, 'Fingers' will have reflected that this was probably not the ideal speed to be jumping fences several feet high.

At the second last, rather than leap majestically over like a salmon heading up stream, Quartz Starr jumped half heartedly, as though there was no fun in this race any more, his underbelly hit the birch at the top of the fence and 'Fingers' Marling was dumped unceremoniously onto the mud on the landing side. Quartz Starr also managed to land safely on the far side of the fence and trotted off to find a healthy strip of grass to munch on.

A ghostly figure now set fire, with a zippo, to those twenty pound notes that I was counting in my imagination. I held my head in my hands.

"Shit!"

The dream was over. I would not be going to Singapore after all. A mud splattered 'Fingers' Marling ran off in pursuit of Quartz Starr, eventually grabbing his reins and although Quartz Starr was now facing towards the fence he had just attempted to jump, 'Fingers' put a foot in the stirrups and started to re-mount him. Whilst all this chaos was ensuing, Mistral Flagship was clumsily, wearily, jumping the third last fence. I had no idea what was going on. I needed guidance from Dad.

"What's 'Fingers' doing, Dad?"

"What does it look like he's doing, he's getting back on!"

"Is he allowed to do that though? You told me if my horse fell, I'd lost."

Dad eyes were transfixed to the screen. He answered hurriedly.

"Yes, that's because jockeys don't normally bother getting back on the bloody horse, that's why! They're normally too concerned that the horse might be injured or because the rest of the horses are already two fences down the track by the time they catch theirs, but there's nothing wrong with Quartz Starr and he's still in the lead, so we've still got a chance!"

Just as Dad said this, Mistral Flagship jumped the second last . The tortoise was now beating the hare.

"Turn him around, 'Fingers'!" Dad urged along with a dozen other punters in the bookmakers who were showing a renewed interest.

Mistral Flagship was moving further and further away, probably leaving a trail like a gastropod, carousel horses moved faster. Quartz Starr did not appear to like the sight of another horse passing by, he turned around and with 'Fingers' now back on board, they shot after Mistral Flagship like Tornado and Zorro. Mistral Flagship jumped the last fence like it had done a third circuit of the Grand National course.

"We're going to catch him!" Dad shouted. "WE ARE GOING TO CATCH HIM!"

So much for keeping a low profile!

With every stride, Quartz Starr was gaining ground, but it was hard to tell whether it was all too late. Quartz Starr jumped the last fence awkwardly but at speed. The commentator sounded like he was going to have a heart attack. Several people in that bookmakers looked likely to die with him, including Dad.

"Quartz Starr is closing on Mistral Flagship here! 'Fingers' Marling is not looking his normal self-assured self as he pushes Quartz Starr along and rides for dear life! He only has one foot in the irons and it looks like his saddle has slipped too, boy will he be sore when this one's over! Quartz Starr is gaining ground though! Mistral Flagship can see the winning post, he has less than half a furlong to go, but he is looking like he's on a treadmill, everything is moving, but he is not going forward! Here comes Quartz Starr, it's going to be close, it's going to be ever so close! Both jockeys push their mounts forward, they want this win! Here comes the line….MISTRAL FLAGSHIP, QUARTZ STARR….. QUARTZ STARR, MISTRAL FLAGSHIP! IT'S TIGHT! PHOTOGRAPH! PHOTOGRAPH!"

Everyone in the bookies breathed out simultaneously! What a race! Dad was convinced we'd won it.

"He's won. Won by a nose!"

Caroline was equally sure Dad had it wrong!

"Your horse only went past mine after the line! Mine won!"

I had absolutely no idea which one had won!

"I thought it was a draw! Can you have a draw in a horse race, Dad?"

"You can, it's called a dead heat."

"Do we still win if it's a dead heat?"

"Yes, but not as much."

"Enough to get me to Singapore?"

"I think so, hopefully we'll find out in a minute! Just stop asking questions, Richie, or we'll miss the announcement!"

Within seconds of hushing me, the commentator announced,

"The result is coming through from Wincanton. Number 3, Mistral Flagship, beats Number 2, Quartz Starr."

Dad's head sagged. I smiled a rueful smile. Caroline rubbed her hands and cheered in that deafening high pitched tone of hers! I knew my dreams of going to Singapore were over. My immediate thoughts were for my father though, not for me, he looked visibly shaken as he said a hasty farewell and rushed back off to work, no doubt trying to catch up on the several hours he had missed. That was the least of his worries now though, until he paid that money back, I knew he would be constantly looking over his shoulder. He would certainly be making no shortcuts through unlit passageways!

Caroline offered to take me for a pint of Guinness in "The Buck".

"You were going to lose anyway," she explained, "whether I had the other horse or not was immaterial. At least I have enough money to help you drown your sorrows now!"

Once our stomachs were lined with about three pints of Guinness, I angled the conversation away from Donna and her bust up with Caroline and told her where Dad had found a hundred pounds from to back the two horses.

"Kiffer!! Dad borrowed money off Kiffer!!! Does he have a death wish?!"

I shrugged.

"Looks like it!"

"They'll beat him to a pulp until they get that money, you know that don't you?"

I nodded. Caroline looked down at her handbag that was sat on the table.

"You want me to give Dad the £150, don't you, Richie?"

"I don't want you to do anything. I just think it would be safer to owe you money than Kiffer."

"But I'll never get it back!"

"You'd never get Dad back if he was made into a kebab or an ice cube!"

That night, when we got back to Mum and Dad's in Aughton, after Mum had gone to bed for a read, Caroline slipped Dad the £150. She was at liberty to point out,

"I have completely saved your arse, Dad! Listen to this, because I mean it, if I ever, EVER want to come to the bookies with you again, I expect to be welcomed with open arms, OK?!"

Dad gave Caroline a hug.

"That would be fine, love, but I've learnt my lesson today. Me and the bookies have gone our separate ways."

Caroline went back to Durham that weekend and patched things up with Donna. Donna continued to be possessive and Caroline continued to hate it, but, as I kept telling her, we all have our faults, we either learn to accept them or move on to someone who has other faults that are more tolerable!

Quartz Starr went to the Cheltenham festival the following March and despite his fall at Wincanton, he went off favourite again. This time he fell at the second fence and 'Fingers' Marling did not have the opportunity to get back on board. Two years later, once Paul Mullins sorted out his jumping, he won the King George on Boxing Day and the Cheltenham Gold Cup in March. Dad insisted he did not have a penny on either time, although Dave at the Dog & Gun's son, Joe, won an absolute fortune!

The afternoon of the failed double ended my gambling career as soon as it had begun. I also conceded that my pursuit of Kelly was over. What I didn't appreciate, on that day of the gambling disaster, was that every cloud has a silver lining and although the pursuit of Kelly was over, the pursuit of Jemma had just begun!

Kelly

"Oh my God! Who was that?! That absolutely reeks!"

"Eugh! Was that you, Danny?"

Danny did not confirm or deny that he was the perpetrator of the vilest smell that I had ever been subjected to. The worst thing was, I was several hundred feet up in a cable car, so there was just no escaping it. I covered my mouth and nose in a similar fashion to three of the four Londoners in their early twenties, that I shared the cable car with, whilst the fourth, Danny, an unshaven, dark haired, unattractive guy, just sat back with his arms folded, admiring the odour his backside had produced. His three friends laughed through their gagged mouths, they thought it was hilarious! Laddish humour was beyond me!

I was in a particularly bad mood as my body was aching! I had been in Singapore for over six months now and had decided it was time to move on. It was a wonderful place, spotlessly clean with amazing shops that I could not afford to shop in, but I had managed to get a job in a backpackers hostel just off Orchard Road, the main retail and entertainment area of Singapore, so had survived without eating into my savings. The majority of the backpackers that came through the hostel had been over to Sentosa Island during their stay. Sentosa was meant to be a beautiful island full of entertaining tourist attractions and fantastic beaches. I particularly wanted to see 'Fort Siloso', one of the restored coastal gun batteries from World War II when British ruled Singapore was trying to defend itself from the Japanese. Before I left Singapore, I knew I must go to check it out. The reason I was aching was that I decided to head over there by cable car, from Jewel Box, the iconic hilltop destination at Mount Faber. I thought I was in fairly good shape, but the torturous ascent up Mount Faber had proved me wrong!

Once I arrived at Jewel Box, I took five minutes to grab a bottle of water and sit in the shade out of the blazing Singapore sun, then bought my return cable car ticket to Sentosa Island. Trust me, it was infuriating to then share a cable car with four idiotic Southerners, who were spoiling my enjoyment of the lush greenery and stunning coastal scenery below, by acting worse than chimps at a tea party. To further darken my mood, halfway across, at its highest point, the cable car stopped. After five minutes without moving, the chimps grew restless.

"We're going to be stuck up here until we starve or die of dehydration," one said positively, "they'll get it going again after a few weeks and once each cable car gets to Sentosa, the doors will open and a load of skeletal remains will spill out!"

"I know how to get us out," genius Danny said and began rocking from side to side, making the cable car rock forwards and backwards.

"Cut it out, Danny, you dickhead!" said the quietest of the four, a guy who's black hair was poking out of a New York Yankees baseball cap.

"Scared Woody?"

"No, but you're frightening this young lady!"

"Sorry, love!" said Danny, half-heartedly.

"It's OK. You seem to be determined to kill me one way or another, either by suffocation or choking after that disgusting smell or now that's failed, you try to dislodge our cable car and make us fall a thousand feet to our death! Did they leave you out in heaven, when God was dishing out brain cells?!"

Other than Danny, the boys erupted again into laughter. I was pleased that I had managed to come up with a reproach straight out of the Jemma Watkinson text book. I had certainly learnt to look after myself since Mum died, or I suppose, since the moments before Mum died.

Once they had stopped laughing, the cable car started moving again and a conversation ensued.

"I take it you are English. Whereabouts are you from?" one of the two at that time nameless characters asked.

"Yes, I'm from Ormskirk."

"Where's that?" he asked looking puzzled.

"It's a market town in West Lancashire. If you head North from Liverpool, towards Preston, Ormskirk's pretty much on the way. Have you ever been to Southport?"

"No."

"I have," Danny piped up.

"Well, you will have passed through Ormskirk to get to Southport."

"Right," Danny said, not really feigning any interest, "we're from Richmond in Surrey."

"What are your names?" I asked, "I'm Kelly."

"Hi Kelly! I'm Andy, but everyone calls me Woody!" Woody took my hand and shook it. The other three did not have much to write home about in the looks department, but Woody was an attractive man. You could tell there was a load of bulging muscle underneath his T-shirt. He had an Italian type look, a very dark complexion. His brown eyes seemed to sparkle when he looked at me.

"Danny!" said the Phantom Farter.

"Pete," said the pale redhead who looked like he'd burnt.

"Scotty," said the final lad, the smallest of the bunch, who had boyish features and smooth skin. Scotty was the type of lad who would look good in make-up. Pity he'd missed the 1980's boat. I thought he must be the youngest of the four, but it later transpired that he was, at twenty three, the eldest. The others were all twenty two. They were all school friends who had graduated, worked for a year and were now spending twelve months travelling the world. They had been away from England for four days. If Pete didn't cover up for the remaining 361 days, he would have no skin left by the time he arrived back home.

"Are you backpacking?" Woody asked.

"Not really. Just travelling. I haven't even done much of that! I went to Holland six months ago for a couple of weeks, then came here to Singapore. It's been great, but it's time to move on."

"Where are you going next?" Scotty enquired.

"No idea!"

"We're going to Hong Kong on Saturday. You could always tag along with us, if you wanted." Woody suggested.

I had had a lot of offers like this over the previous six months. Given the offers were generally made by young men and normally after the briefest of conversations, I deduced they were made based on my looks rather than my personality.

"You don't know me! I might be a murderer for all you know!"

I used this one a lot. Sick, I know, but it amused me.

"You couldn't be any worse to travel with than Danny!" Pete replied.

"Yes, if we can cope with his farts, we can cope with anything!" Woody added.

"Are you travelling alone?" Scotty asked.

"Yes."

"How come?"

"No-one my age was allowed to come. I have very liberal parents," I suppose not having parents, one being dead and one being an escapee, made them fairly liberal.

"How old are you?" Woody asked

"Nearly eighteen."

"Bloody hell! You're brave, travelling around alone as a seventeen year old female," said Danny.

"I told you, I'm a murderer!" I said with a sarcastic smile.

"You could come in useful. We can get you to strangle Danny then, if he keeps delivering those 'silent but deadlies'!" Pete said.

"You should definitely come with us! We could do with some female company. We need a sensible head to keep us in check! If we start to annoy you, you could just move on alone, but you'll grow to love us, I guarantee it!" Woody said, flashing me a lovely smile.

Of all the groups that offered to accompany me on my travels, this four had not exactly made the best initial impression, but the more I spoke to them, the more I warmed to them, especially Woody. We stuck together around Sentosa and once we hit the beach, Woody's bronzed body and six pack sealed the deal. Richie seemed a distant memory to me now, sometimes I could hardly picture what he looked like. It was time to fall in love again and time to have some fun. Three days later, the five of us flew to Hong Kong Kai Tak airport. It was a pretty scary landing as the airport was surrounded by high rise buildings and it seemed like the pilot had to weave his way in and out of them. Woody held my sweaty palm throughout. We were an item by then and, if truth be told, we were already an item by the time we took the cable car back to Jewel Box.

Jemma

"Oh my God! It's Richie! I can't believe you've come! Thank you so, so much!

You've come all this way to see me, how can I ever thank you?!"

Richie sat facing me as I said this in the most sarcastic tone I could muster. I'd been in Styal prison for six months before he had the decency to pay me a visit. Like everyone else, he had left me to rot.

"Screw the lot of you!" I thought.

"I'm sorry, Jemma," Richie said, bowing his head a little.

"What for?"

"What?"

"What are you sorry for?"

"Not visiting."

"No, you're not. Have you been ill again?"

Richie started mumbling and his body language was closed and uncomfortable.

"No. It's just been difficult. There's been a lot going on in my head, what with Kelly disappearing and various different things at home. I wanted to come but…."

I cut him short.

"As far as I'm concerned, Richie, if you haven't been ill, you've got no real excuse, have you? You can't really be sorry for not doing something that you genuinely did not want to do! I don't want you here. Could you please leave."

Richie looked surprised.

"Seriously? Its taken me bloody ages to get here!"

"I'm absolutely serious, Richie."

I was going to say 'deadly serious' but given I was in Styal for manslaughter, death was a topic I tended to avoid. Richie stood up to leave, half of me wanted to stop him, that same half wanted to hug him like I had hugged him in Ormskirk (which was never going to happen with half a dozen guards looking on) but the other half was bitter and twisted and had found a scapegoat.

"I'll go then."

"What made you come anyway, Richie? A guilty conscience?"

Admittedly, I was not expecting the response Richie came back with.

"Actually Jemma, if you must know, it was a guilty conscience that has been keeping me away!"

"What?"

"Jemma, either I can explain or I can bugger off home. I can't do both."

Despite everything, I was officially intrigued. I needed to keep the tough outer layer on display though. At all times in Styal, I needed to be tough.

"Yes you can! Sit down. Explain to me what you meant by what you just said. If it makes sense, you can stay, if it doesn't, you can bugger off home!"

Richie sat back down. We faced each other across a wooden table, like every other

con and visitor in there. It was like a mass congregation of 'The Invisible Chess League', as it felt like a chess board and pieces should be on the table. Not that every prisoner at Styal could play chess, some of them would have struggled to play

Tiddlywinks!

Richie looked at me as though he needed to see through my eyes and into my soul. I'm not into romantic clichés, but when he sat there, looking at me, that was genuinely how I felt.

"Jemma, you know exactly what I meant! I felt guilty visiting you. I went out with your sister. Your sister was…is….the only girl I have ever loved. For some reason, I found myself developing feelings for you too. Feelings that, for so many different reasons, were wrong for me to have. Maybe they developed because of my cancer. Maybe they developed because of your arrest or because Kelly disappeared, but they were developing and that felt wrong. I needed to keep away. I needed to sort things out in my head."

"Richie, if you had visited me for an hour a week, you would have had another twenty three hours that day and twenty four hours every other day of the week, to get your head sorted. I needed you to visit me and you didn't come through for me. Not for six whole months!"

"Needed me to?! I'm nothing to you apart from your sister's ex and some guy you thought you screwed at Joey Birch's party when we were fifteen."

I shook my head.

"Richie, if that was your attempt to eek out a confession of love from me, then I must say, that was pathetic!Just ask me! You've had cancer, I'm being detained at Her Majesty's Pleasure for killing my mother. Do you not think, both of us are beyond playing games? Had I started developing feelings for you from the day we collided in Ormskirk? Yes. Did those feelings grow whilst I was in Risley? Yes.Am I completely pissed off with you now for abandoning me for the last six months? Too right I am!!"

"I've tried to explain to you why I've not been. I'm sorry, Jemma."

"Richie, your explanation is not good enough, nor is your apology. I had convinced myself that there was something between us. It didn't feel right to me either, because of your love and my love, for Kelly. There were feelings there for you though, feelings I couldn't suppress. Weird, inexplicable feelings as though destiny had wanted me to be with you and care for you. Then all this happened.

Now, I'm thinking I read it all wrong. If I was destined to be with you, you would have kept visiting me over the last six months."

"Broken glass can be replaced, Jemma."

"Would there be any point though, Richie? I'd always just feel like your consolation prize. You may have had feelings for me, but they are outweighed by your feelings for Kelly. How is Kelly by the way? Any idea where she is?"

Richie swept his fingers through his blond hair.

"Singapore!"

"You're joking!"

"No. Amy had a phone call from her."

"Did Amy not tell her that the 'Mystery Of The Murdered Mother' has now been solved and she can come home?"

"I don't know. Maybe she thinks that if they arrested you, they could arrest her too."

"They won't, Richie. They'll have closed the files on this one."

"It's not me you need to tell, Jemma. It's Kelly."

I smiled at him.

"I might just struggle to do that! I don't think the prison wardens will get a kitty going to fund a trip to Singapore! Have you not thought of going?"

"I thought about it, but it didn't happen."

"Why?"

"It's a long story but when you get out, if my Dad ever gives you a tip for the horses, just ignore it!"

"I will."

"Any idea when you will get out?"

"No. I'm being a good girl so hopefully I won't be here forever. They can't let a killer loose after six months though. The Ormskirk Advertiser would be crammed with letters from outraged right wingers! Still, I'm not ready to come out yet, I'd miss all the girls in here too much!"

Richie and I sat and chatted amiably throughout that visit. I needed to catch up on what was happening in the outside world. I wanted to know if anyone was outraged by the guilty verdict. I had secretly hoped there was a "Free the Ormskirk One" campaign being run by my MP but Richie confirmed there was nothing of the sort. I don't know what I expected really, as to a great extent, I wanted to be found guilty, to take the heat off my guilty sibling.

It was comforting to be able to speak to Richie like an old friend. After confessing our feelings for each other I wondered whether it would be awkward, especially once I took the conversation down the 'it would never work' route, as Richie had done very little to persuade me I was wrong. Perhaps he agreed that the ghost of his relationship with Kelly would always haunt us. Still, at least he had finally come and I could finally stop hating him for not visiting.

Just as visiting time was coming to an end, Richie was putting his coat on and I was looking at him enviously, wishing it was me heading back to a loving family, he threw me another curveball.

"Jemma, do you hate me a bit less now?"

"I didn't hate you, Richie, I was just mad at you!"

"And are you now?"

"Less so."

"So do you no longer think its destiny that we should be together?"

I thought he was mocking me.

"Shut up, Richie?!"

"I'm being serious. Do you think its destiny that we should be together?"

I was shocked how pleased I felt about him not being playful, but did not know how to react. Richie had taken the pin out the grenade and thrown it towards me. I picked it up and launched it back.

"Do you?"

"Who knows! Time will tell us. All I do know is that I will keep coming here every week until you get out, as a friend and if fate decides he wants to pair us up, how can we argue with fate?!"

"Do you promise, you'll visit?"

"I promise."

Richie smiled at me. I had forgotten how handsome he looked when he smiled. I supposed I had pretended I hated him, but the reality was that my love for him had not needed to be rekindled as it had never died.

As I headed back to my cell, I just wanted the days to pass, to see if he was a man who kept his promises. I soon found out he was. As for destiny, she played with us for a while, but she knew in the end she was never going to be able to keep us apart!

Richie

Finally, after what seemed like forever, Jemma was out of prison. For over a year, I had visited her every week, without fail and now the wait was over. The wait for Jemma anyway, the wait for the bus wasn't. We had been standing outside Styal prison for fifteen minutes and Jemma, naturally impatient anyway, but more so having just been released from prison, was getting fed up.

"So, Richie, why exactly have you not managed to get yourself a car?"

"I've told you this! What would be the point in me having a car, if I can't drive it?!"

"Still got that multi-tasking problem? Brake, clutch, accelerator, gears, can't do more than one at once thing?!"

"Don't you take the mick! I don't ever remember you passing your test!"

"Yes, but I've got a better excuse than you though, haven't I? I've been banged up!"

"I have tried to pass! I failed last time for not being completely stationary at a 'STOP' sign. Fifty metres from the test centre, I was! I'd driven perfectly before that too."

Jemma laughed. It was comforting to see that the cloud above her was moving away.

"I don't think you'll get any medals for driving well for fifty metres!"

"I meant fifty metres from the end of the test, not fifty metres from the start!"

I looked at Jemma and she was smiling knowingly at me.

"You knew what I meant!" I laughed. "Anyway, here's our bus!"

Over the previous twelve months, the bizarre love triangle that had previously existed between Jemma, Kelly and myself, had just become a platonic straight line between Jemma and I. Kelly was completely out of the equation, she had not made contact with myself, Amy, Jemma or anyone else from Ormskirk throughout that year. She may well have still been in Singapore or, for all I knew, she could have been back in England. I'd sometimes be in a pub or walking along a busy street, see the back of someone's head and be sure, when they turned around, that they were going to be Kelly. I was always wrong. As time passed and as the friendship between Jemma and I grew, the less it mattered.

Probably to my parents relief, I never made it to Manchester Polytechnic. Helen and Jim were always the ones who merited a place at University, Caroline and I had less intellect, but I would argue, more personality. After eighteen happy months at Andy's Records, I managed to get a new job as a 'Customer Adviser' at the Red Rose Building Society in Maghull, a train journey from Town Green each morning of one whole stop! Learning about mortgages and investments was nowhere near as interesting to me as music, but the wages were half as much again, so I was prepared to learn about endowment policies, term assurance, repayment mortgages, personal equity plans and the likes, if it meant I had more spending money each month. At our branch, there were six staff in total, five women and me, but the average age of the ladies must have been well into the late forties, so it was more like working with five mothers than five potential new girlfriends.

During Jemma's final days in Styal, the barren romantic years returned. I had no romantic successes but equally no romantic failures. This may have seemed strange considering I was a decent looking lad in the prime of life, but it was easy to explain. To put it bluntly, I was head over heels in love with Jemma. Each time I visited Styal, the bond between us seemed to grow and I had absolutely no interest in pursuing anyone else.

At some point early in that 'Styal' period, my brother, Jim started dating Amy Perkins. Initially, this seemed really weird, especially when they barricaded themselves into my bedroom, when Mum and Dad were out for the evening, as unfortunately I knew what they both looked like naked and had mental images even more disturbing than the ones I'd had about Caroline's heart shaped bush! They were noisy too, so if I was ever in the house with them, whilst Mum and Dad were out, I made sure my personal stereo was close at hand!

As the months passed though, I stopped thinking of Amy as the girl I once saw naked and just saw her as Jim's really friendly girlfriend. My weekly visits to Jemma, also shamed Amy into overcoming her fears about prisons and during Jemma's last few months in Styal, Amy would visit a couple of times a month. I think Amy was subjected to a Jemma Watkinson tongue lashing the first time she visited, as I had been, but once she had overcome that first obstacle, it became plainer sailing. Once Jemma's release date was announced, Amy arranged with her Mum and Dad for Jemma to go and live with them on release. Martin, Amy's brother, was training to be an actuary in London, so his room was going spare. Most parents would baulk at the thought of having an ex-convict staying in their home, but Amy's parents were not most parents, they were extraordinarily sweet parents, so apparently agreed to Amy's request without objection.

What the future held for Jemma and I, I did not know. On her release, we shared a hug, I kissed her forehead, but we did not act like a boyfriend and girlfriend would act. We had been very close friends, there was no doubting that, the doubt was just whether we would now make the next step. Two years earlier, my relationship with Kelly had appeared to be an obstacle, but too much water had passed under the bridge now for that to still be the case. It was just that if we made the leap from friends to lovers, I knew it would be impossible to revert to friendship if things did not work out.

Jemma was not Amy, she was a far fiercer creature! I was certain I did not want to rush into anything, although I suppose it could hardly be described as "rushing", given that we had met platonically every week for the last two years. I was just keen to avoid another "me and Amy" type scenario, where we ended up feeling awkward and embarrassed.

Jemma and I had talked about fate and destiny. I did not believe in "que sera sera", however, I realised you could steer fate in a direction, but if you forced its hand, it would buck you like a frightened horse.

We arrived at Amy's Mum and Dad's three hours after leaving Styal, a journey that involved taking two buses and two trains! It should have been a forty five minute drive! I needed to pass my driving test! We walked to Amy's from Aughton Park train station and as we reached Amy's road, we laughed as we saw a "Welcome Home!" silver banner draped over their porch! We rang the bell, Amy answered, squealing with delight and then gave Jemma an almighty hug before showing her through to the lounge where Amy's Mum and Dad and Jim were waiting. Amy's Mum and Jim had party poppers which they pulled the string of, as Jemma arrived and Amy's Dad popped the cork on a bottle of Cava! I am sure not too many ex-cons, released after serving their manslaughter sentence, have something similar laid on!

"Welcome back to Ormskirk, love," Amy's Mum said. "the place has not been the same without you!"

Mrs. Perkins went over to Jemma and hugged her. I noticed Jim and Mr.Perkins did not follow suit, but both did seem genuinely pleased to see Jemma.

"Welcome home, Jemma!" said Mr.Perkins, as his wife pulled out of her hug,

"Our home is your home for as long as you need it to be."

"Thanks Geoff!"

"How was Styal?" Mr.Perkins asked.

"Well, it rained for the first few days, but after that it was great!"

Jim and I chuckled, but the Perkins family lived in a shiny, happy world so did not quite grasp Jemma's black humour. It was an old joke, our grandfather used to use it when people asked him about the Stalag prisoner of war camp in World War II. The Perkins family just looked confused, so Mr.Perkins poured the Cava and our minor celebration kicked off. Before handing Jemma a glass of Cava, Mr.Perkins checked whether Jemma was OK with alcohol. I could never quite figure out why he asked this, I suppose it was in case Jemma had said,

"I'd better not, it turns me into a psychopath!"

Mr & Mrs. Perkins were so pleasant, they would probably just have limited Jemma to half a glass on that basis!

Throughout the afternoon, irrespective of who I was conversing with, I found my eyes drawn to Jemma. My brain could be very logical about not pushing things and allowing them to run some sort of natural course, but I was twenty one years old and overloaded with testosterone, sperm and desire! The calm, pleasant, easygoing side of my character would say all the sensible things about biding my time, but the lustful, passionate side would find my eyes focusing on Jemma's breasts, just like I had done aged eleven in the Rachel Cookson infatuation stage, thinking how much I would love to see them emerge from underneath that blouse and bra. Those thoughts were pretty much echoed as my eyes wandered further down Jemma's body! Given I had been celibate for two years, this reaction was hardly surprising, although I did resist the temptation to run over, wrestle Jemma to the floor and chance my luck! After all, the Perkins' lounge carpet already held some uncomfortable memories!

Jim and I stayed at the Perkins house for a couple of hours, before jointly deciding it was time to make a discreet exit. Jim had once described Amy's Mum and Dad as, "more twee than Tweety Pie!", so he wasn't keen on hanging around for too long and I didn't want to either, as I was sure I would ruin my own 'playing it cool' tactic, if I stayed in Jemma's presence for any longer. I headed over to Jemma, who was deep in conversation with Mrs.Perkins and Amy and politely tugged at the back of her shirt. I let the conversation run its course, then Jemma excused herself and moved a few steps away with me. We faced each other, Jemma looking up at me.

"Jim and I are going to get going."

"Arrrr….do you have to?"

Jemma's eyes were a little red. Two glasses of Cava were probably taking effect. I doubted Cava was freely available at lunch time in Styal.

"We best had. You need to get yourself settled in."

"It's not like I've got six suitcases to unpack, Richie!"

I knew this. I had carried Jemma's only small bag of clothes and belongings back from Styal.

"I know but Jim's keen to get going and I said I'd go with him. He's a bit uncomfortable around Amy's Mum and Dad!"

"Why? Do you not like them either? Geoff and Doreen are lovely!"

Jemma said this at a drunk persons volume. Mr & Mrs Perkins naturally turned around. Great! I could now feel a little awkward with every member of the family!

"We're going to go!"

I no longer felt the need to explain any further.

To say Jemma looked despondent, would have been an almighty exaggeration but she did look disappointed.

"When will I see you again now then?" Jemma asked.

"When do you want to see me again?"

I am sure without the two glasses of Cava, Jemma would have spotted I was testing the waters. Her ability to get the better of me was at an all time low. At that very moment, Cava was Jemma's sophistication Kryptonite!

"Now! I want to see you now! I don't want you to go!"

Playing hard to get when you've not had sex for two years and you are looking straight down at possibly the best pair of breasts ever known to man, attached to a beautiful, dark haired, blue eyed goddess is very, very difficult!

"I need to go, Jemma! Jim's waiting!"

"Let him wait two minutes, Richie! I've waited two years!"

"I know, but what harm will one more day do?"

I took a step back. If truth be known, I was now 100% sure something would happen between Jemma and I, and sooner rather than later. Neither of us had any patience and it seemed we were both keen to get things kickstarted. I was prepated to wait one more day though, as I did not want anything to happen at Amy's house. Jemma was less keen on waiting.

"You never know what might happen in twenty four hours in our crazy world's though, Richie!"

"True. We're going to have to chance it though. Come here, give me a hug and I'll be around tomorrow about twelve. We can have some lunch and then properly celebrate your freedom!"

Jemma took a few steps towards me and we hugged each other tightly.

"See you tomorrow, Richie Billingham! I shall be counting the minutes!"

I broke out into a wide grin. I know she was drunk but it was still flattering to have someone that stunning making a play for you! Given Jemma's rather loud comments, I let Jim thank Mr & Mrs Perkins on our behalf and we headed home on foot.

Before we were halfway home, Jim, typically blunt, wanted to discuss what was happening between Jemma and I.

"You're going to shag her, aren't you?!"

"Who?!"

"You know very well who! Jemma. She was all over you! All those years in prison must have done something to her brain!"

"I think it was the drink. She won't have had a drink for more than two years."

"So! Sometimes the drink just stops us playing games. I will repeat, she was all over

you!"

"I'm not going to pretend I'm disappointed!"

"Do you like her then?"

"Of course I like her! Who wouldn't?!"

"Her Mum for one!"

"I've told you, Jim. She didn't do that!"

"I'm not so convinced."

We walked on a little in silence. I could have explained to Jim why I was so sure that Jemma had not killed her mother, but I still felt it would be a betrayal of Kelly. A couple of hundred metres down the road, Jim broke the silence.

"If you had a straight choice between the sisters then, Jemma and Kelly, who would you choose?"

"I haven't got a straight choice, Jim! Kelly's probably got a couple of kids to some bloke from Singapore by now!"

Jim persisted.

"But if you did have that choice?"

"I've no idea, Jim. Jemma, maybe."

"Really! Do you think you can handle her? She's feisty!"

"I'd like to think I could handle her!"

"If you get a house together, make sure it's a bungalow!"

"Cheeky get! Believe me, one day you will find out that Jemma was innocent."

"I hope I do."

There was the briefest of pauses before Jim added,

"So, Richie, when are you going to make a move?"

"Jim, I've no idea!"

"Well, I'll tell you what, to encourage you to get your skates on and Jemma's kit off, if you shag her by this time next month, I'll buy you a bottle of whiskey!"

"And if I don't?"

"You buy me one!"

"I'm not betting on that!"

"Coward! Whether you bet or not, this time next month I'm going to quiz you, Richie! Its my duty as a little brother, I'm going to have to quiz you!"

"Shut up!"

Over the next month, I took a lot of stick from Jim, but it was lighthearted banter so I didn't mind! Looking back now, it was one of the best months of my life. No illnesses. No complications. Just fun, laughter, opportunities and love. I have precious memories of that month. Precious memories that will stay with me for the rest of my life.

Richie

It was a simple game. A silly game that we would never have played, if we hadn't been drinking, but we had been drinking and we did play it and it drove me wild. Nothing had previously fuelled my physical desire for Jemma as much as that game. I had always found Jemma attractive, but I had not properly appreciated how much I wanted her until then. By the end of the game, I was drooling more than Pavlov's dogs and could not remember feeling so in awe of a woman since seeing Olivia Newton-John in black spandex pants in Grease in 1978!

I had called round at Amy's at lunchtime the day after Jemma's release. The look of concern on the faces of the Perkins family when they invited me in, contrasted with the look of joy on Jemma's face as she came down the stairs and saw me in the hall. I think Mr & Mrs Perkins did not want a young man leading Jemma astray so soon after her time in jail, but were too polite to point this out to her. Too scared too probably! Jemma just wore a simple pink t-shirt, blue jeans, high heels and a brown leather jacket,but everything Jemma wore seemed to accentuate her curves. She was so hot, I was scared to touch her in case I was scalded.

"Where are we off to then?" Jemma asked excitedly

"I thought we could go down to The Café Bar for lunch and then perhaps head into Southport for a few drinks. Is that OK?"

"Sounds good to me!" Jemma replied.

After a delicious pasta lunch and a shared bottle of wine, we walked through to Ormskirk bus station and hopped on a double decker to Southport. Having seen Jemma's performance the previous night after two glasses of Cava, I was wary of Jemma being fall over drunk by mid-afternoon, so I made sure I had two glasses to every one I poured for her. As a result, I felt a little sick on the bus journey over and was happy that the sea breeze had a sobering effect! If I had been a little less nervous, I would have slowed down the pace of my drinking, but anticipation led to the pace increasing! We did an 'L' shaped pub crawl, dropping in on each pub and bar on Lord Street, before nipping into McDonalds for a milk shake and following Eastbank Street up to "The Old Ship Inn". I remember being told there was an Andy's Records in Southport, but I couldn't find it. I made a mental note to look next time I was there and sober. By the time we reached "The Old Ship Inn", we had probably had a drink in half a dozen bars and, as a result, Jemma was beginning to transform into the tactile lady she had been the previous day. This time around though, I had fallen down the rabbit hole with her, into a new world of drunken debauchery or at least that was the world I was hoping for! Jemma was now drinking at my pace, although I was having a pint of Stella each time she had a vodka and diet coke, so my lead in this drunken marathon remained undiminished!

Conversationally, with alcohol loosened tongues, we were covering off plenty of subjects and I was using the opportunity to get a few historical issues off my chest. I was happy to confess to Jemma that although I had always thought her looks were "gobsmackingly stunning", at school, I had found her brash, over confident manner tiresome and annoying. Jemma admitted that, on reflection, she had been an easy character to dislike, but insisted she had changed for the better since. I concurred!

"Mind you," Jemma warned, "I am never going to be quiet, so if you're looking for a quiet girlfriend, you best start looking elsewhere!"

Conversations that touched on us being boyfriend and girlfriend seemed to be happening more and more frequently now. We also chatted about my relationship with Kelly and Jemma's with Ray. I explained that although Kelly had meant the world to me, I was probably just swept along by the new emotions and that even if Kelly hadn't left, it probably would have just fizzled out over time. Admittedly, I wasn't 100% sure that this was true, but felt it was the right thing to say to Jemma!

Jemma explained that after perfecting the role of the precocious brat at school, her relationship with Ray, who was several years her senior (she did say how many years but I forget!), was her attempt to show her new found maturity, but ultimately, she was not attracted enough to him to justify staying with him.

"We were like Arthur Miller and Marilyn Monroe!" Jemma explained, which led me to believe my drunken marathon lead was now definitely being eaten into! I bluntly told her that I thought Ray was such a big arsehole, he could have probably managed to fit the moon up his backside and still leave space for the sun. Jemma insisted he wasn't all bad. I was not, and remain, unconvinced.

The drinking game that changed the whole dynamic of our relationship began, and finished, at "The Old Ship Inn". On walking through the door, we put a few songs on the jukebox, including "Suedehead" by Morrissey and Jellyfish's "The King is Half Undressed" before heading to the bar. Jemma decided we should order half a dozen vodka shots and then play a drinking game she dubbed "Three Yeys or a Nay".

"Three Yeys or a Nay" was almost simple enough for me to understand despite my inebriated state. One of us would ask the other one questions, that had to be answered truthfully. If we could answer three questions with an honest "Yes", then the person questioning would have to down a vodka shot. If any question was answered "No", the person answering would have to take a shot. As a lad, it was the sort of game you would only agree to play if you were drunk and with a pretty girl.

Jemma decided that if she was asking the questions, every question would have to start, "If I was your girlfriend......" and obviously, if I was asking the questions, each question would have to start, "If I was your boyfriend....".

Half a dozen vodka shots purchased, we took three each and carried them over to a table near the jukebox, to play our game and listen to our music which we were hoping was going to be on next after Metallica's "Nothing Else Matters" – people always seemed to pick the long tracks on the jukebox, I guess they were trying to get full value for their 50p! I wasn't that tight, I just picked what I liked.

Jemma decided she would start the questioning and, like mental foreplay, it all started in a gentle, straightforward manner.

"If I was your girlfriend, Richie Billingham, would you send me flowers?"

For most people this would probably be a nice, easy one, not for me. I pulled a face. I didn't like flowers, they took ages to grow, flowered for hardly any time at all and then died.

'Here's a bunch of flowers, they're pretty much dead already, put them in a vase and watch them droop!' – was my take on flowers.

I would have said "No" – but the point of the game was to try not to. I hedged.

"Sometimes."

Jemma frowned.

"It needs to be a 'Yes' or a 'No', Richie!"

"Well sometimes is a 'Yes'!"

"Not really!"

"Ask the question in a different way then!"

"OK. If I was your girlfriend, would you send me flowers every Valentines Day?"

I felt compelled to tell the truth.

"No."

"Take a shot then," Jemma insisted.

I downed the first straight vodka.

Half jokingly, Jemma added,

"I'm offended, Richie! Why wouldn't you send me flowers every Valentine's Day?"

I looked at Jemma's beautiful face. It was hard to believe she had just spent two years in jail.

"Valentine's Day would be my day off, Jemma! The other 364 days a year, I would be romantic so I'd need a day off on Valentine's Day! It's a commercial rip off anyway, just to pressurise men who sit on their arses all year and do nothing for their wives to make a token effort. My romanticism would be spontaneous!"

"Arrrr! Aren't you sweet?! You should have said that first, I might not have made you take the forfeit! Can I ask another one and you answer again?"

"Go on. Oh good, Suedehead."

The introduction to one of Morrisey's classics kicked in through a very poor sound system.

"If I was your girlfriend, would you wear make up if I wanted you to?"

Weird question.

"What do you mean?"

"OK. If I was your girlfriend and we lived together and you were going out with your mates and I wanted to dress you up in women's clothing and send you out with the lads wearing it. Would you do it?!"

"Why would you want to?"

"To test the boundaries of your love for me! To see if there were any boundaries to your love. Would you do it?"

"Not a chance! No!"

"So there would be boundaries?"

"Of course there bloody would! If you wanted to make a complete arse of me, then sorry, I'm afraid I'd have to draw the line!"

"Luckily for you, I wouldn't want to make an arse of you nor would I want you to wear make up, but a 'No' is a 'No'! Take the forfeit!"

Once again, I did what I was told. Vodka number two gone! Down in one! I was now aware that I was pretty smashed. Not only that, I was starting to feel that it was a stupid game and that I didn't want to play it.

"I don't like this game," I moaned, "it's daft. Can we stop?"

Jemma was having none of it!

"Come on, Richie! I'm enjoying it!"

"Yes, because you're just asking asking stupid questions that I can only answer 'No' to!"

"Well you ask the questions then!"

"I will!" I replied. Game on! Jemma looked confident.

"I'm ready for you!" she said, rubbing her hands.

"If I was your boyfriend and I developed an addiction to cheeseburgers and cream cakes and as a result, I became a bed ridden eighty seven stone hippo and I then asked you to climb in to my specially made bed so that my humungous eighty seven stone frame and my sixteen bellies could make love to you," I paused for breath, "would you get in?"

Jemma did not even hesitate!

"Yes."

"You liar! You would not!"

"I would! Looks aren't important to me, I went out with Ray remember!"

I thought about it.

"I can't argue with that!"

"Ask me another."

If I was going to lose this game, I thought I might as well get some sort of enjoyment out of it. I decided to go down in a blaze of glory. All the testosterone fuelled questions that had crossed my mind in the last two years but had dared not ask, were now going to get their one and only vocal outing.

"OK….if I was your boyfriend, would you satisfy every single one of my desires?"

"Yes, absolutely!"

"Absolutely? No matter how mad or bizarre they were?"

"Yes!"

"Be warned, Miss Watkinson, if I ever become your boyfriend, I will be reminding you of this conversation and I'll hold you to it!"

"You can!"

"So, I could do pretty much whatever I wanted to do to you and you would be fine with that?!"

"Yes."

My imagination was running wild. Now I was turned on.

"As much as I like that answer, Jemma, I am finding it hard to believe! You may have a good poker face, but the aim of the game is to tell the truth, not to be a convincing liar."

"Look, if you were my boyfriend, I would trust you enough not to make me do something I did not want to do. So, yes, I would satisfy every single one of your desires, because I trust you."

Wow! Things were looking up for me! I still needed to get Jemma to say 'No' though! I decided Jemma would be nailed on to be a possessive type.

"If I was your boyfriend, would you let me sleep with another woman, with your prior knowledge and consent, if you did not feel up for it?!"

"Yes."

"You're taking the piss now, Jemma! That's a lie!"

Jemma shook her head.

"No, it isn't! If you were my boyfriend, you would not want to sleep with another girl and I would always be up for it, so of course I would let you sleep with another girl, if you really wanted to, but I am telling you now it would never happen!"

"And you expect me to believe that?!"

"It's the truth. I don't particularly care if you believe it or not, it's the truth! You asked me three questions, I answered them all honestly with a 'Yes", you need to down another shot, Richie!"

I took a third glass and a third vodka followed its Russian brothers into my bloodstream.

"I'm still not convinced you're playing fair!" I said in a voice that was becoming increasingly slurred.

"Don't accuse me of cheating! Remember what happened to your brother when he accused me of cheating!"

Kelly was not this tough! I was a little intimidated by Jemma, but I also found her strength of character an attractive quality.

"I wouldn't dream of accusing you of cheating, Jemma!"

"I hope not!"

"You're obviously just bloody good at the game!"

"Not at the game, Richie, I'm just bloody good!"

"We'll see!"

I drunkenly winked at her a couple of times.

"Will we now! Don't count your chickens before they flutter!"

"Before they flutter?!"

"There was some crazy, posh old bird in Styal, who used to say that!" Jemma explained.

"Anyway, all I'm saying is," I was speaking in that slow, deliberate way that drunks do, "that it's no good claiming your engine purrs, if you're not going to let me drive it!"

"And all I'm saying is," Jemma replied, "if you have a top notch engine, underneath an outstanding body, you only want it to be driven by an excellent driver! Are you an excellent driver, Richie?"

I think I would have ruined the moment if I'd have confessed to jerking and stalling all the time, so I came up with a line that would not have been misplaced on 'Blind Date!'

"Hand me the keys, lift up your bonnet and I'll make more than your engine purr!" Jemma feigned shock and disgust!

"Did you really just say that?!"

"It could have been worse!" I replied, "there were lots of other cat like phrases that nearly came out!"

"Well, I'm glad they didn't!"

"Me too! Certainly not the way to charm a lady!"

"Is that how you see me, Richie, as a lady?"

Jemma's face suddenly looked quizzical and serious. I was concerned that I was now a little too drunk for things to get deep and meaningful. I tried to continue the playful conversation.

"If I was your boyfriend, I would see you as a lady!"

Jemma was having none of it, she remained serious.

"But now though, Richie, despite everything that's happened, everywhere I've been, you still see me as a lady?"

I had random drunken thoughts. A fit lady! A fit lady who's my friend. A fit lady who used to be a cow but who's now very nice. A little scary, but very nice.

"Yes, I see you as a lady," I was not sure where this was going, "does that mean I don't have to have another forfeit?"

Jemma grabbed me. Admittedly my recollection is hazy, but I am sure she did the grabbing. She made the moves. She kissed me forcefully. There were tongues. There were spectators – we were in the middle of a busy pub on a Friday night, after all. Nothing mattered. Just Jemma. Just me. Just us. It wasn't romantic, but it was passionate and in those early days, that's all Jemma Watkinson and Richie Billingham were all about.

Kelly

I was sitting on some steps at the harbourside, in the Central area of Hong Kong Island, looking over Victoria Harbour towards Kowloon, one late afternoon. I was in my own little world, taking a few sips from my Diet Coke and wondering when I was going to hear back from a couple of jobs I'd been interviewed for, when I heard a voice.

"Sprechen Sie Deutsch?"

"Pardon?"

I looked up to see who was asking the question. It was a young European man, in his early twenties. He wasn't great looking, I remember he had long shorts on and despite having blond hair on his head, he had masses of dark, wiry hairs on his legs. He smiled at me and I remember immediately thinking he had a cheery disposition. Looks wise, he reminded me of the chubby, blond haired Hitler Youth Austrian in the Sound of Music. The one who kissed Liesl. Even as a child I remember thinking she was too good for him, even if he was a year older. What was his name again? Rolf?

No, it couldn't be, my mind was thinking about Australia a little, so I must have added Rolf Harris into the mix! This young man standing over me definitely bore no resemblance to Rolf Harris! He wasn't tying a kangaroo down on the harbour's edge! Anyway, I digress. The young, European who looked like Liesl's boyfriend, switched to English, in that seamless way that makes me embarrassed of my poor foreign language skills.

"Oh, sorry, you are English, right?"

"Yes."

"I'm sorry, I don't know why I asked if you could speak German! I suspect most Europeans in Hong Kong are going to be British, after all, you sort of own the place!"

"For now!"

"That's right, until '97, then the deal ends, I believe."

"Yes, then it's back to China for Hong Kong!"

"And back to England for the British here?"

"Maybe. I certainly won't be here in '97, so I'm not too worried."

"Do you live here now then or are you just travelling through?"

"A bit of both really. I met some lads…", I wasn't sure whether he would understand the term 'lads' so I re-phrased, "….some young men, when I was in Singapore and came over here with them, but after four weeks, they moved on to Australia and I stayed here."

"On your own?"

"Initially yes. I had started work in a hotel over in Kowloon and decided I wanted to stay. I'd had enough of the young men really, so didn't want to be traipsing around Australia with them! They farted too much!"

I made him laugh.

"I think the English word 'fart' is a funny word!"

"What's the word for fart in German?"

"'Pupsen' would be 'to fart'!"

"That's funny too!"

"Yes," he smiled, "I suppose it is! So, how long is it since these young men left you?"

"Twelve months."

He looked genuinely concerned for my welfare.

"So you have been here all alone for twelve months?"

"No, not really," I re-assured him, "I've worked in two hotels and a hostel, so I've met a few friends along the way. Are you working here?"

"No, no, I'm backpacking. I was backpacking in Indonesia and Vietnam with my girlfriend, but here in Hong Kong, it is just me."

"Has your girlfriend gone back to Germany?"

"Oh, I'm not German, I'm Swiss."

I was surprised, largely down to me knowing very little about Switzerland.

"I thought they spoke French in Switzerland."

"In the western side, French is the main language, but mostly German in the rest. Some Italian and Romansh too in some parts."

I should have asked what Romansh was, but I didn't! I wrongly presumed it was Romanian!

"Well, I never knew that!"

"Now you do!"

"Your girlfriend," I asked again, "went back to Switzerland then?"

No, no, she's still travelling. She just found another boyfriend to travel with!"

"Oh, I'm sorry! Poor you!"

"No, I'm happier on my own! She wasn't a farter like your young men, just, you know, fewer arguments!"

"I don't know," I smiled, "I argue with myself some times!"

I realised I still did not know his name or him mine.

"Sorry, I'm Kelly."

I stretched out my hand and we shook firmly. He sat down on the wall next to me.

"Pleased to meet you, Kelly! I'm Christian!" he replied, "do you mind if I sit with you a while and watch the darkness win his battle with the day?"

"Be my guest! It's nice to have some company. Your English, is great!"

"Do you think so? It could be better!"

"Well, it's a damn sight better than my German! I only know pupsen!"

"Hopefully not a word you would be wanting to use too often!"

"No!"

And that was how two lonely European souls came together in Hong Kong.

Richie

Our three remaining vodka shots soon began their transition to urine. We decided we would knock them back and head off to somewhere else. Trying to be the 'Big Man', I knocked two of them back and left the other for Jemma to polish off. Jemma wanted to return to the bar at the back of the 'Scarisbrick Hotel, where we had been earlier, as she thought it would be buzzing in there by now. As I had finally managed to kiss Jemma, having desired such an occurrence since my body produced swimmers, I was in no rush to go anywhere fast. In fact, as I was well aware that I had had more than enough to drink, all I wanted was a deserted bus shelter in which to re-ignite the passion. At the outset of our relationship, what Jemma wanted Jemma got, so I struggled to my feet and headed to the exit with her, ready to move on to the 'Scarisbrick'.

As we opened the door of the pub, a howling wind invited itself in and rain swept along the road in swarms, like King Kong was standing over us with a giant watering can.

"We're going to get soaked!" Jemma shouted but was almost drowned out by the wind and rain.

"We can do it in stages!" I yelled back, "just keep diving into the shop entrances!"

I wondered whether Jemma would spot my alterior motive, but if she did, she did not seem to mind! Every doorway we stopped at, I pounced, cupping her face in my hands and kissing her passionately. On the third or fourth pit stop, I let my left arm off its leash and like an excited ferret, it found its way up Jemma's top. As I tinkered under Jemma's bra like a straight Liberace, my blood supply seemed to surge to a central point vertically down from my bellybutton! Those breasts felt amazing and I remember thinking that Jemma could always hire them out to the National Health Service as a natural remedy to brewers droop! Not that I would have allowed that to happen, although I pictured an orderly queue outside Amy's Mum and Dad's every Friday and Saturday night after closing time, full of male drinkers of all ages ready for their medicine!. Admittedly political correctness was the last thing on my mind at this stage of inebriation!

"Your boobs are fantastic!" I blurted out post-kiss, "you hide them well!"

"They're actually quite literally a pain!" Jemma revealed, "they give me backache!"

"What size are they?" I enquired. I had no idea how bra sizes worked, I knew womens dress sizes were six, eight, ten, twelve, fourteen etc, but bra sizes were beyond my comprehension. I just asked so I could ring Caroline the following day and seek confirmation that they were freakishly humungous! This was dependent on enough brain cells surviving through the night.

"32D".

"Wow!" I replied. I had no idea what 32D meant, but all the same, 'wow'!

After several further stops, several more kisses and a couple more feels under Jemma's top, we arrived, saturated and satiated, at the 'Scarisbrick Hotel'. The 'Scarisbrick' is an unusual hotel, in that it successfully manages to cater for both the younger and older generations. It has a traditional hotel bar in a room to the left of the entrance reception, playing music by crooners from the fifties, whilst at the back of reception, there is a boxing ring shaped bar, in the centre of a large room, normally packed to the rafters with the under forties, who dance along to the loud, modern music that blares out. The boxing ring bar is full of bar staff who's CV must include a modelling contract and a twelve month spell in the circus where they need to have mastered the art of juggling. Each glass has to spin twelve times and touch the ceiling before a drop is served. In the reception area, Jemma and I surveyed the damage to our bodies inflicted by the wind and rain.

"I'm absolutely drenched!" Jemma moaned, stating the obvious, as droplets of rain were taking it in turns to drip off her hair and zig zag down her face like it was a ski slope.

I was in no mood for negativity. Positive thoughts only! Drink does that to me initially, in those pre-hangover hours, whilst my brain is still in its expanded state.

"Come on Jemma! Who cares?! I still love you and think about it, a few weeks ago, you were stuck in Styal, would you not have given your right arm to be outside on the rainy streets of Southport on a Friday evening?"

I think Jemma missed most of my motivational words, she just picked up on one section.

"You love me?!"

"I love you! Yes!"

I was going to say, I'm not 'in love' with you yet, but I love you, but then I stopped myself throwing a negative into a positive. I loved her, that's all Jemma needed to know.

Having dried ourselves as best we could, we went through to the back bar and it was indeed crammed with young, lively drinkers and barmen spinning bottles and ringing bells to indicate pretty girls had just paid them a flirtatious tip. On Jemma's insistence, I headed straight to the bar, to get her another vodka and diet coke. I was considering getting myself a blackcurrant and soda, to give me an opportunity to dilute the Stella and vodka, but unfortunately Jemma accompanied me to the bar .

Within twenty seconds, a highly tanned, highly moisturised, highly arrogant barman, nodded at me to indicate that it was my turn to give my order. As we had struggled through to the bar, I noticed he had treated his stunningly sexy previous customer rather differently, leaning right over the bar to let her whisper in his ear. Chivalry was alive and kicking in Southport.

"A vodka and diet coke please and a blackcurrant and soda!"

I shouted to be heard over the James track "Laid" which was encouraging a healthy bout of singing from the clientele.

"Hang on! Hang on! What are you having?" Jemma questioned.

"A blackcurrant and soda!"

"Oh no you're not! If I'm drinking, you're drinking!"

Jemma rocked a little as she said this, as though there was a tiny earthquake who's epicentre was below her feet.

"I've just had five of those six vodkas, Jemma!"

"It's not my fault you're crap at 'Three Yeys or a Nay!'"

"Yes it is, you made the bloody game up!"

Jemma looked at the barman, who would no doubt have abandoned my request by now, if the prettiest girl in the bar was not by my side.

"Get him a double vodka and coke!" Jemma shouted firmly.

"Thanks Jemma!" I said sarcastically.

The barman knew who to obey. He went off in seach of vodka and cokes, leaving the blackcurrant and soda feeling unwanted and praying that one of the old drinkers from the next generation bar, may wander in by mistake. Once the barman returned, I paid him and took the drinks from him, despite this, the whole time he gazed only at Jemma. He received the tip he deserved off me. There was no bell ringing!

As we walked away from the bar, to allow several thirsty drinkers to take our place, we found ourselves, face to face and toe to toe with two unkempt characters, who looked like they were tag team wrestlers. They would have been the 'Laurel & Hardy' of the ring, as one of them looked like Ollie with a beard and without a top hat, whilst the other looked like Stan's anorexic grandson. Like the barman, their focus was on Jemma rather than me, but this time, the look was vengeful rather than in admiration or desire.

"Well look who it is!" said the scale breaker of the pair. "No wonder this country is in a mess, when scum like you are free to roam the streets."

"Morgan, good to see you again!" Jemma said calmly to the rotund scruff.

"You too, Cam! Richie, I don't know whether you remember these two gentlemen from my mother's funeral. Morgan and Cameron, this is Richie."

I wasn't sure what to say. Handshakes were definitely inappropriate. I hesitated long enough for Southport's impersonators of Syd Little and Eddie Large to pick up the conversation.

"We would never have set foot in your house that day if we'd have known what you did!" said Morgan.

"Bollocks!" replied Jemma, "two words that can prove that statement wrong…. FREE BEER!"

"Unlike you, Jemma, we have some morals! Everyone in Ormskirk is disgusted that you're out of jail," said skinny Cameron, "I nearly wrote to my MP."

"And then it dawned on you, that you can't write!" Jemma responded.

Cameron sneered at Jemma. I half expected him to get a bow tie out and spin it around or come back with an idiotic response that led to an admonishment from his fat friend, who would then implement a slapstick punishment. Unfortunately, the other half was right, as he just continued to sneer.

"Life should mean life for murderers!" Morgan interjected aggressively.

"I wasn't sentenced to life, Morg!"

"Well, you should have been! Life for a life. Your mother was our friend."

"That says a lot!" Jemma replied.

"Anyway," I said, the alcohol having started to kick in further, "Jemma did not kill her mother!"

I should have kept my sticky beak out. Jemma could have handled the pair of them single handedly. Drinking and kissing in the same night, had obviously thrown rational thought out the window.

"How would you know, pretty boy?" asked Morgan, as he took a swig from his bottle.

"I just know."

"Because she told you," said Cameron, "and because you're wanting to get into her knickers, you believe her! How stupid are you, pretty boy? If she told you she shit golden eggs, you'd believe her!"

I smiled sardonically back at the pair of them.

"Jemma does shit golden eggs! Has she not told you? Twice a day. I collect them. I make a bloody fortune at Easter!"

"Fuck off smart arse!" Morgan said, his face was reddening and he was almost growling now.

I couldn't help myself.

"You'll find it's Jemma's arse that smarts. She's the one who lays the golden eggs! In fact, thinking about it, I forgot to collect them one week, a few years back, I heard her mother slipped on them. They were on the stairs."

I didn't see the punch coming, but I heard it whistle past my left ear. Morgan, as I suspect is stereotypical for a twenty stone beast, obviously packed a lot of power in his punch, but not a huge amount of accuracy. Having failed to connect with his punch, he lunged towards me and I did what any self-preserving coward would do, I ran, pushing my way through the throngs of people. It was like a scene from the end of a

Benny Hill sketch, but without the breasts, as I was chased around a circuit of the bar, by two furious thugs, shaking their fists.

As I reached the starting point from which I fled, having literally come full circle, I collected Jemma by the hand, as she had stood motionless and bemused throughout."Quick, let's get out of here!" I urged. "Your Mum's mates will probably tie me up and torture me by singing 'Blue Ridge Mountains of Virginia'!"

Jemma and I ran out of the bar, through reception, out the front entrance and into a wet and windy Lord Street. Turning left, we sprinted along the pavement, gaining an ever increasing lead on our pursuing pair, before taking a left into one of the side streets, packed with amusement arcades and then an immediate right into a road lined with bed and breakfast guest houses, the majority with neon blue "vacancy" signs lit up.

"Have we lost them?" Jemma panted.

"I've no idea! Quick nip in here!"

We jogged up the path of the nearest 'B&B' which had a picture of a palm tree in the bay window and a sign above the front door saying, "Tropical Paradise Guest House". Even in the near darkness, it was evident a lick of paint would not go amiss. As we entered, 'Tropical Paradise', a white poodle, with a pink bow around its neck, ran up to greet us, wagging her tail. The long, narrow hallway smelt damp and the wallpaper was a 1970's floral design, that was peeling at the corners. There was a reception hatch on the left wall, that was closed and on the right, a staircase with a carpet that was patchy rather than threadbare. Southport had some great Guest Houses but this wasn't one of them.

"I need to go and dry off, again!" Jemma moaned, "and I could do with a wee after all that excitement! Do you think we lost them?"

"I think so."

"Me too! Morgan's done ten years for murder, when he was in his twenties. He strangled his ex-girlfriends new boyfriend."

"Now you tell me! You've never been out with him, have you?"

"NO!"

"Good!"

In spite of my brush with death, my penis was still sending cryptic messages to my brain.

"Given a convicted murderer is chasing us, do you think it'd be an idea to book in here and just lay low for an hour?"

The irony of hiding from one convicted killer by laying low with another, had not escaped me.

"Why not?" Jemma shrugged. "Let me go and find a toilet first!"

Jemma headed up the creaking staircase and not wanting to give her the opportunity to have a change of heart about the room, I rang the bell, on a small wooden table, outside the closed hatch. The bell was next to a handwritten sign that said,

"We are tending to the needs of our other guests right now. If you require our assistance, please ring the bell and we will be with you as soon as we can."

Within a minute, a small lady with wizened features emerged from a door at the end of the hallway. She must have been well into her sixties, wearing a pink dressing gown, fluffy pink slippers and tight rollers in her hair. She moved towards me in tiny steps, almost shuffling, puffing on a cigarette as she moved. She was like a miniature steam train. As she slowly approached, the door of the 'Guest House' swung open and my heart skipped a beat whilst my head turned. Thankfully though, I was not confronted by Morgan and Cameron, but a tall, moustachioed, dark haired gentleman, clad head to toe in black leather. In all likelihood, he had just finished his Freddie Mercury tribute act in a local pub.

"What are you after, luvvies?" said the smoking dwarf with a heavy Liverpudlian accent.

"Do you have a double room, please?" I asked politely.

"Now look love," she replied, "I'd love to give you a double room, I'm dead liberal me, but I can't. Honestly I can't. It's me husband, Frank, he'd have me guts for garters, if I let you pair share a double room. Have a twin or two singles, but not a double, love. He just doesn't like gays. Says its not natural. He says you shouldn't be putting square pegs in round holes.

I'm not like that. If God had have given me a son, I'd have wanted him to be gay! Clean, tidy, polite, good taste in films and shows and theatre, love your mothers, tidy nails….what more could a mother want?!"

I was completely dumbfounded. I looked at her, then looked at the fifty something year old Freddie Mercury clone standing behind me. Luckily, at this point, Jemma started to come down the stairs.

"I'm not with him" I exclaimed, "I'm with her!"

I pointed towards Jemma, who was halfway down the stairs. I'd like to think if I had been gay, I wouldn't have chosen someone who could have slotted right into the Village People, if you pardon the pun.

The landlady took another drag on her cigarette, which was now little more than a filter.

"Sorry love!" she cackled, "I though you and Magnum P.I were together!"

Our leather clad friend stayed mute, just smiling pleasantly.

"Now, it was a double room you wanted, wasn't it love?" Scouse Hilda continued, searching around for the guest book, "I know we've got Tropical Beach available for £18 a night or Tropical Heat for £16. Which do you want?"

"What's the difference?" said Jemma as she arrived alongside me.

"Tropical Beach has an en-suite bathroom and a radiator. Tropical Heat is up in the attic, so you have to use the communal bathroom, there's no central heating in the attic either, so its fan heated."

"Tropical Beach, please!" Jemma and I both responded simultaneously.

As the smoking antique went in search of the keys, Jemma whispered,

"Good move! I've just been in the communal bathroom. It stinks! There's a floater in there too….and before you say it, neither the smell nor the floater belong to me!"

Several years later, Jemma and I were out for the evening with two of our friends, Dogger and Sandra. After too many wines and gins and amarettos, the conversation sunk to the depths conversation often sinks to, when drink affected. We began talking about losing our virginity and subsequently where we first slept together, as a couple. Sandra confessed their first time together, was in a sauna at a sports club when things turned steamy for more than one reason.

"What about you two? Where were you?" they asked.

"Tropical Beach in Tropical Paradise," I stated, without even a hint of irony.

Jemma

"Richie! Move your head! QUICK!"

Richie was kneeling on the floor with his head nestling in pubic hair on the rim of the toilet in the "Tropical Paradise" Guest House, Southport. I would have loved to have taken the moral high ground from that day forth, constantly reminding him how I had sobbed heartily into my concrete pillow after he had thrown up moments after we made love. Sadly, the moral high ground was a place I did not get to trample. Richie had hurriedly dashed from the bed, with the desperate message,

"I think I'm going to be sick!".

Seconds later, my brain sent a message to my throat and mouth that my stomach was refusing to forward my food and drink to my colon, to package it up ready for delivery at my rear end and had instead decided to return it to sender. Thus, I found myself kneeling down next to Richie, like two commode devotees, retching and allowing my partially digested lunch to join Richie's for a midnight swim. As the bile and the putrid stench left me, my eyes filled up and I started to cry.

Richie offered his sympathy.

"Hey Jemma, don't cry! It's not sad, its funny. Look at the pair of us! I've been sick too, its OK."

"That's not why I'm crying," I said as I wiped my mouth and prepared myself for a second bout of vomit, "I'm crying because I'm a bad person. I hate myself, Richie. I really hate myself!"

My hearty sobs continued. I don't think I'd cried this month since Jon Voigts character died in "The Champ" and little TJ tried to wake him up.

"Well, that's ridiculous, Jemma! You're a great person!"

As expected, I threw up a second time.

"No, I'm not Richie, I'm a bad person. That's why I've just spent nearly two years in prison. That's why I've just slept with my sister's ex-boyfriend. I should not be having sex with you. You do that sort of thing with my sister, not me. This isn't right."

"Jemma, it is right."

"Well how come we both keep feeling so guilty about it? Sometimes you feel bad about it, sometimes I do, sometimes we both do. If it was right, we wouldn't be feeling like this. Should I be jumping into bed with my sister's ex the moment I'm out? No, I shouldn't!"

"Jemma, its not yesterday that I went out with your sister, its three years ago. Kelly is just a memory to me now, whilst you're here, sharing a toilet with me, having the most bizarre, backwards midnight feast! Now is not the time to feel bad about Kelly any more. We've done that. Let's move on."

Grabbing a rough looking towel to wipe my mouth, I replied,

"Richie, I don't know whether I can. You will always be Kelly's ex. Maybe it will always feel wrong."

"I know where you are coming from, because at times it still feels wrong to me, but other times it feels like the best thing in the world and it feels like the best thing in the world more. We are not bad people. Jemma, you have just sacrificed two and a half years of your life for a crime that we both know you did not commit. You allowed yourself to carry the can for your sister's actions, so don't feel bad about falling in love with someone she abandoned three years ago."

I vomited a third time. Not much came out. It was just retching now. It was becoming humiliating.

"I didn't say I was falling in love with you, Richie!"

"Then tell me you're not!"

"I'm not! Falling implies that I'm still in the process of falling in love. Listen carefully to this, Richie, as I don't flatter people often, but I have fallen in love, Richie. Every second I spent in Styal, I was just thinking about the day I could come out and spend time with you. That's why it all feels so weird. I should feel fantastic now. I don't. I just feel guilt."

Richie rubbed my back as I continued to retch!

"Look Jemma, when you're sober, you are going to have to straighten this out in your head. If you think you can handle it, I think we will be great together. If you don't think you can, we can just call it quits, no harm done."

"Except that I have slept with you for a second time!"

"Second time?"

"The first was at the Birch's party."

"That wasn't me, Jemma."

"Yes, it was! Anyway, do you know what it is that is stopping me just going for this."

"What?"

"Fear."

"Fear of what?"

"Fear that I could be completely in love with you and then one day, Kelly will come back, she'll click her fingers and you'll drop me like a stone."

Even though I stunk, I looked dreadful and had vomit on my chin, Richie placed his hand on my cheek and turned my face towards him, before saying,

"That won't happen, Jemma. I promise you, that will never happen."

Jemma

From the day I stepped out of prison, to the day we were married, life was almost perfect. Granted, I had my moments of feeling tetchy, hopeless, in despair and totally fed up but I think God gave women stormier waters, as we are the ones who have everything thrown at us in life. God gave men calmer seas because he knew once their seas started to get choppy that their boats would sink! To be fair, Richie is one of the few exceptions to this rule, when God made Richie, he put some of the sterner stuff in.

My relationship with Richie kickstarted from when I left Styal. In spite of the initial doubts, as each day passed I became increasingly convinced that I needed Richie in my life. I needed him as a friend, as a lover, as a calming influence and as a motivator when times were tough.

Six months after leaving Styal, I moved out of Amy's Mum and Dad's place and started to rent a smart, terraced house in Mill Street, Ormskirk. My old school, Ormskirk Grammar was at the top of the road, so if I was ever at home on a school day, it was really busy between half eight and nine and then again between half three and four, but on the whole, despite the odd can of Coke and Mars bar wrapper finding its way on to my path, they seemed like good kids. I could have thrown a few buckets of water over some buck toothed, metal mouthed minxes, but I was hormonally challenged at that age too, so I refrained from running the taps.

Finding work was difficult. Once your curriculum vitae has a prison sentence for manslaughter on it, getting employment is tricky! Luckily, there are kindhearted souls around though who are prepared to give people like me a second chance in life. I started off working in a mobile café that was parked just off the M61 in Chorley. The bloke who owned it, Eric, was an ex-con himself from old Skelmersdale, he had served two years for handling stolen goods back in the sixties and once he went straight, he learnt to appreciate how difficult it was for ex-cons to get a foothold on the jobs ladder, so he started employing them. Eric used to drive across from 'Skem' to pick me up at Amy's Mum and Dad's at six o'clock every morning and his café would be open from half six to half two each day. Most truckers and drivers were after sausage, bacon, eggs and burgers, so Eric had noticed over the years that he only had to be open for breakfast and lunch as by mid-afternoon, business began to tail off. It was certainly different to working in a bank, but I enjoyed it as everyone who stopped seemed to be an interesting soul with a bit of time to tell a story.

As I managed to get through six months with Eric without killing anyone or stealing anything, I was able to graduate to a job "waiting on", in a coffee shop in Ormskirk, 'Caffeine Corner'. Eric had given me a glowing reference and although providing middle class housewives with carrot cake and coffee wasn't overly taxing, it gave me a bit of cash, which originally allowed me to offer Amy's Mum and Dad some keep, (which they refused to accept) and subsequently allowed me to rent a place of my own. When I moved into Mill Street, I gave Richie the option of moving in with me, but he turned it down. He said he would help me with the rent, as he knew I would struggle to cover it alone, but he didn't believe in living with someone before marriage. I kept asking every day from the day I visited the house for the first time until the day I moved in!

On the day I moved in, Richie was helping me unpack everything and I found myself becoming a little irritated with him for not taking the plunge with me.

"How very 1950's of you!" I told him, once Richie had again re-iterated his feelings that it would be wrong for us to live together before marriage.

"I'm old fashioned with things like that!"

"So you'll get home from work, have your Mum cook your tea, give her your dirty laundry to wash and iron, pass her your plates to wash and then you'll nip on the train here, have a couple of beers, watch TV, screw me and then nip back home to check whether your mother has hung your jacket up and pressed your trousers for the next day! Don't try and fool me by saying you're a traditionalist, you just know how to get your toast buttered on both sides!"

"No, its nothing to do with that! I just have values, that's all!"

This grated with me.

"Are you suggesting I don't?"

"No! Stop trying to turn this around! I just don't think we should live together before we are married."

I softened a little each time he said this as there was an implication that we would get married. I decided to check out whether the implication was intended.

"So, do you think we'll get married?"

"I'd like to think so. Do you?"

I just gave him my sexiest smile.

"I'll give you my answer when you're on one knee. Not before!"

"A man needs to know he's going to get a good response before he asks!"

"Well you'll know, because if I ever think we haven't got a future together, I'll dump you!"

"Come here!"

Richie grabbed me and gave me what started out as a playful bear hug and developed into a kiss and then ultimately resulted in sex on my unmade bed. When I think back to those days now, the one word I would use to describe our sex life would be – frequent! Not necessarily long sessions, but regular, repetitive sex sessions. Back in the day, before life wears you down, I wasn't a girl for saying 'No'! Richie also had an ability back then to re-charge his batteries in next to no time! It was start, stop, start again ten minutes later. Once you have kids, it becomes start, stop, start again same time, same place, next month!

Despite Richie refusing to sacrifice the joys of his mother's cooking for a place with me, he spent almost every evening at Mill Street and our weekends were pretty much love-ins that John and Yoko would have been proud of. The train journeys Richie was taking on a daily basis, to and from work in Maghull and to and from my house in Ormskirk, were becoming a bind, so he enrolled in an intensive learner driver course and after one failed attempt, he managed to pass second time. Fifth time overall! We celebrated like we had won the pools and he bought a lime green Toyota Carina that set him back £500. Richie bought it from an eighty year old man with failing eyesight and reactions and it was the type of car designed with the more mature driver in mind, but it was reliable and took us to places without us having to rely on public transport, so it added a new dimension to our lives. We could now go to places like the Lake District and the Yorkshire Moors, that we had never tackled by train.

Richie and I both loved walking in the countryside. When you are cooped up in a café all week, the last thing you want to do at weekends is go shopping, you want to be out in the open air. One sunny spring Sunday, Richie drove us up to Ambleside and from there we had a wonderful walk up Loughrigg Fell. After a couple of hours walking, we sat down on a bank, looking down upon Loughrigg Tarn and Richie opened a wicker picnic basked he had brought our lunch in. He took out two plastic champagne glasses and a miniature bottle of champagne.

"Wow! You've come prepared, Mr Billingham! I am impressed! Look at this view, isn't it amazing!"

"It is," said Richie, he looked red faced and a few beads of sweat had gathered on his forehead, "but it needed to be after lugging this picnic basket up here!"

"Be a man! It's a picnic basket not a suitcase!"

"I get no sympathy from you, do I?!" Richie said in an amused tone.

I lay back on the bank so my whole body was resting against it and put my hands on my head.

"This has got to be the most beautiful spot in the whole world!" I said as Richie forced the cork off the champagne bottle. It flew up in the air and down the bank, Richie ran down after it, keen not to litter such a clean and picturesque place. He strode back up with the cork in his hand.

"I'm glad you said that, a bit of an exaggeration maybe, but I'm glad you said it!"

"Well, it's definitely my favourite place in the world!"

"It might be mine too, in a minute." Richie replied cryptically. He passed me a plastic glass of champagne.

"Cheers!"

"Cheers!"

"It is just an amazing place to be though, isn't it? It makes you appreciate how lucky you are to be alive and to have the freedom to come somewhere like this. Look how the tarn reflects the trees and the clouds in the water and everywhere is just so green and bursting with life. It just gives you a brilliant buzz being here, doesn't it?"

"That'll be the champagne!" Richie responded with a giggle.

"Don't be daft! I just think its fantastic. In a way, it makes me think about everything that's gone on in my life so far. Vomit Breath was an idiot but I didn't help the situation being a hardnosed, stroppy little madam either. When she was using my face as a punchbag, Kelly, Tut and I should have thrown a sack over her head, bundled her into Tut's car and driven her up here. We could have shown her this view and tried to educate her that there's more to life than fighting, fags and booze."

Richie shook his head.

"Your Mum was beyond educating, Jemma. If you'd have brought her here, she would have taken out a bottle of whiskey and a pack of fags, drank and smoked herself silly, then gone in search of the nearest offie, leaving her bottle and fag packet behind. She was a nasty piece of work and she was never going to change."

"She didn't deserve to die though."

I had thought about Vomit Breath a million times since she died. She was a horrible woman but I blamed myself completely for her unnecessary death. Although I sometimes tried to kid myself that I was wrongly punished for Kelly's misdemeanour, the reality was somewhat different. If I had not been waving a knife at Vomit Breath that evening, that sorry episode would never have happened. The guilt and responsibilty lay squarely at my feet. I should have run away or reported her to the police. On reflection, I fully deserved the punishment I received.

"No," said Richie after a pause, "but if she hadn't been a child beating, evil cow of a woman, she would still be alive. Anyway, nothing can ever change history. You can regret what happened, but you can't change it."

"True, but it can change me. It has changed me."

I decided the conversation could become too morbid and the huge high I was feeling could be taken from me if this conversation continued. I changed the subject.

"Do you think we'll bring our kids up here?"

Richie smiled the broadest smile I think I had ever seen him smile.

"I'm not supposed to know yet whether you'd marry me and here you are talking about our unborn children!"

"You can have children without getting married, you know!" I joked.

"I can't! Stand up."

"Why?"

"Don't question me, just do it. Stand up."

I was a little worried.

"I've not been lying in dog poo or anything, have I?"

I stood up. Plastic glass of champagne still in my hand.

"No, nothing like that. Put your glass down." Richie insisted as he got to his feet too.

I did as I was told. This was the moment for me that everything changed. The moment that drew a line under the 'Agony Years' and started the 'Ecstasy Years'. Richie went down on one knee.

"Jemma Watkinson," Richie looked right into my eyes, his pupils were enlarged, "will you do me the immense honour of becoming my wife?"

There were no doubts. Nothing to ponder. I just had an intense feeling of joy.

"Definitely. Nothing could make me more proud!"

Richie had a box in his hand. My immediate feeling was one of fear. Richie was not the most artistic of men, I could imagine his choice of engagement ring being something unconventional but not necessarily something pleasant on the eye. I did not have too long for fear to set in, Richie flicked the box open and inside was a hula hoop crisp. He slipped it on to my ring finger.

"I didn't want to choose an engagement ring for you. I thought, seeing as though you'd be wearing it for the rest of your life, you should choose it yourself. Get something you really love. For now though, this will have to do. If you're hungry, you can always eat it!"

I started to laugh and cry simultaneously. Everything was perfect. The sun shone brightly, we sipped champagne, I trembled with delight.

"One thing I forgot to ask!" I said once my jangled nerves began to settle.

"What's that?" Richie enquired.

"Have you asked my father's permission?" I questioned, keeping a poker face.

Richie looked at me with a furrowed brow.

"Your father? I have no idea who your father is!"

"Neither have I and neither has he!!"

"Do you want me to show you how he did it?"

"Did what?"

"Created you!"

"Here?"

"Why not?"

I looked around there was no-one in sight.

"True! Why not?"

So the first thing we did as an engaged couple was make love on Loughrigg Fell. It was also the second thing we did and the third! I told you, we were frequent back in the day!

Jemma

It was a Wednesday night. "Caffeine Corner" had been quiet all afternoon, it had been deadly boring and I was due on. Richie had been working on one of the cashier tills in the Building Society because two of the women had been off sick and there was a one hundred pounds discrepancy on his till. It was short too, which he said was worse. Thus, we were ripe for a row. Coronation Street had just finished, we were in the lounge at Mill Street and before the next programme started, I just mentioned matter-of-factly, that we needed to book Christ Church soon otherwise it may be booked up for the big day. Cue, argument!

"No way, Jemma, absolutely no way!"

"What do you mean, 'no way'?!"

My legs had been resting on Richie's on the settee, I took them off!

"I refuse to get married in a church!"

"Hang on a second, who's wedding is this?" I enquired, upset that Richie was making unilateral decisions.

"Ours," Richie replied reluctantly, before adding, "not just yours!"

"I didn't say it was just mine, but should we not be making decisions together, compromising on certain things, to keep each other happy?"

"Jemma, I'll compromise with you about everything, in fact, there is no need for us to compromise, when it comes to this wedding, you can do exactly what you want and I'll go along with it, with one exception. I am not saying my vows in a church. If you make me do that, I'll be carrying a placard with 'Here Under Protest' written on it!"

"Why?"

"Jemma, you know why! I'm an atheist!"

"But I'm a Christian!"

"No, you're not! You're a half hearted Christian! When was the last time you went to church?"

"I've been to Christ Church several times since I came out of Styal and when I was in jail, I went to chapel every day."

I know Christians have been accused by non-believers of sometimes adopting a superior attitude, but Richie was the one with the superiority complex. He looked at me as though I was a twelve year old who still believed in Father Christmas.

"Why would you of all people believe in God, Jemma?!"

"What do you mean 'YOU OF ALL PEOPLE'?!"

"Well, you haven't been treated very fairly in life, have you? Beaten by your mother, jailed for a killing you didn't commit, it doesn't seem your prayers have been answered!"

"But look at me now! OK, my life was tough, but I came through it and now I am getting married to you. Who's to know God's influence on that?"

"I know!" Richie replied, "There wasn't any influence! He doesn't exist!"

Richie was often a stubborn man. If he knew something or at least felt he knew something, he refused to back down, even when he turned out to be wrong.

"Richie, if you know categorically that God does not exist, why are you wasting your time persuading me? You should be out and about explaining things to all the incredibly intelligent people who are Christians and continue to believe because they have read the Bible, understand it and have a true faith. People far more intelligent than you."

"Jemma, just because there are intelligent Christians, that does not prove a thing! There are intelligent people who believe in every religion under the sun and there are intelligent atheists. I just don't see there being a man on high, who looks down on everything we do, keeping score and ultimately punishing us for bad behaviour like the world's Headmaster! Also, you can supposedly only get into heaven if you believe in God, so there must be millions of cavemen and early aborigines in Hell feeling pretty hard done to, because no-one taught them about God. He also seems to punish every other species other than man, which seems more than a little harsh given he created everything. God gives the majority of humans eighty years on earth and then an eternity in heaven, but gives caterpillars a matter of weeks, but tries to placate them by allowing them to fly around a bit at the end!"

Richie was in full flow now, but in a supercilious way.

"Richie, you can trivialise Christianity if you want to, but I've read the Bible, several times over and it gives my life meaning. I have faith in Jesus Christ and I have faith in God. Have you ever even read the Bible?"

"No. Not in full. I've read bits."

"Well, how can you just dismiss it then, when you've not read it?"

"I haven't put my hand in a fire either, but I still know its's hot!"

"What?"

"Sometimes you only need a basic understanding of something to realise how it works."

"That's just complete rubbish! How ridiculous! You cannot decide there's no God when you haven't read the Bible!"

"Hypocrite!"

Richie enjoyed this type of argument. I would get annoyed but he would just find it all very entertaining. The advantage I had over him though was my persistence. I would not back down.

"Richie, why am I hypocrite?"

"Have you ever read the Qur'an?"

"No."

"OK. You just said I couldn't possibly dismiss Christianity if I haven't read the Bible. If that's the case, how can you dismiss Islamic faiths, if you haven't read the Qur'an?!

Read up on every religion, Jemma, before you decide the Christians are right. Make an informed choice, like you're telling me to do! Who knows where you'll want to get married then, you may want to marry in a mosque or a synagogue. You're just siding with the only religion you've ever been taught about! That's not being broadminded, it's just jumping on the bandwagon!"

This was one of those arguments were no-one could win, as neither of us was ever going to agree with the others viewpoint. I didn't want to win the battle though, I wanted to win the war. I wanted to get married in a church!

"To repeat.I have read the Bible. I understand and believe the general message within it and I want to get married in a church. Can you not respect my wishes?"

Richie gave me the look he had once given me, when I had burst out laughing and spat some of my soup out, around his parents dinner table, when his Mum had said her soup had been made with a lot of "cumin".

"This is like, 'there's a hole in my bucket, Dear Liza,!' Why would I respect your wishes, if your wishes involve me getting married in a Church?! That would mean that you would not be respecting my wishes!"

"Why are you so against getting married in a church, Richie?"

"I'd feel like a hypocrite getting married in a Church. Devoting my life to you in front of a God that I don't believe in!"

"So what? Why would you be bothered? If you don't believe in God, it's not as though you'll be punished in the afterlife, as you don't even believe there is one! I'd feel like I betrayed God, if I didn't get married in a Church."

Richie pulled another face. This one was his "AS IF!" face.

"Betrayed God!" he scorned, "did you not betray God when you lied under oath at your trial?"

"I did not lie!"

"You did not tell the truth, the whole truth and nothing but the truth, so help you God!"

"I did."

Admittedly, I did not say this convincingly.

"Did you mention in court that you just happened to see your sister pushing your mother down the stairs?"

"Maybe not."

"Maybe…not." Richie paused between the two words for dramatic effect.

"But it was an altruistic lie." I added in my defense.

"God might not see it that way, Jemma."

Admittedly, at this stage, I was losing this battle.

"Don't give me that! You don't even believe in God, Richie!"

Richie laughed smugly, "I think the safest option would be for us to get married in a Registry office. I wouldn't want my bride to be getting struck down by a lightning bolt, sent by a vengeful God, as she walks down the aisle!"

Richie tried to grab me in one of those bear hugs that always ended up in sex. I resisted. I was not in the mood!

"Don't be trying it on. If I don't feel you love me, you won't be having sex again this side of the twenty first century!"

"You've just got a cob on because you're losing the argument!"

"No, I'm not! You forget God forgives those who repent of their sins and I have truly repented of mine. I have absolutely no doubt that I have been forgiven in the eyes of the Lord. We are getting married in a church and that's that!"

"Oh not, it's not!"

"Oh yes, it is!"

The pantomime continued into the early hours and then again in the days that followed. Twelve months later, Richie and I were married at Christ Church, Aughton with a reception at the Briars Hall, Lathom .Richie did not carry a placard revealing that he was "Here Under Protest!"

Richie

Jim and I stood propping up the bar or to be more accurate, the bar managed to take our weight and prop us up.

"I'm going to bed!" I slurred, letting go of the side of the bar tentatively, like a novice ice skater would let go of the edge.

"NO! NO! NO! NO!" Jim stated, pulling me back by the shirt collar, "this is your stag do, Richie, I'm your best man, you're going nowhere! Look at your mates, they aren't falling by the wayside, they're driving hard!"

Jim did one of those funny forward, circular rotations of his hand, like a master of ceremonies would do in olden times when announcing a returning knight to the Queen. In this case, there were no returning knights, just eight deranged friends, pogoing around a Copenhagen dancefloor in frenzied fashion, to the sound of Vic Reeves and The Wonderstuff's version of 'Dizzy'. They were gathering up helpless Scandanavian women like a tornado in the desert would gather up tumbleweed.

"Jim, I've partied hard with these boys for the last thirty six hours. My bed is calling me now. Please just let me go!"

"No! What sort of brother would I be, if I let you go? This is your stag do! Hopefully your only stag do! By Monday, it will all just be a memory. You need to breathe in the vibes, savour the moments, for soon your friends will scatter and you will be left with a fat wife, spoilt kids and an enormous mortgage!"

"Thanks for that! Jemma's not fat."

"Not yet! Wait until she's married! Women feast on contentment!"

"Anyway, I'd still love Jemma if she was fat."

"No, you wouldn't! Why do people say that and pretend to be nice?! You'd only love her until someone younger, prettier and skinnier gave you a nod and a wink!"

I stared at Jim like he was a lunatic, which he was.

"Does Amy know all about your bizarre judgements on the female species?"

"Yes. Amy's aware that she's the luckiest girl in the world!"

"I bet you tell her often enough!"

"Every day, mate! Every day!"

Jim was still the misogynistic, chauvinistic pig, he had been since he was a teenager or so he would have you believe. The truth was, when Amy was around, he would do anything for her. Amy was most definitely the one who wore the trousers.

"Jim, seriously, I need to go to bed!"

"Richie, this place will be shutting up shop in half an hour, the boys that don't pull will be ready to go home with us then. Let's go and join them or at the very least, have another pint at the bar. My treat!"

"It isn't a treat though, is it Jim?!" I protested, "I must have had thirty pints since we got to Denmark! If I have another one, I might drown!"

"Stop being so melodramatic! These are your last days of freedom! Enjoy them!"

Jim still had the capacity to infuriate me like no other.

"Will you shut up about it being the last days of freedom, Jim! I'm lucky to be be marrying Jemma. She's a bloody good woman, loyal, passionate, interesting, beautiful, sexy….every day is an adventure and I'm thankful that something or someone brought us together. I love her, Jim. In fact, I don't just love her, I adore her!"

Jim feigned a yawn.

"Bog off," I continued, "anyway, can we not just get out of here? If none of these maniacs manage to pull a desperate Dane, their attention will be turning to me in half an hour. I'm the stag and I've had nothing depraved done to me yet. Remember what they did to 'Dogger' in Brighton? Tied him to the lamppost naked in the middle of the gay area, didn't they? Covered him in flour and then wrapped him in clingfilm! They didn't collect him until the following morning and it was barely morning either, because the pissheads overslept! His willy had the girth of a baby worm when they untied him!"

Jim smiled knowingly at me.

"Richie, I don't know why you're saying 'they', from all accounts you were one of the perpetrators!"

"Exactly! That's why we have to flee now!"

"We could go here!"

Jim dug deep into his trouser pocket and found a crumpled flyer which he handed to me. Due to the darkness, my drunkenness and the flashing lights, it was difficult to make out. There seemed to be a cartoon on one side of the flyer with a semi-naked Danish version of "Jessica Rabbit". On the other side, it said something along the lines of,

'See the best of what Copenhagen has to offer, in the flesh. Two free entries with this flyer'

"Why would I want to go to another club, Jim?"

"It's a lapdancing joint!"

"A what?"

"You pay for naked lovelies to dance for you!"

"I can't be arsed Jim, I just want to go to sleep!"

"Richie, you get married in three weeks, you may never see a naked woman again!"

"Jim, are you off again?! Of course I will, Jemma! That's the only naked body I want to see."

"Not necessarily."

"Eh?"

"I told you, women feast on contentment, once they are full, they don't need sex. Sex for women is all about their uncertainty and the desire to feel wanted. Once they know they are wanted they stop playing the game. A cat only plays with a mouse until it kills it."

I laughed.

"You talk some crap, Jim! You obviously don't know Jemma! She has a lot of sexual energy. It probably built up whilst she was in jail."

"There was a bloke at work who was going out with a right horny minx, but he says from the day he got married, he never saw his wife naked again. Not once!"

"Who?!"

"Ben Scott!"

"Ben Scott from Moss Delph Lane?! He's got four kids!"

"I know he has, but he created them in darkness! She was another one that went chunky after the wedding so she made him switch the light off!"

"Are you trying to put me off getting married?"

"No, but I do reckon the old jokes right!"

"Which one?"

"The one that says when a bride gets into the church, she sees three things, the aisle, the altar and you and that's what she's thinking…..I'll alter you!"

"Jim, I am not going to the lapdancing joint!"

"Why?"

"I'm tired and I'm skint!"

"Skint! Don't worry about that! I'll pay!"

"You're going to pester me until I agree to this, aren't you?!"

"That's what brothers do!"

"Dizzy" finished and before my mates had chance to draw breath, the DJ put on Carter The Unstoppable Sex Machine's "Only Living Boy In New Cross" and as the frenzy continued, Jim and I snuck out.

The lapdancing bar was rather amusingly called 'Nipples and Tipples' and was in a seedy looking road on the edge of the city. I have no idea what part of the city it was, there just seemed to be bikes everywhere, so Jim and I managed to find two that were not locked up, mine actually had a basket and a bell on but I was past caring and I followed Jim as he weaved his way across the city. Jim seemed to know exactly where he was going, which probably meant he had made a strategic plan to go lapdancing all along and had mapped his route out. We dumped the bikes one hundred metres from the club and sauntered up a slight hill to the entrance. We handed our flyer in to two tough looking bouncers in penguin suits and were directed down a staircase that seemed to descend forever. By the time I reached the bottom of the stairs, I was half expecting to see a horned devil with a multitude of sinners, shovelling coal into a roaring furnace. Once I reached the dimly lit club though, I did see the sinners but there was no horned devil, although Jim was most definitely a horny devil. On arrival, we stood at the bottom of the staircase, looking like naughty schoolchildren. Lapdancing joints were not commonplace back then and, despite the drink, I had not felt this embarrassed since I had charged into my parents bedroom as a fifteen year old, to find my mother's head at the top of the bed and my father emerging sheepishly from the bottom end.

A tall, leggy lady with bright hazel eyes and a black 'bob' came towards us wearing little more than a beaded thong and a bra, barely large enough to cover her nipples. She looked like she had escaped from a James Bond movie, probably wanting to escape the shackles of its 'PG' rating. She spoke English with a mid-atlantic drawl.

"Hello Gentlemen! May I welcome you to 'Nipples and Tipples! My name is Marianne and I host the parties here. As you can see, we are very busy this evening, our beautiful ladies are being admired by many men. We currently only have tables available in our VIP area, 'The Lounge'. Would you gentlemen be interested in taking a table in 'The Lounge'?"

Jim was excited by this prospect.

"VIP! Absolutely! It's my brother's stag do, I'm going to be his best man, so I need to make sure he has a great night!"

Jim was talking to Marianne's breasts which seemed to be having the same effect on him as a hypnotist's watch. Marianne was probably totally dis-interested in the fact that it was my stag do and Jim was going to be best man, but she politely played the game.

"Well, you have come to the right place for a great night!" She turned to me, "I am assuming you are the brother, right?"

"That would be me!" I replied. Those breasts were drawing me in too. I tried to keep my eyes off them so as not to render myself as a stereotypical male.

"What is your name?" Marianne asked smiling.

"Richie."

"And you brother is…?"

"Jim."

"Well Richie, I really hope you and Jim enjoy spending time with our beautiful ladies here tonight, but please remember, no touching the ladies! Please save your touching for your wedding night!"

"I think Jim is going to be enjoying this experience more than me!" I said pointing at my brother who was staring around in every direction like a meerkat on sentry duty, as scantily clad women moved through in all directions. It was like a Heathrow terminal purely for drunken businessmen and strippers!

"Gentlemen, follow me!" said Marianne, leading the way through the throng and the thongs. There were a feast of gyrating hips attached to pretty young women of all hair colours and ethnicities. We passed through two sets of curtains, until we reached an area that was minimalistic but looked like the budget had been stretched a little for this section. Chandeliers replaced disco lights, tables were glass rather than wooden and cigarette stained. It looked like the same club but classier. The same could be said for the women. The ladies appeared more sophisticated, a bit more sassy and chic and on the whole, the men looked older, balder and no doubt richer. Jim and I bucked the trend. Marianne saw us to our seats.

"Can I get drinks for you two gentlemen?" Marianne asked.

"Can you get us a bottle of champagne, please!" Jim piped up.

"Any preference? Would you like me to run through what we have or maybe get you a price list?"

"No!" Jim insisted, "just bring us a top quality champagne and two glasses!"

"Jim!" I whispered, "should we not get a price list? It could cost you a fortune!"

"Hush brother! I am proud to be buying a fine champagne for my big brother! Sod the expense!"

Marianne went off to find the bottle of champagne with the biggest mark up and as she departed, our table was soon welcoming an African-American stunner that is difficult for me to describe. Difficult for me to describe, not because she was incredibly glamorous, but because my intense drunken state trigerred night time narcolepsy and cataplexy, if such a thing existed. We were sat on a semi circular sofa that arched around a glass table, faced with a woman that could have walked straight off the runways of Milan or Paris, but all I needed to do was sleep. I remember her coming over and I remember her asking if anyone would like a dance but I slumped into a foetal position on that sofa and from there on in, the night was, how I imagine one long LSD trip to be, I was totally aware of my bizarre surroundings, but I was totally incapable of reacting to them. I could hear Jim asking for drink after drink, joking with the lapdancers, having them sit on his knee, which given the no touching rule, I imagine came at a price, but I was too out of it to pick myself up. After a long period of impersonating a giant foetus, but probably making myself look like a giant faeces, Jim propped me back up.

"Mate, do you remember when you first met Kelly?"

I nodded. The ability to speak had now temporarily been withdrawn.

"It was at The Birch's party, wasn't it?"

I nodded once more.

"And you said that if you hadn't been out with Kelly, your opinion of Jemma would never have changed. Right?"

I nodded less vigorously third time, as it was beginning to make me feel sick.

"Well, do you remember how you managed to get to the Birch's party that night?"

"Taxi," I mumbled, surprising myself that I had some sort of deep, confused voice.

"That's right, Richie and who paid for that taxi? It was me, wasn't it?"

"Uh-huh!" I groaned. 'Just let me sleep', I thought, 'please let me sleep!'

"Well, I need the favour repaying. These girls need to be paid for the fine work they have done already and the work that they are yet to do."

I turned my head to look at them. There were a lot of them. Five, six, maybe more, I am not sure what was real and what was a double triggered by my weary brain.

"OK." I responded. "My credit cards are in my wallet…I'll pay."

"Good boy!"

Jim allowed me to slump back down but five minutes later some random female voice asked if I could sign a form. I heard giggles and mock flirtation and music and champagne corks, but all I wanted to do was sleep, which was not altogether easy, as every time I managed to start to doze, I was prompted for another signature. Eventually, Jim realised he was in no fit state to continue and hoisted me up and told me that it was time to hit the road. For his own amusement, once we were outside, Jim put me back on a bike, but after dropping off it to my left once and to my right once, he decided enough was enough, put a big, chubby, brotherly arm around me and steered me back to our hotel.

The following lunchtime, myself, Jim and the eight others were in a mini bus, all looking paler than Casper, heading towards Copenhagen airport when my mobile phone rang. It was one of those sturdy mobiles that were just coming into regular use back then and was big enough to double up as a bed for a Chihuahua.

"Hello," I croaked in a voice that needed its next dose of water and paracetamol.

"Hello, is that Mr.Billingham? Mr. Richard Billingham?" a male voice asked.

"Yeeeerrrsss", I groaned as if it was painful to even say three letters.

"Its Middleland Bank Visa here, Mr. Billingham. We just wanted to check that you are currently in Copenhagen?"

"I am," I replied, "but how did you know?"

"There was some unusual activity on your credit card last night, sir. We just wanted to ensure it was not a fraudulent transaction?"

"I haven't used my credit card whilst I've been here!" I protested. "There must be some mistake!"

"It was at 4.30 am this morning, at a place called 'Nipples & Tipples'?"

"Oh yeah!" I said feeling my pale skin turn crimson, "that was me!"

"That's fine sir," said the voice, "enjoy the rest of the trip."

As soon as I put the phone down, it started to ring again. I started to panic and without answering it, I began feeling for receipts in my pocket. I dug out the full contents of every pocket.

I prodded Jim who was snoring next to me. He didn't move. I flicked his nose as hard as I could. Jim and his ruffled hair sat up. He looked jaundiced.

"What?" he asked, not sounding as exuberant as he had in the club.

"How much in pounds is four thousand krone?" I asked.

Jim paused for a few seconds to think.

"Just under five hundred quid."

"Shit!" I said. "SHIT!"

"What's up, Richie?" someone asked.

"Last night, lapdancing." They were the only words I could manage to get out.

"Richie, forget about it." Jim said, "We had a great night. If you had stayed awake, you would have loved it, it was a Leonard Cohen themed lapdancing club. The manager was a big Leonard Cohen fan, so every girl had a name based on a song of his. Marianne, Suzanne, Chelsea. Iodine, Janis…what an amazing place! If you had to pay five hundred quid, just for a brief glimpse of it, then it was worth it. Don't stress! It's a stag do, these things happen. Put it down to experience!"

"Jim, if it was just five hundred quid, I could just about it handle it! But its not just one receipt for four thousand krone, its….." I said counting the receipts out onto my lap, "…….one, two, three, four, five, six, seven, eight! That's almost four grand! I didn't even see a fucking tit!"

My bad language was back but this time, I allowed myself this luxury. As I was kicking off, we went into a tunnel,

"Look out the window, Richie!" I heard Andy "Dogger" Woodward shout.

"Why?" I asked, "I can't see anything, its dark, I can only see myself."

"Well, at least you've seen a fucking tit now!"

The mini bus erupted into laughter and I was left to contemplate whether I could hide the fact that I had lost four thousand pounds in my sleep, from Jemma, for the rest of my life!

Brad

I'm a big bloke now. I'm forty and Tyrene says if I keep supping the tinnies at this rate it won't be long before I'm forty stone! I'm nineteen stone right now and if I had a dollar for every time Tyrene called me a "big, fat, lazy bastard", I could charter a yacht and sail to the Whitsundays and we live in Perth! These days, when I have a shower, I lose half the water in those ripples of fat on my belly and I've got bigger tits than a Pommie cricket ground on a sunny day.

I've not always been big though. When I was a young bloke, I was a bit of a catch for the young pretty girls and I must say, Tyrene was a looker in her day too, before the fags and the drink took effect. I met her when I was twenty seven and she was twenty four, over in a bar in Melville. I'd had a string of girlfriends before Tyrene. Only loved one of them though and she was a Pom! Her name was Kelly, I remember meeting her, back in '94, like it was yesterday…….

Horizontal bungee would not normally have been my idea of nightclub entertainment. I was in Cairns at a nightclub called "End of The World", schooner in hand, watching a load of young blokes with bike helmets and knee pads on, sprinting towards a beer on a table at the far end of the dancefloor, with a bungee rope tied round their butts. Joel, Brett and myself were letting our hair down, having reached our final destination after seven weeks backpacking around Australia. We had taken in Adelaide, Melbourne, Canberra, Sydney, Brisbane and loads of fantastic places along the way. We toured the MCG in Melbourne, crossed the Harbour Bridge and checked out the Opera House in Sydney. In Brisbane, we went water ski-ing, scuba diving at Airlie Beach, visited a strip joint in Surfers Paradise and in Cairns, I wanted to finish with a bungee jump. A proper one.

I was standing on my own watching these bungee guys. Both Brett and Joel had already disappeared with young women, in their attempt to add another used prophylactic to Cairns sewerage system. These bungee guys were sprinting along, like demented athletes, to within a metre of the beer, before the rope became taut, then it would catapult them back to their starting point, usually along the ground. OK, it was pretty funny, but there was no way I was having a go!

I was about to finish off my schooner and head back to Caravella, the backpacker Hostel where we were staying. I didn't fancy heading to bed though. We were in a dorm and I had already scared the girl in the bunk next to me that morning, as I had woken up to find my 'snake in the grass' had found its way through the gap in my PJ's. She looked aghast and impressed in equal measure! I thought maybe if I headed back there I could watch the World Cup soccer on the big screen out the back, if a game was on. I had watched the Italy-Ireland game there with a load of Poms and Irish and the atmosphere was great, especially when the Irish scored.

Just as the last drops of the amber nectar disappeared down my laughing gear and I was about to set back off to the Esplanade and Caravellas, I was stopped in my tracks by the next bungee contestant. They had obviously run out of daft blokes willing to give it a go, so a young woman had stepped up to the plate. A woman who, up to that point, must have been the finest looking woman I had ever seen. It's hard to explain what it is that makes a woman attractive, but whatever magic it is, Kelly had it. I suppose you'd call it a magnetic beauty. A sexual aura. There is just no way, fifteen years on, I can describe her in a way that will do her justice, but as a starting point, the fact that she still looked incredible wearing a bicycle helmet says bloody loads! Kelly, who would have been about twenty three at the time, was wearing a white t-shirt with a silver heart on it and her breasts were pushing firmly against it with her nipples prodding against it like a pair of concealed pistols. As a bloke, I can't say this was something I noticed often in women, but with Kelly, I was immediately aware that her skin was perfect. It looked as though someone in heaven, had been smoothing and polishing it, like a prize bowling ball, before sending her to earth. The DJ announced her arrival,

"And now we have our first female contestant of the evening. What's your name and where are you from?"

"My name is Kelly and I'm from England."

There was a mix of boos and cheers. I cheered, not because she was a Pom but because she was bloody gorgeous.

"Nice to meet you, Kelly. Good to have you here. Whereabouts in England are you from?"

"A small town called Ormskirk."

"Hornchurch," the DJ incorrectly repeated, "I've heard of Hornchurch."

"No! Orms – kirk!" Kelly stated.

"Can't say I've heard of that place! Anyone famous from Ormskirk?"

"The Beatles!" Kelly answered with a mischievous smile.

"Strewth, really?" said the DJ genuinely surprised, "I thought they were from Liverpool?"

"It's near Liverpool. Less than twenty miles away."

"Right! And were all 'The Beatles' from there?"

"No," Kelly replied, "just Paul and John. Ringo and George weren't. Penny Lane is in Ormskirk and Strawberry Fields. They were originally called 'The Quarrymen' and then 'The Ormskirk Beatles' before shortening it, to just 'The Beatles'!"

"Wow! Seriously?"

Kelly started laughing.

"No, I'm just joking! No-one famous is from Ormskirk. Not as far as I know!"

"Well, maybe Kelly, you might put it on the map. Your name is Kelly, right?!"

"Yes. That bit was true!"

"So, having just made me look a fool, do you think this horizontal bungee will make a fool out of you or do you think you can reach that elusive beer over there which none of the blokes have managed to get to?"

"I'll certainly give it my best shot!"

"Atta girl! Lets get a bit of a chant going for Kelly! KEL-LY! KEL-LY! KEL-LY!"

The whole crowd in 'End Of The World' started clapping and chanting or at least the male contingent did, the females probably looked at Kelly like she was a dingo in a sheep pen. Kelly looked better than she ran! The DJ, no doubt raging after Kelly's bogus story about 'The Ormskirk Beatles' must have taken great pleasure in her cord tightening about ten feet from the beer, she lost her balance and bounced back to her starting point like a speedboat on a choppy sea! The male clappers gave Kelly another round of applause, purely based on effort rather than attainment. If she weighed then, as much as I weigh now, I guess the applause may have been muted. She kept smiling despite the bumps and bruises.

For the next half an hour, I became a bit of a stalker, as I just could not help following Kelly's every move. As I have said, I was a bit of a looker then, tanned, muscular, fit, so I was used to being chased by women rather than chasing them, but Kelly was something a little bit special. She appeared to be with a couple of other girls and the three of them were laughing and smiling and looking as happy as a croc chewing Captain Hooks arm. Three schooners and alcohol-induced Dutch courage later, I made my move. I found out later that Kelly was on her way to the John, but all I knew at the time was that she was finally on her own, so when she walked past me, I gently took hold of her hand.

"Fancy doing a real one?" I asked.

"A real one?"

"Bungee. I've just travelled all the way across Australia and my intention when I finally arrived in Cairns, was to do a bungee. It would be heaps better and heaps more memorable if I did it tied to you!"

"Is that how Aussies chat women up? Suggest they get tied up and throw themselves off a cliff?!"

"It's not off a cliff! It's at 'The Cairns Bungy Tower', I'm going to register tomorrow. Fancy coming with me?!"

Kelly's face reddened and her smile re-emerged. She had a fantastic smile and Christ did she have fantastic lips! I imagined, when I saw her lips, that Kelly had been in the Hunter Valley, standing barefooted in a barrel, crushing grapes to make wine, with a load of other backpackers and then she had dropped something and had to swim to the bottom of the barrel, but no-one else noticed so they trod on her lips! Crazy I know, but that's what I imagined!

"Go with you to do a bungee jump?! Tied together?"

"We wouldn't have to be tied together. We could each do it alone if you wanted! The site's out in the rainforest. I've never been because, as I said before, I'm from Perth, but it looks great on the photos. Come and have a gander tomorrow if you like, you don't have to jump, just see what you think. Then you can go home to England and tell your mates and your folks that you did both a horizontal and a vertical bungee!"

"What's your name, crazy Aussie?"

"It's Brad!"

"Brad! I'm Kelly! I don't think I'll be telling anyone in England about my exploits, I haven't been home for over six years! I spent a fair bit of time in Hong Kong and then

came here over three years ago on a working visa that has long since expired"

We didn't need to shake hands, I was still holding hers.

"So be nice to me Kelly or I may get the authorities to send you home!"

"You wouldn't dare! I know already you aren't that nasty! I promise I'll be nice to you as long as you are nice to me!"

"I already have been. I was cheering you on before! I gave it a good,

'ONYA KELLY!!!'

Kelly's forehead creased. She was puzzled.

"On you, Kelly! What does that mean?!"

Kelly started laughing at me. I didn't know 'ONYA' was an Aussie expression, I just thought it was said by people who could speak English.

"Do you not say that in England?! If you're cheering someone on, do you not say, 'Onya Charles!' or 'Onya Diana' or 'Onya Whoever'?"

"NO! What does it mean?"

Kelly sounded real posh. It was like speaking to the Queen!

"I don't even know what it means! I guess it means 'Good on yer!'"

"Good…on…you?!"

"Cripes Kelly, you're posh!"

"I'm not posh!"

"You bloody are!"

"I'm not! They'd call me common in England!"

"Well, you're a lot posher than me! Anyway, how about it? Are you going to come and do the bungee? Some Kiwi called AJ Hackett started it up. It's really safe. No-one has ever had a bad injury doing it."

"But a million have died!"

"No, honestly, Kelly, no-one's died. It's just fun! An adrenalin rush!"

"No offence, Brad, but I don't fancy being in the record books for being the first one to die from doing this bunjee. It may be safe, but I don't think my heart would cope."

"You'd be fine!"

"Thanks Brad, but no thanks. Horizontal bungee will do for me!"

"Come on, Kelly, be a sport! You just go up some platform and then dive off into some water underneath. It looks awesome! If the guys at the top get your weight just right, your head dips in the water at the bottom!"

"What if they don't get your weight right, do you drown or does your head smash on the rocks at the bottom of the water?!"

"I told you, you ain't gonna cark it, Kelly! Your head just doesn't go in the water if they get your weight wrong! Look, if you don't want to do it, don't do it, but come and watch me. You can just veg out side."

"Will they let you jump tomorrow?"

"I think so."

"How would we get there?"

"By car. I've got my own. She's called Lizzy, like the Queen! She's taken me and my two mates, Brett and Joel all across Australia. She's a beaut!"

"Can I bring my two friends, Dani and Nicole? They're from Western Australia like you. They're stopping in my dorm in Caravellas on the Esplanade."

"You're stopping in Caravellas! So am I!"

"I think everyone Under 30 stays there, Brad!"

"Whereabouts in W.A are your friends from?"

"Melville in Perth."

"You're kidding me! I'm from White Gum Valley! Just up the road! Do they play golf?"

"I have absolutely no idea, Brad! Not an immediate topic of conversation amongst three girls!"

"S'pose not. It's just I'm in Royal Fremantle, if they play, I'll probably know them! Small world, eh?!"

Kelly pointed them out, they were on the dancefloor dancing to some song by Chocolate Starfish. It was the same two girls that Kelly had been with before, I didn't recognise them.

"Recognise them?"

"I'm not sure. Anyway, whether I know them or not, they're welcome to come along too."

"Great. Let me introduce you to them!"

"Bonzer! I'll just get you a drink first. What are you drinking?"

"That'd be lovely. Vodka and diet coke. Do you dance? Whatever the next song is, you're dancing with me! Deal?!"

"Only if you do the bungee!"

"Good try, Brad, but no chance!"

The following day, Kelly watched as I did my first ever bungee. I almost shit my pants but acted like it was a stroll in the park. Dani and Nicole did one too, tied together!"

That night, Dani, Nicole and I bought Kelly a bungee t-shirt on which we scrawled with one of those permanent markers,

"She came, she saw, she bottled out!"

We sat on their balcony that night smoking dope, not the brainiest thing to do given it was against the law in Queensland, but it must have relaxed Kelly, because after Dani and Nicole went inside, as the night grew cooler, she gave me a long, lingering kiss.

Three days later, Brett and Joel headed off to Alice Springs by Greyhound coach minus one friend who they called every name under the sun, as me and the car stayed on with Kelly and the girls! My seven week adventure became a seven month one as I fell in love, big style and toured the Northern Territories with Kelly, before making an about turn and heading back towards Sydney. Eight months later, Kelly and I did a tandem bungee at Kawarau Bridge, Queenstown, New Zealand! She loved it! Four weeks after that, it was all over and I headed back to Perth and Kelly headed to back to England. I can never quite remember what split us up but I remember something happened whilst we were at Franz Josef Glacier and that was that.

I loved every minute I spent with that girl and I must confess occasionally, when Tyrene isn't really doing it for me, and the big boy ain't working how he should, I close my eyes, picture Kelly and its like mental Viagra! Works every time!

Jim

When Amy and I were married, I was nervous about being centre of attention for the day, all eyes being on my ugly mug, but I was not at all nervous about the speeches. Let's face it, as a groom, you hardly have to say anything, you just have to trot out the bog standard pleasantries,

"Thanks very much to the bridesmaids, what a wonderful job they did and I'm sure you will all agree, they looked pretty as a picture!"

"I'd like to thank my wife (pause for cheers) for being so gorgeous and marrying a toe rag like me!"

"Here are some flowers for the mother and mother-in-law, we are both ever so grateful for all your help, love and support in making today so special….BLAH, BLAH, BLAH!!"

Easy stuff!

A best man's speech is different. When the speeches start, the invited guests aren't bothered about the father of the bride speech ('my little princess is all grown up but I'm not losing a daughter, I'm gaining a son') or the groom's speech but, they want to be entertained by the 'Best Man'. As a 'Best Man', you need to be amusing but not abusive, drop in a few "in" jokes for the lads on the stag-do and make the groom embarrassed and proud within the duration of your speech. I picked Richie to be my "Best Man" and he did a fine job. He ripped me to pieces a bit, told jokes about my ugliness, my reputation as a serial shagger until I met Amy, mentioned the tragic "Goth" years and reminded everyone that I was an annoying little shit of a brother for many a long year. It was all said in an endearing tone though and he managed to pull things back by talking about how I turned into a world class brother and friend. When it was Richie's turn to get married, I was the obvious choice and although I am sure he was sorely tempted to go with someone less obvious, he asked me all the same! It was an honour.

Richie's wedding was at Christ Church, Aughton, with a reception afterwards at Briars Hall in Lathom. Richie had been promoted in the Building Society where he worked to 'Branch Manager' and six weeks before the wedding, he was told he would be getting posted to a flagship branch in Nottingham City Centre. Both Richie and Jemma were excited by this prospect and they knew once they returned from their honeymoon in Sorrento, their new life in Nottingham would start the following day.

Mum did not take the news about Richie and Jemma's relocation as enthusiastically as they did! She cried buckets, so much so, you would have thought his posting was on the other side of the moon, not a two hour car journey up the road! Richie was no doubt her favourite! Personally, I had mixed feelings, Richie, Jemma, Amy and I saw a hell of a lot of each other, but I knew we would still see them when they were in Nottingham and by all accounts, it would be a great place to visit.

Jemma and Richie's wedding went like clockwork. Vows were exchanged with glistening eyes. Infectious smiles spread like veruccas. The only rather strange aspect to the whole day was that the bride's side of the church was virtually empty. Kelly, Jemma's sister had disappeared abroad several years earlier following Jemma's arrest and had lost all contact only months later. Jemma's mother had obviously died in the incident that had led to the arrest and her father, by all accounts, could have been any drunk in the North West of England. As 'Chief Bridesmaid', Amy took on the role of giving Jemma away.

Once the church service finished, photographs were taken and everyone enjoyed a Champagne toast on the lawn at Briars Hall on a cloudy but warm and dry day. The bride, groom and guests subsequently sat down for the meal, although I hardly touched mine and before I knew it, it was time for the speeches. Due to the lack of family on the Watkinson side and the whole host of family on ours, the speeches were made by Caroline, Richie and myself! It was certainly unique that the only three speeches being made were by three siblings, but when a replacement for father of the bride's speech was discussed, my Mum and Dad and also Amy, shied away from doing it, so Caroline, who lives with her female partner, Donna and is unlikely to have a traditional wedding of her own, was desperate to be involved.

Caroline's speech was all I would have expected it to be, touching and witty. Cal and Richie always had a close bond throughout our childhood and she spoke warmly about listening to LPs in her room and then spoke about how much she had grown to love Jemma. This was a common theme, everyone in our family, including Richie, once thought Jemma was a right royal pain in the butt, but had had a change of heart over time. Quite rightly, given she was replacing the father of the bride, Caroline devoted most of her speech to Jemma and she did it impeccably, although more than a few eyebrows were raised amongst guests of all ages when she jokingly said that both her and Donna loved Jemma so much that she was welcome over to theirs for a threesome any time! The Vicar almost choked on his chocolate mint!

Richie's speech was brief but he brought the house down in laughter and a subsequent standing ovation with an awful "A Cappella" version of Elvis Presley's "Can't Help Falling In Love". Before I knew it, it was my turn.

The moment I stood up to speak, the nerves evaporated and the adrenalin kicked in. I was no longer nervous, but excited. This was going to be great!

Jim

"Bloody hell! That was a sorry attempt at singing, wasn't it?! I don't think my ears will ever be the same again. Torture!

Right! There are eight thousand ways I could start this speech, but I'll just simply begin by saying, Ladies & Gentlemen, Boys & Girls, we now reach the moment of the day that I know some of you have been looking forward to for some time and Richie has been dreading since the second he asked me to be "Best Man"! The reason Richie has been dreading it, I think, is because he knows if I make a lot of boobs, he'll end up paying for it in the end!

I noticed a few chuckles over there from the boys from the stag do! Over there at the back! Those guys were taking bets before on what Jemma and Richie's first dance will be tonight and amazingly, the odds on favourite is Tina Turner's "Private Dancer"! Maybe one of them can explain to the rest of you later why that is! Unless you want to explain, Richie…."

I turned to Richie, on cue, he shook his head,

"…thought not! Anyway, whilst I'm talking about the guys from the stag do, let me tell you a story! Several years ago, mine and Richie's Dad, the strange looking bloke to my right, who is twitching for me to hurry up so he doesn't miss the three o'clock at Royal Ascot, went over to Canada for his cousin's wedding . In Canada, Dad tells me, the best man is not really called upon to make a speech, he just acts as a 'Master Of Ceremonies', therefore he just introduces friends of the bride and groom to say a few words. On that basis, I want everyone to give a huge hand to Andy "Dogger" Woodward, a good friend of Richie's, who accompanied him on his stag do and is very keen to say a small speech. The floor's all yours, Dogger!!"

Everyone cheered and clapped, with the exception of one man! Poor 'Dogger' nearly stuck his head in his pint of lager and drowned himself! Everyone turned and stared at him, and, totally unprepared, with the applause still ringing out, he took to his feet,

"Erm…bastards….sorry, that slipped out…its just these Billingham brothers have a habit of stitching me up and guess what, they've done it again! As you can probably tell, I wasn't expecting to be doing much this afternoon, other than drinking beer and eyeing up the one bridesmaid I am officially allowed to look at, my wife, Sandra. So, Jim's caught me off guard here!

Right, all I will say is that, despite once tying me naked to a lamppost in Brighton and abandoning me, an ordeal I will never get over, despite that, I have a lot of love for Richie. He's one cool guy. As for Jemma, well she's turned out to be a million times nicer than the bitch we all both fancied and hated at school…."

There was a collective sense of disapproval amongst the audience,

"…what? Don't tut! It was meant as a compliment! Jemma is a great girl these days! In fact, so much so, if I could have chose a wife for Richie myself, Jemma would have been the one!

So, can everyone please be upstanding and raise their glasses to today's happy couple, 'Richie and Jemma'!"

Everyone stood. "RICHIE and JEMMA!"

'Dogger' sat himself down, necked about half a pint of lager in one go and I continued.

"**Can everyone please give 'Dogger' a round of applause for being my scapegoat there! I have to be honest, I wasn't expecting his speech to go any further than 'F OFF!"**

Everyone gave 'Dogger' a pleasant round of applause. Other than committing the cardinal sin, 'Thou Must Not Slag Off The Bride On Her Wedding Day!' – he had done pretty well.

"**Thanks, Dogger! OK, before I get back to taking the mickey out of my big brother, I just want to say a few words about the newest** addition to the Billingham family, today's blushing bride, Jemma. My wife, Amy, has been friends with Jemma for more years than they care to admit, so I could, at this point, pass the buck once more and get Amy to stand up and do this part of the speech. That, however, would not be the best idea I've ever had! Whilst I don't really care how much I cheese 'Dogger' off, it may not do anything for my future sex life if I sprung a speech on Amy, so I'm going to have to do this bit myself. When asked about Jemma, Amy said the following...."

I took out a piece of paper.

"...Jemma is quite simply the best friend a girl could have. She's fiercely loyal, incredibly forgiving, strong minded, passionate and truthful. Everyone knows that she spent some time in prison and those who don't know her, would wrongly assume this makes her a bad person. This could not be further from the truth. Jemma is one of those rare people who is as radiant on the inside, as she is on the outside. Richie is a lucky man to have her."

Jemma stood up and walked over to Amy and gave her a quick hug and kiss, before returning to her seat.

"Thanks for that Amy! I really do have to re-iterate what Amy and 'Dogger' think. The more I get to know Jemma, the more I understand why Amy and Richie think so much of her. Most important to me though, is how she makes my brother feel and I know he thinks Jemma makes every second of his life worth living. Jemma, you look fabulous today, your dress is perfect and you do look truly stunning. For making my brother, the happiest man alive, I salute you. So, could I ask everyone to be upstanding once more and raise their glasses to our gorgeous bride, Jemma!"

Everyone took to their feet, their chairs scraping on the floor and reminding me of the days back at school when the Headmaster came into class. There was no toast then though, just apprehension. This time there was only joy.

"Jemma!"

"OK. As much as I love you, Jemma, it's time to move on to your cute little husband. My brother, Richie!"

There was a mumbled 'hurrah' from the boys on the stag do.

"When we were little, as my Mum and Dad are only too happy to testify, there was not a great deal of love lost between Richie and I. In fact, it would be fair to say, that we hated each other like Russians and Americans! Our ideologies were different about everything. He liked Laurel & Hardy, I liked Harold Lloyd. Richie liked Dukes of Hazzard, I liked Starsky and Hutch. I liked Tiswas, but wasn't allowed to watch it as Richie liked bloody Swop Shop! We just had nothing in common! I was quiet and shy, Richie was fairly outgoing. I preferred my own company to that of groups, Richie was always in a gang. I could make things, Richie could break things! I was studious, Richie was sporty. I liked to go to sleep in a dry bed, Richie preferred to sleep in puddles he managed to create in his sleep! I won't dwell on this point, as I would like to think I will still be alive by midnight, but as a nine year old child, I took great delight in being given the top bunk whilst Richie had the bottom one. This wasn't always the way it was, but Mum finally took pity on me after several evenings of yellow showers! As I say, I won't dwell on this, but Jemma if you and Richie ever go on an overnight train and have to share bunk beds, I strongly advise you to take the top bunk and I would also recommend that you borrow these………"

I stuck my hand under the top table and pulled out a man sized nappy, with a massive safety pin in the front. I threw it across to Richie. I also took out a golfing umbrella and threw that across to Jemma.

"Richie, you know how I promised I would not mention the bedwetting? I LIED!"

There was a general good humoured murmuring. I let it die down and then continued,

"OK, Richie will be pleased to know that's the bedwetting done. Well, at twenty six, I hope it is! The next childhood thing I need to cover off is Richie's early interest in women and one, in particular, a certain Rachel Cookson.

Rachel wasn't the greatest looking girl at Town Green, was she Richie? Don't get me wrong, she wasn't ugly either, but at an age when certain bits of a girl's body were capturing Richie's attention for the very first time, Rachel Cookson had two major attributes! He was a shrewd boy! So much so, guess where he took Rachel on his first date?"

Some heckler shouted out, 'A Dairy Farm!'

"No, not a dairy farm, but I like your thinking! Richie took her to Park Pool swimming baths. He wanted to see those boobs bobbing on the water like 'weebles!' There were a few flaws in his devious plan though, weren't there, Richie?! Tell everyone the main one!"

"She couldn't swim!" Richie reluctantly admitted. The guests smiled or laughed. Jemma bowed her head and shook it in mock displeasure.

"That's right! Rachel could not swim! So, Rachel dragged her armbands and her brother, Barry on the date and Richie dragged me. Did the date go swimmingly, Richie?"

"No!" was Richie's curt response.

"Tell everyone why!"

"Jim and I got kicked out the baths before Rachel got there!"

"And tell them all why that was!"

"If I remember rightly, you were going to tell Rachel that I was a bedwetter, so I punched you!"

"That's right! We ended up fighting in the deep end during the disco swim, so some burly lifeguard chucked us out! So, seeing you missed out, I've brought something else for you…."

Once again, I delved under the table, this time I dug out the skimpiest pair of adult Speedos I could find in the shops and a pair of armbands.

"Jemma, Richie, if you want to have any dates at the swimming baths, you may need these. Richie, would you like to try these Speedos on, now?"

"No!" Richie replied, "but it'd make my day if you put them on!"

"Swiftly moving on! Richie and I got over the altercation at Park Pool, I had the reconstructive surgery on my nose and we gradually started getting on better. Not well, I might add, just better! Then, one day when we were in our late teens, something major happened in both our lives and completely changed how I saw my big brother. Richie, as I am sure you all know, was diagnosed with testicular cancer. Up until that point in our lives, I had always taken Richie for granted. He was just the slightly older brother, who I would try and wind up every day. Richie was a constant in my life though and once he became ill, all be it for a short period of time, I recognised for the first time really, how important he was to me. I stopped focusing on the negative side of his character like the vanity, the fact that he was a lot beter looking than me and the fact that I always felt that Mum and Dad and our sisters, Helen and Caroline liked him more than they liked me. I stopped focusing on that and started to notice the good points like his bravery and his ability to be respectful towards women, which I only really learnt once I started dating Amy. Anyway, thankfully, after an operation, the cancer was removed and

our family learnt an important lesson about the fragility of life and how much we loved our brother. These days, as adults, Richie and I are the best of friends. It probably helped that our wives are best friends too, so we have spent a lot of time as a foursome. Richie is a brilliant guy and I know Amy and I will miss Richie and Jemma enormously when they move to Nottingham. To ensure he fits in, I bought him a couple of things…."

For the final time, I rummaged under the table, this time dragging out a Brian Clough mask and Robin Hood and Maid Marian outfits.

"Put the mask on, Richie! You can save the Robin Hood and Maid Marian outfits for whenever it takes your fancy!"

Richie did as instructed. Several mates and members of the family took the opportuntity to take a photo. I took a sip of water.

"One final story. Richie deals in mortgages these days and most of his customers come into the branch but he also has to do the odd call to customers houses. Last year, he pulled up outside a smart, four bedroomed property in Lydiate and was greeted at the door by a very pleasant but ugly man who welcomed him and showed him through to the lounge. Above the fireplace, was a big, framed photo of someone in their robes, receiving their degree. Richie decided it would be good to make pleasant chit chat.

'Is that your brother?' Richie asked.

'No' replied the man, ' that's my wife!!!

Then trying to make good out of a cringeful situation, Richie continued digging his hole,

'Oh, its just that she looks like you!'

Fantastic!

Well, that's it from me. I am really proud and delighted to be Best Man today for Richie and Jemma. It is an honour. I wish them a long and happy life together. Could everyone please be upstanding for one final time and raise your glasses to the bride and groom. 'Jemma and Richie'!

"JEMMA AND RICHIE!"

I sat down to loud cheers! I took two minutes to take everything in and then set about getting absolutely battered! The wedding was on the Saturday, my hangover was so bad, by Monday morning, I still couldn't open my eyes!

Richie

Like every man, I am a flawed human being. My biggest flaw in adult life, has been that my happiness has been dictated by the amount of sex I manage to have. Around the time of my wedding and honeymoon, I was happier than Imelda Marcos in a shoe shop. Before my marriage, married male friends had dampened my sexual expectations. Several, including Jim and Dogger had warned me that their brides were too emotionally overcome, too tired and too drunk to make love on their wedding night.

"I couldn't even play with the little fella myself, as it felt like cheating." Jim moaned.

I had no such issues. Jemma's sexual appetite had always been as strong as mine, but from our wedding night onwards, for the next couple of years, I was the one who went to bed of an evening sometimes just hoping to sleep. Don't get me wrong, most times I would eagerly encourage any remote signs of foreplay, but if my body had shed its reproductive load on several consecutive nights, and sometimes the following morning too, my aching ball would cry enough. Being kicked in the scrotum and being asked to go to work on an empty sack, create an uncannily similar reaction from your non-electric organ.

On our wedding night, I was blissfully unaware that this problem would arise. We stayed at Briars Hall Hotel on the night of our wedding, but as Jemma was fearful that some of our exuberant friends would trash our room, as an act of bizarre amusement, we had to leave an hour before the end in a taxi, circle around a little, park up, change from our wedding clobber into hooded tracksuits and then sneak back into the hotel.

As soon as I put Jemma down from carrying her over the invisible threshold, our sexual adventures began. By the time we arrived back from Sorrento, I felt like an Olympic gold medal winning marathon runner, exhausted but elated. Funnily enough, the day that sticks in my mind most from our honeymoon, was our sole day off! We woke late, had coffee on our sunlit balcony as housemartins travelled busily back and forth to feed their young in the nest above, then decided that as the Bay of Naples looked like a mill pond, we should take a boat trip over to the isle of Capri. We were in the hills a mile or two up the cliffs from Sorrento so we took a taxi down to the harbour and I remember pointing Vesuvius out to Jemma on the way down.

That day, was one of those perfect cloudless days, ideal for slapping on the sun lotion, putting a cap on your head and heading out on the Tyrrhenian Sea. The views back to Sorrento as we departed and arrived back were breathtaking, as were the views of Capri as we arrived at the Marina Grande. We had a full day on the island from mid-morning to early evening, but the highlight of the whole holiday for me was going into 'La Grotta Azzurra' ('The Blue Grotto') in a little rowing boat. This is a small cave that you have to get into by hiring out a boat and then ducking down to avoid having your head taken off at its entrance point. The cave itself is not much bigger than a very large swimming pool, but the water colour in there, is just the most intense blue that you will ever see. It reminded me of one of those Radox baths I used to have as a kid, around at my Nan's. It was like my Nan had been there and tipped a few million boxes of the stuff into the sea! As it was such a sunny day, the sun poured in through the entrance like a torch. Whilst the boatman circled around, Jemma held me tightly with one hand and dipped her other into the water.

"This is just a fairytale!" she said and started to cry with tears of joy.

It was the high point of a brilliant honeymoon. An unforgettable moment.

Eighteen months, almost to the day later, I arrived home in Hucknall, to our semi-detached house, after a mortgage filled day of cavity wall ties and retentions in Nottingham city centre. As soon as I arrived on our bumpy drive, which had a small, scattering of snow on it, Jemma opened the front door clutching a white, plastic contraption, which at first glance, I thought was a toothbrush minus its head. It was unusual for Jemma to greet me as soon as I arrived. When I had been 'going out' with Kelly, at the end of the day, she would often stand at her doorway and watch me until I disappeared from view, but making a big fuss at arrival or departure was just romantic schmaltz to Jemma, so it immediately struck me as odd that she had been awaiting my arrival. As I stepped out my Peugeot 306, in my long winter coat, the snow flakes circled around me like midges. It was mid-December.

"Had a good day?" Jemma asked not really managing to feign an interest.

"A day underwriting mortgages is not quite the same as storming an embassy for the SAS, but it pays the bills."

"Right, right," Jemma replied in a manner that indicated that if I'd said I'd spent the day trying to milk a zebra she would not have batted an eyelid, "come and sit down, honey, I've made you a cup of tea!"

"How did you know when I'd be home?" I asked. I normally left the office when I was comfortable that I had a clear desk, I could arrive home at any time between half five and seven. That night, it was probably nearer the latter.

"I didn't! This is the second cup! The first one went cold and I had to throw it away!"

"Right!"

If I'd been more in tune to women's things and the workings of the female body, I'm sure I would have twigged what was coming, but I'm a man, selfish by design and all I deduced was that Jemma was acting differently and more attentively than usual. Normally it was, "Richie, you're home! Stick the kettle on!"

That evening though, my arrival had been prepared for in advance.! Something was definitely up! Our credit card balance sprang to mind!

We headed inside. I took a seat on our sofa, an old one of my Mum and Dad's that they had passed on to us. Jemma passed me my tea, let me take one sip and then blurted out,

"Do you not have any idea what this piece of plastic is in my hand, Richie?"

"I haven't the foggiest," I said, "it looks like a miniature spirit level!"

On closer inspection, I had concluded it was not a toothbrush.

"No, it's a home pregnancy kit!"

I felt my bottom twitch and my shoulders sag, weighed down by a responsibility that I was not sure I could cope with.

"Do you think you might be pregnant, Jemma?"

I tried to look excited but Jemma has said since I just looked petrified.

"No, no!" Jemma said, a tide of relief swept over me momentarily.

"I know I'm pregnant!"

Jemma sprang up and did some weird celebratory dance as if she was Eve.

"Look," she said pointing at the plastic thing, "two blue lines! I rang Amy, she said the tests can give a false negative, but they can't give a false positive! I'm pregnant, Richie! Can you believe it, I'm pregnant?!"

"Brilliant!" I said, sipping my tea again, actions speaking louder than words.

"You don't look like you think it's brilliant, Richie! Where's my hug?!"

I realised I was not reacting how I should be reacting. I was in the perfect marriage and my wonderful, beautiful, gorgeous wife was going to have a child. My child. I stood up and hugged her. In fact, I stood up and gripped her like she was my mother, I was ten years old and she had just announced she was leaving me and from this day forth, I would have to fend for myself.

"What's the matter?" Jemma asked.

"It's my childhood," I said, "it's just ended!"

"You're twenty eight years old, Richie!"

"But I've only ever been responsible for me, Jemma. What if I don't turn out to be the Dad I have always hoped I'll be?"

Jemma looked at me intently. There was love and trust in her eyes.

"If you're half as good a father as you are a husband, you'll be an amazing, Daddy!" she re-assured me.

Jemma didn't understand though. How could she? I didn't even try to explain. I was not spontaneously questioning my parental abilities, I was questioning my mortality. I had had testicular cancer. I had had an orchidectomy. What if I died? How good a father would I be then?

Jemma

There are a lot of myths about pregnancy, one of which is that pregnant women "glow"! I found out first hand that you do not "glow", most of the time you just look and feel crap. Sympathetic people tell you that you look "fantastic" and that "you are glowing", because they know you have enough on your plate, so it would be heartless for them to be honest and tell you that you look bloody awful! I felt a bit like the local freak show, Hucknall's version of the 'Bearded Lady', when I was pregnant, as random people would ask if they could feel my belly. One day, some bloke who I didn't know asked if he could feel my belly and I said,

"Only if I can feel your dick!"

It was a reaction meant to indicate that he was being plain rude and crossing a line, but he just said,

"Sounds like a good deal to me!"

Women who enjoy being pregnant are normally women who have a vacuum for a personality and enjoy being centre of attention for once in their sorry lives. They normally have a dozen kids so they can develop a fan base, as the rest of the world, outside of their gene pool, just don't like them! The whole science of pregnancy and childbirth is amazing, but for me anyway, the nine months I went through, culminating in the agony that is childbirth itself, is purely an unpleasant means to a very pleasant end, when you are passed the newly born child. I am a Christian, but I do sometimes think, if there is a God, why did he not create women with more expandable vaginas and a less painful process of delivery!

The first two weeks of "known" pregnancy were exciting and pain free and it all even seemed beneficial at that point, as I skipped one of the heavy periods I usually have. My periods had always been, from my late teens onwards, in perfect twenty eight day cycles, so as soon as I was a couple of days late, I nipped into Boots and bought myself a pregnancy test. I was so excited and so convinced that I would be pregnant, that I also bought a "Week by Week" guide to pregnancy, even before I peed on the stick! I started reading it on the bus back to Hucknall from Nottingham and the first thing I discovered was that you mark your pregnancy from the first day of your last period, so as far as the books are concerned, you are classed as two weeks pregnant by the time you conceive! No idea who came up with that one!

Morning sickness kicked in about Week Seven. Once again, I don't know which genius decided to call it "morning" sickness, but I had a twenty four hour a day ability to throw up. The nausea was the worst bit, I used to speak to Amy on the phone every night, as she was three months further along her pregnancy than I was and was also one half of the only couple who actually knew before twelve weeks that I was expecting. Amy was, having been through it herself, brilliantly sympathetic and had the ability to relate to everything I was going through. When I was worried about my almost constant nausea and daily vomiting, Amy told me not to worry as her midwife had told her that morning sickness was just a sign that her placenta was developing in a healthy way.

Work wise, during my pregnancy, I was doing a cleaning job at a small hotel on the outskirts of Nottingham, right on the banks of the River Trent. I worked 8am to 2pm, six days a week. I made and changed beds, tidied rooms from top to bottom and cleaned the bathrooms. Working in the hotel persuaded me that I wanted a baby girl rather than a baby boy! Women would have make-up and clothing strewn around their bedrooms, but it was the untidy toilet habits of men that put me off them! Richie would often wee kneeling down, poo with the taps running so I could not hear the plops, go in the garden to break wind and clean any toilet mess up after him, but I learnt that this was by no means the norm. A lot of businessmen who stayed at our hotel, would look at the mess and just leave an apologetic note and a tip.

One day, I saw a pale faced, businessman in his forties leave his room, kitted out in his suit and carrying a briefcase and when I went in there, it absolutely stank. The bath was an inch deep in thick vomit which he had tried unsuccessfully to wash down the plughole, the toilet was smeared in faeces that he had barely managed to get below the seat and in the bedroom, the bed had been stripped and it smelt like he had been dunking the sheet in a bucket of urine. There was a note left on the sideboard that simply said,

"Sorry about the mess. Heavy night!"

On top of the note, he had left a five pound note and three one pound coins! He must have surveyed the damage in the bedroom and in the bathroom and thought,

"It's a real mess in here! Really bad! It's worse than a fiver's worth of mess, but maybe not quite a tenners worth!"

I told the manageress and the man in question was billed for a further night as his room was deemed unfit for occupation for the next day. I'm sure if that man's mother was still alive and she had heard what he'd done, she'd have been ashamed. If Richie and I did have a boy, I was definitely going to teach him some manners and some decent toilet habits!

At thirty two weeks pregnant, I called it quits at the hotel and started preparing our home for the new arrival. It was an exciting but expensive business, as we had to buy a car seat, a 'Moses' basket in case we decided that we didn't want the child and would put it in a basket and float it down the river, a cot, a pram, baby clothes and all this was on top of converting our spare room to a nursery. I seemed to be pregnant forever and the arrival of the baby felt like something that Richie and I would talk about endlessly but would never happen.

Just before I packed in work, the dreaded stretch marks came and by the time I eventually went into labour, they had arrived all over my medicine ball of a belly like a hundred jelly worms tattooed under my skin. They were gross and Richie's sex life died on the spot once I saw them in the mirror. I have to feel sexy to have sex and if I feel repulsed by my own body, its hard to get in the mood! His sex life was given a mini-revival when I was several days overdue and Amy advised that her and Jim had triggered Gracie's labour by indulging in a sex session. I let Richie start, but unlike Mastermind, I did not let him finish, as I had visions of the midwife doing an 'internal' and emerging with Richie's sperm all over her gloves! His sex life flatlined again after that and I'm sure Richie thinks that it was never the same again, which to an extent is true.

Sex did not start my labour. Prostaglandin did! I was ten days overdue with swollen ankles, feet, legs, arms, face and belly. I was so big, Richie nearly rolled me into hospital. A few days earlier, the Doctors and Midwives had said if the baby had not arrived naturally by the Monday, that I should come back in after the weekend and they would "get things started". All that weekend, I was willing the baby to get moving, but other than Braxton Hicks, nothing happened, so on the Monday morning, Richie and I traipsed in to Nottingham City Hospital and a cheerful, young midwife inserted a pessary on Monday afternoon, which she said would ripen my cervix and induce labour, although she did warn it may take some time! She wasn't wrong! "Proper" labour started about thirty hours later!

In the ante-natal classes that I had attended and Richie had usually avoided, the Midwife often discussed birthing plans and encouraged us to make one, but I didn't know where to start, as how can you plan for something you don't know how you are going to cope with. You could plan that you are not going to have any drugs whatsoever and then halfway through decide its all too much and you need an epidural. The Midwives kept telling us that every pregnancy and labour is different, so it just seemed senseless to plan. All I can say is, however painful I imagined childbirth to be, it was twice that bad! During several contractions, I actually thought that I was going to die from the pain because it was so intense! No mother ever tells you that when you are glowing! After I came out of hospital, I felt like knocking on every mother's door on our street and saying,

"You bitches kept that to yourselves, didn't you?!"

In labour, I survived until I was about five centimetres dilated on gas and air. The contractions were coming more and more regularly, so the second I had the vaguest hint of an oncoming contraction, I would snatch the mask from Richie, breathe in and out desperately through it and then toss it on the floor once it passed off. Richie would then scramble around on the floor, picking it up ready for the next one! Some friends of mine have slagged off their partners during their labour, but Richie did all I asked of him. Ultimately, the male is pretty helpless in the whole event and if he can manage to be supportive without you wanting to rip his head off, then that has to be deemed a success. Richie pretty much struck the balance right between interfering and sitting back on his arse and doing nothing. I'd say he was involved but not pushy.

My main support through the labour was my midwife, Niamh, who was originally from Dungannon in County Tyrone, Northern Ireland. She said she had moved over to England in 1993, after two civilians were killed in her area, after they had mistakenly been identified as IRA members. Niamh said she had not known them personally, but it signalled to her that it was time for a fresh start. Richie said the following day that Niamh was obviously on the Catholic side of the religious divide. He understood it all better than me. For me, if you believe in God, you should all just be respectful to each other, it seems ridiculous that you would kill someone for sharing the same Christian faith but choose to practice it, in a slightly different way. I said this to Richie and he said the problems are deep rooted and he only had a basic understanding of it himself. All I know is that Niamh was lovely and there for me when I needed her, she was encouraging, knowledgeable and superb at her job. In the times, I just felt like giving up, she would say things like,

"Well, I don't think that baby of yours is going to let you give up! Come on now, Jemma, you're doing really well, you seem so in control, it's hard to believe you are having your first baby!"

I thinks she must have blinked each time I threw the gas away!

The best thing about Niamh, was that she did not try to lead the birth by bullying me into doing things I did not want to do, she was just there as a guide. A mentor. The fact that she was so relaxed definitely did not lead to me being relaxed too, but I was probably calmer because she was there.

Given the drama I have experienced in my life, I was expecting my childbirth to be riddled with complexities for both myself and the baby, but I had what Niamh described as a "wonderful, problem free labour."

If only it had been pain free too! Once I got to five centimetres dilated the gas and air started making me vomit. To help me through, Niamh suggested Pethidine, which she explained was a fast acting, analgesic drug. I was happy to try this, as I was not coping well with the gas and I was frightened of having an epidural, so this seemed like a sensible solution.

All in all, I think the Pethidine helped me cope with the contractions until I got to the stage that I was ready to push. Someone, probably Richie, told me relative to the size of the pelvis, humans have the biggest heads of any mammals, so getting the baby's head out, stung like mad.

I reached a stage where I felt an almighty urge to push, Niamh confirmed that I was fully dilated and I just felt overcome by this increasing pressure. Richie always tells the story to friends that I was literally howling with pain, noises were coming out of me the likes of which he had never heard from me or anyone else, for that matter!

"Just keep going, Jemma! You're almost there!" Richie encouraged from between my legs. All along, he had said he would stay at the top end throughout, but curiosity had got the better of him and he had dropped down to the business end. He was so fascinated, he could have done with a miners lamp, as he was looking right up my insides,

"I can see the baby's head!"

"Ooooowwwww!" I screamed.

"Keep going Jemma! Almost there! Keep pushing!"

"It's alright for you!" I said in between grimacing pushes, "it feels like you're burning my labia with a blow torch!"

For the last half hour, Niamh and Richie turned into my cheerleaders and they both must have said,

"Just one more push!" a dozen times each.

Eventually though, the final push arrived and Niamh passed the baby on to my chest.

"Congratulations Jemma and Richie! You have a beautiful baby girl!"

Melissa Kelly Billingham was born at 9.52pm on Monday 7th June 1999, weighing seven pounds, three ounces, which I think they said was 3.3 kilograms. She was, and still is, the most stunningly beautiful creature that God has ever created.

Richie

Jemma was already in bed when I came in. The lights were off but my side of the bed was closest to the door, so I just clambered in, snuggling in close to her. Jemma was facing away from me. I put my hand inside her pyjama bottoms and felt her cold, sexy backside against my palm.

"Good night, Richie!" Jemma stated pleasantly.

I took my hand out and reached over to kiss her.

"Good night honey!"

There was a silence that lasted maybe thirty seconds.

"Take that thing off me!" she stated firmly like a policewoman tackling a snake.

"What thing?" I innocently protested.

"Richie, you know very well what thing!"

"You used to love it!"

"I used to have a decent night's sleep without one baby crying every two hours and the other one sneaking between us at six o'clock in the morning! I'm knackered, Richie!"

"So am I, Jemma, but I'm still attracted to you."

"It's different for girls, Richie!"

"Sounds to me like you've gone off me!"

"Richie, it sounds to me like I'm absolutely knackered. Now good night!"

"Good night!"

I left it for a few seconds, sulking, before adding,

"Have we had sex this year?"

"It's been about three weeks, Richie."

"We used to have sex about twenty times in three weeks."

"Yes, and as a result of that we had two children and as a result of them, I'm knackered. Now for the last time, good night!"

As a mark of protest, I got back up out of bed.

"Where are you off to now?" Jemma asked.

"To watch TV. I'm not tired."

"Why did you come to bed then?"

"You know why I came to bed."

"Maybe at the weekend, babe, if I'm not so tired."

"I heard that one last week, Jemma and the week before."

"I can't help being shattered. I don't know what you expect."

"The odd night of affection!"

"You get the odd night of affection!"

"Whatever Jemma!"

I grabbed my dressing gown from behind the door and headed downstairs, trying to choose between Playmates and the Playstation as I went. The Playstation won this time, but I knew if another fruitless weekend passed me by, the allure of the football management games would soon diminish. I felt miserable. At that point, I felt like I had a wife and children that I adored but for the first time in our marriage, I started to wonder if this was just a one way thing. Maybe Jemma no longer felt the same way about me. It all felt wrong. I was married to someone who treated me like her brother. Maybe if I spoke to someone else about this, another bloke with kids, I could get a better perspective on things. Maybe if everyone else with kids was the same, I'd feel better.

Maybe I should speak to Jim or 'Dogger'. Yes, that's what I'd do, I'd speak to one of those guys, but first of all I needed to get Accrington Stanley back into the Premiership!

Jemma

"I don't know how you do it, Jemma!" Amy said, as she wiped Gracie's nose. We were in Ormskirk at one of the soft play centres where a hundred under fives ran around in all directions like a herd of cats. Gracie was a beautiful thing, with jet black curls and a gappy smile, she had managed to avoid her father's looks, but she did have an innate ability to create more snot than a bucket of snuff.

"You just manage," I replied, speaking in a barely audible shout, as the din of a hundred children is louder than the roar of a Wembley crowd, "two kids under three is hard work, but what can I do? I just have to get on with it and cope as best I can. Melissa's very good, she'll play with her dolls or watch the TV, it's just this fella who causes all the trouble."

I pointed at Jamie who was now six months old. He was all chubby cheeks and rolls of fat. He was sat up in his pushchair watching the older children, wishing he was old enough to throw plastic balls at other kids heads. I gave him a rusk to take his mind off his lack of mobility. Jamie was born by caesarean section due to being breech and from labour to date, he'd been difficult! He was a poor sleeper, he'd struggled with colic, wouldn't latch on to the breast, everything that had been straightforward with Melissa became difficult with Jamie. He was adorable, but "problematic" was his middle name.

"No!" Amy yelled back as loud as a whisper, "I was talking about you and Richie! How do you do IT?!"

I contained my smirk, I was pretty open about sex, but Amy and I had not discussed it for a long time and all of a sudden I felt we were both teenagers again, talking about "doing it" over a bottle of Thunderbirds or Asti Spumante.

"Are you asking me who takes what position, Amy?!"

"No! Don't be daft! I'm not interested in the graphic detail, I just mean you've got both Melissa and Jamie, so you've obviously done it at least twice in the last three years and at least once in the last eighteen months. How do you find the energy for sex? Since I had Gracie, I hardly have the energy to switch the light off!"

"Surely you must do it from time to time?" I asked, bizarrely intrigued given the thought of Amy and Jim in sexual mode was not a pleasant one.

"If the first time is Christmas 1998 and the second time is Easter 2000, then yes, we do it from time to time!"

"Bloody hell! I thought we were bad!"

"Why, how often are you?" Amy asked, before Gracie, who had wandered off after blowing her nose came back, offering her tissue to her mother as though it was a snot filled boomerang.

"Gracie, be a good girl and take your tissue to the bin," Amy commanded.

"Once or twice a month." I answered.

Amy was taken aback.

"Once or twice a month! Even now? You dirty cow!"

"You need to speak to Richie, he thinks he's hard done to!"

"You must be joking!" Amy laughed, "Richie needs to get some perspective from Jim! Once or twice a month! That's like every other weekend!"

"Every other Sunday night to be precise!"

"Is it "proper" sex too?"

"Proper sex?"

"Drink, starter, main course, afters, coffee?"

"Not really. More like quick kiss, dips his little finger in to check if it's going to hurt to squeeze the big boy in, if he thinks it will, out comes the K-Y, then he clambers on top, asks if he's squashing me, if not, half a dozen thrusts, a quick groan, asks if I need a tissue then says goodnight.

I can't really be bothered to be honest, but three minutes of thinking of England is better than a whole month of self-pitying moans. I love Richie with all my heart, but making love needs to be atmospheric and when you've got two kids under three, there's more atmosphere on the moon than in our bedroom! It's OK feeling sexy when you've got no kids, but for the first twelve months after they're born, your nipples drip and you stink of milk or baby vomit, then after that, they start tottering around everywhere and by the time you get them to bed, you just want to go too. I wear crap clothes, I never have time to do my hair or my make up, my bits and my stomach still bear the scars of childbirth. There is just nothing sexy about motherhood!"

Amy nodded in agreement. Gracie returned from disposing of her tissue,

"Mummy, can you play with me?"

Amy was not interested in playing with Gracie, I think she was delighted to hear everyone else in the world was not having passionate sex whilst she abstained.

"Gracie," she said, "leave Mummy to talk to Auntie Jemma for a minute. Go and play with Melissa over there in the ball pit. Good girl…"

Gracie waddled off.

"It's not like that for men though, is it?" Amy said seamlessly reverting to adult conversation like all good mother's do, "I mean, if it was about atmosphere for men, every heroin addicted hooker would be out of business. It's like fulfilling a need in men, like drinking or eating or having a wee."

"Exactly, but you're not fulfilling that need of Jim's…"

"No," Amy said, "but it doesn't stop him though! He just does it to himself! He used to stay up later than me and get himself excited by someone on the TV or the internet, but he doesn't even bother doing that now. He comes to bed with me and just lies there next to me, pushing and pulling!"

"How romantic!"

"I'm used to it now! Rather him than me! Jim just says if I'm not game, he'll sort himself out!"

"I don't even think Richie plays the home games."

"Come off it!"

"No, no, I don't think he does. I've never seen him."

"You've never seen him breathe in oxygen, but it doesn't mean he doesn't do it!"

Melissa who had played like an angel for the last half hour toddled towards me looking like she had something on her mind, as her normally smiling face was wearing a slight frown.

"Mummy, I need a wee wee!"

"OK honey," I said standing up, "Mummy's coming!"

"Not something Mummy does very often!" Amy chipped in.

"Look who's talking!" was my retort.

Amy stood up too and accompanied me on our slow trek to the 'Ladies', as I pushed Jamie's pushchair along with one hand and guided Melissa through the bedlam with the other.

"Do you think they're happy though?" I asked.

"The kids?"

"No, our husbands."

"I'm sure they are. Every mother with young kids will be exactly the same as us. Maybe not as harsh as me, but certainly Richie's lucky to be greasing his pole twice a month!"

"I've told him once the kids leave home, we might even get back up to once a week!"

"Only another twenty years, eh?!"

"It'll soon go though, Amy. Mark my words, it'll soon go. Richie will be backing out then because of his arthritic hips and his dodgy back!"

"I won't be doing it when I'm old! I shall retire from sexual activity at forty five!"

"I thought you already had retired!"

"This is just a sabbatical! A long one!"

"Poor Jim! He's going to be starching those sheets like a teenager for the rest of his life!"

I left Amy in fear of her sheets and guarding Jamie's pushchair as I took Melissa in to the toilet.

"Wait until you're Mummy's age!" I said to her. "Life gets very complicated."

Richie

"SHE BUYS YOUR PORN! You're pulling my leg, Dogger!"

"I swear on little Jake's life that I'm not! My porn collection has not cost me a penny! If Sandra goes to the supermarket, she'll say 'Do you want me to pick up some porn whilst I'm out'?"

I gave Dogger a quizzical stare.

"Is that not a little bit odd? Is Sandra into seeing other women naked?"

"I don't think so. She just knows what effect it has on me. If I'm tired and not really in the mood, she knows it'll give me that little bit of zest, you know, turn David Bruce Banner into the 'Incredible Bulk'!!"

"Great! I am now picturing your green penis!"

"Surprisingly, it is not really green!"

"Sorry but I am always going to imagine you have a green penis now! How old is Jake now then?"

"One in August."

We were outside at the courtyard in the Buck. Dogger, myself and a pushchair containing his little son, Jake who was fast asleep. We were using the quiet time to sup a couple of quick pints of Guinness and catch up. Sandra and Jemma had gone shopping. I took a big swig of my drink and continued my questioning wearing a creamy moustache.

"And Sandra is just as sexually charged now as she was before Jake was born?"

"She's worse."

"In what way 'worse', Dogger?"

"She used to want it three or four times a week, it's pretty much every night now."

I almost choked on my Guinness.

"And you call that 'worse'?!"

"It's hard work when you're knackered, Richie!"

"POOR YOU!" I said in both a sarcastic and mildly aggressive way. It was pent up anger caused by a lack of what Dogger was getting far too much of!

"Sandra just went like that after she recovered from the birth. She worried that with her breasts sagging and her stretch marks, that I might not be attracted to her any more. It's insecurity really."

"I wish Jemma was insecure. When the girls come back from shopping, I'm going to tell Jemma she's bloody ugly and I find her repulsively unattractive!"

"Don't think it'll work, mate! Different kettles of fish, Jemma and Sandra."

"Maybe it's not them. Maybe it's us," I replied, "maybe if I had a green knob too, Jemma might want it more often!"

"It's not that! Jemma's self-confident and self-assured, you should have married a needy bird!"

I reflected on his point briefly.

"I'm happy with my marriage, Dogger, it's just the sex rations that are hard to take."

It was Dogger's turn to take a long, reflective drink of his pint. He put it down and his face looked more intense and less amused.

"You see, Richie, that's where we differ. I would not consider myself to be overly happily married."

This was a complete shock to me. Sandra was not the world's most attractive woman, but then Dogger was hardly Mel Gibson either. He was punching above his weight with Sandra and with the fringe benefits, I thought he had a cheek to complain.

"Dogger, your glass isn't half empty here, mate! You are having sex every night! Your glass is so full, its contents are spilling over the sides!"

Dogger shook his head.

"You're wrong, mate. The sex is just there to make up for our other deficiencies. We have very little in common. We barely talk to each other. To be honest, I find her a little bit thick! Then there's the problem that she is the most possessive woman in the world, if I even slightly turn my head when we walk down the road, Sandra's nostrils flare and she's like,

"What are you looking at her for? Do you know her?"

Last week, we were walking past the Sixth Form block at the Grammar just as they were all coming out at half three and I swear I didn't even look, but Sandra was like,

"Put your tongue back in, she's a child, Andy!"

I thought how much I would have hated that. One thing I definitely wasn't, was a hen pecked husband.

"We went down to Kent the other week to visit some of Sandra's family," continued Dogger, he was getting it all off his chest now, "so they could see Jake. It must have taken about six hours to get there and the whole way down was either silences or trivial chit-chat about Jake. We just don't have anything to say to each other any more that does not revolve around the baby."

"Bet you got a shag when you went to bed that night though!"

I was trying to lighten the mood. This was supposed to be a rare opportunity for an enjoyable pint with a mate and it had all gone pear shaped. It was my fault, I started it. Dogger preferred to continue with the sombre stuff.

"That's not the point, Richie! My sex life is great but I would swop in a heartbeat to have a relationship like you've got with Jemma. I see how you two are together, you make each other laugh, you have lots to talk about or even argue about. I would love a relationship like that. A relationship where you are passionate about each other. Any passion Sandra and I have is solely reserved for the bedroom. It's great that Sandra likes sex, but that and Jake are our only bonds. There needs to be more in a relationship than just an active sex life and a shared love for a child. It feels like Sandra and I don't love each other, we just need each other."

This felt like Dogger had opened up a wound and we were just sat there as all the blood and guts spilt out. He was an emotional haemophiliac.

"Dogger, I understand where you are coming from, mate. I just don't understand why we can't have both the good things from your relationship and the good things from mine. A brilliant relationship both mentally and physically."

Dogger blew out.

"It's the kids, mate, they're hard work. At least your sex life will return to normality as Melissa and Jamie get older. I just think Sandra and I have more to worry about."

"I hope these things sort themselves out for both of us, Dogger. I just want everything to be right."

Having seemingly calmed down a little, my statement fired Dogger up all over again.

"Do you know what your problem is, Richie? If something is 99% right, you dwell on that 1%. Stop doing that! Stop thinking about all the things that aren't right and start thinking about all the things that are. Jemma's fantastic, Richie! You have two lovely children. Be grateful for everything you have. There are a lot of miserable, lonely, single people out there who would swop with you in the blink of an eye!"

Dogger was cross with me, but I still thought he had no right to be.

"So says the man who has sex every night!! Pot, kettle, black, Dogger mate! Pot, kettle, black!"

Kelly

Sometimes clarity does not exist in a relationship. Your perspective is clouded by a desire for the relationship to succeed. It is only once you analyse the relationship from a safe distance of time away, that you can accurately judge whether it was a good one or a complete disaster. With hindsight, my relationship with Brad Hughes, should not have lasted beyond a few crazy days in Cairns. The problem I had at that stage in my life was that I was incredibly lonely. Touring around the world sounds wonderful to the 'stay-at-homes', but it can be a lonely existence. There is a general consensus that in life you should not just "settle". Don't just make do with something or someone mediocre, you owe it to yourself to look for something better. This isn't always true. People chase dreams when sometimes they need a reality check. If you are ugly as sin with the intelligence and conversational skills of a gnat, no matter how hard you try, at some stage you are going to have to accept that Tom Cruise is not going to be the man for you! In Australia, subconsciously, I must have done my reality check. Brad was no Prince Charming, but he was company and I was lonely. Richie used to call this his "Black Jack Theory". On that basis, I would have scored Brad a sixteen. A safe option but not a great one. The fear of loneliness dragged that relationship along for seven months in Australia and a further three in New Zealand.

A chance meeting at 'Franz Josef Glacier', on the west coast of New Zealand's South Island changed everything. It opened my eyes to the fact that Brad and I had no future. Using Richie's analogy again, I suddenly became aware that the cards that I held were two eights rather than an Ace and a King! Our trip to the glacier resulted in the death of our relationship and although we managed to tolerate each other long enough to get the "Ute" we had been travelling in, up to Picton, for the ferry crossing to Wellington, once we arrived in the North Island, I bade Brad farewell and he travelled on in the "Ute", whilst I stayed in a hostel for a few days before heading off to the fragrant smells of Rotorua.

I am sure as I grew older, I also grew less tolerant! I was definitely more laid back as a child and young adult. Mum was a complete fruitcake, the winner of "World's Looniest Lady" for twelve years running, but her erratic, drunken, aggressive behaviour did not seem to irritate me as much as it irritated Jemma. Jemma herself had more than her fair share of 'hissy fits' and 'teenage tantrums', but I seemed to tolerate her too. I just kept everything bottled up until that one life changing night. If Mum had not made the transition from verbal abuse to physical abuse, I would have probably headed off to University and married Richie. We would have settled somewhere in English suburbia, a stone's throw from a country pub, with our four children and two cocker spaniels. Mum kept pushing Jemma though until that night when I quite literally pushed back.

By the time I was with Brad, I was no longer tolerant. When I met him in Cairns, I liked his confident charm and cheeky smile. I also liked the fact that he was Australian, as all my previous boyfriends had been European, so I figured variety was the spice of life. Seven million Aussie blokes to choose from though and I went for Brad! An error on my part but he wasn't all bad, he was an adrenalin junkie, which I loved as my natural state had gone from risky to cautious and I found with Brad, I'd push the boundaries back out.

The problem I had with Brad though, was that early in our relationship, even after the first few weeks, I started to find his traits and mannerisms irritating. In fact, some qualities I liked at the outset, were the ones I found most irritating as time passed. When our relationship started I liked the fact that Brad was tactile. He would think nothing of seeking out a full blown kiss on the middle of Cairns Esplanade. I remember finding it cute that he thought so much of me that he wanted the world to know. When he tried to do the same thing in Brisbane, a couple of months later, I remember asking him, firmly, to keep his wandering hands off me!

Brad's snore was another thing I bizarrely found cute initially. If we were in a hostel, often in a mixed dormitory, it felt like he was comforting me, even when he was asleep. That was what I thought for the first few weeks. Several months later, when we had worked our way down to Sydney, it became so irritating I felt like smothering him with a pillow! I managed to talk myself out of murdering him, I already had one death on my conscience, a second and I was well on my way to being a mass murderer!

On the long list of "Irritating Habits of Mr.Brad Hughes", sexual noises would also rank very highly! As well as the sexual mutterings which made him feel more like my coach than my lover, he also came out with sexual babble of the cheesiest order. He said things like, "I'm going to be your dentist and give you a good filling!" and "The Snake Is In The Grass!", it was the biggest turn off ever! To add further insult to injury, at climax, he would make a bizarre noise like a mouse! It seemed like he was trying to stem a grunt, but what came out his mouth, whilst his fluids were departing, was pretty much a high pitched, mouse like, "Eek"!

As we had spent the majority of our nights in hostels, we were normally booked in to a dormitory, which meant that sex was off limits, even tactile Brad drew the line there, but in Coffs Harbour, Brad had pre-arranged for us to stay with an old University friend, Shane, and it was in Shane's spare room that the mouse first appeared. At that point, admittedly, I found it endearing, despite several of his other habits driving me crazy by then, as I just thought that Brad was being discreet, not wanting to disturb his friend with an ejaculatory yell, but in Churchtown and Queenstown in New Zealand, we stayed in hostels that had double rooms available and I was less sympathetic when "Jerry", as that cry became known, re-appeared.

I know I'm horrible, but it was not just the physical and nocturnal habits I found irritating. Brad drank more than than any other human being I had met since Mum died and at a speed that would even have impressed Mum, if she had remained amongst the living. He also ate junk food like he believed rationing was imminent and farted like he believed the smell of his gases could be bottled and sold as an aphrodisiac. How he wasn't fat, I really do not know, but somehow he managed to stay in shape.

Brad had a collection of annoying habits, but until we reached Franz Josef Glacier, I did not consider them to be significant enough to want to end our relationship. I have mentioned all the negatives, but there were positives too, the main one being, as I said, that he always looking for the next thrill. He even persuaded me to do a bungee jump at Kawaru Bridge in Queenstown, something I never would have dreamed that I would do and I am sure I would not have done, if Brad had not coaxed me into giving it a try. It was the biggest rush I have ever had and when I sat in the boat at the bottom, looking back up at the bridge I had just thrown myself off, I just could not believe that I'd done it. I have always said that my middle name is "Risk", which reflected that I would take bold options in life, not that I would take life threatening options! This time, "I came, I saw, I bungee jumped!"

Brad was really excited about visiting the Franz Josef Glacier. It was a glacier that was around eight miles long and sloped down from the Southern Alps to around three hundred metres above sea level Every photo looked spectacular and Brad really wanted to do a day's hiking on the glacier itself, saying it was a once in a lifetime opportunity and we owed it to ourselves to do it. I may have been persuaded but he said exactly the same to me about bungee jumping and as a result of Kawaru Bridge, I was totally skint! A day's hiking was going to cost over one hundred New Zealand dollars (about forty five quid) and I had not done more than the odd days bar work since I had met Brad, so I had no choice but to opt out. I told Brad that I would be happy having a wander around Westland National Park, where the glacier was located,but I must admit, when I waved him off early that morning, I was more than a little jealous. His tour was not only taking him onto the glacier, but also into it too, there were photos of previous hikers squeezing in between tight crevasses between two sheets of compact ice.

As it turned out, I actually had a lovely day on my own, as I meandered around the park. It was a chilly day and I was thankful that I had purchased a lime green sock hat in Queenstown, that clung to my head like a joey to its mother's pouch. By mid-afternoon, my feet were aching, so I sat myself down on the valley floor, with a book and a flask of coffee, occasionally looking up at the immense glacier that spilled its way down to the valley floor like freezing lava.

Coach parties came and went, which I did not take too much notice of, as I was immersed in my book, but at one point I felt someone peering down. My immediate thought was that it was Christian, my Swiss ex-boyfriend, as we had met in similar circumstances on Hong Kong Island. I looked up to discover that this time it was actually a young woman that was staring intently at me. This was unusual. Men staring down had been commonplace throughout my travels, but not women. For men, an attractive young woman reading was too good an opportunity to miss out on, as they could use the book as an excuse for a glib chat up line, so, over the years I had had to politely respond to the likes of,

"Any good?"

"I've read that! It's good isn't it?!" – this usually transpired to be a lie, or "I won't spoil the ending!"

A woman staring at me was different, there was no hidden romantic agenda. I returned the stare. There was a vague familiarity about this lady. She looked like an athlete, I wondered briefly if she was a famous runner or tennis player. She was in her twenties, was girl next door pretty, with straight black hair and skin littered with brown freckles. She was wearing a long pair of shorts, hiking boots and a thick sweater. It was her bronzed, muscular calves that made me think that she was an athlete.

"I know you from somewhere!" she announced with a Northern English accent, "are

you from Ormskirk?"

"Yes, I am! Small world! I recognise you too," I said, "I just can't think where from though! It'll come to me in a minute!"

"Did you go to Cross Hall?" she asked.

"No, Ormskirk Grammar."

"Town Green?" she asked, meaning the Primary school.

"No! Greetby Hill!"

She scratched her head.

"This is going to drive me mad! How old are you?"

"Twenty three," I answered.

"I'm twenty five. Maybe I've just seen you around Ormskirk. Stood next to you in a bar?"

"I doubt it. I moved away quite a while ago now."

"This will come back to me!" she insisted, "My name's Anna, by the way, Anna Eccleston."

The name meant nothing to me.

"I'm Kelly. Kelly Watkinson."

"That's it!" Anna announced excitedly, "you went out with Richie Billingham, didn't you?! I remember meeting you once on Clieve Hill,

I was walking my dog with my Mum. We stopped to talk to Richie and he introduced us to you!"

I felt my cheeks flush. I remembered that day. Richie and I had been fooling around a little at the 'Sunny Road' and had spotted someone coming so had dressed in a hurry and then I was mortified when it turned out that Richie knew them.

"I went to school with Richie. He's lovely Richie, isn't he?"

"He is. Lovely guy."

"I went to Primary School with him and the Grammar. I always had a bit of a soft spot for Richie! He was my first love! We used to chase each other all over the playground when we were in the infants! I remember kissing him behind the annexes on the school field! Sloppy kisser!"

I took the jibe personally, so defended Richie,

"He's improved!"

Anna Eccleston's eyes suddenly lit up as the penny dropped regarding my family history.

"Shit! You had all that stuff going on with your family, didn't you?! Did your mother not die?"

Anna was not one to beat around the bush! I had two choices at this point, I could politely make my excuses and leave Anna or I could finally, after several years, find out what had been happening in Ormskirk since I had fled.

After Jemma's arrest, I had phoned and spoken to Amy, but as time passed, paranoia kicked in. I kept thinking the police would be tracing my calls and wherever I was in the world, Interpol would catch me if I made a call home. In the first couple of years, it was particularly hard not to give in to temptation and phone Jemma on her birthday or at Christmas, but I had no idea where she would be living, I knew she could possibly be in prison and I feared any attempt to trace her would ultimately lead to my arrest too. For all I knew, Jemma may have had to tell the police exactly what had happened that night. In over five years, I had not heard any news about Jemma, Richie or Amy, I needed to know what Anna knew.

"My Mum did die, yes. She fell down the stairs."

"That's right or she was pushed. Your sister went to jail for it, didn't she? Her name's Jemma, isn't it? She argued that she was asleep but the prosecution argued that she was pushed. I used to read about it every week in the 'Ormskirk Advertiser'.

The jury agreed with the prosecution, didn't they? What did she get, three years?"

I felt numb. About a year after I left, I had phoned Amy and she had told me that Jemma had been jailed for my crime. The overpowering feeling of guilt that I had had back then, had now returned.

"I'm not sure, I just know she went to jail."

Anna Eccleston almost wet herself with excitement.

"Oh my god! That's right, you disappeared, didn't you?!! I have just found Ormskirk's version of Lord Lucan!"

I was not delighting in my notoriety in quite the same way as Anna. Anna was having the same capacity to irritate as me as Brad.

"What are you going to do, Anna? Administer a citizens arrest? Call the local police and claim the reward money?"

Anna look at me like I was deranged.

"No!! But I will buy you a few drinks and you can tell me the whole story. I don't think the police are overly bothered where you are these days, there will be a stamp on that file saying 'Solved', but I'm bothered. I'd love to know what really happened. I'd gladly buy a few drinks for the only living person, with the exception of Jemma, who knows the truth."

If Anna was right and the police file was closed, there was no way I was ever going to tell her what really happened the night Mum died. Having said that, I fancied having a few drinks. It was a luxury I could not afford and a few drinks with someone from Ormskirk who could fill in a few gaps for me, seemed really appealing. I played along.

"Buy me a few drinks, Anna and I may well tell you! We'll have to leave now though, my boyfriend will be back from the glacier in a minute and he knows nothing about any of this and I would prefer to keep it that way!"

"Deal!"

Anna helped me gather up my things and we ran off in search of the nearest bar. Poor Brad apparently waited for ninety minutes for my arrival, but we were only re-united once I stumbled back into the hostel at midnight. By then, Anna had told me enough for me to not care too deeply about how Brad was feeling. I did not want to hurt Brad, but in the whole swing of things, it mattered little. I knew it was time for me to start my journey home.

Richie

As a baby, Jamie was not good at going to sleep, in fact, that is putting it mildly, the truth is, Jamie was an awful sleeper. This was particularly hard for Jemma and I as we had been lulled into a false sense of security by Melissa, who was a terrific sleeper. We thought the phrase, "sleeps like a baby" was an accurate one until Jamie arrived. Jamie fought sleep. Every night Jemma and I took turns to battle with him, but for short term gain we made the ridiculous decision to rock him off. This set the mother of all precedents and from six months to twelve months old, Jamie would not fall asleep at night without a thirty minute rock session that Guns 'N' Roses would have been proud of! Every night, the routine was bottle of milk, wind his back, rock him off. If we did not persist with the rocking for at least thirty minutes and then attempted to put him down in his cot whilst he was half asleep, Jamie would kick, scream and howl and the half-hour rock session would need to be re-started. How a child that could not yet speak or walk could dictate terms to two adults, I really do not know, all I do know is that Jamie managed it.

The whole routine was waring. One night, Jemma or myself would have the privilige of bedtime reading with Melissa who was as loveable a three year old girl as you could possibly imagine. Fairy stories and handsome princes were always the order of the night, whilst by default, if we were not cuddling in with Melissa, we would be battling with Jamie. Melissa's bedtime routine always lasted less than ten minutes, Jamies's was always more than half an hour. If I had not been there at conception, I would have struggled to believe he was mine!

On the nights Jemma put Jamie down, she would eventually come downstairs feeling exhausted, irritated, dismayed that she was not a better mother and at odds with herself. If it was my turn with Jamie, I had almost identical emotions although I obviously questioned my ability as a father. The fact that one or other of us was always trying to curb depression and high blood pressure, did not bode well for harmony in the late evening, child free slot. Our nerves were too frayed for rational and coherent conversations. Silently vegging out in front of some banal nonsense on the television became standard practice. We lost the art to converse.

On one particular evening, it had been my turn to deal with Jamie and, having emerged victorious but battle scarred after a particularly arduous routine, lasting almost an hour, with tears from one side and almost tears from the other, I arrived in the lounge seeking nothing like peace and quiet. What I walked into was nothing like peace and quiet!

Jemma was sat on the nearest two-piece suite to the television. She had changed into her pyjamas already. The days of skimpy, silk pyjamas had long gone, these were pyjamas designed to cover every ounce of flesh below the neck. It was sometimes hard to believe we were in our twenties not our fifties. I threw myself back on the other settee. We had two, two seaters. In the days before Jamie, we would have cuddled together on one, we now had one each. As soon as I was sat, Jemma switched the TV off with the remote. A tell tale sign. Switching the TV off in the evenings in

our house was equivalent to taking swords out their holsters. It meant one or other of us was ready for verbal conflict.

"He's a bloody nightmare at the moment, isn't he?" Jemma began.

"Too right. We need to do this 'tough love' thing, Jemma. The controlled crying that Jim and Amy did with Gracie, when she was playing up at this age. It worked for them. We just can't go on like this, Jamie's eleven months old now, he's getting too big to rock off. If we don't get it sorted, we'll still be doing this when he's thirteen!"

"Lucky we've only got one like him," Jemma said, "imagine if we had two!"

"I know," I replied, "thank goodness Melissa's as good as gold."

"I didn't mean, Melissa. I meant, imagine how bad it would be if we had another baby and that baby was as difficult as Jamie? That would be hell on earth."

I could feel the tremors coming, but was still unsure as to why this earthquake was about to erupt. I attempted to douse the flames but it was futile, a bit like standing on the edge of an erupting volcano with a bucket of water.

"Not really something we need to worry about right now, Jemma, given the circumstances."

The circumstances I was referring to were our monk and nun-like existence. In the last few months, our once a month sex had dwindled to once every few months.

"I think you should have a vasectomy, Richie."

My natural state is calm. Admittedly though, when pushed, I do have a tendency to overreact. I don't just think I was being pushed here, I was being manhandled! I became as prickly as a porcupine sandwich.

"Is this your idea of a joke, Jemma, as I'm not finding it very funny?"

"No, I'm serious, Richie. Jamie has changed us. We're always on edge these days, but we are just about managing, we wouldn't manage if we had a third child though. You need a vasectomy."

My ears were now doing their own opinion of a volcano. Lava was spilling out along with the steam.

"Am I missing something here, Jemma? Surely a vasectomy is a measure that allows sex but protects against the risk of pregnancy. Given we have a 'no sex allowed' policy in this household at the moment, what is it that we are protecting against? Are you fearful of landing on the wet patch if I have a saucy dream?"

Jemma switched the TV back on. This annoyed me even more.

"What do you think you are doing, Jemma?"

"I wanted a reasonable conversation," she said, "if I'm going to have to listen to your 'poor celibate me' speech again, I may as well watch TV."

"Hang on! I have the 'Poor celibate me' speech because I AM CELIBATE!"

I stood up and switched the TV off again from the power button then returned to my settee.

"On that basis," I continued, "my argument is a consistent one. Your argument, however, is a completely shit one! Your argument is,

'Richie, given we never have sex, how about you have a vasectomy?!'"

I do not know if it is all women or just Jemma, but if an argument is being lost, Jemma has an ability to make it about something completely different, to somehow attempt to shift the balance of power back in her favour.

"I know very well why you don't want a vasectomy," Jemma announced moodily.

"So do I, because we don't have sex!"

"No, no, Richie, do not pretend that's it!"

"I am not pretending anything, sweetheart."

I used the word 'sweetheart' in derogatory tones.

"Yes, you are! The real reason you do not want a vasectomy is because you want more children."

"Believe me, Jemma, the last thing that I want is for you and I to have more children."

"Oh I know that," Jemma said, "you want children with someone else."

"Jemma, you are just being fucking balmy now!"

Neither Jemma or I tended to swear. If you swear all the time, its impact is diminished. If you rarely swear, when you do, whoever you direct your profanities towards knows you mean business! I was at the end of my tether. Jemma persisted with her non-sensical logic.

"I know you, Richie. Better than you know yourself. The reason you don't want a vasectomy is in case we split up and you end up with some young, pretty, childless woman."

"That's just complete crap, Jemma! The reason I don't want a vasectomy, is because I do not want some doctor to take a pair of scissors to my balls, to inflict unnecessary agony, rendering me spermless, a result which you already inflict painlessly every night by your abstinence."

"Your ball." Jemma stated heartlessly, reminding me that one of my testicles was as real as the tooth fairy.

"Thanks!"

"Richie, as well as the fact that we are always shattered, have you not considered that the fear of pregnancy may also be playing a part in my lack of sexual appetite?"

"Don't use that as a new excuse, Jemma! Once I was snipped and there was no going back, I am sure I would end up discovering that the bedroom was still passion free. You would not be interested whether I was a Jaffa or not!"

"Why would you want to go back to being a sperm maker? See, you're planning ahead! Planning life with your second wife."

"Jemma, you are just insane!"

"No, I'm not. We don't want more kids, so if you had a vasectomy and it did not result in more sex, why would you want it reversed? Not for more kids with me, we've established that!"

"Jemma, let's get one thing straight. Having kids with someone else had not crossed my mind for one single second until you brought it up. That is not what I want. What I want is to get our marriage back on track. To be like we used to be. To enjoy each other's company, feel very positive about life and yes, sometimes, have a bit of passion. Is that too much to ask?"

"Sometimes it is. Life is a struggle sometimes. Most of the time. Richie, you have an escape, you go off to work every morning and can completely forget about everything at home for eight or nine hours. I can't. I have to clean the dishes, clean the toilets, wash and iron the mountain of clothes, vacuum, change nappies, struggle to get Jamie off for his afternoon sleep, entertain Melissa, feed them both, which is a battle in itself and then when you arrive home, I have to feed you and be all happy and cheery and act like a dirty little whore if you are up for a shag! Get real, Richie! You need to start taking a dose of reality every day!"

"Does our life have to be this miserable?"

"Richie, our life is not miserable. We have two beautiful children, one of whom is very hard work. He is not doing it because he is a vindictive little sod, he is doing it because he knows no different. I don't think our life is miserable, it's just pretty tough, but it will get easier once we sort Jamie out. It would also get easier if you started helping me more around the house, instead of just playing on the Playstation and complaining that I'm not wanting sex every day."

"Jemma, if you need more help around the house, all you needed to do was ask."

"I shouldn't have to ask, Richie."

"I'll help."

"Good. And the vasectomy?"

"I'm not having a vasectomy. I'll tell you what, once we start having sex three or four times a month and we are actually running a risk of pregnancy, then I'll have a vasectomy."

I don't know how we managed it, but sometimes, just when it looked like the argument had finished, we managed to kickstart it again. Jemma did not take kindly to this suggestion. Her mouth sagged at both ends.

"Is that your way of blackmailing me into sex, Richie?"

"If I have to blackmail you into sex, Jemma, I would rather not bother."

"Good!"

On cue, Jamie started crying again. I dragged myself up off the sofa and was all set to go to tend to him, but could not resist one parting shot.

"You know what, Jemma, maybe you are right. Maybe I should preserve my sperm for my second wife, some young beauty who is happy to see me each night rather than be sick of the sight of me like you."

Jemma did not take the bait, she just struck back.

"Best of luck finding a young beauty who would be interested in you! Divorced, two kids, lazy, crap in bed! They'll be queuing up!"

Kelly

"So she did just fall!"
"Absolutely."
"But Jemma did play her part, because she did have a knife."
"Only to keep Mum away."

Anna and I were sat next to a roaring fire in the bar area of Anna's hotel, drinking Sambucas. I had told her the whole story of Mum's demise, from the very beginning, Mum's life of drinking and partying, the various one night stands and stepdads, how she had turned on Jemma and began regularly beating her. Every minute detail was discussed. I just changed one little bit. In this version of events, I managed not to charge out of my room like a wild bull, I just stayed in there, frightened and sobbing.

In this parallel universe, Mum fell as she had been drinking all day, so had lost her footing and tumbled, she did not die because I had pushed her. I preferred this version! Anna seemed to like it too. Hopefully, she would be as much of a gossip as she appeared to be and when she flew back home, she would spread the word that Jemma Watkinson was innocent and so was her sister, Kelly.

"Do you not feel guilty?" Anna asked as she made circles on the table with her Sambuca glass.

"What about?"

I needed to clarify what Anna was asking. I did feel guilty, incredibly guilty, about killing my mother, but Anna didn't know she died at my hands, so I had to establish what else I might be feeling guilty about.

"Abandoning your sister. From what you have told me, Jemma was the main victim throughout. She had to endure the beatings, she had to protect you from your mother, yet when the chips were down and she needed you most, you abandoned her. You let her face the trial alone. If you had testified, told the court everything that you've told me, Jemma would not have gone to jail."

I thought about the question. I had to dilute my real answer, as my real answer was that I did feel guilty, but given the circumstances, I really should have felt a lot worse. It was all my doing, yet Jemma went to jail. I should have been far more supportive than I had been and I should have made more effort to right my wrong, but I had done nothing. I had made no effort to contact Jemma at all. If I was completely honest, I would have confessed that I did not even think about Jemma all that often, I had just tried to put the whole incident out of my mind. For the first time in many years, I was overcome with a sense of guilt and a desire to see Jemma. A burning desire.

"Are you OK?" Anna asked. I hadn't answered her question and probably wore a troubled expression.

"Yes, sorry! I was miles away," I explained, "my mind was taking me back to that night with Mum and Jemma. Yes, I felt guilty, but I was just a seventeen year old girl, totally out of her depth. I was scared of facing the police, my Nan even warned me not to come back after Jemma's arrest, as I had already fled to Holland by then. I started to panic, started thinking illogically, I even had it in my head that I may end up jointly charged with Jemma. I did not think, at the time, that my return would have made things easier for Jemma, all I knew was that they would make things a lot harder for me. With hindsight, I should have been braver. There's no doubting I let Jemma down badly. I should have gone back, but I didn't and that's something I'm going to have to live with now."

Anna polished off the rest of her Sambuca. Mine was already empty.

"To be honest, I think you did let her down. At least, you did it inadvertently. You didn't think you could help Jemma, you just went into self-preservation mode. It's understandable, as you said you were only seventeen."

"Do you know what jail she's in?" I asked.

Anna gave me a puzzled look.

"What do you mean? She's not in jail now! She's been out for at least two or three years! I saw her in Woolworths once, not long after she was released, then I'm sure I saw her in a coffee shop in Ormskirk too. Waiting on."

"Do you know whether she still lives in Ormskirk now then?"

"I'm not sure. I've been living in Didsbury for the last eighteen months so I was only nipping back from time to time to see my Mum and Dad. I didn't know her anyway, so it's not like I would really look out for her. I just spotted her a couple of times after her release because she had become a bit of a celebrity figure."

"Celebrity?"

"No, I suppose that's not the right word," Anna corrected herself, "I suppose I mean she had become well known. Notorious."

"Do people hate her then?"

The guilt I had managed to stave off for five years was now growing by the second.

"Hate would be a bit strong, but the general impression was that she should have served longer. I remember the Ormskirk Advertisers front page headline after her release was, "Killer Back On Our Streets". I could understand the mild hysteria, the general consensus was that she was guilty."

"Did you think Jemma was guilty, Anna?"

"Until today I did. She was found guilty. It was natural to think she was guilty, but I did have a nagging doubt, that's why I wanted to hear the truth from you. Can I get you another drink, Kelly?"

"I'll have another Sambuca please."

Anna headed back to the bar. As she queued, I had some more time to reflect. What had I been doing? What had been the point of spending my life running around the world? I had been running away, but by the looks of things, no-one had been chasing. I had been oblivious to what Jemma had had to deal with. As children we had been so close. She must hate me now, I thought, she must really hate me now.

When Anna returned, putting the two Sambucas down on the table, my desire to be back in Ormskirk continued to grip me. I needed more information now. I was almost desperate for it. Romantically, I had had several boyfriends, since I ran away, but had any of them matched up with what I had at home? No. Not by a long way. Not only had I left a loving sister behind, a sister who had been jailed for me, I had also left a boyfriend. A boyfriend who had adored me. I felt overcome by my emotions. I had screwed everything up, big time. Richie was "the one", I was sure of that now and I abandoned him. I needed to know what had happened to him in my absence. I felt nervous, scared almost, to ask Anna for the answer, but I knew I needed to.

"Anna, you know how you said you didn't know Jemma, so you didn't really know what she was up to. Well, what about Richie? You went to school with Richie, you still used to run into him after that, I know that myself as we both saw you on Clieves

Hill. What's Richie up to these days?"

I tried to ask in a manner which indicated that I was interested rather than intrigued, but those nerves I felt kicking in, had really taken hold, so I had become a little jittery. I was scared how Anna might answer this. I suddenly felt overwhelmed by a feeling that my destiny decreed that Richie and I would return to each other's arms, like a couple from a fairytale. I knew Anna could destroy this vision by telling me that Richie was already with somebody else.

Anna laughed to herself a little.

"Sorry, Kelly! I don't really know what Richie is up to either. I've not seen him since I ran into both of you together on Clieve Hill. I just laughed because, without him knowing, Richie brought me here!"

That struck me as such a bizarre thing for Anna to say. I needed to understand what she meant

"In what way?"

"Around the time Jemma was arrested, maybe just after, my Dad had an operation. It was nothing major, just a routine hernia operation. He was in Ormskirk Hospital, just for a few days, then he came out and after a few weeks he was fine, driving me around everywhere like he had been doing before! Whilst Dad was in Ormskirk Hospital though, my Mum had been to visit him and she had seen Richie, in his dressing gown, in another Ward. Mum asked me if I knew why Richie was in hospital and I didn't have a clue, so she rang Dot, his Mum. They knew each other from 'Maghull Operatic'. Poor Dot burst into tears as soon as Mum rang, spilled her heart out. That's when we found out about Richie's cancer."

Richie's cancer? My first thought was that I must have heard her wrong. My second was that Anna was obviously somehow getting things confused.

"His cancer? What cancer?"

"You know, his testicular cancer."

"Anna, Richie never had testicular cancer around the time Jemma was arrested. I only left England just as Jemma was arrested. Richie was fine."

As I said this, every memory of Richie suddenly started flashing through my brain. I remembered how everything had been really intense and then, for no apparent reason, he had backed off. Then there was that time when Jemma was with him at Coronation Park, when I saw them together. Could this be the missing link to everything that had confused me so much at the time? Surely not. We told each other everything. If Richie had been suffering from testicular cancer back then, I am sure he would have told me.

"Kelly, he did!" Anna continued, "I told you, Richie brought me here. After Mum found out, she used to ring Dot every week, to see how Richie was doing. He was in hospital when Dad was in, because he had to have a testicle removed. Richie came through it all though. The cancer did not spread and he was OK, but it was a massive awakening for me. What do they call it? An epiphany. For someone my age, someone I had been to school with, to have a life threatening illness, really brought home to me how fragile our existence is. None of us will be here in a hundred years and fate decrees how much time we have. I realised I was wasting mine, so when I found out about Richie's cancer, that's when I started saving for this trip. It took me four years, but eventually I went to Spa Travel and booked myself on a "Round The World" trip with just a backpack and a passport to keep me company. Richie's illness inspired me to travel. I would not be here now if it was not for him."

I tried to speak but I was temporarily mute. A tear gathered in my eye and then rolled down my face like a tyre on a hill. Within seconds, my voice returned.

"Anna, it's been lovely speaking to you, thank you for everything it has meant a lot to me. Please believe me, Jemma was innocent and I let her down. I need to go now."

Both Anna and I stood up. I gave her a hug.

"I know it's upsetting for you to hear about Richie's cancer," Anna said, "I totally understand. Did you really not know?"

"Enjoy the rest of your trip," I said without answering.

Did I really not know? Did I have an inkling? I quizzed myself, tried to search my subconscious mind, but no matter how much I searched, the answer was always going to be 'No'. If I had known about Richie's cancer, I would never have left him. Never.

Anna was tactful enough not push for an answer.

"You enjoy the rest of your trip too," she replied, "hopefully we will run into each other around Ormskirk at some point in the future!"

"That would be nice!" I answered genuinely.

I was in a hurry to go. I needed to get back to our hostel to see Brad. I had to finish things with him. Finish things straight away. I wasn't supposed to be with Brad, I was sure of that now.

Somehow I felt I had been destined to run into Anna. Destined for her to tell me about Jemma and about Richie. I felt the urge to finish things with Brad, as I felt I should not be with him, should not be with anyone, except Richie.

I knew now that I had to get back in touch with Richie. I needed to see him. I knew now that it was my destiny to meet back up with him. Meet back up and I knew exactly where and when we would meet. If Anna's destiny from Richie's illness was to travel, mine was to return. To return to Richie and to meet up, just as we had agreed we would. We were going to meet again, just like we said we would when we were teenagers, at midday, on the 4th July, on the "Sunny Road".

RB

It was my destiny. I know it probably sounds ridiculously slushy for a man to say this, but I have concluded that everyone in life has "one true love". Now, I am not saying we all end up staying with our perfect partner, there are too many divorce statistics to prove that theory wrong, but at some stage in life, we get an opportunity to be with our ideal partner, some of us seize it, others fluff their lines.

There is one thing I am certain about. I am certain Kelly Watkinson is my ideal partner. I am also certain that now I have found her, I will never, ever let her get away. Other people may fail to seize their opportunity, but not me. I know I am destined to be with Kelly Watkinson until my dying day.

Kelly

Procrastination is a failing of mine! Often, I make snap decisions, decide I am going to act on impulse and then, once I have time to rationalise, I start thinking I have made the wrong decision, get caught between one thing and the other and end up going around in circles like a one armed canoeist.

When I came across Anna Eccleston in New Zealand, I felt 100% certain that I needed to head home, meet up with Richie and re-kindle the fires of a love affair that should never have burnt out. My destiny was mapped out. I was going to finish with Brad, head up to Auckland and then jump on the first flight to the United Kingdom. Once there, I would immediately track Richie down, he would be euphoric, we would sprint into each other's arms on a sun drenched "Sunny Road", make love at dusk in a field of corn or sunflowers and then live happily ever after. Using Richie's 'Black Jack Theory' we would be the unbeatable twenty one.

That is not what happened!

I finished with Brad. That bit was easy. Admittedly though, when we parted in Wellington, it felt a little strange. Relationships are crazy things really. At one point, you like someone enough to spend all your time with them, let them see you naked, allow them to touch you in places out of bounds to all others and then, further down the line, if that person is not 'The One', you decide you do not want to spend any time with them at all any more and hope you do not run into them again for the rest of your life! That is how it felt in Wellington, like I was consigning Brad to merely a memory.

Once Brad moved on in our "Ute", I spent an enjoyable few days in windy Wellington, a beautiful city that I would love to return to, with its amazing coastal views, unique charm and fantastic, scenic cable cars. From there, I headed up by coach to Rotorua in the Bay of Plenty, internationally famous for its geothermal activity, with its steaming mud pools and geysers. I worked in a hostel in Rotorua, for three weeks, for a bit of pocket money and adjusted to the town's eggy aroma that gave off the impression that the local teenagers never tired of the stink bomb gag!

After three weeks, I left Rotorua in a rental car with three Scottish girls from Bishopbriggs, who had been in Australia but then spent a month in New Zealand, touring around both islands and were on their way up to Auckland to return the car and then head home. I paid my share of the petrol, enjoyed their company and my abiding memory of them is that they introduced me to a Wirral band called Pele, as they constantly played their two albums, "Fireworks" and "Sport Of Kings" over and over again. I remember them winding the windows down, opening the sun roof and screaming out the words to a song called 'Megalomania' at the top of their lungs! As the song was not one I knew at the time, it was like observing a deranged ritual!

Things like that you just don't do when you are travelling alone!

In Auckland, I just chilled, enjoying the last few weeks of a time in my life I knew I would always look back upon fondly, 'The Travelling Years'! I read constantly, I remember reading books by John Irving, Amos Oz, Milan Kundera, Josef Skvorecky (who's books I particularly enjoyed) and every afternoon I would go to the cinema. The best film I saw was "Once Were Warriors", which began an obsession with New Zealand film that I retain to this day. My favourite film of all time is 'Whale Rider' which even when I say the name of it, makes me cry! 'Once Were Warriors' comes in a close second. Those weeks were delightful and life is wonderful when you have time on your hands but ultimately, the most cherished moments are moments shared with a loved one and at that time, my lovelife was merely my past and my future, but not my present.

Sorry, I did not explain why I was chilling out in Auckland rather than desperately jumping on to a flight to London, basically, I had no choice! On my first day in Auckland, a cheery, elderly male travel agent with a neat, grey beard told me he could not get me on to a direct flight to London for six weeks. Sensing my disappointment, he told me that he could, however, get me on a flight after three weeks to Tahiti, then a subsequent flight to Los Angeles and then finally a third flight to London. His logic was that I could stop for ten days in Tahiti and ten in L.A and still be home as quickly as I would be by taking a direct flight, but the stopovers were an opportunity not to be missed. He was right! It worked out about $250 dearer and I arrived back in the UK almost penniless but I knew, in all likelihood, the closest I would ever get to Tahiti in the rest of my days would be playing a David Essex CD! Sometimes there is more to life than money.

Leaving New Zealand and flying to Tahiti was bizarre as I travelled twenty two hours backwards in time. I felt like a smalltime Michael J.Fox. I left Auckland at ten o'clock at night and due to travelling through the international time zone, I arrived in Papeete in Tahiti at five in the morning on the same day! I thought how exciting it would be to do that on New Year's Eve, 1999! Welcome in the new millennium at a massive party in Auckland or even Sydney and then hop on a plane to Tahiti and re-live the day again! Two Millennium parties for the price of one, or probably for the price of ten but it would have been worth it!

If I'm honest, when I arrived in Tahiti, and again when I arrived in L.A, I half expected to be delayed because some new adventure took me away from my intended path. Surprisingly, I did not end up living in Bora Bora for two years with a Tahitian, bronzed Adonis or twelve months in Venice Beach with a surfer dude! No complications crossed my path though, as I did not welcome their presence, my life had already been complicated enough, my focus was purely on Richie. I spent ten days on the Tahitian island of Moorea, sleeping in a two man tent alone, on a beachside campsite. Once I reached Los Angeles, I found myself a cheap motel by 'LAX' and spent the ten days doing the touristy bit, I did the 'Walk of Fame' visit on Hollywood Boulevard, took a stroll along Sunset Strip on Sunset Boulevard, went to see the Hollywood sign in the Hollywood Hills and went to Mulholland Drive and took the best photo of my trip, a panoramic shot of Los Angeles, taken with a cheap camera I picked up in a supermarket for ten dollars! Three weeks after leaving Auckland, I arrived, as intended, at Heathrow airport.

For a long, long time I had dreaded reaching 'Passport Control' at Heathrow. Mentally, when I pictured my arrival back in the UK, I always imagined a strong hand on my shoulder and an armed policeman with a German Shepherd leading me to a holding cell, before facing a belated trial for murder. Reality was more straightforward. A young, stern lady with a pale complexion and her hair tied back in a bun, like someone from a John William Waterhouse painting, beckoned me forward. I handed her my passport, she studied my photograph and then began my interrogation.

"You've been away a long time," she said in a monotone voice as she flicked through my passport pages with the various visa stamps.

"Yes," I replied timidly, "almost six years".

"Did you miss the rain too much?"

"The people," I answered, "I missed the people too much."

Then, handing my passport back she said,

"Nice people or not, give it a week and you'll be wishing you were away again!"

'Welcome to London!', I thought as I put my passport back in my handbag. I was free to go. There was no real interrogation, I was welcomed back to my home country like any other seasoned traveller. Welcome back but you should have stayed away! I had spent far too much time fretting about my return, Anna had been right, no-one was interested in me. The other thing that Anna had mentioned though, was that Jemma had a certain notoriety in Ormskirk following Mum's death. As I stood at the luggage collection, I began to ponder what a return to Ormskirk could mean. If I headed there and took root, would I always be the victim of whispered accusations?

I am not a brave person. My default mode is cowardice. Being back in England, although I could feel its emotional pull for some time, was already scaring me. For six weeks, all I had wanted was to be back in England and to begin my search for Richie, but now I was back I was not just apprehensive, I was petrified. Questions kept filling my head. What if Richie did not want to see me? What if he had a girlfriend or a wife or even children? Was it right that my intended search was focused on Richie rather than

Jemma? After all, Richie had been no more than a teenage sweetheart, Jemma had virtually raised me single-handedly and had suffered more at my selfish hands than anyone. I made a decision. A cowardly decision. I did not want to subject myself to any abuse in Ormskirk. I also began to worry how Richie would react. Maybe the wisest thing to do was to test the waters first. I decided the safest option would be to stay in London for a while, take stock, not rush into any rash decisions I may regret for the rest of my life.

Despite my uncertainties, in my positive moments, I was still convinced my future was with Richie Billingham. I decided the best way of re-establishing contact would be to send Richie a letter. I procrastinated. By the time I posted the letter, I had been back in London for five weeks. I had even managed to find myself a job, in Dillons bookstore in Gower Street, right in the heart of Bloomsbury. As a result of having a job, I was able to sign a tenancy agreement on a flat, albeit a modest flat, it was cramped, had one bedroom and was above a bookmakers, but it became home and it was convenient as it was only one hundred metres from Ealing Broadway tube station. Every morning, I would jump on the tube to Holborn on the Central line and then take the Picadilly line, one stop north to Russell Square. I loved living in London, everything seemed to be done at Roadrunner pace, it reminded me so much of Hong Kong. Everyone seemed to live in their own private bubble, rudeness was the norm, particularly on the tube, when everyone seemed to go about their robotic personal routines like worker ants, but at least everyone that came into Dillons tended to remove their mask of isolation and wanted to befriend me. I adored working there, but understood it was just a stop gap until I returned to Richie.

I had no idea where Richie was living, so once I had finished my letter, I posted it to his parents house. My theory was that they were unlikely to have moved and I was certain Dot would pass a letter addressed to Richie straight on to him. In fact, I could picture her peering over his shoulder as he read it! The letter I sent was a relatively short, simple letter. The main reason for this was because I had spent weeks trying to write it and on that final night, I had thrown at least a dozen previous attempts in the bin and was down to my last piece of writing paper! I was determined to complete the task that night though and post it the following day, so despite it being two in the morning, I made a final attempt. Previous aborted letters had been lengthy, explaining in the finest details where I had been, who I had been with and why I had come back, but on that final note, minimalism was the key. The letter read as follows,

Dear Richie,

I expect you will recognise my handwriting straight away. If you can get through this whole letter without tearing it into a million tiny pieces, it will mean everything to me. This is about my thirtieth attempt at writing, the previous twenty nine all ended up in the bin, as I wanted to write you the perfect letter, but I think I am beginning to realise, no matter how many times I write this, I will never get it right. It is impossible to justify a six year absence from someone you love. I hope sending this to your Mum and Dad's was the right thing to do and that it has arrived with you safely.

So how are you? It's been so long since we saw each other, it's difficult to know what to say. Over the last six years, I have seen more of the world than I ever dreamed I would. I appreciate more than I ever have before what a wonderful planet we live in, but places don't make lives special Richie, people do. I came back hoping for a miracle. Hoping you are in a position to give me another chance.

Do you remember the promise we made each other on the 'Sunny Road'? I desperately hope you can. We said we would meet, every year, on the 4th July, at midday, as long as the sun was shining. I am hoping it has been wet and miserable on the 4th July for the last six years, but I know now, this year on 4th July, the sun will be bursting out over the hills.

I am sure by now you have realised I am single! I've never been married nor have I had the children we always talked about having together. Truthfully, no-one has ever matched up to you, so every romance has been fleeting. I have loved too many, probably because deep down I loved one person too much. You are the person I loved too much, Richie. I just worry that my chance has gone though. I want to be with you and for it to be like heaven on earth, but perhaps after everything that has happened, that is more than I deserve.

I know you may have a girlfriend these days or even a wife, but if you haven't Richie, please take a chance, meet me back on the 'Sunny Road'.

Well Richie, I haven't got much paper left, so I will have to leave it there. I cannot tell you how much I hope to see you on the 4th July. Our recent past has been apart, but I very much hope that our future is together.

Love
Kelly. xxx

The following day, I popped the letter in the post and then on 4th July, I headed up to Ormskirk, hoping, after six years, to meet Richie again, on the 'Sunny Road'.

Richie

In Melissa and Jamie's pre-school days, Jemma and I had become very poor at finding the positives in our relationship but excellent at pinpointing each other's flaws. One day, a disagreement about unwashed dishes had become an argument, once again, about sex. I felt harshly treated sexually, so as soon as an argument began, I would use it as an opportunity to highlight my frustrations. Admittedly, I did labour the point. Jemma's counter argument was that we were normal sexually but I was irritating her by constantly absconding from household chores, despite promising change. I remember this particular argument took place on a Saturday afternoon in our kitchen. I was suited and booted, as I was having to work one in every two Saturday mornings in the branch, so had not long returned from my morning shift. Jemma was still in her dressing gown, Melissa was having an afternoon nap and Jamie was in his high chair, smearing rusks everywhere he could possibly get to. Blood pressure and speaking volumes had already been raised.

"That's bollocks, Jemma! Count myself lucky?!"

"Ask him then!"

"I am not asking my brother when he last had sex!"

"Why not? You said Jim used to tell you all the time when he was having sex, why not just ask him if he's getting much these days?"

"I'm not asking him."

"Because you know he'll say he's not getting any! Amy told me that they have not had sex for ages!"

"How does that make me lucky?"

"You get more than your brother!"

"So what! Just because you have managed to find one couple who have had sex less than us, that does not mean I do alright! If I ran the London Marathon against 30 000 other people and I came second last, would you say I'd done alright?"

Jemma gave me a look that indicated all frying pans needed to be hidden.

"So, Richie, what you are telling me is that you have conducted a sexual survey amongst 30 000 women, each with two pre-school kids, each with a husband who does bugger all to help around the house and you are telling me 29 998 of them said they had sex more than once a month?!"

"Of course I haven't, but I bet they do! Dogger was saying him and Sandra are at it like rabbits!"

Jemma sighed.

"Well, why does that not surprise me? Have you ever thought there is a correlation between dull women and active sex lives?"

I was tempted to remind Jemma of her hypocrisy. When Jemma and I were regular partners in nocturnal dips, I doubt she would have found herself dull.

"Sandra probably uses sex to make up for her personality, looks and intellectual deficiencies." Jemma continued, "Would you rather I was as dull as dishwater and attached to you like a leech, like Sandra is with Dogger?"

"No!"

"And…now answer this honestly…would you rather have sex with me once a month or sex with Sandra every day? Don't just think about how you would feel during the sex, think about how you would feel the second after you finished when you had to cuddle up to Sandra with an empty sack!"

"Sex with you once a month!"

I answered immediately and emphatically.

"See!"

Give Jemma her due she was smart. If she had not tagged on the final sentence, my answer would have been debatable. The most common sexual phrase I had heard from friends whilst I was growing up, normally from friends justifying a dalliance with a less than beautiful woman, was,

'You do not look at the mantelpiece when you are poking the fire'.

If I had sex with Sandra every night, I could close my eyes and pretend it was Jemma or Nastassja Kinski or Anna Friel or whoever I wanted it to be. At least the fire would be on. Once the fire has burnt out though, you want someone you love to keep you warm. I loved Jemma, I never stopped loving her, but I wanted the physical side of our relationship to be an important aspect of our bond and these contant digs about housework were annoying me.

"Anyway, I do help around the house, Jemma! We've talked this through before and I promised I would help more and I have!"

"Richie, you haven't! You went out this morning and I came down with the kids and I thought you had thrown a party whilst we slept. There were breadcrumbs everywhere, cereal packets out, a half empty bowl of cereal, a banana skin, a plate with a crust on!"

"I was rushing!"

"Clear up as you go then! Anyway, its not just that. When did you last clean anything in this house?"

"I wash the car and mow the lawn."

"Not exactly 'in' the house, Richie. I do appreciate you doing those jobs, but when you think about it, it isn't all that much, is it? The garden's tiny and its your car! Even if you washed your own dishes, it would be a help."

"I'll do it!"

"Seeing is believing. You could play a bit less golf as well."

This was pissing me off now!

"Hang on a minute, Jemma, when did you turn into my mother?"

Jemma gave me a look.

"I hope the frustrations you have with your mother are a little different to the ones you have with me, otherwise Sigmund Freud was right!"

"You know what I mean, Jemma. Clean up after yourself! Stop playing golf. You'll be telling me to tidy my room in a minute!"

Jemma smiled.

"Well, you could tidy your side of the bed and your wardrobe!"

"Are we not on an equal footing in this marriage any more?"

"To be honest, Richie, I don't think we are. Only one of us has grown up."

"Don't be ridiculous!"

Jemma started pottering around the kitchen doing insignificant jobs as she spoke.

"Show me you're a grown up then. Sacrifice something for this family."

"Like what? A chicken!"

"Like golf."

"I need to play golf, Jemma, it's good for business."

"What?! Playing golf on a Sunday morning with Jim and Dogger helps business, how?"

"It improves my golf, so when I play with business contacts I can get round without making a fool of myself."

I had only taken up golf since Jemma and I had married. Jemma hated me playing. Before the children, I had tried to involve Jemma, but she said she could not see the point in a game where you just hit the ball as far away from you as you possibly can and then spend the next few minutes walking after it.

"OK. Give up watching Everton then! How does your Everton season ticket help business?"

"It improves my social interaction skills!"

"Bull! One of the two needs to go. We need a family day every weekend."

"Everton are only at home every other weekend, Jemma!"

"Yes and you work alternate Saturday mornings. You work the weekends that you don't go to Everton! Richie, I love you but seriously, you are not pulling your weight for our family at the moment."

"Two words spring to mind!"

"I hope they don't start and end in 'F'" Jemma said feistily.

"Conjugal rights."

Jemma stopped pottering and turned to face me. She looked pale, tired and the first few signs of wrinkles were appearing around her beautiful eyes.

"Richie, just help me out a little, that's all I'm asking."

"Jemma, help me out a little. I'm a man. I have needs."

"Richie, I'm a woman, I have needs too. I need someone to help me run this family. Melissa and Jamie need you to be a better father."

That hurt. Being described as a bad husband is hard enough to take, being described as a bad father was a low blow. I was emotionally wounded.

"Jemma, I'm scared we're drifting apart."

"Then turn your boat around, Richie and paddle towards me."

"I'm trying to. I just feel the undercurrent is taking you away."

All our previous arguments had never gone beyond the sex and the housework debate, this was covering new ground. Jemma opened up too.

"Do you know what I think sometimes, Richie?"

"What?"

"That our relationship, in the early days was based too much around sex. It set expectation levels that were never going to be sustainable once we had children, but because we used to have sex every day, you think we should still be having sex every day."

"I don't want sex every day. Just more than one night in thirty."

"How often did you have sex with Kelly?"

It was not untypical of Jemma to go off at a tangent. It was her style.

"Do you really want me to be answering that?"

"Yes. More or less than once a month?"

"I don't know. Probably more."

"Much more?"

"No. Probably not, but I wasn't married to Kelly."

"So what! You used to see her all the time though. The opportunity was there. You didn't expect to have sex all the time because that's not what fuelled your relationship. Maybe your relationship with Kelly was built on love, whilst the foundations of our relationship were built on lust."

"Jemma, that is one of the craziest things you have ever come up with!"

"Is it though? Compare the two of us, Kelly is classically pretty, whilst I'm more old fashioned sexy. Kelly's confidently timid, I'm ballsy. I can understand why you were attracted to Kelly, but sometimes I think maybe you were just attracted to me by desire. Now the passion has been stripped out of our relationship, I wonder whether there is enough left here to sustain your interest and sustain your love."

I kissed Jemma on the lips. It wasn't a passionate kiss. It was the type of kiss you give each other when you say goodnight and you both know there will be no sex on the way. A peck.

"You're wrong, Jemma", I said, "you are so wrong!"

I continued to argue that Jemma had totally misread things, but deep down, at that point in our relationship, I thought she had it just about right.

Roddy

"Do you not have a mirror in your house, Kelly"

I was on a lunch break with Kelly Watkinson, the most beautiful woman in the world bar none and I could not believe what I was hearing. Four years she had worked at Dillons and in that time, I had just discovered, she had not had a serious boyfriend, not once. I knew she hadn't in the six months I had been there, but I had presumed she had been getting over a serious break up, but I was wrong. Not one steady bloke in four years. I wanted to find out why. No, I needed to find out why!

"What do you mean?" Kelly asked.

Some girls play on being coy and dumb, but that was not Kelly's style, she was just genuinely pleasant. If she said she did not understand what I was getting at, she did not understand. There were no hidden agendas. Kelly Watkinson was, in effect, my boss. I was a "Sales Assistant" at Dillons and Kelly was "Assistant Manager", she ran the store one day a week and for an hour every day, when Nicholas, the manager, was having his break. I had debated whether 'going out with my boss' was something I could cope with. It was a short debate. The answer was an emphatic 'yes'. If they wanted to relocate me to a Dillons igloo, selling books to Eskimos in the North Pole, I would do it if it meant I had a chance to be with Kelly. Every glimpse of her just took my breath away. I could handle insignificant complications.

"I just meant 'Look at yourself. Kelly!'"

I said this with a cheeky smile.

"This is not a come on in any way, shape or form," I continued, "but you must know you are stunning. No other word would be fit to describe you, other than stunning. Why are men not just queuing up?"

It was a come on! Kelly was not just out of my league, she was 20 000 Leagues above me. If there ever came a time when my feelings were reciprocated, I did not want Kelly to be in any doubt about how I saw her. She certainly wouldn't be now!

Following my flattering, but entirely truthful comments, Kelly smiled at me, not coquettishly more an amused smile, as though my comments were incomprehensible to her. I did not care too much about the nature of Kelly's smile, all I knew was that when she smiled back, it induced feelings in me that should have solely been reserved for thirteen year old girls, upon receipt of a smile from their favourite boy band member. My God I had it bad!

"Thank you, Roddy! Believe it or not, before the last four years, I had a lot of boyfriends!"

Why would that be hard to believe?

"So what changed?" I asked.

They say opposites attract. I was hoping that saying was true. I was sat opposite Kelly who was beautiful, smart, thin, fairly shy and Northern and there was me, Roddy Baker, rough and ready, pretty thick, not great looking, sturdy and more Cockney than the Bow Bells themselves.

"My outlook changed," Kelly said as she crossed her legs. I was so infatuated with her, every single move she made just drove me crazy.

"In what way?"

"I fell in love again."

"Who with?" thinking whoever he was, he was a muppet. If Kelly Watkinson fell in love with you, why on earth would you not just grab the opportunity with both hands? I decided on the spot this guy was a moron.

"His name's Richie."

I hated that name. I didn't know anyone called Richie, but from that moment forward, I hated that name. I instantaneously changed his name to 'DICK'!

"And where is Richie?"

I said 'Richie' but thought 'DICK'!

"Roddy, it's a long story! A very long story!"

"I'm all ears!"

"Roddy, stop being so cheeky, there's not enough time to tell you the whole story now!"

"Yes there is! There's fifteen minutes before the end of our lunchbreak! I will not say a word during those fifteen minutes. I'll just listen. Come on, Kelly! Fifteen minutes will cover it!"

We were in the staff kitchen, just the two of us. I used to go to bed every night praying I'd have the same lunch break as Kelly. It was a child-like crush, but I loved the way Kelly made me feel and I wanted more of it. Kelly laughed her lovely, feminine, attractive laugh.

"Is it possible for Roddy Baker not to speak for fifteen minutes?"

"Try me!"

And so the story began……

Kelly had had a crush on this bloke, Dick, since she was thirteen and had been drinking cider at a bus shelter, spotted by a copper, rescued by her sister and dragged to some party where she had met Dick.

Kelly had ignored him for years after the party, because she thought he'd knobbed her sister (I bet he had too!) but after some poncey karaoke outside her bedroom window, she had let him off.

Kelly and Dick started dating, it was all slushy-wushy and then Kelly's mother, who was more than just a bit of a pisshead, had died and Kelly's sister ended up getting arrested and charged. Fearing arrest herself, Kelly buggered off to travel the world, abandoning Dick..

Several years later, Kelly bumped into some girl she half knew in New Zealand. This girl knew Dick. The girl told Kelly what had been happening with Dick, he had been really ill with cancer and even had to have a bollock off. Kelly felt awful about Dick being ill whilst she was away, even though he had recovered, so she had decided it was her destiny to be with Dick. So she travelled back to Britain, but for some girlie reason, decided not to go and find him, but instead she decided to write him a letter.

Kelly posted this letter off but despite not hearing anything back, every 4th July, she travelled up to some 'Lovers Lane' that they used to shag on and she waited for him like an abandoned dog. She had been back for four years and every year Dick did not show. In my mind, this was probably down to the fact that he had not received the letter in the first place or he had, but was shacked up with some other Goddess, so did not give two hoots about Kelly's declaration of love in her letter. Either way, I concluded that Dick probably did not care a jot whether Kelly was dead or alive, yet here I was, totally infatuated and prepared to take a bullet for her. Which one of us was she interested in? Typical! For a while after that story was told, the Spin Doctors "How Could You Want Him When You Know You Could Have Me" became my most listened to tune. No idea why!

At the end of the story, with three minutes still before the end of lunch hour, my anger, I supposed spawned by jealousy, could contain itself no longer.

"Kelly, this Richie, may or may not know it, but he is, without doubt, the biggest loser in the entire world, because he has lost your love. Don't demean yourself by ever going back there again. There's plenty of decent blokes out there!"

And I'm one of them, Kelly, I'm one of them!

Kelly looked solemn.

"Do you not think though, Roddy, that everyone has one person that they are destined to be with?"

"Who do you think I am, Kelly? Barbara Cartland? Of course not!"

I did though. I felt I was destined to be with Kelly. Destiny does not always prevail. I felt like Buttons to Kelly's Cinderella. Buttons lusts after Cinderella, but she buggers off with Prince Charming! I hate Cinderella! She's a bad role model. She bases romantic feelings on looks and money when there's a perfectly good, poor bloke there with a fine sense of humour. In my mind, Cinderella is a class traitor.

"I do." Kelly replied, almost dewy eyed.

"So are you just going to sit on this road, once a year forever then? When you're eighty, hobbling along the road on your walking stick, he will probably drive past you in his sports car, with a twenty five year old dolly bird on each arm!"

"No," Kelly replied, checking her watch to see if lunch time was officially over, "this July I am heading up there for one last time. I'm putting my heart in the hands of fate. If Richie's there, it's meant to be. If he's not, I am not going to track him down. Five years is long enough."

'Five years is four years too long!' I thought. If I was Kelly, I reckon I would have gone up there just the once.

"Oh well!" I said jokingly, "if he's not there and you need someone for that rebound relationship, just let me know! I'll drop everything, including my pants!"

"What are you like?!!" Kelly laughed as she stood up to leave the staff kitchen. She thought I wasn't serious, which was what I wanted to imply, but in truth, I was deadly serious. I decided at that moment, to make an addition to my prayers. From then on, each night, I continued to pray that every day I would have the same lunch hour as Kelly, but I also prayed that, come 4th July, Prince Dick Charming did not turn up on the "Sunny Road".

Charlie

In life there are winners, there are losers and then there are people who spend their life ducking and diving, flitting from the edge of heaven to the edge of disaster and back again. I was one of those people.

I was into my horses. Horse racing enthusiasts love horse racing. They have an in depth understanding of the "Sport of Kings". They care what happens to horses. They mourn the death of a racehorse as though it was a family member or a close personal friend. They have an encyclopaedic knowledge of the horse racing calendar. The National Hunt crowd go racing in tweed, some of the flat racing chaps will go in top hat and tails. From the moment they emerge from the birth canal, they have an awareness of horse racing terminology, such as 'lost an iron', 'on and off the bit', or 'off the bridle'.

I was into my horses, but I was not a horse racing enthusiast. I was a gambler. I belonged in a smoke filled, tacky bookmakers in any town or city throughout the length and breadth of Britain. I have never sat on a horse in my life. The terminology baffled me for years and to be frank, if a horse died, I only cared if I'd had money on it. Why should I have been sentimental about horses? They eat horse in France and apparently despite their size, they are far less intelligent than your average dog. My interest in horses was purely a financial one. I was not in love with horses, I was in love wth gambling. When the horses won for me, gambling was my best friend. When the horses fell at the last fence when still in with a chance of winning or got touched off by a nose when I had lumped on large, gambling became my worst enemy. I knew every bookie in Ormskirk, most in the North West of England and some from further afield. Whenever any of them drove past me in their Audis and Mercs, I always thought, 'I paid for that!'

Gambling was my drug of choice. Nothing could beat that adrenalin rush from outwitting the bookies, handing them a tenner in the morning, then collecting a couple of hundred back in the afternoon. Obviously,like 98% of gamblers, the bad days far outweighed the good, but you have to be optimistic to gamble, no matter how bad a day you have had, no matter what financial losses you have had to endure, you always think things will be different the next day. Every race is a puzzle with an answer.Unfortunately, during 1996, my losses were always going to be re-couped the next day and then the next day and then the next day. The sun was always going to be coming out the following day. Sadly, the more I lost, the more I put on to try and win it back. Somewhere along the line, you should just call it a day and limit your losses, but that's hard for gamblers to do, as I say, we're an optimistic bunch, the next big win is always so close you can smell it.

Kiffer entered my life through gambling. I met him initially, a few years before that fateful 1996, in the Dog & Gun, in Aughton. It must have been about 1990, I did not know it was Kiffer at the time, I only knew him by reputation back then, not by looks. Had I known, I would not have borrowed a penny off him. He was only a young guy back then, not much older than my daughter, Helen, but he was already building up a reputation as a headcase. Stolen cars, drug deals, turning dirty money clean – Kiffer had his dirty fingers into a lot of crooked pies, but when I first met him, I just presumed he was a flash young bloke with a bit of money, a bit of money that he was prepared to lend to the likes of me.

I was a Sales Rep in insurance, covered a big area around North West England across from Liverpool to Manchester and then the whole way up to Carlisle. Sometimes it was great, but in hard economic times, some people would rather have enough money for their daily pack of fags than their life cover, so if their policies lapsed, I had to deal with the insurance brokers who had their commission 'clawed back' off them. At times it was stressful, during these times I relieved my stress by nipping into the bookies during my lunch hour and then I tended to stop off for a pint of brown bitter on my way home. The 'Dog & Gun' in Aughton was my usual haunt and my mate, Dave was often there. Dave was a milkman, he would generally start his round at three in the morning, so if he wanted a couple of pints, he tended to nip out to 'The Dog' late in the afternoon or early in the evening. Dave is into his horses too, at the time, his son was an up and coming National Hunt jockey, who was making a name for himself on the 'Point to Point' circuit, so often Dave would pass me a tip. One Friday afternoon, Dave was sat in 'The Dog' having a pint of mild and as soon as I walked in, he said,

"Charlie, I was hoping you'd come in! I've got a surefire winner for you tomorrow at Newton Abbott, 'Red Nosed Knight'. You need to lump on, Charlie, our Joe says it will win by a distance. The trainer apparently has it in peak condition and it's stepping up to three miles on good ground for the first time. He says it will definitely stay. It'll be a real bookie basher for you, this one."

"Dave, I'd love to lump on," I said, "you know there's nothing I like better than a decent bet, but things are pretty tight right now. Its hard enough having four kids, but with one at Uni, it's even tougher. I'm just going to have to put a few quid on this one."

"Our Joe doesn't get these tips wrong very often!"

"I know that, Dave, but what can I do? Unless I rob a bank, I just can't afford to."

This was the moment I met Kiffer. He arrived like a fairy godfather or, with hindsight, like a Godfather. Kiffer was sat at the other end of the bar, drinking a Mexican bottled lager with a slice of lime in the top, not a standard tipple of choice in 'The Dog'. He wasn't tall, but thick set, with a couple of days dark growth on his face and sporting the latest designer tracksuit. He spoke with a soft Liverpool accent.

"What's the story then, Gents?" he asked.

Dave immediately clocked who he was and became uncomfortable and hesitant.

"I was just…erm..telling my mate here, Simon, about a horse that's running tomorrow."

"Going to win then, is it? Worth a bit of a punt?"

"I think it might do quite well," Dave replied, suddenly a lot more cautious about its chances.

"What did you say it was called?"

"Red Nosed Knight."

"And are you boys both backing it?"

"Erm….just a small wager," Dave answered shakily, "you never know what can happen with horses, unreliable creatures. I might just put a fiver on for a bit of an interest."

Not knowing who this guy was, I wondered why Dave had become a bumbling idiot.

"What about yourself?" Kiffer asked turning his attention to me.

"I'll have a few quid on, but I was just saying to Dave, things are tight, so that'll be it."

"What if they weren't tight?" Kiffer asked as he glugged his drink through the lime, "what would you put on then?"

"A bit more. Dave's lad gives us the tips and they are normally spot on."

"Are they now?" Kiffer said with a great deal of interest.

"Begginer's luck!" Dave explained.

"Don't be harsh on the lad, Dave! He knows his stuff!" I added. I didn't know I was potentially creating an issue for young Joe, only after, when Dave told me about Kiffer and I was reminded of the conversation, did I cringe. Luckily, as far as I'm aware, Kiffer never did make contact with Joe, although whenever he is unseated when riding a favourite, I do wonder whether Kiffer had advised him that it if his girlfriend wants to continue looking pretty, it may be in his interest to fall off.

"So," Kiffer continued, "how much more if things weren't tight?"

"I've no idea. This all very hypothetical, as they are pretty damn tight right now. I have four kids in their teens and twenties. Cost me a fortune."

"I understand," Kiffer said empathetically, "I have a two year old daughter myself, Melanie, she's my little angel but she costs me an arm and a leg. Luckily, in my game, I can afford to spoil her, but I understand everyone is not as lucky as me."

"What is it you do?" I asked.

"This and that."

Dave threw me a warning look but at the time, I thought it was some sort of nervous tick.

"Like what?"

"I help people. Good people who need a helping hand. People like yourself, Charlie."

I concluded that he had obviously heard my name earlier. I realised he knew my name but I did not know his.

"Sorry, what's your name?" I queried.

"Simon Cunnington."

"Pleased to meet you, Simon" I said. I got up, walked over and shook his hand.

"Always good to meet new people," he replied.

The name Simon Cunnington meant nothing to me. Fifteen minutes later, when he announced he had better get going, as he had a small matter to attend to, Dave revealed that Simon Cunnington was 'also known as' Kiffer.

"So, go on then, Simon, explain how people like you help people like me."

"Simple economics, Charlie. You want to have a tidy bet on a horse tomorrow, but can't afford to. I provide the financial backing to allow you to place your bet and if you win, you give me my money back plus 50% on top for allowing the transaction to take place."

The idea sounded interesting but the costs sounded prohibitive.

"50%! So if you give me £100, I have to give you £150 back? No thanks!"

"Think about it though, Charlie. What price is this horse of yours?"

"I've no idea. Dave what sort of price will this horse go off at?"

By now, Dave really did not look like he was wanting to be part of this conversation. Normally, he drank at a very leisurely pace, but his pint of mild that had been almost full when I had walked in, was virtually gone.

"I'm not sure, Charlie, with it going at a new distance and on better ground, there are a lot of unknowns. I'd guess about 5-1."

"OK then, Charlie. The way it would work, is that I would give you £100. You would back the horse at 5-1. It wins. You collect £600, pay me back £150 and you get to keep £450 without ever having to place a penny of your own money. How good is that?"

It sounded too good to be true. I needed to investigate the potential catch.

"What if it loses?"

"Just pay me back when you get the money, there would be no rush, you look like a man I can trust. You could just pay me back the next time you get paid, or if you want, I could lend you a bit more next time you get a tip and you could pay me back from the winnings from that one. I'm a fair man, Charlie. A very fair man."

I have subsequently learnt that if a man has to tell you he is a 'fair man', he probably isn't one.

"So what do you reckon, Charlie? Want to borrow a hundred notes?"

A deal was done and Simon Cunnington took out five crisp twenty pound notes from a wallet crammed full of them. It felt great, but admittedly not half as good when Dave told me who I was dealing with. As luck would have it, Joe was right, "Red Nose Knight" won by a distance at 9-2 and I pocketed £400 after paying Kiffer back, the following evening in 'The Dog'.

"I knew I could trust you!" he said with a smile, "I could tell."

This should have been the end of my dealings with Kiffer, it wasn't, it was just the beginning. I knew his reputation, knew he was not doing this through generosity of spirit or to win a knighthood for services to mug punters, he was a businessman and a ruthless, vicious businessman at that. I just got greedy.

To be fair, the first few horses I backed, having borrowed Kiffer's money, all won and then, when the next couple didn't, Kiffer was patient and understanding. Kiffer said there was no panic, he knew I was good for it and if I ever wanted any more, the same 50% increase on capital borrowed terms would apply. I had a couple of County Court Judgement's that Dot did not know about, so it was not as though banks were falling over themselves to lend to me at better rates, so the simplest way for me to get hold of money was via Kiffer. Caroline, my daughter, bailed me out once, but other than that I was always good for Kiffer's money, that is until that spell in 1996, when the wheels well and truly came off. Day by day my losses were just getting bigger and bigger and eventually rather than asking Kiffer for more money, I just decided it was best to keep a low profile and avoid him. Kiffer was not the only person I needed to avoid, I needed to avoid all my creditors too, as I had managed to rack up a series of debts I could no longer afford to pay.

Our postman, Tom, used to turn up between seven and seven thirty every morning, so I used to wait for him and once he had parked his bike at the top of our drive, I would sneak out, collect the mail, stuff any bills in my pocket and then leave the rest on the kitchen table so Dot could deal with the Reader's Digest subscriptions and the junk mail. Saturday June 8th 1996 was Derby Day at Epsom. The 'Derby' was the big race of the flat racing season. The top three year old horses would race over one and a half miles of the undulating Epsom Downs. I felt lucky that morning, I had yet to pick my horse but thought I was due a big winner and there was no better time to get it than Derby Day. I had woken early, with sunlight creeping through the curtains and the birds singing their same old songs. It required less sneaking on a Saturday morning to collect the mail, as Dot used to like a lie in at weekends. Just after seven, I was looking out the landing window and I saw Tom arriving at the bottom of the road, through the passageway that linked our road to the main road. I quickly crept down to the porch and as he parked his bike up, I followed my normal routine, unlocking the door and quietly going out to meet him halfway down the drive.

"Morning, Charlie!" Tom said cheerily, "got your Derby horse picked?"

"Not yet," I responded, taking a bundle of mail off him, some looking, as usual, like threatening letters, "I'm waiting for my Racing Post to arrive, the kid who brings it isn't an early bird like you!"

"I was going to ask you for a tip!"

"Well, Tom, the only tip I can give you is not to bet! It's a mug's game!"

"Doesn't stop you!" he said laughing and climbing back on his bike before cycling away.

I turned back around with my body pointed back towards our front door, with my head down, examining the post, seing what damage was being inflicted today. Credit card bill – that's for me! Gas bill – mine! Personal loan company – missed payment letter – I'll have that! Catalogue company – Dot's. Junk mail – Dot's. Then there was a handwritten letter, who would write us a letter? Hang on, it wasn't addressed to us, it was addressed to our Richie – Dot could have that too, she would remember to pass that on to him. I stuffed the bills in a back pocket of my jeans and was carrying Dot's letters in my hands, when I heard a voice.

"Good morning, Mr.Billingham! And what a lovely morning it is for a drive! Perhaps you'd like to join us?"

Without turning, I looked over my shoulder. Standing there, outside a big, black limousine, were two of Kiffer's henchmen, Kevin, who was known as 'The Smirking Giant' and Bobby who was known as 'Muscles'. I turned around to face them.. It was 'The Smirking Giant' that addressed me, in his chirpy Wirral tones. He was only in his late twenties but had gone to work for Kiffer after a failed attempt at professional kickboxing. He was allegedly given his nickname because no matter what nasty job Kiffer gave him, torturing people, killing people, disposing of bodies, he did it with a smile all over his face. The 'Giant' bit was self-explanatory, he must have been almost seven foot tall. My dealings with him had always been pleasant but I had a feeling in my gut that this was about to change.

"Good morning, Kevin! I'm just off in to get dressed, I'm heading out soon, tell Simon I'll be around later with his money!"

I turned my head back, ready to walk slowly towards the door, at a pace that betrayed my internal panic, but Kevin's next words made me give up the ghost.

"No problem, Charlie! I need the money now though. Where do you suggest we go to get it, your Helen's or your Caroline's?"

"Kevin, let's not do this here," I was whispering loudly so Kevin could hear me but the neighbours couldn't. I kept imagining Dot was also staring outside from the front bedroom window.

"Charlie, get in the car, mate."

"Not now, Kevin, I need to nip into Ormskirk, go to the Building Society to get Simon his money."

"That's good," Kevin replied, "we'll give you a lift."

"It's too early now."

"Charlie, we're not in a rush mate. Kiffer wants his money."

Time to come clean.

"Kev, I don't have it."

"I know that, Charlie. Get in the car!"

Shit! Without another word, I stuffed the letters meant for Dot into my back pocket, walked down the path and climbed into the limousine. Kevin followed me in, on the kerbside of the limo, 'Muscles' entered from the roadside. To no great surprise, I was confronted by the smiling face of Kiffer, looking smarter than usual, cleanly shaven and wearing a white, Ralph Lauren shirt and black trousers.

"Morning, Charlie! I hate early mornings, always seem to put me in a bad mood. Early mornings and misplaced trust – a lethal combination."

The engine started and the limousine moved away. I remember looking back at my house, through the blacked out windows, wondering whether I would ever return or whether that would be my final image of our family home. I tried to look calmer than I felt. I had a horrible feeling I was now on my way on to a 'Missing Persons' list, destined to be found ten years later, in a shallow grave, by a man walking his dog in remote woodland.

Richie

"We think he's a vampire, Mum, he only seems to stay awake when it's dark outside!"

Jamie was flat out in his pushchair. Jemma had taken Melissa to Manchester Opera House to see some Australian band that are on children's TV, catering purely for pre-school kids, so Jamie was my responsibility for the day. We had moved back to the North West from Hucknall, when Melissa was six months old, as my old Regional Manager from my days in Maghull had offered me a new Manager's role in Wigan. The branch itself was no bigger than the ones I'd worked in before, but I was also given the authority to oversee seven agencies in the Lancashire area. It was more money, a better car and a far superior bonus package, so there was no decision to be made. We loved Hucknall but it was time to head home!

We bought a three bedroomed, new build detached house in Standish near Wigan, only thirty minutes from Manchester and twenty minutes from Ormskirk. Thus, whenever I was responsible for looking after Jamie or Melissa or both of them, without Jemma, I tended to take them to my Mum's! On this Sunday morning, Mum and I had taken Jamie to the park, bought him a "99" from the ice cream man and then taken photos of him after he smeared it all over his face! On the "push" back to Mum's, he had fallen asleep, so once we were back, Mum had made us both a coffee and we were able to enjoy a rare chat that did not have to be interspersed with baby talk every couple of sentences.

"It's your fault he's a bad sleeper," Mum was saying, "you were a nightmare when you were a child! Often I would come to bed at eleven o'clock when you were three or four and James would be flat out, yet you would still be up, playing with your Space 1999 toys or playing football with your soldiers! You only started sleeping properly when you were a teenager, probably all the masturbation wore you out!"

"Mother!"

"Well, that's what teenage boys do, is it not?"

"I didn't, I was a good, clean boy!"

"I remember your sheets telling a different story!"

"Mum, how did you manage to get on to teenage boys sexual habits?! I was talking about sleep deprivation! Jamie's been really hard work. A lack of sleep is not an aid to a happy marriage."

Mum looked concerned

"You and Jemma are OK though, aren't you?"

"Jemma and I? Oh yes, we're fine. We could just do with a bit more sleep, that's all."

"Well, if you ever need a babysitter to take them both over night, you only need to ask."

"I'm sure we will take you up on that soon. It's just that Jemma hasn't wanted to burden you with Jamie, because he doesn't sleep for longer than a couple of hours at a time."

"Do you know what Jemma's problem is? She sometimes thinks too much about other people's problems and not enough about her own. I have to admit, when you first told me that you and Jemma were going to get married, your father and I had our reservations, only because of all that stuff with her Mum, but we were wrong, Richie, she's a fine wife and a wonderful mother to your children. You are very lucky to have her."

"I know, Mum, I know."

I said it, but at that time, I was not feeling particularly lucky. People have a tendency to do that. They make judgements on your marriage from how it appears from the outside. Jemma was great with the kids, tolerated my mother and father's foibles very well, so from Mum and Dad's perspective, she was near perfect. They were oblivious to how things were behind closed doors. Jemma and I had a limited sex life, spent a fraction of our lives together and seemed to bicker constantly when we did share a room. Marriage problems are like cycling on hills, it's very easy to go downhill, but once you hit the bottom, its an awful lot harder to get back up. I did not want to burden Mum with all this, for the time being at least, I was happy for her to think that everything in the garden was thornless.

"What about things with you, love? That testicle of yours OK?"

Jemma and Mum had a similar way with words, although Mum's openness was due to a lack of tact and diplomacy, Jemma was just blunt. Having had five years of follow-ups at the hospital, following my testicular cancer, I had been given a clean bill of health and very rarely thought about my prosthetic friend these days.

"It's fine, Mum. Everything is in working order."

"I check your Dad's balls every few weeks, but they seem to be the same little hairy things they've always been. They're not growing or anything."

"Good, although Dad is probably more prone to prostate cancer these days, Mum. You should be putting on the rubber gloves and shoving a finger up his back passage as well!"

"Bloody hell, Richie and you say I'm tactless!! I'll leave that to the Doctor, my days of shoving a finger up your Dad's back passage are well behind me!"

"Too much information, Mum!"

"You started it! Anyway, whilst we're talking about privates, has Jemma not persuaded you to go to the testicular barbers yet, Richie?"

"To trim my pubes?"

"Don't be so ridiculous! You know exactly what I mean! For the snip!"

My Mum did a cutting sign with two of her fingers.

"She hasn't persuaded me yet! That production line is still in working order. As you know, I was forced to close one of the factories a number of years ago and cut the work force in half, but the other little guys are still beavering away!"

The double entendre was intended, my Mum and I shared a warped sense of humour.

"Still churning them out, eh!!"

I laughed.

"I am not sure many men have such detailed conversations with their mothers!"

Mum laughed too.

"Because they are not lucky enough to have a mother like me!"

"I suppose not!"

"Do you want a scone, love? I made them this morning!"

"That'd be nice!"

"Butter and jam?"

"Yes, please. I'll just nip to your loo before I eat."

Mum stood up to go and make the scones, I followed her out the room to head to the loo. Before I went, I nipped into the porch to check on Jamie who was flat out in his pushchair, looking like butter wouldn't melt. I then headed upstairs to Mum and Dad's main bathroom, there was a downstairs toilet, but there was a low ceiling in there and I tended to forget post-pee, so the upstairs bathroom was a safer option.

Every time I went back to Mum and Dad's, for nostalgic reasons, I always looked into the old bedroom that I used to share with Jim. Dad now used it as an office, but he had never got round to having a proper clear out, so a lot of our stuff was still there. I peered in and then decided, given I wasn't too desperate for a wee, that I would have a little look around whilst Dad was out. I sat at his desk, he was a right scruffy bugger, he had work papers everywhere. All the top drawers were full of Dad's work stuff, but a lot of mine and Jim's stuff was stuffed into the bottom drawers, so I pulled one or two open and started to look through.

One drawer was full of my old Roy of the Rovers comics. When I was seven, I had announced to Mum and Dad that I no longer wanted the Beano every week, but instead wanted Roy Of The Rovers. I have no idea what happened to my copies of the Beano but once I started receiving the 'Roy Of The Rovers', I would not throw any away. This hoarding has continued from that day forward, after Roy of The Rovers, it was Shoot, then Record Mirror and then Q! As I opened the drawer, the top copy was the classic issue when Melchester Rovers emulated Dallas and Roy was shot by Elton Blake. The front cover had a black border, hinting at the possibility of Roy dying and 'Get Well' wishes were inside from many stars of the day, including Eric Morecambe. I was momentarily excited that this issue could be worth a few quid until I remembered that I had taken the middle pages out to blue tack the poster of the footballer in the middle on to my bedroom wall. I don't even remember which footballer it was, I did that every week, so I had four years worth of 'Roy Of The Rovers' comics all with the middle four pages missing!

I opened a second drawer. It was full of old photographs . I started to flick through them, they were stereotypical family albums of the seventies and eighties, mainly containing photos of Helen, Caroline, Jim and I with bad haircuts and dodgy clothing. Someone had arranged them in some sort of chronological order, so there were the baby photos, then the naked paddling pool shots, then the children's party photos with the magicians, Jimco and Fredco and then the teenage year shots, Helen playing 'Simon & Garfunkel' on her 'Frisco Disco', Caroline crimping her hair, Jim looking like the bastard child of Johnny Cash and me looking like I thought a Kappa kagool was the coolest fashion item ever invented. I laughed when I saw one photo of Caroline with a mass of blonde curls, cuddling up to a very youthful Nick Birch. That was a collector's item, as Caroline had been with Donna, her girlfriend for years. By this point, Caroline had still not officially 'outed' herself to Mum and Dad, which was ridiculous, as Mum and Dad had long since guessed and always put the pair of them in a double bed when they came over from Yorkshire to stay.

A third drawer was full of school reports. Jim and Helen's reports were at the front, I presumed this was because they were the academic ones and would have had the better reports. The 'lesser' reports of mine and Caroline's were probably hidden away at the back. I pulled the drawer out as far as it could go, as I did so, I could see something behind the drawer, it seemed to be some post that had fallen down the back of the drawer, probably because at some point the drawer had been overfilled. The first thing that struck me was that the postal items seemed to have blood on them. I put my arm in, behind the drawer and felt around, there seemed to be quite a few of them so I pulled them all out, one by one. It was crumpled old post. There were thick droplets of blood on each of them, I thought it was all junk mail at first, but as I looked at them individually, I discovered some were old, opened bills and reminder letters, addressed to Dad. The very last one I came to, was in a white envelope, handwritten and I squinted to make out the name behind the blood, it was addressed to me. As soon as I realised it was addressed to me, my heart started pounding, as I knew who it was from. I was about to open it when I heard a shout from downstairs, "Richie, what's taking so long? Are you having a poo? I've made you another coffee, it'll go cold!"

"I'll be down in a sec, Mum," I yelled back, "I'm just having a root around my old room."

"Tidy it up whilst you're in there!" Mum shouted, "it's a pig sty, but your father doesn't allow me to clean his precious office! It's the one room in the house that is always a mess!"

I was about to tear open my letter and then I stopped myself. I needed to get things straight in my head first, wanted to understand who knew what, so I gathered up all the bloodied post and took it straight downstairs. I was bursting for a wee by now, but it could wait.

Mum was already back in the lounge.

"Have your coffee, Richie, it'll be ready to drink."

I put the letters down on the coffee table in front of Mum. I felt like a detective, presenting the evidence to an accomplice to a murder to gauge her reaction.

"Mum, what are these?"

Mum leaned forward to take a closer look.

"They're letters. They've got blood on Richie! Are you OK?"

"It's not my blood! What are they?"

"I've no idea."

"They're letters and bills from 1996," I picked up the one in the white envelope, "this one is addressed to me, it's from Kelly."

Mum took the envelope out of my hands and studied it.

"How do you know it's from Kelly, if it isn't open?"

"It's her writing."

Mum passed it back to me. I could tell she really wanted me to open it there and then, but Mum was a right old nosey parker, always had been and now I had established she knew nothing about it, I wanted to open it in private.

"Open it then!"

"I will, Mum. Just not now."

Mum understood.

"You mean, not whilst your interfering mother is around! I know! What are these others?"

Mum began to pick up each piece of junk mail and then each bill. She studied the opened ones carefully.

"These are final reminders, Richie! I don't understand, your father always says we don't have any money worries."

"Did you have any in 1996?"

"Not that I know of. It doesn't make sense, some of these bills are from credit card companies that I still use, as a second card on your father's account."

I didn't understand what Mum meant.

"So?"

"Well, if the bills weren't paid, they wouldn't let us carry on using the cards, surely?"

"Maybe it was a temporary problem back in 1996," I said, "maybe Dad sorted it."

Mum seemed flabbergasted by this whole revelation. I was less so. I knew Dad had borrowed money off 'Kiffer' in the past. Men with money do not borrow from loan sharks like 'Kiffer'.

"Maybe".

I could tell Mum was furious. I knew Dad was going to walk straight into a row when he came home.

Mum placed everything back on the coffee table, so I picked them up again and started sifting through them, trying to make some sense out of this mystery.

"The thing I don't understand though," I said, "is why he's hidden an unopened letter for me and some stuff about H.R.T and catalogues for you, as well as all the reminder notices?"

"And", Mum added, "why does everything have blood on?"

As Mum's question lingered in the air, we heard the sound of a key penetrating the front door's lock and then the sound of a front door opening.

"Dorothy, I'm back!" my Dad announced warmly.

Dad had been over to see his brother, Billy in Wavertree. My Mum and Uncle Billy had never seen eye to eye, so she had opted out of joining Dad, making the excuse that she needed to stick around to help me with Jamie. I thought they probably didn't get on because they were too similar, both too outspoken.

"We're in the lounge," Mum shouted back, and then she whispered to me, "now this is going to be interesting!"

Charlie

Kiffer's black limousine was parked up on Clieves Hill overlooking miles of greenery in every direction. I had chosen the destination which seemed very much like the final request of a condemned man. I used to take the kids to Clieves Hill when they were little to give Dot a break from them. It was our picnic spot. I used to call it our "Sunny Road".

As the limo had moved off from our house, I had calmly asked Kiffer,

"Where are you taking me?"

Kiffer just smiled, as though he was a sweet, friendly guy and said,

"Where would you like to go, Charlie?"

"Clieves Hill," I'd said, "I'd like to go to Clieves Hill."

If I was going to die, I wanted to go somewhere that brought back some happy memories.

"Well, that's where we'll go then," Kiffer said doing his finest impression of Jimmy Saville, "Marcus, take us to Clieves Hill, please."

Marcus turned left at the top of our road and headed towards Clieves Hill.

"Can I get you a drink, Charlie?" Kiffer continued in his jovial manner.

"No, I'm fine thanks."

"What do you think of the motor, Charlie? She's a beauty, isn't she?"

"Very nice."

This old pals act was not going to last long, this was surely just an act before he started electrocuting me or removing my teeth, one by one with pliers. Whilst he was being pleasant though, Kiffer wanted to recount a story of his entrepreneurial endeavours.

"I was from a poor upbringing, Charlie. Eldest of seven kids, five boys and two girls. My Dad was a docker, a drinker and a hard man. He used to drown people's unwanted kittens. My mother was, and still is, a frail woman, five foot tall in heels and as soft as oven baked butter. Every rags to riches story has a lucky break and my lucky break came in the form of death, my father's death, I would not be the wealthy man I am today, if my Dad had not died of a heart attack at forty three years old, when I was just a boy of fifteen. Once Dad died, someone needed to step up to the plate, to keep the eight of us fed and as the oldest, I knew it was my responsibility. I left school within a week of the funeral and started labouring, but it was long hours for crap pay and I knew we were never going to survive on what I was bringing in.

A couple of weeks into the job, I sat down one evening with Mum, to talk about how we were going to make ends meet. In the course of that conversation, it came out that Mum had been left about a grand from some shitty little life policy Dad had. I persuaded Mum, and bear in mind that I was only fifteen years old at the time, that the only way we could survive, would be if she handed over that grand to me and I put it to work. She trusted me, Charlie, with the only money she had.

That's when I started lending money. I packed in labouring, started going door to door in our road. During the day. I offered to lend housewives or 'doleys' money until the next childrens allowance payment came in, or the next dole money or their husband's next pay packet. That's how it started, lend twenty quid, a week later get £25 back, no paperwork, everything done on trust.

As time passed, my confidence grew. I stopped just lending to the housewives and unemployed folk of our road in Walton and began to branch out. I started moving further and further afield, always the same tactics though, short-term loans, small sums, always less than £100 a time and re-claim the loan plus 25% extra, within a fortnight. I always managed to get my money, until I came across Kenny Beagrie.

Kenny Beagrie was a long distance lorry driver. Kenny's problem was that when he wasn't working, he was a total pisshead. A twenty pints a day man. He was in his early fifties, divorced, someone told me his wife went off with his best mate whilst he was on a job to Berlin, fat, balding, heavily tattooed and not a great looker. This man loved to drown his sorrows, so he had come to me to borrow £100 with a promise that he would pay me back after a four day work trip to Northern France. He did pay me back too, good as gold. Three days after arriving back though, he was knocking on my door again, asking for £200 this time. £200 was more than I had ever lent to an individual before. Kenny explained he had a ten day trip sorted down to Madrid, which would be paying handsomely and he'd pay me back as soon as he arrived home. He said he'd make it worth my while and would pay me £300 back. I got greedy, Charlie, I had seven others to feed as well as myself, so against my better judgement, I ran with it.

A couple of weeks later, when I had heard Kenny was back from Spain and had been spotted in several local pubs, I called round at his house one Saturday lunchtime. He opened the door, stinking of booze,

"What do you want?" he said to me.

"I've come to get my £300." I told him.

At this point, Charlie, he made a fateful error. As you know, I am the best, politest man on earth to people who treat me right, but if you cross me, I can be a mad fucker!

"What £300?" he said. Could you believe that?! He was denying all knowledge.

"I lent you £200 a fortnight ago, Kenny. You said you would give me £300 back, when you came back from Madrid. I want it, Kenny."

"Fuck off, Cuntington! I owe you nothing. I only leant money off you once and I've paid you back. Now piss off and let me get back to bed."

"Borrowed money." I said, it annoyed me when people muddled up their lending and borrowing, "you borrowed money, you did not lend it, you borrowed it. Give it me back!"

"Piss off!" he said.

Kenny Beagrie slammed his door in my face. Kenny Beagrie was a fool to cross me, Charlie. I knocked on his door again, he opened his door and I stared him straight in the eye.

"You'd better give me that £300, Kenny!"

He started pushing me, Charlie! He came straight out his front door, into the road and started prodding my chest. No-one prods Simon Cunnington.

"Or what Cuntington? Or what?" Kenny Beagrie was saying, "look at you! Fifteen years old and a seven stone weakling! I told you to PISS OFF! If I ever see you around here again, Cuntington, I will take great pleasure in kicking every last bit of shit out of your skinny little body!"

I went home, Charlie, took stock and ran with Plan B. I filled a bag with stones and half-bricks and about one o'clock in the morning, I went round to his road and sat on the floor, about a dozen doors down, on the other side of the road. About two o'clock, Kenny Beagrie staggered up his road, I'd heard he used to go to "The Melrose" for lock-ins, so I knew he'd be coming back legless. I watched him struggle with his key in the door, but didn't make a move, I just watched him. I saw the lights in his house go on and then ten minutes later, saw them go off again. Half an hour later, when I was sure he'd be fast asleep, I started banging on his door, making a right old racket. Once again, the lights came back on. I could hear him muttering,

"What the fuck's going on? It's the middle of the fucking night!"

The hall light came on and then he opened the front door with just a dressing gown on.

"Cuntington! I warned you not to come here!" he sneered.

"I want my money, Kenny!" I said.

"There is no money!"

Kenny Beagrie tried to shut the door., but he was drunk, rotten drunk and his reactions were slow. As he tried to push it shut, I kicked it open and before he knew what was happening, I swung that bag of bricks and rocks and it hit him, right on the top of his head. For a split second, he just looked at me, like I was insane, then he put his hand to his head, inspected it, his hand was full of blood and he just dropped to the ground like a tall tree beaten by a lumberjack.

I went into his house. Shut his door behind me. Went upstairs, found his bedroom, then found a brown envelope in his bedside drawer, opened it, saw there was about a grand in there, stuffed it in my pocket and then left. I had gloves on, so left no fingerprints and threw the bloodied bag with the rocks in, into the Mersey. I heard the next day that Kenny Beagrie had been found dead.

I must admit, Charlie, I felt no guilt. If that fucker had paid me back his debt to me, he would still be alive now. Same goes for everyone since. I'm not looking for trouble, I just need a deal to be honoured, to be shown the respect I feel I deserve."

As Kiffer's story finished, we came to a stand still at Clieves Hill. Perfect timing. I think I had been duly warned. Kiffer's henchmen disembarked, as did the driver, leaving Kiffer and I alone in the limo.

"Tell me what's happened, Charlie. You're a family man, like me. Explain to me how things have spun so far out of control."

"It's the horses, Kiffer. I've had some bad luck. Real bad luck."

Kiffer was unsympathetic.

"Bad luck Charlie or bad judgement?"

"Both I suppose, Kiffer. I'll win it back though, I always do."

"It's nice to hear you so confident, Charlie, it really is, but remind me how much you owe me?"

"I've borrowed four grand, Kiffer."

"Four grand, so at today's rate of exchange, that's six grand you owe me, Charlie, isn't it?"

"I'll get it you, Kiffer."

"I know you will, Charlie! How exactly will you get it me though, Charlie, that's what

I want to hear?"

"If I could just borrow another grand, Kiffer, I reckon I could turn it all around."

Kiffer allowed himself a little chuckle.

"That's good, Charlie! Really good! Who's lending you that, then?"

"I was hoping you would, Kiffer."

"Me?! I'd love to mate, but as we've just said, you owe me six grand already. I can't afford to be throwing good money after bad. If I gave you another grand, that would be seven and a half grand that you'd owe me and that's a significant amount of money. Too much to lose.

As far as I can see, Charlie, the only luck you seem to be having right now, is bad luck. I operate my business just like a bank, so if I decide you are getting in to a situation where it is becoming increasingly unlikely that I am going to get my money back, I have to resort to Plan B."

I started to feel very uncomfortable. Kiffer had already told me what plan B was.

"You won't get your money by killing me, Kiffer!"

That was the switch he needed. Good Godfather, became Bad Godfather. Kiffer lunged forward, grabbed me by the hair and pulled my head down towards the floor. He gripped a thick bundle of hair with his left hand, I was passive, there was no point in me fighting back, with his right hand, he delivered a barrage of upper cuts to my nose. It immediately started dripping thick blobs of dark red blood.

"I don't believe you're in a position to start fucking lecturing me on what to do and what not to do, Charlie! Believe me, if I want to kill you, I will kill you! Simple as that!"

My blood was dripping on to the floor of the limousine, I didn't have a handkerchief or a tissue, nor did I want to ask for one from Kiffer. I took the letters I had earlier stuffed in my pocket and used them to wipe my nose and wipe the blood up off the floor.

"I'll get you your money, Kiffer."

"You've got twenty four hours, old man!"

Twenty four hours! I felt like a dead man walking now! Six grand in twenty four hours was, barring a lottery win, near on impossible.

"I'll get it, but I need more than twenty four hours."

Kiffer was not known for having a soft centre.

"I don't care what you need, Charlie. What you have is twenty four hours and after that if you do not have my six thousand pounds, I will bring you back here and I will get the boys to start snapping your bones, starting with your legs and moving upwards until they get to your neck."

I think I gulped so loud it was audible back home.

"Boys!" Kiffer shouted, "come and get this old fucker out of my limo!"

The 'Smirking Giant' and 'Muscles' appeared, dragged me out of the car and pinned me face down on the 'Sunny Road' Muscles sat on my back, he had been smoking a cigarette which he now decided to extinguish by stubbing it out on the back of my neck. As the heat burnt into my skin, I yelled out,

"What the bloody hell are you doing that for, Muscles?"

Matter of factly, he replied,

"It's my job, Charlie! If you think this is bad, wait and see what'll happen to you in twenty four hours time, if you don't get Kiffer his money."

As Muscles was talking, with his knees digging into my back, the 'Smirking Giant' was rifling through my pockets, taking my wallet out, then he removed the chain I had on around my neck. I began struggling at first, but Muscles had a sharp knife in his other hand and each time I struggled, he pressed the blade into my neck so that it drew blood. I could feel it, trickling down my back like Castrol oil. I decided motionless was a better policy and remained still as the 'Smirking Giant' removed my watch, it was only when he began prising my wedding ring off my finger that I regained the struggle.

"Come on lads!" I protested, "I've had my wedding ring for thirty years!"

"It's a deposit, Charlie," Muscles explained, "If we get the money off you, depending on what sort of mood Kiffer's in, you might just get it back. If we don't, you'll never see that ring again and we'll be straight around to your house. We'll strip it bare like a swarm of locusts in a barley field and then, in all likelihood, we'll come looking for you. We like you Charlie, but Kiffer has a reputation to maintain, there's no point being sentimental in our game."

"How am I supposed to get six grand in twenty four hours, when you've just taken my wallet with my last fifty quid in it and my watch and wedding ring, the only two things I own that I could pawn?"

Muscles stood up, taking the weight off my back. I stayed on the floor for a few seconds as he'd knocked the wind out of my sails and I needed to regain some composure. Once I felt a little better, I pushed myself up onto my feet. By the time I was upright, Kiffer's henchmen were back in the limo. The engine started. The electric window came down and Kiffer put his head out of the window,

"Twenty four hours, Charlie, the clock is already ticking. It's time to sink or swim. If you need any motivation just remember Kenny Beagrie. Everyone pays me back, Charlie, everyone!"

The limo sped off leaving a trail of dust in its wake. I began my lonely walk home, continuing to dab my bloody nose and cigarette burnt back, with the morning's post. What I needed to figure out, and quickly, was how on earth I was going to get hold of six grand by the following morning.

Kelly

Paul Newman, the legendary Hollywood actor, when asked by journalists about his long and happy marriage to Joanne Woodward, in the fickle world of Hollywood, allegedly responded by famously saying, something along the lines of,

"Why go out for hamburger, when you have steak at home?"

In my life, I had steak at home, but I must have kept putting it in the freezer, as I had a habit of totally forgetting it was there, thinking I had nothing in and then going out and picking up something to stop me from starving! For five years though, I did starve myself of love, as I thought there was potentially the juciest fillet steak ever coming my way. Once you haven't been fed for five years though, you realise someone may have pinched your meal and it may be time to just start eating and time to stop being so bloody fussy!

As July 4th approached, I pondered whether there was really much point travelling up to Ormskirk again. Over the last four years, the journey up to our "Sunny Road" had not led to an emotional re-union and, despite having optimistic moments, most of the time I just could not see how this time would be any different.

In my mind, there were two possible outcomes that could have happened in relation to the letter I had sent to Richie's Mum and Dad's. Either Richie had received it and had decided it was no longer in his interest to meet me because his life had subsequently moved on OR he had not received it and his life was just continuing along the same path, oblivious to my heartfelt appeal. Irrespective of which of those scenarios was the right one, there was nothing to suggest Richie would turn up. My problem was, some romantic notion was telling me to give it one last shot.

I was still working at Dillons, a job that I had thought was temporary, had kept me in gainful employment for over four years. I was enjoying it and although I was never going to become a millionaire from my wage there, I did not ever wake up dreading work. Twelve months earlier, life at Dillons have become more interesting when a new employee, called Roddy Baker, started. Roddy soon became my closest friend both in and out of work. I had overheard some of the other staff saying that he had come into retail as a complete career change from what he had done previously. For a while, I did not know what that other career had been, but it was blatantly obvious that he had not read a single book since leaving primary school! Roddy just survived on his sense of humour. We used to have lunch together most days and I would always finish lunch in higher spirits than when it started.

"If this is a career change," I asked Roddy one lunchtime, "what was it you did before?"

"I was a Headmaster." Roddy replied stoically.

Men often think that women are easily fooled, but you would have to be the world's most naïve person to think Roddy had been a Headmaster, he looked far too youthful and the only Queen's English he spoke, was the English of the 'Queens' in Soho. Not that he was camp, I'm just saying he had a strong London accent. Really strong.

"If you used to be a Headmaster, Roddy, then I used to be a bloke!"

"Kelly! Now you come to mention it, I've always wondered why you had such a massive Adam's apple!"

"Sod off!" I said playfully.

"I swear, I was a Headmaster for six years. Swear on my Mum's life."

Roddy did not look any older than about twenty five, but he was making his statement with such conviction, that a small part of me started to believe there must be an element of truth in what he was saying.

"At which school?" I enquired.

"School? What are you on about woman?!! No school! I was a Headmaster at Bobby's Barbers in East Ham! Six years cutting hair, I got so bored even selling books for a living seemed like a decent option."

"Do you know anything about books?"

"Not a thing! I just know that you open them, read everything inside and then you're done, Bob's your Uncle, Fanny's your Aunt!"

That was typical Roddy! He was always upbeat, always cracking jokes, never took himself too seriously, it was a joy to be around him, as he would always make me feel good about myself. If Roddy had been in the mirror on the wall, Snow White would not have been the fairest of them all, I would have stolen that prize. I knew how Roddy felt about me, as he would consistently tell me, but it was not a reciprocal attraction. If I had given Roddy even the slightest inkling that I was interested, he would quite literally have grabbed the opportunity with both hands. I was sure that would not be happening though. I knew I wanted my future to be with Richie. I made it abundantly clear to Roddy that my interest was purely platonic and he should not entertain any ideas that further down the line we may become an item. I told him it was never going to happen. I told him that if I ended up marrying Richie, he could be a pageboy!

As July 4th, approached, the butterflies in my stomach, the pounding heart and the erratic breathing returned, like they had in the weeks before my visit North, in each of the last four years. I felt like a silly, lovestruck schoolgirl again, which, given every visit so far had failed to deliver Richie, seemed very optimistic of my internal organs.

The routine I had followed on the four previous trips to Ormskirk had not changed. I felt like a Crimewatch actor, re-enacting the same scene every twelve months. Each year, I would travel up by train from London Euston to Preston, then take another train to Burscough, stop at a hotel between Ormskirk and Burscough, called the Beaufort and then on the morning of the 4th July, I would make a four mile walk up to the 'Sunny Road'. I did not mind the walk there, it was always filled with both nervous excitement and optimism, but the lonely trudge back after a no show from Richie was always tough.

This time around, I had decided it was time to do things differently. Rather than book into the Beaufort, I decided to book into the West Tower Hotel in Aughton, which was a lot more expensive, but only half a mile from the 'Sunny Road'. The other more radical thing I decided to do, was to journey up with a companion. I decided, all things considered, it would be a good idea to bring Roddy up with me.

Over the last four years, I had always avoided going into Ormskirk whilst I was on my annual pilgrimage to the 'Sunny Road'. I did not want to risk public humiliation or arrest by the local constabulary still looking for the fleeing accomplice from Mum's murder. The main reason I avoided Ormskirk though, was to steer clear of a face to face confrontation with Jemma. The repercussions of crossing Jemma's path scared me more than the thought of being arrested. Jemma had been responsible for most of the positive aspects of my childhood and it was the guilt that I felt that had led to me avoiding her for so long. I did not know how I could possibly rebuild the bridges that I had burnt, so thought the least complex solution was complete avoidance. The longer I avoided her, the guiltier I felt and the more certain I became that she would now hate me.

The issue I faced though was that each year after Richie failed to turn up, I had no emotional support and the long walk back to the Beaufort Hotel and the subsequent trip home had been heartbreaking. Romantically I felt like I was just torturing myself by pursuing something that probably should have been consigned to the 'happy memories' part of my brain, but I just could not help doing it. Journeying up and down with Roddy I thought would ensure my spirits would not sag irrespective of circumstance and if Richie did not turn up, I would finally close this Chapter of my life and allow another one to begin. Americans called it 'closure' and that's what this one last trip to the 'Sunny Road' was for me – 'closure'.

One lunchtime at Dillons, Roddy and I were discussing our imminent trip to Ormskirk.

"I love spending time with you, Kelly, you know that, but the one thing that makes me feel uncomfortable about this trip, is the thought that Richie will finally turn up this year."

"Why does that make you feel uncomfortable?"

"Two reasons. One, I'll just be stuck on my Jack Jones looking like a gooseberry, but secondly, and more importantly, I don't want to lose you as a mate."

"Roddy! You'll never lose me as a mate!"

"I might if I punch this Richie bloke for not having the decency to turn up for the last four years!"

"You wouldn't do that!"

"I'd be tempted. I didn't mean that though, I mean if you two fall into each other's arms like a pair of lovebirds and everything goes swimmingly, you might decide to move back up North. If that happens our little lunch time chats will come to end and I'll be lonely working here with all these stuck-up arty farty types!"

"I wouldn't start worrying about all that stuff just yet, Roddy! Richie hasn't shown up for the last four years! We'll probably just go up, have a trip to the 'Sunny Road', have a look around, sit and have a picnic and then come back down."

"If he does turn up, what would I do with myself? I ain't hanging round watching you kissing him, I'll be jealous!"

"You can kiss him too if you like!"

Roddy gave me a look of being a little vexed with me.

"You know what I mean!"

"You could just go back to the Hotel for a bit and I'd meet you there an hour or two later."

"Maybe all this just isn't worth the bother, Kelly. I mean if he hasn't shown up for four years, why give him a fifth chance?"

"I don't know. Part of me thinks, for some reason, that Richie is going to show up this year."

"He won't."

"Is that what you think Roddy or is that what you hope?"

"Both!"

"Well, we'll never know unless I go, will we?"

"I still think the money we are wasting on this search for Prince Charming could be put to better use. You and I could just go out on an almighty piss up and drink to Richie's health."

"Roddy!"

"What?"

"Richie's had cancer."

"So? All the more reason to drink to his health!"

"I suppose….anyway, don't be trying to talk me out of it, it's just something I feel I need to do. One last time."

"You probably said that last year, Kelly!"

"I didn't! I swear this is his last chance. If Richie isn't on the 'Sunny Road' by ten past twelve on the 4th July, I'll move on and never mention his name again."

"Can I quote you on that?"

"You can! Start the tape recorder."

Roddy pretended to press play and record on an imaginary tape recorder and then held an invisible microphone up to my mouth.

"Make your statement, Kelly Watkinson!"

"I, Kelly Watkinson, hereby announce that if Richie Billingham is not on the 'Sunny Road' by ten minutes after twelve o'clock on the afternoon of the 4th July 2000, I promise and swear on my own life and that of my best friend's, Roddy Baker's, that I shall never ever mention the name Richie Billingham again, throughout the term of our natural lives…..OK?"

"Ideal!"

Charlie

By the time I arrived back from my enforced visit to the 'Sunny Road', Dot had left for work. Dot worked part-time in an old people's home as a care assistant and this included a 'ten until four' stretch on a Saturday. She'd left me a key under a plant pot in the front garden, which was our usual emergency hiding place and a note on the kitchen table that read:-

Charlie,

God knows where you have disappeared to, but give me a ring at work to let me know that you are OK. There's a pork pie in the fridge for your lunch. Don't forget to put the tea in, like I told you last night.

Love Dot xxx."

Panic was beginning to set in. I kept talking to myself, telling myself to keep calm, panic in the morning when all avenues had been explored and I still did not have the six grand. Deal with everything in bite size chunks, I told myself. Firstly, ring Dot, tell her that you are OK, then once that's out the way, scour the house for money, building society passbooks or anything else that is potentially worth a few quid.

Dot was easily comforted. As a gambler, I was used to having to create stories to explain unusual absences, so just rang her and matter-of-factly told her that I had wandered down to the newsagents to pick up a few newspapers, then, as it had been a beautiful morning, I had decided to take myself down to the park, sit on a bench and have a pleasant read in the early morning sun. Dot was only half listening, there were probably things going on in the background at work and all she was concerned about, before I put the phone down, was that I put some sauce in a casserole dish and put it in the oven for our tea.

Once Dot's mild concerns were addressed, it was time to see what we had in the house that I could utilise to make me six grand. The first place I headed were the drawers next to Dot's bed where I knew she kept the Building Society passbooks. I had no idea how much money we had in those accounts as I did not contribute to our savings at all, but knew my wages paid most of the bills, so thought there may be some savings that Dot had put away. I was the type of person who lived for the day, Dot was the type who always believed in being prepared for a rainy day. I needed that money now, it was pissing down!

I rifled through the drawers like an anxious, drug addled burglar, pushing all the crap that Dot had gathered out the way, for some reason, tights, knickers, credit card bills and passbooks were all in together. The first passbook I found was a Girobank account, I flicked through to the most up-to-date balance, £13! Shit! What did Dot do with her money? I knew mine went the way of the bookies, but where did Dot's go? There must be others, I thought,

"Come on, Dot! Don't let me down!" I said to myself, "My life depends on this!"

I started throwing everything out that drawer, feeling my blood pressure rising. Then I saw a second passbook. Temporary respite. Birmingham Midshires, how much was this? I flicked through the pages, £1-12.

"Fucking hell!" I cursed, "Fuck! Fuck! Fuck! Fuck! Fuck!"

I was a dead man. A dead man. I pulled the whole drawer out and tipped its contents on the floor. The last remaining passbook in that drawer was a Halifax one, that sat there, shinily, gleaming at me like the gold in a treasure chest.

"Six grand!" I pleaded aloud as I leafed through those pages, "if it's not six grand, I'm screwed!"

Why I kept reminding myself of my own predicament, I have no, but fear does strange things to the human mind. I reached the final page, "£487-20." Better than the other two, but I knew it was nowhere near enough to keep Kiffer sweet. I was, by now, breaking out in a cold sweat. I imagined myself waking up in a coffin, hammering on its lid, six feet below the ground, hopelessly screaming for help as I died for a second time. I needed to leave a letter for Dot, I told myself, let her know that I wanted to be cremated. I did not like the idea of being stuck in a confined space or the idea of my body just being left to rot, having said that, if Kiffer's mobsters murdered me, they weren't exactly going to pop around to my house, ring the doorbell and hand my battered body over to Dot. I doubt they would listen to funeral requests either. I needed to find something in our house, anything, that I could sell.

I started running around the house feeling like a contestant on Mike Reid's show, "Runaround" that the kids used to watch when they were little, as I'd run into the lounge and then decide that was the wrong place to be, so would run over to the dining room. There was nothing in the lounge that was sellable other than the TV and the settee and they weren't going to get me five and a half grand and they weren't things you could find an instant buyer for either. The same problems existed with the goods in the dining room too, I wasn't going to make a quick fortune by selling a dining room table and chairs. The gravity of the situation and the hopelessness of my search began to kick in. I was hunting for something I just wasn't going to find. I just stood there yelling and began punching myself in the head. Then the tears came. My life was over.

As the tears continued to pour, I dropped onto my knees and began to pray aloud,

"God, if you can hear me now, I need your help. I've been a fool, a complete fool and I've neglected you, I've neglected my family and I have made a complete mess of my life so far. You have given me so many things, a good marriage, great kids, but I've not appreciated them, I've just been selfish, thought of no-one other than myself and taken everything and everyone in my life for granted.

I'm scared now though, God. I don't want to die. If you can help me through this God, I promise I will change. This is my road to Damascus moment, God. I promise you it is. I'll make a deal with you, God, if you can somehow find me six grand, by tomorrow morning, I will never gamble again. I'll never take anything for granted again, I'll be a better and kinder man. I'll come to church, not just at Christmas and at weddings and christenings, I'll come every Sunday without fail. Just help me, God. I don't want to die, God. Six grand, that's all. I'll even pay it back, over time, to the local church. We can do this, God, if you help me, we can do this! Just give me a sign, God. If you do, I swear, it'll change me forever. I know I've never done a thing for you, but help me through this and I will! I swear I will. AMEN."

Now I know some people laugh at me when I tell them this, tell me I'm talking rubbish, but I don't care. I swear, as soon as I stood back up, I felt different. Completely different. I felt like I was being guided. Something, I don't know what, told me to go to the bathroom. I don't mean said it out loud, I just meant it was like a sixth sense, telling me to go to the bathroom. I no longer felt scared or nervous. I felt self-assured. Something told me everything would be OK. I felt like an angel had taken me by the hand and was calming me and leading me in the right direction. Then, when I reached the bathroom, I was certain, as sitting there, on the side of the sink, next to the toothpaste, were Dot's rings, her engagement ring and her eternity ring. Before, when I wasn't thinking straight, it had totally slipped my mind that Dot always took those rings off for work. Apparently rings can be a great breeding ground for germs, plus, Dot always pointed out, jagged rings could always catch one of the old dears when she was lifting them or washing them. Dot only ever wore her wedding ring for work and left the other two at home. I knew, just knew, that these rings were going to be my salvation. Somehow, these rings were going to save my life. I put both of them in my pocket, picked up my car keys and set off for Ormskirk.

Charlie

Kubilay Turkyilmaz. A Swiss footballer of Turkish descent - ever heard of him? On 7th October 2000, he became the first person in World Cup Qualifying history to score a hat-trick of penalties. Heard of him now? Thought not, it was against the Faroe Islands! I love Kubilay Turkyilmaz! I love him more than any other footballer that has ever walked this earth. I love him more than Bobby Charlton, more than Geoff Hurst, more than Bolton's greatest, Nathaniel Lofthouse, scorer of 255 goals in 452 games for the mighty Bolton Wanderers and thirty goals in thirty three games for England. Kubilay Turkyilmaz surpasses all of them, in my book. Why, you may ask? What's so good about Kubilay Turkyilmaz? Simple answer…Kubilay Turkyilmaz saved my life. Kubilay Turkyilmaz and God anyway……………………………………….

A grand. Lunchtime on Saturday, 8th June 1996 and I had a grand in my pocket. Normally, a grand in my pocket meant that I had just had a big win on the horses and it was time to treat the boys in the pub to a round on me or the family to a meal out. Not this time. I knew this time, that a grand in my pocket by day break would almost certainly mean death.

I had stooped to an all time low. The theft of the savings and personal belongings of my wife had netted me that thousand pounds. The Halifax account was fortunately in joint names, so I had managed to withdraw all but £12 from that account and I had also visited a pawn shop in Burscough Street, to receive £525 for two rings worth more than five times that. I understood that if my plan did not come off, Dot would no doubt kill me before Kiffer's henchmen came calling.

I was still five grand short. It was, without doubt, crisis time. In a time of crisis, I had little choice but to resort to what I knew best. Gambling. Gambling, the very thing that had created this whole mess, was now the only thing I had to rely on to save my life. In fact, that was not strictly true, I had faith too. Faith was going to be the thing that would make this gamble different from every bet I had previously placed. From a personal perspective, this was the bet to end all bets. Prior to this one bet, I had always hoped or thought I was going to win my bet, this time, I knew I would win. There was a spiritual difference. An Almighty difference. I had repented of my sins before God and I knew God was going to allow this one final sin, to clean my slate and cleanse my soul. This was one final, Almighty bet. I was going to pick one horse in the Derby at Epsom and put the whole one thousand pounds on it to win. I had decided now was not the time to be cautious. Somehow, I knew, God was going to guide me through this. God would ensure that I was a winner.

I parked up in the car park by the bus station, with more adrenalin flowing through my veins than I had ever felt before. Could this have possibly been the Holy Spirit? I needed to go to Stanley Racing and pick the right horse. It was still only late morning, so I decided I would pick my horse, refrain from placing the bet, head out for lunch, take time to ponder and deliberate, then return just before the race, if everything still felt right, to invest my thousand pounds.

By eleven thirty that morning, I was in Stanley Racing in Ormskirk, praying fate and faith would lend a hand. It was busier than a normal Saturday morning in there, not Grand National busy, but certainly Cheltenham Festival busy, so I found myself having to make pleasant chit chat with part-time punters who I had not seen for a few months, all looking for a bit of guidance. I was genuine when I told them I had yet to decide. Some punters like to keep their cards close to their chests, but I was not one of them, it defied logic, it was not as though the horse knew my money was down and would suddenly feel additional pressure to perform. I just told people that they could copy my bets if they liked, but if they did not have big enough balls to choose for themselves, then they did not have the right to come whingeing to me if things worked out badly.

As soon as I looked at the racecard for the Derby, on the wall of Stanley Racing, that euphoric feeling that had never been far away since my "Roads To Damascus" moment, came hurtling back. Something weird happened. Every horses name seemed to shrink so they became impossible to read, with one exception, DUSHYANTOR. As the others shrank, this one was magnified to ten times it normal size. It was as if God was imprinting the name on my brain, DUSHYANTOR. I had a look at its form, its breeding, its jockey, its trainer and its odds and amazingly everything seemed right. I was so excited my body started shaking like God was using me as a rattle.

"Thank you Lord!" I whispered. "Thank you!"

Dushyantor, second in the Dante stakes at York, fantastic pedigree, ridden by the sublime Pate Eddery, trained by the wonderful Henry

Cecil and priced at 5-1, meaning if I placed the full £1000 on this horse, I would collect £6000 when it won. I just felt destiny was well and truly on my side. I felt so confident, I nearly filled out the betting slip and ran to the counter waving my thousand pounds in the air. There was definitely no way I was going to change my mind. I felt the engraver could start putting the name Dushyantor on to the trophy already.

I stopped myself. Was this certainty or optimistic excitement? I had to be sure. My mindset had been that I would follow a set routine, choose a horse, go and have coffee and lunch, then return to place the bet. If God wanted me to change horses, I was sure this would give him ample opportunity to give me a sign. I decided against placing my bet there and then, but bade my fellow punters farewell convinced I would see their faces again on a regular basis around town and that in twenty four hours time, I would be feasting on a Sunday Roast rather than providing a feast for some underground insects. I had the winner. Dushyantor. No doubt about it. I had the winner.

I went over to Taylor's coffee shop for my lunch, I just had a baked potato with cheese and a black coffee and read the papers. I always started a newspaper from the back, the sports pages and all the tabloids were full of hype about England football teams first game in the European Championship against Switzerland, that was kicking off at three o'clock at Wembley. This was the first time England had hosted a major football tournament since the 1966 World Cup. Would this be the year to end thirty years of hurt? The tabloids suspected it was, I suspected not. Venables was a good manager, but we were still emerging from one of the most disastrous spells English football had ever known and I thought this tournament had arrived a bit too soon for us. We had not qualified for the 1994 World Cup and automatically qualified for this because we were hosting it. The Derby was at 2.25pm, so if I picked up my six grand after that, I could go and have a pint or two in "The Buck", "Bowlers" or "Disraelis" and cheer the boys on.

By two o'clock, lunch eaten, coffees drunk, newspapers read, I was ready. It was time to go to work. Time for my lifesaving bet. Time for the last bet of my life, that was a guarantee, win or lose, it would be the last bet. If I lost, there would never be another opportunity. If I won, I had made a deal with God and I needed to stand by that. I had read the Bible, God didn't seem to sympathise too much with the people who crossed him, just ask Noah who he went for a pint with after the floods or ask Lot what he had on his fish and chips. This was it. My time had come. It was quite literally do or die. Bring it on! I gathered up my plates and mugs, put them on a tray and returned them to the ladies in the kitchen, put my newspapers under my arm and headed to the door. As soon as I took one step outside Taylor's, on my short journey to Stanley's, I heard a familiar voice,

"Dad!"

To be honest, despite its familiarity, I didn't take too much notice, probably a third of the people in Ormskirk were answerable to that name.

"DAD!"

It was deeper and louder second time, followed by a high pitched,

"Charlie! Charlie!"

I looked over and making their way through the crowds were our Jim and Amy.

"Shit!" I mumbled to myself. "Could you not have distracted them, God?"

Jim and Amy, holding hands, were sidestepping market day shoppers, heading towards me with faces full of smiles. I did not look quite as gleeful, I felt they could be signing my death warrant.

"Dad! How are things? All set for the Derby?"

This was a catastrophe! There was no way I wanted Jim anywhere near me when I placed my lifesaving bet. How could I explain to him why I was putting a grand on Dushyantor?!

I tried to lie.

"I think I'll give the Derby a miss this year, son."

Jim automatically thought I was joking.

"Good one, Dad! That would be like Father Christmas saying he fancied a night in front of the TV on Christmas Eve! No really, what've you picked?"

"I haven't even looked, son."

Amy then did her impression of Inspector Jean Darblay from Juliet Bravo.

"What's that you've scribbled on your paper, Charlie?"

I looked down at my Daily Mirror. As well as having nervously scribbled moustaches, beards and cross-eyes on every male and female character, I had written, Dushyantor, hundreds of times, all over the front and back cover. Normally with Dot, I had a bit of time to think of excuses, this time I felt really on the spot.

"Erm…Dushyantor…it's a new cream."

"What sort of cream?" Amy asked.

"For my piles," I answered. Nosey bitch deserved that!

"Oh!"

Jim laughed.

"Take no notice of him, Amy! Dad's taking the mickey out of you! It's a horse in the Derby! It won't win though."

"What's going to beat it, then?" I challenged Jim.

"Shaamit. Nailed on."

"Shaamit!" I said like it was something I'd stood in, "that's got no bloody chance!"

"It'll win!" Jim insisted.

"Amy, don't let him put any of your money on that thing," I advised, "it's got no worthwhile form, it's not even run this season!"

"Michael Hills, good young jockey." Jim explained.

"Damon Hill is a good racing driver, but he couldn't get a tractor to win the Grand Prix!" I countered. This was standard banter between Jim and I. Normally, I loved it, but on this day, it definitely had a less lighthearted edge. That would have been down to me.

"Where are you watching it?" Jim asked, "Amy was going to do a bit of shopping, see if she can pick up a few bargains off the market, so I was going to head up to Stanley's for an hour. Is that where you were heading?"

"No, I was going to go to Woolies to buy a Neil Sedaka CD," I lied, "but seeing as though you are heading to Stanley's, I'll head up there with you."

I needed to shake Jim off somehow. I suppose I could have just made my excuses and gone to another bookies, there were a few scattered around the town, but Stanley's was my home territory, my lucky bookie, so I did not want to go anywhere else. Up until this point, I was convinced God was on my side, but now I felt the devil had joined the game. I felt like God had handpicked 'Dushyantor' for me and now the devil was trying to sabotage the plan and stop me placing this bet.

Twenty minutes later, I found myself standing next to my youngest son in Stanley Racing, wishing he would faint. I wanted a spade that I could knock him out with. Everything I had suggested to get rid of him in the previous twenty minutes had failed.

"Should you not go and give your wife a hand?" I asked.

"She'll be fine!" Jim replied.

"Can you not just nip over to the other bookies to check the other prices?"

"It's not worth the energy for a tenner bet, Dad!"

"I think I've forgotten to lock my car, be a good lad and run over to the bus station for me and check it, will you?"

"Piss off!"

Five minutes before the race started, as the horses were heading across Epsom Downs to the starting point of the 217th Derby, I was in a blind panic. I had a grand total of £10 on Dushyantor to win at 9-2. One thing I knew for certain, was that if my horse won, Kiffer would not be accepting a £55 downpayment on a debt of six grand! It had just been impossible to get the bet on with Jim following my every move. I felt like I was slowly suffocating. The grains of sand in my egg timer were dropping fast. I could hardly breathe and not just because the fumes from a hundred gamblers fags were polluting the air.

"£10 each way on Shaamit at twelves!" Jim was saying, "if this comes in, I'll buy the pints during the England game!"

I felt faint. The blood drained from my face like someone had pulled a plug out of my neck.

"I need the toilet, Jim."

Jim took a proper look at me and realised I would go undetected in a milk bath.

"Are you OK, Dad? You look awful!"

"I'm OK."

"Do you want me to come with you?"

"NO!" I said rather too forcefully, "what are you going to do? Wipe my arse?"

"Catch you if you faint."

"I'll be fine."

I headed towards the toilets. I thought I was going to vomit, everything was swirling. I entered the cubicle, which, in a bookmakers, is never the most salubrious of locations. Gamblers have a poor aim or are always in too much of a rush to line their shot up. There was urine all over the seat and the stale aroma of a hundred previous craps, some of which still graced the porcelain. Luckily, there was a window in there. A half opened window. A window, just about big enough for me to squeeze out of. I opened the window as wide as it could possibly open, pushed myself up on to the window sill and squeezed myself through. This measure was done from desperation rather than calculation. I did not even consider what was on the other side, which turned out to be a four foot drop to a muddy puddle and I fell like Humpty Dumpty into the middle of it, belly flopping into a three inch pool of mud. There was no time for self-pity though, so I picked myself up and ran through Ormskirk towards the nearest alternative bookies, looking like an overfed swamp creature. I tried to sprint but its hard to run when you are a fifty something, fat waster, caked in mud. I waddled across looking like a rhino and moving like a penguin. With two minutes to spare, I pushed opened the door of Ladbills. Everyone gets paranoid at times, thinks other people are staring at them, but this was not paranoia. It was impossible not to stare at me, my whole front, from my forehead to my shoes, was caked in mud.

"Shit!" someone said, "Augustus Gloops escaped from the factory!"

I disregarded the comments, picked up a betting slip and a pen, and wrote out

'2.25 EPSOM - £990 WIN – DUSHYANTOR'.

Typically, there was a queue. All three staff members were serving clueless punters. Everyone else in the queue stepped back and let me through. Managing to ignore my impression of a maskless bog snorkeller, the three staff members busied themselves with the idiots at the counter. The first one was a twice a year female punter, who probably only bet on the Derby and the Grand National, she was asking Vera how to complete her slip. Secondly, Graham was helping old Ernie, a doddery ninety something who punted in copper, to count out his pennies and then Suzy was trying to find a price on a horse for 'Mardy Martin', an idiotic regular punter who would argue a horse with a dick the size of Gibraltar was a mare. Martin was arguing some no hoper should be piced at 250-1 rather than 200-1, which was immaterial as in five minutes it would no doubt finish last.

"This is fucking ridiculous!" I said to the Zander, the South African punter stood next to me, looking almost as twitchy as me, "it's Derby Day, they should take more staff on! Martin, if you want to give me your two quid, mate, if that bloody donkey wins, I'll give you the £500 myself!"

Martin uttered something under his breath. I could see on the screens that the first horses were being led into the stalls, I dug my muddied wedge of notes from out my pocket, just as old Ernie shuffled away from the counter, clutching his betting slip in his withered old hand. I strode to the counter, about ten of the horses were in the stalls. I pushed my betting slip and money across the polished counter towards Graham.

"What's this?" Graham asked surveying my dirty notes.

"That would be legal tender, Graham."

"Where in? Trampsville? We'll never get these banked."

"Of course you bloody would!"

"Well, I'm not accepting them!"

"Graham! The race is about to fucking start!"

"No need to speak to me like that, Charlie!"

I had lost it. I may as well have passed this moron a loaded revolver and asked him to shoot me.

"Yes there fucking is! I need this bet on!"

I am sure even God would have had to use all his powers not to swear at Graham, he was, and I am sure still is, a pompous prick.

"Well take it somewhere else and see if they'll accept it!"

"I can't, the race is about to start!"

"Well, you should have got here earlier then, Charlie, shouldn't you? They haven't changed the time of the race. You could have come here any time this week, but you come in two minutes before the start, stinking to high heaven and then kick off because we won't accept your money that looks like its been stored up your arse! Piss off, Charlie, I've real customers to serve!"

I snatched my cash and betting slip back off him and moved away from the counter as the stalls opened and the Derby began. I felt like Graham was my very own Judas, I had asked him three times to put my bet on and each time he had denied me. I hoped Graham's bowels would all spill out at Akeldama too!

Seething, I walked straight out of Ladbills, still cursing to myself and walked the seventy five yards up to Stanleys. I went in and started to push through the crowds to get to Jim, but when they saw the state I was in, they parted like they were the Red Sea and I was Moses. I went and stood right next to Jim, but he was too embroiled in the race to notice my unkempt appearance.

"Bloody Shammit's lost this already!" he moaned, "it's about eighteen horses back!"

"What about Dushyantor?" I asked.

"I think that's one of the two behind it!"

The cloud of dejection that felt like it had been about two feet above my head, pissing urine and faeces on to my already filthy body seemed to move off and be replaced by Johnny Nash, merrily singing, "I Can See Clearly Now" into my ears! Maybe I had this all wrong, maybe the devil was trying to encourage me to back Dushyantor and God had sent Jim and pompous Graham to stop me losing everything.

Counting your blessings is like counting sheep, just when you've counted them, they jump over the fence and disappear. As the horses rounded Tattenham corner, into the final straight, some of the horses at the front, decided they were knackered and some of the ones at the back, decided they fancied the idea of a sprint downhill, so the complexion of the race changed in the blink of an eye and of the eight horses that still had a chance, Dushyantor and Shaamit were two of them. With a couple of furlongs left, Michael Hills and Shammit made me eat my pre-race words about tractors, as they shot off like Champion the Wonder Horse in pursuit of a thief. Jim clenched his fist.

"I've won this Dad! I've won this!" he was saying.

There was only one horse that could steal the crown from Shaamit now and that was Dushyantor. The race suddenly seemed to almost stop and advance frame by frame. Pat Eddery had angled Dushyantor onto the outside of the rest of the weary pack and was making a desperate lunge for Shaamit. After three furlongs downhill, the last half furlong at Epsom is back uphill, and a pretty steep uphill climb it is too, so stride by stride, Dushyantor was closing in.

"Go on SHAAMIT!" yelled Jim.

"Shift your bloody arse, SHAAMIT!" I yelled twice as loud as Jim, his head jerked momentarily away from the screen and towards me, in bewilderment, as he knew I had backed Dushyantor. Little did Jim know that if Dushyantor won, I would feel like I'd lost five grand and an escape route, but if Shaamit won, I had a second chance. I kept expecting Dushyantor's nose to elongate like Pinocchios and flash past the winning post a nostril hair ahead of Shaamit, but it did not happen, despite tiring as it headed back uphill, Shaamit clung on gamely to become the 1996 Derby winner. Jim was ecstatic, he had not only found the Derby winner, but by finding me had saved my life, temporarily at least, not that he knew that.

As Jim raced excitedly to the counter to collect his winnings, I toiled with a new dilemma. What would I bet on now? Once Jim left Stanleys, I would place the new bet there, as the staff knew me well enough to accept my muddy notes, but what or who should I bet on? Jim solved that riddle.

"Bloody hell, Dad!" he shouted over, "what's happened to you? Have you been rolling in cow pat again? You best go and get yourself cleaned up before the match!"

The match! England versus Switzerland. Three o'clock start. It was becoming increasingly obvious, Jim was carrying out God's work here, he was definitely steering me towards the righteous path. He had not managed to rescue me yet though, just provide a reprieve, but the football would be my salvation.

What would be a sensible bet at around 5-1 to turn a grand into six?

Shearer first goal? No, that was too optimistic, he had not scored for England for a year.

England to win? Too short a price and I didn't fancy them anyway.

Switzerland win then? The price was 7-1. Seemed like a reasonable bet to me, but a draw was more likely and a draw was not going to be a decent enough price to turn my thousand pounds into six thousand pounds.

What about a correct score bet then? 0-0. Loads of England games finish 0-0 but more often than not when we are away from home.

What about 1-1 then? The price was 13-2. If it was 1-1, I would win £7500 from £1000. That seemed like a good bet to me. A nation's false hopes riding on our first trophy win for thirty years, surely we could be trusted to completely cock things up at the first hurdle. 1-1 seemed like a plan.

"Jim, I'm just going to buy a T-shirt off the market before the England game starts.

Where are you watching it?"

"The Buck. What are you drinking, Dad? I'm buying!"

"Guinness. See you up there in ten minutes."

I ran off, bought myself a t-shirt, then doubled back to Stanley's, entering from the back entrance, probably just as Jim left from the front. I was right, they did accept my dirty money. £990 on England 1 Switzerland 1 at a price of 13-2. Any other scoreline and I was a dead man. As I placed the bet, Kubilay Turkyilmaz was probably doing little warm up sprints on the Wembley turf, unaware that, as Switzerlands centre forward, he was all that now stood between me and a bullet to the brain. I did not realise at the time, but despite my new found Christian faith, I was now relying on a Muslim man to ensure I was still alive at Christmas!

Richie

My Dad was trying to speak but nothing was coming out. I don't think he knew where to start. Mum was standing in the lounge, hands on hips, awaiting her explanation as to why Dad had stashed a load of old bills, relating to large scale credit card debts and a letter from Kelly to me, in a drawer in his office.

"Charlie!" Mum said impatiently, "I don't really care what this is to do with, I just want the truth. The truth, Charlie, not some story you cobble together, off the top of your head, to get you off the hook. The truth!"

"Dorothy, what's the point in raking up the past? This is all old news now. I've changed. You know I've changed. God has changed me. My lies are consigned to history now."

"Good. Just tell me the story then, Charlie."

"We had problems, Dot. Financial problems. Problems I had created by my gambling."

"Why did you not tell me?"

"I didn't want to worry you."

"OK. So I know the gambling has stopped, but what about the financial problems, do they still exist?"

"No."

"Thank goodness for that! What about the letter from Kelly to Richie, why were you hiding Richie's letter?"

Dad gave Mum a look which was a mixture of confusion and "don't be so ridiculous".

"I wasn't!"

"Richie, show him the letter."

I held up the blood smudged envelope.

"I've no idea," Dad replied genuinely, before adding, "hang on, it probably arrived in the post on Derby Day 1996!"

I looked at the date stamp on the envelope, sure enough, it was stamped 7th June 1996. I knew from the years spent living with Dad, that Derby Day was in June.

"That's the date on it, Mum," I confirmed.

"What was the significance of Derby Day 1996, Charlie?" Mum asked.

"You should know this, Dot."

"Remind me!"

"Derby Day 1996 was the day God revealed himself to me, the day I became a better man."

I stood up off the settee. I had heard Dad's story about God showing him the light before and to me, it always sounded a little crazy! I had never heard the full story, but quite frankly, I didn't want to either. Dad had been a self-absorbed, devious, selfish gambler and a few years ago he'd changed, he had become a Christian, a born again Christian. As an atheist, I was not interested in what had triggered the change, I was just happy that he had become the father that he had not been throughout our childhood, a proper husband to Mum, a man who now cared about keeping her happy and a proper father to his children, who would now listen to what we were saying, without drifting off to a world of galloping hooves mid-sentence. It was time for me to go.

"Mum, Dad, I'm going to head to your toilet and then I'm off home!"

"Do you not want to hear what your father has to say?"

I gave Mum a kiss.

"Not really."

Dad came over to me and gave me a hug.

"I don't have to explain everything to our Richie, Dot, he understands me."

"That's right, Dad, I do…I'll see myself out. I'll give you a ring in the week, Mum."

I didn't really understand. Sometimes I didn't really understand myself, let alone Dad. As far as I could see, we were all just brains with limbs and senses. Why we thought the way we did, acted the way we did, was unfathomable. How anyone of any religion or anti-religion could claim to comprehend the meaning of life or death, was, in my humble opinion, giving their own brain too much credit. All I wanted from life was to be happy without making anyone else unhappy. This seemed a simple enough task, but I was failing to achieve it. I felt I was failing in the most glorious of ways. I had a beautiful wife and two beautiful children, but I felt something was missing from my life, not something spiritual, something physical. To me, religion and testosterone have their similarities, they both lead you on a path away from logic. Having said that, if Dad had reached a point in his life, through his belief in God, whereby he was happy and was not inflicting unhappiness on anyone, then I was genuinely delighted for him.

Once I drove away from Mum and Dad's, I parked up a couple of hundred metres up the road to open Kelly's letter. Dad had spent the last four years telling everyone he had been on a path laden with thorns until God had picked him up and shown him a more righteous path. In a totally different way, maybe I was on the wrong path. As a teenager, I had developed my "Black Jack Theory" whereby I felt we were all chasing perfection. Perhaps for me, Kelly was my perfect partner, would I ever have married Jemma if Kelly had not gone away? Perhaps my marriage to Jemma had just been a rebound thing, a ricochet on to the wrong path. Was I being true to myself to stick with Jemma if I was only ever going to feel like I settled for a mediocre relationship? Jemma must have felt something similar, as at least I was eager to re-ignite the passion, whilst Jemma just seemed to pour cold water on the embers. I put my hazard lights on and tore open the blood stained envelope.

As soon as I opened that envelope, memories flooded out. As I read through the letter, feelings I felt I had long since buried, raised their heads back above the ground. It was a cryptic letter. A letter short on detail, but strong on intent. In July 1996, Kelly had wanted to meet me back in Aughton, back on the "Sunny Road", like we had always talked about, back when we were teenagers. The letter was four years old now, I felt my opportunity had been and gone, I could almost smell the burnt bridge. I wondered whether Kelly had turned up that day and I also wondered what had happened to her since? Four years was a big time span in anyone's life. It was now 2nd July 2000, almost four years to the day that Kelly suggested meeting up. I pondered whether it would be worth just taking a journey over to the "Sunny Road" at midday on the 4th July, just on the off chance that she might be there. I chided myself. What would be the point in that? This was all ridiculous. OK, my relationship with Jemma had probably reached its nadir, but if I was going to even consider leaving that relationship, the worst thing

I could possibly do, is start a relationship with Jemma's sister! It would be crazy. Kelly is my children's auntie!

The problem I had though was that the same thought kept returning into my mind. A morbid thought. I had had a reminder when I was diagnosed with testicular cancer that I was mortal. We only had one life and it was a short one so we had to make the most of it, maximise the opportunities presented to us. Could I honestly say I was doing that married to a woman who seemed to lack any desire for me? For all the negatives that would surround me rekindling my relationship with Kelly, further along the line, perhaps there was an opportunity to be really happy. To coin a phrase would it be 'short-term pain for long-term gain'? I felt there was only one way to find out. I needed to go back to the 'Sunny Road' on the 4th July, just to see if Kelly was there. Just to get an indication of how she was and what she was up to. Just a journey to see an old friend, I told myself. I kept telling myself that, I was not committing a crime, it was just a journey to see an old friend.

Jim

Thinking back now, I have to say it was one of the most bizarre experiences in my whole life! I did not have a clue what was going on! England were leading Switzerland one-nil in a drab start to the 1996 European Championships, when for some reason, my father swapped his allegiances from King and Country to the landlocked European neutrals.

Mark, one of the barmen at The Buck, was out from behind that prison cell of a bar, to collect some glasses and to get a proper look at the footy. Everyone in there was downbeat, it had been a dire game and to make our suffering even worse, in the 83rd minute, the ball was booted at Stuart Pearce's hand, inside the box, from close range and a penalty had been awarded. A Switzerland penalty was not in the script for a triumphant start to Euro '96. Everyone was crestfallen except one man. My father.

"What's going on with your Dad?" Mark asked. "Why is he so made up? Is he part, Swiss?"

"He'll have a hole in him like Swiss cheese, if he doesn't sit down!" some irritated England fan warned.

"Sit down, Dad!" I pleaded.

"Does he make watches or fondue sets or penknives or something?" Mark suggested.

"No," I replied, "he's not Swiss and he has absolutely nothing to do with Switzerland. I haven't the foggiest idea what goes on in that man's head!"

"Well," Mark continued, "he certainly seemed Swiss when he screamed handball as soon as the ball struck Pearce's arm. He was pointing to the spot before the referee!"

I looked back over at my Dad, to see what he was up to now, hoping the bloke who was threatening to make him into Emmental had managed to calm down. Dad was fidgeting nervously in front of the screen, he had gone so close he was blocking several people's views and was literally pulling clumps out of his own hair, chuntering to himself as Kubilay Turkyilmaz placed the ball on the spot,

"He's going to miss this! I know it! He's going to miss it!"

Dad clasped his hands and looked up to the heavens or at least to the ceiling of "The Buck"!

"Remember our deal, God?" he said to the ceiling, "I'm on your side now, remember?! See me right, God! See me right!"

Turkyilmaz was all set to strike. He stood in the little semi circle on the edge of the box, I don't know what its called, our Richie was the one into football in a big way, I just watched the big games in the pub. The Swiss striker was ready, but so was the English goalkeeper, the moustachioed, David Seaman, who stood on his line with big gloves and a positive focus.

"Come on Seaman!" someone shouted at the TV like a bored housewife who had consented to sex when she was tired and ready to sleep.

"He'll miss this!" I shouted over at Dad.

"He better fucking hadn't!" Dad replied, "HE BETTER FUCKING HADN'T!!"

Turkyilmaz ran up. A long run up for a penalty. This was not one of those Spanish jobs where they just take one step back. Seaman stared intently, all set to spring, cat like, on to the oncoming ball. Dad crossed himself. The run up towards the penalty spot could not have lasted more than three seconds, but it was during those three seconds that the penny dropped or given the circumstances, the Swiss franc dropped! All of a sudden, I understood. Dad was in trouble. Big trouble! Big trouble which would, given the sweat on his forehead and the hair in his fists, only be getting bigger if this penalty did not go in. I am a proud Englishman. I may not have a bulldog tattoo on my right arm, but I cried in 1990 when Gazza was booked. I thought St George's Day should be a Bank Holiday. I waved my Union Jack at the TV on 29th July 1981 when Charles and Di were married. I sang the National Anthem with more gusto than any other Englishman and knew the verses that were never sung, the ones about scattering our enemies and confounding their knavish tricks. I was English and proud of it but in those three seconds, my loyalties were no longer for my country, they were solely for my idiot of a Dad, who had no doubt fucked up royally this time.

"Score," I whispered, just as Kubilay Turkyilmaz struck the ball with his left foot, "please score!"

There was an almighty groan from the four corners of The Buck as Seaman flopped to his right and Kubilay Turkyilmaz, with pinpoint accuracy, stroked the ball into the keeper's left hand corner! With less than ten minutes to go it was England 1 Switzerland 1! Risking a beating from two hundred Englishmen and women, Dad pulled the front of his newly acquired T-shirt over his head and zig zagged around the tables and chairs with his enormous beer belly and two hairy man boobs on display.

"Bloody hell, Ursula Andress has got hairy tits these days!" shouted someone, which was a mightily impressive shout as I didn't think anyone other than me in 'The Buck' would have been aware of the former Bond girl's Swiss heritage.

"Sit down, you tosser!" someone else shouted, "I swear, if Switzerland score another, I'll break your bloody neck!"

"Don't worry!" Dad shouted back from under his T-Shirt, if Switzerland score another, I'll break my own!"

Charlie

Sometimes in life, you have to reach a dead end before you realise you are heading the wrong way. I had been a gambler for over thirty years, I had won a few battles, but lost every war, yet I just kept going. It was total lunacy. Only once my life was on the line, did I understand the seriousness of my addiction and make a deal with God to stop. I had lost a lot of money, but just as importantly, I had sacrificed a lot of time. If I am careful, I still believe I can get Dorothy and I back to the financial status that we would have enjoyed if I had never completed a betting slip, but I will never get my children's childhood back. I pray every day that I live long enough to somehow make it up to them. I have vowed to treasure my grandchildren in a way that I never have with my own offspring.

That evening, back in 1996, following the final whistle in England's one-all draw with Switzerland, a new Charles Billingham was born, as the greedy, sinful, materialistic, liar, died. I must admit, I was more than a little excitable when Kubilay Turkyilmaz equalised for Switzerland and uttered some of the final profanities to leave my lips, but once the final whistle went, God gave me a composure I have managed to maintain to this day. I collected my £6682-50, asked the ladies in there never to mention the win to a living soul, then after brief stops at WH Smith and the pawn shop to reclaim Dot's rings, I headed home. Once home, I hid the plastic bag full of notes and all the mail from that morning behind a drawer in my office, to avoid Dorothy's detection and the rings were returned to the bathroom as if they had never had a journey out.

I did not want to lie to Dorothy, but at the same time, I did not want to have to tell her that we had six grand in cash, but every single penny would be needed to make a small dent in our overall debt and would prevent a local gangster setting his henchmen on to me.

Sure enough, the following morning, as I looked out of the front bedroom window, Kiffer's crew were there, standing menacingly outside Kiffer's limo, in the road at the top of our drive. There was no doubt they would have been anticipating an act of aggression that they would need to carry out, to teach another bad debtor a lesson. As Dorothy snorted her way through her dreams, I slipped into my office, collected my plastic bag full of bank notes and another plastic bag I had prepared for them, then went outside to confront Kiffer and his band of merry men. I pitied them. A new chapter in my life was set to begin, but they were still entrenched in their violent lives. I knew I would not be betting again, God had reached out to me and I was not going to let go of his grasp now, but these men before me would continue to threaten, to intimidate and to kill. Sometimes God can only be found if you open your eyes.

I walked towards the limo, presuming, like twenty four hours earlier, that all four of them would be there. Kevin, "The Smirking Giant" and Bobby aka "Muscles" were standing outside the limo, chatting and attempting to look like James Dean whilst smoking a cigarette. Marcus, the driver, had his window down and his arm draped out, whilst Kiffer was no doubt sat in the back, contemplating what words to grace me with before setting his pack of wolves on to me. I felt empowered as I knew the last thing that they would be expecting, would be for me to repay the debt. The whole six grand. I knew they would be expecting a frightened, desperate, hopeless man who would try anything to save his skin. When "The Smirking Giant" and "Muscles" spotted me heading along my path, one plastic bag in each hand, they quickly dispensed of their cigarettes and stamped them out. Their break was over, they were back at work.

"What the fuck's in those plazzy bags, Charlie?" The Smirking Giant demanded.

"Money and a gift for each of you", I replied calmly and with a smile.

Trust is not a word in a mobsters dictionary.

"Fuck off, Charlie! We weren't born yesterday! Drop the fuckin' bags where they are and step into the limo." Muscles commanded.

I dropped the bags at the end of the drive, it was a breezy day, but they were both too heavy to blow off.

"You'll need to pick them up though lads, there's six grand in one of those bags and a gift for each of you in the other!"

"Yeh right and I suppose Kylie's keeping your bed warm, Charlie!"

"Have a look if you don't believe me!"

I opened the limo door, climbed inside and one of the two henchmen slammed it behind me. As expected, Kiffer was sat there, he was on a mobile phone organising a purchase of shares with his stockbroker, but was just rounding up as I sat down.

"Good morning, Charlie! Are you well?" Kiffer asked jovially as though we were two friends out for a trip together.

"Never better thanks, Simon! And I mean that, never better!" I replied, ensuring he was fully aware that I was no longer intimidated. He had his thugs in his corner, I had God in mine.

"Good," Kiffer managed a half smile, "that either means that you have my money or you have perfected your poker face. For everyone's sake, Charlie, I hope you have my money."

"Poker was never my game, Charlie!"

"So where is it?" Kiffer asked politely. I was already aware he could move easily from good thug to bad thug.

"The money? It's in a plastic bag outside. Kevin and Bobby made me drop it on the path. I suppose in your game, you worry about what people might be carrying, but you've nothing to fear from me. I even brought each of you a present!"

Kiffer's smile became a full one. The whole scene was being played out like something out of a gangster movie where everyone is perfectly amiable, then someone takes out a handkerchief and a gun with a silencer and blows brains out, even wearing God's armour, this was still a concern.

"Did you hear that, Marcus?" Kiffer was saying to his driver, "Charlie here has gone and bought us all presents, isn't that nice?"

"Lovely!" Marcus commented from the front. He turned and gave us a golden toothed smile.

"It is, isn't it?!" Kiffer said. "Like an apple each for the teachers!"

The passenger door opened again. Muscles stood there open mouthed.

"You're not going to fuckin' believe this, boss! He's only gone and brought the fuckin' money!"

Kiffer was emotionless.

"All of it?" he enquired.

"We don't know yet boss, but there's shitloads in there!"

Muscles shut the door again and returned to counting the money.

"It's all there." I told Kiffer.

"I'm sure it is, Charlie, haven't I always said you are a man I can trust?"

"I don't remember you saying it yesterday!"

"Nice guys don't play in our playground, Charlie."

There was a brief silence. A calm one rather than one where I felt increasingly threatened. Kiffer broke it.

"Go on…tell me where you got it from!"

"Simon, it doesn't matter where I've been, all that matters now is where I'm going and where I'm going, I won't be seeing you. I think it's time I started playing in that other playground, the one where the nice guys play."

"People like you and I, Charlie, we don't belong with the nice guys. We live for the rush. Nice is boring."

"Nice guys aren't often found face down in a ditch though, Kiffer or in a brown sack in the Mersey. In this seedy life I've led, I was always going to cross paths with you eventually. Our lives were like a Venn diagram, as long as I kept drinking and gambling, there was always going to be that intersection. From today though, my life changes. Changes for the better. Gambling, drinking and loan sharks have no further part to play in my life. I'm moving on."

"You'll be back, Charlie. You'll miss the buzz. We're born gamblers, Charlie. We're chancers. You'll be back!"

"Maybe not. Maybe one day you'll come looking for me, not to threaten me or do me over, I mean if you want to change direction in life too."

On cue, the limo door opened once more. This time it was "The Smirking Giant" who stuck his enormous frame inside. He was smirking too, from one side of his face to the other.

"Here you are boss! A present from Charlie! He's bought us all one!"

The Smirking Giant threw a Bible into Kiffer's lap.

"A fucking Bible, Charlie! What am I going to do with a fucking Bible?! Smash people over the head with it?!"

"Or even read it," I answered.

"Me and God are on different sides, Charlie! He hates what I do, but the devil, he admires it. When I die, Lucifer will pat me on the back and welcome me home!"

"Just keep it," I said, "you never know, one day you may turn to it, you may feel like you need it!"

"I doubt it Charlie!"

"Well, keep it anyway. Just in case."

Muscles pushed his head through next to his colleagues,

"He's good for the whole six grand, boss!"

"Good."

"Am I free to go?"

"You've always been free to go, Charlie!" Kiffer said, "this is a limo, it isn't the fucking Hotel California!"

"I'll leave you guys to it then!"

Kiffer tossed me my wedding ring and then I made my way towards the open door.

"Look after yourself, Charlie! There's something about you that I fuckin' like! Balls of steel! There's not many of us left with balls of steel!"

I stepped out the limo, the hoodlums climbed back in and our lives moved on in different directions.

I felt dirty after that confrontation, so I undressed myself in the bathroom and ran the shower. I looked at myself in the mirror. I was a fat, ugly middle aged man. I hated everything I had allowed myself to become but as I said, sometimes you have to reach a dead end before you realise you are going the wrong way.

Roddy

Kelly was so excited, she was almost wetting her pants. This annoyed me. I lived a double life around Kelly. To her face, I was, what is technically deemed a good mate, I was upfront about finding her attractive but she did not know the true depth of my feelings. I idolised her. This was why it was so hard watching her pace around excitedly in a field in the middle of rural Lancashire, in nervous anticipation of the arrival of another man. A man that I knew only too well that she wanted to be romatically linked with.

"Kelly, will you stop bloody fidgeting! This bloke has not turned up in previous years, so don't you be getting all soggy knickered about him showing up today!"

"Why shouldn't I be excited, Roddy? I have a good feeling in my bones about today!"

I remember immediately thinking about how I'd have liked to have given Kelly a good feeling in her pubic bone. I understood how Dexy's Midnight Runners felt about Eileen.

"Well, I hope for your sake he turns up!"

"But from a purely selfish perspective, you'd rather he didn't?"

"We've been over this, Kelly, I'm not being selfish, I just think you can do so much better than chase after a man who no longer seems to care. That's all."

Kelly came over to me and gave me a hug. She was very tactile with me, which messed up my mind even more, to be honest, but equally I craved that intimacy. Class clowns can have a deeper side and enjoy a good cuddle!

"Roddy, you are only being protective because you don't know Richie. I spent my teenage years growing up with him and I can't recall a moment that he was anything other than lovely."

There is nothing more soul destroying than a platonic friendship with a Goddess. I looked at my watch.

"Lovely or not, he's late."

"Why, what time is it?"

"Five past twelve. How long, in addition to the four years you've already given him, are you going to wait?"

"Look around you, Roddy! This scenery is stunning and the weather is wonderful, why do we need to rush off? We can stay here as long as we want!"

We both knew this was a lame excuse for staying.

"We can, but that would make you a sad and desperate woman. This is meant to be last chance saloon, Kelly, let's not start giving him extra lives. You said you'd only give him until ten past twelve. Maintain your dignity."

Kelly looked at me like a puppy begging for a biscuit.

"Ten more minutes?"

"Five…hang on, what's that on your nose, Kel?"

I could see instant panic setting in on Kelly's face.

"Roddy, what is it? Is it snot?"

"Snot! Why would it be snot?!"

"I get hayfever! I blew my nose before, did I leave some on my face?"

"Yes, you did!"

"Shit! Where is it? On this side?"

Kelly ran one of her fingers down the left side of her nose.

"No, no, it's on the tip."

Kelly continued to search with her finger.

"Where Roddy? I can't feel it! Bloody typical this! I am about to see the love of my life for the first time in years and the first thing he's going to see is a big bogey dripping off the end of my nose!"

"Do you want me to get it?"

"No I do not!" Kelly stated firmly.

"Why?"

"It's a bogey! My bogey! It would feel wrong you getting it. You'll be offering to wipe me after I've had a wee soon!."

Kelly was like the Queen to me in this sense, in that I did not like to entertain the idea of her having a wee.

"I don't think I will. I'll get that bogey though! Come here!"

"No! Roddy Baker leave my snot alone!"

I tried to grab Kelly and she dodged me playfully. I pursued her long enough to get her in a playful bear hug and she giggled, a little hysterically, then, out of the blue, things turned serious.

"Roddy, stop!"

"It'll be off in a second."

"No, seriously, STOP."

"Why?"

I turned to look over my shoulder. In the distance, I could see someone approaching from the top of the road, down the hill, a couple of hundred metres away. Even from a distance away, you could see he was tall, presumably good looking and attractive.

"Is that him?" I whispered as though he was two metres away.

"I think so." Kelly whispered back, "have I still got snot on my nose?"

"No."

"Did I get it off?"

"No."

"How come?"

"There was no snot. I was just getting bored, so I invented it…are you OK?"

"I'm crapping myself. What am I going to say to him?"

"You can start by saying 'hello'!"

"It's pearls of wisdom like that which convince me I was right to bring you!"

"Don't insult me or you'll have my snot on you in a minute. Shall we stop whispering?"

"OK."

Kelly still whispered her OK, but I resumed normal tones.

"I thought you said he was a big bloke, he only looks about an inch tall!"

I made a gap between two of my fingers, closed one eye and showed Kelly how he could fit between them.

"Very funny! Somehow I think he might grow to over six feet tall in a minute."

"Really?! You best watch out, Kelly, if he keeps growing at that rate, he'll be as big as King Kong by the end of the day. He'll have you in one of his hands and there'll be a load of two seater planes flying round his head on the Sunny Road!"

Sometimes Kelly didn't understand my sarcastic humour.

"What?"

"Have you never seen the 1930's Kong film with him battling planes from on top of the Empire State building?"

"No."

"You haven't lived!"

"Roddy, can you just be serious for a minute and show me some support. He's getting closer, is it too late to run?"

I would have loved it if Kelly had run, but I knew those words would never become an action.

"Deep breaths, Kelly! Deep breaths!"

"Do you think this is one big mistake, Roddy?"

I could have been vindictive, but it wasn't in my nature, especially where Kelly was concerned. Something within me would always prevent me from doing anything to upset that girl. Nothing has changed there!

"No, Kelly it's not a mistake. You've said yourself, it's something you have needed to do. You have felt the need to see Richie again and here he comes!"

"Thank you, Roddy!"

"What for?"

"For being you. For being the best friend a girl could have."

I was beginning to accept that's all we would ever be. Just good friends.

"No problem. It's time for me to make a sharp exit!"

Kelly tried to cling on to my arm.

"No, Roddy, don't go! I need you here!"

"No you don't Kelly, you're a big girl now."

"Well, at least stay and say hello."

"No."

"Why?"

"Kelly, this isn't about me, it's about you and Richie. I need to leave you to sort this out for yourself. Good luck Kelly!"

I headed off in the opposite direction from which Richie was arriving. In truth, from my perspective, it was not about Kelly and Richie at all, it was just about me! I was trying to look and sound magnanimous, but really I just didn't want to meet Richie Billingham. I was happy with the mental image I had created of "Dick", good looking but vain and self-obsessed and I knew it would be harder to character assassinate if I genuinely liked him. Rather than take the chance, I scarpered. That was one reason anyway, the other was more obvious, it would have broken my heart to see Kelly, the girl I worshipped, being romantic and affectionate with anyone other than me.

When I was a child, my Dad, now dearly departed, used to sing a song to me every time I was feeling a little low. It was called "Spread A Little Happiness", Sting did a version of it in the eighties, but my Dad told me that it was originally from the twenties, from a musical his grandfather had seen called Mr.Cinders. My Dad's grandfather used to sing it to his Dad, my grandfather used to sing it to my Dad and when I was a kid, Dad sang it to me. Hopefully, one day, I'll have a child of my own to sing it to, to keep up the "Baker" tradition. Anyway, the reason I'm telling you this, is that on my way back to the hotel, from Kelly's 'Sunny Road', I sang that song to myself to try to cheer myself up. It worked a little, but not a huge amount. Only Kelly could have blown away my bad mood and patched up my broken heart, but way back then, to be frank she just didn't want to. All hope seemed lost. I was pretty sure on that depressing trek back to the hotel, that Kelly Watkinson would never be mine.

Jemma

Melissa was always smart beyond her years. When it was time for her to start school, she was more than ready. Nursery had been good for her, as she had been a very clingy child at first, frightened at the idea of spending time away from her Mummy with strange adults and children who did not understand the concept of sharing, but she adjusted. It was a slow process, but six months into nursery, the tears stopped and Melissa began skipping in, every morning.

By Easter of her second and final year at nursery, things began to change, as Melissa began to find it less challenging.

"I'm bored of playing baby games with the little ones", Melissa announced one day on our journey home, "I'm a big girl now!"

The lack of mental challenges was not the sole reason that Melissa fell out of love with nursery. A second reason was the company she had to keep there. Jamie, her younger brother, had started and even in those formative years, Melissa had deduced that any place Jamie was, was not a cool place to be! Jamie was not smart beyond his years! He was smart enough to know how to cause trouble, but not clever enough to know when to stop! Prior to Jamie starting at nursery, toddler group had been an embarrassment, as he bit his way through more children than any child since Vlad the Impaler's pre-school days, but no amount of telling off or solitary confinement in his room or on the 'naughty step' led to a realisation that his behaviour needed to change. The aforementioned biting was often accompanied by kicking, pushing and even punching, which led to mothers aiming looks at me that should only have been directed at sluts and whores! I was just a mother of a poorly behaved child! It was not my fault…or maybe it was, I was consumed with guilt that it was my genes that were the issue. Melissa was kind, caring and intelligent, like Richie, maybe Jamie was strong minded, stubborn and troublesome, like me or even more scarily like my mother! I bet Vomit Breath had sunk her yellow gnashers into a fair amount of flesh over the years! Maybe Jamie was becoming a mini Vomit Breath. Now that was an uncomfortable thought.

When the children were little, my relationship with Richie was definitely tested more than it had even been before. I would imagine there comes a time in every relationship where it has to be worked at and to be brutally honest, at that point, I closed my eyes to the problem and made no effort at all. All my effort to get through from one day to the next with minimum damage, was concentrated on the children, especially Jamie. Going from no children to having one, is a culture shock when you are so used to doing what you want to do, whenever you want to do it. It is a major shock to lose that spontaneity. All of a sudden, everything needs planning with military precision. You cannot go anywhere without the formula, the bottles, the baby food, the cot, the car seat, the nappies, the changes of clothes, the pram, the toys and the dummy! Then, when you have two children, you don't even have the ability to pass the baby over to your partner for some "me" time, as there is another one that needs looking after too! Once you have two children, you appreciate how easy it was when you just had one! Richie and I would not have coped with a third child, especially not if the third was a similar type to Jamie, so I was always on at him to have a vasectomy. Admittedly, this was like putting a cape under the nostrils of a wounded bull! Richie used to say that asking him to have the snip was like telling a bald man that he needed to have a haircut!

With hindsight, I appreciate things were not great in our marriage at this point, but I am not saying that the blame lay squarely with me. It was our collective fault. Looking back, we failed to communicate properly. Richie was happy to moan about his lack of sexual opportunities and I was equally happy to criticise him for not providing enough of a helping hand around the house, but we were not adult enough about our own situation to subsequently talk through proper solutions. We should have been talking about how Richie could help me more and as a consequence, I could be energised and could then try harder to find time for Richie. It was not just sex that Richie was crying out for, it was physical and emotional affection. We had transformed from a tactile couple to a couple who could find time to hug our children but not each other. "I love you", came to be something we said rather than something we meant.

On 4th July 2000, everything changed. Love, health and money are all alike in that you do not appreciate what you have until you no longer have them. I still do not enjoy thinking back to the events of that day, but they happened and nothing can change that now. All I would say, is that it is only in moments of adversity that you can truly understand how strong or weak a relationship is. We were like a building feeling the full force of an earthquake. 4th July 2000, tested whether our relationship was structurally sound or had already begun to subside, collapsing around us, leaving only memories of what used to be and scattered debris.

Very recently, Dorothy, Richie's Mum, said something to me which turns out was a quote from a seventeenth century Frenchman called Jean de la Bruyere. She simply said, "Out of difficulties grow miracles". Back in 2000, no day had ever been as difficult throughout our relationship as 4th July. That day turned everything on its head. Perhaps saying that subsequently 'miracles grew', would be stretching the truth a little, but it is certainly true to say that everything that happened that day, changed the relationship I had with Richie, and also with my sister, Kelly, forever.

Richie

It all felt very peculiar. Sitting on the "Sunny Road", looking across to the Welsh hills one way and Blackpool Tower the other, with the adult version of my teenage sweetheart sitting by my side on the grass verge. It was all a little difficult to take in. Part of me felt like a time machine had transformed me back to the era of the Birch's party. I felt young again inside but old on the outside. To an extent, it was like being one of those old dears they feature in the national papers who stumble across their first true love, seventy five years after first getting it on and get married in their nursing home wearing a veil, false teeth and incontinence pads! There was definitely still an attraction, there was definitely still a spark, but there was something uncomfortable about it all. I was on the adrenalin rush of the old drug but I knew the following morning I would feel like shit! The following morning at the latest. I was already starting to make myself feel sick with guilt, the fact that I had slid my wedding ring off my finger and into my jeans pocket was no doubt a contributory factor!

We had spent the first five minutes together making mundane conversation as old friends who are trying to rekindle that old energy do.

"You look well!"

"What do you do these days?"

"Where are you living now?" etc.

Inevitably the conversation was going to come around to marital status. Kelly's marital status from four years previous had already been established in her letter and I was assuming not a great deal would have changed otherwise she would not have been here, but mine was still a mystery to her. She would be asking about it, I knew that, I just did not know how I would answer. I knew I wasn't going to be telling the truth, I just wasn't sure whether I would be running with the white lie or the outright lie. I had slid my wedding ring off whilst making that judgement call.

Kelly still looked fantastic. Her face had thinned slightly since her teenage years and the odd line had crept tenderly onto her face, but she remained slender, porcelain skinned and those green eyes continued to mesmerise me like they always had. Emboldened as the familiarity of the conversation and company returned, I asked a straight question, figuring attack was the best form of defence.

"So who was the guy?"

"Which guy?" Kelly asked puzzled.

"The guy who did a runner as I arrived!"

"Oh! That was just Roddy!"

"A boyfriend?"

"No, just a friend. He'd like to be my boyfriend and he's a lovely, lovely person…"

"I sense a but."

"But I want to be loved not worshipped. It would be a long way down from that pedestal."

I shrugged. I wasn't in total agreement. At that point, I felt adoration from Jemma would have resolved many of our problems.

"Kelly, maybe you would enjoy being in a relationship with someone who feels that strongly for you. I used to adore you."

I blushed a little. There was no need.

"Yes but that was mutual, I don't think I could ever be that emotionally passionate about Roddy."

"So you're still single then, Kelly?"

"Yes, I said in my letter that there have been a number of ships that have passed in the night but none that I have taken to port. Well, it's been a dry dock since then!"

"That analogy is not meant to be sexual is it?!!"

"NO! Richie Billingham! You and your dirty mind!"

We were smiling at each other, slightly lovestruck but that was just old feelings, I guess. Nothing more than old feelings.

"So, you have no children, Kelly?"

"No. No marriage, no children, I am destined to die a lonely old spinster! Me and my dry dock are going to have to get used to that."

"Yes, there's nothing down for you, Kelly! I mean look at the state of you! In no time at all you'll be eighty six, sitting on the prom at Blackpool, feeding breadcrumbs to pigeons! How old are you? Twenty six?"

"Twenty seven."

"Past it either way! Your best years are behind you, Kelly!"

"Honestly, sometimes it feels that way!"

"Don't be daft!"

"Well, life seems to have lost its sense of fun a bit recently, that's all."

"Yes, because you spent years travelling around the world. Normality isn't going to seem quite as much fun as that! You are a beautiful, independent woman, enjoy your life. Maybe this Roddy isn't the guy for you, but there will be plenty of others for you to choose from."

I could not believe I was trying to encourage Kelly to go out and find someone. When I had made the decision to meet her, I thought I would be trying to lie and cheat my way back into a relationship with her, but everything was stopping me – personality, guilt, Jemma, the kids, everything.

"I'm sorry, Richie! You just seem to get me to open up, to reveal how I am really feeling. You were always good at that, that was one of the things I liked about you, Richie, you were always so open and honest."

"Go on, ask me who I'm married to?!" I thought to myself.

"So anyway," Kelly continued, "enough of my moaning on. Tell me a bit more about what you've been up to. Are you married?"

Spooky!

"Am I married?"

"It's not a difficult one, Richie! You must remember! I noticed you don't wear a wedding ring, but that doesn't necessarily mean you aren't married, so are you?"

"I'm sorry," I stuttered, "yes, yes, I'm married."

"OH!" was all Kelly said. The fact that I was married seemed to catch Kelly off guard. I think because I was there, on the 'sunny road', she was at least expecting me to say I was separated or divorced, but I was nothing of the sort. I was married. It was one of those uncomfortable moments that seemed to last forever.

"How come you don't wear a ring?" Kelly continued, regaining her composure and continuing as though her letter to me had never been sent and we were just two old friends meeting up.

I decided it was time to come clean. To an extent, anyway.

"I do wear a ring. I just slipped it off before. See, it's here in my pocket!"

"Why did you take it off?"

I sighed.

"Oh, I don't know. When I finally received your letter, which is another long story, involving my Dad and his gambling, when I finally received it, my marriage wasn't in a happy place."

"I'm sorry."

"No, no, it's not your fault. It's my fault really. Anyway, I liked the idea of meeting up with you. I suppose realistically, I didn't expect it to be anything other than an afternoon spent together, but I just thought it would be nice to go back in time for a while. You know, to pretend we were seventeen again, sitting here, just the two of us, like we used to, watching the world go by."

"We can still do that."

"I know, but to an extent it feels like a betrayal now."

"So your wife doesn't know you're here?"

"No…there are a lot of things we don't talk about, Kelly."

"You need to."

"I know."

"Do you have children?"

"Yes, two children. A girl and a boy, Melissa and Jamie."

"Really! That's lovely, Richie, congratulations! How old are they?"

"Melissa's nearly five and Jamie's nearly three."

"Do you have any pictures with you?"

"Yes, in my wallet."

I took my wallet out and carefully withdrew two photographs, one showing Melissa before a friend's party dressed in a fairy outfit, a mass of blond curls and little white teeth, whilst the other was of Jamie, in a pirate outfit with an eyepatch, beard and sword, looking cheeky and mischievous.

Kelly studied the photos for a minute before handing them back.

"They're both gorgeous, Richie! You must be very proud of them. Melissa will have the boys all chasing her when she's older!"

"Thanks! I'm sure I'll be the protective father, throwing teenage boys out the house and administering a chastity belt which can only be unlocked on her wedding day or when she's twenty five!"

"Is she a real Daddy's girl?"

"To be honest, she's more of a Mummy's girl."

"Really…", there was a brief pause, "where did you meet your wife, Richie?"

Sometimes the line of questioning made me feel like Kelly knew very well who my wife was and was just asking me these questions to make me squirm.

"I've known her for a long time, Kelly, she was in my year at school."

"Honestly! Wow! I'll probably know her then! What's her name? Was Jemma friendly with her?"

I'm glad she asked me two questions as it enabled me to focus on the latter.

"No, she wasn't a friend of Jemma's."

That much was true.

"I might still know her. What was her name?"

"Gillian."

A lie.

"Gillian what?"

"Gillian Billingham!"

"I meant before she was married to you, smart arse!"

"Gillian Sorensen"

Kelly scratched her head.

"I don't remember a Gillian Sorensen."

Surprisingly enough!

"Well, she wasn't a friend of Jemma's."

"Do you love her, Richie?"

"I do love her, yes."

"Then how come you are here?"

"Oh, I don't know….like I said before, I just wanted to be seventeen again for an afternoon. I just wanted to disentangle myself from all my commitments temporarily and just feel free."

"Are you happy?"

"Depends on what you mean by happy. I have children I love, I have a wife that I love, I have a job that does not involve getting shot at or digging coal out of the ground, but for some reason, I don't know why, I feel like I'm missing something."

"I know what that something is, Richie."

"Don't say God! My Dad's a born again Christian, he'd tell me it's God!"

Kelly laughed. It was a familiar laugh, stored in my memory banks from those halcyon days of old.

"I wasn't going to say God! I was going to say the chase. You miss the adrenalin rush of the chase. The feeling of new love and all its endless possibilities."

Was this what I was missing? I thought for a while.

"There's probably some truth in that. That's not what I miss the most though. I miss the woman I married. The spontaneous, cuddly, witty, passionate, live life for the moment, woman I married. She died when the children were born. Sometimes…often…I just want her back."

"Richie, it's selfish of you to want that. She's a mother now. It's not all about you any more."

"I know that. There's a tale told amongst men that you should not do anything early in a relationship that you are not prepared to do for its entirety. If you start off buying flowers and chocolates, you have to do it forever otherwise your wife or girlfriend will start accusing you of not loving her like you used to because you used to buy her flowers and chocolates.

This is the same but the other way around. My wife should not have shown me all those vibrant characteristics she had, if she was going to box them up and put them away once she had children. I know I'm sounding like a selfish, stereotypical male but she's a different woman these days. Various events have taught me to value my life, Kelly, to live every day like its your last but my wife does not have that mentality. She's just consistent these days. A steady person. She's changed and I did not want her to."

"Maybe she wanted you to change and you haven't."

"I have changed, but I've never forgotten who I used to be. That's my wife's problem. She's forgotten who she used to be. Anyway, I'm the one moaning on now, I'm sorry I didn't mean to. Let's talk about you again. Going back all those years, why did you really go and why did you take so long to come back? Jemma needed you."

Whether that was a clue or not to the secret I was hiding, I'm not sure, but Kelly stood up.

"You know what, Richie, let's not go there. I think I need to go now."

"Hang on, Kelly! What's the matter? I'm sorry if you don't want to go over all that, we don't have to. After so long not seeing you, I don't want to leave you on a sour note."

"It's not that, Richie. I left because I was scared and I didn't come back because I was a selfish bitch who was protecting number one but that's not why I want to go."

"Then why?"

"We just shouldn't be doing this! When we were kids, we talked about sitting here and talking things over, but you said it yourself, Richie, from your perspective this is a betrayal. I contacted you because every relationship I've ever had has crumbled to dust eventually and I wanted to re-kindle the hearts and flowers of our 'Sunny Road' days, but we are no longer teenagers, Richie. You aren't the boy I used to love. You're more cynical, tougher and your problems are not our problems any more, they are yours and your wife's. They are your families problems. Go home and stop looking at the hurdles as something that's stopping your marriage, just look at them as something to get over. Marriages only fail because people stop trying and start focusing on the negatives. For the sake of your children, Richie, do not stop trying."

Everything Kelly said seemed to make sense. I felt overwhelmed with guilt.

"I'm sorry, Kelly."

"What for?"

"Turning up."

"Don't be."

"No, I am. I turned up for selfish reasons. To make me feel excited again.. To temporarily resurrect those feelings I had during "the chase" as you so succinctly put it. I only thought about my feelings though, Kelly, not about my wife's or my childrens or about yours."

Kelly smiled sympathetically.

"I came here for my own selfish reasons too. I didn't want to move on with my life still wondering about what had happened to you. Wondering what might have been. Wondering if you were my "Black Jack"! I have been given my answers today, Richie. I can move on with my life now in the knowledge that you weren't. You were a lovely boyfriend for me to have as a teenager but that's it."

"I feel the same. My wife is my "Black Jack" and I'm hers, we just need to work things through."

"Richie, I genuinely hope you do. You sound like you want to, which has to be a massive step."

"Thanks Kelly! Where are you staying?"

"West Tower."

"Can I give you a lift back? I parked my car at the top of the road and walked down."

We carried on chatting on the short walk back to the car, climbed in and set off towards West Tower. Setting off is the last thing I remember. For a long while, try as I might, I could not remember a single second of that journey until we came to a stand still. I didn't think I ever would.

The problem I had, was that I could recall the twenty seconds following on from that. I remembered them in the day, I remembered them at night and I remembered them in my dreams. Those memories will be with me until my last breath. Constantly haunting me, constantly making me question why it had to happen. Nothing will change though. Everyone tells me it was not my fault, but how can I be sure? As I say, until we came to a standstill, I could remember nothing.

Richie

There was a buzzing in my head. A buzzing noise like you used to have on television channels at night, when they went off air, high pitched, constant, irritating. I opened my eyes, there was smoke drifting up from my bonnet, but it was also managing to edge its way into the car through the shattered windscreen. My immediate reaction was to put my hand to my nose, as that's where I sensed pain. I was expecting blood but at that stage it was still gathering pace internally on its journey to my nostrils, like water to a waterfall.

It was only then that I saw her, laying on my concertinaed bonnet. It was a young woman. Was it Kelly? I tried to tilt my head around to check the passenger seat, but the intense shooting pain in my neck and shoulders stopped me. A gentle sobbing that punctuated the high pitched shrill re-assured me.

I looked again on the bonnet. The woman was on her side, facing away from us, her lower body, dressed in light blue faded jeans, was pressed against the broken windscreen. Without moving my neck, my eyes journeyed up her body, she wore a white, flowery blouse which was speckled with blood and glass and her head, with a mass of straight, long blonde hair, was tilted backwards at an angle which immediately struck me as uncomfortable. She did not move.

"Kelly, are you OK?"

"I can't get out, Richie, I'm stuck!"

Kelly's voice was quiet and trembling, but I was relieved that she was still next to me and not the mysterious, lifeless, body on the bonnet.

"Please don't let me die, Richie. I'm so scared. Please don't let me die."

Before I passed out, I heard the distant sound of an ambulance siren.

Jemma

I was trying to wash the dishes in the kitchen and I heard the familiar sound of a little girl.

"OW!"

Melissa came wandering into the kitchen, looking like she was about to burst into tears.

"Mummy, Jamie punched me!"

I was getting sick of this. I stormed into the lounge.

"Jamie, have you just punched your sister?"

"Well, she took Thomas and Diesel off me, when I was playing with them."

"Did you, Melissa?"

"He was being noisy with them. I couldn't hear Dora."

Dora The Explorer was blaring out of the TV. My tolerance levels were at zero. I needed a good night's sleep to re-charge but it was only early afternoon.

"Right! I've had enough of this fighting. Why can you not just be nice to each other? Both of you, upstairs! Five minutes in your room!"

Melissa bowed her hand and stomped away.

"It's always his fault," she complained, "Jamie always gets me into trouble!"

"It's both your faults, Melissa. You shouldn't have taken his toys off him!"

"He was annoying me!"

Melissa disappeared upstairs. Jamie had not moved from the carpet in the lounge. He had started to play with Thomas and Diesel again.

"Jamie! Upstairs!"

"NO!"

"Upstairs NOW!"

"NO!"

"Get up!"

"I am playing with my toys!"

"Oh no you are not!"

I made a grab for him and put him into the fireman's lift position. Jamie began kicking and screaming, as per usual!

"Get off me!"

"No, you are naughty, cheeky little boy and you are going in your room!"

I put my foot on the first stair and the doorbell rang.

"Shit!" I muttered to myself. Our front door was glass, whoever was at the door could see straight in, so could see me carrying Jamie. I could not exactly pretend I was out.

"Right you, I said to Jamie. Sit on the naughty stair whilst I see who's at the door. If you speak, you go in your room for ten minutes."

"That's not fair!" Melissa shouted down from her bedroom, "why does Jamie get to go on the naughty stair when I have to go in my room?"

"Just shut up, Melissa!" was my non-parental reply.

I quickly checked my appearance in the hallway mirror, which was a complete state, before turning, seeing two policemen standing outside and opening the door to see what they wanted.

"Good afternoon! Does a Mrs. Jemma Billingham live here?"

"Yes, that's me."

I was trying to think what crime I could actually have committed. Speeding? Noise pollution? Failing to control a minor? Ever since I had been in prison, the presence of a police officer made me feel uncomfortable.

"Mrs. Billingham there has been a road traffic accident on Mill Lane, involving your husband, Richard Billingham and your sister, Kelly Watkinson."

This seemed preposterous.

"Are you sure? I haven't seen my sister for almost ten years. She's abroad as far as I know."

"All documentation on her person seems to indicate that Miss Watkinson was involved."

This seemed like the weirdest crash ever. For me not to have seen Kelly for ten years and then for Richie to have crashed into her. It was bizarre.

"Are they OK?"

"Your husband has concussion and cuts and bruises. Miss Watkinson's condition is more serious, I'm afraid. They have both been taken to the accident and emergency department at Ormskirk hospital."

"Is Kelly alive?"

"Yes. She has life threatening injuries though, Mrs Billingham. We could take you to the hospital, if you would like us to."

"What about my children? I have two under fives."

"Do you have a neighbour or a family member you could leave them with?"

"Yes, I'll ring Richie's Mum and Dad. They'd be here within twenty minues, could you wait that long?"

"That would be fine, Mrs.Billingham."

"Did they crash head on?"

"Yes, the other car appears to have been travelling at speed around a bend and it has caught your husband's car, head on."

"So you think it appears to have been Kelly's fault?"

The policemen looked confused.

"No, Mrs.Billingham, it appears the other car driver may have been at fault although that is just an assumption at this stage, we are not really in a position to apportion blame."

"But you just said Richie's car was hit head on. I'm sorry I don't understand."

"Mummy!" Melissa shouted, "can I come out now? I need a poo!"

"Yes, Melissa. Out you come."

The second policeman tried to clarify matters.

"Mrs. Billingham, your husband and sister appear to have been turning off Mill Lane into West Tower, they were hit head on by another vehicle. Tragically, a young lady in the other car was pronounced dead at the scene. The driver of the other car and your sister, both have life threatening injuries."

"So my husband and my sister were travelling in the same car?"

"Yes, Mrs. Billingham. Your husband was driving, your sister was in the front passenger seat."

"Please come in. I need to phone Richie's parents."

Kelly

I needed to get away from there. Married. Not just married, married with two kids. I looked blankly at the photos Richie passed me of his children and stared right through them whilst thinking, "What A Fool I Am!!" I had been turning men down over the last four years believing I had already found "The One", which was about the most stupid thing I could have possibly done given I had not been in touch with Richie for almost ten years. Why did I fool myself into thinking he would be waiting for me? It was all madness. First degree lunacy. During my celibacy, Richie's wife had been giving birth to her second child. Roddy had been right all along. He had tried to talk me out of making a fool of myself, but I just wouldn't listen. I had behaved like a silly little girl wanting Prince Charming to come back with my glass slipper. It was cringeful! Was it not about time I grew up? I passed Richie his photos back telling him his daughter was gorgeous, she might have been, then again she might have been a three headed bullfrog and I'd have said the same thing. I hadn't really looked.

To my credit, I snapped out of the reality induced haze. I wanted out of there but there was a little bit of me that was intrigued to hear about Richie's family life. It's lucky there was, as Richie was only too happy to pour his heart out about his troubled marriage! I listened intently and passed on what I thought was sensible advice about getting his problems sorted and working hard to save his marriage. Richie was a good man, a little bit battered and bruised around the edges emotionally, but a good man and he deserved some happiness in his life. Why I thought I would be delivering that after so many years away, heaven only knows.

As we sat there chatting away about his relationship issues, it dawned on me that I no longer had any romantic feelings for him. I was not jealous of his wife's situation. I did not hear him talking and wish it was me who had children with him. I think the second he said he was married, any feelings I had or misplaced ideas of romance had just evaporated. Richie did not seem to want to be there either. I think for him the idea of meeting up was exciting but the reality of it was less so and all he felt was guilt and as he described it "a sense of betrayal". We had belonged together as teenagers but not now.

Once Richie stopped talking about his wife and brought the conversation around to questioning me about my disappearing act after Mum's death, I decided it was time to go. Perhaps I owed him an explanation, but I felt we had reached a point where we were not putting our past behind us, so there seemed little point in raking some of it back up. I had been selfish, scared and had totally abandoned my sister, I knew that, Richie knew that and I am sure Jemma knew that too, we could talk about it until the cows came home, but the facts would remain the same. I just needed to go. Consign Richie to my history as a fond memory.

I still had one further mistake left in me. I should have just declined Richie's offer of a lift back to West Tower, but for some reason unbeknown to my logical side, my emotional side felt an urge to get back to the hotel as quickly as I could, to tell Roddy how he had been right all along and it had been a terrible idea. I also wanted to know about Richie's cancer and why he had felt the need to hide this from me. It was about a mile to West Tower which would take me fifteen minutes on foot, but only three in the car, so I plummeted for the latter.

During that short journey we chatted pleasantly like the old friends we were. Richie was asking when I would be heading back down to London and I was asking after his Mum and Dad. As the road neared West Tower, it narrowed into a single lane and I remember Richie steadily breaking and indicating right.

It came out of nowhere. I know nothing about cars so can't describe it very well, I just remember hearing its engine a split second before seeing it. It was a dark red car. Sporty looking. If I close my eyes, I can still picture them like a photograph, two young looking teenage boys in the front, two teenage girls in the back. One of the girls had really long, fair hair. Loads of it. My brain can still piece it all together, split second by split second, flicking from one frame to the next like a cartoon. Richie's car slowing, then indicating, a loud engine noise, the other car and the teenagers inside, brakes screeching, the impact sound of metal on metal, the sound of shattered glass, something flying towards me – a large object, me instinctively ducking, a teenage girl's face hitting the windscreen in front of me and for a second I swear our eyes met before her twisted body sagged, more glass shattering, silence and stillness, a constant, high pitched sound in my ears, Richie asking if I was OK, realising I was trapped, reverting to type and being consumed by fear and thoughts only for myself, begging not to die, hearing an ambulance siren, trying to speak to Richie again and realising he was not responding, going into shock. By shock, I do not mean shock like some sort of emotional surprise, I mean going into circulatory shock or as I have heard the doctors describe it since, hypovolaemic shock. As I slipped out of consciousness I remember thinking this was it. The End. My thoughts returned to Roddy. If my body was found here, next to Richie's, what would he think? He would think Richie and I were together. Roddy would get it all wrong. He would never know he was right, Richie now meant nothing and as he had kept saying, we should never have come.

Richie

"Daddy looks like a stormtrooper!" Melissa said, unusually for a five year old girl, she was into Star Wars and to her, the brace on my neck looked highly amusing. Melissa, Jamie, my Mum, Dad and Jemma were gathered around my hospital bed as I sat upright, propped up by several pillows. My injuries from the crash had been relatively minor, whiplash, a broken nose and seven stiches to a head wound. The only reason I was being kept in hospital overnight was due to the concussion I had suffered earlier.

"Are you sick, Daddy?" Jamie asked.

"No, Jamie, I'm fine. Daddy's just been in a car that bumped into another car, so he's hurt himself, but I'll be coming home tomorrow."

The way parents alternate between the first and third person when talking about themselves to their children, does not really help children to master the English language, but we all do it!

"Will you be a stormtrooper tomorrow?" Melissa queried.

"I think I'll be a stormtrooper for a couple of weeks, Melissa."

"And will they give you the helmet too?"

"I don't think so, Melissa!"

"Do you want me to ask for you?" Melissa suggested. She was used to getting her own way by using her charm and beauty and had rarely seen me get my own way, so probably concluded she would be more likely to achieve the goal on this task than I would.

"That's very kind of you, Melissa, but no, I do not want you to ask!"

"We get to stay at Gwanny Dot and Gwandads!" Jamie announced, as though my accident had been a worthwhile sacrifice for their adventure. A trip to a hospital and sweets and biscuits at Granny Dot and Grandad's was pretty exciting stuff for a three year old.

"I know, lucky you! I wish I was going to Granny and Grandad's instead of having to stay the night in hospital!"

"But you may see people die!" Jamie said excitedly.

Given neither my Mum or Dad were getting any younger, I was going to respond with a tongue in cheek, 'so might you!' but thought better of using my black humour in the circumstances.

"Jamie!" Jemma scolded, "that's not a nice thing to say."

"I think you've had your fair share of luck today, Richard," Mum said, "more than your fair share!"

Mum was a glass is half full type of person. You could argue I had had my fair share of bad luck, by all accounts I was not the one driving like a lunatic. I just crossed paths with him.

"Yes, God has certainly been looking out for you today, son" Dad added.

This statement from my father should not have set me off, but I had been through a lot that day and was becoming tetchy and irritable. This was partially down to the ordeal anyway, but also because I had yet to have the "Kelly" conversation with Jemma which I knew was imminent. It was not a conversation I was looking forward to.

"Don't say that, Dad!" I snapped.

"Don't say what, Richie?"

"Don't praise your God for saving my life. What did he do, decide to cause a crash but then have the grace not to kill me off, just kill some of the other poor sods like that young girl on my bonnet? Mum's right I was lucky, this was down to luck not divine intervention."

"You don't know that, Richie."

"Dad, will you just give it a rest! Just for once can you stop preaching?! You don't know enough to preach! I know today was down to luck and anyway, why would your God save me but let millions of young Christians die all over the world?"

"Millions of young Christians?"

"In Africa, in third world countries across the globe, even in Britain young Christians die in car crashes or children of Christian families die of tragic illnesses, why would your God allow someone who worships him to die young, but allow a heathen like me to live?"

"He isn't just my God, Richie, but to answer your question, I do not know why God does what he does. I don't really see that it is my place to question him."

"Yes, it is. You only find the answers by asking questions. But do you know why you don't think its your place to question him, Dad?"

My father had kept cool throughout this conversation, to my shame I had overheated.

"Richard, stop arguing with your father!" Mum said trying to douse my flames.

"I'll tell you why it is, Dad! Because you're not a bloody Christian!" I said in a virtual shout.

"Sssshhh! Richard! Mind your language in front of your children." Mum chided.

"I am a Christian." Dad insisted.

"No, you are not. You are just a flawed individual with a gambling addiction who did not have the strength of character to give up on his own, so you've invented a pretend friend as your emotional crutch."

"You are so wrong, Richie," Dad said. I felt like I had hit a nerve. I began to feel a little guilty for launching this tirade.

"I'm not saying there isn't a God, Dad, I'm just saying don't use him as the reason for everything good that happens, but then relinquish him from responsibility when things go wrong. If you're saying God saved me today, you are also saying he killed that young girl. God's to give and God's to take away."

"I don't think this an opportune time to have this conversation, Richie."

"Why not? I'm not having a go at you, I'm just telling you how I see it. As far as I'm concerned you deserve a lot of praise for giving up the gambling. It was you who gave it up, Dad, God did not do it for you."

"God helped me through it."

"How?"

"Will you two boys give it a rest? Richard, leave your father alone. If he believes, let him believe!" Mum was getting all red in the face.

"No, come on Dad, explain it to me. How did God help you stop gambling?"

"God gave me the strength. I could not have done it on my own. I've tried so many times and failed, Richie."

"You never had any faith in yourself, Dad, but by putting your faith in your fictitious God, you gave yourself the confidence to do it."

"Why are you being like this, Richie? I am a better man now than I have ever been and that fact is undeniable. I don't really care what you think has brought about this transformation, because I know God has been there for me when I have needed him most."

"No he has not!"

It took a five year old child to get me to back off.

"Stop arguing Daddy!" Melissa reprimanded me, "stop being mean to Grandad!"

"I wasn't being mean to Grandad, honey, we just have different opinions on something."

"Do you still love Grandad?"

"Of course I do!"

"Well, if you love someone, you do not do mean things to them, that's what you always say to Jamie!"

"You're right, Melissa, but I did not do a mean thing to Grandad!"

"Yes you did! You spoke to him in an angry voice!"

"Don't worry love," said my father to my daughter, "your Daddy has just had a horrible day, he hasn't made Grandad sad. Grandad understands."

"Right!" said my Mum clapping her hands, "I think it's about time me and your Grandad took you two back to ours! There's some ice cream and chocolate at ours with your name on!"

"Chocolate and ice cream with our names on! Brilliant!" said Melissa, "I've never seen chocolate or ice cream with my name on!"

"Well you will at our house!" Mum said smiling, "Come on kids! Give your Mummy and Daddy a kiss goodbye! Be gentle with your Daddy though, Jamie!"

The children came over and tenderly kissed me on the cheek, Jamie following Melissa's lead, then both gave Jemma big hugs and kisses. My father then came over and kissed the top of my head before my Mum very gently kissed the tip of my nose as if she was kissing it better, like when I was a child.

Mum and Dad both hugged and kissed Jemma warmly. The bond between the three of them had grown so close an outside observer would have thought Jemma was their daughter rather than me being their son.

Mum sometimes rubbed Jemma up the wrong way with her bluntness, but Jemma adored her.

"Thank you so much for everything today," Jemma said to my Mum, "I don't know whether I would have coped without you!"

"Come on Gwanny!" said Jamie, pulling on the back of my Mum's blouse, "we need to go and have the chocolate with Jamie on!"

"How are you going to manage that?" Jemma whispered to Mum.

"Don't worry, we have raspberry sauce, my grandchildren will be having ice cream with their names on! Jemma, I'll ring you tomorrow to see if they'll let him out."

"Mum, I will be coming out tomorrow whether they like it or not!"

"You just take it easy, Richard. If the Doctor's tell you that you need to rest, then you need to rest. What's another day when you have the whole of your life ahead of you?"

With that, Mum and Dad led the children out the ward and Jemma returned to sitting on a chair at the side of my bed. I knew what was coming next. The interrogation. It was time to get everything out in the open and once we took everything to pieces, I just hoped we could put it all back together again.

Roddy

It was like a scene from a soap opera. Kelly was in intensive care, attached to various wires, drips and breathing apparatus. The Doctors had said she had swelling on her brain (they called it an "Edema") and the next forty eight hours would be critical. In soap operas, the scenes normally played out with a five minute awakening, a declaration of love, a relapse, a flatline on the cardiograph and then a crash team arriving to work tirelessly, but ultimately unsuccessfully, on the body. I kept visualing those scenes with Kelly as the leading lady and then hated myself for even imagining Kelly dead.

Death had already claimed two victims from this tragedy. The driver of the other car, an eighteen year old boy called David and a seventeen year old female passenger called Vanessa had already died. Vanessa died at the scene, David several hours later at Ormskirk hospital. Grieving family and friends were littered around the hospital but I tried to keep my distance in case sorrow was infectious and their mourning subsequently became mine. Death scares me. I see it as a journey to permanent oblivion. I fear my own death, but then, as now, I feared Kelly's death more.

As the minutes and hours passed in intensive care, I would not leave Kelly's side. There were no family memebers rushing in to visit her. Since we had begun working together, I was Kelly's family and I was wary of abandoning her, even for a few moments, for a toilet break, in case those moments turned out to be her last. Kelly needed someone there who loved her, just to be there for her, just to hold her hand.

When I was little, I used to play with my toys silently. I didn't talk to them or make them say things to each other. There was just silence. My parents thought this was odd and I remember one day, when I must have been about seven, my Mum asked me why I did not speak to my toys as I played with them.

"Because they can't hear me!" I replied.

For the first twenty four hours in that hospital, I did not say a word to Kelly because I felt she could not hear me. As I say, I held her hand as I somehow felt she would be able to sense that it was me, but other than speaking to the hospital staff, I said nothing. I listened though. I listened to Kelly's breathing and I also listened intently, to what the Doctor's and nurses said to each other and to me about Kelly's condition. It is not an environment of putting arms arounds shoulders and re-assuring you that everything is going to be alright. The consultants are so blunt that you think some of them stop understanding that they are dealing with real people. I even asked one of the nurses if all the staff learn to stop caring. They don't.

"The day I stop caring will be the day I stop coming in," was her response.

In those first twenty four hours, the impression was that I needed to hope rather than to expect Kelly to recover. Surgery was mentioned. Two consultants discussed doing a "decompressive craniectomy" which sounded like something you would perform on a scubadiving stork with the bends, not on a person.

One consultant, after clarifying that I was Kelly's boyfriend, an honour I had bestowed upon myself to receive more information, had explained things in layman's terms. She explained that Kelly's brain was injured from the impact from the other car and had swollen. The Doctor's concern was that the pressure in Kelly's brain could mount, pushing the soft brain tissue against her hard skull, stopping her blood from circulating properly and potentially causing permanent damage. What I read into this, was that Kelly's life was in danger and even if she did survive, there was no guarantee that the old Kelly would be back. The hospital staff brought me a blanket that night and allowed me to sleep in a chair by Kelly's bed. I only slept in snatches though, as I kept replaying those soap opera scenes then realised I was within a dream and shook myself out of it.

The following morning I changed tactics. My logic was probably completely wrong medically, but in the same way I had persuaded myself as a kid that if I watched the whole of the "Country Life" butter advert my whole family would die, I persuaded myself that if I did not speak to Kelly her brain would continue to swell and her death would be all my fault.

I started talking and would not stop. Constantly re-assuring her that only good times lay ahead. I wanted to persuade her brain to stop seeking the self-destruct button and look forward to the good times that were around the corner.

"Kelly Watkinson! Open your eyes and look at the state of me! I look like someone has been rubbing a balloon against my head! This ain't the comfiest place you've ever brought me to! But look at you! If you get through this, Kelly Watkinson. No…let me say that again, WHEN you get through this Kelly Watkinson, I reckon the NHS are going to get you to model their gear, because somehow you even manage to look good on a bloody ventilator! You're somethin' special, Kelly, you really are!

I heard your crash from my bedroom in the hotel. I know you're going to call me a big soft girl when you're better, but I'd had a bit of a cry. Don't tell no-one. I ain't known for being soppy. The boys in the pub will take the piss! I just hated leaving you with Dick. I can't describe it, Kelly, it just felt wrong on every possible level. I just went back to my room and started blubbing. Me, crying over you, even before all of this?!! It's ridiculous, isn't it? We're only supposed to be friends! I just couldn't help it though, Kelly. I know you don't have the same feelings for me that I have for you, but right now I would gladly be 'just good friends' for the rest of our lives, as long as you get yourself better. I would even be happy seeing you with someone else, as long as you were happy, that would make me happy. I ain't going to be jealous, I'll just be happy for whoever it is. If you're happy Kelly, I'm happy.

It won't be Dick your marrying though, will it? He's already married. You probably know that now, don't you? He's in here, in this hospital. He's got a gorgeous wife as well, would run you a close second, Kelly! Bloody cute kids too. They should be modelling clothes in catalogues they are that cute. I saw them all coming in last night to see him, that time I nipped out for a jimmy riddle. The only time I nipped out for a jimmy riddle! I was bursting, Kelly! He ain't going to die, old Dick! He's pretty OK, just let you take the hit, he did. Knobhead! I hope he told you he was married. I mean, what was he even doing meeting you in the first place? He's married! Why should he have two women, when some of us can't even get one?! It ain't right that, is it?

I reckon I'll always blame him for this. If he hadn't shown up, those two kids would still be alive and you wouldn't be in here, all wired up, teetering on the brink. Do you know what I wish? You'd really tell me off for this one, Kelly! I wish it was Dick that had died in that accident instead of those kids. OK, I know that's not a nice thing to say, especially because he has a family and those gorgeous kids don't deserve to grow up without their Dad, but I hate him, hate him for what he has done to you. I even wish he'd died when he had cancer. None of this would have happened then. His pretty wife would have married someone else. Someone else who didn't go off for secret rendezvous behind her back.

No, no, forget I said that. I don't really mean any of that. How can I wish someone dead who I don't even know? He might be the kindest man on the planet for all I know and his wife might be a right crazy bitch! Like Mr Rochester! See, I've been reading! I thought I'd read Jane Eyre to impress you. I didn't tell you that, did I? I was just waiting for an opportunity to bring it into our conversations. I didn't like it though. A book about ugly and mad people, what's that all about?! I ain't got nothing against Richie boy. Not really. It's just that I love you so much, Kelly, it sometimes brings out the deep rooted caveman in me!

"She, my woman, you leave her alone!!"

If only you were my woman, Kelly. If only, eh?! There's a lot of if only's at the moment. If only I'd trusted my instincts when Richie showed up. If only I'd stayed with the pair of you. If only you hadn't got a lift in his bloody car. If only that other car hadn't been coming the other way. Too late for if only's now. It's all happened. If only I'd just done one thing differently though, I probably wouldn't be here now, at your side in hospital, talking complete crap!

I reckon one day we might laugh about all this Kelly. Maybe one day when we are sat next to each other, in an old people's home, holding hands, colostomy bags touching, seventy years wed, we might have a right old giggle about this then. We might laugh until our false teeth fall out. Silly young fools doing stupid things that brought us together. In seventy years we might laugh, but not right now. I just feel like crying again now, Kelly! Sobbing my little heart out! Please don't get worse. I couldn't bear it if you got worse. I really couldn't."

I took a hanky out to wipe my nose. I had tears and snot everywhere. I took a moment to re-compose.

"I heard a nurse say your sister's coming in, in a bit. That's a turn up, isn't it? Can't avoid her now, like you have been doing, can you? Don't worry though, I'll make sure she's nice to you. Maybe all this will bring the pair of you back together. Close again, like you said you were when you were kids. Maybe there'll be a happy ending. That's what we all need right now, isn't it Kelly? A happy ending. A happy ending where you become good friends with your sister again and maybe even a happy ending where you learn to fall in love with me. If you did, Kelly, I would squeeze every last drop of enjoyment out of every single second of your life.

Do you know what? I think you know how much I love you, Kelly and the reason I think you keep me at bay is because it scares you. You don't think you can live up to the reputation. I tell you what though, you're going to get better and I am going to earn your love. I am going to give you the confidence in yourself to love me, knowing you deserve my love. I'm telling you now, everything is going to be perfect. A proper happy ending for all concerned. You just need to get rid of that fluid now! Come on Kelly! How hard can it be to get rid of fluid? I used to get rid of a bit of fluid every night when I was a teenager and from where I did all my thinking too! Just get better, Kelly! Your happy ending is all wrapped up and waiting. Just come and get it whenever you want.

Jemma

Fuming was probably too mild a word. Absolutely livid probably did not go far enough. Once Dorothy and Charlie had disappeared with Melissa and Jamie, it was time to discover what the hell had been going on. I vowed to maintain my composure.

"So…have you had a nice day, Richie?" I asked with a soupcon of sarcasm.

Richie gave me his look. The look that swore and began and ended with the sixth letter of the alphabet.

"I've had better."

"Funnily enough, I have too. Kelly's in intensive care, did you know that?"

"No," Richie breathed out heavily, his day had just become even worse.

"That surprises me or maybe it doesn't. I'm really not sure if anything surprises me any more. Can I just ask, how was my sister before she was hit head-on, whilst travelling in my seat in our car?"

"She was OK. A little fed up, but OK."

"Fed up?"

"Because life was not turning out to be as exciting as she'd hoped."

My next statement was spontaneous and I regretted saying it, but I have always been the outspoken one.

"Well, she'll be delighted now then, won't she? Nothing like a fatal car crash to liven up a boring existence!"

"Jemma, I wouldn't have thought Kelly would be seeing it quite like that."

I had already broken my vow.

"Come on Richie! Look at the evidence! Brought up by her sister because her alcoholic mother was neglectful and abusive. Killing her mother at sixteen, then running off around the world, for God knows how long, whilst her sister is wrongly accused of the murder and is then found guilty and serves her prison sentence. Then, several years later, returns for secret meetings with the very same sister's husband and during one of the meetings, is involved in a fatal car crash that now threatens her life….not exactly dull, is it?!"

"I suppose not."

Time to ask the sixty four thousand dollar question.

"Have you been having an affair with my sister, Richie?"

As the words left my lips they did not seem real. This was a question for an episode of a Jerry Springer show, it should not be a question I should be asking my husband. I was half expecting all my fears and dreads to be coming true, but Richie did not become tearful and apologetic, begging for a second chance, he just looked me in the eye and replied,

"No! It wasn't like that Jemma."

I was relieved but still unconvinced.

"Then what was it like?"

"It was a one-off meeting. A meeting that changed how I viewed my marriage."

From my perspective, the first sentence was a good one, the second one just antagonised me. I did not want to hear that a secret meeting with my long since disappeared sister had resulted in a shift in how Richie viewed our marriage. I wasn't even sure if he meant this as a positive or a negative. I did not intend my response to be rhetorical, it just came out that way as I spoke.

"For better for worse. For richer, for poorer. In sickness and in health."

"Jemma, do you want me to tell you everything, absolutely everything, warts an' all?"

I could feel myself welling up. I am a tough cookie on the outside, I have to be, I have had so many years practice at it. I am conditioned to having a strong outer shell, but it can be penetrated. At that moment, I did not feel like being tough, but I knew for my childrens sake more than anything else, I needed to be. Richie did not see even a hint of a tear. Adrenalin kicked in.

"Richie, as things stand, I am looking for signs of life in our marriage and I can barely feel a pulse. I trusted you. I thought you were an honourable man. A man worthy of bringing up my children, in a manner that I was not brought up myself. You are no longer the man that I thought you were. I think you had better tell me everything, warts an' all and let's see where that takes us. Maybe I'll think you're less of a prick once you've finished. I wouldn't count on it though!"

"I wanted to feel loved, Jemma."

I was always unimpressed when Richie went into self-pitying mode! Life with kids is busy and I did not have time to dedicate to massaging his frail ego nor did I have the inclination to moisten up as often as an East European whore on a Friday night in the Reeperbahn.

"Richie! Don't make this about my failings! If you're just going to go over the same old boring ground about needing the physical side of a relationship to feel loved, then to be frank, I'd save your breath. My life is about caring for my family and especially my children, it is not about pampering you and screwing you every time the mood takes you. We've been over and over this and it bores me, Richie."

"Jemma! Shut up!"

This caught me off guard.

"I beg your pardon!"

"Just shut up! We have spent the last couple of years bickering and sparring, but not really talking and definitely not listening. We both just keep thinking about our next line to come back with. For once, let me just speak. If you can just listen and then I'll completely shut up and you can then say whatever you want back. OK?"

"OK."

"So you'll let me speak without butting in, Jemma?"

"Yes, go on, talk away. I'm all ears."

"Right, when we were at school, I've told you before, I used to hate you. I thought you were an outspoken, pompous, arrogant bitch, who liked nothing better than her own reflection. I thought you were gorgeous on the outside but ugly within."

"Charming!"

"Jemma, stop butting in!"

"Carry on then!"

"OK. I didn't like you at all, but it wasn't based on factual knowledge, it was based on assumptions. As you well know, I started "going out" with your sister, Kelly and initially, as I got to know you better, my opinion didn't really change. You remained outspoken but I didn't really care much whether you were nice or not, as I only had eyes for your sister.

My opinion of you, only really started to change once I found out I had cancer. I obviously didn't have any intention of crying on your shoulder, but that's exactly what I did when I literally bumped into you in Ormskirk. You were a whole host of things that I did not expect you to be, warm, caring, comforting, emotional, passionate, tactile and understanding. My opinion of you tilted into positive territory for the first ever time, but then it was only after Kelly ran off and you were arrested that I began to understand you. I saw that you would go to the ends of the earth and back to support the only person you really loved. In Kelly's absence, I got to know you better and the more I knew you, the more impressed I became. Against my better judgement, I found myself falling in love with you. The physical side of our relationship came later, but that was not what made me love you, the lovemaking was just a reflection of how intense we had come to feel about each other.

The intensity of what I felt for you did not waiver, it just grew and grew relentlessly. We got married. We had kids. Both of us love Melissa and Jamie with all our hearts, that fact is not debatable, but as time passed, it began to feel that there was not enough love to go around. It wasn't just the sex that dwindled away, it was that sense of togetherness. We would do everything for the kids and nothing for each other. We just got by and one thing I felt having cancer had taught me was not to just get by, to live each healthy day as if it is a bonus. Jemma, I've stopped doing that. I understand our parameters are more constrained now because of the age of our children, but we are not making the most of every opportunity. We definitely aren't.

Last week, out of the blue, when I was going through some of my old things at Mum and Dad's house, I came across some bills and letters of Dad's from four years ago. It turns out, Dad had some financial problems and had hidden these bills away, but had also unknowingly hidden a letter from Kelly addressed to me. I opened it and pretty much told me that she was back living in London, working in a book store but through all her years of travelling around, Kelly had never found her true love. She started to ask herself whether this was because she was destined to be with me. Kelly suggested we should meet up, over on Clieves Hill, at midday on the 4th July, at the place we used to call our 'Sunny Road'.

So, despite being four years late and despite being married, I felt inquisitive. I thought maybe she had a point. I played around with the thought that maybe I wasn't feeling as happy as I should be feeling with a partner I had chosen to spend the rest of my life with. I wanted to feel more loved, more inspired, less inadequate and I thought maybe the reason I was not feeling as happy as I wanted to feel, was because I was married to the wrong sister. I decided I would go to the 'Sunny Road' at midday on the 4th July just to see if Kelly was there and despite being four years late, to my astonishment, she was there waiting for me."

This was painful listening for me. Part of me wanted to put my suffering to an end by jumping in, but I said I would listen and I intended to do just that. At that stage, I could still see no future for our marriage, but I needed to hear everything, so I managed to hold my tongue and let Richie continue.

"The thing is Jemma, when I saw Kelly standing there, my heart did not skip a beat, I did not feel like this was my date with destiny, I just felt like a complete fool. Kelly isn't my one true love, the person I want to be buried next to, or at least have my tombstone next to, to signify who I shared my life with. You are Jemma. Meeting Kelly just underlined that fact and I just chatted with her, often about us, more than anything to get a neutral perspective. It was a daft thing to do and perhaps my original intentions were not as honourable as they should have been, but all I wanted to do whilst I was there and all I have ever wanted to do really, is to get things right with you again."

"Does Kelly know who you are married to?"

"No, she knows I'm married but not who to."

"Why did you not tell her?"

"As I said, I wanted a neutral perspective on our relationship and if I'd have mentioned that I was married to you, I wasn't sure how she would react and what sort of perspective she would have given me."

I thought Richie was trying to cover his tracks. As far as I was concerned, he did not tell her because he thought there would be no opportunity of getting into her knickers if he let that one slip out.

"Did you kiss her?"

"No, I did not kiss her and before you ask, she did not kiss me either. I think both of us had briefly played with the idea that meeting up could be the pot of gold at the end of the rainbow, but once we arrived, all we discovered was wet grass."

"Am I allowed to speak now?"

"Say everything you need to say."

"You said a lot of the right things then, Richie, but I still feel pissed off. Sometimes you annoy me, Richie, in fact sometimes you drive me bloody potty, but not once have I ever thought anyone else was my pot of gold at the end of the rainbow, except you. Once you read Kelly's letter, you should have popped it in the bin and come back to reality where you have three people who you mean everything to. I cannot believe you were prepared to jeopardise the future happiness of your children on the basis that some teenage romance might lead to a few more shags than you are getting now. OK, the children aren't always perfect, especially Jamie, but their love for you is totally unconditional, as is mine, I don't go out looking for a handsome prince because you've left socks on the landing, boxer shorts on the bedroom floor and used tea bags in the sink. I believe you when you say that nothing happened, but the fact that you even bothered to turn up in the first place to see Kelly, still means that you are not the man I thought you were."

Arguments are ultimately futile if all parties to the argument are not going to see things any differently once the argument ends. If you put a Jew, a Muslim, a Christian and an atheist, in a room together, they will enter the room and leave the room with the same deep rooted views they had already formed. This argument was similar in a way, as I felt Richie had crossed the line by so much that he could barely see the line in the distance behind him. Richie, however, felt he had been wrong to consider crossing the line, but had ultimately sat on it for a while before jumping off it in the right direction. We could debate the point for the rest of our lives and our opinions would not change so ultimately you could say the debate was futile. Sometimes though it just feels good to vent your spleen.

"Jemma, why do you think that people have affairs?"

"As someone who has not even considered having an affair, that is a hard question for me to answer. How about you tell me, Richie?"

"No, humour me. You tell me."

"Opportunity, desire, an escape from the daily grind…there's a whole host of reasons."

"I agree. Ultimately though, it is about wanting more than they have already got. Wanting someone better looking or more exciting or more intelligent….someone who makes them feel better about themselves. No-one has made me feel better about myself than you, Jemma. I want something and someone I've already got. I just think we need to recharge our batteries, not swap them for new ones. This has never been more obvious than today"

"Richie, I can't help feeling how I feel about this. You keep saying that meeting Kelly was a good thing, it wasn't!"

"Look Jemma, I am not perfect, I am not saying I am, but don't be trying to send me on a guilt trip over meeting up with Kelly because I'm too busy having a guilt trip about being in a car crash where two people are dead and from what you've said, one more, your sister, could still die.

I am not saying meeting up with Kelly was a good thing, how can it be when it played its part in that crash and those deaths, but if you take the subsequent crash out the equation, when I met with Kelly, I felt good because all it showed me was how I feel about you.

If I'd have spent the last six months having secret trysts with Kelly and had been tasting the juices of her desire, then I'd deserve all the shit you cared to throw at me, but being totally frank, I do not have an ounce of guilt about this. Not one! Now, if you want to make a big deal about me meeting for a chat with your sister, be my guest, but let's get one thing straight here, I love you more than anyone else ever has or ever will and any frustrations I have are because the woman I adore does not want to go anywhere near me."

I sighed again.

"Richie, you're doing it again, trying to push the blame for your actions on to me."

"No, I'm just saying Jemma, that in my simple mind there's a couple of issues but it doesn't seem to be the most difficult riddle to solve. It just seems that there's a river that's run between us, so I'm left on one river bank and you are on the other, we just need to build a bridge that meets in the middle. Now if you think you're doing everything you can already to make this marriage work then fair enough, but I think we could both be doing more."

"No, I agree with you. It's just…."

"Just what, Jemma?"

"It's just the whole Kelly thing. If she dies, her last moments were spent with you and if she doesn't there's this messy love triangle thing that needs sorting out."

"No, there isn't! I don't love Kelly, I just love you."

"I know that, but I love you and Kelly, Kelly loves you and me and she doesn't know we're married. I just hope it's a problem that all three of us get to sort out."

Richie took hold of my hand in his.

"Jemma, Kelly does not love me. If you'd have seen her today, you would understand that."

"Richie, I might not have seen her for ten years, but I know her well enough to know that if I tell Kelly that you and I are married, to Kelly that will be the greatest act of betrayal I could have ever committed."

"Given everything that's happened, she has no right to say that."

"She'll say it though. God willing, she'll say it."

Roddy

Kelly's accident was the biggest ordeal I had ever had to face in my life and for the first twenty four hours after the crash, I was her solitary visitor. The following day, the nurses told me in the morning, that Kelly's sister, Jemma was due to visit late in the afternoon, so I was caught off guard when a familiar faced visitor arrived unannounced shortly after lunch. Richie's wife was not a visitor I had been expecting and as she pulled up a chair to sit on one side of Kelly's bed, whilst I sat on the other, I had no idea where our conversation would go or how I would handle it. I did not have the slightest idea what she knew or didn't know, but had an uneasy feeling that somehow I was going to put my foot in it.

"How is she?" Richie's wife asked sounding genuinely concerned.

"Still not good." I said as we watched Kelly breathe through a ventilator, "They have induced this coma on her as the Doctor's are concerned about the swelling on her brain. It's too early to tell apparently, how well she is going to come through this, or even if she is going to come through it. I need her to come through though. Kelly, if you can hear me, keep fighting, do you hear me, you have got to keep fighting!"

I blew my nose again. I was not being as tough as I felt I should be. My eyes were redder than a hayfever sufferers when chopping onions in a field of freshly cut grass. I made an effort to compose myself with Richie's wife present, as it felt wrong to be tearful in front of her.

"How's your husband?"

"My husband?"

She seemed taken aback that I knew she had a husband.

"Yes, I saw you visiting yesterday, with your family, your little boy and girl. You're a very eyecatching family. How is Richie?"

"He's fine. Pretty much. Do you know Richie? Do you know why he's in hospital?"

"I know of Richie, but I don't really know him. I know why he's in hospital though."

"And sorry you are?"

"I'm Roddy. A friend of Kelly's."

"Pleased to meet you."

We extended arms over the bed and over Kelly's unconscious body and shook hands. I could feel my throat drying. It suddenly dawned on me that the only possible reason that Richie's wife could be visiting Kelly was because she wanted to know what her husband was doing in a car with her. Given Kelly was unconscious, the only way Richie's wife could acquire any answers would be by interrogating me.

"How do you know of Richie then, Roddy?"

There was no point in me lying. Richie was conscious after all and had no doubt offered an explanation to his wife already, she was obviously trying to establish whether his story was true. I could be a good liar when it came to playing a practical joke, but in these circumstances, I decided any questions Richie's wife asked me, I would answer honestly. I might spare her some of the grisly details, but I would be honest.

"I know him through what Kelly has told me about him. Also, I was over on the other side of Aughton with Kelly when your husband arrived to meet her yesterday. I didn't speak to him or nothing, but I saw him. I left him with her and then I saw him with you yesterday, when you and your kids were visiting."

"But you don't know who I am?"

This struck me as a strange thing for her to ask. I used to be mates with a lad called Garry Barrons, a great little footballer, who joined Crystal Palace as a schoolboy. He made his way through the ranks and when he was sixteen, he signed as a "YTS" player, then when he was eighteen, he turned professional and must have played about twenty games for Palace reserves. If I ever went clubbing with him or even down the pub, that would be his line,

'Do you know who I am?'

Garry Barrons was a nearly man. That's who he turned out to be, he just didn't know his own answer when he asked the question. Anyway, Richie's wife asking the same question, was a bit weird.

"Look", I said bluntly, "to be honest with you, I don't really know who you are and I don't really care who you are. I know you are Richie's wife, or at least the mother of his kids…"

"Wife," she stated.

"Ok, wife. Anyway, I know you're his wife, but if you're someone famous, I can honestly say I don't know you. I don't watch soap operas, I don't watch the news, I only really watch sports with men in, if I'm honest, so whoever you are, doesn't really mean much to me.

I'm sorry that your husband has been in a crash, but he's the lucky one. Kelly's not been anywhere near as lucky, so my thoughts are just about her right now. Don't get me wrong, I'm glad your husband is not in the same mess as Kelly, but you need to talk things through with your husband really, not with me."

"I know. I understand that. That's not why I'm here."

"Good. I'm not being funny, it's good of you to take the time to come and visit Kelly, but if you want to find out what she was doing with your husband, he needs to be the one to tell you."

"I know that. I just needed to see Kelly. See how she was."

A nurse came in, her name was Lucy, I had spoken to her before on this shift and on her previous one. She had done the late shift the night before and the early one that morning, so it seemed she was constantly working. Lucy pottered around, checking charts, traces and figures, signed some forms and then struck up a polite conversation with Richie's wife and I.

"She's a fighter, isn't she?" Lucy observed.

"She is," I replied.

"Can I get either of you a drink? Mrs. Billingham?"

"No, thanks!"

"What about you, Roddy?"

I needed something for my dry throat.

"I'd love a drink, Lucy!"

"What would you like?"

"I'd love a cup of tea."

"No problem. How do you have it?"

"Milky. Two sugars."

"Fine. I'll pop that back in to you in a few minutes."

"Wonderful! Thanks Lucy!"

As soon as I said Lucy I began to doubt whether I had her name right, then convinced myself I was 99% sure she was called Lucy. The nurse whose name was probably Lucy, left.

"You work with Kelly, then?" Mrs. Billingham asked after a momentary silence. I figured that Kelly must have told Richie that she had travelled up with me and he must have told his Mrs. I felt quite flattered that I had been discussed.

"I do. We're best mates at work. Best mates full stop really. I love the bones of her and I'd say she loves the bones of me too, just a little differently."

I seemed to reveal the lovesick puppy to anyone who asked really. Random strangers in pubs and at bus stops had heard me pour my heart out before about Kelly, now I was doing the same to a random stranger in a hospital intensive care unit.

"So you'd like to be more than friends, but Kelly wouldn't?"

"In a nutshell. I think I'd be a bit of a rollercoaster ride, but how does she know whether she'd like it or not if she doesn't buy a ticket?"

"Maybe if Kelly gets better, she'll appreciate how you've been there for her through a difficult time. Women like that. As teenage girls, we are stupid, we go for the bad boys, but the older we get, the more we come to realise that reliability is a good thing. Women like men who keep the faith through thick and thin. They like men who will fix the leak in a sinking boat rather than just abandoning ship."

I guessed Mrs.Billingham was talking more about her own situation than about mine. Kelly and I didn't have a leaky boat, we'd never even set sail.

"There would be nothing I would like more, Mrs.Billingham, but I can't see it happening. I ain't all that bothered right now though, priority number one is just to see Kelly better again. I want her to outlive me. If I had one wish, that's what it'd be, for Kelly to outlive me. Whether or not Kelly and I ever get together is immaterial, we will always be friends, no matter what, so I do not want to live my life with a huge void in it, which there would be if Kelly died. I suppose it's a selfish wish really, but I think Kelly could cope better without me than I could without her."

"God bless you, Roddy, that's a lovely thing to say."

"Thank you."

"That's how I feel about my husband."

I didn't do much of a job hiding my surprise.

"You do?"

"Don't look so surprised, Roddy! Just because he was in a car with Kelly yesterday does not make him a bad man or a man that's unlovable. He's a lovely man but even lovely men make mistakes sometimes. In my eyes, he's made a whopper but that doesn't mean I'll stop loving him. I've made a few mistakes of my own through the years, even bigger whoppers and Richie has always been close by to throw me a lifeline and stop me from drowning so I'm not abandoning him now because he's made a mistake of his own. Bizarrely, I think once I calm down about his breach of trust, we'll have a better marriage. We will both not want to return to a place in our relationship were things could turn out like they have in the last twenty four hours."

I felt close to this woman. She was both beautiful and interesting which I had always found, other than with Kelly, to be mutually exclusive.

"I hope everything goes great for you, I really do. Last night, I saw the grieving family and friends of those two poor kids that died and it breaks my heart just thinking about them. At least Kelly's still here fighting and your husband has cuts and bruises and a tail between his legs, but those two kids are just memories to their friends and family now. I know that eventually happens to us all, we die and just become a loved one's memories, then once all our loved ones die, we just become an image on a photograph or a record in a census, but not at eighteen years old, that's just wrong. Teenage bravado does not deserve a death sentence, does it?"

"No. The girl that died was just a victim of getting in the wrong car and sitting in the wrong seat without a belt on."

"I know. The paramedics said that Kelly actually having her belt on is what has given her a fighting chance. If she hadn't put that on, I'd be at the mortuary now, not sitting here talking to you and wondering how I'm going to tell Kelly's sister later, when she comes in, that the sister that she has not seen for ten years, only has a fifty-fifty chance of survival. At least she's got that fifty-fifty chance though, without the belt there'd be no hope to cling to."

"Kelly will pull through, she's spent her whole life fighting and I'm sure she won't stop now."

I was perplexed. How would Richie's wife know that Kelly was a fighter? Did she literally mean a fighter? Perhaps Kelly and Mrs. Billingham had fought over Richie in the past? I briefly imagined them in a boxing ring, with the big red gloves on and me acting as a referee, running through the Queensberry rules. I didn't have too much time to think about that though, as the kindhearted nurse from earlier returned with my sugary, milky tea and a grey haired, bearded gentleman with glasses who looked important. Turns out he was.

"Here's your tea, Roddy! I'll just pop it over on the side here," the nurse said with a half-hearted, tragic smile which she had probably perfected through years of witnessing families turmoil at the bedsides of their sick relatives.

"Thanks! That's lovely!" I replied.

"Mrs. Billingham," the nurse continued, "I've brought Mr. Lapinski in to see you. He's here to discuss the operation."

Mrs. Billingham immediately stood up from her chair and shook Mr. Lapinski's hand.

"Very pleased to meet you," Mrs. Billingham said, adopting the nurse's tragic smile.

"I wanted to discuss the options we have," Mr. Lapinski said in a heavily accented East European voice, "as next of kin, you need to be fully aware of what choices we are faced with. Do you have a few minutes to talk this over now?"

"Yes," Mrs. Billingham replied, "could we go somewhere private?"

"Of course we can, please come through to my office and we can talk things through there."

"Thank you!"

Mr. Lapinski led the way followed by Mrs. Billingham. I could not work her out at all. One minute she seemed cold, then warm, then she'd say something that I just couldn't fathom. At that point, I had her down as pleasant in an odd sort of way. I had also had a sense, throughout our conversation, that she had been hiding something and I now felt that I knew what that was. She had lied about her husband's condition, he was obviously in far worse shape than she had let on. If the consultant was talking over options with her, this wasn't about whether Richie needed a plaster or a bandage, it was something much more important, much more serious.

"Goodbye Roddy" she said before she exited, "it was lovely to meet you! Thanks for everything you've done. I hope to see you again some day, in more pleasant surroundings!"

"No problem, hope to see you too!" I replied not really understanding why she was grateful to me or why she would want our paths to cross again. My lack of intellect was a frustrating handicap! Mrs. Billingham followed Mr. Lapinski out the door. The nurse checked over a few charts again at Kelly's bedside.

"Is her husband in a bad way?" I asked the nurse.

"No, no, Mr. Billingham is absolutely fine. He is the only one to have come out of the accident with relatively minor injuries."

"And he hasn't taken a turn for the worse?"

"No, not as far as I'm aware," the nurse said trying to figure out whether she had missed something, before adding, "in fact, definitely not, he only went home a couple of hours ago."

"Then why does the consultant need to speak to her?"

"Oh right! That wasn't about Mr.Billingham, that was about Miss Watkinson here."

I still didn't get it.

"I'm sorry, you've lost me. Why would they need to speak about Kelly?"

"As Kelly's next of kin, Mrs.Billingham will have to give her consent for the Doctors to operate."

I laughed in a confused, panicky manner.

"No, no, there's been some mistake! Mrs.Billingham isn't Kelly's next of kin, Kelly's sister is. She's due in here soon. The Doctor's will need to speak to her sister, not Mrs.Billingham!"

The nurse looked at me like I had just won the 'Village Idiot' award and my village was London.

"Roddy! Mrs.Billingham is Kelly's sister!"

"No! Kelly's sister's name is Jemma. Jemma Watkinson."

"Well, I'm sure that would have been her name before she got married, but she's Jemma Billingham now."

"Fuck! She's Jemma! Kelly's gonna love that!"

"I'm sure Kelly is perfectly aware who her sister is, Roddy!"

"Sorry for swearing! It just slipped out. I just didn't know Kelly's sister was married to Richie!"

"Yes, I guess that's why they were in the car together, because they're family."

'You guess wrong!!' I thought to myself.

The nurse finished off her duties and as she was making her way out, I felt the need to ask her something.

"Tell me something, nurse.."

"What Roddy?!"

"Are the majority of blokes from Ormskirk ugly?"

She smiled at me.

"A lot of them are! Why do you ask?"

"It would just explain a few things, that's all!"

"Saying that!" the nurse continued, "I shouldn't really say that! My husband is from Ormskirk!"

"Do you have any sisters?" I asked.

"No. Just two brothers."

"Probably a good thing," I said, "probably a very good thing!"

Kelly

Following the crash, time and consciousness arrived in snippets. I remember the impact, I remember being trapped in the car and I remember passing out in a manner similar to that I experienced when I was given gas as a child to extract a rotten tooth. That horrible feeling of drifting into an unwanted, nauseous, unconscious paralysis. The next eight days passed like snapshots. Each snapshot seemed to contain Roddy. He was ubiquitous both in my dreams and in my conscious state. I felt no pain but did feel a mixture of emotions coursing through my veins, amongst them guilt over how I had treated Roddy. He was a constant in my life but I had failed to appreciate how important he was to me. Sometimes its those we love the most that we treat with the least amount of thought, as we know their love will not die, irrespective of what we do. I would have liked to have told Roddy this, as he sat patiently by my hospital bed, but speech was frustratingly beyond me and those fleeting periods of consciousness did not provide ample time to write down a heartfelt message. I could hear Roddy though. I couldn't be sure how often what I heard were actual words spoken and how often the words were just created by my drugged-up, delusional state, but in all instances, Roddy was urging me to be strong, encouraging me to fight and revealing the extent of his love for me. In the past, I had always found his revelations of love to be inappropriate but now I found them humbling. I wasn't sure if I could ever love Roddy how he loved me, but for the first time ever, I wanted to try.

I had no comprehension of time, but I was becoming aware that as it passed, my periods of awareness were growing longer. I was told later that the swelling on my brain had become so severe that an operation to reduce it was discussed and agreed, but miraculously, through a combination of IV fluids, medication and oxygen therapy the swelling came down and my slow recovery began. Five days after the crash, I was able to start having brief conversations with Roddy, then longer conversations and then one afternoon, I awoke to find that Roddy was not perched in his usual seat, but he had been replaced by a ghost from my past, my sister, Jemma. At first, I was overwhelmed and unable to speak, Jemma and I had been through so much since we last saw each other and I really did not know how she would feel about me. I had been plagued by guilt ever since I had abandoned her and let her face the trial for Mum's murder alone. I had spent years deliberately avoiding her because of how I had behaved, but this time there was nowhere to hide. Jemma had found me and I could no longer run away from my failings.

"Kelly, how are you feeling?"

I could not answer her at first and then when I did speak, it was not a response to the question. This moment was about so much more than the crash.

"I'm so sorry," I cried, "I truly am so sorry."

Jemma just started at me like she had been taking lessons in stoicism from Shakespeare's Brutus.

"What's done is done, Kelly. I'm not angry with you. I'm just grateful you've survived the crash."

"Jemma, you should be angry! I let you down."

"Kelly, it was a long time ago! You were a child. Whether you had run away or stuck around, I would have taken the blame for Vomit Breath's death. I wish you hadn't spent the years that followed avoiding me, but you did what you did and we can't do anything now to bring that time back. All we can do now is move forward, move forward and just try to remember the good things from the past. We are family, Kelly. We need to forgive each other for our past failings and start afresh."

In principle, it all sounded very easy but I was sceptical, not about how Jemma would view me, but about how I would view myself.

"Every time I see you though, Jemma, it'll just be a reminder of how weak I've been. How I've let you down. You might say you've forgiven me, Jemma, but I'll always be worried that deep down you haven't and also that I haven't forgiven myself. I've been so weak, Jemma, that's why I've avoided you, because I know I've been so weak."

"Kelly, you nearly died in the car crash! I only have one sister, one surviving family member from the old family of my childhood and I've spent the last ten years wondering whether I would ever see you again. Wondering when we would get to speak. Over the last week, as I've watched you battle for your very survival, I had to face the fact that the answer may be never. You're a fighter though, Kelly, no-one can doubt that. Our childhood was one long battle and everything that happened in it, led to the moment when you came to my rescue and Vomit Breath died. OK, I wish you hadn't run away but you did what you did to our so called 'Mother' out of love for me, so I still have a lot to thank you for as well as to forgive you for and as I've said, I have been waiting for this moment for years on end, so let's not dwell on the past, let's move forwards."

I propped myself up more erectly in the bed.

"Jemma, it's easy to say all that but it doesn't work like that! My character and personality are derived from my memories and the fact that I treated you so badly is a stain on mine. I can't just skip merrily along and forget Mum died, forget I killed her and pretend I didn't run away and leave you to pick up the pieces. I've spent over ten years trying to forget and no matter where I was, whether it was Hong Kong or Australia or London or wherever, it has been impossible to forget what I've done. It is a curse that I will have to live with until the day I die."

Jemma did not do self-pity. Throughout our childhood, she had always been about dogged resistance rather than 'if only's' and my 'woe is me' speech, spoken from a hospital bed following a serious car accident failed to draw sympathy from her. It just riled her.

"Look Kelly, you need to stop making everything you've been through such a burden on you. Our past is not meant to be a burden that weighs heavily on us. Didn't someone famous not say that 'if something does not destroy me, it makes me strong'? Well, you need to start adopting that attitude! Look at everything you've come through, an unpleasant upbringing, Vomit Breath's death, this car crash and whatever else you've had to put up with over the last ten years, but you're still, just about, in one piece. You are a fighter, Kelly! Count your blessings!"

"I try to Jemma, but sometimes it's hard."

"Kelly, when you were a little girl, probably about six or seven, you noticed you weren't enjoying the same happy upbringing as some of your little friends who had Mummy's and Daddy's who walked them to school, hand in hand, kissed them goodbye and turned back up at half past three to collect them. You had no Daddy and a Mummy who, most mornings, was still nursing a hangover in bed and was usually back on the booze by half past three, plotting the next one. Do you remember, you used to get all worked up about it and, as a result, your body stopped working as it should? Remember, when you used to get constipated? You would go days and days on end without having a poo. I wouldn't let you flush the toilet because sometimes you would tell me you'd been, even when you hadn't, so I demanded to see the evidence! Seven or eight days would pass and nothing would come out, you'd just hold it in and hold it in and then eventually, when you could keep it in no longer, it used to sting like mad. It was a vicious circle. You became so scared of having a poo because it hurt so badly, that you would clog up inside again and we went on and on with this for months.

One day, Vomit Breath was getting ready to go out and she was waiting to get into the bathroom, but couldn't because you were locked in there. You'd locked the door and Vomit Breath was banging on the outside, cursing like a sailor, screaming at you to hurry up and get out! You were in there crying with the pain of moving your bowels with all your insides clogged up, so I turned up outside the door, told Mum to leave you alone, explained that you had been constipated for a week and tried to make her understand that this was a painful process for you. I was wasting my time, it was like trying to persuade Hitler not to move his troops into Czechoslovakia! Vomit Breath just kept banging on that door, yelling at you to get out.

I remember saying,

"Leave her alone! Kelly tries to avoid going to the loo, so when she does go, it hurts her like mad!"

Vomit Breath, not even realising that she was being profound, just scowled and said,

'Kelly needs to realise that in life you have to be able to deal with all the shit that happens to come your way!'

In Vomit Breath's sorry existence, that was probably the only sensible thing that she ever said! Twenty years later, she's still right! Nothing has changed! Kelly, I'm not asking you to forget everything, but just don't let it impact on your future. You're a gorgeous looking woman with a warm heart and I'm sure men are drawn to you like ships to rocks, so go out and find someone who will love you and adore you and make you happy."

It was only at this point that I noticed Jemma's engagement and wedding rings resting proudly around her finger.

"Like you have, Jemma?"

"Pardon?"

"Like you have? I've just noticed your wedding ring. Is that what defines happiness, do you think? Having a man that adores you? Maybe it does. Maybe that's why I don't feel happy. I have a good job. I have a reasonable amount of money, but I'm not happy. Has having a man that adores you made you happy?"

"Not just a man, Kelly, a family. I have a daughter now called Melissa, who has inherited her Auntie's good looks! She's five years old, loves baking cakes, dressing up and sharing hugs. Then there's Jamie who's three. Jamie's just one big bundle of energy. He never stops. He's into everything and I mean everything! He's still only a toddler but he's taken more blows than a heavyweight boxer, if there's a wing mirror or a door handle, or a corner cupboard that he can crack his head on, somehow he'll find it! He's just too busy to look! Too busy to sleep too!"

"I'd love to see them, Jemma! Will you bring them in here?"

"Once you're a little better, I will. I don't think you are quite ready for Jamie just yet!"

"Of course I am! Bring him in!"

"I will Kelly, in a few days."

"I'm excited already! How long have you been married, Jemma?"

"Seven years."

"What's your husband's name?"

Jemma could have lied, she could have just altered one word in that conversation to preserve the status quo, but she chose not to. She just came right out with it.

"Richie."

Surely not? Maybe it was a co-incidence. Surely after all that she had just said, she would not do this to me.

"Richie? Not Richie Billingham?"

I was numb with shock. I was beginning to regain some self-belief, some hope for the future until this moment.

"Yes, Kelly. I am married to Richie Billingham. The man you were with in the car, when it crashed, is my husband."

Richie

I don't know why, but one day it just came back to me, weeks later. I was heading out for the evening with Jemma, waiting for her to come downstairs and all of a sudden the last words that Kelly said to me before the crash just came back to me.

I could picture myself back in the car with Kelly. I was slowing down, ready to turn into West Tower and we were just talking away, saying amicable goodbyes and then Kelly said, out of the blue,

"Richie, can I just ask you something?"

"Fire away."

"Why did you never tell me you had cancer?"

I wasn't expecting it. I was expecting something about Jemma, maybe something about that night at the Birch's when Kelly accused me of sleeping with her, but I was not expecting the cancer question. I hesitated, not sure how to respond. I was going to tell her the whole story, how I had met with Jemma and how she had comforted me and urged me to tell Kelly all about it, but I had panicked and not managed to get the words out, scared of revealing the truth. It felt like a good time to tell her, to piece things together for her, so I was about to say,

"Jemma told me to tell you everything, but I did not have the courage to. I was scared." but I only got as far as,

"Jemma told me….." and then out of nowhere came the other car, swerving around the corner at enormous speeds. Before I had the time to answer Kelly's question, our worlds and our cars collided, leaving two lives behind us on that quiet road.

Jemma

I needed to say it. I had nothing to be ashamed about. I had married a man I had fallen in love with and when we did fall in love, he was not married, he did not have a girlfriend, he was bloody single! I knew Kelly would go potty but what did she expect, the world to stand still until she came back like something out of a fairytale? As soon as I mentioned that I was married to Richie, Kelly laughed, but it was not an amused laugh, it was more a disapproving, sarcastic laugh.

"It's all about one upmanship with you, isn't it, Jemma?"

The tables had turned now. Kelly's whole approach had been 'Please Forgive Me' but now it was, 'You've Wronged ME, Bitch!' Her tone was more aggressive, her manner more confident, Kelly knew when she had to fight her corner and she had shown me before that she was a pussy cat when things were going her way and a tiger when they weren't. I knew she would think she had the upper hand morally now, but that was bullshit and I was not going to apologise for anything I had done.

"One upmanship? How?"

"You always have to get in on the act. Go one better than me."

"Kelly, I married Richie because I loved him."

"That's garbage, Jemma! There are twenty million men in Britain between the ages of sixteen and sixty and you just happen to fall in love with the ONE, the ONLY ONE, that ever meant anything to me. Both choosing the same man out of twenty million?! That's some co-incidence, Jemma! I remember you even said that if Richie was the only choice you had, you wouldn't even bother. There's no two ways about this, you did this to get at me!"

I loved Kelly, but she had it all wrong and it was annoying me that she could, after everything, accuse me of stooping so low.

"Married someone and had two kids with him, just to get at a sister that I haven't seen for years and for all I knew may never see again! Don't flatter yourself, Kelly!"

"The reason you were attracted to him though, Jemma, was because he was mine! Ever since the Birch's party when we were teenagers, you have always made sure you bettered me!"

"You're talking rubbish, Kelly!"

I could feel myself doing the 'Big Sister' thing. I know I shouldn't have done, but sometimes when we are put back into familiar territory of yesteryear, we revert to type. Kelly did not take well to being patronised.

"I am NOT talking rubbish! Ever since the Birch's party, you have tried to better me! At the Birch's party, I start talking to Richie, we hit it off, next thing I know, you're telling me you shagged him! You saw me talking to him, let me tell you how much I liked him and then you went upstairs, slipped your knickers off and asked him to come inside to play. Literally!"

I protested but not very well.

"Kelly, it wasn't like that! I was smashed off my head. I thought it was Richie but it might not have been!"

"Are you trying to make yourself sound like less of a whore, Jemma, because if you are, you are making a crap job of it?!"

The simple solution here would have been to slap her, but slapping a patient sat up in a bed in intensive care would not have looked good at all! I just bit my tongue.

"Then, Jemma, when I was absolutely besotted by Richie, when he was my total world, I found you cuddled up with him in Coronation Park."

"He had cancer, Kelly!"

"I know now he had cancer, but I didn't know it then. You could have told me. Do you think I would have disappeared like I did, if you had told me? Of course not! That's why you didn't tell me! You let me go, so you could have Richie all for yourself. Richie even told me, before the crash that he was going to tell me about his cancer but YOU told him not to! Everything has always been about you going one better than me. Even when I killed our mother, you had to go one better, take the blame and play the innocent victim in bloody prison!"

"Kelly, I was in prison for a murder that I didn't commit, how is that playing the innocent victim?"

"You orchestrate things though, Jemma! That night, when Mum died, when I pushed her down the stairs, would I have killed her if you hadn't been waiting for her to come in, with a knife in your hand? For years and years, I have felt guilty for destroying your life but I didn't destroy your life, did I? You are here playing happy families with the one man I truly loved and the kids you have created together. I have not destroyed your life, you have destroyed mine and you know what, I think that's what you wanted to do. Mission accomplished, Jemma!"

"All of that is complete bunkum, Kelly! I don't know why Richie would have said I stopped him telling you about the cancer, because the opposite is true. I begged him to tell you."

"You expect me to believe that?!"

"It's the truth. I don't care whether you choose to believe it! IT IS THE TRUTH! I did not do anything ever because I hated you. I did everything because I loved you and then, when you went away, I grew to love Richie too. There is no sinister sub-plot. We both loved Richie, but at different times."

"I don't believe that, Jemma! I believe I loved him and so did you, but not at different times, I reckon the two overlapped. Do you know what, knowing what I know now, I wish I hadn't come out of my room that night. In those few seconds when I charged at Mum, my life was ruined. I wish I'd have just stayed in the safety of my room, left the pair of you to slug it out."

"Kelly, you don't mean that!"

"Oh but I do! Can you go now? I despise you, Jemma. I can't believe it has taken me so long to see through you, but I'm so glad that I have! Can you leave me alone now, Jemma. Forever!"

"Kelly, this is stupid!"

I moved towards her but she turned over in bed and faced away from me.

"Kelly, I am not going to stand here and grovel. I'll leave now and one day, when you've grown up a bit and come to realise that the whole world does not revolve around you, track me down and apologise. I am overjoyed you survived the crash, but whilst the Doctor's are doing their medical checks on you, Kelly, get them to do a reality check too, because you could do with one!"

"Just go, Jemma."

"I'm going! I'm surprised at you, Kelly! I always knew you would be annoyed with me for marrying Richie, I just didn't think you would be so pathetic!"

"Keep away from me, Jemma!"

"I intend to."

"And next time you have sex with your husband, look in his eyes."

"Why?"

"To see whether you see your reflection in them or an image of me."

Richie

Melissa was sat on my knee, in the lounge, watching Dora The Explorer and Jamie was running around the house, pretending to be a firework, when the front door slammed.

"What a bitch!" I heard Jemma say to herself in the hall, "after everything I have done for her! The cheeky bitch!"

I gathered Melissa up off my knee, placed her back down on the settee, she was fully concentrating on helping Dora find Diego so she barely noticed I'd moved and headed to the hall, closing the lounge doors behind me.

It had been raining relentlessly all day, so Jemma was shaking her umbrella off in the corner and removing her coat with her other hand.

"That woman has a bloody cheek!" she growled, this time for my benefit.

If I hadn't managed to involve myself in this mess, I would have made some jokey, sarcastic comment about it not being a teary re-union, but as I had been partially responsible for the mayhem in our personal lives, I kept my expression serious and my attitude sympathetic.

"I'm sorry it didn't go well, Jemma. What's Kelly have a problem with?"

"Me, basically!" Jemma said as she hung her coat at the bottom of the staircase, "she thinks I married you to get at her!"

"You didn't even know where she was when we got married!"

"I know! It doesn't make sense. Do you have a tattoo on your arse that says 'Property of Kelly Watkinson', because that's what she seems to think?!"

"No, just the one on my willy that says blow here to inflate!"

Jemma gave me a look that said 'Men In The Doghouse Should Not Tell Rude Jokes'.

"Very funny," she said as if it wasn't, "by the way, did you tell Kelly that you were going to tell her about your cancer, before she ran away, but I stopped you?"

"NO! When?"

"When you met her before the crash?"

"No. As far as I knew, Kelly didn't even know I had cancer. I've never told her."

"Well, take it from me, she knows."

"Right….I suppose there's a chance I may have told her when I was driving her back to West Tower before the crash, but I have no recollection of that journey and I don't see why I would have done. It's a random thing to come out with, 'By the way, did you know I used to have testicular cancer, I was going to tell you but Jemma stopped me!' There's just no way I would have blamed you for not telling her, you told me to tell her!"

Jemma threw me a quizzical look.

"There's no way you could have had an alterior motive?"

"What alterior motive?"

"I don't know, a romantic or physical one?"

"What? Slag you off to get her to sleep with me?! No, absolutely not! We've been through this over and over again, Jemma! It was not a romantic meeting, by the time we got in the car, I just wanted to drop her off and come back to try and kickstart a better relationship between you and I. I had no reason to lie about my cancer or to say you told me to keep quiet."

"OK. Kelly's got it in her head though that I told you not to tell her. That's not the only thing that she's pissed off about though. She's pissed off about Mum's death and even about us sleeping together at the Birch's party."

"Kelly needs to get a grip. The world does not owe her a favour. Anyway, I didn't sleep with you at the Birch's party!"

Jemma sighed.

"Let's not start that one off again, Richie! We both know you did!"

There was little point arguing. I had failed to persuade Jemma in the past that I was not the perpertrator and the penetrator of that crime but she would not believe me. I only ever entered into an argument these days if I thought there was a potential victor, this one was always going to end in stalemate.

"Fine!" I conceded.

"She's making me feel like a bad person!" Jemma continued, there was no stopping her when she went off on one, "Kelly is the one with feelings for my husband not the other way around, yet I am the one who's supposed to feel bad! I was prepared to put that issue to one side and move on, but instead, bloody Kelly wants to dredge things up from donkeys years ago! I am not a bad person! I'm a good mother! I am not a bad wife, even if sometimes you think I am! I'm a caring person and in my life there's no-one I've cared for more than Kelly, yet I get it all thrown back in my face."

People don't say things like 'I am a good person', unless part of them has an element of doubt about whether it's true. Its called fishing for re-assurance. Jemma started to sob. I tentatively moved over to her and gave her a gentle hug.

"Why does everybody hate me?" she asked between cries.

"No-one hates you, Jemma!"

"Yes they do! Kelly hates me! You hate me!"

"I don't hate you, Jemma!"

"You nearly left me for my sister because you think I neglect you!"

"Jemma, I screwed up! You know I screwed up, I know I screwed up. I would never have left you, Jemma, I was just being an idiot. I'm sorry."

"Do you think we will make things right again?"

"Of course I do! We have a fantastic marriage. We just steered off course for a little while, that's all."

Jemma took her head out of my arms and looked up at me tearily.

"So when you make love to me, you won't be thinking of Kelly?"

"No! Definitely not! You're the only one for me, Jemma!"

"Kelly said you'd be thinking of her."

Jemma sniffed.

"Kelly lashes out when she's hurt, Jemma, you know that."

"I do too. It's a Watkinson trait. Richie, I'm sorry too, you know."

"What for?"

"For lacking imagination. Since the kids have been born, I have felt so lucky to have them that I have forgotten that I am also so lucky to have you."

Romantic gush was not something that Jemma had ever really spoken. This was a rare moment!

"We're lucky to have each other, Jemma!"

"I know but we've let our lives and our relationship become one monotonous treadmill. Every day from now on, we need to work together to make things more fun. We allowed things to go stale between us. I promise I will never let that happen again. Never!"

I kissed Jemma on the forehead.

"Neither will I, honey. Neither will I!"

Roddy

I had deliberately made myself scarce to give Kelly some time with her sister. I nipped down to the nearest pub from the hospital, 'The Ropers Arms' for a quick pint of lager. There was a sign up in there saying 'Free Pints Of Lager For Pensioners - As Long As They Are Accompanied By Both Parents'. My Dad had just retired after forty years working in Ford Dagenham and my grandparents are both still alive, so I said to the landlord that I'd drive them all up, so they could all get pissed at his expense! There's no chance they'll come up here, my Nan's incontinent and my Grandad has dementia so they keep him to a routine, but I just wanted to see the look on the landlord's face!

A couple of hours later, when I ambled back cheerily to the hospital, I went into the Ward to hear a gentle sobbing which I could soon see was Kelly. I wanted to be and tried to be sympathetic but by this stage in affairs, I was tired and my nerves were on edge.

"Kelly! Kelly! Why are you crying? Come on! It's alright!"

I gave her a hug. As I pulled away, Kelly kissed my cheek.

"Roddy, it's not alright, Jemma hates me!"

"She told you she hates you?"

"No, I told her that I hated her, but only because of everything she's done. She married my boyfriend!"

This whole saga was becoming tiresome. I felt I was turning into Kelly's doormat. Kelly's dramatics about some tosser from ten years back who didn't give two hoots about her and had a good looking wife and kids of his own, was now getting on my tits.

"Kelly, you haven't got a boyfriend!"

"I know, but the only boyfriend I have ever had in the past that still means something to me, Jemma married! She knew how much Richie meant to me. She's just done it to get at me, to get her revenge on me for leaving. I even think the hatred she has, may have built up when we were children. I think she spent so much time as a kid having to look after me, that she grew to resent me. Did I tell you about the party we went to when we were teenagers when she slept with Richie?"

About a million times, I thought. Change the bloody record, woman!

Someone had knocked my 'Infatuation with Kelly' button to OFF. I felt that day that I had gone from being totally in love, completely in awe of Kelly's every move to cynical, rational and blunt. I reckon the way she was behaving, it had to happen at some stage. OK, she had been through a massive trauma, but it ain't that hard to be decent in any circumstance.

"Kelly, just hush for a minute, will you. Look, we're friends, aren't we?"

"That's a daft question, of course we are."

"Good friends?"

"Yes."

Kelly said that 'Yes' slowly and suspiciously, like she knew something more was coming but she didn't quite know what it was.

"And over the last few days, since you've come around after the accident, would I be right in thinking your attitude towards me has changed a little?"

Kelly stopped crying.

"In what way?"

"Well, either you have been a complete prick tease or you've started flirting with me in a way you've never done before."

"I have?"

Kelly feigned innocence but she knew she was guilty as charged.

"You know you have! Asking for kisses after hugs, gazing really intently at me, smiling at me all the time. You're acting differently around me. Why?"

"Because I feel differently."

"How?"

"Everything that's happened to me has taught me how important you are to me."

"Do you reckon?"

"Definitely."

"Can I tell you how it feels to me?"

"Go on."

"It feels like you're grabbing hold of me, not because you love me, but because I'm all you've got left. I'm like your oasis in the desert right now, but it feels like you're trying really hard to do it, rather than it coming naturally. To me, it feels like you'll get off your camel in the desert, fly back to England where water flows out of every tap and soon enough forget that you were ever thirsty!"

"Roddy, that's not true! It's not fair of you to say that!"

I was sticking to my guns on this one.

"Of course it's bloody fair of me to say! Try listening to yourself sometimes, Kelly! I may not read many books, but I know what a narcissistic bitch is and you are in danger of becoming one! You go on and on about Richie! You've just said your sister only married him to get back at you and only shagged him when you were teenagers to get at you and only went through childbirth TWICE to get back at you in Outer Mongolia or wherever you were! How conceited are you, Kelly? For fuck's sake Kelly, their relationship is not about you and if you ever want to think about having a relationship with me, don't make it about them!"

A nurse came over and told me to mind my language and keep my voice down. I continued in a whisper.

"I'm not here to be your crumbs of comfort. If you want to be just friends with me, that's fine, I can handle that, let's just be friends, but don't even bother entertaining the idea of a romance between us if you can't go into it wholeheartedly. I ain't putting up with you talking crap about Richie all day!"

I barely had chance to finish my sentence when Kelly reached forward in her bed, placed her hands either side of my mouth and gave me a big smacker! I was too shocked to kiss back!

"What did you do that for?!!"

"I was being wholehearted! You're right Roddy, sub-consciously I've been playing games and life's too short for that. I think I love you Roddy Baker and I want us to give this a go."

"So you'll drop this whole boring Richie thing now?"

"Consider it dropped."

"And you're going to make up with your sister?"

"One step at a time, Roddy!"

"No! You've just said yourself, life is short, why waste any more time playing games. We need to find out where your sister lives and when you're better, before we go home, we need to get everything sorted out."

Richie

My relationship with Jemma took several giant strides back in the right direction after the crash. I made more effort to understand what Jemma wanted from the relationship, I helped more with the household chores such as dishwashing, ironing, washing and drying of clothes and joined in with difficult side of parenting such as disciplining and bearing bad news, such as breaking the catastrophic news to Melissa that she cannot have an ice cream from the second ice cream van when she has already had one from the first. I had always been the type of Dad that allowed Jemma to do the majority of the trickier elements and just did the fun stuff, but after the crash we worked as a team. For her part, Jemma understood my physical needs more, but despite her best efforts there were still problems on that score.

When I reminisce about this period of time now, I refer to it as our "Morrissey" period. This is because our sex life went through various levels of activity that linked to songs. When we first got it together, I called this our Bill Medley & Jennifer Warnes period, because sex was exciting and frequent which links to their song, "I Had The Time of My Life". Then, following the wedding and when Jemma was first pregnant with Melissa, daily sex became weekly sex, which normally happened on a Sunday night, so this was our "Blondie" period because of their song "Sunday girl". Once Melissa arrived and then Jamie, sex became less and less frequent so this became known as our "Sandy Denny" period after her song "Solo" and finally, the "Morrisey" period was after the crash when sexual regularity was not just every Sunday night, but was at least attempted every day, so the brilliant Morrisey song, "Every Day Is Like Sunday" defined this period!

Everything should have been perfect as for the first time in a long time I was getting what I wanted, but it still wasn't. The obstacle to good, wholesome, enjoyable sex in your thirties, when you have two children, is that the desire to avoid pregnancy returns to peak levels only previously endured in late teenage years. Sex becomes a threesome, but not a threesome involving two females and a male or two males and a female for that matter, a threesome between a man, a woman and a condom. At least when condoms were used in teenage years, I had a body to be proud of, so almost all sexual activity took place in daylight or at least with the lights on. In our thirties, Jemma was wanting to hide her stretch marks, her "Spaniel's ears" breasts and a vagina that had been torn, stitched and battered from a double helping of childbirth and I was equally happy to hide man breasts that felt chunky enough to lactate and a belly that resembled Demi Moore's on the cover of Vanity Fair. Thus, the act of condom placement in late teens is simple, as the procedure is carried out in full visibility and with an instrument that stiffens to diamond quality hardness at the mere mention of the word "knickers". In your thirties, however, condom placement becomes like an adult version of 'It's A Knockout'! Each time I tried it, I was sure I could hear Eddie Waring saying, "He's a poor lad!" or "Aye..Aye…! It's an awkward one, the boy's got to deal with it!"

After horseplay that lasted no longer than a five furlong sprint, one or other of us would jump off the saddle then fumble around in the darkness in the forlorn hope of finding an elusive silver wrapper before its intended recipient shrank from a recorder shaped instrument to the size and girth of a tin whistle that could no longer play a tune. Pretty often, by the time all safety equipment was in place, everything was small or dry and the very outcome you were trying to avoid, would, by default, become physically impossible.

I clearly remember the last night I gave up all hope of retaining one fully functional testicle. Jemma and I had bribed the sixteen year old girl who lived opposite us to snog her boyfriend's face off in front of our television rather than her own, so we had nipped down to 'A Passage To India' in Ormskirk, to enjoy a quality curry and a bottle of wine or three. On our return home, we drunkenly paid our teenage guests more money than they deserved, politely escorted them off the premises and raced up the stairs excitedly in anticipation of blind passion.

We took turns to brush our teeth and empty our bladders in the en-suite, a ritual that led to foreplay involving kissing but not oral sex. Jemma switched off the lights then we each stripped our own clothes off in the darkness before the games began. I followed a well rehearsed routine, kisses without tongues, kisses with tongues then a finger dip to check whether spit on a fingertip would suffice to grease the playing surface or whether a proper lubricant would be necessary. On this occasion, the wine had acted as a successful aphrodisiac and the landing area was as damp as a field of mushrooms, so no artificial juices were required. Feeling sufficiently enlarged, I clambered on top of Jemma, prodding around under her bellybutton, trying to find the pearly gates and the entrance to heaven. In my inebriated state, I was failing miserably so twisted over with my back to the mattress, pulling Jemma on top of me and leaving her to position herself correctly. She did so with ease and then gyrated her pelvis around in circles, making noises that I knew were borne out of sympathy rather than fulfilment.

Within a minute, my thoughts moved from passion to fear, as I knew all the mini-Richies were gathering in their millions for their pre-match warm-up, like a mass of miniature triathletes.

"Whoa! Whoa! Whoa!" I called out like a bus conductor who's spotted a passenger riding without a ticket, "Hang on! Hang on! You're going to have to get off!"

Jemma had obviously genuinely begun to enjoy it, as she sounded frustrated.

"Already?"

"Jemma, if you fizz the cola up in the can and there's a hole in the top, it can quite easily spray out a little….if you're happy to have another little Jamie running around in nine months time, you stay right where you are!"

Jemma lifted herself off muttering something about not running around in nine months time, but I didn't quite catch it as I had begun my search for the child catchers. I opened my top drawer next to my bed and immediately found a couple of empty condom packets. My first instinct was paranoia, 'who's been using them?'

but then reality kicked in and I realised I was a lazy bastard and amongst my crimes was failing to dispense of discarded condom wrappers. After much fumbling around in the dark, I realised I was making no progress and my sunflower which had been proud and tall only seconds earlier, was now starting to droop as it faced away from the item it worshipped.

"Can I switch the light on?" I pleaded.

Jemma groaned and sighed,

"Go on, but hurry up, I'm tired!"

Female disclosure of tiredness mid-sex is a danger sign. It is warning you, that although you have managed to get your plane on the runway, you still might not get it up, up and away. I switched my bedside light on and as Jemma turned away from the light, I hurriedly pulled my middle drawer open and sitting there was a whole new packet of condoms that I had bought from the supermarket the week before. Supermarket condom buying is a careful process, as you always have to select the check out aisle that will cause the least embarrassment and the most respect. Generally, I select the lad in his mid-twenties or the very ugly older lady who's opinion does not bother me. If I buy Jemma's sanitary towels, I would avoid the mid-twenties guy and go for the mid-twenties woman, as I want her to appreciate that I am a chilled out, modern man. Anyway, the problem the new condoms presented, was that not only were the condoms wrapped up, but so was the box, so I had to unwrap twice and then wrap once before I was ready for action. After a painfully drawn out process, I managed this, but I had to unwrap twice and then wrap twice too, as once I had my thumb and forefinger in place and started to roll, I only got through one rotation and things came to a standstill. Inside out! Shit! Shit! Shit! Shit! Shit! Why does this always happen to me?!

"Are you wanting sex tonight?" Jemma asked, "as Mr.Sandman seems to be putting out the fires that were burning earlier."

Hastily, I put the condom on, but by now there was not much left to wrap up and the condom looked like it had performed the penises version of a facelift reversal, as its skin had gone from taut and stretched to wrinkly and tired looking. I was giving up hope.

"Are you still awake?" I enquired.

"Just about," was the reply, "but you won't be needing that condom soon as I'll have been through the change!"

I grabbed my willy at the pubic hair end and gave it a few hopeful shakes. Nothing stirred. In frustration, I peeled the condom off and carried it to the en-suite knowing at least I would have the small consolation of making it into a water bomb.

"Goodnight Richie!" Jemma murmured with her face buried in a pillow.

"Goodnight babe!" I replied.

"Vasectomy it is then?" Jemma stated rhetorically.

"Vasectomy it is," I agreed, "vasectomy it is."

Kelly

Once I was out of hospital, there was no reason to hang around in Ormskirk. Whilst I had been on the critical list in intensive care, Roddy had booked himself a few emergency days holiday, but once I was on the mend and moved to a standard ward, he reluctantly headed back down to London. Once Roddy left, the hospital seemed a lonely place and the seven days I stayed there after his departure passed like months. We spoke each day on the phone, but I was anxious to get back to Ealing and back into work, to see whether this had been the relationship I had been searching for. Harping back to Richie's 'Black Jack Theory', I may have had 'Black Jack' for some time, but had forgotten to turn my cards over.

The one thing I knew I needed to do before I left for London, was to meet up with my sister. Whilst he was in the hospital with me, Roddy had consistently stressed that I had been in the wrong to react the way I did with Jemma. His opinion was that I had no right to complain about Jemma marrying Richie given that I had effectively ended my relationship with him, the moment I had fled to Amsterdam. I could see his point, but it still seemed odd to me that Jemma would marry the man she claimed that she hated most in the world. I did not, however, want to be perceived by Roddy as petty and narcissistic and felt that if I could show him that I had offered to make peace, he would view me in a better light.

Meeting Jemma for an apologetic chat was not entirely straightforward though as I had no idea where she lived. This puzzle was solved by a friendly male nurse, called Matthew, who worked nights on the ward. Late one night, when I was struggling to sleep, I had recounted to him, parts of my story about my estrangement from Jemma, conveniently forgetting to mention that the moment that triggered my disappearance was when I killed my mother. I told Matthew that I was anxious to see Jemma again, as I had said some unkind things to her, when she had visited intensive care and I had been remorseful since. Matthew was a sucker for a sob story from a pretty girl, so took Jemma's full name and date of birth from me then re-appeared the following night clutching a piece of paper with a printed copy of the electoral roll register for Richard & Jemma Billingham. Two days later, I was released from hospital and just needed to decide whether I was going to visit Jemma to kiss and make up or to scratch her eyes out!

Jemma

It was not a re-union straight out of a Hollywood movie. That morning, I had dropped Melissa off at school, then taken Jamie up to nursery and watched as all the other children scattered like rainwater on a puddle, as he approached. I warned Jamie to 'be nice' which was a bit like warning John Inman to play it straight. Free from children, I drove up to the chemists.

Over the previous few days, I had noticed that I had been passing a bit of blood and on inspection, could feel the offending pile, another battle scar from childbirth, so wanted to nip up to the chemists to buy some cream. I would not consider myself to be overly prudish, but cream for piles ranks up there with tablets for threadworms in the cringe factor stakes. You just feel as though you might as well be wearing a T-shirt that announces,

"My poo is not looking how it should."

As I left the chemists, with a face the same crimson colour as my toilet bowl, Kelly was stood outside, waiting for me. Given I had left Ormskirk hospital, a week earlier, with her insisting that if she never saw me again it would be too soon, this was one hell of a surprise.

"Kelly! What are you doing here?"

"I've come to see you, Jemma."

"At the chemists?"

I have read before about sisters having a sixth sense, but for Kelly to know that I had gone to get cream for my sore bum, seemed too inspired.

"I didn't know you were going to the chemists! I found out where you lived, so was just heading there from the train station and bizarrely, on my way, I saw you get out your car and head into the chemists, are you OK?"

Kelly gestured at the bag I was holding, with the cream inside.

"This? Oh, it's just vitamins for the kids. Need to keep the coughs and colds at bay."

"Right," said Kelly, sounding even with that one word like a childless woman, before adding,

"Jemma, we need to talk. I said things at the hospital that I had no right to say. Can we go somewhere to talk it through? I want to put things right."

"Come back to mine."

"Is it just number thirty one, down that second road on the right?"

"It is, but just get in the car, save your legs."

Kelly hesitated,

"I'd rather walk, Jemma, if you don't mind. I've got a thing about cars at the moment."

Given the car in question was a courtesy car to replace the one that Kelly had nearly lost her life in, I can't say I blamed her.

"OK. See you up there in a few minutes. I'll put the kettle on."

Richie

I was naïve. I thought when you made an appointment to see your GP about having the snip, they just booked you in and that was that, I had no idea that they had a moral duty to emotionally torture you first. Dr.Whiteside eyeballed me like this was 'Who Wants To Be A Millionaire?' and I had just provided a very uncertain answer.

"So, you are absolutely 100% sure about this, Richie? I do not do vasectomies myself, but if I do refer you over to Dr.Allison, in Leyland, I know that he makes a larger cut into the vas deferens than most other Doctors, specifically to ensure the procedure is not reversible. So even in later life, if you decided that you wanted to change your mind, it would be virtually impossible, there would be no turning back."

To me, this seemed like an unnecessary warning. Women are tough, so they may have unwanted pregnancies and subsequently endure a painful labour, but men, on the whole, are weak and have a lower pain threshold, so there is no such thing as an unwanted vasectomy. If a man is prepared to have his privates tampered with, by a Doctor wielding a scalpel, a lot of thought has already gone into the decision making process."

I levelled with Dr.Whiteside.

"Dr.Whiteside, I have two perfectly healthy children, Melissa and Jamie, who are now coming up to six and four. They are fantastic children, but at the same time, they are a handful, more than enough for any parents. Both Jemma and I are one million percent sure that we do not want any more children."

Dr.Whiteside fidgeted. He did not have his customary dickie bow on, if he had, I am sure that would have been twiddled.

"Have you given any thought to how you would feel if your circumstances changed?"

This was a relevant question, I guessed. Dr.Whiteside had probably arranged many vasectomies for men who subsequently divorced and re-married a new wife who was keen to have children with her seedless spouse. In the midst of our marital troubles, this had been relevant to me, but now with our marriage through its difficult stage and on firm ground, I knew we would never allow ourselves to experience those times again.

"Jemma and I have a strong marriage, Dr,Whiteside. I suppose like all couples, we have had our good and bad times, but we will never, ever split up. We know having a vasectomy is the right thing for us to do."

"OK," Dr.Whiteside said, "but what if something tragic happened? You know as well as anybody that life can deliver ill health at any time without warning."

This seemed like a strange line of questioning. We were wanting a vasectomy not IVF treatment.

"Like what?" I asked, confused.

"I think when having a vasectomy, you have to picture the worst case scenario and ask yourself whether, in those circumstances, you would regret the vasectomy?"

"Like if Jemma died?"

"Or one or both of your children," Dr.Whiteside helpfully added, "can you be sure that if anything ever happened to Melissa or Jamie, that you would not want more children?"

I thought this was an outrageous question.

"My children aren't goldfish, Dr.Whiteside. If one of my children tragically died, I would not want Jemma to pop another one out, in the hope that in a few years time, nobody would notice! Irrespective of circumstances, Jemma and I would not want any more children."

Dr. Whiteside looked relieved, like a man who was compelled to ask the questions, but was thankful that the verbal jousting had come to an end.

"I am sorry I had to ask, Richie, but before I refer you to Dr. Allison, I have to be absolutely certain that you are aware of the finality of having a vasectomy."

I gave him an understanding smile.

"I know its your job to ask, but we are certain about this."

"OK, that's fine. My secretary will put the referral in place and Dr. Allison will be in touch. He normally carries out the procedure a couple of evenings a week."

"How long is the waiting list?"

"It varies, it can sometimes be a couple of months, but I believe it's not as long as that currently. I would expect you to receive a date that is in the next four to six weeks. Is that going to be OK?"

"That's fine. The sooner the better as far as we're concerned."

"Obviously, if you do have any second thoughts, then please make sure you cancel the appointment, as soon as possible."

Bloody hell! Change the record!

"Honestly Doctor, that won't be happening! The next nappies that Jemma and I will be changing, will be our grandchildrens!"

Jemma

Throughout the conversation, there was an undercurrent. I had welcomed Kelly into my home, given her a guided tour of my house and even promised she could walk down with me to pick Jamie up from nursery, but I could feel tension in the air. I thought Kelly was trying her level best to be pleasant, but she seemed to be forgetting how well I knew her, forced pleasantries were always going to be apparent to me. After an hour of slogging through our time together with niceties, apologies and tactful reactions, I tired of playing the game.

"Kelly, I appreciate you coming here today, it means a lot to me that you felt the need to put things right, but is this what we are resigned to now?"

"What?"

"Bullshit conversations where neither of us really speaks their mind in case it triggers off World War Three."

"I don't know how to answer that, Jemma."

"Answer it honestly."

"I think this is the best we can hope for. Look at the photos around your house, Jemma, it's not as though this time you just kissed or even screwed my boyfriend…you MARRIED him! I wish I was one of those incredibly nice people, the type that doesn't resent being double crossed, the type that can put their past behind them and move on, but that's not me. I'm not that nice."

"Why aren't you? As a child you were the nicest person anyone could possibly meet, you were placid, calm, cheerful and loving, what has happened to change that?"

"Do you even have to ask, Jemma? Mum died. I killed her. The only person I ever felt truly loved by betrayed me in the most devious of ways. We are a product of circumstance, Jemma and circumstances have changed."

"Your version of events is distorted though, Kelly. Nothing happened between Richie and I when you were together, it all only happened long after you left."

"That's a lie!"

"No, it's not!"

"It was all happening between you and Richie whilst I was still around."

"Kelly, I promise you it wasn't!"

"Jemma, it did!!! Maybe not physically, but emotionally it did. Before I left, Richie told you that he had cancer, he didn't tell me…. and neither did you."

"That was to protect you!"

"To protect me?! I didn't want protecting! I just wanted the truth. When I saw you in the park together, you could have just said,

'Kelly, it's Richie, he's got cancer…..', but you chose not to. You chose to rank people in order of importance to you and I came off second best. You hardly knew Richie and you put him before me, your own sister."

"Kelly, I wish I had told you."

"No, Jemma, don't continue to lie to me. I have been a victim of your lies for too long. You don't wish you'd told me at all. If you had told me that day, that Richie had cancer, we wouldn't be sitting here in your middle class palace, sipping percolated coffee in fine china mugs, looking at photos of the offspring you conceived with my boyfriend. Keeping your mouth shut was part of your long-term strategy, don't insult my intelligence by suggesting anything else.

If you'd have told me that Richie had cancer, Richie would never have been available, I would have helped him through that ordeal and who knows, you may have been visiting Richie and I, and our children."

"Kelly, how much of a bitch do you think I am?! None of this was pre-meditated, it just happened. Not like your visit here today, you said you came here to put things right, but that's not what you planned at all, is it? You came to finish what you started in hospital."

"Jemma, I came to try to get things to a level where we can be civil to each other. Having brought me up, I felt I owed you that much, but let's not kid ourselves, we aren't going to be best mates. That's impossible now."

I thought this through for a few seconds. On this point, there was no real reason to disagree.

"Do you know what, Kelly? I agree with you. To an extent I understand the point you are making and if I put myself in your shoes, I can understand why you are bitter. I mean if I'd have buggered off and you'd been the one who was jailed, then I'd come back to discover you'd married my ex, I'd feel like you do now, well and truly pissed off!

I promise none of this was done to get at you though, believe me we just fell in love, but knowing how you feel about Richie, it's probably best you don't spend too much time around us, it'd only complicate matters."

"Jemma, you're right,. Looking back, I just wished I'd been aware of the whole situation before the crash. I mean when I met him, Richie wasn't even wearing a wedding ring, so I didn't even know he was married, let alone who he was married to."

"I agree, Kelly. Richie should have told you."

"Maybe then we wouldn't have made love."

"I beg your pardon!"

"I'm just saying, if I'd have known he was married to you, Jemma, I wouldn't have let him make love to me on the 'Sunny Road'."

"Don't even try that one, Kelly! I know nothing happened. I know you want to get back at me, but is making up lies really the way forward? Have some respect for yourself!"

Kelly smiled sardonically.

"Is that what Richie said, Jemma? That nothing happened! Bless him! He probably didn't count it as proper sex, I mean it probably only lasted thirty seconds. He was in and out before I could say, 'Dick Billingham'."

I had been a fool. All this was too raw for Kelly to forgive me. I even half think she had come looking for me to try to put things right, but the house and the photos and everything else, just allowed the hatred to bubble up inside. We needed time apart. Time for her to accept who I was married to.

"Get out, Kelly!"

"I'm sorry, Jemma! Sometimes the truth hurts."

"The truth! This is just a pack of lies!"

"He told me his wife didn't let him anywhere near her. He said she'd been up for it all the time before the kids, but now she came out with every excuse under the sun to get out of having sex. There was no intimacy left in their relationship. They were just like brother and sister, is what he said. That was his excuse for coming so quickly. He said he was totally out of practice. I told him not to worry. I told him together we'd put it right, teach him a bit of endurance. Back in the day, when he put his mind to it, your husband couldn't half make me come, he was my first and still the best lover I ever had. That's why I wrote the letter. No-one else compared. At least I got to feel him inside me for one last time!"

I should have kept my cool. I knew she was lying, but Richie had obviously been mouthing off to her about me, that was what made me so mad. Kelly was wanting to get a reaction and that's exactly what she got. I shouldn't have done it, but I slapped her right across the face, a real tennis backhander it was, the full stroke. Kelly was unfazed. She put her hand to her face, to feel where I had caught her, but she just smiled at me again and proceeded with the onslaught.

"Let's just hope I bleed now, Jemma. I'm already a couple of days late. The Doctors warned I might be late, with the trauma of the crash, but who knows, it could be down to the pitter patter of tiny feet. How would that feel, Jemma? Wouldn't it be lovely to have a little brother or sister for Melissa or Jamie, without the agony of childbirth. I mean you're too posh to push now, aren't you?

It's amazing when you think about it, isn't it? Life created from just thirty seconds of unbridled passion between YOUR sister and YOUR husband. It felt better afterwards though, I mean we both really, really needed it."

I was starting to question my faith in Richie, but I was determined not to let it show.

"I don't believe you."

"I tell you what then, when he gets in tonight Jemma, tell him who popped in for coffee. Don't accuse him but just throw in a little line about me mentioning I might be pregnant and watch his face drop. When it does, you'll know exactly who the liar is and I can assure you, it's not me!"

"Get out of my house, Kelly!"

"He'll never love you like he loved me, Jemma. Whatever happens, I'll always be his first."

"Just get out!"

"Thanks for the coffee. I'll pop the scan photos in the post. I'm sure Richie will be dying to see them…..I'll see myself out."

I let her go. I was fuming, not with Kelly as much as Richie. He was in big trouble. I vowed when he got back in that night, I was going to kill him.

Jemma

I was so ready for a blazing row that I had already shipped the kids over to Richie's Mum's in anticipation. I just told Dot that I had a surprise planned for Richie and with her being a diamond and him being 'favourite offspring', she agreed without a moments hesitation. Dot was one of the only people that could handle Jamie. She was very firm with him, but he seemed to respect her for it. Dot was insistent that Richie and I should implement her strong armed methods with Jamie but would not have it that we had tried and failed. She was an interfering busy body but a lovely one at that! She wasn't content with just knowing I had a 'surprise' planned that night either, but when she pressed me, I just told her I wanted to book a taxi and take Richie for a pasta and a bottle of wine. It was a Friday, so Dot said she'd keep the kids and drop them back off on Saturday afternoon.

Most nights Richie was back from the Building Society by about six, but to compound my fury that night, by seven o'clock, there was still no sign of him. I poured myself a glass of white wine and then another and by the time I heard the key in the door, I was on my third large glass. It was almost half past seven. I heard Richie put his briefcase down in the hall.

"Why haven't you phoned to say you'd be late?" I shouted through.

"Sorry love, there was a till discrepancy. A fiver down. Stopped back for ages running through the tills trying to find it, but I couldn't. If you give someone a fiver less than you should, they soon tell you about it, but give them a fiver too much, it just goes in their arse pocket!

It's quiet in here, isn't it? Where are the kids?"

"At your mother's?"

Richie came into the lounge all suited and booted. I was as mad as hell with him, but boy he looked sexy after a few glasses of wine.

"Why are they at my Mum's? We're not supposed to be going out are we?"

"No, I needed to speak to you."

Richie laughed a little falsely to himself.

"Can you not talk when the kids are here?"

"Not properly, no."

Richie failed to appreciate the level of my fury. He walked over to the television and switched it on, grabbing the remote control and putting some 'Sports News' channel on. He's lucky I didn't grab a chair and smash the TV screen into a million tiny pieces, but managing to control myself a little, I just snatched the remote contol off him and switched the TV off.

"Oi! I was about to watch that!"

"Did you not hear me, Richie, I said I needed to speak to you?"

"About what."

"Kelly."

Richie sighed.

"Jemma, it's been a long day and a long bloody week. It's the weekend, the kids aren't here, can we not just make the most of a bit of peace and quiet, just for one night and we'll talk about Kelly tomorrow?"

"No, Richie, we can't. She's been here today."

"Kelly has? To our house? What for?"

"To tell me things."

"Like what?"

"Things I didn't know. Things you never told me!"

"Such as?"

"Such as you taking your wedding ring off when you met up with her!"

"Jemma! This is just a small, insignificant piece of information about that day. Why rake this up again now? Its behind us. What good does it do dredging up tiny fragments of new information?"

The time was right to drop the bombshell.

"Tiny fragments of new information like Kelly's pregnant?"

I watched to see how Richie would react. I had hoped he would smile or laugh hysterically, but he didn't, he reacted just as Kelly predicted he would, the colour in his face drained away and he muttered an obscenity,

"Shit!"

My fury continued to mount. I had forgiven him for meeting up with Kelly, tried to put the incident behind us, but once again he had lied to me. It would impossible to come back from this one, my children and Kelly's child would be siblings. I needed to lash out. I had, what I can only describe as an out of body experience. I looked down on myself for a couple of minutes and saw this crazed, demented, wronged woman. I grabbed Lladro, Nao, pottery, photograph frames, anything I could get my hands on really and threw them, as hard as I could, against the walls. I was crying, screaming and wailing language that would have made a docker blush.

Richie left me to it at first, I wasn't throwing anything at him, I hadn't even thought of doing that, so he just stayed on the settee looking as placid as ever. He allowed all my favourite ornaments to be smashed to smithereens, but as soon as I picked up a surviving piece of Lladro and took aim at the television, he stood up, grabbed me by the wrist and restrained me.

"What do you think you're doing, Jemma?!"

"You cheating, no good, bastard! Get out my house!"

"Jemma, will you calm yourself down, you complete muppet! If Kelly's pregnant its not my baby! Not unless my sperm have been swimming around inside her like a load of bewildered goldfish for about the last twelve years! I have heard of slow swimmers but that's taking the piss!"

"You said you didn't sleep with me at the Birch's party…and you did!"

"For Christ's sake, Jemma, I didn't! I didn't get Kelly pregnant either, OK?"

Richie let go of me with a bit of a pissed off push.

"Why did you say 'shit' then, when I said she was pregnant?"

"Because I crashed a car, didn't I, with her unborn baby inside. If she loses that baby, that's another victim I'll have to deal with, as well as those two teenage kids."

"Promise me you're not lying to me, Richie. Promise me you didn't sleep with Kelly."

"I promise you I didn't. I'll even swear on our children's lives."

I surveyed the damage .

"Why did you not stop me smashing everything up?"

Richie smiled.

"Because I hate all the bloody Lladro!"

"Noticed you saved the tele!"

"I'm not soft!"

"Richie, go and grab a brush and shovel from the kitchen, seeing as though you drove me to it, you can help me tidy up!"

Richie went into the kitchen and then shouted through.

"Where is it?"

"Under the sink."

"OK. You'll have to do the cleaning though, Jemma! I'm still in my school uniform."

Richie always referred to his suit as his school uniform. He thought children never really grew up, they just pretended better. I looked at the mantelpiece where my Lladro had been, I had just proved his point about not growing up, but the pretence was still in need of some work too. Richie came back in and passed me the brush and shovel. He had definitely improved around the house, but it was still not difficult for him to find excuses to pass the workload on to me. In this instance though, he had plenty of justification. I went down on my hands and knees and started brushing.

"Who's baby will it be then, do you think, if it's not yours?"

"Did Kelly tell you it was mine?"

"Yes."

"If anything had happened, could she even know she was pregnant by now, if I'd have slept with her before the crash?"

"Possibly, if she was late for her period now, she'd have a good idea."

"There won't be a baby though, Jemma, she'll have just said it as a way of getting back at you for marrying me. I suppose for us, because we've been married for a fair while, it's old news that we're together, but for Kelly, it's still raw. I don't approve of what she's doing but I can understand it."

"True, I hadn't thought of it like that. Do you think in time she'll move on? She's Melissa and Jamie's only blood relative on my side of the family, other than me. I was going to take her with me today, to pick Jamie up from nursery but then she kicked off so I sent her packing."

Richie got down on his hands and knees and started helping me with the broken pieces.

"Not like you Watkinson girls to kick off!"

"Yeh right! I suppose at least there's an element of subtlety about Kelly's kick offs whilst I just go ape! Richie, I'm really sorry I thought you were capable of sleeping with her."

Richie took my hand.

"Jemma, I should never have betrayed your trust by turning up to meet her. I always knew I was in the wrong, I just didn't want to admit it to you."

I squeezed Richie's hand back.

"Richie, I'm glad you went. Its helped us sort our relationship back out. We needed a crisis, I don't think we'd have undone the knots without one. Fancy coming to bed?"

"It's not even eight o'clock! What about the mess?"

"You can wear a condom!"

"Very funny! This mess."

"Come back down in five minutes and clear it up!"

"You're on form tonight, Jemma! Ten minutes! I'm getting better!"

"Come on then, we can even make a bit of noise with the kids not being here!"

"Go easy on the noise or I'll be back down in two minutes!"

"OK. Make sure you put your party clothes on as soon as you're ready to go and put it on properly, not inside out or back to front."

"I'm not sixteen!"

"I'm not saying you are, I'm just saying its an art form you haven't mastered."

"That reminds me, I went to the Doctor's last night."

"For your check up?"

"No, although I need to sort that out soon. I went to book a vasectomy."

"You're kidding me!"

"No, I decided to take the bull by the horns or to take the horn from the balls!"

Sometimes, if you spend a couple of years chipping away, the walls do come down! I was delighted. I knew I did not want any more children and I knew there would be no pangs of regret, no broodiness, my childbearing days were over. Pregancy was my second biggest fear behind death.

"You brave thing, Mr Billingham! About bloody time!"

"I needed to pluck up the courage!"

"Well come upstairs and I will make sure that your bravery is suitably rewarded!"

Richie

I sat on the toilet, with my trousers and my boxer shorts pulled down to my knees, with my thumb and my forefinger of my left hand, placing and maintaining my penis on my left thigh.I just looked at my scrotum in despair. I cupped my right hand underneath and I shuddered when I felt it. How could I have missed it? HOW COULD I, OF ALL PEOPLE, HAVE MISSED IT? I felt so stupid. I used to be so obsessive about checking. I used to drive myself mad wondering if it all felt the same today as yesterday. Why did I stop doing that? This could cost me my life, not only that it could cost my wife a husband and my children a father, just because I had been lazy about checking. Knobhead! I've already been given a second chance by fate and a third chance as I survived a fatal car crash. Why did I keep expecting fate to save me from my own neglect?

I was shaking. I didn't want Jemma to see me like this. Things had settled. We needed some tranquillity in our lives. We did not need another rollercoaster ride. It was always rollercoaster rides with us. Someone else should not have been pointing this lump out to me. I should have been spotting this. For fuck's sake, this was my job to check. A two minute job. No-one was asking me to climb Everest. A simple bathroom routine, that's all it needed to be and I had failed to see it through. Idiot.

What should I do now? Should I tell Jemma? Last time, I had not told Kelly, but had that been the right thing to do? Did I regret that? Probably not, but this time it was different, Jemma hasn't recently killed anyone. I was going to have to tell her. What will she think? She'll think I am a fool. I am a fool. It's like crossing the road witout looking, you just don't do it. What an idiot!

What if this time I'm not as lucky? What if I die? What will I go through before I die and what will I go through after? Nothingness. What is nothingness? Is it possible to have nothingness? Is there any existence without a brain and without your senses and without a heart and lungs? I had always thought not, but could there be any way you could be aware that you were trapped inside infinite nothingness? Could there be a God? Should I have heeded his warnings? I was scaring myself now. What was life like before I was born? I'm really not ready to die. Nowhere near ready. Don't let this happen to me, let me cling on. My children are still babies.

I told myself off, 'Stop doing this to yourself'. It might be curable, I knew from last time, that in most cases it was. This could just be a wake up call. A warning sign. Another lucky escape. It didn't feel like it though. If you play Russian Roulette for long enough, you eventually find the bullet.

Until now, why had I always felt so immortal? I looked at it again. It was still there. Could it not just go away?

Roddy

Perfection only exists as an image when seen through rose tinted spectacles. I saw just as much of Kelly before her crash as I did after, but the defects that had probably always been there, became more apparent after the crash, once I had made the transition from friend to 'boyfriend'. I didn't find Kelly's defects abhorrent, in fact it was quite the opposite, I found them strangely re-assuring. In a relationship, you want to be on an even keel, not looking up at someone on their pedestal.

The Richie thing had always been an issue for me. To an extent, I knew I was the understudy, taking the place of the guy who had been designated the role, but had chosen not to take it up, so I was hoping Kelly would resolve her issues with Jemma quickly, but without any desire on either sisters part, for regular contact. At that stage, I still felt I was punching above my weight and when you feel that way, you don't want a prize fighter circling the ring.

Several days after Kelly's crash, I had no more holidays to take, so had come back down to London to return to work at Dillons, whilst Kelly continued her recuperation in hospital. I did not feel comfortable leaving her up there on her own. Our relationship had crossed over from platonic to mildly physical, in that we had kissed, but I did not have enough faith in myself or our blossoming relationship, to think that it would continue to flourish from a couple of hundred miles apart. I was wrong. We have Alexander Graham Bell to thank. We spoke to each other every evening without fail and after seven long days, Kelly told me excitedly one evening that, all being well, she would be discharged the following day and would be making her way home to Ealing.

The following evening, about half past six, my phone rang. I knew it was Kelly. I was ready to pick it up after the first ring, but let it ring a further half a dozen times, as I didn't want to appear overly anxious. Once I picked up, the emotion in Kelly's faltering voice automatically made me assume that our relationship had somehow managed to crash in those dangerous sixty one seconds after take off.

"Hello."
"Roddy, it's Kelly, I'm home."
"Great. Everything OK?"
A pregnant pause. I asked again.

"Kelly, what's the matter? Is everything alright?"
Another pause.
"Kelly?"
"No, Roddy, everything isn't alright. I've done something stupid."
"How stupid are we talking?"
"Very."
"What was it?"
"I don't want to tell you over the phone, Roddy."
That did not sound good.
"Do you want me to come around?"
"Yes…don't hate me, Roddy, you're all I have left."

I wanted to tell Kelly that I couldn't possibly hate her, that I had loved her since I had first clapped eyes on her and I would continue to love her until my spirit died, but masculine pride stood in my way.

"Depends what you've done, Kelly!"

Richie

"We're home!"

Jemma and Melissa came through the door not looking like they had had their best ever trip to the cinema. They looked emotionally drained. Jemma had wanted to accompany me to the surgery for the vasectomy, but some things a man has to do alone, so she had left Jamie with my Mum and Dad and taken Melissa to see a special showing of the 'Titanic' movie.

"Was the film good, Melissa?"

"It was very sad!"

I was sat on the settee and Jemma came over and gave me a sympathetic peck.

"It was actually a bit too sad," Jemma explained, "we weren't expecting that, were we honey? Both Mummy and Melissa did a lot of crying, but I have been trying to explain to Melissa on the way home, that the boy in the film was only pretending. He has not really died."

"They just had to pretend he has gone to heaven, but he hasn't really." Jemma added.

"Good," I said, "I'm pleased about that."

"Melissa, how's about you go and get your pyjamas on, sweetheart." Jemma said.

"Can you come up with me, Daddy?"

"No," Jemma said, "Daddy is feeling a little bit sore after his operation, so we need to be nice to Daddy. It would help Daddy, if you were a very kind little girl and went upstairs on your own and put your pyjamas on."

Melissa was a crowd pleaser.

"OK," she said before running up the stairs.

Jemma waited for Melissa to disappear before she began questioning.

"How was it, babe? Are you really sore?" she enquired in a tone fit for a three year old or a man who has just had a scalpel to his scrotum.

"Not good."

"Agony?"

"Jemma, I couldn't have the vasectomy."

Jemma's tone went from overly sympathetic to overly pissed off.

"What do you mean you couldn't do it, Richie?"

"There was a complication, Jemma, I couldn't go through with it."

"You mean you bottled it! I had a feeling you might! When I dropped Jamie off at your mother's, I told her I had a feeling you wouldn't be able to go through with it. I knew you'd get squeamish about it and then wriggle out of it. You men are just pathetic! You're bloody lucky we're the ones who have to give birth! We can't just call a stop to it when our bits are about to go through pain. We just have to tough it out. Have you re-arranged it?"

"No, it's not as simple as that."

"I bet it isn't! They're probably busy dealing with real men who have the guts to go through with it. They probably don't want to book you in again in case you do the same thing again. Honestly Richie, you are a big girl's blouse!"

"Jemma, it wasn't me that cancelled the vasectomy. If I could have done, I would have had it done. I'm not saying I'm brave, but I'm a little bit braver than you give me credit for."

"Was someone sick?"

"I don't know. Possibly."

"Richie, stop being so mysterious and just tell me what's happened!"

"They found a lump, Jemma."

"A lump?"

"A lump on my right testicle. My only testicle."

"How could they find a lump? You check."

"Jemma, with everything that's been going on in our lives recently, with the kids being born and the crazy sleeping hours, then the things that have gone on between you and I, I just haven't checked. I haven't even thought about checking."

"But you have already had testicular cancer, Richie! Surely you, of all people, should be checking!"

"I know that, but I haven't checked."

"What do they think it is?"

"They're not sure. I need to go for checks. It could just be a cyst."

"Let's hope so. Bloody hell, Richie! I can't believe you didn't think to check!"

"Jemma, I have spent years checking but then after a while, when everything is OK, you forget what you went through, you just don't check as much, then you don't check at all. You having a go at me isn't going to make me feel any more stupid than I already do."

"God, Richie, I hope you're alright."

"So do I. Last time I went through it, it was cancerous, but it all turned out OK, even if the news isn't good, there's been so much progression medically over the last ten years, I am sure I'll be fine. I just want to know what I'm dealing with."

I was doing my best to persuade us both that this was only a minor problem, but I failed miserably on both counts. A fulminologist will tell you whether or not lightning strikes the same place twice, but I knew myself cancer could. It had gatecrashed my body before and I had no doubt it was back. I had a bad feeling about this, a feeling that it would not be as simple this time around. I knew I had to be tougher though. I was a teenager last time around, this time I was a married man with children. I would not be collapsing in floods of tears, I would be strong and whatever it threw at me, I would defeat it. If cancer was looking for a fight, it had picked on the wrong man.

Roddy

Thirty minutes later, I was knocking on Kelly's door, having persuaded myself that I'd now have to listen to some story about her sleeping with some handsome young Doctor or even worse, with Richie. Nothing disastrous would have surprised me. I was mentally prepared.

Kelly opened the door wearing her dressing gown. It was a white, silk thing with red hearts plastered all over it. It looked like something a boyfriend would have bought her at Christmas. I immediately imagined her flashing at me like a dirty old man, opening up each side of the dressing gown and pulling them wide apart like wings, exposing her naked breasts and pubic hair, before sexily urging,

'Feast your eyes on this, big boy!'

That didn't happen! Kelly's eyes were red and her nose was damp and running, even after the crash, I had never seen her look so vulnerable.

"Hi Roddy! Come in, can I get you a tea or a coffee?" she asked.

"Go on then Kelly, I'll have a nice cup of tea. Put the kettle on and you can start telling me what all this is about. Two sugars please."

Kelly had converted me to tea. I was more of a coffee drinker before. I think it's Northern tradition that you can't retire for the day until you have had your quota of ten cups. It's an unwritten law once you are North of Birmingham!

Kelly looked at me with those big, sorrowful green eyes.

"Roddy, I'm scared to tell you. I know I need to, but I'm scared. I need to tell you because I need you to carry on being the friend you've always been, the person who I can tell anything."

I noted the use of 'friend'. This did not sound good. This sounded very much like Kelly was teeing up a return to us being 'just good friends'. I put a brave face on it.

"Kelly, you told me years ago what happened to your mother and I will not mention that to a living soul until my dying day. If you can tell me that, you can tell me anything, despite what I said on the phone, whatever you tell me, we will still be friends."

Seeing Kelly in the flesh made it so much more difficult to play the tough guy.

"It's different telling you things now though, Roddy. Everything's changed."

Seemingly Kelly wanted to wait until the tea had been brewed and poured before she broke the news. I'm not sure what her logic was with this, maybe she thought that a sugary drink would lessen the shock, maybe she just liked the drama, I don't know, all I do know is that I had to suffer five minutes of bookstore chit-chat before we finally moved out of Kelly's kitchen with two mugs of tea and a plate of biscuits in tow and sat down on the sofa. The teapot was abandoned in the kitchen with a knitted purple tea cosy wrapped around it to keep the cold out. At long last, it was time for Kelly to open up,

"I went to Jemma's this morning…."

Murder sprang to mind. If Kelly had killed a second member of her family, I think even my love for her would have been tested.

"….I know you wanted me to. I know you thought it was important to do that, to put things right with Jemma. That's why I went, Roddy, honestly it was, but just seeing her again brought all those angry feelings back."

"Why?"

"It'll just sound stupid to you, Roddy."

"Try me."

"When I met Richie, the other day, almost straight away, I knew he wasn't the man that I wanted to spend the rest of my life with. Time changes people and we had both moved on from where we had been as teenagers. Having said that, I didn't want him to be married to my sister!"

"That doesn't sound stupid, Kelly! No-one in your shoes would want that to happen, but it has happened. It's how you deal with it that matters."

"I knew you'd say that, Roddy, but that's easy for you to say as an outsider. Back when I was in love with Richie, properly in love, when we were teenagers, he didn't tell me he had cancer but he told Jemma. It feels like she hatched a plot to steal him off me and when I went round to her house, it just felt like she was evidencing how her plot had worked. I was bombarded with photos of Jemma, Richie and their kids. When you've spent years abroad, dodging the authorities ater commiting a crime to save her skin, you don't want to return to England to discover the sister you helped has married the boyfriend you left behind."

'Change the record, Kelly!' I thought. Maybe she was going over and over this to illustrate why she had killed her sister!

"What did you do, Kelly? Obviously it was something and that's why you are so upset, but what was it you did?"

"I struck back, Roddy. I needed to get some sort of revenge. I needed Jemma to feel the way I feel, hurt and double crossed….."

I had a good idea what was coming.

"….so I told her I'd slept with Richie, that afternoon on the 'Sunny Road'."

I knew that's what Kelly was going to say. The problem I had though, given the dramatics, was that I did not know how Kelly was going to answer my next question,

"And did you?"

It was a question I had to ask. The answer meant everything to me. There was no real reason for me to place so much importance on it, but in those few seconds, I felt my destiny was dependent on her reply. The short answer meant we had a future, the three letter one meant we were over before we had begun. Kelly's emotional baggage would be too heavy for me to carry, if she'd slept with Richie before the crash. I knew if that was the case, if I tried to lift it, the weight would break my back.

Richie

Jemma was sound asleep. I watched her for a while, her face was buried deep into her pillow and her legs were tucked into her chest. She looked untroubled. I was jealous of her tranquillity as I could not sleep. I was troubled. That afternoon, we had been to Clatterbridge hospital for our first appointment with a new consultant urologist, Mr.Mollon. As a teenager, I thought my consultant looked ancient, this time though, he looked so young that his facial hair seemed to have been drawn on with eyeliner. Jemma said he must have been thirty, but if he was, he had moisturised twice daily since nursery. He was a small man, a little smaller than Jemma, with curly brown hair and smokers or poorly brushed teeth. His mannerisms were those of a man who had traded his nicotine patch for a gram of speed, he was twitchy and excessively upbeat, which I found a little irritating!

Mr.Mollon was incredibly positive about my prognosis, but the bare facts were that he was the bearer of bad news. A series of tests had revealed that I did, as suspected, have testicular cancer, but alarmingly I also had secondary cancer in my lungs. My internal bells continued to ring as Mr.Mollon went on to tell us that as far as testicular cancer goes, it is banded into three stages and I had Stage Three, the most progressive. This time around I would not be escaping chemotherapy. The reason for Mr.Mollon's optimism despite my harrowing news, was that statistics were on my side. 85% of testicular cancer sufferers, who needed chemotherapy, went on to overcome their cancer, so the scales of death and recovery were tilted in my favour. I remember Mr.Whiteside, my GP, had previously said though, that only one in twenty five testicular lumps turned out to be cancer and mine turned out to be that one in twenty five. I was not going to take anything for granted, but I could not have been more determined to avoid being in the 15% that lost their battle. I owed it to Jemma, Melissa and Jamie to remain positive at all times.

Due to the progression of my cancer, Mr.Mollon explained that it would be necessary for me to complete three or four cycles of chemotherapy. He explained, to my great relief, that I would not have to be admitted to hospital, but I could have my chemotherapy as an outpatient. This would involve three days of being drip fed a cocktail of drugs called BEP (Bleomycin, Etoposide and Cisplatin- with the "P" being the platinum from 'cisplatin').

After three days of chemotherapy, there would be some respite, but on Day 9, I would need to go back to hospital for further drugs and then back again a week later, Day 16, for even more. My body was then allowed another week off without being pumped full of anything, but after that week's rest, the cycle would start again. Mr.Mollon expected the whole course of chemotherapy to take between two and three months.

As well as the treatment, we also discussed the side effects, but to me it was an overdose of information, so I was grateful when Mr.Mollon handed me a leaflet on chemotherapy and its side effects. As Jemma lay there sleeping peacefully, I was flicking through that leaflet anxiously, which explained how my body may react to being pumped full of drugs. Risks of infection, reduced production of platelets (which help blood to clot and stop bleeding), anaemia (low blood cell count) potentially leading to tiredness and breathlessness, nausea, vomiting, hair loss, hearing problems and diarrohea, to name but a few. Ironically, I did remember Mr.Mollon saying that the chemotherapy may harm our chances of having any further children! I couldn't complain too much about the vasectomy trip though, as I was not put through the pain of a vasectomy and more importantly, that trip to the Doctor's may well have saved my life.

That evening, I had made the dreaded phone calls to friends and family. It's amazing how guilty I felt about my cancer returning. I felt as though I had let everybody down. When I reflected on those feelings, I think it was because all our loved ones have to go through the emotional turmoil that comes with serious illness, all because I failed to keep checking myself. I had the same pitch in my mind for everyone I spoke to, Mum and Dad, Jim, Helen, Caroline, old school friends, work colleagues – they all received the same initial patter. A few pleasantries, ask how they are, then I hit them with,

"Now listen, I do not want you to panic, but I thought that I needed to tell you that my cancer's back….."

Once again, Mum, Helen and Caroline all cried. Mum did her usual and asked a thousand further questions, but she was wonderfully supportive. Dad, a changed man since my last bout of cancer and a change for the better too, offered to pray for me and said he would encourage the Vicar to ask the congregation to pray for me too. It would be wrong to feel anything but grateful towards those kindhearted people, but I wondered whether the 15% who didn't make it, lost their lives because of a lack of prayers? Whether they did or they didn't, in my eyes God did not come out of it looking good! Reminds me of the footballers who cross themselves as they take to the field of play, to thank God for making them millionaires. The same sportsmen tend to overlook the fact that the same God might have just allowed millions of their fellow countrymen to live in poverty or thousands to be killed by natural disasters like floods, earthquakes and tsunamis. Religion has been diluted through the centuries into something synthetic, but whether there was any truth left from the carcass the powerful had fed on, I would find out whenever fate (or God) decreed. If Dad is right and I'm wrong and there is a God, Dad will be thoroughly miserable for eternity as all his friends and family are non-believers so they won't make it in!

As well as breaking my bad news to our friends and family, Jemma and I also had to decide how to deal with breaking the news to our children. We discussed our need to maintain a normality for Melissa and Jamie and to leave it as late as possible before letting them know that I'm not well. I would only tell them once it reached a stage that I could not keep it from them any longer. This may have meant telling Melissa before Jamie, but we decided to just let events develop and take stock of the state of play at regular intervals.

Jemma also felt uncomfortable about mentioning the "C" words, cancer and chemotherapy. She said each time either word was mentioned, it sent a shiver down her spine and we discussed alternatives we could use. Jemma suggested we make an acronym from the letters 'BEP', the drugs we hoped would save my life and use that instead of constantly referring to 'cancer' and 'chemo'. The best she could come up with was 'Black Eyed Peas', but when I spoke to Jim on the phone, the conversation led on to an alternative acronym as he thought 'Black Eyed Peas' was a stupid acronym as I had no interest in the band or their music and I should find something more relevant to me. When prompted for a suggestion, Jim came up with 'Boring Evertonian Prick!!' .Admittedly, it made me crease up with laughter, but if I was looking for an inspirational acronym, that certainly wasn't it either! I eventually came up with, "Beating Every Problem", which I thought was relevant and motivational, as it was exactly what I intended on doing.

That night was the beginning of erratic sleep problems that would hound me throughout my treatment. Each night, Jemma slept soundly. I once said to her, only half joking, that this was because she wasn't as worried as me, but she saw it as a reflection that she had exhausted herself from worrying during every waking second. She probably had a point.

I started 'Beating Every Problem' at Clatterbridge Hospital the following Monday, Tuesday and Wednesday. A new battle for survival had begun.

Roddy

Kelly looked at me aghast.

"Of course I didn't sleep with him! I told you there was no attraction! Why would I sleep with Richie if there was no longer any attraction?"

"You managed to persuade Jemma that you did!"

"I don't know whether I did persuade her. I just wanted to place a seed of doubt in her brain that maybe her perfect marriage was not quite so perfect, so I told her that I'd slept with Richie and a result of this, I was now pregnant."

I have to admit this vindictive side of Kelly was not a side I liked at all. I would not have wanted her to be the type of girl who was so weak that she did not have the backbone to fight her corner, but there's a big difference between fighting your corner and punching your opponent in the face even before the bell has rung.

"Kelly, who do you think you are destroying here?"

"What do you mean?"

"Well, who are you destroying and who are you benefiting by saying that you are pregnant?"

"I don't understand what you mean, Roddy!"

"Look Kelly, it's simple. You're trying to get back at Jemma for marrying your ex-boyfriend, but no-one is getting anything positive out of this at all. You're not feeling good about yourself, look at the state it's left you in and if Jemma does believe you, that Richie has fathered your child, it may not only destroy their marriage, but it could destroy the lives of their two children. Do you want that on your conscience?"

Kelly sniffed.

"No."

"So what are you going to do about it?"

"I'm not apologising to her, Roddy. If I do she's totally defeated me!"

"Kelly! Jemma hasn't tried to defeat you! She may have fallen in love with someone she wasn't supposed to, but that doesn't make her a bad person. You need to get over yourself and move on! There are only losers in this game you're playing, Kelly."

"I know. I'm an idiot. I don't even know what you see in me, Roddy!"

I moved over and gave Kelly a comforting cuddle.

"Kelly, you're a mixed up woman but I've always been able to see through that. I love the bones of you. Always have. Always will."

"And you think I should apologise to Jemma?"

"Ring her and apologise for saying you were pregnant. You must admit, Kelly, that was a pretty low stunt! Don't try to patch up all your differences though, you can't put everything right in one go. Just make a start."

"OK. I'll do that, I'll give her a ring."

"When?"

"Tomorrow."

"Why not now?"

"Because you're here! I want a bit of privacy."

"You will do it though, tomorrow, no backing out?"

"No, I promise I'll ring!"

"It'll make you feel better about yourself."

"I know. It's hard though, Roddy. I used to idolise Jemma. She was my big sister and she cared for me more than anyone else. It's just been a shock discovering she has her flaws like the rest of us."

"Speak for yourself, Kelly! Have you not realised yet that I'm perfect?"

Kelly puckered up and kissed me on the lips.

"Perfect for me, Roddy! I'm starting to realise that you're perfect for me!"

Mavis

Richie Billingham was a great boss. In fact, let me re-phrase that, Richie Billingham was the greatest boss I ever had in thirty five years in the Building Society industry and I had loads!

When he was given the role of Manager in Wigan, Richie must only have been in his late twenties. Staff always feel apprehensive when a new boss starts, but even on his first day at work, the five of us were immediately enamoured by his cheery disposition, his big booming smile and his energy and enthusiasm for the role. Richie also made us feel for the first time in a very long time, like we were a team, a team who were all dependent on each other. Our branch became a tremendous success, North West 'Branch of the Year' three times in five years and National 'Branch of the Year' once. Richie managed several agencies too and their figures went through the roof as well. If Regional or National Managers came to the branch, any plaudits handed out to Richie were immediately accredited to the team. No targets felt unachieveable with Richie at the helm, we all went home each night looking forward to the next day and whilst Richie was boss, the staff turnover was zero.

Richie's last day will be one of those days that will stay with me forever. Up until that day, we were all oblivious to the illness. We later discovered that there were people in Human Resources that knew and Howard Robinson, our Regional Manager was also aware, but us girls in the office knew nothing. We wrongly thought everything was as good as ever. Richie kept the charade going until his final afternoon, then in his own inimitable way, unleashed hell!

Mid afternoon on that final day, I remember making teas and coffees, handing all the girls drinks out and then taking Richie's coffee into his office. Richie always volunteered to do his turn at making the drinks, but they were vile, like dishwater, so eventually we took him off the rota. It would not surprise me in the slightest if this was a carefully executed plan! Anyway, that afternoon, I went into his office, carrying his coffee and placed it down on the mat on his desk. Richie was on the phone, but he gestured for me to sit down, so I took a sat on the other side of the desk, facing him. Bearing in mind, up until this point he had been the consummate professional every step of the way, I was astounded by what I heard.

"Hello. Could I speak to Mrs.Alridge please? It is Mrs.Aldridge. It's Richie Billingham from Red Rose Building Society here, are you OK to speak for a couple of minutes? You are. Good!"

Nothing unusual so far, just a stereotypical conversation I would hear Richie having, day in, day out.

"Mrs.Aldridge, you have been a regular customer of ours over the last five years. You have your ISA with us, you have your savings account with us, until you paid it off, you had your mortgage with us and I just wanted to say that in my fifteen years in the Building Society industry, you rank amongst the most unpleasant customers I have ever had the misfortune to have to deal with…."

I could not believe my ears!

"No, no, Mrs.Aldridge, you did hear me correctly. I did say UNpleasant. Do you ever smile Mrs.Aldridge, because I have often seen you pulling a face like someone's anal sphincter is vibrating right next to you, but even on a sunny day in summer, I have never witnessed the merest hint of a smile from you. You moan about your pension, you moan about the heat, the cold, the rain, the sun, the snow, the frost, the waiting times, the interest rates and the cost of everything. You never say please or thank you, I just wanted to phone you to say you are a rude, unlikeable character, Mrs. Aldridge and….you've never been so insulted….well maybe that's because people in this country witter on behind people's backs rather than say things to their face….you will have been insulted just as badly, Mrs.Aldridge, you just didn't get to hear about it. Goodbye!"

Richie grabbed a pen and crossed out some writing on a piece of paper.

"Richie, what are you doing?"

"It's my lottery hit list, Mavis. I always said that if I won the lottery, I would ring everyone on this list and tell them exactly what I really thought of them!"

I felt a temporary buzz of excitement.

"Richie, are you telling me that you have won the lottery??!! How much have you won?! Don't tell me it's millions!"

I felt if anyone I knew won the lottery, it would be Richie. Everything he touched seemed to turn to gold. His work record was impeccable, his wife was drop dead gorgeous, his children were stunning, they all had personalities to match, it would just be typical if he won the lottery too. Or so I thought.

"Mavis, I haven't won the lottery! If I had, I'd have walked out of here and never come back and between you and I, that's what I'll be doing at the end of today."

Now, I was worried.

"Why, Richie? What's the matter?"

Richie looked at me solemnly.

"I've got cancer, Mavis. I'll sit all the girls down before I go home and I'll talk it through with them, but before I do, I've got twenty three more customers, one former boss and an ex-boyfriend of Jemma's to phone, to let them all know what I think of them! I've already phoned fifteen in the last hour and you know what Mavis, it's been the best working hour of my life! Very therapeutic! I figured that over the next few months, I'd be telling my nearest and dearest how much they mean to me, but before I did, I wanted to rid my body of any hatred I might be bottling up!"

"Are you dying, Richie?"

I thought he must be. How could he be leaving forever if he wasn't dying?

"I hope not, Mavis! I've got to start chemotherapy next week, but if I get over this, I want a totally fresh start, I've loved working with you and the rest of the girls, but I just don't enjoy the job itself any more. Life is short, Mavis and if I'm not enjoying what I'm doing, it's time to make a change."

"What will you do?"

"I'm not sure, I might go back to college and re-train. I'm going to beat the cancer into submission first and then have a really good think about it after that."

"The girls will all be devastated."

"That I'm ill or that I'm leaving?"

"Both. We've never had a boss like you, Richie. All the others have been out to boost their own careers and haven't given a damn about impressing those graded below them, all they have cared about is impressing the people above. You value us, Richie and that's been really important to all of us."

"Thanks Mavis! I'll knock you off my lottery list!"

Richie pretended to scrub me off his list! He then picked up his phoned and dialled,

"Hello, could I speak to Ray Walker please? My name? It's Mr.Billingham from Red Rose Building Society…No, he won't know what its regarding….tell him I'm running a course on bigotry and would like to know if he wants to attend. He's been recommended!"

Whilst he waited for Ray Walker to come to the phone, he took a sip of his coffee. I stood up, ready to get back to my work. Richie covered the mouthpiece.

"Mavis, please don't mention this to the girls yet. I will speak to them all after we close and let everyone know exactly what is going on."

I nodded, then as he was connected to Ray Walker, I slipped out leaving Richie to it.

At ten past five that evening, Richie called us all into his office, asked us all to take a seat and broke the news to the five of us that he had had testicular cancer as a teenager, had a testicle removed and recently it had returned in the other testicle but had spread this time and he now had secondary lung cancer. He said he had spoken to Human Resources and would now officially be taking a break but unofficially, he would not be coming back. It was testament to Richie that the only dry eyes in the office belonged to him. As the Branch Supervisor, I felt it was right for me to take the lead, so I stood up, walked over to Richie and hugged him tightly, not saying anything just holding on. It felt to me like my son had cancer. The other four ladies followed suit, hugging Richie and kissing him tenderly on the cheek. Once we had all managed to regain our composure, I made a brief speech on behalf of the girls, thanking him for everything he had done to make our office the best place in the world to work and wishing him well in his fight against cancer.

At six o'clock, Richie locked up, handed me his keys and walked away. We all visited him at home, at a party held in his honour and at hospital during his illness, but it was heartbreaking watching the old Richie fade away. He never returned to the office, but still every time I'm there, I feel his presence. He left us all with a million happy memories and all the people that made it on to his lottery list need to have a good look in the mirror, because if you were hated by Richie Billingham, one of the loveliest men that ever lived, you should be thoroughly ashamed of yourself.

Melissa

My Daddy is sick. He has lost his hair. Mummy said Daddy was losing his hair anyway, before he was sick, so it didn't really matter. Daddy is still happy sometimes but he is too tired for work, so stays at home.He lays on the settee a lot and watches television which is good because I can give him a kiss as soon as I get back from school. Mummy says Jamie does not understand that Daddy is sick, so he is still being naughty. He runs around the house a lot and still shouts lots too and cries when Mummy or Granny Dot says its time for bed. I go to bed when Mummy or Daddy or Granny Dot tell me. Mummy says I am a very good girl. Daddy says Jamie is a little bit naughty. He is not, he is very naughty.

Daddy has to go to the hospital sometimes now for his special injections. When he comes back from the hospital, Mummy says he is not our normal Daddy as he feels very tired and very sick and very grumpy. Mummy says when Daddy has been to the hospital, the best way we can help Daddy, is by playing nicely away from him. Sometimes Jamie does not listen to what Mummy says and jumps on Daddy when he is in bed. This makes Mummy and Daddy cross. Mummy slapped Jamie's legs once, very hard, after Jamie did this, but afterwards she said she was very sorry and she should not have done it.

On some days, Daddy does not lie down. He walks around like normal Daddys and plays with us and tells us he loves us. Mummy says Daddy tells us he loves us so much, so we never forget how lucky we are to have a Daddy like him. Daddy should just say it to Jamie, as I think Jamie would forget, as he always forgets where he has hidden my dolls.

Sometimes Mummy cries when Daddy is in bed. She says she is just being silly, but I heard Mummy tell Granny Dot that she is scared. I think Daddy might look scary in bed with no hair.

One day soon, I hope Daddy is better and not sick any more, then he might not be tired and his hair on his head might grow again. If it grows, Mummy might not be sad any more either. When Daddy gets better, I want to take my Daddy to watch Everton. I do not like football, it is boring, but Daddy likes football and if Everton won he would be very happy. I just want Mummy and Daddy to be happy all the time.

Jemma

It was early evening in Autumn. The clocks had just gone back and it was a damp, drizzly night. Dead brown leaves were swirling around our path and reminding us winter was on its way. October is the worst month of the year because it progressively reveals more of the six months of misery ahead. This time though, we had more than the winter to worry us.

Richie and I walked into the house in silence. Richie's Mum and Dad, Charlie and Dot, were sat on the edge of the settee in the lounge and as we walked through, they looked up at us expectantly.

"The kids are asleep," Dot said in a tone that re-assured and also permitted us to disclose our news, "what did the consultant say?"

I wasn't ready to get into the whole saga the second we walked through the door, so I looked for a distraction.

"Let me make a cup of tea, Dot and then we'll have a chat about it. Do you both want one?"

"Yes please love!" said Dot answering for both her and Charlie, "make a pot though, love, it never quite tastes the same when you make it in the cup."

"Richie?"

"Yes, please."

I suppose I was being too optimistic to hope a pot of tea would be enough to stem the flow of Dot's questioning. She was not prepared to wait.

"Is it good news though?!"

Dot asked this in such a desperate tone, that I felt so sorry for both her and Richie, when he answered,

"No, Mum, it is not good news."

As Dot digested this information, I made my way out to the kitchen, turned the kettle on and popped three teabags into the pot. Whilst the kettle was boiling, I nipped back into the lounge. We had two, two seater settees in the lounge, Charlie and Dot were on one and Richie had parked his bum on the other. I sat down next to him, ready to deal with the diagnosis.

"What did he tell you, love?" Dot asked.

I turned to Richie, he looked pale, I think this was more as a result of shock than as a result of the cancer taking hold.

"It's spread Mum, they can't treat it to get rid of it now, they can only treat it to slow its progression."

"Are you telling me its terminal?"

"I wish I wasn't Mum, but I am. Jemma and I were referring to the 'BEP' as "Beating Every Problem", but it turns out, "Ball Exceptionally Poorly" would have reflected things better.

Dot closed her eyes and rubbed her face with an intensity that made it look like she was going to take the skin off.

"Oh no, son! Oh no!"

If this routine was meant to stop the tears from flowing it failed. Charlie put his arm around her and with his other arm reached into Dot's handbag and took out some tissues. He passed them to her and she snorted noisily. With Dot in no fit state to speak, Charlie took up the parental questioning baton.

"Did they give you any indication how long they think they can keep it at bay, Richie?"

"Six to twelve months, Dad."

Richie's response led to Dot sobbing more heartily. I allowed her this outpouring of emotion this time, but knew if it continued, I would have to have strong words. Going forward, for Richie's sake, she would need to be stronger than this.

"We're hoping, Charlie, that Richie may be able to trial new drugs or treatments that may buy him some more time," I said, letting him know that we weren't abandoning all hope, "we aren't giving this one up as a lost cause, are we Richie?"

"No. This is my life, it isn't like chasing after a bus. If I miss this chance, there isn't going to be another opportunity five minutes later. This is my only chance. We'll keep fighting until the bitter end."

I squeezed Richie's hand.

"I'll go and make the tea."

As I stood up and went to the kitchen, Dot moved settees to give her son a hug. A tiny part of me was jealous of Richie as he had a proper, compassionate family. If Vomit Breath had lived and I had developed cancer, she would have just sneered and muttered something about what comes around, goes around.. It would not have destroyed her life, I am pretty sure it wouldn't have even destroyed her evening.

Whilst sharing a hug with his mother, I heard Charlie ask him a question,

"Have you given any thought to anything you would like to do? I mean, is there anywhere in the world you'd like to go? Your mother and I don't have a great deal of money, but we have an overdraft facility and credit cards. If there was somewhere, anywhere, you'd like to go for a family holiday whilst you are still in good enough health to enjoy it, just let me and your mother know and we'll book it that day."

"Thanks Dad, but we couldn't do that."

"Honestly son, you could. If you wanted to take the kids to Disney World, it would be on us. It would be our pleasure to pay for you, Jemma and the kids."

I could tell from the kitchen that Richie was choked but he maintained his composure.

"That it so kind of you, Dad and I'm really touched that you would do that for us, but it's just not possible. No travel company are going to allow me to travel without charging an absolute fortune for insurance. Anyway, if I ended up in hospital over there, it wouldn't only be expensive, it would also be traumatic for the kids. Travel has never been important to me anyway, Dad, family and friends are the important thing and I am the luckiest man in the world with mine. I just need to savour every second I have with you all now."

I hurried back in with the teapot and mugs. As I did, Charlie walked over to Richie, stood over him and placed a comforting hand on his shoulder.

"I am very proud of the man you have become, Richie."

"We both are." Dot added.

"You must do what you say though and keep strong, determined and hopeful," Charlie continued, "I hear people recounting stories at church about friends who have been riddled with cancer, who have ended up cured by the power of prayer. Miracles do happen, Richie. We don't know what plans God has for us."

I was about to say something but was becoming better as I grew older at showing restraint. In my feistier days, I would have asked Charlie what sort of sick God would make a young man suffer like this and then strip him away from his own family, leaving his wife to cope alone with two small children. Surely there's a serious design fault there from the Almighty? Now though, I chose not to speak. To an extent, if I had spoken out, I could have been accused of hypocrisy as I had my own, less vocal faith and I was praying regularly myself, pleading with God to help us. If Charlie was right though and God did have his own plans for us, was there really any point praying? Did we have the power to change God's mind?

"Your Dad's right," Dot added hopefully, planting another kiss on her son, "you need to believe that you will get better. Do everything that the Doctors tell you and more. Go on to the internet and see if there are any other cancer sufferers who have overcome the disease and see what they have done. Leave no stone unturned, Richie."

I felt like telling Dot that she wasn't exactly singing from the same hymn sheet as her husband! Charlie seemed to be saying put your faith in God and Dot seemed to be saying don't rely on God, sort it out yourself! As a couple they had done so much for Richie and I though, so it would have been inappropriate of me to pass comment. Perhaps I was being a bit harsh anyway. Perhaps what Dot was saying was, with God's help and with your own steely determination, there were still grounds for being optimistic. I poured the tea and tried to temporarily lift the mood.

"Were the kids good?"

Dot immediately brightened up a little.

"They were excellent, weren't they, Charlie?"

"They were great. Our grandchildren always are!"

"Jamie spent most of the evening making paper aeroplanes with his Grandad," Dot said, now showing signs of a smile, "and Melissa and I played Connect 4. She doesn't like losing, does she?"

Even Richie now seemed to get a bit of a colour back in his face.

"No, Mum, she's very competitive! We don't want to teach her that it's wrong to be competitive, as we think it's a good thing in this day and age, but at the same time, kicking the Connect 4 over and throwing the pieces around when she loses, which I imagine is what Melissa did, cannot be tolerated either!"

"That's exactly what she did!" Dot chuckled, "Several times!"

"Dot, you should have stopped beating her!" Charlie said with a smirk, "I think Melissa gets her competitive streak from your mother, Richie!"

Charlie winked over at Richie.

"No, no, don't let her win, Mum! She needs to learn. Fight to win but lose with dignity!"

"Well, she's halfway there." I added.

It was left to Richie to round this conversation off.

"The thing is, Jemma and I are very competitive too. Jemma's had to learn from an early age that if you don't fight hard in life, there are some bad people around who will make your life hell. On the other hand, I've had a great upbringing but had three siblings to compete against and then, in my working life, have always enjoyed the battles with other Managers and other branches. Both Jemma and I, in our very different ways, are used to coming out on top in the end.

I suppose that's why the cancer diagnosis hurt so much today. We are used to winning. We are used to overcoming every obstacle, so to be told that the cancer has spread and that there is nothing more they can do to get rid of it, well…that just feels like the ultimate defeat."

Roddy

It felt like payback time. All those years when I had not managed to get a girlfriend or had one who was determined not to put out with me and then became as dirty as a coalminers face after a twelve hour shift, once we finished. My luck had been so bad, I could have taken Alanis Morissette to the theatre and nothing would have happened! With Kelly though, things were really taking off. The barriers that she had initially put up because of previous romantic experiences, had all come down and when laid bare, both physically and emotionally, she was one hell of a woman! I was on cloud nine! The paranoid voice in my head kept telling me that sometime soon, someone or something would come along and push me off it, but I decided that if I lived my life as if disaster was around the corner, sooner or later it would be, so I just kept enjoying the moment and the moments just kept coming!

Nine weeks into my relationship with Kelly, my life changed forever. It was a joyous moment, the proudest moment of my life, but it arrived into my ears in a less than joyous manner. It was a Saturday morning. Kelly was in her bathroom in Ealing and I was laying on her bed, naked and star shaped after a heavy Friday night out and a follow-up sex session on Saturday morning. If we had sex on Friday night when I was full of beer and then again on Saturday morning when everything was still recovering from the previous outing, I could fool Kelly twice over that I was good at this game! After this particular Saturday morning session, I watched euphorically as Kelly's naked bottom bounced along to the bathroom, saw the door shut in front of me, heard the urine jets go into maximum thrust and then a minute later heard that anxious, shrill yelp!

"Oh my God! I don't believe this!"

As a man emboldened by nine weeks of making love to a bewitching, fascinating woman, I had this primitive cry down to either being some kind of post-coital orgasm or I thought perhaps my girth had somehow managed to damage Kelly's internal lady parts. I was completely wrong! Kelly opened the door looking panic stricken.

"What's the matter, gorgeous?"

"Roddy, you are not going to believe this! I'm pregnant!"

Dot

My son was dying. Life challenges you in all sorts of ways, financially, emotionally, spiritually, yet we soldier on, making the best of every day but nothing can ever prepare you for losing a child. I was sixty three years old, Richie was thirty two, it did not really feel like he had had a proper life, just the beginning. To watch as that life was slowly pulled away from him just felt dreadfully wrong. He should not have been going to his grave before me. It felt like someone was playing a sick joke on me and I wanted to tell them to stop, but I couldn't.

As a teenager, Richie had been diagnosed with testicular cancer. He had a testicle removed but the cancer had not spread and after a scare that had rocked our family to its foundations, normality prevailed and Richie went back to living a normal life. He married a lovely girl called Jemma, who I was wrongly a little wary of at first, because she had had a chequered past, but Jemma turned out to be perfect for Richie, I could not have handpicked a better match and they had two children together, Melissa and Jamie, who are the apple of their Granny's eye.

One rare, sunny summer's evening, I was sat in our lounge watching Emmerdale when the phone rang. I had been out in the garden earlier in the evening, doing a spot of weeding, so Charlie had recorded Emmerdale . I remember I nearly didn't answer the phone as it was all kicking off in the Woolpack and then I remembered that I could pause it, so that was what I did. It was Richie.

I recall that he was very upbeat, very concerned about me worrying too much, but he calmly explained that his cancer was back. This time, he explained, he had a little bit more of a fight on his hands as the cancer had spread and was now in his lungs.

"Don't worry though, Mum!" he said to soothe my nerves, "With medical advances, they will put me right in no time!"

I am a quizzical mother. I am not one to be content with just knowing the big picture, I wanted minor detail. I asked Richie question after question about his illness until my thirst for knowledge was satiated. Richie needed chemotherapy, he was going to Clatterbridge on the Wirral to have it and despite it being what the Doctors called 'Stage Three', the consultant was confident he would beat it.

Once I had acquired enough medical information, I needed to establish its emotional impact.

"How's Jemma?"

"Shocked, upset but strong, Mum. Like always, Jemma is strong."

He was right. Jemma's mother was a common, drunken, abusive, no good, who had given her a torrid time as a child. Jemma had always needed to be tough. Sometimes, inadvertently, Jemma could be so tough that she could make comments to me that were a little upsetting, but I bit my tongue, I had to make allowances for the upbringing she had had.

"And the kids?"

"We aren't going to tell them just yet, Mum. We want everything to remain normal for them, until it gets to a stage where it can no longer be."

"Like when?"

"Like if I lose my hair. They will have to be told why I'm losing my hair, not necessarily Jamie, but we will have to tell Melissa."

I had not even thought about Richie's hair. I welled up at the thought of him losing all his beautiful hair, but I would not let myself cry. If my darling son was being brave, I would try to be too.

"I know you and Jemma will do things exactly the right way for those children. Make sure Jemma knows that if she ever needs a break from them, even just for a couple of hours, I am always only a phone call away."

"We know that Mum. Thank you!"

"Have you told James, Helen and Caroline yet?"

James is Richie's brother, Helen and Caroline are his sisters. As a child, James and Richie used to fight constantly, not always physically, but my goodness they knew how to argue! As they grew older though, they became very close. Richie and Helen were never particularly close but were always courteous to each other, whilst Richie and Caroline were constant companions at one stage, but they headed in different directions romantically and geographically, so did not see much of each other as adults. When they did see each other though, they still giggled like a pair of teenagers.

"I've told Jim," Richie replied, "but I'll ring Helen and Caroline after you."

"Don't forget, Richie! They'll never forgive you if you forget!"

"MUM! I'm ringing around to tell people I have cancer! I am hardly going to forget!"

"I'm just reminding you, that's all!"

Richie could be a bit sharp with me at times, but it was impossible to take it personally as he always managed to follow it up by sweet talking me! This was no exception.

"I know you are, Mum and that's why you jointly win, "Best Mum In The World", along with Jemma, because you care so much about all of us, but don't worry, I'll make sure everyone knows what I have and I'll let everyone know that I'm going to beat it!"

Those final words still make me cry, "I'll let everyone know that I'm going to beat it." The cancer was so aggressive, he could not possibly beat it, it could only beat him.

One afternoon that Autumn, Richie and Jemma had to go over to see their consultant, Mr.Mollon, at Clatterbridge Hospital. I volunteered to babysit and suggested to Charlie that he should come with me. He agreed reluctantly, for a born again Christian, he could be very grumpy! That afternoon and evening, Melissa and Jamie behaved the worst they have ever behaved for Charlie and I. Maybe they sensed there was something strange going on with their parents and it sent everything out of synch. They were both absolute terrors! It felt like Richie and Jemma had force fed them all the wrong "E" numbers to make them hyperactive. They were off their rockers! Melissa insisted that she should be allowed to play 'Connect 4' and when she lost, she would turn into the Incredible Sulk, lifting the board up and tossing it around the room like a caber. Jamie wanted to make paper aeroplanes, but he didn't want his Grandad to make them, HE wanted to make them! He would not be shown how they were made either, so he ended up making paper balls! If Charlie tried to show him what to do, he would just stick his fingers in his ears and hum very loudly!

"Do they not smack these children?" an exasperated Charlie asked.

"No. No-one smacks their children these days, Charlie! There are other ways of disciplining them"

"Well, getting them to sit on a step is obviously working wonders with these two!"

The good thing about manic children is that they eventually wear themselves out. By half past seven, Charlie and I had those kids bathed and in bed and by twenty five to eight they were both fast asleep. As we sat ourselves down wearily on the settee, I warned Charlie,

"Don't you dare tell Richie and Jemma that those kids were anything other than perfect."

"Dot, give me some credit! I wouldn't dream of it!"

Half an hour later, Jemma and Richie were back. We did tell them the children were as good as gold, but it hardly would have mattered that night what we had told them. That was the night we all discovered Richie's cancer was terminal.

Jim

Mum rang me before Richie did to say it was terminal, she knew I would be in bits, but didn't want me to fall apart when I was speaking to Richie, so rang me first, allowing me to bawl my eyes out and then she told me I owed it to my brother to be strong.

Mum explained that she'd only just come back from Jemma and Richie's and that they'd had a long day at the hospital, so not to expect a call until the following day. There was no way I could sleep after that. I went into Gracie's room for a while and just watched her sleeping, she was six years old and was turning into such a pretty young thing and was doing brilliantly at school, I was so proud of her. My sobbing nearly woke her up a couple of times, so in the end, after five minutes or so, I had to go out. Just being in that room made me realise what Richie had to face. Like me, his children meant everything to him and now he was going to miss out on their futures. It really did not bear thinking about. I broke the news to Amy too and she seemed to cry for Jemma and the childrens loss, whilst I cried for Richie's. We had rare and meaningful sex that night, but after we had finished, Amy settled down to sleep but I couldn't, so went downstairs and watched re-runs of Cheers and Rising Damp.

By the morning, when the night had passed without sleep, I decided I needed to see Richie face to face rather than have him discuss things over the phone, so at half past six, I left a note for Amy, dressed and headed over to Standish. I arrived on Richie's doorstep just after his milkman. Richie was opening the door in his dressing gown, ready to collect the milk.

"Jim, what are you…oh, I take it Mum's told you? Come in!"

Driving over, I pictured it being more emotional than this. I pictured Jemma opening the door and me going upstairs to see a bedridden brother and neither of us speaking, just giving each other a bear hug through wave after wave of tears. It was much more every day routine than that though, I followed Richie into the hall, then into the lounge where Melissa was, watching grown men on the television in different coloured tops, singing daft songs and pretending to be imbeciles whilst silently totting up their bank balances. There were sounds filtering down from upstairs, Jemma was obviously trying to wash Jamie's hair in the bath and he sounded as though he was more than a little unhappy about soap getting in his eyes. Tortured hostages made less noise. We each sat down on a settee.

"Mum did tell me, Richie, I'm so sorry."

"What are you sorry for, Jim?" Richie said matter of factly. "It's not your fault."

I wanted to tell him that I had thought perhaps it was. Perhaps if I had dragged him to the Doctors when we were teenagers, he may not have had the problem recur. I just let him wait and wait. I shouldn't have let him do that. We didn't go down that route though, I just mumbled,

"I suppose not."

"Can I get you a cup of tea or coffee, Jim?"

Richie asked as though it was just another normal day, not one where he was waking up to a death sentence for the first time in his life.

"No, no, I don't want a drink, Richie. I just wanted to see you. I need to know if there's anything I can do."

"Like what?"

"I've no idea! Anything you want, Richie, you're my big brother, anything you want, I'd do it for you."

"Well, there is one thing but it's a little crazy…no, I couldn't ask."

"No, come on, its me you're speaking to, your brother! There's no need to be shy!"

Richie looked uncomfortable with whatever idea he had.

"I think there is…"

"No, honestly, Richie, there isn't! Tell me!"

Richie stood up.

"Not in here, Jim," he gestured over at Melissa who was still hypnotised by the television crazy men, "come into the kitchen with me."

We moved in to the kitchen and stood face to face.

"Tell me!" I urged.

"OK…I've never had a three in a bed," Richie whispered, "and before I get too unwell, I'd like to have one."

When I said anything, I didn't quite mean anything.

"With me??!!"

"Not with you, Jim, you daft git! Why would I want a three in a bed with you?"

"I've no idea, Richie! You looked awkward about it! We're very different, I don't know how your mind works!"

"Believe me, my mind does not work in a way that involves having a three in a bed with my own brother! Who was the third party?"

I pointed upstairs.

"And what exactly were we going to do, Jim, take it in turns?"

"I've no idea Richie, it was your gig!"

"No it was not!"

Man, did I feel relieved!

"What has this got to do with me then?"

"I need your consent."

I didn't understand.

"What do you mean?"

"I want a three in a bed with me, Jemma and Amy."

"My Amy?"

Richie nodded. Was I hearing this right? Richie was never into Amy. Just before Amy and I got together he had his chance but he turned her down.

"Seriously?"

"If it's OK with you, Jim. I've spoken to Jemma about it and she's not into things like that, you understand, but to grant a dying man his final wish, she's said she'll go along with it, just the once."

It was my turn to feel uncomfortable. I did not like this idea one bit, but it was Richie, my brother and he was dying. I felt duty bound to grant him his wish too, like Jemma had, but I could see another stumbling block.

"Look Richie, if that's what you really want…"

"It is Jim!"

"Well, if that's what you really want, I can't say I'd be happy about it, but I would go along with it. The thing is, you may have a problem with Amy, sex isn't really her thing these days and she's never been into any kinky stuff, so I can't…"

Richie interrupted me.

"Jim, don't worry about that, Amy's fine about it!"

"She is?"

"Oh yeh, Jemma rang her last week…"

"Last week? You didn't know you were dying last week!"

"I knew I was ill though. She just said name the time and place and she'll be there. She said she might have to have a glass of wine or two to lower her inhibitions, but she reckons once she has, she'll be fine."

"OK." I said through gritted teeth.

I was furious with Amy. She hadn't even discussed this with me and she agreed last week! Before the bad news! I knew it wasn't quite an infidelity, given the circumstances, but she could have at least talked it through with me first.

I could tell Richie was warming to the idea as he talked about it. His bald head suddenly seemed to be glowing.

"So, I was thinking maybe this Friday night, Jim. I'm most comfortable in my own bed, so I was thinking maybe if Amy could come here. Would you be able to drop her off?"

"You want me to be here, Richie?"

"Well, I get very tired these days, so I'd probably want to get things kickstarted early in the evening. If I did, our kids may still be up, so I was thinking you could look after them downstairs. Bring Gracie as well, if you like."

The cheeky bastard was asking me to keep his children entertained downstairs, whilst he kept my wife entertained upstairs! I was beginning to lose my cool.

"Hang on a minute, Richie!"

"Jim, don't worry, it won't be for long, as I say, I've never had a threesome before so I would imagine it'll all be over very quickly. Has Amy got any sexy underwear?"

"Why?"

"Well, that could make it quicker again. Also, if you have a Marvin Gaye CD, bring that, preferably, 'Let's Get It on'!"

I knew he was dying. I knew I should be the bigger man, but I just could not allow this. Dying wish or not, I'd have to live with it forever. This was too much. It was sordid.

"Hold it right there! I am not going to let this happen! I forbid Amy to do this! I know you're ill and everything and you're my brother and I love you, but this is just totally wrong! It's alright for you, you're buggering off, but I would never be able to look Jemma or Amy in the eye again!"

Richie shook his head and looked at me with disgust.

"So, you're telling me that you won't even babysit for ten minutes?"

"NO!"

"Well that's not very fair, is it?"

"It's not about the bloody babysitting!"

"Well, what is it about then?"

"You know very well!"

"No, I don't!"

"It's about you wanting to have sex with my wife."

Richie was non-plussed

"Well you should have said! If that's whats bothering you, Jim, I'll just watch Jemma and Amy then."

"NO!"

"I could film it, you could watch it later. Balance out the score. I get to see Amy, you get to see Jemma!"

"NO! Richie, don't be so disgusting! You're starting to creep me out now! I didn't know you were like this."

"Like what, Jim?"

"Like a pervert."

"Are you calling me a pervert, Jim?"

"Well if the shoe fits…"

I thought Richie was going to punch me. It felt like that date at Park Pool when we got kicked out for fighting, like Richie just needed half an excuse to lamp me. It was like he was looking down on me for not having the same weird desires.

"Do you know what I think, Jim?"

"Don't say I'm a prude, Richie! Remember when we were the kids, you were the prude, not me! You were the one into romance when everyone else was into doing it. Bloody hell, look how things have changed! Maybe it's the drugs you're taking. Maybe they've warped your brain!"

Richie's face broke into a grin so big, if the sun had have shone at that moment, I would have been blinded by his smile, rebounding back off it.

"I was just going to say, I think if there's a more gullible brother on this planet, I would be very surprised!"

I still did not get it.

"What??"

"I'm just joking, Jim! Look at the state of me! Bald, skinny, do you really think I'd be wanting a threesome in my state!"

I started to feel a bit of a fool.

"Well I don't know, do I?"

Richie came over and rubbed my hair like a Dad would do to a son he was proud of.

"Thanks Jim! That's really cheered me up that! Do you really think Amy would have agreed to a threesome with me and Jemma?!!"

"Possibly, if there were a couple of free glasses of wine involved!"

"Wait until I tell Jemma! Do you know, I've waited more than twenty five years to get you back for all that bedwetting stick!"

"Hang on! May I remind you that your wife once broke my jaw!"

"Oh yeh, she did, didn't she?!!"

We continued to joust and laugh about the old times. I went into Richie's house with a deep frown and left with a broad smile. Richie said that the only way he could think of dealing with the illness, was to find some dark humour in it. Sometimes its hard to find humour in a joke played at your expense, but I loved this one. It was like the old days, when we were kids and we had our whole lives ahead of us. If only that were still the case.

Jemma

I was shocked by what Richie was saying. We were sat in an Italian restaurant called the Café Bar in Ormskirk, discussing funeral arrangements. By this point, Richie had made the decision not to have a third session of chemotherapy. Following the first session of chemotherapy, he had had a second session of palliative chemotherapy, but when a third session was discussed, Richie and I were told the survival benefits were likely to be weeks or months rather than years, so Richie made the decision, with my consent, not to have it. Not all the family supported this decision. Helen and Dot, in particular, felt for the sake of our children, that Richie should not be giving up the fight. I think it was more down to the fact that they did not want to let go. I cannot pretend I was delighted with Richie's decision either, but it was his decision and he felt that he would rather try to find some quality in his final days than battle through them with chemotherapy. I still think there is no right and wrong decision on this, it is purely an individual choice.

Richie had lost a lot of weight. At that stage, he was down from a well toned fifteen stone to a thin looking eleven, but he was wanting to make every effort to get out and about whilst he still could. I think he only ate one small slice of pizza that day. The thing that had shocked me was the music Richie had chosen for his funeral.

"'You'll Never Walk Alone', is that not a song Liverpool fans sing?"

I didn't know much about football, but even I knew that.

"It is. I've spent thirty years roundly booing it!"

"Then why have it at your funeral?"

"Because I was an idiot to boo it! I've had so much time to think and reflect recently and it's just struck me as pathetic that I would boo a bunch of people who want to sing a 1940's Rodgers & Hammerstein classic at the top of their voices."

I was oblivious to the history of the song.

"I thought it was a Gerry & The Pacemakers song?"

"They covered it in the 1960's, Jemma but its from the film, Carousel. Have you never seen Carousel?"

"No."

"Right, after we've finished this coffee, let's go into Ormskirk and we'll buy Carousel on DVD. We can watch it tonight. Anyway, in Carousel, Billy Bigelow dies during a failed robbery and his wife Julie starts singing it after he has passed away, she's too overcome to finish it off though, so her cousin Nettie sings it to her."

"Not much point watching it now, Richie! You've just spoilt it!"

"I haven't, there's a lot more to it than that, as you will see when we watch it later. The point is it's a great song but because every time it's played, I associate it with Liverpool Football Club, I boo it. Back in 1989, after the Hillsborough disaster, the FA Cup Final was fittingly between Liverpool and Everton at Wembley. I could have gone to the game, but as you know my world was being tipped upside down at that point with Kelly leaving and having cancer, so I just went to 'The Buck' with Dogger to have a few pints and watch it in their front room. Dogger isn't really into football, but because I was supporting Everton, he said he would as well. Just before the game kicked off, Gerry Marsden from Gerry & The Pacemakers went on to the pitch and sang an emotional rendition of 'You'll Never Walk Alone'. It was less than two months after the Hillsborough tragedy and Liverpool fans held up their scarves and sang, the odd Everton fan did too, but most just kept a dignified silence. In 'The Buck' it was the same, Liverpudlians stood up and sang, Everton fans sat down and were silent, but Dogger, not aware of the etiquette and a big fan of the song, wanted to stand up and sing.I pulled him back down and told him to shut up!

That's just ridiculous really, isn't it? I was incensed enough to kiss Ray on the day of the tragedy, because I felt he had insulted the Hillsborough dead, but less than two months later, I wouldn't allow one of my best mates to sing a song, on a day celebrating their lives and mourning their deaths, because of some stupid, tribal prejudice. Every Evertonian, out of loyalty to the city they're from, should have held up their scarves and sang that day. I didn't and if playing 'You'll Never Walk Alone' at my funeral, in some small way, makes amends for that, then the thought of that, makes me happy. Dress me in a suit and put me in an Everton blue and white coffin, but make sure everyone, including Everton fans, Manchester United fans and Glasgow Rangers fans, sing that song."

"Do you want the Gerry & The Pacemakers version?"

"No. I love the version in Carousel, but an even better one in my opinion is by a Norwegian lady called Sissel. That's the one I want playing at my funeral."

"Will your Evertonian and United mates not be annoyed with you?"

"Jemma, I'll never know, will I?!! It's just a song though. A very emotive song. It doesn't belong to Liverpool Football Club, if it belongs to anyone, it would be Richard Rodgers and Oscar Hammerstein, they wrote it."

"So you're absolutely sure about this?"

"Jemma, I have never been more sure about anything in my entire life."

Dot

"For Christ's sake, Dot, do you even know what palliative treatment is?"

Jemma and I had always had a great relationship, some wives struggle to get on with their mother-in-laws, but Jemma and I had always had a brilliant friendship, but as Richie's illness progressed and both of us became more anxious about his worsening condition, we started to disagree. Melissa and Jamie were starting to spend more and more time with Charlie and myself, as Jemma was spending more time with Richie at hospital, which was totally understandable, but one evening, when she was picking up the children from our house, Jemma announced that Richie had opted out of a third session of chemotherapy. We were having a coffee together in the kitchen and Jemma just dropped it into conversation as though it wasn't that big a deal. Well, it was a big deal to me! I thought this was virtual suicide and told Jemma as much, telling her she may as well take the lid off the coffin and throw him straight in.

"I know it's not going to cure him, Jemma, but how could you let this happen? It could give him an extra six months! Six extra months for the children with their father."

"No, Dot, six extra months with you and Charlie as Richie spends all his time in bed or on an Oncology Ward. At least without the treatment, he may get a chance to spend some quality time with his children. Time that they will hopefully remember fondly for the rest of their lives."

I was dismayed and furious. My son and his wife seemed to be giving up as soon as the going got tough.

"Jemma, have you persuaded Richie that this is the right thing to do, because let me assure you, it isn't? You can't just let him die!"

"Dot, first of all, this was Richie's decision……"

"And yours."

"No, Dot, it was Richie's decision."

I was getting flustered. How could he be so stupid? Maybe it was because he was ill.

"Is he well enough to be making such a momentous decision, Jemma?"

"Dot, his brain is functioning fine. He's had chemotherapy not a lobotomy! Let him be the master of his own destiny. He is thirty two years old, Dot. He's not a child!"

"He's my child!"

"Yes, but what are you going to do? Grab his hand like he's a very naughty boy and drag him up to the hospital?"

"If that's what it takes!"

"Don't be so ridiculous, Dot!"

"Believe you me, Jemma, I'm not the one being ridiculous!"

"Oh yes you are!"

"Oh no, I'm not!"

Jemma laughed sarcastically.

"Dot, I'm not playing pantomime games with you. It's Richie's decision and that's that."

"As his wife, you should be persuading him to do the right thing!"

"Dot, you are right, he is MY husband. This is the worst thing I could ever have to face, but through it all, I am going to support him every step of the way. If Richie wants to die with dignity, he will face no hostility from me."

"Even if you are betraying your children?"

Jemma came right up to me. She was so close, I swear at one point our noses even touched.

"How dare you say I am betraying my children, Dot! Thank you very much for looking after them, but I think it's about time I took them home to their father."

I replied angrily and almost shouting.

"Whilst you still can!"

"That's right Dot," Jemma shouted back, "whilst I still can!"

Jemma marched into the lounge, grabbed Melissa off her Grandad's knee and picked Jamie and his toy cars off the lounge carpet. She put their shoes and coats on them in record time and frogmarched them out the house and into her car. After she had strapped the kids in the car, she stared at me venomously and spat out,

"Just back off, will you, Dot! I know it's in your nature to interfere, but just this once, for everyone's sake, just BACK OFF!"

With that, Jemma slammed the rear car doot shut, climbed in herself, revved her engine, then sped off up the road. I was distraught and Charlie annoyed me by coming across all knowing and stating that,

"Perhaps Jemma has a point."

Two hours later, whilst my nerves were still frayed, the phone rang.

"Hello."

"Dot, it's Jemma."

I wasn't ready for another argument.

"Hello, dear," I said frostily.

"Look Dot, I'm sorry everything turned a little angry earlier, understandably emotions are running high. Believe me, if it was just down to me, Richie would be having this treatment, but I don't just love your son, Dot, I know him too. He is a very stubborn man. If he has made a decision, there is not a chance that you or I will change his mind. If he does not want to have any more chemotherapy, we cannot change that fact."

"I wish we could, Jemma."

"I know you do, Dot, but I was thinking, what we should do, is to look to channel our energies into doing something positive."

It was a point I could not possibly argue with.

"Like what, Jemma?"

"Remember when Charlie offered to pay for a holiday for us?"

"Yes, I'm sure that offer still stands, but is Richie well enough to travel?"

"No, he isn't, but can you remember what Richie said? He said he wanted to spend the time he had left surrounded by the people he loved."

"I remember."

"Well, maybe you and I should arrange a party for him. Think of all the people you would invite to his funeral and let's arrange something where Richie gets the chance to see them. You invite family and family friends and I'll invite all our other friends."

I have to admit, my initial reaction was a little dubious. I was not totally convinced that this was a good idea.

"Will people not think it's a bit strange, Jemma? Having a party when your husband and my son is dying? Should we really be having fun?"

"Celebrating, Dot. We should be celebrating. All the people that are closest to Richie, should be celebrating the fact that they have had the opportunity to know him and that they will get the opportunity to see him one last time. Even if I say so myself, I think it's a brilliant idea! It'll give him a lift, I know it will."

I thought about it. Jemma was right.

"OK, let's do it! I could book Ormskirk Cricket Club, that would fit about a hundred in, would that be OK?"

"That'd be ideal, Dot. Try and book it for three or four weeks time. Time enough for people to make arrangements, but hopefully Richie will still be well enough to enjoy it then. When you speak to people, tell them to park up Brook Lane rather than in the car park, I'd like it to be a surprise for him, but if Richie spots a load of cars he knows, he'll realise something is going on."

The idea was already starting to grow on me. I could see it being a lovely night and a night Richie would thoroughly enjoy. I felt awful about arguing with Jemma. I now understood that she would have had nothing to do with the decision not to have further treatment.

"Jemma, you do know that you're a wonderful wife!"

"Not for much longer, Dot, sadly, not for much longer."

Kelly

The numbers had been half punched twenty or maybe even thirty times, but then nervousness had got the better of me and I had cancelled each call. The final time though, I had been courageous, punched in the whole number, battled with myself not to hang up, listened to the tone and wiped sweat from my brow.

"Hello."

I gulped.

"Hello, is that Jemma?"

"It is, Kelly."

I was relieved. My biggest fear was that Richie would pick up. I knew he would have subsequently heard all about what I had said.

"Jemma. I'm just ringing to say I'm so, so sorry."

"How did you know, Kelly? Have you spoken to Amy?"

I was immediately puzzled.

"Know what?"

"That the cancer is back."

This was a horrible conversation. It made no sense and once it did, I knew it would not be any better.

"What? Who's cancer? Richie's cancer?"

"Yes. How come you didn't know? You just said you were sorry."

"I meant for saying I was pregnant. I've been wanting to ring you for ages, Jemma, but I've been putting it off and putting it off. I wasn't pregnant and nothing happened between Richie and I on the 'Sunny Road', but I guess you always knew that, didn't you?"

"I did."

"Is it testicular cancer again?"

"It is, but he has secondary lung cancer too."

"Is it bad? Is he having chemo?"

"He was having chemo. Not any more."

"Why?"

"He has too many tumours on his lungs, Kelly. It's a particularly aggressive form of cancer. Richie's dying, Kelly."

"Dying? He can't be. It's less than twelve months since I saw him. He looked great."

"Believe me, Kelly, he doesn't look great now."

"Jemma, I'm so sorry. I truly am so, so sorry."

Not that I deserved it after everything I had put her through, but somehow, Jemma found it within herself to offer me a further gift of her compassion.

"Look Kelly, Dot and I are arranging a party for Richie, he probably only has months, possibly weeks left now and we thought it would be a lovely idea to have a party for him, where he gets to see his old friends one last time. I know more than anyone how important you used to be to him, so it would be wrong of me not to ask you. Would you come, Kelly?"

"When is it?"

"Next Friday."

"Could Roddy come too?"

"Roddy? The bloke in the hospital."

"Yes. We're together now. He'll drive me up."

"That's fine. It's at Ormskirk Cricket Club. Get there for seven thirty, I'll bring Richie in just before eight. I've been telling everyone to park up the road so Richie doesn't recognise the cars, but I guess you guys can park right next to the entrance, if you like!"

"OK, that's great. Thank you Jemma."

"It's OK. See you on Friday."

"No, Jemma, thank you, really, thank you."

"Lets just start afresh on Friday. I'll look forward to seeing Roddy again. He seemed like a good guy."

"He is. Jemma…."

"Yes."

"One last thing…"

"Go on…"

"It won't just be Roddy, I'm bringing. I'll be carrying our other guest, Jemma, I'm pregnant."

"Congratulations. Are you happy, Kelly?"

"Jemma, I'm ecstatic. Present telephone conversation excepted, I am the happiest I have ever been. Roddy is a fantastic man, he'll be a fantastic father and every day I wake up, I just feel so lucky."

As soon as I said it, I knew I shouldn't have. The line went quiet and then I could hear some gentle sobbing. Despite everything she did for me, I always managed somehow to make Jemma's life difficult. I felt guilty. Even when I didn't mean to rub her nose in things, I still managed to.

"Jemma, Jemma, are you there? Sorry, I didn't think."

"It's OK. I'm really happy for you. I'll look forward to seeing both you and Roddy on Friday night."

It was my turn to start crying.

"Jemma, I promise I'll never hurt you again."

"Kelly, thank you for saying it but you can't promise that! Believe me, even if you do, I'll still love you. You're my sister and no matter what happens that won't change. My love for you is unconditional."

"I know I haven't always shown it Jemma, but I feel the same way too."

"See you on Friday, Kelly. Tell Roddy to drive carefully."

Caroline

Donna and I had gripped hold of each other's hands when Richie had arrived at the door and then disappeared. We had been standing close enough to the entrance to glimpse his arrival and his subsequent swift departure.

"Cal, that didn't even look like Richie," Donna whispered in my ear.

"I know what you mean," I whispered back, "his skin looks like its been in the bath for a week. Maybe this is cruel, putting him through this. Do you think I should go and have a word? We've always been close."

"No," Donna replied, "Jemma and your Mum have gone after him. If someone else goes, he'll start feeling crowded."

"They might be trying to coax him in though. I wouldn't do that. I'd tell him if he wants to bugger off home, that's fine with me."

Fortunately I didn't go out. Mum and Jemma did coax him in and there was this awkward period where everyone did not know how to react, it was a party for a terminally ill man who had just shown everyone that he was a reluctant host. No-one had any experience of how to act in those circumstances. There was some minor acknowledgement of his return, but everyone, probably rightly, gave him time to find his feet in there. That must be how celebrities feel all the time when they go to parties, everyone is aware of their presence but most people pretend to ignore them as they feel its bad form to be too in their face.

Donna and I kept a particularly low profile. We didn't really feel like we fitted in too well to family events anyway. We were the odd lesbian misfits. Old family members wore cloves of garlic to deter us from going anywhere near them. We just bought a few drinks and sat in the corner and chatted amiably to anyone who ambled over for a natter.

About twenty minutes after he came back in, Richie struggled over to us. There were two small steps between Richie's starting point and our table, but his body was so badly ravaged by cancer, they must have seemed like Grand National fences to him. He sat down on a stool, breathless.

"Bloody hell, Richie!" I said as I reached across the table to kiss him, "we drive all the way over from Yorkshire and you nearly bugger off before the first song has finished!"

"I'm sorry about that! Once that door opened, I saw the pair of you and I just bolted!"

"Really?" Donna asked sincerely.

"Well I did see you, but that's not why I legged it. If you could call that feeble attempt to run 'legging it'!"

"Why did you?" I asked.

"I didn't want people to pity me, Cal."

"You're dying of cancer, Richie! People are allowed to pity you! No-one pities someone they hate!"

"Anyway," Donna joined in, "why do you give a toss what anyone else thinks? Most people here just want to have a good night and see that you have one too. Don't let anyone spoil it for you, Richie, you just enjoy yourself, hun."

"Thanks Donna! I intend to. Are you still looking after my big sister?"

"We look after each other, Richie. We still fight like a pair of boxers at a weigh in, but we're old enough now to know it's all in the name of love."

I took hold of Richie's hand. It felt cold. As kids, he always had warm hands, that was one of the many things I remember about him. Warm hands.

"You never bloody told me about Kelly being up the duff! I hope that wasn't the last act of a knackered testicle?!"

Richie laughed. It was a strange laugh. His shoulders moved up and down but no sound came out, like his body was too tired for that now.

"Don't even go there, Cal! I can assure you it wasn't mine, I didn't even know anything about it until Jemma whispered something to me as I came in."

"The first time or the second?" Donna asked.

"The second."

"Damn! It would have explained everything if it had been the first. Jemma whispering, 'Kellys pregnant!' and you legging it. Sherlock Holmes would not have taken long to figure that one out!"

Richie smiled shyly.

"I hate to disappoint you ladies, but the baby belongs to the gentleman sat with Kelly. His name's Roddy. I spoke to the pair of them for a few minutes before, he seems a good lad, the type I'd go for a pint with, back in the days I was well enough to go for a pint."

"We'll go over and interrogate him later, Donna, won't we?" I said, "Check him out for ourselves, we won't take your word for your innocence!"

"We've got test tubes," Donna added with comedy timing, "we'll take a sperm sample!"

"You two wouldn't even know what sperm looked like!" Richie countered.

"A DNA test then!" Donna laughed., "we'll pull his hair out!"

"I should have kept you some of mine!" Richie said.

It was all silly banter. Richie went on to say he had requested Nirvana's "Heart Shaped Box" for me and I said I had requested Chumbawamba's "TubThumping" for him, a jokey reference to his childhood bedwetting. Richie soon moved on to speak to others, giving Donna and I each a clasped hand shake before he went on his way.

Later in the evening, Richie took the stage and gave a wonderfully emotional speech, danced a slow dance with Jemma and before we knew it the night was over. Donna and I were two of the last to leave. We had drunk shedloads and were more than a little messy. Richie stood on the dancefloor making sure he said goodbye to everyone. Full of beer, I gave him a massive hug, cried and said,

"I love you so much, Richie Billingham. No-one has ever made me laugh like you do and no-one ever will!"

Richie hugged back,

"Piss off you big oyster diver! I've done enough crying for one night, don't get me started again!"

As we slumped on to the backseats of the taxi, Donna looked at me and slurred,

"Do you know what, Cal, your brother Jim is alright, but your brother Richie has to be the best brother that ever lived."

And he was.

Richie

OK, this is going to be tough!

First of all, I owe you all an apology. As you could probably tell, I did not have the foggiest idea that this party was taking place tonight and once I did know, as you will have noticed, I did not want to come in. Now let me make one thing clear, that is not a reflection of how I feel about any of you, it's a reflection of how I feel about myself right now. This tired, bald, skinny man does not feel like me, it feels like a pale imitation of my former self and I did not want your abiding memory of me to be this emaciated, nine stone weakling.

It was Jemma that persuaded me to come in. She felt it was important for you to see me and equally important for me to see all of you. As has often been the case in our marriage, I was wrong and Jemma was right. I cannot possibly tell you how much tonight has meant to me. My dear mother has always said to me that you can tell a lot about a man by the quality of his friends and if that is the case then I am the most brilliant, wonderful man that has ever lived. Words cannot describe how grateful I am to all of you for coming here tonight and for the friendship you have offered me throughout my life. From the bottom of my heart and the heart of my bottom, I thank you!

I feel a bit like Yul Bryner at the moment, because to an extent this feels like I am speaking to you all from beyond the grave. To have advanced warning of your demise, in a way, is a great thing, as you get the opportunity to say your goodbyes to everyone you love, but all things considered, I still wish I could have slipped away in my sleep aged ninety three. Although I said it was something I really felt uncomfortable about, could I ask all of you to have a good look at me. A really good look. The reason I ask, is because this dying body that is just about managing to stand before you, is a victim of my laziness and forgetfulness. It's far too late for 'if onlys' now, but if I'd have regularly checked for lumps, none of us would be at this "Pre-Funeral" party tonight. Fellas, please don't ever make the same mistake as me.

With regards to thank yous, I have already done a collective one, so I am only going to do one more. I just want to thank my amazing wife, Jemma. I am not scared of death itself, it comes to us all, what I hate though, what I really, really hate, is that death will take my wife and my children away from me forever. We take things for granted in life. We get upset when trivial things don't happen the way we want them to. At times in my marriage, I have failed to appreciate how incredibly lucky I have been to spend the last twelve years with Jemma. Jemma is the strongest, most loyal, most beautiful woman I have had the privilege of knowing. I am ashamed that I did not appreciate that fact for every second I have had with her. I would have loved to have grown old with her and watched those beguiling blue eyes smile out from an old ladies face, but it was not to be. To quote Elizabeth Barrett Browning,

"I love you not only for what you are, but for what I am when I am with you. I love you not only for what you have made of yourself, but for what you are making of me. I love you for the part of me that you bring out."

Now I know tonight has been a little unorthodox, but I want to continue with the theme of doing things a little different. Many of you were at our wedding reception at Briars Hall and witnessed our first dance, well now, whilst I still have the strength to get around a dance floor for three minutes, I want you to witness our "Last Dance".

Jemma knows nothing about this, but I asked the DJ earlier whether he has a lovely song by Natalie Merchant called 'My Beloved Wife'. The song is about an old widower looking back on the fifty wonderful years he spent with his wife before she passed away. Every emotion in the song expresses how I feel about my beloved wife, Jemma. I love you so much Jemma and will never stop loving you!

DJ, if you could start the music and Jemma, if you could be good enough to steer me round the dancefloor for the duration of the song, I will be eternally grateful!

Thanks once again everybody, please feel free to join us on the dancefloor, enjoy the rest of the night and I hope the rest of your lives are filled with health, wealth and happiness.

Richie

My family are around me now. Mum, Dad, Jim, Caroline, Helen and Jemma. Sometimes I forget where the kids are and I panic and ask for them, but in moments of clarity I remember they are with Amy. Better there than here.

I can feel Jemma holding my hand. She keeps talking. Keeps trying to soothe the pain, constantly re-assuring me everything will be fine, but I only hear some of what she says now as I slip in and out of consciousness

I know I'm in hospital. I know they have put me in a side room, away from the moans and groans of people with minor ailments. I know from the strange sounds emanating from my body that this is the end. When you make love, you reach a stage when you know the orgasm is coming and nothing can be done to stop it. That's the stage I have reached with death now, it is coming and there is nothing I can do to stop it.

I want to sit up for one last time. I want to tell Jemma there is no pain, just haze. Tell her not to worry. I try to move, to hoist myself up, but nothing happens. Nothing at all. I release a deep sigh. There feels like there's little air left in my lungs now. I'm checking out, I know I'm checking out. I'd love to stay, but I have already lost my grip on the cliff, I'm just waiting to hit the ground.

A tear drips on to my face. I look up and Jemma's tear filled eyes are looking right down at me. I try to smile to comfort her, to tell her not to be sad, that it will all be OK, but even my lips are barely moving now. With all my might, I try to squeeze Jemma's hand and although I think I manage to tighten slightly, I'm not sure it's enough for her to notice. I feel her kiss my dry lips. I feel a depth of love I have only felt before when I witnessed the birth of my children. I want to tell Jemma that I feel more for her than anyone has ever felt for another human being, but I can't. I'm so glad that I have been given the time to tell her before. I only wish I had been given more time to show her.

My body jolts. It feels different, but I understand that it's a new phase. Not long now. I look at Jemma one last time. She gradually disappears like the picture on an old television screen. I feel sadness. Overwhelming sadness, then that fades too. All I can see is a tunnel, three dimensional, bizarrely reminiscent of the 1970's credits to Doctor

Who. I'm moving along it. A bright white light at the end is forcing me towards it like a magnet. This is the end. The very end. I thought I would love Jemma forever but forever is over. What lies beyond the light? God only knows.

Lightning Source UK Ltd.
Milton Keynes UK
178311UK00001B/262/P